Adeptus Major

Adeptus Major

ALEX MYKALS

Cavalier Press
2005

Adeptus Major

Copyright © 2005 by Alex Mykals

All rights reserved. No part of this publication may be reproduced in any form or by any electronic or mechanical means including information storage and retrieval storage systems without permission in writing from the publisher, except by a reviewer, who may quote brief passages in a review. The characters portrayed in this work are fictional, and any resemblance to any person living or dead is purely coincidental.

ISBN 0-9746210-8-0

9 8 7 6 5 4 3 2 1

Front and Back Cover Designs and Map of Atlantis
by Lúcia A. de Nóbrega

Published by Cavalier Press, LLC
P.O. Box 6437, Falls Church, VA 22040
Web site http://www.cavalierpress.com
Printed and bound in the United States of America

To my Mom and Dad.
For Everything.

part one

"This power came forth out of the Atlantic Ocean, for in those days the Atlantic was navigable; and there was an island situated in front of the straits which you call the Columns of Hercules; the island was larger than Libya and Asia put together and was the way to other islands and from the islands you might pass through the whole of the opposite continent which surrounded the true ocean... Now, on the island of Atlantis there was a great and wonderful empire, which had rule over the whole island and several others...

"But afterward there occurred violent earthquakes and floods, and in a single day and night of rain all your warlike men in a body sank into the earth and the island of Atlantis in like manner disappeared and was sunk beneath the sea."

~Plato, *Timaeus*

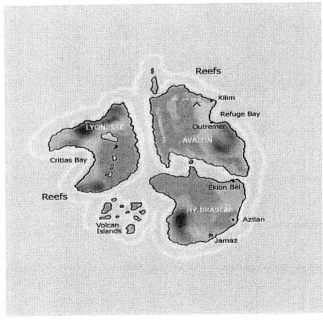

the island nation of Atlantl

chapter one

The young woman blinked and squinted as she turned the corner out of the shadow of the buildings into bright sunlight. She paused a moment to catch her breath and get her bearings. Someone bumped into her from behind and she stumbled. The offender offered a brief apology in French before hurrying on and the woman shrugged as she looked out over the Marseilles harbour.

"Now, which way was it?" she muttered, looking up and down the harbourfront before catching sight of a landmark she recognised. "Ah, there we are." She headed off down the street at a near jog, wincing as she looked at her watch. *Damn, Ally, you are so late.*

She felt sweat beginning to soak her shirt as she dodged around other pedestrians and winced again internally. She cast a wistful glance at the other women on the street, many of whom were outfitted in the unofficial uniform of southern France: tight shorts and the briefest of bikini tops—if that. Ally blushed at one woman wearing even less. *Yeesh. Still, that looks a lot cooler than what I'm wearing.* She looked down at her own T-shirt and mid-thigh shorts. *The ultimate in geek chic.* She pushed her glasses up further up her nose, continuing to rub her hand through short brown hair. *At least I don't have a bunch of pens in my pocket.*

Dodging her way through the crowd, Ally finally recognised the café that was her destination. Catching sight of the person she was going to meet, she eased her way through the tables and into a seat opposite, relieved that the umbrella overhead was providing some shade. "Hey, Chorus," she said as the stocky man looked up, smiling. "Sorry I'm late."

"Ally, hi." The young man grinned, his teeth brilliantly white in his very dark face. "Don't worry about it. *Ga gona mathatha.*"

"Yeah, one of the showers at the hostel broke just after you left. And, of course, then everyone wanted to shower. And there's also a whole lot of activity on the streets for some reason."

"I was talking to our waiter and he said that there's some VIP showing up today. The Crown Princess of Atlantis, I think he said. Or Atlantl, if you want to use their own term."

"Oh yeah, I heard something about that," Ally said. "Going to *le Centre de la Vieille Charité*, I think. It's a museum."

Chorus nodded at her French. "Not bad, Ally. *Ton accent s'améliore.*" Ally looked blank. "Your accent's improving," he translated. He looked up as the waiter approached. "So, what would you like?"

"*Un croissant, s'il vous plaîs,*" Ally requested. "*Et un,* um, *thé glacé?*"

"*Et pour moi . . .*" Chorus rattled off a long series of instructions in French while Ally scowled.

"I hate it when you do that," she complained. "It's not fair. Anywhere we go, we're there two weeks and you can talk like a native. You're a freak, you know that, right?"

Chorus' eyebrows rose. "Hey, it took me three weeks to learn Thai! Besides, you're one to talk, *zarbi*! Just because I'm a Savant–"

"Idiot savant," came the muttered interjection.

"–there's no reason to be insulting. Besides, would you wanna trade?"

This question inspired an emphatic headshake.

"Good, then shut up. So, what do you think? Do you want to go visit a museum? I read that the one the princess is visiting has a really good exhibit. And, hey, if we get there around noon, we'll be in a position to ogle some royalty. It'll do you some good to fantasise about being some princess' knight in shining armour, *chérie.*"

Alleandre looked uncomfortable. "I dunno if I want to go ogling right now. I mean, Annie–"

"Damnit, fuck Annie. Or don't fuck Annie. *She* broke up with *you.* By phone. While you were on the other side of the planet from her, no less. She's not the centre of your life any more. Now, you *are* going to come with me to this museum." Chorus pointed at her commandingly. "Ogling is optional."

Alleandre dragged a hand through her short chocolate-coloured hair. "Okay, okay, I'll go! What's '*zarbi*', anyway?"

"Weirdo."

"Gee, thanks."

ॐ   ॐ   ॐ   ॐ   ॐ

Colonel Sir Arthur Ramirez, Knight of the Temple and Master of the Heir's Guard, was not happy. Partly, this was due to physical discomfort. Someone–who was going to be looking for a new job, and possibly a new head, once Sir Arthur found out who it was–had misplaced both Sir Arthur's custom-fitted body armour *and* his backup. So the Master had been forced to borrow a set belonging to Corporal Ariman Tresca.

Corporal Tresca was a massively built black man whose head and shoulders tended to brush the edges of any doorway he walked through.

chapter one

Unfortunately, while Sir Arthur lacked over a foot of Tresca's height, he often had to actually turn sideways to get his shoulders through doorways.

And so Sir Arthur had the uncomfortable sensation of being squeezed, rather like a large tube of toothpaste.

However, eighteen years in the Imperial Marines and another thirteen in the Atlantlan Guard allowed him to ignore the mere physical discomfort and concentrate on the primary cause of his unhappiness.

"Eagle three, this is Anthill, report status, over." Sir Arthur cupped his hand over his ear in an attempt to hear the voice coming through his earbud.

". . . gle Th . . . Sa . . . gain . . . er."

Sir Arthur directed a glare around his command centre, a medium-sized room in the *Hôtel Delcourt*. "Someone talk to me. Why can't I hear Eagle Three? Dicky, is it hardware?"

Major Theodora "Dicky" Nixon, a rail-thin dark-haired woman, who nevertheless was one of the only people who could take down Sir Arthur hand-to-hand on a semi-regular basis, replied, "Negative, sir. I checked everything myself. Whatever it is has taken out Three's primary and *both* backups. It's either a bug in the decryption software on our end, or something's jamming us." She shrugged. "Jalal is checking the computer now."

"Well, tell him to hurry up. We're scheduled to move in ten, and if—"

"I've got it, sir," Corporal Tresca rumbled. His commander spun to face him as he pointed to a map of Marseilles on his computer screen. "It's the building, sir. It uses a dedicated-frequency radio transmitter on the roof to communicate with another office across town, and its transmission frequency is almost smack in the centre of our bandwidth. Sniper Team Three's almost sitting on the antenna."

Sir Arthur exploded. "Goddammit, why didn't anyone catch this before? When I find out who—" He stopped and visibly gathered himself. "Too late now. We don't have time." The bodyguard turned to his second in command. "Dicky, contact Eagle Two. They have line of sight with Three. Tell them to go visual. Eagle Three is now under condition Red One."

Major Nixon's eyes widened, but she nodded and began speaking quietly but clearly into her radio. Condition Red One would allow the two-man sniper team to fire on any target that both members considered an imminent lethal threat, without reference to command. This was not a responsibility to be given lightly, especially on foreign soil. Still, Sir Arthur trusted the judgement of all the people under his command.

He was already issuing more orders. "Tresca, shut down that transmitter. Call the building, call the management, get them to turn it off. Cut their power lines if you have to."

As Corporal Tresca reached for the phone, Sir Arthur tried to sigh deeply, but was prevented by the constricting mass of the too-small body armour under his silver and purple uniform. He settled for rolling his shoulders, eliciting an alarming series of creaks and groans from the already-stressed material. "I'm off to meet the Princess. This had better be all that goes wrong today."

On the roof of a tall building overlooking *le Centre de la Vieille Charité*, a black-clad figure cradling a powerful scope-equipped rifle watched carefully as a light flashed from Eagle Two's position on top of the building across the street. After counting the flashes and decoding their meaning, he turned to his companion, and said, "They've given us Red One authorisation." He then used his own signal light to flash a confirmation back to Eagle Two.

His companion nodded solemnly before switching her gaze back to the street below.

Behind them, the bodies of Sergeant Abdul al-Latif and Corporal Miroslav Garner, Royal Atlantlan Heir's Guard, the two-man sniper team codenamed Eagle Three, lay cooling on the rooftop.

Evelynne Sophia al-Heru deMolay, Crown Princess of Atlantis, stood in the high vaulted lobby of the *Hôtel Delcourt*, and looked longingly at the bright sunshine out the huge floor-to-ceiling windows that fronted the hotel. Maïda, her lady-in-waiting, had been briefly called away to deal with some minor catastrophe involving flowers and seating arrangements. The bulk of Evelynne's Personal Guard had yet to arrive, so she stood alone daydreaming in the middle of the floor while a large number of people did the million-and-one last minute things that needed doing.

Only ten more days. Hooray. I wish it were over now. Oh well, suck it up, Princess, as Patrick says. Once this is over you can go to the Summer Palace and sunbathe for a week. She caught a glimpse of herself in one of the mirrors lining the lobby and was torn between resignation and appreciation over her appearance.

A mass of flame-red hair had been elaborately coifed into a pile on top of her head. Several jewelled pins held it in place and Evelynne knew from experience that nothing short of a tornado would ruin Maïda's masterpiece. Not even the weight of the coronet that, since her recent nineteenth birthday, Evelynne was now legally entitled to wear.

chapter one

Below the hair, both almond-shaped eyes, a legacy of Evelynne's Egyptian grandmother, took in the full effect. Her lightly tanned face was surprisingly free of freckles, another gift from her grandmother. Brilliant blue eyes were currently surrounded by a heavy layer of kohl designs, more to hide the dark rings of fatigue under them than for any real desire for makeup. Her lips were covered in an equally dark shade of kohl, with small designs at the corners of her mouth, which gave the impression of a quirk of a smile. Below the face, a dark blue dress started at the shoulders, showing just a hint of cleavage, and ran down to the ankle, and though Evelynne's genius of a tailor had assured her that it would be as comfortable as possible to walk in, she was still dreading the prospect. Still, aesthetically Evelynne had to admit the arrangement was quite pleasing.

Isis, only ten more days, she repeated to herself like a mantra. *Only ten more days. I wonder if I can convince them to skip the Switzerland trip.* Even as she thought it, she knew it would never happen. Both the diplomatic considerations and her own sense of duty would ensure that she finished the tour with grace.

A sound behind her made Evelynne look back, and she saw Colonel Ramirez coming towards her. As he walked determinedly in her direction, a path through the throng spontaneously opened, and in no time the bodyguard arrived at Evelynne's side.

"Sir Arthur," Evelynne said gravely.

"Your Highness," Sir Arthur responded, just as gravely.

There was silence for several seconds, as they both stood there solemnly.

Evelynne cracked first, as usual. Her lips twisted in an effort to control herself, an attempt doomed to fail as a very un-princess-like snort erupted from her chest, followed by a giggle. It took her a few minutes to regain her composure. "Goodness, I needed that. Thanks, Uncle Arthur," she said, around a few extra giggles that managed to escape. She sighed. "I was trying to get Maïda to go to this thing in my place, but she refused. Could you please arrest her as a traitor to the Crown, or some such thing?"

Sir Arthur's mouth had quirked into a hint of a wry smile. "Somehow I think people would notice that the Heir had suddenly aged forty years overnight, Your Highness. However, I understand how you feel. This trip has not been easy on me, either." He grimaced, thinking about his most recent troubles, and Evelynne winced in sympathy with him, knowing that however hard this was on her, it was ten times harder on those in charge of her security. "As for Maïda—oh dear, I guess we're leaving now," he said. "No time for any arresting at the moment, I'm afraid."

Evelynne scowled at her bodyguard, until Maïda's voice came suddenly from behind her, making her jump. "Don't frown, Highness, you'll ruin my makeup. What did Sir Arthur do now?" The short, motherly woman looked at her charge disapprovingly.

"He's been showing his disloyalty by refusing to arrest you. And what do you mean, 'your makeup?' It's on *my* face!"

"Yes, Highness, but I'm the one who put it there. Therefore, it is my makeup. You may keep your face."

More than one attendant was somewhat shocked as they heard the princess mumbling about "traitors," "dissidents" and "beheadings" as she was escorted towards the car.

🙞 🙞 🙞 🙞 🙞

"You've never been to Atlantis, have you?" Chorus asked as he and his friend walked along the busy street.

"No," Ally replied, looking up from where she was searching through her fanny pack. "I didn't think you had."

"No, I haven't. I'd like to visit some day. I'd love to learn Lantlan. It sounds similar to Xhosa or San. All those clicks and glottal stops. And have you heard them do that whistling thing? It sounds so exotic."

"Well, maybe once we've done with Europe we can head there from Portugal. Or maybe go to Egypt first and head across North Africa and leave from Morocco." Finally discovering the lip balm she was looking for, Ally paused a moment to apply the cinnamon-scented substance. The tall woman held out the fanny pack to her friend. "Would you mind putting this in your backpack? I'm getting way too sweaty carrying it."

Chorus took the item and placed it in his pack. "So, that's why you're sweaty, eh? And here I thought it was all the scantily clad females everywhere around here," he teased, receiving a baleful glare. "Really, Ally, you're way too—what's the word? Uptight. You need to get laid, badly."

Alleandre avoided his gaze as she blushed furiously. "Why would I want to get laid badly? I'd rather be laid goodly," she rallied valiantly, though the effort was spoiled by the ever-deepening colour of her face.

Chorus' eyebrows rose. "What's this? Was that a sex joke I heard coming from your lips? Will wonders never cease? You've been corrupted, Ally." Seeing her red cheeks, he decided to let up a bit. "Well, it does you good."

"Say, isn't the museum down there?" Ally asked in an effort to change the subject, indicating a street just ahead.

Chorus allowed her. "I think so. Look at all the people." The streets had been getting steadily more crowded and the police presence was becoming more obvious. "I guess the Europeans just love royals, eh?" He looked at his

chapter one

watch. "Yeah, they should be coming along any time now. Come on, let's see how close we can get."

≈ ≈ ≈ ≈ ≈

Evelynne sat back in her seat as the car was driven slowly down the street and she waved to the crowds lining the sidewalks as she passed. The sun was shining brightly from overhead, although air conditioning kept the car cool.

"Explain the logic behind this car to me again, please," she requested out of the corner of her mouth, speaking to Sir Arthur, who was sitting in the front passenger seat. "This is a convertible. Convertibles should be, by definition, open to the air. Not enclosed in a bubble. I feel like I'm in a fishbowl. Do you want to see my goldfish impression?" Her eyes never left the crowds and the smile never left her face. It was at times like this that she wondered whether she had any other expressions.

"Please, Your Highness," replied her bodyguard. "It's policy when travelling through foreign nations." His tone was distracted. There was something nagging at the back of his mind, and he was trying to isolate what it was. It was like trying to remember a name on the tip of the tongue; no matter how hard he tried, it wouldn't come.

"Anthill, this is Crown. Status report," he murmured into the mike sewn into the collar of his uniform.

Major Nixon replied, "Crown, Anthill. All units report green. Exception: Eagle Three. They are still silent in condition Red One. Tresca is in contact with the office building and estimates shutdown of the transmitter in two minutes. Auxiliary units report ready."

"Understood, Anthill. We're approaching the museum now." He frowned and then decided to trust his instinct. "Anthill, I am authorising an increase of one alert level, across the board."

Back in the command post, Major Nixon and Corporal Tresca looked at each other across the room. They were both long-time members of the Colonel's command, and had learned to trust his hunches. Still, there was protocol to follow. "Crown, this is Anthill. Confirm Alert Plus One All."

"Confirm Alert Plus One All, Anthill. I've got a feeling."

The car slowed even further as it pulled up in front of *le Centre de la Vieille Charité*, an old stone building that had once been a hospice and now housed an excellent museum of Mediterranean history. Evelynne sighed as she looked out of her rolling fishbowl at the group of people waiting to greet her at the top of the stairs and resisted the urge to curl her mouth into a set of fish lips. "Well, here we go again," she sighed.

Sir Arthur smiled at his charge in the rear view mirror. "Here we go again, Your Highness." He spoke one last time into his mike, "Crown is exiting the vehicle."

❧ ❧ ❧ ❧ ❧

"Well, we're definitely getting close," Chorus commented. "Come on, let's try to get just a little nearer," he suggested, keeping a grip on Alleandre's hand. Not that she really needed him to help her through the mass of people, he reminded himself, but old habits died hard.

The crowd, while peaceful, was still enthusiastic, which made for a steadily increasing concentration in both density and energy. The police manning the barricades remained alert, though the spectators were well behaved.

Suddenly the two friends found themselves against a barricade, mere feet from the road and less than fifteen metres from the steps of the museum. "Wow, this is great!" enthused Chorus. "We can see everything from here!" He turned a suspicious gaze on his companion.

Ally noticed. "Hey, I didn't do anything," she protested. "We're just lucky to get this spot. Honest."

Chorus looked sceptical, but decided to take her at her word. "Look," he said, pointing up the street. He almost had to shout over the noise of enthusiastic onlookers, to which was now added the wail of approaching police sirens. "I think that's them."

Sure enough, behind an escort of three police motorcycles, a blue convertible rolled into view, bearing the white and blue flag and circle-cross of Atlantis and surrounded by six people in blue uniforms, five men and a woman who jogged alongside the car as it moved. Unlike a real convertible, however, the car was fitted with a plexiglass canopy within which three people were sitting. The driver was dressed in a smart blue uniform and looked decidedly military, though his face was unremarkable. The other man in the front seat was very distinctive, with a body shaped as though some god had taken an ordinary man and then pushed down on his head so that he was almost as wide as he was tall. His face wore a forbidding expression and Ally could see his lips moving as he talked.

Both of these people, however, paled beside the young woman smiling and waving in the back seat. As the vehicle passed to pull up in front of the museum steps, Ally caught a glimpse of a vision of flaming red hair surmounting a strong, yet delicate face, exotically painted, with a wide, generous mouth. In the few seconds it took for the car to drive past her and Chorus, Ally could have sworn that the princess' eyes met hers

chapter one

with an almost audible click and Ally found herself waving, without ever remembering raising her arm.

Then the royal vehicle was past, pulling up to a stop several metres away and a number of important-looking people started moving towards the car.

Chorus turned to his partner with a low whistle on his lips. "Wow, did you see her? She is *hot*!"

"She's gorgeous . . ." Alleandre murmured, before looking up at her friend. "I mean," she said, flustered, "I've seen her in pictures before, but she looks better in person. That is—" She glanced back in the direction of the car, then back at her friend. "Oh, shut up," she muttered, looking anywhere but at him.

Chorus just smirked. "So, going ogling was a good idea, eh? Come on, you can say it."

"Fine," she grumbled, still avoiding his face. "Ogling was a good—" Alleandre broke off suddenly, her eyes fixed on the top of a building across the street.

❧ ❧ ❧ ❧ ❧

The car pulled up in front of the museum. Evelynne said a little prayer of thanksgiving as the sirens of the police escorts were finally silenced and Sir Arthur exited, walking around the car to open the princess' door. Looking up through the canopy at the brilliant blue sky, she made one last bid for freedom.

"Jose," she addressed her driver, "how about just swinging this car around and heading out of the city? We can head for one of those lovely beaches just down the coast. Come on, what do you say? Sir 'Protocol' Arthur, here, refuses to let me go."

"I'm sorry, Your Highness. I think he'd shoot me if I tried."

"We're surrounded by a quarter-inch of bulletproof glass," Evelynne said. "Besides, if you do I'll give you his job."

Incredulous eyes stared at her in the mirror. "I'm sorry, Your Highness, is that supposed to be an incentive?"

Evelynne was still smiling broadly as she was assisted from the car by Sir Arthur, but Jose could hear her cursing him under her breath as she got out.

"Traitorous coward," she murmured. It was the mildest of her epithets.

Sir Arthur's eyebrows rose as he helped his ward out of the convertible. "Should I be worried, Your Highness?" he asked in a low voice.

Evelynne sighed. "No, I'm just adding another name to my List," she explained. She gave him a brief grin before slowly walking forward to meet the Mayor and other dignitaries who had assembled to greet the Atlantlan Heir.

Her bodyguard let her move a few paces ahead as he fell back into a less obtrusive position, his eyes never ceasing to sweep the crowd. He observed the other members of the Heir's Guard with approval as they likewise kept a vigilant watch for any trouble. His earbud gave the soft chime signifying a transmission from the control centre.

"Crown, this is Anthill. We have shut down the transmitter. Attempting to contact Eagle Three now." The following silence seemed to last forever as Sir Arthur's inexplicable unease grew stronger. The relief when his earbud chimed again was short-lived. "Crown, we cannot raise Eagle Three," came Major Nixon's calm voice. Only years of association let Sir Arthur detect the faint worry in it. "We are trying aga-"

And Sir Arthur *knew*. He didn't know how he knew, but he *knew*. Eagle Three was dead, and the danger directed at his charge was only moments away. The knowledge flashed through his brain in a split second and training took over as he bellowed into his open mike, "Zulu! Zulu! Zulu!"

He saw the members of his team, startled in spite of their vigilance for the briefest of moments, cursed the too-small body armour restricting his movements and slowing him, knew it was too late and saw something moving at incredible speed from the crowds on his left towards Princess Evelynne, just as the first shot rang out.

      ફ   ફ   ફ   ફ   ફ

The surrounding crowd, the police watching them, the sunshine, Chorus: they all disappeared as Alleandre's entire concentration centred on the two small figures on top of the office building. With preternatural clarity she saw them looking down through telescopic sights at the dignitaries below. She reached out with her mind and, in an instant, heard their thoughts, knew their target below, and felt a finger begin to pull a trigger. Only one would fire, she knew, the other saving her fire for the unlikely event that the first assassin missed.

The mental connection snapped suddenly, as it always did, but Alleandre was already reacting. The rest of the world rushed back into her consciousness as she desperately focussed her mind on the distant weapon and channelled. It was at extreme range, but the force needed was small, simply requiring the rifle barrel to move a few inches; Ally knew it had worked when the 'pop' of the gunshot echoed simultaneously with a louder 'crack' as the bullet struck the stone of the building instead of its intended red-haired target.

chapter one

There was no time for triumph, however, as Alleandre had already focussed again, this time on herself, channelling energy, propelling herself over the police barricade towards the young woman. Ally felt the strain, as she pushed herself harder than she ever had needed to before, but grimly persevered. She literally flew past a large, bulky man who was already turning towards the princess, his hand reaching into his jacket. *The bodyguard*, a part of Ally's mind recognised.

The princess was still ducking instinctively when Alleandre careened into her, sending her onto her back with a thump that knocked the breath out of her, just as a second bullet tore through the space where she had been a moment before. The bullet took a large chunk out of the stone step nearby. Then Evelynne's startled blue eyes were looking up into Alleandre's grey ones, and the princess was caught by their intensity, aware of the press of the body above her.

Even as she acknowledged that the body beneath her seemed to be largely unhurt, Alleandre's mind was already focussing one more time, this time reaching for an ability that she had developed mere weeks before. She channelled desperately, weaving her energy into an aura around her body, less than an inch from her skin. She held strongly to the focus, feeling it snap into place with a strength she could feel in her chest, just as the third bullet arrived.

Alleandre felt the impact of the bullet between her shoulder blades, gratified when the aura held and stopped the projectile, leaving it lying against her shirt. Her satisfaction lasted a fraction of a second, however, as she felt yet another bullet pass through her aura. Though its force was considerably attenuated by her aura, it still had more than enough energy to penetrate her skin and burning pain erupted through Alleandre's right shoulder. Through the haze of pain, Ally saw an answering expression of agony bloom on the face of the princess and realised that the bullet had passed right through her own body and into the one below her.

Fighting to remain conscious, Ally struggled to maintain her focus, and felt a last bullet enter her aura, just before an explosion of agony in the middle of her back dragged her down into oblivion.

chapter two

Evelynne lay in the back seat of the car and listened to the wail of the siren and blare of the horn as she was sped toward the hospital. The reassuring bulk of Sir Arthur's body was under her head as he cradled her, murmuring assurance and keeping a steady pressure on her left shoulder. The princess was vaguely aware that her wounded shoulder was hurting more than she could ever remember anything hurting before, but the pain was strangely distant, as if muffled.

I'm in shock, she thought calmly. *It is a rather . . . unpleasant sensation.* Looking up at the blue sky, she reflected, *It's very . . . bright. So that's what it's like to get shot.*

With extreme clarity, Evelynne's memory replayed the preceding events.

Getting out of the car aided by Uncle Arthur. Feeling his hand give hers a reassuring squeeze before directing her towards the waiting dignitaries. Looking up at them, seeing the genuinely welcoming smile on the face of Mayor Dubois as he starts down the steps to meet her. Offering her hand to shake, seeing the twinkle in his eye as he brings it up to kiss the back. Turning to greet his wife as he introduces them.

Hearing with shocking suddenness Uncle Arthur's voice bellowing the ultimate code word, "Zulu, Zulu, Zulu." Zulu: imminent terminal threat to the protectee. Immediate Red Three authorisation. The thought barely registering before the step not two metres away seems to explode with a crack, showering the area with stone chips. Turning instinctively towards her bodyguard, barely noticing a large shape moving rapidly toward her. Feeling the sudden impact of the shape with her chest. Falling backwards, sudden shortness of breath as the wind is knocked out of her. Hearing an odd whistle just before another step explodes, much closer this time. Experiencing real fear now. The warm pressure of another body above hers. Looking up into incredibly intense grey eyes, the fear disappearing immediately, leaving behind a totally illogical sensation of complete safety. Cinnamon. A weird prickling sensation running over her skin, followed by a grunt from the person on top of her. I saw her in the crowd. *Seeing the jaw clench, and renewed determination etch the soft-featured face above. Then a choked-off scream—her own, as pain explodes in her left shoulder. Seeing the pale face, inches from hers and the intense focus in the grey eyes falter, then renew for an instant. The person above her stiffens momentarily, as the eyes go blank with shocking suddenness and then is a limp weight, crushing her.* Please don't die.

Oddly, her memories after that point were much less clear. Evelynne vaguely recalled the weight being rolled off her, though she had tried desperately to hold onto the warmth and security. Then Uncle Arthur was there, asking her something she couldn't make out. The next thing she knew she was in the car, looking up into the warm sunshine.

I knew we should have gone to the beach, she thought fuzzily. There was something wrong with the thought, though. *But then I wouldn't have met her.* Her thoughts seemed to be coming slower now and the pain was steadily increasing. *Shock's wearing off. I don't think I want to be around when it goes. Maybe I'll sleep now. Tired.* She could hear, from far away, Uncle Arthur's voice urging her to stay awake but couldn't seem to find the energy to respond as she slipped into unconsciousness. *Please don't die.*

❧ ❧ ❧ ❧ ❧

Jean, the elderly on-duty security guard at *l'Hôpital Métropolitain de Marseilles*, had never expected to receive the call to clear out the trauma rooms—now. Still, he had rallied and had complied with commendable efficiency. Not that it had been easy. The patients, along with some of the staff, had naturally picked up on the tension running through the guards and rapidly-arriving police, and the security staff had been forced to remove a few of them bodily. Still, the trauma room was now clear and just in time, as the first of the police escorts pulled up, closely followed by the Royal car.

Nurses helped Sir Arthur manoeuvre the princess' limp body onto a stretcher. Dr. Martin, on call for just this kind of emergency, demanded an immediate report from the bodyguard.

"Single gunshot wound to the upper left quadrant," Sir Arthur said concisely and gruffly. "Entry and exit wounds seem fairly clean. Looks like it went right through."

Dr. Martin noted his patient's pallid complexion and quick, shallow breaths. "When did she lose consciousness?"

"Two and a half minutes ago. She looked like she was going into shock before then."

The doctor nodded. "Probably. What type of bullet was it?"

"Unknown. It came from a sniper rifle of some kind, though, and a couple of others took chunks out of the museum. Large calibre."

chapter two

They had arrived in one of the operating theatres. One nurse fixed an oxygen mask over the unconscious woman's nose and mouth; another began to draw blood, while a third began to cut away her long blue dress.

"I heard there's another GSW coming in?" Dr. Martin asked, while shining a light into Evelynne's eyes.

Sir Arthur nodded, though Dr. Martin wasn't looking. "Someone knocked Her Highness down and then shielded her with her body."

"One of your men?"

"No, a civilian. Female. It looks like the bullet went through them both."

The doctor's head came up at that. "*Merde*, a hero. I hate heroes." At Sir Arthur's questioning look, he explained, "Heroes always die so easily."

After that Dr. Martin ignored Sir Arthur to direct his full attention to his patient. The bodyguard looked on for a moment, then, satisfied that his charge was in adequate hands, beckoned to two other Guardsmen standing nearby and ordered them to remain on full alert with the princess. As the Guardsmen took up their posts, Sir Arthur made his way towards the hospital entrance, as an ambulance pulled up, bearing the mysterious heroine.

As he moved, a loose, flapping sensation around his lower back reminded Sir Arthur that one of the fastenings on his borrowed armour had finally given way under stress. The reminder just added to his already foul mood. *When I find out who lost my suit, I swear to God they're going to be guarding the bilges—from the inside—on the dirtiest, most decrepit garbage scow I can find until Atlantl rises again.*

The unknown woman was just being unloaded from the ambulance by another team of paramedics, and the Guardsman was shocked at how small she looked. He hadn't got a good look at her at the museum, since his focus had been purely on getting Evelynne to the car, but now he was able to see and analyse. She was a tall woman, probably six feet, but her slenderness could be seen in her arms and legs, which were exposed by the shorts and T-shirt she wore. He wasn't able to see the woman's face, since she was currently strapped tightly facedown to a board. The reason was horribly evident in her wounds.

The hole in her right shoulder Sir Arthur knew to be a match to the one in Evelynne's left. Its rate of bleeding was being controlled by a paramedic applying pressure to it. The other bullet wound had been left to bleed almost freely, with only a light bandage applied to control it, and the location made Sir Arthur wince. The bullet had entered right in the middle of her lower back, and the bodyguard had seen and treated enough battlefield wounds to know why nobody was trying to staunch the bleeding. *If the bullet's still in* there, or if the spine is broken, any pressure will definitely sever the spinal cord. A lot of blood had been lost, if the gurney's sheets were anything to go by. *Blood can be replaced,* thought Sir Arthur pragmatically. *Spines cannot.*

As the group of medical staff rushed in through the doors, Sir Arthur stepped up to Lieutenant Martinez, who had ridden in the ambulance. "Susan, what do you have for me? Who is she?"

Martinez could only shrug her shoulders and spread her hands helplessly. "Chief, I don't know. She's about one point eight metres, sixty kilograms, brown hair, grey eyes, early twenties. That's all I could tell just by looking at her." She shrugged again at her superior's raised eyebrow. "No ID, no driver's licence, no passport, nothing. She had about 28 Euros in her pocket and a receipt from a restaurant where she apparently had breakfast this morning. That's it. Everything else is what you saw."

"*Paka!*" Sir Arthur swore. "Just what I need." He pinched the bridge of his nose. "A *fretin* Jane Doe hero."

"Yes, sir," Martinez said, with a half-smile of grim sympathy. "How is Princess Evelynne, sir?" she asked in a lower voice, real concern in her words.

"I'm not sure. They were just examining her a few minutes ago. I'm going to find out. Follow me," he ordered, turning and marching back inside.

They met Dr. Martin coming the other way. The doctor held up a hand before they could speak. "She's going to be fine. The bullet passed cleanly through her shoulder. There was some blood loss and muscle damage, but no arteries were nicked and no bones were broken." He indicated the window through which they could see the princess being prepared to be moved. "We're taking her up for some scans right now, just as a precaution." Dr. Martin quickly forestalled Sir Arthur's question. "Don't worry, the area's been secured."

Sir Arthur and Lieutenant Martinez both relaxed minutely. "What about Jane Doe?" asked Martinez. At the doctor's blank look, she explained, "The mystery woman."

The doctor shook his head. "I don't know. She's been taken up to the operating room already. I've also ordered full blood and viral workups, including AIDS tests on both of them, since there was some blood transfer." A nurse waved to attract the doctor's attention. "If you'll excuse me, I have to go."

The doctor walked briskly away as Sir Arthur let out an explosive sigh, then turned to Martinez. "Susan, I'm assigning you to Jane Doe for now. Stick with her. Get a couple of Guards to relieve you when needed. I want to talk to her as soon as she wakes up. Go."

chapter two

Martinez sketched a salute and turned to leave, but paused as Sir Arthur spoke again. "And Susan? Remember that she did our job for us today. You know what that means."

The Lieutenant did. Jane Doe had just been adopted.

☙ ☙ ☙ ☙ ☙

The hospital chair was, naturally, hard and uncomfortable, but Sir Arthur had endured much worse things in his career and ignored it as he kept a tired watch over his charge. She lay on a simple bed, as an intravenous line fed medication into her system and a battery of leads monitored her vital signs. Sir Arthur wearily watched the screen of the silenced monitor as it displayed reassuring information on Evelynne's pulse rate, respiration and blood pressure.

At least he had managed to get out of the blasted body armour. Though it was technically against procedure, the Guard figured that if anyone was well-equipped enough to get to him through the fourteen other Guardsmen outside, a simple body suit wouldn't be enough to make much difference. Sir Arthur had also managed to catch an hour's sleep, nodding off in the hospital chapel when he went there to pray.

Evelynne's lady-in-waiting, Maïda, had been safely installed on a cot nearby, where she was now sleeping. She had been escorted into the princess' room after bullying her way through six members of the Heir's Guard. Upon seeing her ward, she had burst into tears, and Sir Arthur had been forced to hold her and awkwardly console her as she cried herself out. Then she had pulled herself together and taken charge of the more domestic details, bringing a few flowers into the otherwise stark room and arranging for food to be delivered to the Guardsmen still on duty. She had forced Sir Arthur to eat; her forbidding expression had left the Knight unwilling to resist her. She could give drill sergeants instruction in intimidation if she wanted. Eventually, though, she had succumbed to the lure of sleep.

Knowing himself to be at less than optimum efficiency, Sir Arthur had handed over the preliminary investigation to "Dicky" Nixon. So far she had only reported what he already knew. One would-be assassin was dead, taken out by a quick-thinking member of Eagle Two. The other assassin was presumed wounded, based on blood found at the scene, but had managed to escape. That was bad enough, but the two Guardsmen of Eagle Three, Sergeant al-Latif and Corporal Garner, were dead–shot at close range from behind–the person he was charged to protect with his life had been saved by an unknown civilian, and both of *them* were wounded. Now, at 7:30 in the morning the day after the attack, the only thing he was truly grateful for was that both were in stable condition, though Jane Doe's situation was still serious.

He sat in the spartan hospital room and prayed earnestly as he watched Princess Evelynne sleep. *God, Evelynne almost died yesterday. I ask that You watch over her and heal her. Our Father, Who art in Heaven . . .*

A light knock on the door announced the arrival of Major Nixon, who peered into the room. Sir Arthur ignored her until his final *Amen* and then joined her outside in the waiting room where a television was playing silently. Sir Arthur watched as the screen showed a scene of large numbers of people placing flowers at the gates of a building. The caption read *Londres, Angleterre* and the Guardsman recognised the Atlantlan Embassy. The scene shifted to another, almost identical, but this time the caption identified Berlin, Germany.

"It's been like that all morning," the Major said quietly. "There are rumours that Her Highness is dead."

"She isn't." Sir Arthur's tone was challenging. "And she won't be."

"I know, sir. It's just the media. An assassination's more sensational. Even the States have toned down their usual anti-Atlantlan rhetoric. CNN still managed to imply that it could have been rebels out to topple our government, though."

"Government or regime?"

"Sir?"

"Listen to the words they use. Calling it a government or administration means that it's good and friendly; they're being diplomatic. A regime is evil and hostile." He shrugged. "Semantics. Technically they both mean the same thing."

"Ah, so for the Americans it's the British government, the German government, the Japanese government . . ."

". . . the Cuban regime, the Iranian regime, the Atlantlan regime. A subtle, but rather clever, form of propaganda."

"Except, of course, that only one's enemy uses propaganda. One's own government publishes only the truth."

Sir Arthur smiled for the first time in what seemed like forever, and patted Major Nixon carefully on the shoulder, mindful of their relative masses. "Now you're learning. I'll make a stateswoman out of you yet." Turning serious once more, he asked, "So, what do you have for me, Dicky?"

"Not much yet. The dead shooter is a white male, no identification. We're working on it. The biggest question I have comes from our preliminary ballistics report." Dicky held out a file, but Sir Arthur waved it away and gestured her to continue. "Chief, why aren't they dead?"

chapter two

Her superior's eyes snapped to hers. "What the hell do you mean, Major?"

"I mean that according to what we know, they shouldn't be alive. The recovered weapon is a modified Israeli-made 7.62 mm Galil sniper rifle. It's easy enough to obtain and even modify on the black market. It fired rounds that were likely custom made; some kind of bound hollow-point. We ran a test at the precinct, fired a round at an inch of armour steel. Chief, we had to dig the bullet we fired out of the wall behind the plate."

For the first time since she had known him, Dicky saw Sir Arthur's face display naked shock. "*Jesu Christe*," he whispered.

"That's not all, Chief," Major Nixon continued.

"Isn't that enough?"

The Major's smile was tight. "Not quite. The gun was equipped with an ultraviolet laser targeting scope. There should have been absolutely no way the shooter could have missed the first time." She took a deep breath. "In short, Chief, instead of lying in bed recovering, both of them should be lying in a morgue with holes in them big enough to put your fist through."

Sir Arthur shook his head in an attempt to rid himself of the horror of that image. "Well, however it happened, I'm glad they're not. Needless to say, I'll want absolutely everything for my report. Do you have any clue who our Jane is?"

"Not yet. Nobody matching her description has been reported missing so far, although the police stations are chaotic."

"Well, keep trying. You know where to find me."

❧ ❧ ❧ ❧ ❧

Evelynne deMolay swam reluctantly upwards towards consciousness. She groggily knew that waking would bring pain, and light, and noise, and it was very tempting to remain oblivious. She opened her eyes.

Oh, God. Yes, there it was: a dull persistent throbbing throughout her shoulder, bright fluorescent lights stabbing through her brain and the noise ... Actually, it was blessedly quiet, which the princess welcomed with relief. Still, the other two elements more than made up for the lack of one and she couldn't hold back a soft groan as a slight movement changed the throb to a stab.

Instantly, a face appeared in her field of vision, fuzzy at first, then resolving into Maïda's visage. A moment later, Evelynne recognised her bodyguard's face as it appeared before her as well. Maïda's eyes were damp with tears, and even Sir Arthur's normally impassive face bore a very slight expression of relief.

"Highness?"

"Evelynne, are you awake?"

Both of the faces spoke simultaneously, shattering the blessed silence.

"Oh, Isis," Evelynne croaked. "I'm dead. I'm in hell and I have two of my very own personal demons to torment me for eternity."

On cue, Maïda snorted. It was a weak snort at best, though, as she buried her face in Evelynne's uninjured right shoulder and held her tightly.

Sir Arthur's voice was suspiciously husky. "Evy, how do you feel?"

"Ouch. Did you catch the *sa-kim* that skewered me? What happened anyway?" Suddenly, the entire memory came flooding back. "Is everyone else okay? Did anyone die? Is the cinnamon woman all right? Do you know who she is?"

Maïda's head came up. "Cinnamon woman?"

Evelynne blushed unaccountably. "The woman who saved me," she explained. "She smelled like cinnamon."

Sir Arthur spoke calmly. "No civilians were killed," he said, deciding not to burden her with the knowledge of the two Guardsmen's deaths just yet. "The Mayor's wife was cut by some flying chips of stone and a few people were hurt in the panic, but nothing serious. You were hit once," gesturing to her shoulder. "As for the woman, we still don't know who she is. She had no identification. She was hit twice, once in the shoulder and once in the back." Seeing Evelynne's distressed expression, he strove to reassure her. "She's stable for now. The bullet to the shoulder went through with minimal damage–" He still wasn't sure how that was possible given the ballistics report. "–and the other barely grazed her spine." The princess paled. "There's still swelling against her spine and it's too soon to know exactly what the long-term damage will be, but the doctors are optimistic. Unfortunately, she's still in a coma." He didn't mention that neurological tests seemed to indicate some kind of *grand mal* seizure had taken place, a finding that had greatly puzzled the neurology specialist.

An older woman doctor entered just then, in response to Sir Arthur's earlier summons. She had a kind, motherly air, reminding Evelynne of a slightly younger, thinner and taller Maïda, and smiled as she noticed that her patient was awake. "Your Highness, it's good to see you with you eyes open. I am Dr. Corbeil. I've been looking forward to meeting you. *Naturellement*, I would have liked it to be under better circumstances. How are you feeling?"

"I hurt, I'm scared and I'm tired. When can I get up?"

Dr. Corbeil looked taken aback by the abrupt question. "Get up, Your Highness? You've only been in that bed for twelve hours and it's been less than twenty-four since you were sh–injured. I really prefer if you could stay here for a while yet. Maybe get some more slee–"

chapter two

"And I'd prefer to get up and see the woman who saved my life yesterday." Evelynne's temper, normally mild, flared.

"Highness," Maïda tried to calm her. "Please, you were seriously hurt yesterday. Rest for a while. When the doctor says it's safe—"

Evelynne interrupted, "Please, Maï-ma. I need to see her." She turned to Dr. Corbeil. "Please. I need to know she's safe."

Maïda turned to the doctor, but any further discussion was interrupted by Sir Arthur's barked, "What?" Waving a hand to still the other occupants of the room, he turned his attention back to his earbud. "Say again . . . you're sure? It's confirmed? The British Consulate? Good . . . you've searched him? Fine, bring him up to her room. I'll meet you there." Turning back to the room, he addressed three pairs of curious eyes. "Well, one mystery may be solved. Someone has arrived who claims to be able to identify our Jane Doe. I'm going to meet him now." Pointing a stern finger at Evelynne, he ordered, "You are not getting out of that bed until the doctor says so." At her imminent protest, he raised a hand and shook his head. "In this situation, I outrank you, Highness." Pointing at the doctor, he continued, "And she outranks me. She's in charge."

Evelynne was devastated. *I need to see her. It's important. I don't know why, but it is.* She looked up to plead her case with Dr. Corbeil once more as Maïda finished a whispered consultation with the doctor.

"I think we can work out a compromise," Dr. Corbeil said.

ഊ ഊ ഊ ഊ ഊ

Princess Evelynne lay back and tried to look as dignified as possible. She still felt foolish and was sure she looked as ridiculous as she felt, being pushed down the corridor by two of her Guardsmen, safely ensconced in her hospital bed. *Isis, I feel like I'm on some kind of royal palanquin. All I need now are two fan-wavers and a bunch of scantily clad young slaves feeding me grapes.*

The doctor's compromise had been simple: move the princess to the same room as the soon-to-be-identified woman, which was more than large enough to accommodate them both. Sir Arthur had bristled at first, but had been persuaded when Evelynne pointed out that it was easier to guard one room than two.

Up the corridor ahead she could see the Master of her Guard talking to a distinguished looking young man in a business suit, and a well-built dark-skinned man with a distinctly worried look. In contrast to the smartly dressed people around him, he was wearing shorts and a rumpled T-shirt, which looked as though he had slept in them. As she was pushed closer, Evelynne caught the tail end of their conversation.

"–and so I'll let you get on with trying to contact them," Sir Arthur was saying to the man in the business suit. "Just remember, absolutely no press releases until we authorise them. Understood?"

Assuring Sir Arthur of his discretion, the man shook his hand and was escorted out by a Guard.

Turning to the other man, Sir Arthur caught sight of Evelynne's little procession and addressed her instead. "Your Highness, this gentleman claims to be a friend of our young heroine. May I introduce–I'm sorry, sir, I'm afraid I missed your full name."

The black man smiled. "My full name? Keitumetsemosimanewapula Tladi." At his audience's stunned expressions, he conceded, "Please, call me Chorus. Everyone else does."

"I certainly will," Evelynne murmured. Shaking her head, she asked, "You say you know . . ."

"Her name is Alleandre Tretiak."

"Tretiak?" Maïda questioned. "That doesn't sound like a French name."

"It isn't," replied Sir Arthur, holding up a passport. "She's a Canadian, visiting as a tourist. According to Mr Tladi, here and the number of stamps in her passport, she's taking a trip around the world."

Addressing Chorus again, Evelynne said, "You're travelling with her?"

"Yes, ma'am–I'm sorry, is there some title I should be calling you by?"

The princess actually chuckled, despite the pain that flared when she did so. "As you can see," she said, indicating with her right arm her still bedridden position, "I am hardly at my most regal at the moment. I think we can dispense with the formalities for now." Both Maïda and Chorus smiled at that and the Guardsmen stifled smiles, though Sir Arthur looked vaguely disapproving. "You were travelling with . . . Alleandre? Are you her husband?"

The question surprised a laugh out of Chorus. "Goodness, no! Ally's a l–lovely friend I met up with a few countries back," he finished awkwardly.

The answer made Evelynne feel better for some reason. "Good," she said. "I mean it's good that you're her friend. Otherwise we still wouldn't know who she is."

Chorus smiled self-deprecatingly. "It took me long enough to get here. When I realised I had all Ally's ID, I went to the police, but the stations are really busy right now for some reason. After getting the run-around for six hours, I went to the British Consulate, but of course they were closed by then. I managed to get back just as they opened, and they got in touch with

chapter two

your staff here." He swallowed, looking guilty. "I'm sorry I didn't get here sooner."

"The Consulate will inform the Canadian Embassy in Paris and try to contact Ms. Tretiak's parents," Sir Arthur added. "In the meantime, though, I'd like to get you settled into your new room, Your Highness." A glance at the doctor, who had been silent throughout the exchange, was met by a firm nod. "Good, then let's get you out of this hallway. Her Highness has asked to be put in the same room as Ms. Tretiak," he explained to Chorus. "She's right through here."

☙ ☙ ☙ ☙ ☙

The first thing Evelynne noticed about the silent body in the bed was the lack of vitality. Gone was the intense, vibrant woman who had protected the princess with her own body. In her place was this pale shell, somehow smaller than her six feet of height. She was thin, Evelynne saw, made even thinner by the stark white expanse of the bed and the machines monitoring her life signs. Tubes leading from an oxygen tank entered her small nose and her short brown hair was unkempt. Evelynne had a strong desire to comb it with her fingers. Alleandre Tretiak would never be considered classically beautiful, especially now, but . . .

There was still something there, some ineffable energy, some underlying force of will, which told anyone looking that the woman was still there, underneath it all, just waiting for the right time to emerge.

"Oh, the poor child," breathed Maïda and Evelynne realised that the woman in the bed was indeed young, probably near Evelynne's own age.

"How old is she?" Evelynne asked Chorus quietly.

"She turned twenty last month," he replied in a hoarse voice. His eyes glistened with tears. "We were in Athens. I actually persuaded her to go out to the *tavernae* and nightclubs. She got absolutely plastered on ouzo." He wiped a hand across his eyes. "Jesus, Ally, you always have to be the fucking hero, don't you?" Maïda frowned at him. "Pardon the language."

Evelynne's bed was placed to the left of Ally's, leaving about four feet between them.

"You really should sleep, Your Highness," Dr. Corbeil urged.

Evelynne wanted to protest, but could feel her already depleted energy ebbing away.

"Rest. We'll let you know when she wakes up."

Evelynne muttered a sleepy acquiescence and dropped into sleep, listening to the reassuring sound of breathing in the bed nearby.

chapter three

When Evelynne woke again, the room had been transformed. While still lacking a window–Sir Arthur wasn't about to put his charge anywhere she could be seen easily–Maïda, at the head of a small army of conscripted hospital employees, had managed to turn the sick room into something closer to a hotel room. Care had been taken to keep the vital monitors and other medical equipment clear, but some pictures and a few discreet vases of flowers added much-needed colour to the previously bare room.

Evelynne was surprised that it had all been done without waking her and even more surprised when she glanced at the clock on the wall to find that a full day had passed since she had closed her eyes.

Her first action on waking was to check on the young woman in the bed beside her. She was gratified to see a bit more colour in Alleandre's well-tanned face and that the energy that had seemed so hidden before seemed stronger and closer to the surface. It also looked as though the young woman's brown hair had been combed and Evelynne was oddly disappointed that she hadn't been able to do it herself. *Maïda again,* she guessed, puzzled at her own reaction.

The Guard sitting beside the door noticed that the princess was awake and spoke softly into her collar mike. The speed with which Sir Arthur and Dr. Corbeil entered the room made Evelynne think that they had been just outside. Her bodyguard looked as though he had been able to rest in the last twenty-four hours, as well as change into a new uniform. His freshly shaved face, though still lined with stress, looked marginally more relaxed.

"Your Highness," greeted Sir Arthur, and the relief in his voice, though almost inaudible, came through clearly for someone who knew him as well as she did. "It is very good to see you with us again. Dr. Corbeil and I were just discussing your recovery," he said, confirming her suspicion.

"*Oui,* Your Highness. I'd like to check your injury again right now, if that is all right."

"I suppose so," Evelynne said, wincing as the wound in her shoulder reminded her of its presence.

"Also, Your Highness, your father called several times while you were asleep," Sir Arthur added. "He has expressed his wish to speak with you as soon as you are able. With your permission, I will set up the call immediately."

The princess' response was immediate. "Please, yes. I want—I need to talk to him."

Sir Arthur nodded his head. "Certainly, Your Highness. We should be ready by the time the doctor has finished her examination. I will bring the equipment here." He quickly took his leave.

Taking her mind off the upcoming talk with her father, Evelynne turned her eyes to the still, silent figure of Alleandre beside her. The doctor was carefully removing the bandage from Evelynne's shoulder when the princess asked in a soft voice, "Is she going to be okay?"

Dr. Corbeil spared a compassionate glance at the woman in question. "I believe so, Your Highness. Ms. Tretiak is a very lucky girl. There does not appear to be any damage to her spinal cord, although there is still some swelling around the wound. Doctor Riel believes she will recover fully, but any injury involving the spine is uncertain. We will know more when she wakes from the coma." At Evelynne's entreating gaze, she said gently, "I'm afraid we have no way of predicting when that will be, Your Highness. She will wake when she wakes."

"Has anyone—Ouch!—talked to her parents?" Evelynne asked.

"I'm not sure, Your Highness." The doctor carefully probed the wound, wincing in sympathy at the pain it was causing. "The young man who identified her has been back several times. He appears very concerned." A strangled gasp escaped her patient as the doctor touched a particularly sensitive area. "I'm sorry, Your Highness. I'm going to rebandage you now."

Evelynne's breath was coming in sharp gasps as Dr. Corbeil wrapped her shoulder again. Finally it was done and the princess relaxed with a sigh. "Would you like a painkiller?" the doctor asked.

"Ugh. No, I'll live."

"Indeed, Your Highness," the doctor mimicked Sir Arthur's words, just as Evelynne's bodyguard re-entered the room carrying a laptop computer and several accessories.

"I have everything here, Your Highness. I will set it up now."

Alleandre rose towards consciousness and almost gave up when the pain became too intense. Fighting the urge to give in to the welcoming darkness, she set about trying to contain the pain, controlling it. *Pain is a mechanism built into organisms by millions of years of evolution to inform us when something threatens our survival. It is a stimulus, information sent to my brain by my body. My*

chapter three

mind acknowledges the information and therefore takes away the brain's need to process it. Without processing, it is no longer pain, merely data. Data is painless. Pain is a mechanism . . . The mantra continued, as she worked to control her body's reactions, taking the pain and locking it into a corner of her mind, acknowledging its presence, but no longer considering it to be important. Then she was able to turn her thoughts to other things. It was a tricky balancing act. On the one hand, ignore the sensation too much and the control would slip as her concentration waned. On the other, too much attention would give the pain the power to move to the fore. Either way, the agony would cease to be an abstract concept and become a true sensation once again.

For the moment, though, the balance held, allowing Ally to take stock of her current situation. With her eyes still closed, she first concentrated on her body. Her head felt surprisingly clear, with only the barest hint of a headache. There was something in her nose and when she breathed in, the headache would subside slightly before she exhaled. *Oxygen, pure,* her brain translated. Her mouth felt anything but pure, though; more like a mass of Parmesan cheese that had been left long enough to evolve a complex civilisation. The civilisation had fallen and the rotting remains were lying in Ally's mouth. The disgusting sensation was relegated to the same corner of her mind as the pain and the young woman continued her analysis.

The data that her brain was translating into pain seemed to be centred around her right shoulder and Ally shied away from the area, deciding to leave it to last. The rest of her upper torso seemed to be fairly intact, though it ached in sympathy with her shoulder and it felt like there were several small objects stuck to her in various positions. Ally's right arm was strapped to her side and felt quite stiff. Her left arm was lying free on the bed and the back of her hand itched. A very slight movement of her fingers told Ally that there was foreign object stuck in her hand and she could feel it shifting slightly as she moved. *Needle, probably intravenous line,* she decided. Taking the data she had collected so far, she concluded, *Hospital.*

Moving farther down her body, Ally avoided another concentration of pain, this one in her back, and had to conclude that, other than this, her lower torso felt relatively whole. A most uncomfortable feeling in a very intimate spot left her confused until her mind extrapolated on *'Hospital'* and came up with *'Catheter'.* The acute embarrassment she felt threatened to disrupt the young woman's concentration, and she fought to keep it under control. *Of course it's a catheter. And before you start getting embarrassed about someone . . . seeing you, it was probably a doctor or nurse. A professional. Someone who's seen . . . that kind of thing thousands of times.* Ally wasn't sure if the last part made it better or worse.

Satisfied that her body was more or less functional, Ally turned her attention to external stimuli. Her ears picked up the sound of two people speaking softly nearby. Straining slightly, she was able to identify her friend Chorus' deep male voice, along with a lighter female one that was somehow familiar. Ally thought she recalled the female voice speaking to her at some point when she was asleep, though she couldn't remember the words. At the moment, both voices were engaged in conversation and Ally decided to listen for a while before revealing her awareness.

"So how did you get the name Chorus, anyway?" the woman was asking. "Don't get me wrong, I'm glad you have it, since I would never be able to keep Keitum–whatever straight all the time. But why 'Chorus'?"

Chorus laughed. "Keitum-whatever. Ally called me the exact same thing the first day we met. By the way, it's Keitumetsemosimaniwapula. In Setswana it means 'Thank you for the boy of the rain'. I was born during a thunderstorm. Which is funny, really, since my last name, Tladi, means 'thunder'. Doubly appropriate, I suppose. Anyway, when I was in elementary school in Botswana, my teacher was a British woman called Mrs. Douglas. She was asking us our names the first day and when she got to mine, she said, 'Goodness, it sounds like you have a chorus in there.' None of us knew what a chorus was at the time, but the nickname stuck."

The feminine voice giggled, immediately picking up Alleandre's spirits with its light, cheerful sound. "I can imagine. Well, if you see Mrs. Douglas again, tell her that the world thanks her."

Ally couldn't stand not knowing who the unknown voice belonged to and opened her eyes. Blinking rapidly at the sudden light, though it was actually quite dim, she tried in vain to focus her eyes. Two fuzzy figures–one dark, one light and topped with fire–were situated near the end of her bed. Ally assumed they were sitting, since they were both too low to be standing. The rest of the room was a uniform white, with blotches of blurry colour here and there.

Still blinking, Ally reflexively reached for her glasses.

Her low, choked scream instantly drew the attention of the two sitting figures. Both were at Ally's side a moment later, Chorus beating Evelynne, as the princess had to manoeuvre her wheelchair around the side of the bed.

"Ally, can you hear me?"

"Alleandre, what's wrong?" They spoke simultaneously.

Ally didn't answer them. Her eyes were shut tight, her entire body was tense and the tendons in her neck stood out as she bared her gritted teeth in a near soundless scream. Her breath came in short, sharp gasps.

chapter three

Chorus looked quickly over to Evelynne and blurted, "I'm getting the doctor." He was gone before he finished speaking, wrenching the door open and yelling for help.

Evelynne nodded, never taking her eyes off the woman before her. She held Ally's clenched left hand gently in her own. The force of Ally's fist had caused the IV needle to pull out and a small trickle of blood crept out from under the tape holding it in place. Sitting forward in her wheelchair, ignoring the strain it placed on her own wounded shoulder, Evelynne used her other hand to carefully stroke the distressed woman's forehead. She kept up a steady stream of comforting words. "Ally, it's okay. You're safe here. It'll be all right. The doctor's coming. Breathe, Ally . . ." The woman showed no signs of hearing her, and Evelynne had to hold back her own sobs as she saw tears leaking from between Ally's clenched eyelids.

It seemed like hours, but was really less than a minute before Dr. Corbeil swept into the room accompanied by a pair of nurses, Chorus and Lieutenant Susan Martinez, who had been on duty outside. Taking one look at the now crowded room, the doctor started barking orders. "You and you," she snapped, pointing at Chorus and Martinez, "out. You," she pointed at Evelynne, paused as though considering, then continued, "can stay. But move back; let us in."

Reluctantly, Evelynne let go of Alleandre's hand and backed her wheelchair out of the way, allowing a nurse to take her place. Ally was now keening softly in pain, punctuated by gasps for breath. Through her own tears the princess watched as the nurse performed a quick check of Ally's vitals.

"Pulse is 145, blood pressure is . . . off the chart."

"I can see. I think it might be a spasm. Help me lift her to check," Dr. Corbeil ordered. As gently as possible, the doctor and nurses rolled Alleandre part way onto her side, careful not to twist her spine. Quickly examining Ally's back with her fingers, the doctor shot off an order for some type of medication, the name of which Evelynne wasn't able to catch. A syringe was passed to the nurse on the left side of the bed and the contents were quickly injected into Ally's uninjured arm. "It's a combination of muscle relaxant and painkiller," the doctor explained to Evelynne, who was watching with worried eyes. "It should take effect very soon."

Sure enough, Alleandre seemed to be slowly relaxing. After a questioning glance to Dr. Corbeil for permission, Evelynne took up her post by Ally's side, once again taking hold of her hand and stroking it gently. The hand was no longer clenched so tightly and it relaxed further under Evelynne's ministrations. Ally's breath was slowly evening out into a more comfortable rhythm. As the minutes passed and the medication acted on the young woman's system, Dr. Corbeil watched her patient's vital signs carefully and Evelynne continued her comforting.

Finally, Alleandre relaxed completely and opened her eyes. Every muscle in her body pulsed with a dull ache and her throat felt raw, but at least the sensation of someone driving a red-hot spike into her head and down through her spine was gone. She had desperately tried to contain the pain, but it had been too much to control. Panicking, she had tried to fall back into unconsciousness, but even that had been denied her, remaining tantalisingly out of reach on the other side of an invisible wall. Finally, all conscious thought had fled, leaving behind only the pain.

Now thought had returned and Ally reluctantly opened her eyes. The first thing she saw were two blue eyes, made brilliant by the tears shimmering in them, looking into her own. They were close enough that Ally's nearsighted vision could make them out quite clearly, although the room behind was a group of fuzzy blobs. A feeling of *déjà vu* swept her. *I've seen those eyes before*, she thought, but her tired brain couldn't find the energy to make the connection. Ally briefly considered reaching out to just take the information from the mind behind the eyes in front of her, but couldn't. *No energy. Besides, it's against your rules.*

The owner of the eyes was speaking, and Ally forced herself to concentrate on the words. "Ally? Do you feel better?"

Evelynne wanted to kick herself for saying something so stupid. *She's no longer screaming in agony. Of course she feels better! Just don't ask her if she's okay. You know the answer to that one.* Her guilt chose that moment to cut in. *Yeah, she got shot saving your life.*

Princess Evelynne deMolay! Alleandre's memory finally identified the young redhead before her. She looked quite different without her makeup and with her mass of wavy flame-red hair tumbling across her shoulders. If anything, Ally thought, she was even more attractive out of her regalia. *Of course, she'd probably be even* more *attractive in nothing at all.* The thought slipped out before she could censor herself, letting Ally know that despite the damage to her body, her libido was still active and paying attention. *Shit, I've been spending too much time around Chorus.* Realising that she was staring, Ally sought to reassure the princess that she wasn't a vegetable. "Hello," she croaked, wincing at both the sound of her own voice and the pain that erupted in her throat. "Ouch." *Great, now you sound like an idiot. Way to go, Ally,* her libido mocked. The rest of Ally's mind, too tired to put up with it any more, told it to shut up.

The young woman's words had alerted the doctor, who now sought to capture Ally's attention with a gentle hand on her face. "*Bonjour*, Alleandre,"

chapter three

she said in a soft, concerned voice. Ally tore her eyes away from Evelynne's and peered blearily at the motherly sounding woman beside her. She was just too far away for Ally to make out her features. "Do you know where you are?"

Ally hesitated while her tired brain protestingly dredged up the answers. "H'spital," she whispered hoarsely. "M'seilles."

The blob above her seemed to smile. "Good. Now, do you know who you are?"

Even her tired brain found this one easy. "All'ndre Tr'tiak. Fr'm C'n'da." She turned her head back to Evelynne. "Hurts," she whispered. "Tired. Sl'p now. Stay," she mumbled as she let the blackness—not as deep as before, but more welcoming—pull her down.

Evelynne watched as Alleandre slipped back to sleep. "I'll be right here," she reassured the unconscious woman. "I'm not going anywhere." Still holding Ally's hand, she reached up to carefully tidy her brown, sweat-soaked hair. "I'll be here when you wake up."

Chapter Four

The second time Alleandre woke up, she was much more wary. She slowly rose out of unconsciousness, at each stage prepared to fall under again if necessary, but inexorably drawn by a soft voice speaking nearby. While a dull pain was still present, centred on the middle of the young woman's spine, the rest of her body felt surprisingly good. Not perfect, but definitely better than her last ill-fated trip to the land of the living.

Having finished her quick appraisal of her own well being, Ally turned her attention to her external surroundings. Still in the last layer between sleep and wakefulness, it took her a moment to decipher the meaning of the words she could hear. Whoever was speaking was just next to her, she realised. Slipping up the last level, which would allow comprehension, Ally listened to the soft, melodious voice and realised that the person—female, she recognised—was reading. It was obviously something humorous, as the reader chuckled, then continued.

Wanting to know the identity of the reader, but unwilling to stop the comforting murmur of words by revealing her awareness, Ally cautiously extended her mind, seeking the correct mental frame that would enable her to see. There was resistance, as she sought the correct shape. It was even more difficult than usual, the mental pathways feeling bruised and tender. *Well, of course they are. You tried to stop at least two bullets.* She vaguely remembered that now. *You're lucky they're not scraping your charred cerebellum off the inside of your skull with a spatula.* Shrugging the thought aside for now, Ally continued slowly expanding her perceptions.

Starting with the obvious sensory input—the voice beside her, the barely audible hum of fluorescent light, the feel of linen sheets, the faint but sharp smell of disinfectant—Ally's mind slowly built her a picture of her surroundings. Finally, after several false starts, the vague mental image slipped into a true vision of her environment.

Despite the fact that her eyes were still closed, the sight was clear and vivid. More clear and vivid, in fact, than her purely optical vision. Even after a year of practice, though, the image arriving in her mind was slightly skewed; nothing that Ally could specifically point out, but just a general feeling of oddness. Alleandre suspected that it was due to the images arriving directly in her visual cortex and bypassing her optic nerves, with their highly evolved adaptations for perspective and distance. The result was a picture where, instead of focussing on a single object, she had the strange sensation of looking at all the objects nearby at the same time. A slight shift in perspective would enable her to see the opposite side of an object—or, stranger still, both sides at the same time. The result felt decidedly unnatural and unreal.

Practice had taught Ally to adapt to, or at least ignore, the sensory shift, and once she was sure that the sight was secure, she focussed her mental gaze on the young woman seated beside her. Fiery red hair tumbled around her slim shoulders. One arm, the left, was bound in a sling. She was seated in a wheelchair at the left side of Alleandre's bed. She was reading aloud from a small paperback book, awkwardly using only her right hand to turn the pages. There was another bed in the room, and its unmade state showed that it had been recently occupied.

The colour of the hair sparked a memory, of gentle words and hands in the aftermath of terrible pain. *Princess Evelynne,* Ally's brain supplied. *What was she doing here before? And why is she still here? Shouldn't she be surrounded by bodyguards or something?* A quick mental scan showed that, except for the two of them, there was no one in the room. *And what is she reading, anyway? It sounds familiar.* Shifting her perspective so that she could see the book, Ally got another surprise. *That's my book! It has that little torn bit in the corner. Why is the Heir to the Atlantean throne sitting in a wheelchair reading one of my own books to an unconscious woman in a hospital room?*

Alleandre could feel the strain that maintaining the sight was placing on her energy. Deciding that no new information could be obtained in that manner, she allowed the vision to fade, letting her awareness collapse back into her more mundane senses. The switch left behind the familiar feeling of vertigo and slight nausea, this time accompanied by a mild ache behind her eyes as Ally's brain protested the strain on her still-healing neurons.

Pushing away the pain, Ally opened her eyes, blinking rapidly as the light stabbed at her retinas. Squinting, she could just make out the princess, who was seated just far enough away that she was outside Ally's range of clear sight. To Ally's short-sighted gaze, Evelynne existed merely as a pale, red-topped blob, darker blotches taking the place of facial features. Ally was disappointed that she couldn't see the brilliant sapphire eyes that she remembered.

Deciding to announce her presence, Ally spoke up.

Or tried to. What actually emerged was a rough croak, her throat informing that it had been far too long since any sort of liquid had wet it.

chapter four

It was still enough to catch Evelynne's attention and she broke off in mid-sentence.

"Ally?" she asked, relieved when she saw grey eyes looking back at her with awareness. "Can you hear me?"

Ally tried to speak again, but once again only an unintelligible croak issued from her lips and she swallowed convulsively against her dry throat.

Realising the problem, Evelynne put down the book, pressed the button to summon the doctor and picked up the plastic water cup and straw lying on the bedside table. Raising the straw to Ally's parched lips, she held the cup steady as the woman in the bed sipped.

All too soon, though, Evelynne was taking the straw away. When Ally made a small noise in protest, she said, "I'm sorry, but the doctor said not to give you too much. You haven't had anything in you stomach for over five days."

Though disappointed, Ally understood. "Thank you," she said, with as much earnestness as her hoarse voice would allow.

Evelynne smiled, ruefully. "Actually, I wanted to thank you," she said softly. "You saved my life. I don't know how I'm ever going to repay you for that, but I swear that if there is *ever* anything I can do for you, you just need to ask." The princess let out a sigh. "I really don't know how I'll ever be able to truly thank you. None of my words seem strong enough." She paused a moment. "I Owe you my Life, Alleandre Tretiak." The words were deadly serious and filled with an undercurrent of hidden meaning that Ally couldn't interpret.

Alleandre was a little uncomfortable at the attention. "Your Highness," she started to rasp.

"Please," Evelynne interrupted. "Call me Evelynne. That's what my friends call me. I'm hoping that, given the circumstances, I can add you to that list." She indicated her current state with a little chuckle. "Besides, I hardly look like a "Highness" in this delightful little hospital number." She gestured again to her wheelchair. "And they seem to have misplaced my throne."

Ally couldn't help but laugh, though her mirth didn't last long as the movement caused a spike of pain to lance through her abdomen. She gritted her teeth and waited it out, consciously attempting to relax the tense muscles. When she opened her eyes again, she could see Evelynne's worried face looking at hers. Ally realised that Evelynne had leaned forward, allowing Ally to fully focus on the princess' features, and had also taken hold of her hand, gently rubbing the back of it with her thumb.

God, she's gorgeous. The thought crossed her mind before Ally could stop it. She remembered earlier thoughts, in the aftermath of incapacitating pain. *I can't believe I thought that then. In that situation. I know I'm not a masochist, so I hope that was whatever medication they gave me doing the talking,* she thought. *It was,* another part of her answered, *but this is your real sense of sexual aesthetics speaking. She's hot.* Ally blushed uncontrollably at the thought and then realised that Evelynne was speaking.

"Are you okay?" the princess asked.

"I'm . . . better," Ally replied. "Just please don't make me laugh right now." She stared into the blue eyes less than half a metre from her own. There was something there, some connection tickling the back of her mind, something that felt a little like . . .

The door opened before Ally could finish tracking down the thought and Dr. Corbeil, Sir Arthur and another woman in a doctor's uniform entered. The newcomer was about the same age as Dr. Corbeil, but over a foot shorter and with silvery-grey hair pulled back into a tight bun. Sir Arthur took up a post just inside the door. To Ally, though, they were just a collection of vaguely man-shaped blobs.

"Ally, it is good to see you awake again. I'm Doctor Corbeil," said the doctor. "How are you feeling this time?" Taking out a small penlight, the doctor proceeded to shine it into each of Ally's eyes. She seemed pleased by the response. Putting away the light, the doctor pressed two fingers to her patient's wrist, checking her pulse. "You gave us a little scare last time. Do you remember?"

Ally winced at the recollection. "I remember," she replied, her voice still hoarse. "Much as I don't want to."

"Ah, *oui*, I understand. So how do you feel right now?"

Ally took stock of her body, subtly stretching her arms and wiggling her fingers. She grimaced at the residual ache and stiffness, but otherwise felt much better–aside from the continuous dull throb in her right shoulder and lower back–and told the doctor as much. "I've felt better, but then again, as you reminded me, I've felt worse," Ally answered. "All in all, I think I'll–" She broke off suddenly, and her face drained of colour. "I can't move my feet!" she exclaimed, panic in her voice.

The new doctor gently but firmly pushed Dr. Corbeil out of the way and moved to the foot of the bed. Flinging back the blanket from the young woman's feet, she took one of them in her hands. "Ally, *je m'appelle* . . . I am Doctor Calinot," she said with a thick French accent. "I am *neurologue*–How do you say? Nerve specialist. You have bullet enter near spine. I think there is no damage to . . . spinal cord. There is . . . swelling, it push spinal cord.

chapter four

Now I check your nerves." Despite her halting English, the doctor's tone served to reassure Ally, pushing back her panic.

Ally gave a short, sharp nod.

"Before start, though," Dr. Calinot continued, turning and pointing at Sir Arthur and Evelynne, "you two, *sortez*."

Alleandre started to protest Evelynne's removal, then stopped, uncertain. *Do I want her to see this? Does she want to see this? She's a princess; am I allowed to ask her to stay? Why do I want her to stay?* Before she could answer even one of these questions, Sir Arthur had come forward to collect the princess. Before leaving Ally's side, Evelynne gave her hand a final squeeze of encouragement and whispered, "I'll be right outside." Ally didn't know why the statement reassured her so much.

Then the two Atlantlans were out the door, leaving Ally to the competent, but not so tender mercies of Dr. Calinot, while Dr. Corbeil stood nearby, ready to give assistance.

By the time the examination was over, Ally was glad that Evelynne had left the room. The doctor had tested her sense of feeling all the way up both her legs, and the blanket—and underlying hospital gown—had moved all the way up in response. Despite Dr. Calinot's clinical, detached manner, the young woman was blushing beet-red by the time it was over, and her heart was racing. An old, familiar shyness, bordering on outright panic, welled up, and Ally put her willpower to work suppressing the reaction. When the doctor was done she sighed in relief. *At least she was thorough,* she thought sardonically.

Both doctors seemed pleased. "*Très bien*, Alleandre," said Dr. Calinot. "I think you have full—" A whispered question to Dr. Corbeil. "—full sensation in your legs and feet. Now we . . . test movement." Taking hold of Ally's foot once more, she directed, "Now, you move toes."

Obediently, Ally tried to wiggle her toes.

Dr. Calinot frowned. "You are trying?"

"Yes, I'm trying!" Ally snapped, barely contained panic and frustration adding bite to her tone. Ignoring the doctor's sharp glance, she concentrated harder on getting even a twitch from her unresponsive digits. Suddenly she was rewarded as her toes twitched once, spasmodically, in unison. Feeling the movement, Ally relaxed once more, letting out a breath she hadn't been aware of holding.

"*Excellent*," the doctor smiled, though Ally couldn't see it. "Now, *l'autre pied*."

Ally groaned softly, but tried once more. This time it seemed easier and her toes obediently twitched several times in succession.

"It's good, I think," said the doctor with satisfaction, writing notes on Ally's chart. "You have full sensation, some movement. I think *l'inflammation* . . . the swelling in wound is stopping movement. When swelling goes, movement returns." Rehanging the chart at the foot of the bed, the doctor paused to rest a hand reassuringly on Ally's uninjured shoulder. "I make time for *l'examen radioscopique* . . . the X-ray." Her eyes twinkled. "Soon you run, dance, *oui*? Soon." Dr. Calinot smiled reassuringly and left the room.

Dr. Corbeil smiled down at the woman in the bed. "So, it is good news. Doctor Calinot is a very good doctor. If she says you will be running and dancing soon, you will." She looked at her watch. "It will take time to schedule the x-ray. Do you want company now? I know your friend wants to see you and the princess' bodyguard wants to ask you some questions. It is up to you. I can tell them to come back later if you want."

A moment passed as Ally considered. "I'd like to see them," she said, the stress and fatigue of the last few minutes showing in her voice and expression. "But can you give me five minutes alone? I need to . . ." She trailed off.

The doctor nodded in understanding. "I will tell them five minutes and then to knock. You let them in if you want." Leaning forward, Dr. Corbeil rested her hand in turn on Ally's shoulder. "You *will* get better," she said emphatically.

A somewhat shaky smile was Ally's response. "Before you go, do you know where my glasses are? I can hardly see a thing without them."

"I do not know where your glasses are." The doctor frowned. "They may have been lost. Do you have your prescription?"

"If anyone has my fanny pack, it should be in there, with all my other papers."

"I will look and see what I can do. Anything else?"

Ally's blush returned. "Um . . . Can you take out this . . . um . . . catheter?" She was bright red. "It's a little . . . uncomfortable."

Dr. Corbeil strove to contain a laugh, knowing it would only embarrass her patient more. Besides, she sympathised. "I am sorry. Until we get the new x-ray we cannot put you in a wheelchair. Hopefully it won't be much longer. Be patient."

Be patient, hmph, Ally grumbled internally, her blush slowly fading. *You're not the one with the tube up her . . . hmph.* The blush was back.

ತಿ ತಿ ತಿ ತಿ ತಿ

chapter four

By the time Dr. Corbeil left, Evelynne's anxiety had risen to new levels. She had a length of hair in her hand and was nervously twisting it around her fingers. Chorus was also waiting in the anteroom and he wasn't faring much better, but he was able to hide it more. By contrast, Sir Arthur was as calm and collected as he usually was. Dr. Calinot had exited a few minutes earlier, but had refused to answer any questions. Her response to Evelynne's increasingly persistent enquiries had been to say that Dr. Corbeil would speak to them soon.

She hadn't reassured Evelynne much, though, and as soon as Dr. Corbeil came through the door, closing it firmly behind her, the princess was asking her about Ally.

"Doctor Calinot believes that Alleandre will recover," the doctor explained. "We will run more tests to be sure, but things look good now. Not perfect, but good. We will know more after an x-ray."

Evelynne visibly relaxed. "Can we see her now?" She was already moving towards the door, but was stopped by the doctor.

"Alleandre has asked for five minutes alone." She smiled apologetically. "I think she needs some quiet to think and relax. The examination was stressful." The doctor's pager went off suddenly. Glancing at it, she finished, "I have to go now. I will be back. Before you go in, please knock." With that, she hurried off.

Disappointed, Evelynne turned back to face Sir Arthur and Chorus. She went back to twisting her hair. "Well, that was good news. I think. Do you think so?" she asked the two men.

"I'm no doctor, but it sounded good to me," answered Chorus.

Sir Arthur added, "I agree, Your Highness. Of course, as the doctor said, we'll know more when these new tests are completed."

Evelynne let out her breath in a burst, trying to relax a little. "Isis, I hope so. If she's paralysed–" She didn't finish the thought. Turning her attention back to Sir Arthur, she asked, "Has anyone been able to track down her parents yet?"

"No, Your Highness. I must admit I'm getting discouraged. The closest relative we've been able to find is her grandmother living in England and she doesn't know where they are. It's been two days since Ms. Tretiak's name was leaked to the press, so I'd expect them to have seen something on the news by now."

Despite the best efforts of all involved, reporters had discovered the identity of the mysterious "Marseilles Heroine" and her name and picture–a rather unflattering high school photo–were now plastered across televisions and newspapers worldwide. Sir Arthur was actually rather surprised that it had taken almost three days before the facts became known.

"I'm worried too," put in Chorus. "Although I've never met them, from what Ally's said, they're quite close. I really don't think it's that they don't care."

"Well, that's another thing we can ask Ms. Tretiak now that she's awake," said Sir Arthur. The injured woman in the next room bothered him. Having studied the more detailed forensics and ballistics reports, he was more curious than ever about how both the young women had escaped death.

Evelynne looked at him sharply. "You won't be asking anything detailed right now," she declared firmly.

Sir Arthur set his jaw stubbornly. "Your Highness, I have to get some answers now, while the events are still clear. I must–"

"No." Evelynne's jaw was set even more firmly and a fire burned in her eyes. "She has just woken up from a five-day coma. You will *not* ask her any questions that might cause her stress. She was hurt saving *my* life, and I forbid any more distress." Despite her wheelchair and attire, Evelynne was every inch the princess now–and in command. "If you try, I will call Doctor Corbeil and get her to have you removed." As Sir Arthur opened his mouth to protest, she overrode him. "She outranks you in this situation, remember?"

Caught by his own words, Sir Arthur subsided with a scowl. He was a little concerned about the princess' fiercely protective stance towards Alleandre Tretiak. "Very well, Your Highness," he acquiesced grudgingly.

Deflating, Evelynne turned to Chorus, who had instinctively stepped back during the exchange. "Can we go in to see her yet?"

Recognising the princess' still-brittle mood, the young man quickly looked at his watch. "Another two minutes," he replied.

His eyes widened when the princess swore softly.

Precisely five minutes after Dr. Corbeil left, there was a knock at the door to Ally's room.

"Come in," she croaked, her voice still hoarse from disuse.

Ally had spent several minutes relaxing, dealing with her anxiety, adjusting to the dull pain and getting a bit more used to her stubbornly unresponsive body. Concentrating on her breathing, she had managed to attain a measure of mental calm and had pushed the discomfort into an easily ignorable corner of her mind. Her sore, dry throat refused to be ignored, however and Ally vaguely remembered herself screaming the last

chapter four

time she had awoken. The cup of water was tantalisingly out of reach and she didn't want to chance further discomfort by stretching for it.

The young woman had considered using her talents to bring the cup closer, but didn't want to risk more strain on her recovering concentration and mental energies. Even worse would be someone walking in and asking difficult questions about why there was a cup full of water floating in the air above her bed.

Ally had resigned herself to her thirst when the hesitant rapping came at her door. Steeling herself for the coming intrusion into her space, reckoning that at least she'd be able to ask for some water and hoping that it would be the princess who would give her some, she called, "Come in."

The door opened and Evelynne peered around the doorjamb into the room. "May we come in?" she asked softly.

Pleased to recognise the princess' voice, Ally carefully waved her in with her good hand. "Please."

The short flame-topped blob that was Evelynne entered the room, her wheelchair pushed by a much larger purple-and-silver blob that filled the doorway. A slightly smaller, darker blob followed.

As they came closer, the darker blob spoke and Ally recognised Chorus' voice. "Hey, Ally," he said. "How are ya feeling?" He took up a spot at her right side and bent down to carefully give her a hug, mindful not to jostle her too much. As he pressed his slightly bristly cheek to hers, he whispered almost silently, "They don't know anything."

Nodding to signal her understanding before he pulled away, Ally felt a knot of tension loosen inside herself. Though nobody had mentioned anything, she had wondered if anybody had seen how she had saved the princess' life. The odds had been against it, as there was no observable physical link between her talents and their results, but the fear had still been present.

"Hey, Chorus," Ally replied to her friend's audible question. "I'm feeling better now. And I'd feel even better if you'd give me some water."

Evelynne was the one who quickly grabbed the cup and brought it to Ally's lips. "Here you go."

Ally slowly sipped several mouthfuls of water. When she was done, she released the straw and fervently said, "Thank you."

"You're welcome. The doctor told us that your prognosis was good." A discreet tap of a finger on her shoulder reminded the princess of her Guardsman standing beside her. "Oh, yes, this is Sir Arthur Ramirez, the Master of my Guard."

"I'm pleased to meet you finally, Ms. Tretiak," the bodyguard said, touching his fingers to his forehead, lips and breast in salute. "On behalf of myself and the rest of the Heir's Guard, I would like to thank you sincerely for saving Her Highness' life. You did our jobs for us and we can never fully express our gratitude."

Ally was becoming tired of blushing continuously and firmly told the flush to leave. Encouraged by the attention she was receiving, it ignored her and stayed. "Um, you're welcome," she stuttered, then cursed herself for her lack of eloquence.

"I do have a couple of questions I need to ask you. Do you feel up to it?" Sir Arthur ignored Evelynne's cautionary glance.

"Um, I guess so," Ally replied tensing up again. *Does he know anything? Did he see anything? I think he was the closest to us.*

The bodyguard sought to reassure Ally with a stiff smile, but she couldn't see it. "Good. First of all, we've been trying to contact your next of kin for the last five days, but haven't been able to find them. Do you know where they are?"

Ally was startled. "Five days? I've been asleep that long?"

"You were in a coma for four days," Evelynne explained. "You woke up briefly yesterday and have been asleep since then."

"Jeez," breathed Ally, still shocked. *Five days? Why wouldn't Mom and Dad be here? Oh shit, that's right.* "Mom and Dad are on vacation. Dad's a teacher and Mom's a marine biologist. Every summer they pack up everything and spend five straight weeks camping. No phones, no TV, no radio, nothing. This summer they were going to . . . somewhere around Alkali Lake, I think. In the interior of British Columbia. I can't remember exactly where. They left two weeks ago, so they're going to be gone for another three. They don't stay at regular campsites, so I'm not sure how you'll find them." Pausing a moment, Ally continued, "They go into town for supplies every once in a while. That's the only thing I can think of." She gave an apologetic smile.

Sir Arthur returned the smile. "That is actually quite helpful. Instead of searching the whole of North America, we can narrow it down a lot. Thank you." Switching topics, he said, "I have a few more questions if you–"

"That's enough for now," Evelynne interrupted. With a warning glare, she said, "There will be time enough for that later. For now, though, I have a question of my own." Directing her attention back to the woman in the bed, the princess asked, "So your parents might not be home for three weeks?" A nod. "Do you know what you want to do until then?" At Ally's puzzled look, she explained, "Do you want to go back to Canada? I can arrange that if you want. Or you can stay here. My family will pay for anything you need." Ally started to reply, but Evelynne cut her off, wanting to get the next part out before anyone could stop her–though she knew that both her father and

chapter four

her bodyguard would be more than a little angry that she had not discussed her suggestion with them first. "You can come and stay with me. In Atlantl. As soon as the doctors say it's safe, we can fly you out there." Before Sir Arthur could interrupt, she hurried on. "I'm going to be spending some time recuperating myself. I was planning on going to the Summer Palace anyway when I got back. I can arrange for doctors, therapists, whatever you need." Coming to the end, Evelynne sucked in a deep, needed breath.

Ally was surprised, to say the least. "Um," she said eloquently.

Mistaking the hesitation, Evelynne said, "Naturally, you don't have to if you don't want to. Whatever you choose is entirely up to you. Just think about it, okay?"

Ally looked into the earnest blue eyes near hers. "Okay," she said bemusedly. "I'll think about it."

Chorus didn't think she'd have to think for long. He knew what she'd eventually say before Ally did.

chapter five

There were exactly seventeen screws along the join in the ceiling right above Ally's head. They were each about a centimetre across, set about ten centimetres apart and were painted the same off-white colour as the ceiling. They were almost invisible except for the tiny hexagonal holes in their tops and the fact that they were raised just slightly above the level of the surrounding roof, but once one knew they were there, they were quite easy to find.

Ally had found all the screws in the seam within five minutes. That had been fifteen minutes ago and she was beginning to regret the impulse that had made her refuse the sedative the doctors had offered her.

She was once again flat on her back, but was further immobilised by a neck brace and the restraints holding her body tightly to the bed. The doctors had insisted on them before they would let her board the plane. Though Ally had regained full movement in her limbs within two days of emerging from the coma, the muscles and tendons along her spine were still healing and nobody wanted to risk a sudden movement shifting the vertebrae and undoing all the progress she had made.

And, according to Dr. Corbeil and Dr. Calinot, Ally had made excellent progress over the last week. Her mobility had returned slowly but steadily over the course of the first two days, though it had been another two before they allowed her to leave the bed or even sit upright. The last few days of physiotherapy, though painful, had let the doctors predict total recovery, though more work would be needed as her muscles and tendons healed.

The pain of recovery had been more than worth it when Dr. Corbeil finally removed the catheter.

Princess Evelynne had been nearby almost the whole time. Most of the few exceptions had occurred during Ally's physiotherapy sessions, when Ally had requested that no onlookers be present.

The other times that the princess wasn't there were when she was speaking to her father–and Ally was still bemused that Evelynne could speak of the ruler of an entire nation in such familiar terms. The other occasions had been a few private conversations with her bodyguard and lady-in-waiting. These conversations always took place outside their room, although a few of them—especially in the last three days—had been lively enough to spill over into the room through the closed door. From the fragments Ally was able to pick up, Evelynne was supposed to have left two days ago and Ally wasn't sure why she hadn't. When tentatively questioned on the matter, the princess had mumbled something about "obligations" and "trying to push me around," then changed the subject.

Finally Dr. Calinot had pronounced Alleandre fit to travel and Ally had had to announce her decision.

So now Ally was strapped to a stretcher inside the Royal Atlantlan Aircraft *Ptah-Ra*, a medium-sized jet used by the Royal Family. From what little she had been able to see as she was carefully carried on board, the interior was unlike any commercial airliner, but more like a Learjet, as befitted such a prestigious conveyance.

Right now Ally's field of view was restricted to five feet of rather bland ceiling and, just at the corner of her right eye, the edge of a window. Outside that window, she knew, three KR-1 *Dragon* fighter planes of the Royal Atlantlan Air Force were flying escort as the *Ptah-Ra* completed its ascent after takeoff. Ally envied their freedom.

She also briefly envied Chorus, who was at that moment on solid ground. The young man had declined the princess' offer to accompany them, choosing instead to spend some more time touring France. He had promised to visit soon.

After an eternity, the plane levelled off and the pilot gave the passengers permission to move around the cabin once more. He hadn't even finished speaking before Evelynne unbuckled her seat belt and hurried forward to where her new friend was laying. Though she had wanted to, she had not been able to sit beside Ally during takeoff. There were only two seats near where the stretcher was bolted to the floor and they had been claimed by a doctor and nurse in order to keep an eye on their patient's condition.

As Evelynne moved closer, she could see the doctor bending down to speak to Ally while the nurse checked her vital signs. The princess could hear neither the question nor Ally's response, but the doctor seemed satisfied. Looking up, the doctor saw Evelynne's approach and smiled.

"Alleandre's doing as well as can be expected, Your Highness," he said before Evelynne could ask. "She's obviously not as comfortable as she'd like to be, but she says she isn't in any serious pain." He smiled again at Evelynne's sigh of relief. "I'll leave you two alone for now. I'll be back a bit later to check up on you."

"Thanks, Dr. Ryann," Evelynne said, moving closer to her friend as the doctor and his assistant went off toward the back of the plane.

chapter five

In Evelynne's opinion, Ally didn't look like she was doing as well as Dr. Ryann believed. She was pale beneath her tan and Evelynne could see a sheen of sweat across her brow. Her breathing was quick and a glance at the monitor beside the stretcher told the princess that her pulse was slightly fast. Her eyes were closed behind a new pair of glasses. The glasses were small and rectangular, made of a silvery material and fit Ally's facial features perfectly.

Now the eyes behind the glasses flashed open when Evelynne said quietly, "Hey, Ally, are you feeling all right?"

"No," Ally snapped. She immediately felt bad when she saw the hurt in the face beside her. "Sorry," she apologised, adjusting her tone. "It's just that I'm stiff and sore, and I can't move, and I'm feeling a little sick."

"Oh. I'm sorry. Do you usually get sick in planes?"

Ally started to shake her head before the neck brace reminded her of its presence. "No, normally I love flying. Normally, though, I'm not lying down and strapped in. I also think the painkiller they gave me before takeoff is screwing up my sense of balance. I do know it's messing up my brain chemistry. I can't seem to concentrate very well."

She didn't add that just before Evelynne arrived, she had been trying to project her sight outside the aircraft, hoping the sense of total freedom would alleviate her growing claustrophobia. The attempt had failed when she couldn't focus her mind properly, her thoughts scattering.

"I'm sorry," Evelynne said again. She gestured in the general direction of the departed doctor. "Do you want them to give you a sedative so you can sleep?"

"No, I've been doing enough sleeping lately."

"All right. Well, I came bearing gifts. Or *a* gift, actually." Smiling brightly, Evelynne produced a book from behind her back with a flourish. "Tada! *The Light Fantastic*, by Terry Pratchett. Chorus managed to find a copy before we left. Would you like me to read to you?"

Ally returned the smile with a genuine one of her own. Oddly, her nausea and claustrophobia had vanished completely. "I'd love that."

ઌ ઌ ઌ ઌ ઌ

A while afterwards, Evelynne paused in her reading and glanced out the window. "Oh, we're almost at the Avalon coast. I can see the outer reefs."

"Really?" Ally asked. "I wish I could see them." Despite the distraction, the roof of the plane was rapidly becoming boring again.

The princess looked at her sympathetically. "We'll have to fly over them again sometime. They're really quite impressive. You know, sociologists say they're why we're so insular and yet so accepting as a culture."

"Oh? Why?"

"Well, when the island of Atlantl sank about ten thousand years ago—it was just one big island then, remember—it broke up and formed the reefs. There weren't many survivors on the new islands themselves, but of course over time immigrants managed to make their way in. Mostly from North Africa and the Iberian Peninsula, but from other places too. The thing is that the reefs prevented any *large* migrations, or any major invasions, for that matter. So we never had the kind of social friction large migrations cause. Because the reefs are completely impartial, there was no single ethnic majority that managed to take over. Anyone who made it was generally considered by the locals to simply be a new Atlantlan and was accepted as they were."

"That makes sense. But that doesn't make sense if you're insular too," Ally commented.

"Well, not locally, no. But the reefs are as hard to pass going *out* as they are coming *in*, so we never got involved in the conquest and colonisation efforts that the rest of Europe did. We established a few small trading outposts, but for the most part were happy to sit where we were and take advantage of the other nations' trade that had to pass through our waters. We would charge ships for guiding them through the reefs and rent warehouse space for transhipping." Evelynne shrugged. "Now that's one of our largest sources of revenue. Practically all the shipping between the Americas, Europe and North Africa passes through Atlantlan waters. Our customs tariffs are really low, but sheer volume makes it incredibly profitable."

"That I can understand," Ally said. She chuckled. "Just don't try to explain the details of the economics behind it. I've never been able to understand that kind of thing."

"Really? Well, think of it like this . . ."

As Evelynne tried to explain international finance, Ally put on an expression of interest and was just glad that *someone* understood all of it.

Three hours later the plane landed in the Atlantlan capital city of Jamaz on the island of Hy Braseal. Ally had awakened just before landing, mortified to find that she had fallen asleep while Evelynne was reading to her. The embarrassment had only lasted long enough for her to see, out of the corner of her eye, the princess equally fast asleep with the book resting in her lap.

They separated briefly during the landing itself, but Evelynne returned immediately once they were down to help the doctor move Ally out of her stretcher and into a waiting wheelchair. Then Maïda took charge, brushing

chapter five

her short brown hair into some semblance of order. Only Evelynne saw the amusement on Ally's face while Maïda fussed with and clucked at the unruly mass of hair.

"What's so funny?" the princess asked.

Ally chuckled. "My Mom does the same thing whenever I'm at home. Especially when I go out. I keep expecting Maïda to stick a finger in my ear and say, 'Goodness, you could grow potatoes in here.'"

Evelynne's answering giggle turned into a full-fledged laugh when the older woman snorted, then stuck a finger in Ally's ear and exclaimed dramatically, "Goodness, you could grow potatoes in here." When Ally predictably blushed and shot her a reproachful glare, Maïda just raised both eyebrows. "I wouldn't want to disappoint you, dear."

Finally the lady-in-waiting pronounced Alleandre to be presentable. Moving on to Evelynne, it was Ally's turn to laugh as Maïda made a great show of looking in both the princess' ears. When she was done, she announced, "You'll do."

"High praise," murmured Evelynne to Ally as she pushed the wheelchair towards the exit and the ramp beyond.

As they started up the corridor leading to the Royal Terminal, Sir Arthur moved closer to Evelynne and said quietly, "Your Highness, His Majesty is waiting for you in the terminal."

"I thought he was going to meet me at the Palace," Evelynne said, startled.

"As did I, Your Highness." There was a conspicuous lack of disapproval in his tone.

"What about Patrick and Aunt Cleo?"

"Brother Patrick is here, as well, but Her Majesty is not. I am told that there has been an emergency on Avalon. I'm afraid I don't know the details."

"Well," Evelynne breathed, earning a glance from the woman in the wheelchair she was pushing.

"What's wrong?" Ally asked.

The princess shook her head. "Oh, nothing's wrong. It's just that instead of waiting at the Palace, my father has decided to meet us here."

Ally paled. "Here?" she asked, her voice cracking. She cleared her throat. "Now? Oh." A pause. "Do I have to curtsy or something when I meet him? I mean, I've never greeted royalty before."

Evelynne raised an eyebrow. "Hello? What am I? A peasant?"

"Uh, that is–You, um–" Predictably, the blush appeared.

Evelynne chuckled. "You should really get that redness looked at. It seems to be spreading."

☙ ☙ ☙ ☙ ☙

Despite Ally's anxiety—or perhaps because of it—the journey up the ramp seemed to take no time at all. In the room at the top a group of people were waiting. They were all dwarfed by the sheer presence of the large red-haired, red-bearded man at their head.

It was easy to see where Evelynne had inherited her hair. A big man, King Jad Richard ibn Jad deMolay wore a thick, full beard and an unruly mop of shoulder-length hair. Both were a bright orange-red, made even more vivid by the fact that his face was also red in hue; he perpetually looked as though he had just stepped out of a shower. It was a well-known fact in Atlantl that an entire legion of stylists had tried and failed to conquer the King's wild locks. King Jad had finally given up and now simply let nature take its course. A generation of editorial cartoonists thanked him for it, since it made any caricature of him instantly recognisable. Added to his blue eyes, a shade darker than Evelynne's, the combination of hair, beard and size made him look as though he should really be leading some blood-thirsty Viking raiding party, axe in hand and with a woman thrown over one shoulder. Instead, he was one of the most beloved rulers Atlantis had ever known.

"*Za!*" Evelynne took off, dodging around Ally's wheelchair and charging forward on a collision course with the big man, which ended when his strong arms wrapped themselves around her tightly. Evelynne's good right arm held on to him just as tightly and the King's blue and purple tabard was quickly damp with tears.

Finally after long moments, the protests of Evelynne's injured shoulder became too loud for her to ignore and she pulled back from her father's embrace enough to look up into his face.

"Hello, Evy," he said, his voice suspiciously husky. "Good of you to make it back . . . eventually."

The princess ducked her head. "I'm sorry, *za*. I know I should have come back right away. It's just that—"

"No, that doesn't matter now," the King interrupted. "All that matters is that you're home and safe, and that you're going to get better." A movement at his side attracted his attention. "And here is your brother now to reassure you."

The young man in the monk's robes grinned up at his father and down at his sister. Dark blond hair and delicate features characterised his face. With his simple clerical robes, he could not have looked more different from

chapter five

the King and only identical deep blue eyes announced that they were related. As the King's eldest child, once-Prince Patrick had been next in line for the Throne, but had surprised a great many people when he abdicated his claim in favour of a religious vocation. "Reassure you? Not likely. I'm here to tell you that if you ever try anything like this again, God Himself will track you down and spank the living daylights out of you." Patrick turned to his father and spoke in a stage whisper audible to everyone in the room. "Did I get that right, *za*? I think that's what you wanted me to say."

There was a sudden outbreak of coughing in the room as King Jad scowled fiercely at his son. Patrick grinned back, unrepentant, then held out his arms wide for his sister. "Evy, it's good to have you back."

Evelynne returned her brother's hug fiercely. "It's good to be back."

King Jad looked around the room. "Now, where is this young woman to whom we all owe so much? I've been looking forward to meeting her."

On cue, Sir Arthur pushed forward the wheelchair containing the nervous Alleandre. Ally craned her neck up at the red giant before her and hesitantly touched the fingers of her left hand to her forehead, lips and chest in the way Evelynne had taught her. Unsure of what to do afterwards, she let her hand fall awkwardly into her lap. "Er . . . hello, Your Majesty," she stuttered.

The King's eyebrows rose at the surprisingly small-looking woman. Unconsciously he had been expecting someone larger, more impressive. Instead there was this incredibly young girl sitting before him, looking up at him out of slate-grey eyes displaying a large dose of intimidation.

Realising that he was towering over her, King Jad went down on one knee in front of Ally, moving gracefully for someone of his size. With his hands pressed together, the King returned the greeting, touching them to head, lips and breast. Then, ever the diplomat, he extended his left hand. The young woman hesitated a moment, then allowed her hand to be taken. "Hello, *Ishta* Tretiak. You have no idea how glad I am to finally meet you. Speaking as Diarch, We wish to thank you on behalf of Our Dominion for laying your life before the Heir to Our Throne." His voice took on a formal cadence for the last sentence, but lightened once more as he continued, "Speaking as a father, I want you to know that there is nothing I'll ever be able to do to thank you enough for bringing my daughter back safe, if not quite totally sound. If there is ever anything that is in my power to provide, it is yours." Sensing the discomfort level rising in the recipient of his effusive speech, the King backed away, though he remained crouched down.

Guessing that some response was required, Ally stammered, "Um, t-thank you, Sir." She immediately kicked herself mentally. *He's the King; you don't call him "Sir"! You call him "Your Majesty", or . . . or . . .*

The King didn't seem to notice her imagined breach of etiquette. Instead, he beckoned to his son and a rather round man in a business suit. Reaching out to draw Patrick closer, King Jad introduced, "*Ishta* Tretiak, may I introduce Brother Patrick of the Order of the Illuminated Word, my son."

Patrick reached out to give Ally's hand a firm shake. "Hello, *Ishta* Tretiak." He grinned at her. "I must say it's always a little odd when *za* introduces me to anyone. 'This is my son, the Brother.'"

That startled a laugh out of Ally and she relaxed minutely. "Please call me Ally," she said. "And if you think it's bad now, imagine if you become a priest. Then he'll have to say, 'Meet my son, the Father.'"

Patrick, Evelynne and King Jad all laughed. "That's a good one," Patrick said, still chuckling. "I'll have to remember to tell it to Abbot Huro."

Evelynne was pleased. She should have known that Patrick would be able to get Ally to relax. She mouthed a "Thank you" when he turned to smile at her.

Still kneeling, the King next introduced the overweight man, who looked to be in his sixties. "This is Omar ibn Larak, my Foreign Affairs Advisor. He's been helping to co-ordinate the search for your parents, so I thought you might like to meet him."

"*Ishta* Tretiak," the Advisor greeted as Ally found her hand clasped in a large, sweaty palm. "I'm afraid we still haven't managed to track down your parents yet. The RCMP found a store where they had been to pick up supplies, but apparently missed them by less than a day. According to the owner they bought enough food to last several weeks, so it is unlikely that they will be back soon. The police, as well as some park officials are searching, but given the size of the area . . ." He trailed off, shrugging his wide shoulders.

Ally shook her head. "I have no idea exactly where they are. Before he became a teacher, Dad used to lead hiking adventure tours professionally. He's an expert at remaining unfound in the wilderness."

"Ah." ibn Larak looked almost comically crestfallen. "Well, needless to say, we will keep looking."

"And now that we've all met," continued the King, rising to his feet, "we really must get going." He continued speaking in English as a courtesy to Ally. "There is a fairly major diplomatic disaster brewing as we speak." At Evelynne's questioning look, he waved a hand dismissively. "I'll let you in on the details once we get back to the palace."

The group made its way at a brisk pace down the hallways of the Royal Terminal towards the exit. Evelynne, resigned to losing Ally's attentions

chapter five

to her brother Patrick who had taken on the role of wheelchair pusher, walked at King Jad's left side, her right hand firmly held in his larger one. The disappointment showed on her face enough for her father to notice. "Evy, what's wrong? Am I such a terrible second prize?"

He jerked his head behind them, to where Patrick was pushing Ally. Patrick seemed to be monopolising the conversation, though Ally's occasional interjections and their mutual laughter showed that they were definitely enjoying themselves.

Evelynne looked guiltily up at her father. "Sorry, *za*. She's just become a good friend over the last week, and this is pretty much the first time that someone else has taken her attention completely. Honestly, though, I'm really happy to be home."

"Oh, I don't think *Ishta* Tretiak is ignoring you. In fact—" He tilted his head and listened to part of the exchange behind him, then took a quick peek over his shoulder, catching Patrick with a mischievous grin and Ally with a blush. "In fact, I'd be willing to bet my Throne that you are the main topic of conversation."

Evelynne spared a glance of her own, just in time to see Patrick whispering something in Ally's ear. Her brother was grinning evilly as they both laughed, though Ally reddened further and shot an apologetic look to Evelynne when she saw the princess looking.

"Oh, Isis, this is bad," Evelynne said. "This is very bad. I just hope he doesn't really embarrass her. She's very shy."

"I noticed that," King Jad said. "I wouldn't worry, though. Patrick's always known just how far to go."

"Yes, unfortunately," Evelynne replied. Sighing, she decided to put the matter from her mind. "So what's the disaster that you were talking about?"

The King sighed, briefly showing the full weight of his responsibilities. "Last night the Third Escort Fleet escorting the trade convoy to Cuba ran into Hurricane Ida. One of our *Hydra*-class destroyers lost all of its navigational systems, was blown off course and ran aground on the Florida coast just south of Miami. Nobody was seriously injured, but now the U.S. military is trying to get the crew off and their own people on board. We, of course, don't want them anywhere near it, and we're trying to get permission to send in some tugs to pull it out to sea. We don't want them on board because of the sensitive technology and they want to get on board—"

"—because of the sensitive technology." Evelynne frowned. "Wasn't a U.S. spy plane forced down in China a while ago? The Americans raised a huge fuss about Chinese personnel going aboard, didn't they? So why do they think they can board our boat?"

The King shrugged. "They're claiming that since the boat was beached, it's technically a wreck and is therefore the property of the first nation to claim it under international salvage law. We're saying that since the crew is still aboard, it is technically *not* a wreck and is therefore still Atlantlan property." He rubbed his eyes. "The diplomats are just getting warmed up. Your aunt is supervising the negotiations; otherwise she would have been here. She sends her love."

Evelynne nodded. She was used to political obligations interfering with her family's lives. She envied Patrick sometimes for escaping that world.

After several minutes of walking, the procession finally arrived at the doors to the Terminal. Before exiting, the party stopped and the King turned like a general facing his troops. "All right," he said, in English, "there is the usual crowd of press and well-wishers waiting outside. Evelynne and I will be doing a small photo-op." He moved to kneel once more in front of Ally wheelchair. "*Ishta* Tretiak, the press has, naturally, a burning desire to speak to you and take some pictures. Is that all right with you? If you wish, we can shield you from it."

Ally stared at the King with a suddenly pale face. *Press? Photographers? Dozens of strangers staring at me?* Still, Evelynne seemed comfortable with the concept and the young woman had no desire to seem weak. "Um, that'll be okay, Sir," she said faintly.

An expert on interpreting the tone of a person's voice, the King looked at her closely for a moment, then nodded reassuringly and stood. With a single glance at his Master of Guards and a barely seen shake of his head, King Jad conveyed his orders. Taking hold of his daughter's hand once again, he ordered, "Very well, then. Whenever you're ready, Sir Adun."

A Guardsman, whom Ally assumed was Sir Adun, listened intently to his earbud for a moment, then nodded at his liege. "We're ready now, Sire."

Of course. Sire. That's what I should have been calling him. I really hope I wasn't too stupid, Ally thought, desperately trying to avoid thinking of the crowds waiting outside. She felt that she might vomit. *No, you will* not *throw up,* she ordered herself firmly. She set about using all her abilities to suppress her nausea.

The doors opened suddenly, exposing the party to the noise, light and slightly overcast weather outside. *I'm gonna hurl.*

Before Ally could follow through on her internal statement, she was pushed outside, blinking at the sudden brightness. Mentally bracing herself, she was surprised when a group of six Guards formed up around herself

chapter five

and Patrick, effectively blocking them from the view of the people standing nearby. Evelynne and her father, accompanied by another small group of Guardsmen, broke off to the side, towards the waiting cameras. Before they moved out of sight, Evelynne shot a smile back in Ally's direction.

All of a sudden, Ally found her wheelchair being lifted carefully into a stately van emblazoned with the Altantlan Royal crest. As the chair was fastened securely into place, Ally saw that the interior of the van was luxuriously appointed. The young woman started as Patrick climbed into the seat across from her. "A bit of a rush, isn't it?" he asked.

Still dazed, Ally replied, "I thought I was going to have to get my picture taken. I mean–"

The monk cut her off with a raised hand. "Please, Ally, everyone could see that was the very last thing you wanted," he reassured her. "You were turning a most unappealing shade of green. *Za* would never want you to feel uncomfortable, especially for something as minor as a few photographs. I manage to avoid the press because of my religious calling. In a few days, once you've settled in a bit, we'll bring in a single photographer to take a few pictures, and maybe have a short interview. It will be entirely under your control."

"Thank you," Ally said fervently.

The door opened again, admitting King Jad and Princess Evelynne. Once they were settled, the motorcade got under way.

Evelynne sank back in her seat with a weary sigh. Despite the stress that was evident in her face, Ally though she still looked radiant.

"Oh, Isis, I'm glad that's over for the moment," the princess stated. "I admit that I normally love doing that, but I thought they were going to eat me out there."

I wouldn't mind eating–Shut up! Shut up! Shut up! Ally thought.

"Are you all right, *Ishta* Tretiak?" the King asked. "You look a little red."

"She does that a lot," Patrick observed.

chapter six

"Well, I have to admit that I'm happy to be out of there," Evelynne said, leaning back in her seat. "It was wonderful to see *ʒa* and Patrick, but right now I really need a rest."

Ally nodded in agreement. She didn't know how the princess managed to remain sane if the past few days had been any indication of her typical schedule. Numerous interviews; meetings with what seemed like half the population of the island; press conferences; a speech in the Hall of Nobles; another in the Hall of Advisors and more that Ally couldn't even remember right now.

Somehow, though, Evelynne had managed to find the time to be nearby during the single short interview and photo session that Ally had been subjected to. The reporter, an intense but compassionate older man with a long history of covering the Royal Family, had been able to draw Ally out with ease and had left with a promise that the young woman would give a more in-depth interview in the near future.

At last it was over and now Ally and Evelynne, along with Maïda and Sir Arthur, were on their way to the airport, where they would board a helicopter for the journey to the Summer Palace at Kilim.

"I don't know how you do it," Ally sympathised. "I thought that I was the one who was supposed to be busy, what with physio and all. Personally, I think you're nuts. You should think about changing careers. Though I must say," she continued, looking around the interior of their unusual van, "some of the perks are nice."

"True, but there isn't much of a retirement plan. You work until you drop dead." Evelynne gave her uninjured arm a good stretch. "Right now, though, we have two whole weeks all to ourselves. Just you, me, Maïda, Uncle Arthur, Ylan, Emil, James, Kamim, Moses, Latifa . . ." She trailed off. "Okay, maybe not all to ourselves."

Ally looked at her incredulously. "Who are all those people?"

"They are the housekeepers and servants at the Summer Palace," Maïda answered. "Ylan is the Seneschal, Emil is the Master of Servants, Latifa is the Head Cook, James is the Groundkeeper–"

"I get the idea," Ally said hurriedly. "Gee, it's a bit like Cleopatra saying to Julius Caesar, 'It'll be an intimate little dinner. Just you, me and two hundred servants.'" She shook her head. "Do you ever get any time alone?"

"Oh, I find some time here and there," Evelynne answered. "I like being around people, though."

"You'd have to," Ally said.

Sir Arthur had been silent throughout the exchange, though Evelynne was familiar enough with his moods to detect the amusement beneath his impassive expression. "We have arrived, Your Highness," he announced.

The bulk of the Royal Terminal loomed outside. This time the van had driven directly onto the runway, avoiding any onlookers who might be nearby. Sitting on the pad was a large helicopter with the seal of the Royal Family emblazoned on the side.

As soon as the van stopped, the waiting Guardsmen proceeded to carry out the now familiar ritual of lifting Ally's wheelchair onto the ground. She was more used to it now, but Ally still found the procedure extremely embarrassing, even though the people involved were very professional. She had been sorely tempted on more than one occasion to simply lift herself and her wheelchair out. Each time she had avoided giving in to the temptation, but had settled for spending a short time every night in the privacy of her own room free of the constraints of both her wheelchair and bed.

Thankfully, the time it took to extricate the young woman from the vehicle was short and the small party was soon making their way to the waiting helicopter. Evelynne took up her customary position pushing the wheelchair, so Ally was able to spend a few moments simply enjoying the warm sun on her face. It wasn't long before she was being pushed up the short ramp and secured in place within the aircraft.

"I'm so glad I won't be laying down this time," she said fervently, as the helicopter's engines started revving.

Her progress had been such that the doctors had given Ally permission to remain upright during the flight to Kilim.

"It's a good thing that you are," Evelynne said from her seat directly next to Ally. "We're going to be flying over the excavations at Aztlan. I think you'll find it really fascinating. You wouldn't be able to see it if you were horizontal."

The engines reached their highest pitch and the aircraft began to rise with a slight jerk. Ally started at the sudden movement and her left hand involuntarily tightened on the arm of her wheelchair. She was startled again when she felt warm hands gently pry her fingers loose. She looked down to see Evelynne's small hands carefully holding her own larger one.

"Are you all right?" the princess asked.

chapter six

Ally relaxed slowly as her body got used to the movement of the aircraft. "Yeah, I'm okay," she replied. "I've just never been on a helicopter before. It feels different from a plane." She tensed again as the helicopter dipped suddenly in a small downdraft. "I'll get used to it."

"Oh, good," Evelynne said, though she didn't release Ally's hand. "You know, it's a good thing you don't get airsick."

"You have no idea. My mother gets airsick. And seasick. And carsick, unless she's driving. Thank God my Dad has a stomach like a rock. Whenever we used to travel, we'd play 'Rock, Paper, Scissors'. Whoever lost had to sit next to Mom and keep getting her airsickness bags. She has a technique now, though."

"Really? My cousin uses those wrist pressure point things. Does she use those?"

Ally grinned. "Not exactly. She takes a couple of Gravol, about four shots of gin and sleeps the whole way."

"I guess that would do it," Evelynne laughed. "I'll have to suggest it to my cousin Reylinn."

"Of course, she's pretty much stoned for two days after she arrives. On the other hand, if there's a whale involved at all she's got a stomach like a rock. It's the only way she survives working on a boat."

☙ ☙ ☙ ☙ ☙

Some two hours later the helicopter touched down once more on the landing pad at the Summer Palace.

Evelynne looked out the window, startled. "Isis, I didn't realise we were here yet."

While the helicopter's ramp was being lowered, Ally took the opportunity to peer out the window at the small amount of landscape she could see. The landing pad was situated in the middle of a large expanse of lawn. The grass was edged with large trees, effectively blocking the area from prying eyes. Through the trees Ally could see the gleam of sunlight off buildings several kilometres away, and just beyond the town lay the glistening expanse of the Atlantic Ocean.

That must be Kilim, Ally thought. *But where the heck is the Summer Palace?* No matter how hard she searched the area outside her window, the young woman could not spot anything that might even be a shack, much less a mansion. Turning to Evelynne, she asked, "I can't see the Palace. Where is it, exactly?"

The princess gave Ally a curious look, then pointed towards the opposite side of the aircraft, where the ramp was being lowered. "Right over there," she said.

Ally could feel herself reddening. "Right. Of course. Well, don't I feel like the moron. Is there any chance we could just forget I asked that?" She turned pleading eyes to Evelynne's amused face.

"Of course," Evelynne granted magnanimously. Ally's exaggerated sigh of relief was cut short by her next words. "At least until Chorus gets here."

"Oh, God. Please no. You can't. You wouldn't."

Evelynne nodded firmly. "It's only fair. I heard my evil brother telling you all those embarrassing stories about me. I need to have my own conspirator."

"But the story of you holding court with all your stuffed animals in the throne room is just so–"

Evelynne's eyes narrowed. "Finish that sentence. I dare you."

Ally sighed resignedly. "You realise this means war."

The princess' smile was predatory. "Bring it on."

Any further banter was put on hold as the two friends left the helicopter.

Once on the concrete outside, Ally could see the Summer Palace clearly. Set uphill from the landing pad, the building was a synthesis of Arabian and Classical Greek architecture. Constructed out of marble, the Palace sported both ornately carved Corinthian columns along its front face and golden Arabian-style domes set at each end of the building. It wasn't a huge structure, as palaces went, but the front section was at least two stories tall, while the rear was at least four stories. The grounds were set on the hillside leading up from the town of Kilim and behind the Palace to the southwest the land continued to rise, eventually becoming the looming bulk of Mount Sekemat. It was just after noon, so the brilliant sun had yet to sink behind the mountain's mass.

A small group of people had gathered to greet them just beyond the edge of the helipad. There were five that Ally could see. As soon as Evelynne and Ally were clear of the helicopter, two of them–a man and woman in simple grey uniforms–moved forward at the signal of an older man in a more ornate blue uniform bearing the Royal seal to collect the Royal party's luggage. A tall bearded man with the same mien and bearing as Sir Arthur, though wearing a slightly different uniform and a very elderly man in an ornate robe leaning heavily on a cane watched the women approach.

At the sight of the elderly man, Evelynne's face broke into a broad smile, which was echoed in the deeply lined face before her. "Domdom!"

chapter six

the princess cried in Lantlan. "What are you doing here?" Making sure that Ally's wheelchair was secure, she hurried around to hug the old man, who squeezed back with surprising strength.

"Evy," the man acknowledged in the same language. "I'm so glad you're okay." Pulling back, he glared at her with mock severity. "What am I doing here? There's no way I'll let you come to my island without being here to meet you! You're not Queen yet, young lady and I'm still not dead."

Evelynne looked suitably chastised. "I just meant to say that I would have come and visited you. I know you have trouble getting around."

"Hmph. I'll have you know that when I'm dead I'm going to have my body preserved and brought out whenever you're around just to greet you."

"Wonderful image, Domdom."

"Of course, the real reason I always come out to meet you is that I'm always hoping you'll bring some handsome young man that you intend to marry so that I can make him my Heir. You really must hurry up and find one. I'm not getting any younger, you know."

Evelynne grinned again. "Well, I didn't bring you a young man this time, Domdom. However, I did bring you the next best thing." Switching to English, she continued, "Domdom, may I present Alleandre Tretiak of Parksville, British Columbia, Canada. Ally, this is Lord Thomas Baker, Duke of Avalon."

Ally hesitantly extended a hand towards the Duke. "Your Grace," she murmured.

"*Ishta* Tretiak," the Duke replied, taking her smooth hand in his wrinkled one. "Such politeness. You seem to have learned the proper way to address the Nobility, as well. So few foreigners know how to these days."

"I tend to read a lot of fantasy," Ally admitted.

"Indeed." The Duke's brows rose in speculation. "We will have to have a discussion on your favourite authors one of these days. You don't happen to be an Atlantlan citizen do you?"

"Er . . . no."

"Pity. If you were, I could make you my Heir," the Duke joked.

"For now, though," interrupted Evelynne, "as we've established your good breeding, you may as well call him Domdom, like I do."

A little surprised, Ally looked to the Duke for confirmation.

'Domdom' gave a melodramatic sigh. "I suppose if you must. When Evy was very young, she couldn't pronounce 'Thomas', so naturally I became 'Domdom'," he explained. "Young people have no respect nowadays." Turning serious, the Duke continued, "You have most likely heard this many times in the last few days, but I feel that I must say it again on my own behalf. Thank you for bringing Evelynne back to us in one piece. She is very dear to me on a personal level." Slowly and carefully he bent down and brushed his lips against Ally's cheek.

Ally was stunned, but managed to say, "Um . . . you're very welcome."

Standing upright again, the Duke said, "Well, I've monopolised your attention for long enough. I believe there are a few other introductions that must be made."

Evelynne smiled gratefully at the Duke, then turned to the other two men who had been waiting patiently. Indicating the tall man with the military bearing, she said, "Ally, this is Lieutenant-Colonel James Allan, Master of Security at the Palace. Generally speaking, if he's doing a good job, you'll never see him."

Colonel Allan touched his fingers to his heart lightly in salute and gave a brief smile. "*Ishta* Tretiak."

"Colonel." Ally nodded back.

"And, this is Nancu Ylan, the Palace Seneschal. He's in charge of day-to-day operations. If you ever have any complex requests or problems with the servants, he's the one to talk to. Unlike the Colonel, if Nancu is doing a good job you *will* see him."

Seneschal Ylan nodded his head in greeting, though his face remained completely expressionless. "*Ishta* Tretiak."

"Seneschal," Ally greeted.

"All right then," Evelynne stated, "now that everyone here knows each other, let's get up to the house and meet everybody up there. I haven't eaten in five hours and I'm starving."

As they set off for the palace, slowly, out of deference to Lord Thomas' age, Ally asked, "So, er . . . Domdom. You've known Evy for years, right? You must know plenty of stories." Ally grinned triumphantly as Evelynne made an inarticulate sound of outrage.

Unperturbed, the Duke replied, "Oh my, yes. I remember one time when she was learning to speak English . . ."

After the introduction of Emil Leroc, the Master of Servants and Latifa Ammam, the Head Cook and a host of others, Evelynne, Ally and Lord Thomas sat down for lunch. Sir Arthur had left to consult with his Palace counterpart and Maïda had been dispatched to make the final arrangements to the princess' rooms. Latifa was a wonderful cook and for a time there was silence around the table as everyone concentrated on the meal.

chapter six

Ally took the opportunity to examine her surroundings more thoroughly. They were eating in one of the lesser dining rooms, which was still larger than half her parents' house. The stone walls were dyed a muted yellow colour and decorated with portraits of noble-looking individuals. A large window faced east, affording a spectacular view of the lightly wooded hillside leading down to the ocean, while sparing the room from the heat of the afternoon sun. The coolness of the dining room was a welcome relief after the heat outside.

Finally, once the edge had been taken off everyone's hunger, Evelynne spoke up. "So, what sort of things are you dealing with in the Hall of Nobles, Domdom? I've been too busy the last few days to really find out what's on the agenda."

The Duke grew grim. "The Hy Braseal Liberation Army has attacked twice more in the last two weeks. This time two gunmen opened fire in a shopping mall in Po-Matin and a bomb went off in a Req'sal bus station. Altogether fourteen people were killed and over fifty others were wounded. Both times the scum got away cleanly."

"God," said Ally. A glance at Evelynne showed that she was equally shaken. "Who are they? Rebels?"

"Apparently. The odd thing is that until three years ago we had never had any major problems with terrorists. Oh, there was the occasional psychotic or separatist movement, but nothing this organised. Now we have the so-called Hy Braseal Liberation Army, which is very organised, very well equipped and very vocal, especially to foreign media. They claim to be fighting a war against their 'elitist, dictatorial oppressors'. It doesn't matter that Hy Braseal has the highest standard of living in Atlantl." Lord Thomas shook his head in confusion. "It just doesn't make sense."

Evelynne was white by the time the Duke was finished. "Isis," she breathed. "I didn't realise they had escalated things so much." The room was silent again as they contemplated the sombre news. After a few moments, the princess sighed. "I'll have to talk to za to see what I can do to help." Purposely injecting a lighter tone into her voice, she asked, "So what else has been going on?"

Lord Thomas gave an equally forced smile, which became more natural as he talked. "Lord Hassan and his cronies are trying to repeal the Marriage Equality Decision. Again." Now the Duke's smile was feral. "Needless to say, Jason is providing me with wonderful ammunition to fight them."

Evelynne laughed, glad to put the darker subjects behind her for the time being. "I'd imagine he is."

"Pardon my ignorance–again–but what is the Marriage Equality Decision?" Ally asked. She had felt totally lost in the course of the conversation and had decided that her first task would be to read as much as possible on Atlantlan history and politics.

"It was a decision handed down by the High Court about three years ago recognising homosexual, polygamous and polyandrous marriages as fully legal and equal under the law."

"Okay, and who is Jason?"

The Duke answered, "Jason McKendrick is the young man who argued the case. He was actually arguing solely for homosexual marriages initially. His argument was that banning gay marriages was discrimination based on gender, which is prohibited by the Constitution. I was there when he was before the Justicars. He pointed to a very handsome young man and asked one of the female Justicars if marrying him would be considered a desirable possibility. When the Justicar admitted that it would, he claimed that prohibiting another man from doing the same was therefore discrimination based on gender, rather than sexual preference."

"I like it," Ally said.

"From that decision came the one allowing polygamy, since its prohibition was argued to be religious discrimination. Then came polyandry, since only allowing men to marry multiple wives–"

"–was biased against women," Ally completed the thought. "I get it."

"So now Atlantlan citizens are legally allowed to marry whomever they please," said Evelynne.

God, thought Ally. *I think I might move here permanently.*

"Naturally," continued Lord Thomas, "the more conservative Nobles and commoners make regular attempts to overturn the decision. I happen to be at the forefront of those who just as regularly oppose them. Young Jason McKendrick has since been elected my Advisor in Law and helps provide me with the necessary legal arguments. Not too long ago he also married Pedro, the young man whom he pointed out during his case."

"I'd like to meet him sometime."

The Duke smiled. "I'm sure I can arrange that."

"What's happened to the Proposal that Lord Ryers was submitting?" Evelynne asked, changing the subject.

Lord Thomas continued to fill in the princess on the current political wranglings of the nobility. Ally followed along as best she could, but the long days and multiple trips were taking their toll on her still recovering energy levels. Evelynne finally noticed when Ally found her eyes closing uncontrollably for the third time.

chapter six

Breaking off her conversation with the Duke, the princess apologised, "I'm sorry, Domdom. I think we'll have to continue this later. Right now I have to get Ally into bed."

The woman in question woke up just in time to hear Evelynne's last comment and reddened as her libido made a predictable suggestion.

"Of course, Evy." Standing with the aid of his cane and making his way to Ally's side, the Duke said, "Ally, my dear, I will take my leave of you now. You should get some sleep. You're looking a little flushed."

chapter seven

The slow-moving elevator finally arrived at the fourth floor and Evelynne pushed Ally out the doors and into a long, beautifully decorated hallway. The wide corridor had the same off-white stone walls as the rest of the Palace and ran the length of the building. Large windows at either end let in the bright sunshine and made the white marble floor gleam. A number of large potted plants lent vibrancy and tapestries and paintings added colour. In contrast to the other intricately carved wooden doors lining the corridor, the elevator that Ally and Evelynne had just exited was set discreetly into the wall, and once closed, Ally almost couldn't tell that it was there.

Evelynne stopped the wheelchair at a door across from a large tapestry depicting men in armour bearing shields with large red crosses kneeling before an imperial-looking woman wearing a crown. On a shore behind them, six ships were beached, while in the background another five ships could be seen sinking into the ocean.

Seeing Ally's curious gaze, the princess paused before opening the door. "That's the Templars pledging allegiance to Queen Heru after they fled persecution in Europe. They left Europe with eleven ships. Only six survived the reefs surrounding Atlantl to reach shore." She pointed to the lead Knight. "That is Joseph of Aragon a relative of Saint DeMolay, the martyr who was burned at the stake in France. Several years afterwards, he married the Queen and founded the Heru-DeMolay line. My ancestors."

"That's neat," Ally said. "The Templars are still around, aren't they?"

Evelynne nodded. "They're considered one of the most prestigious Knightly Orders in Atlantl. Sir Arthur is a Knight of the Temple. There are quite a number of other Orders."

The princess turned and opened the door. "And here," she said, "are your rooms, Milady."

On being pushed into the room, Ally could only stare. The chamber was huge. Large southward-facing glass doors opened out onto a balcony, letting in both light and heat. In front of the door, two *chaises longues*, a large sofa and three armchairs were set around a low table in the middle of the room. Not far away two more armchairs sat in front of a large empty fireplace. Immediately to the left of the doorway a bookshelf ran along the wall to the corner thirty feet away, where it bent and continued along the next wall until interrupted by another door.

Ally opened her mouth, but nothing came out.

"Is everything okay?" Evelynne asked, worried that Ally was somehow disappointed with the room. "Is there something you don't like? I can get them to change anything you want. If you don't like the furniture–"

"No, no, no," Ally cut her off. "It's just that it–I mean–wow. It's big. My parents' house could fit in here!"

"Oh," said the princess, relaxing. "I guess I'm used to it. This is the *Tiama'apep* Room, as you can probably tell from the décor."

"A wild guess here, but *Tiama'apep* means 'dragon', right?"

"Oh yes, didn't I say that? I remembered that you said you loved dragons, so I thought you'd like this." Evelynne pointed through the west wall. "I'm right next door in the *Sekheru*–um, that is, the Gryphon Room."

The Dragon Room certainly lived up to its title. Murals of dragons of all types covered the walls. Sculpted wooden dragons formed the legs of the furniture and more supported the doorways. Several vases bearing oriental dragons were placed throughout the chamber. On the floor, small dragons were woven into the carpet, threatening to attack the ankles of anyone who walked over them. Possibly the most disconcerting decoration was the fireplace. A large mural of a single dragon took up the wall and melded with the stone of the fireplace, which formed the mouth. Ally could imagine the effect when the fire was lit, leaving the room's occupants looking down the beast's fiery throat. The room was exotic, beautiful and stimulating, all at the same time.

"Wow," Ally repeated. "I like it. And this is my room? Um, this is probably another stupid question, but where do I sleep?"

"Right through there is the bedroom," Evelynne pointed to a second door. "If you still want to, you can have a sleep now."

The reminder of sleep brought the full weight of Ally's fatigue crashing down on her once more. "I think I need to. This new painkiller the doctors have me on is great, but it completely wipes me out. I hate to seem like a poor guest, but . . . I guess you have other stuff you need to do," she finished awkwardly.

"I'd rather be with you," Evelynne said promptly, provoking a shy pleased smile from her companion. She pushed Ally towards the bedroom. "And don't worry about it. You're still healing, so *anything* you need to do–do it."

Much smaller than the main chamber, the bedroom was still quite large. It was darker than the previous room, heavy curtains having been drawn

chapter seven

across the windows. The dragon motif prevailed here as well, but Ally's eyes were drawn to the most comfortable looking–and largest–bed she had ever seen. "Oh, my God," she exclaimed. "That thing's huge! My first-year dorm room at university was smaller than that!"

Evelynne chuckled. "Well, it'll give you plenty of room to roll around. Now, let's get you in there. Are you sure you don't want me to get some more help?"

"Positive," Ally affirmed. "I'll be able to do this."

"Okay, then," the princess said confidently, parking the wheelchair beside the bed. Locking the brakes, she came around to stand before Ally and stretched out her arms.

Ally looked up at her blankly. "What?"

Evelynne was equally puzzled. "What? You said you didn't want anyone else to help you, so I'm it."

"Oh! Um–I meant–that is . . ."

The princess' eyebrow rose. "What, you thought you were going to lift yourself out of your chair and into bed on your own? Not likely." She gave her outstretched arms a slight shake. "So here I am."

Actually, that's exactly what I thought I was going to do. Still, her way looks more fun, Ally thought, looking up at Evelynne's inviting arms. *Damn, I must be tired.*

Giving in, Ally allowed Evelynne to remove her glasses and place them on the small table beside the bed. She reached up and clasped her hands around Evelynne's lower arms, as the princess grasped hers in return. Both of them tensed as Ally was slowly lifted from the chair. Since the doctors had decided that the risk of any damage to Ally's spine was minimal, the care was due more to her still-healing back muscles. The wounds in both Ally's and Evelynne's shoulders had healed to the point where they were more of a painful, nagging inconvenience.

As Ally rose carefully, she wondered how much she would be able to lift herself with her talents without giving anything away. She wasn't sure if Evelynne's smaller frame would be able to handle her larger mass. Her mental debate ended with a decision to just see how far she could go without channelling.

Ally had partially risen and was taking a step forward to clear the wheelchair when her foot caught on one of the footrests. She pitched forward into Evelynne's abdomen. The princess braced herself instinctively, trying to prevent both of them from crashing to the floor, her arms curling protectively around Ally's body. Ally reflexively tried to focus, but fatigue had dulled her mental responses. She was able to prevent both of them from falling, but not stop herself from ending up leaning against Evelynne's warm body, with her face buried between the princess' breasts.

Both women froze. Ally desperately tried to think of a graceful way out of the situation, but her mind remained a stubborn blank. Stymied, she wished that self-immolation was among her abilities and that she could simply disappear in a flame of embarrassment.

Evelynne's mind was blank as well, as she tried to work out exactly what had happened. She looked down at their respective positions. Suddenly she felt a brief, butterfly touch on her breasts and realised that Ally had blinked, her eyelashes lightly brushing Evelynne through the thin silk shirt she was wearing. The princess shivered.

The shudder broke through Ally's stunned mind. Moving slowly, she used Evelynne's arms to push herself upright. Looking anywhere but at the princess, she said, "Um . . ."

Shaking herself out of her own stupor, Evelynne wondered why she could still feel Ally's eyelashes on her skin. Judging by the heat coming off the body of the woman in front of her, her friend was blushing to the roots of her hair. *I wonder how far down that blush goes.* Brushing aside the errant thought, she took charge of the situation. "Okay, then. Let's get you into–I mean–okay, sit down here. Good, now lie down. Let's swing you around. Okay, legs up . . . and you're there." She pulled the blankets up over Ally's shoulders. The woman in the bed still refused to look at her. "Well, that was exciting," the princess said with a little laugh, trying to defuse the situation.

She was rewarded when Ally looked at her with a tremulous smile. Deciding to take the victory and run, Evelynne continued, "I'll be back to check up on you in a few hours. If you need anything before then, just push this button." She showed Ally a small device on the table beside the bed. "Sleep well," she said, and after a final brush of her fingers across Ally's forehead, she left the room, closing the door behind her.

Well, that was more fun than you were bargaining on, wasn't it? Ally asked herself. *I can't believe–No, I can believe–Oh, God. 'Sleep well,' she says. Yeah, right. I'm never going to be able to get to–*

She was asleep in seconds.

Evelynne gently closed the door to Ally's bedroom. Leaning her head back against the wooden surface, she took several deep breaths. *What in the Duat was that?* she asked herself. *Okay, so she tripped. People trip. Sometimes they bump into other people. It wasn't like she did it on purpose.*

She wondered why that thought was somehow disappointing.

chapter seven

Still pensive, the princess made her way through the sitting room and into the hallway. She was so deep in contemplation that when Sir Arthur called her name she jumped a foot in the air before spinning to face him.

"Aah! Don't *do* that!" she barked, placing a hand to her chest to calm her heart. She suddenly realised that her palm was resting where Ally's face had pressed a few minutes before and jerked it away as if burned.

"I'm sorry, Your Highness," Sir Arthur apologised, looking at her oddly. "Evelynne, are you all right? You look a little flushed."

"I'm okay," Evelynne said, reddening further. "I'm just a little warm." Taking herself firmly in hand, she focussed on Sir Arthur's blocky face. "I'll be fine. You wanted to talk to me?"

The bodyguard nodded. "There are two things, actually. First, I've been recalled by the Common Guard. They're conducting the investigation into the incident and I'm needed to clear up some details."

The princess was distraught. "They're not blaming you, are they? It wasn't your fault. You couldn't have done anything more."

Sir Arthur shook his head. "I'm afraid that isn't quite how it works," he said. "You were directly under my protection and I failed to protect you. You may not think that I was negligent or lax in my duties, but that is part of what the investigation will determine. If I or anyone on my team was directly or indirectly responsible for what happened, we will be appropriately disciplined."

"I'll find some way to protect you," the princess promised. "I can talk to *za* and—"

"No, you will not, Your Highness," Sir Arthur said, his tone hard. "If I am found culpable, it is my duty to face the consequences, whatever they may be. The same is true for every member of my team. Regardless of the outcome, you will *not* interfere in any way! That is final."

Evelynne wasn't happy, but she solemnly nodded acquiescence. Despite her initial reaction, she knew that her bodyguard was right. It was his duty to "face the music," as the English expression went, just as it was hers not to interfere. She knew he couldn't expect any less of himself. "Well, I can send you good thoughts," she said. "Even you can't stop me from doing that."

He smiled crookedly at her. "Of course not. I might even let you say a prayer or two to that heathen Goddess of yours."

Evelynne laughed involuntarily. "I just might do that. If I do, does that mean that you'll be going to the Hell that God of yours is so fond of?"

Sir Arthur grunted a laugh, and then returned to business. "While I am gone, Colonel Allan will be in charge of your primary protection. He will remain so until either I return or a new Master is assigned."

"Okay," Evelynne said resignedly. "When are you leaving?"

"Tomorrow morning," he replied.

"So soon? Well then, tonight I'd like you to have dinner with Maïda and me."

"I would enjoy that, Evy. Is *Ishta* Tretiak not going to be joining us?" the bodyguard asked, a little puzzled when Evelynne coloured slightly.

"She was so tired this afternoon that I think she might want to just stay in bed. I'll go and check on her around dinner time." She shook her head bemusedly. "It's still a little surreal to know that she's that main reason I'm alive right now. Most of the time she's just my friend, but then she'll move in just the wrong way and I can see that she's in pain. She never says anything, but then I remember lying there with her on top of me, protecting me. And then it passes and she's my friend again. It gets confusing," she said plaintively.

Sir Arthur patted Evelynne's arm comfortingly. "For now, just let her be your friend," he counselled. "Time will take care of the rest. In fact, Alleandre is the second subject I wanted to discuss with you. The Foreign Affairs Office and the Atlantlan Embassy in Canada have both been swamped with calls either asking about or asking to speak with *Ishta* Tretiak. Many of them are undoubtedly reporters and other spurious enquirers, but at least a few must be genuine friends and relatives. We have managed to get the names and addresses of most of the callers, so what Foreign Affairs would like is for Alleandre to look at the list and indicate which ones she would like to speak to so that the calls can be transferred here."

The princess nodded. "Well, like I said, I'm pretty sure she'll be out of it tonight, but tomorrow I'll get her to take a look at it."

"Excellent. Now, what is Latifa serving for dinner?"

❧ ❧ ❧ ❧ ❧

Alleandre awoke ravenously hungry. She vaguely recalled being woken at some point and offered food, but she wasn't sure if she had given a coherent answer. The curtains were still pulled across the windows, leaving the room dark. There was light leaking around the edges, letting her know that the sun was up.

Ally stretched carefully, feeling disused muscles protest. She fumbled on the bedside table for her glasses and slipped them on. The young woman looked for a clock, but couldn't see one in the darkened room.

Concentrating, she could sense nobody else in the room, though whether she was really alone or if her unreliable sensing abilities weren't working, she could not tell.

Deciding to take the risk, Ally focussed on the window curtains, reaching for them and channelling. She was pleased when her power responded

chapter seven

promptly. Obediently the heavy cloth parted slightly in the middle, allowing bright sunshine to stream into the room.

Wait a minute, Ally thought. *That sunlight is coming from the east! It's morning already? No wonder I'm hungry!* Suddenly the memories of the afternoon before surfaced and she groaned, covering her face with her hands. *I can't believe I did that. I'll never be able to look Evy in the face again.* She warmed in remembered embarrassment. *Of course not,* her libido interjected. *You're going to be spending all your time staring at her–*Ally cut herself off before it could continue.

Her bladder chose that moment to make its demands known, and Ally gratefully seized the distraction. *Okay, so do I push the button and get someone to help me to the washroom?* Through a previously unnoticed door she could see a sink, indicating the bathroom. *I really hate that. It's humiliating. So, my other option is to lift myself over there and get back to bed before anyone arrives. That's kind of risky. Of course, if I just lift myself into the wheelchair, I might be able to convince anybody that comes in that I managed to climb into it from the bed on my own.*

Ally decided to risk the last idea, especially when her bladder began protesting more strenuously.

She first scanned the area closely once more, using all the senses available to her. Satisfied that nobody was about to burst into the room, Ally turned her concentration to her own body. Slipping into the light trance took barely a moment. She visualised the desired response, then set about focussing on turning the image into reality. The sensation of energy being channelled towards that end brought a familiar feeling of exhilaration. The incredibly fulfilling sensation increased as Ally felt the bonds of gravity slipping away. The entire process took less than a second.

Throwing back the blankets with her hands, she allowed herself to float several centimetres above the mattress, revelling in the feeling of freedom that had been markedly absent since her confinement to the wheelchair.

Refocusing on the task at hand, Ally pushed herself through the air towards her chair, moving her body into a sitting position. She lowered herself carefully into the wheelchair and then let go of the focus. Sighing in resignation, Ally adjusted her suddenly incredibly heavy body more comfortably in the seat.

As she was about to push herself towards the bathroom, a light knock sounded on the door. It took Ally a moment to get her heart out of her throat and realise that nobody had actually entered the room and seen her doing something impossible. Letting go of the panic, she called out, "Come in," in a fairly level voice.

The door opened a crack and Evelynne poked her head into the room. She frowned as she took in the empty bed. Then her eyes widened as they fell on Ally sitting in her wheelchair with an uncertain expression on her face.

"Ally, what do you think you're doing?" the princess exclaimed as she strode into the room. "Did you climb out of bed on your own? You know you're not supposed to do that! What if you'd fallen? What if you pulled something? Did you really want to spend another six months in that chair? Well?"

Ally dropped her gaze, chastened. "I just needed to go to the bathroom," she said miserably, "and I didn't want to have to have someone help me out of bed and then onto the toilet. Do you have any idea how humiliating that is? I hate having to depend on someone else to do something as simple as go pee or have a bath. I hate it." Ally hunched her shoulders. "I'm sorry."

Evelynne's hard gaze softened as she looked at the dejected woman. She moved forward and knelt before Ally, taking her hand. "Hey, no, I'm sorry," she said. "I shouldn't have yelled at you. I just don't want you to get any more hurt." She reached out and used a finger to raise Ally's face to her own. "I know you hate it, but it's not forever. Unless you get hurt again and then it might be. I don't want that to happen. I want you whole and healthy."

Ally blushed a little as her mind put its own meaning on the last sentence. She kept her eyes downcast as her head was raised, until she realised exactly where her gaze was resting. Her eyes snapped up to meet Evelynne's compassionate ones. "I know. It's just embarrassing to have someone watch me . . . you know. And no one's bathed me since I was five." *Except for Annie, but let's not go there.*

The princess nodded in understanding. "Is it the nurse? I can get you someone else if you want. Or *I* can–"

"No!" Ally blurted. "I mean . . . It's bad enough having a relative stranger doing it. I can at least pretend I'm never going to see her again. If it was a friend . . . no." *Good God, no. Evy washing me? Nope, no, uh-uh. That would be bad. Very bad. In a good kind of way, of course, but still very bad.*

Evelynne felt an odd pang of disappointment. "Okay. For now, though, will you let me help you into the bathroom? That's all, I promise. I think you've proved that you can get into and out of your wheelchair by yourself."

You have no idea, Ally thought.

Evelynne looked up and frowned. "Who opened the curtains?" she asked. "They were closed when I checked last night."

Oh, shit. "Uh, I guess someone opened them. It could have been one of the servants." *Technically true. Someone could have come in. They didn't, but they could have.*

  е е е е е

chapter seven

Some time later Ally sat with Evelynne eating a well-deserved breakfast of spicy scrambled eggs, bacon and melon.

She had gritted her teeth through another much needed bathing—realising that sleeping in one's clothes was not conducive to a pleasing body odour—and was now greatly enjoying Latifa's very good bacon.

Finally, Ally finished her third helping while Evelynne looked on with amusement. "Oh, that hit the spot," Ally said.

"It's a good thing I know you didn't eat last night or I'd think you had an eating disorder. With the amount you eat and the amount you weigh—"

"It's my metabolism. For some reason, no matter how much I eat I don't gain a pound."

"And western women everywhere hate you for it."

"It's not my fault," Ally protested as they both laughed. "So what's on the agenda today?"

"Well, I thought I'd spend the morning giving you a tour of the Palace," the princess said. "You have a physiotherapy session this afternoon." Ally scowled. "Don't pull a face. You're the one who wants to give up the sponge baths."

"Yeah, I know."

"This evening I figured we'd spend some time together just talking, or watching a movie or reading. Unless there's something you'd like to do."

The Crown Princess of Atlantl wants to watch movies with me. Nobody ever predicted that the class freak in high school would be doing this. "No, that sounds good. I'm easy." *D'oh!*

"Reeeally?" Evelynne drawled, enjoying the flush that predictably spread over her companion's face. She had learned just how much gentle teasing Ally could tolerate. "I'll remember to mention that to Lecherous Cousin Larrel. In the meantime, though, I have a little project for you." She produced a white folder. "These, my dear, are the people who wish to hear the sound of your melodious voice. All the people who have been trying to call you over the last two weeks," she explained, pulling a number of papers out of the folder. "What we want you to do is go over them and let us know which ones should be forwarded if they call again. Some of them are probably reporters, whom you can either talk to or not. It's all entirely up to you."

Ally took the pages and briefly scanned through them. "These people all want to talk to me? There are five pages!" *Aunt Hillary, Grandma . . . Don't know, don't know . . . Mister Waterson? My high school math teacher called? Weird. Don't know, don't know . . .*

Evelynne grinned. "You're popular. I won't even tell you about the Internet fan site that's already been established. Now the information given is name, address and telephone number. That should help you recognise the fakes. The last page lists the news agencies that want an interview. You can choose which, if any, to grace with your spectacular presence."

Ally flipped to the last page. "CBC's *The National?* CTV Newsworld? BBC? LANTA? *Sixty Minutes?* Jesus!" She turned back to the other callers. *My parents' neighbour, Old friend . . . Ugh, old enemy . . .* She suddenly froze on one name. *Annie called? Oh, God. What–?* "What's this number on the side here?" She pointed.

"Oh, that's the number of times the person has called."

My God, Annie's called twenty-two times? But we broke up! Only a few months ago! Ally stared at the name a moment longer. *Still, she never said it was because she didn't love me. She just couldn't handle . . . what I do. She admitted she still cared about me. We went out for two years. Of course she'd want to know how I am.*

"Ally? Are you okay?" Evelynne interrupted Ally's musings. Her friend had been staring at the same page for over a minute.

Ally shook herself out of her thoughts. "No, I'm all right. I was just trying to remember something. Do you need me to do this now?"

"No, whenever you want to. Still, some of those people will probably want to hear from you soon. If you like, you could call them instead."

Ally nodded. "I'll do this list right now if that's okay. I'll call some people this evening."

"That's fine," Evelynne assured her. "Let's go into the library."

"Sure." Ally started marking off names on the list. She hesitated for a long time when she came to Anabel Bourne.

chapter eight

"Ah, Colonel, come in." The swarthy, heavy-set woman waved Sir Arthur into her office. "Please, have a seat."

Sir Arthur obediently entered and carefully lowered his large frame into the chair with relief. The last two days had been spent in endless interviews and debriefings about the incident in Marseilles and even the bodyguard's prodigious stamina was strained. Every single decision he had made, every minute detail he could recall and every insignificant thought he had had: they had all been expertly drawn from him and analysed in excruciating detail. Every minor discrepancy had been pounced upon, instigating a new round of questions. Not even the knowledge that the other members of his Guard detail had already concluded their own debriefings had given him any feelings of relief.

Now his interrogators appeared to be satisfied and their commander, General Dame D'vaya Danun of the Common Guard, had summoned him to her office. The General's sharp eyes picked up Sir Arthur's carefully hidden tiredness. She gave him a tight smile of commiseration. "Colonel, I want to thank you officially for your co-operation in the investigation." She held up a thick file. "The agents have made a note of your willingness to assist." That said, the General relaxed minutely. "Unofficially I want to tell you that the final report will clear both yourself and your team of any negligence or culpability. It will still be a couple of weeks before the report is officially released, of course, but I wanted to set your mind at ease."

Sir Arthur's posture did not change, but the General saw his relief. "Thank you, General. I still lost two good men, though. They were under my command and I feel responsible."

"Of course you do. It's what makes you a good commander. In this case, though, you are not at fault. Forensic evidence shows that Sergeant al-Latif and Corporal Garner were both shot from behind at close range. There were absolutely no signs of a struggle, so it appears they were taken completely by surprise, probably before they had even established their position. What is even more disturbing is the fact that the shooters knew enough of our codes and procedures to give the correct responses when Eagle Two flashed them."

Sir Arthur nodded. "I had considered that. It raises some very troubling questions."

"Indeed. Guard codes are classified Ultra-Top Secret. For someone like Steven Jaspers or his accomplice to acquire the codes requires highly placed intelligence sources, possibly even somewhere in the organisation or in the Royal oversight committee."

"Steven Jaspers?"

"The male shooter. Blood analysis has indicated that the second shooter was female. We identified him a few days ago. Steven Travis Jaspers, thirty-eight, citizen of Gades County, Hy Braseal. We have intel linking him to the Hy Braseal Liberation Army."

Sir Arthur couldn't contain a small gasp of surprise. "The HBLA? *Jesu Christe*. They've never tried anything like this before."

"With this latest increase in terrorist activity that they're claiming credit for, we may have to expect similar attacks. All military and police forces, as well as the Noble Guards and protection details have been warned. We'd like to keep it out of the public arena to avoid a panic, but that decision is King Jad's and Queen Cleo's." General Danun smiled thinly. "But wait, it gets even better. Jaspers' autopsy showed that he was not killed by one of your Guards as we initially thought. The bullet we pulled out of his head matches the one used to kill Corporal Garner."

"You mean he was killed by his own accomplice? But why?"

"We're not sure. Some of my analysts believe that Jaspers was simply a tool, someone to put the blame on, maybe so that we would link the shooting to the HBLA. The problem is that the link is so obvious that it's suspect and anyone planning something this elaborate would know that we'd be wary of making the obvious conclusion. So once again we're left in the dark, with a female would-be assassin–who is apparently the more dangerous of the two–on the loose. The lab is doing everything they can to try to pull genetic information out of the blood sample, but I'm not optimistic."

Sir Arthur shook his head. "I suppose we should be grateful that *Ishta* Tretiak intervened when she did."

The General's expression darkened. "Ah yes, Alleandre Tretiak," she said in a flat voice. "Some questions have arisen about our mysterious saviour as well."

"Really?" Sir Arthur asked in surprise. "I reviewed her background dossier myself. While somewhat remarkable, I didn't find anything that might be considered terribly suspicious."

The General waved a hand. "Oh, I agree, her background *seems* clean. You read about how she saved a number of her classmates from that laboratory fire, then? I agree that such an act, while impressive, is not exactly

chapter eight

unheard-of. However, it's not her background that I'm directly concerned about. I'd like you to take a look at this."

Touching a button on her computer, General Danun caused a portion of wall to slide away to reveal a large television screen. The screen lit up to display a frozen image of a city street, the sidewalk crowded with people. Sir Arthur immediately identified the scene as the street in Marseilles just prior to the princess' arrival at the museum.

"You recognise this?" the General asked. Sir Arthur nodded. "Good. It was taken by a French news team covering the visit." At another button press, the mass of excited people on the screen came to life. The video continued to play silently, until Danun stopped it suddenly. "Right there," she said. A mouse pointer appeared and floated up to indicate a pair of people in the front row. "We've been able to enhance the image–" The General typed a few commands into the computer. "-and . . ." The image, blurred by distance, refocused to reveal the faces of Alleandre Tretiak and Chorus Tladi. "We have identified this point to be just under thirty metres from the spot where Princess Evelynne was hit." The video began playing again and this time a timer appeared in the corner. The panning camera soon left Alleandre and her companion out of view and as soon as they were gone, the image stopped again. "This is the last time that we know her exact location." The scene restarted, now playing at half speed. The camera panned to the princess, already shaking hands with the mayor and turning to greet his wife and then suddenly Alleandre was back on the screen, throwing herself at a startled Evelynne. As they tumbled to the ground, the General stopped the playback for the last time.

Even the imperturbable Sir Arthur looked shaken as the events replayed. It was the first time he had seen a detailed third-person account of the shooting. "She got there just in time."

"Exactly," General Danun replied, her voice grim. "Look at the time index. We lose track of Tretiak at fourteen seconds. The first shot is fired at eighteen seconds. That gives our heroine at most four seconds to travel a straight-line distance of about thirty metres, giving her an average speed of seven and a half metres per second, minimum." She looked at Sir Arthur seriously. "The fastest man in the world runs at about ten metres per second. While those numbers on their own would seem to indicate that Tretiak isn't an Olympic quality sprinter, she *also* had to clear at least one barricade and who knows how many other civilians in order to get a clear path."

"I didn't realise she was that fast."

"It's not her speed that I'm worried about. Maybe she runs in her spare time. What I'm concerned with is her *timing*. She tackled the princess just after the first shot was fired and was hit less than a second later by the third shot. What this suggests to me is that she's either Supergirl, or she knew *exactly* when the shooters would fire."

Sir Arthur looked at his superior incredulously. "Are you saying she was a part of the shooters' plan? She was hit twice!"

"Yes, but the first two shots missed, which should have been practically impossible, given the equipment Jaspers was using. Plus, she survived the next two bullets, contrary to what our experts tell me should have happened. So here is one possible theory: Tretiak is in contact with the shooters somehow, who tell her seconds before they fire. She is prepared and moves instantly towards the princess. She's slightly slower than expected, so Jaspers, not wanting to actually kill Evelynne for some reason, causes his first and second shots to miss. The third and fourth bullets are specially made and aimed to avoid fatal wounds. Once Tretiak is hit, the woman sniper turns on her companion and shoots him."

"That seems a little far-fetched. Why would Alleandre allow herself to be shot?"

"Look at how close she's become to the princess. I can't think of a better way to get someone close to the Royal Family. You know how they are about repaying debts. As to long-term plans, I don't know."

"She was shot in the spine. She could have died or been permanently paralysed. There are lots of safer locations to shoot someone so they'll survive."

"So maybe Jaspers' aim was slightly off." The General rubbed her hands over her face, suddenly showing her fatigue. "Hell, maybe I'm wrong about the whole thing. Maybe she knew about the shooting because she's psychic and she survived the shooting because she's bulletproof. Maybe she's an alien or an angel. Or a devil." Her expression strengthened once more. "Until I know for sure, though, I'll be keeping an eye on *Ishta* Tretiak."

The battle was turning into a disaster and the young, inexperienced commander of the Forces of Light watched helplessly as her troops succumbed to what could only be described as a rout. She looked across the battlefield at her counterpart, who had been expertly directing the Forces of Darkness all afternoon.

"How does the Druid move again?" she asked.

Evelynne sighed. "Either horizontally, vertically or like a chess knight."

"Okay." Ally studied the game board closely again. She reached out and picked up a piece in the shape of a berobed man bearing a sickle and hesitantly advanced it three spaces. With great reluctance, she removed her

chapter eight

hand from the piece and then looked up at the princess. "I can do that, right?"

"Yes," Evelynne confirmed. "But you might have used your move instead to open your Astral portal and bring your other Angel into play. As it is–" She moved a dark piece in the form of a snarling demon forward. "–checkmate."

Ally looked down on the *Vei'Chel* board in resignation. "Of course it's checkmate. Was there ever any doubt?" She leaned back in her wheelchair and shook her head. "That is one seriously complicated game. I mean, chess is bad enough, but no, some genius decided to add another eighty spaces to the board and twenty more pieces per side. Then there are those damned 'portals'. . ." She snorted in disgust.

Evelynne grinned ferally. "So are you giving up? Can't hack it? And here I thought Canadians were so intelligent."

"Are you dissing my country?" Ally bantered back. "Where I come from we don't like uppity foreigners dissing our country. We prefer to make fun of our homeland all by ourselves, thank you very much."

"Blah, blah, blah." Evelynne's hand made a talking motion. "Come on, show me what you've got." She began setting up the board again.

"Oh, you're on, princess. Prepare to win by a narrower margin than last time!"

As she helped to arrange the game pieces on the *Vei'Chel* board, Ally reflected on the events of the last two days. Once she had reviewed the list supplied by the Foreign Affairs Office, Ally and the princess had spent much of the rest of the day touring the Palace. Ally had been awed by the building and fascinated by its history. Evelynne had been happy to play tour guide and had enthusiastically shown her companion every nook and cranny that a wheelchair could access.

Ally had used the evening to get back in touch with friends and family members, spending hours on the phone. The next day the weather had turned rainy, so Evelynne and Ally had spent the day inside, reading, talking and watching movies on the gigantic television in one of the sitting rooms. In the afternoon, Ally had spoken to more people, though there was one number that went undialled.

Today, the weather showed no signs of improving so the princess had taken it upon herself to teach Ally how to play *Vei'Chel*, which was the game of choice among the Atlantlan citizenry. Ally likened the game to "chess squared".

Just as the last pieces were in place and Evelynne was about to make her first move, a discreet knock sounded at the door. Both women looked up to see the solemn form of Nancu Ylan, the Palace Seneschal. "I beg your pardon for the interruption, Your Highness," he said, "but there is another telephone call for *Ishta* Tretiak." He indicated the portable phone he was carrying.

Ally held out her hand for the phone. "Thank you, Ylan. Do you know who it is?"

"Indeed," the Seneschal answered. "It is Ms. Anabel Bourne calling for you, *Ishta* Tretiak."

Ally froze with the phone in her hand and Evelynne looked on with concern as she paled. "Anabel Bourne? Are you sure?"

"Yes, *Ishta*. I believe you designated Ms. Bourne as an individual who should be allowed to speak with you. Has there been some mistake?"

"No, no mistake," Ally said faintly. "I just wasn't expecting her to call again." *Of course you were expecting her to call,* she thought. *She called almost every day that you were incommunicado, and since then you've been avoiding calling her back.*

Satisfied, Ylan bowed to the princess and Ally, then turned and left the room.

Evelynne waited until he had closed the door before turning back to Ally, who was staring blankly into space. "Ally? What's wrong?"

The young woman shook herself out of her thoughts. "Nothing's wrong," she said unconvincingly. She hefted the phone. "I should talk to her. Um . . . Do you mind if I take this in private? It's just . . ."

The princess was surprised. Until now, her friend hadn't minded her being nearby while speaking to others on the phone and had actually appeared to take comfort in her presence. *Still, she's entitled to her privacy . . .*

"No, that's okay," Evelynne said, rising to her feet. "I'll go and—"

"No, stay here," Ally said, waving her back. "I'll go into my bedroom. Although I don't know how long this will be, so if there's something you need to do . . ." Despite her disclaimer, Ally's eyes were entreating.

"All right, I'll just read for a while. I'll be here when you get back," the princess assured her.

Ally sat in the darkened confines of her bedroom. The lights were off and the sky outside the balcony doors was dark with rainclouds, leaving the room gloomy. *I wonder when the rain's going to stop,* she thought irrelevantly. She knew that she was concentrating on the weather to avoid thinking about the upcoming conversation. With an effort of will, she pulled her mind back to the telephone in her hand. The blinking light on its face told her that the caller was still on hold and Ally had a sudden hope that the person on the other end would get impatient and hang up.

chapter eight

As soon as the thought crossed her mind, Ally scolded herself. *Come on, she's halfway around the world. It's not like she can hurt me.* A small part of her countered, *She already did.*

Taking a deep breath and gathering her courage, Ally punched the button that would connect the call. "Hello?"

A heavily accented voice answered, "*Ishta* Tretiak? Anabel Bourne is holding for you. One moment while I connect you, please."

There was a click, followed by silence that seemed to last forever. The reprieve was still over far too quickly and ended when a quiet voice when a mild Spanish accent said, "Ally? Are you there?"

With a final fortifying breath, Ally answered just as quietly, "Hey, Annie. I'm here."

The woman at the other end gave a sob of relief. "Oh my God, Ally, are you all right? I saw on the news about how you were sh-shot, but they didn't say if you were d-dead, and I tried calling the hospital and they wouldn't tell me anything, and then you were released, and I tried calling every day, and they still wouldn't let me talk to you, and—"

"Annie. Annie! Anabel!" Ally finally managed to interrupt the emotional outpouring. She felt incredibly guilty. She hadn't thought about how events might have affected her ex-lover. *Face it, you didn't think about her, period. You were having too much fun with your new friend and didn't want to consider how someone who used to love you was reacting.* "I'm sorry, Annie. When I was in the hospital I was kind of out of it, and since then . . ." She trailed off. "I still should have called."

"I know," Annie said. She had calmed down and her tone said that she knew exactly why Ally hadn't called. Rather than raise that particular subject yet, she asked, "Are you okay now?"

"I'm fine," Ally replied. "Well, not exactly *fine*, but better. I'm still in a wheelchair, but that's only until the muscles knit properly."

"Jesus Christ, Ally, a wheelchair?" The anxiety was back in Annie's voice. "What the hell happened?"

"I was shot twice," Ally said and heard a shocked gasp over the line. "Once in the shoulder and once in the back."

"Oh, hell, are you paralysed?" Annie tended to ask blunt questions when upset.

"No, the bullet missed my spine. The doctors were worried for a while, but now they say I should make a full recovery."

"Oh, good, then I can slap you for not calling and letting me know how you were." Annie's tone turned biting.

"I'm sorry," Ally said miserably. "I just—"

"No, I'm sorry," Annie interrupted, her voice now contrite. "I know why you didn't call. I also wanted to apologise–" She took a deep breath. "–for . . . breaking up with you like I did. I know a phone call is the last way anyone wants to hear something like that."

"It's okay. I–"

"No, I have to say this. You had just caught that serial rapist guy in Australia and that was a truly amazing thing to do. And I know you covered up your part in all that and no one knows it was you, but . . . that kind of secrecy is part of my problem. All I could think was what if he had caught you instead? What if he had hit you over the head and knocked you out? What if, instead of being the hero, you were lying in a ditch somewhere? What if you had overestimated your . . . abilities? I just couldn't handle the thought of having you simply disappear somewhere, and never know what had happened to you. Or you would get into a situation that you thought you could handle and get yourself hurt or killed instead. It was bad enough when you were . . . working here at home. I also knew that, being who and what you are, the chances of something happening were always present." Annie gave a bitter laugh. "And I was right too. Look at what happened. You were shot and almost killed saving someone's life. I'm sorry, Ally, but I need to be with someone whom I can be reasonably sure will come home at the end of the day."

Ally was surprised. She hadn't realised that her ex-girlfriend had been so affected by the potentially hazardous possibilities raised by what she was capable of. "I guess we never talked about that, did we?" she said ruefully. "I know you were never really comfortable with what I could do."

"I know and we probably should have talked about that too. You can blame my Catholic upbringing. 'Thou shalt not suffer a witch to live.'" The quote was an old morbid joke between them. "I hated the fact that you could know exactly what I was thinking and feeling at any time."

"You know I would never do that without your permission," Ally protested.

"I know you wouldn't," Annie said, though the tone of her voice revealed that she was actually less than sure, "but I always knew that you *could* if you wanted to. I should have said something, but . . ."

"I knew you were uncomfortable and I guess I should have brought it up too." Ally sighed. "Well, I suppose we learned a few things to take into our next relationships, huh?" she joked tentatively.

The remark startled a brief laugh out of Annie and the mood of the conversation lightened. There were still hurt feelings and discomfort on

chapter eight

both sides, but also the acknowledgement that such things would fade in time. "I guess so."

Ally put on her best exaggerated "gossip" voice. "So, dahling, are you seeing anyone new?"

"Wellll, there is this really cute Chinese girl who just started in the orchestra. I *think* she's been checking me out. She plays the cello, and–"

"–and you wouldn't mind her fingering your frets."

"Actually, a cello doesn't have frets, but–" Annie paused. "Wait a minute, what the hell happened to the shy, repressed Alleandre I used to know?"

Ally laughed, pushing down the sliver of jealousy that had sprung up when Annie had started talking about the woman who had caught her eye. "Actually, you can blame Chorus. He's a guy I met–"

"A guy? Really, Ally, I had no idea."

"Oh, shut up, it's not like that and you know it. Anyway, I met him just after I left Australia and he's been corrupting me ever since. Between him and Evelynne, it's a wonder I'm as chaste as I am."

"Evelynne? Who's–wait a minute, *Princess* Evelynne? *The* Princess Evelynne? You're on a first name basis?"

"She's the person I've been staying with. Since I saved her life, she and her father, the King, are paying all my medical bills and they invited me to stay here at the Summer Palace."

"*Madre de Dios*, Ally! You're hobnobbing with royalty?" Annie's voice dropped conspiratorially. "Is she as gorgeous in person as she is in all the pictures?"

"More so. She's also smart, funny, friendly, kind, gentle . . ." Ally trailed off as she heard the heavy silence on the other end of the line. "Annie? You still there?"

"Oh my God, Ally, are you falling for her?" Annie waited for the other woman to deny the charge. When the denial was not forthcoming, she said, "Oh God, you are falling for her. Ally, this is bad. She's a princess. Princesses do not date, especially not lower-class foreigners and most especially not other women. And remember, I know you, Ally. When you fall for someone, you fall completely. I should know. Despite everything, I don't want to see you hurt when you finally have to leave, or she marries some 'suitable' prince, or whatever they have in Atlantis."

"I know," Ally said quietly. "I don't want to, but I can't help it. I didn't want to fall in love with you, remember, but I couldn't help it then either. For the moment, she's just becoming a really good friend. When she does move on, I'll wish her the best, mourn for a time and then move on myself. I'll survive." The last was said in a firm voice.

"Well, even though we're not together any more, I want you to know that if you ever need to talk, I'm always willing to listen."

"Thanks, Annie," said Ally. She was still sad that their relationship was irrevocably ended, but happy that they weren't irreconcilably estranged. "Maybe when this is all over I'll come and visit you and your new cellist and you can comfort me."

"All three of us, Ally? Goodness, I know you've loosened up, but I didn't realise you had become quite so . . . licentious." Annie chuckled as her remark was met with inarticulate objections. "I can feel your blush over the phone, Ally. It's good to know some things haven't changed."

        ❦ ❦ ❦ ❦ ❦

Evelynne cast yet another glance towards Ally's closed bedroom door. She had been attempting to read a summary of Countess Abram's proposal but had been unable to concentrate on the document. Every time she tried to focus, the princess' memory would turn to Alleandre's expression just before she had disappeared into the privacy of her bedroom: her friend had seemed scared. Perhaps even terrified.

Ally had answered and made, well over two dozen phone calls in the last two days and Evelynne had seen her excited, eager, surprised, even politely resigned, but she had never appeared frightened. Whoever this Anabel Bourne was, she had affected Ally strongly without even speaking with her.

Evelynne looked up at the door again. It had been half an hour since Ally had gone through it and the princess was considering knocking to see if everything was all right. Before she could make up her mind, the heavy wooden door swung open and Ally wheeled herself back into the sitting room.

The first thing Evelynne noticed was that the near-paralysing anxiety was thankfully gone. There was still a certain brittleness and lingering sadness in Ally's demeanour, but they were eclipsed by her obvious relief.

Ally wheeled herself beside the table and sat staring blankly out the window at the pouring rain. She remained that way for over a minute, until a concerned Evelynne prompted, "Ally? How did it go?"

The woman in question looked startled, then shook herself and refocused on her companion. "Sorry, what was that?"

"I asked how it went. Your conversation." The princess indicated the phone, which was lying forgotten on Ally's lap.

"Oh. Right. Sorry. It went . . . okay. Better than I was expecting, actually."

chapter eight

"You looked like you were upset. Was it someone you don't like? You don't have to tell me if you don't want to," Evelynne hastened to assure her.

"Yes. I mean, no. I mean–it was–" Ally took a deep breath. *Well, here goes...*" That was Anabel Bourne. She was–she is my ex-girlfriend." She held her breath for Evelynne's reaction.

"Oh. Oh! By girlfriend you mean . . ."

"We, uh, used to be lovers."

"Really." Evelynne sat for a moment looking shocked, digesting the information. "I, um–I didn't know you were . . ."

"Gay? It's not like I advertise it. And contrary to certain stereotypes, you usually can't tell just by looking." Ally's tone was bitter.

"I'm sorry, I didn't mean–I just meant that you never told me." Now Evelynne looked hurt. "You could have, you know. I thought we were friends enough for that. You must have known I would be all right with it."

"Actually, I'm never sure of things like that." The bitterness was still present. "Just as you can't tell that I'm gay just by looking at me, I can't tell how you'll react even though I know you." Ally laughed harshly. "I've known people, family even, who are good, kind, generous and loving, whom I've known for years and they've treated me like a freak when they've found out what I am. On the other hand, there are people like a boss I once had, who was the meanest, most ornery jerk I know and he couldn't have cared less who I slept with. I didn't like him and he didn't like me, but at least the reasons he didn't like me were the same reasons he didn't like anyone else."

"But you know how I've been supporting Domdom in his defence of the Equal Marriages Decision! You know I'm–"

Ally's shaking head interrupted her. "It's not that simple. It's very easy to support something like gay rights in the abstract. Most of the family I told you about is very 'tolerant' and 'open-minded'. Actually put them face to face with a homosexual and the reaction can be very different. They usually *act* polite, but you can tell." *At least* I *can.*

"Oh." Evelynne's mind was still trying to process the information she had just been given. She looked up at Ally. The young woman was sitting motionless in her chair, head bowed and shoulders hunched as if to ward off an expected blow. The princess reached out and raised her friend's shuttered face to her own. "Well, I want to officially tell you that I'm okay with it. Look at me," she ordered when Ally refused to meet her eyes. "Now, can you tell that I'm telling you the truth?"

Ally met Evelynne's eyes. In them there was nothing but honesty and compassion. She cautiously reached out with her mind, staying carefully away from Evelynne's actual thoughts, seeking only the barest hint of the emotions behind them. *She wants me to know the truth,* she justified to herself. *Besides, I need to know.* Insinuating herself into the very topmost layer of Evelynne's mind, Ally was surprised with the ease and clarity with which the princess' emotions came through her normally unreliable sense. Foremost was the friendship and acceptance that Evelynne was striving to project through her expression, unaware that they were being sensed in a much more direct and intimate manner. Underneath were true surprise, presumably at the recent revelations and a barely-sensed, odd mixture of confused elation. Ally couldn't deduce the source or direction of the latter emotion and didn't even try as she pulled her mind back as easily as it went forth. She had trespassed on Evelynne's most private possessions enough.

Dropping back to her more mundane senses was always accompanied by a sense of confusion as Ally's mind attempted to separate her own thoughts from those she had been merged with. Shaking off the effects, she looked back into Evelynne's eyes, which were still staring at her earnestly.

"I believe you," Ally whispered, trying to project her own friendship and trust, though her talents did not extend to sharing her own thoughts.

For her part, Evelynne was shaken. For several long seconds Ally had looked at her with an intensity she recalled from several weeks ago, when she had been lying on the hard ground with Ally's body interposed between herself and the bullets that had been aimed at her. This time that intensity had been accompanied by an indescribable feeling of vertigo and it took the princess a moment to comprehend Ally's softly spoken words.

"Good," Evelynne said and proceeded to hug her friend strongly. Ally awkwardly returned the hug as best she could while still sitting in her wheelchair.

Pulling back, the princess strove to lighten the mood. "So," she said, "now I'm curious. You have to tell me everything about this Anabel who was stupid enough to break up with you. How did you meet?"

Ally was relieved beyond words. *This might not be so bad after all.* "Well, she was a dancer at the University of British Columbia when I was studying there and I met her at one of her performances . . ."

chapter nine

The sound of Nancu Ylan opening the front doors to the Palace echoed faintly through the dining room and Evelynne looked up from her lunch in surprise, then over at Alleandre, who was finishing her own meal. The main doors to the Palace were only commonly used to admit guests. The servants and other less prestigious visitors tended to use other, smaller entrances scattered throughout the building.

"I wonder who that is," Evelynne mused. "I don't recall anyone being scheduled to visit us today."

Ally could only shrug, her mouth occupied with chewing a delicious chunk of savoury chicken. Besides, she had another subject occupying her mind and adding a sense of anxiety to her mood. So far she thought she had succeeded in concealing her worry from her companion.

Evelynne actually wasn't fooled by Ally's façade, though she realised that there was nothing she could say to reassure her friend until the matter resolved itself—which would be later that afternoon. So she temporarily dismissed it, turning her attention back to her own lunch.

Apparently the visitors were of sufficient stature to impress the Seneschal, because he arrived at the door to the dining room a moment later. "Lord Thomas Baker, Duke of Avalon, to see you, Your Highness," he informed. "Shall I show him in?"

The princess broke into a huge grin and Ally looked up with interest. "Of course, Ylan, you know he can always see me." Inwardly she shook her head in resignation. Seneschal Nancu Ylan was incredibly efficient and highly skilled at his job, but he was also almost obsessive about formality and protocol. The only time she had ever seen him crack a smile was the occasion that his grandchildren had visited.

Characteristically solemn, the Seneschal bowed and held open the door. The Duke, leaning heavily on his cane, entered, carrying a long, cloth-wrapped object under one arm.

"Domdom," Evelynne cried, rushing forward to envelop him in a hug before he could even walk a few steps. "It's good to see you again so soon. I didn't know you were planning on visiting today."

"I wasn't intending to," he replied, looking fondly at Evelynne, "but a couple of things came to my attention and I decided to take the time." He gave a little wave to Ally, who waved back. "As a matter of fact, I come bearing gifts." He turned back to the door and called, "Come in, my boy, I think there's someone who would like to see you."

"Chorus!" Ally exclaimed as her friend walked through the doorway, quickly wheeling herself around the table. "What are you doing here?"

The young man bestowed a brilliant grin. "And hello to you too, Ally. I'm doing fine. How are you feeling?"

Ally flushed in embarrassment. "Sorry. Hi, Chorus. I just meant that I thought you were going to spend some more time in France. I wasn't expecting to see you so soon."

"Well, it turned out that France wasn't nearly as exciting without you and Her Highness to keep me company." Turning to Evelynne, he said, "Good afternoon, Your Highness."

Evelynne wagged a finger at him. "It's Evelynne, remember? *Dumela*, Chorus. *O tsohile jang?*"

Chorus' eyebrows rose as the princess greeted him in his native tongue. "*Ke tsohile sentle.*" Switching to Lantlan he asked, "*Ki so liver'o* Setswana, *Urmata* Evelynne?"

"*Mi* Alleandre *re-al'a wei arat,*" the princess answered in the same language, pointing to Ally. Switching back to English, she remarked, "I didn't know you spoke Lantlan."

Lord Thomas answered, "It seems our young Mister Tladi has something of a gift for languages. I'm sorry, Evelynne, but could we sit down? I'm afraid my leg has been bothering me all week."

"Of course, of course," the princess said, scolding herself. "Here you go." She settled the Duke into a chair beside Alleandre and then reclaimed her own seat, while Chorus took another.

The Duke gave a relieved sigh as he relaxed into the chair. "*Ishta* Tretiak," he said, turning to Ally, "it's wonderful to see you doing so well. You were looking decidedly flushed the last time we met."

"It comes and goes," Chorus murmured, earning himself a deadly glare from Ally.

"Thank you, Your Grace," Ally answered politely. "I've been feeling much better."

"Now, Alleandre," the Duke said, waving a rebuking finger, "what did I say last time? None of this 'Your Grace' nonsense with me. If you persist in doing so, I shall be forced to consistently refer to you as *Ishta*."

"*Ishta?*" Chorus asked, his voice startled as the word registered.

"It's a title," Ally answered his question. "It means basically the same as 'Miss' or 'Ms' in English."

chapter nine

Chorus shook his head. "No, I know what it means and it's not quite 'Miss' or 'Ms'. It's a much more respectful designation, isn't it?" He directed the query to the two Atlantlans. "Sort of almost-nobility?"

"Why, yes, in a manner of speaking," Lord Thomas answered. He spoke to Ally. "I thought you knew. *Ishta* is a title of respect bestowed upon a person–a woman, actually–considered to have performed a great service or impressive deed. A man is given the title *Enku*. Traditionally, if the title is given by someone of high rank, it is also used by all persons of lower rank."

Ally stared at him incredulously. "So you mean that because the King called me that–"

"–His Majesty was announcing to society at large that he held you in the highest respect, and that everyone subservient to him–which actually encompasses all citizens except the Queen–should do likewise. I assumed you were aware of this."

Ally turned a stunned but vaguely accusing gaze to Evelynne. "Why didn't you tell me about this?"

The princess' expression was apologetic, but her words were not. "It never crossed my mind. To someone from our society," she said, "it was simply a natural courtesy. I guess it just never occurred to me that much of the western world does not possess such ways of indicating respect. I've been referring to you as *Ishta* Tretiak for a while now."

Ally looked quite stunned by her apparently sudden rise in stature, and Lord Thomas decided to take pity on the poor woman. "Alleandre, my dear, my spies tell me–" A conspiratorial glance at Evelynne. "–that you are leaving your wheelchair for good sometime soon."

The young woman shook herself out of her daze, and replied, "Well, I'm not sure about permanently, but I'll be weaned off it for the next while. According to my physiotherapist, I should be able to get around with a cane. I should only need the chair if I'm going to be out for long periods. He's hoping that once my muscles heal completely, I'll be as good as new." She didn't add the doctor's warning that if the muscles refused to heal properly, she might be forced to use a cane for the rest of her life. On the other hand, had the bullet hit only two inches to the left, even the cane would not have been an option.

"Well then, in honour of the occasion, and with the hope that its use will be short, I would like to present you with this." Lord Thomas took up the long, thin, cloth-wrapped object beside his chair and handed it over to Ally.

Ally took the package in surprise. "Thank you, Your . . . um . . . Thomas," she finished, when the Duke raised a warning eyebrow. "You really didn't have to."

"My dear, I am a Duke. I am frequently forced to do things that I do not want to do. It is a pleasant occasion when I can do something simply because I wish to do it."

"Thank you," Ally repeated, admiring the cloth in which the gift was wrapped. It was a rich green colour and the shimmer of the material, along with the texture under her fingers, told her that it was silk. The cloth was held in place by a pair of blue ribbons. Carefully untying them, Ally gave a small gasp as the cloth fell away to reveal the object within.

It was a cane, carved from an almost midnight-black wood, which Ally tentatively identified as ebony. The carving had been fairly rough, leaving the natural shape of the wood almost untouched. It had been smoothed and polished to a brilliant shine, however, and inlaid with a reddish metal. The metal formed loops and swirls across the surface of the cane, and the light shining on the pattern was hypnotic.

"Oh my God," Ally breathed. "That is beautiful." She peered closer at the designs. "Is that . . ."

"That's oricalcum," Lord Thomas confirmed. "It's a naturally occurring gold-silver-copper alloy found only on Atlantl."

"Thank you so much," Ally said. "It's absolutely wonderful." She handed the cane to Evelynne, who examined it with an appreciative eye.

The Duke smiled, pleased that his gift was being so well received. "Thank *you*. I made it myself."

"Really?" Everyone looked at him in surprise.

He nodded. "After I injured my leg in the War, I was less than thrilled with the ugly cane the hospital gave me. So I decided to make my own. I've been making them ever since. That particular one I made about fifty years ago and it became one of my favourites. Unhappily for me, I am somewhat shorter now than I was then and the cane is now too long to use comfortably. I reckon that you, Alleandre, are tall enough to use it."

Ylan had come to the doorway and made a discreet gesture to Evelynne. She nodded in acknowledgement and then turned her attention back to the rest of her guests.

"On that note, I have been informed that Doctor Willes has arrived and is waiting for Ally to continue her therapy. Ally, do you want company?"

"I'll go with her," Chorus said. "We can catch up. If you want me to, that is."

"That would be fine," Ally agreed.

☙ ☙ ☙ ☙ ☙

chapter nine

"So, Ally," Chorus said as the pair made their way to the gymnasium, "How has it been, hanging out with the royals?"

"Very interesting," his companion admitted. "I think I was half expecting all of this aristocracy to be stuck-up snobs, but all of the nobles I've met so far have been really friendly people. You know, you've met Lord Thomas. Li-Han, Baroness Outremer–she's the ruler of this barony–came to visit a few days ago. A first she was kind of stiff and formal, but Evy managed to get her to relax and she turned out to be really funny."

"Evy, huh? Well, it sounds like the Baroness wasn't the only one. She's managed to get you to open up too, hasn't she?" Chorus said. It took a moment, but he was rewarded by Ally's trademark blush. "Oh please, Ally, not everything is a double entendre."

Ally sternly told her flush to recede, wishing she had more control over her body's reactions. Unfortunately, that wasn't one of her talents. "Then stop making innuendoes. Besides, she knows about . . . you know."

Chorus looked startled. "She does? How did she find out?"

"I told her."

"You told her?"

"Well, I got a phone call from Annie–"

"The bitch."

Ally winced. "Please don't call her that. We actually talked some things out."

"Sorry."

"Anyway, afterwards Evy was there and I needed to talk to somebody, so I told her. She was okay with it."

"Well, that was fast. You've only known Evelynne for a few weeks." Chorus paused for a moment. "So have you shown her what you can do yet?"

This time it was Ally's turn to look startled. "I beg your pardon?"

"You know. Have you given her a demonstration?"

Ally was rapidly turning a beet red colour and making choking sounds. Her wheelchair had stopped dead in the middle of the corridor. "A demonstration? Of that? Are you nuts? I–she–" A pause. "Wait a minute, what are you talking about?"

Chorus was confused. "I was talking about your . . . abilities. What were you talking about?"

The young woman was slowly returning to a more normal colour. "Oh, I meant that Evy knows that I'm . . . you know . . . gay."

"Oh. Oh! Okay, then. So she doesn't know . . ."

Ally shook her head vigorously. She started pushing her chair down the hallway again. "No, *that* I haven't told her about. I'm not really planning to any time soon, either."

"Understood," Chorus acknowledged. A wicked grin slowly crept across his face. "So you haven't given her a demonstration?"

"No."

"In either area?"

"No!"

"Maybe someday, huh?"

"Maybe somed–No!"

"Okay, fine. Just checking."

☙ ☙ ☙ ☙ ☙

" . . . and so the Count is hoping that by gaining approval to open the mine, he can create up to five thousand new jobs. He's been having a hell of a time meeting his minimum employment obligations the last few years." The Duke was filling Evelynne in on a few of the less publicised political manoeuvrings of the Hall of Nobles.

"The environmentalists won't like that," Evelynne mused. "He's caught between a rock and a hard place. Although what if–" She was cut off by a knock. Both occupants of the room looked up to see Chorus standing in the doorway. Evelynne looked behind him, but couldn't see Ally anywhere. "Chorus, is Ally all right? Where is she?"

"Ally is fine," Chorus said, easing the princess' concern. "In fact, I thought that, given the situation, it might be more appropriate to do something a little more formal." He turned his head and seemed to be listening to someone out of sight beside the doorway. "I've just been ordered to hurry up and get the show on the road. So without further ado, may I present . . . Alleandre Tretiak!" He stood aside with a flourish to allow Ally to enter the room.

Evelynne's concerned face brightened as Ally walked carefully through the doorway. Then her brain suddenly comprehended exactly what it was seeing. Ally had *walked* through the doorway and was now standing uncertainly just inside the room, leaning heavily on the cane in her left hand.

"Sorry about that," Ally said, a quirk of a smile on her lips, "but Chorus insisted."

"And well he should have," Evelynne confirmed, quickly standing and hurrying over to her friend. "This is wonderful. You're able to . . . stand . . . up . . ." She trailed off as she got closer and looked up–and up–into Ally's face. "Isis, you're tall," the princess blurted.

chapter nine

Chorus broke into delighted laughter. "I told you," he said. "I told you she'd say that."

Evelynne was chagrined at her outburst. "It's just that I've never seen you standing," she explained. "Until now, I've always been taller than you. Um, just how tall are you, anyway?"

Ally was flushing under the intense scrutiny. "About six feet," she answered. "Six one on a good day."

"That would explain it," the princess murmured. Ally topped her height by at least six inches.

"Um, do you mind if I sit?" Ally asked. "I've just walked all the way here from the gym, and I'm feeling a little . . ."

"Of course." Evelynne shook herself out of her musings. She was having a difficult time reconciling the Alleandre before her with the small-looking woman she had first seen in the Marseilles hospital. *Now she looks like a hero,* the princess thought. Taking Ally's right arm, she led the tall woman further into the room and settled her carefully into a seat. Ally sat back in the chair with a heartfelt sigh of relief. "Are you in pain?" Evelynne asked.

"A bit," Ally admitted. "But it's a good kind of pain. Mostly muscles I haven't used in the last three weeks." She closed her eyes for a moment and then opened them to look at Duke Thomas. "Thank you for the cane," she said. "You're right, Dr. Willes was going to give me this really ugly plastic and metal one. This one is much better."

"I'm glad you like it, my dear. It looks like I brought it just in time too."

"And you look good with it," Evelynne said. She smiled proudly at Ally. She wasn't sure why she was feeling so proud of her friend, but chose simply go with the feeling. "Tonight we have to celebrate! Domdom, you are staying for dinner, aren't you?"

"Oh, I might be persuaded to join such beautiful and charming company for a meal." His smile took in Chorus as well. "Latifa is still creating her masterpieces, I expect."

"Of course. She's told me that the day I don't like one of her meals is the day she resigns and takes holy vows. So far the Churches have been saved from her."

☙ ☙ ☙ ☙ ☙

Ally stood in the darkness of her bedroom later that evening and revelled in the sensation of being on two feet once more.

Dinner had been a very pleasant and entertaining affair. Maïda had been convinced to join the rest of them for the meal. During the meal, Evelynne and Chorus had teamed up in an effort to get Ally to blush as much as possible, so veiled suggestions, innuendo, double entendres and embarrassing stories had been used to great effect. Ally had valiantly defended herself as best she could, until Lord Thomas had entered the fray on her behalf, launching a salvo of stories starring a certain young princess until the opposing forces had retreated in disarray. Maïda had been a double agent, launching sneak attacks at both sides, usually when they least expected it.

Ally grinned. It was the most fun she had had during a meal since . . . She blushed, grateful for both the darkness and the lack of company, as an image of Annie in a very culinary position presented itself for her examination. She blushed harder as Annie suddenly morphed into Evelynne. *Okay, that's enough of that,* Ally thought. *I'm just feeling good. I'm out of that damned chair, I've just enjoyed a good meal with good friends, and I have a lot of energy to burn. And right now there's only one way to burn it.* The image of Evelynne presented itself again hopefully. *Okay, two ways, but that's not going to happen.* A different image of a more solitary nature presented itself for consideration. *Okay, three ways. But those two are not an option.* The second image smirked knowingly to itself and slunk away to bide its time.

Her decision made, Ally went to the doors leading to the balcony outside her bedroom. Opening them as quietly as possible, she slipped outside, taking care to remain in the shadows. Once on the balcony, she slowly stood completely upright, no longer leaning on her cane. Long unused muscles in her back and legs protested, but she ignored them, enjoying the slight pain as she stretched. When the healing muscles in the centre of her back registered their own complaints with a much sharper pain, Ally stopped.

Satisfied, she opened her mind to her surroundings. The mental energies of everyone within a hundred metres of her position slowly coalesced in her perception. Ally smiled as she recognised Evelynne's mind a few rooms away, bright and strong. Ally was surprised that she could recognise the princess so easily, considering the short time they had known each other. She couldn't read thoughts or emotions in this state, but by checking the princess' position against her mental map of the Palace, Ally realised that Evelynne was in her bathroom. She firmly squashed the temptation to extend her perceptions and see exactly what Evelynne was doing.

Putting all thoughts of the princess out of her mind, Ally made a final check of the presences nearby. Satisfied that nobody was in a position to see, she withdrew her mind, then focussed and channelled once more.

A moment later the balcony was empty.

chapter ten

A single slice of sunlight snuck through a crack in the drapes of Princess Evelynne's bedroom to illuminate the figure slumbering in the bed. The princess slept on, oblivious, until the invading beam crept upward enough to strike her directly in the eyes.

Disturbed by the light, she waved her hand in a futile attempt to brush it away. When the attempt failed, she slowly came more awake and additional sensory stimuli began to clamour for attention: the warmth of the bed, the texture of the sheets, the faint sound of birdsong and the strong aroma of fresh coffee. It was this last stimulus that provided the final push to drive the princess into full wakefulness.

Opening her eyes, Evelynne blocked out the bright light with a raised hand, then turned to look at her bedside table, where, as expected, a small carafe of freshly brewed coffee sat waiting. She smiled. Nancu Ylan was a saint, she decided. Every morning he would bring in a pot of sweet coffee and somehow he was never loud enough to wake her.

Evelynne indulged in a long, sinuous stretch, pleased when her shoulder issued only the faintest protest. *Life is good,* she decided. The supper while Domdom was visiting had been extremely entertaining. Ally, freed from her wheelchair, had been in a good mood, so much so that the War of Teasing that had broken out had failed to cause her to withdraw completely. Her friend had blushed extensively and predictably, but had valiantly rallied. Once Domdom took part on Ally's side, Evelynne had found herself doing a fair amount of blushing of her own. *Dear Isis, I can't believe he dragged out that story of me wandering into the men's changing room at his gymnasium when I was six. That anecdote should have died a long time ago. Oh well, it was in a good cause.*

Satisfied, the princess called Maïda to confirm the day's plans, then looked at the clock. Eight fourteen. They had all retired quite early the night before, so Evelynne decided to see if Ally was awake yet and then take both her and Chorus for breakfast. She walked the short distance to the suite next door, nodding a greeting at the servants she saw along the way.

Opening the door to Ally's sitting room, Evelynne saw that her friend had apparently not yet left the bedroom. She briskly walked over to the appropriate door, knocked perfunctorily, and entered.

"Rise and shine!" she said. "I hope you're decent, becau—Eep!" She froze.

Ally wasn't decent. Or she was very decent, depending on one's point of view. She had obviously been in the shower and now stood motionless, in mid-step and leaning on her cane, halfway between the bathroom and the bed. Her stunned brain could not decide whether to dash back into the bathroom or forward to the bed, where the clothes that were laid out explained the reason for both women's unmoving states.

As Ally's logical side desperately tried to make a decision that would end the standoff, her sense of modesty awoke with a vengeance to create a deep flush that started at her upper hairline and spread steadily downwards. Evelynne watched its progress in fascination. *So it does go all the way down.* Suddenly realising she was staring, the princess tore her gaze away, trying to look at anything but the woman in front of her. Her eyes found Ally's hooded cloak, draped over the back of a nearby chair. *That needs cleaning,* she thought irrelevantly. *It's got pine needles on it.*

"Uh . . . um . . . I just–ahem." Evelynne's voice broke. "I just came to see whether you were up yet . . . which you are . . . and . . . um . . . see if you wanted something to eat . . . I mean breakfast," she concluded hurriedly. "So I'll go now, and see you when you come–I mean when you're dres–when you're ready. To eat that is. Breakfast." She took a deep breath and took another glance at Ally before quickly turning away again. The other woman hadn't moved a muscle. "Um, yeah. So . . . bye." The princess made an inglorious retreat, fumbling for the doorknob to close the door on her way out.

Safely back in the sitting room, Evelynne sank into a large overstuffed armchair. *Oh Isis,* she thought. *Oh crap. Crap, crap, crap, crap, crap. This is not good. She'll never be able to look at me again. I just didn't think that . . . I just didn't think, period. That'll teach me to go into someone's bedroom without knocking. That has to be the worst thing that can happen to a shy person like Ally. I know she's body-conscious, and for me to burst in while she's . . . in her all together.* Evelynne buried her face in her hands. *And what a nice all together it is.* The rogue thought startled her when it inserted itself into her consciousness. *What the heck? Where in the Duat did that come from? It's not like I'm attracted to her or anything. After all, she is a woman. Very obviously a woman.* A memory of the recent scene confirmed the conclusion. *I'm not . . . attracted . . . to . . .* Evelynne's thoughts whirred. *Oh Isis, Jehovah and Allah. I am attracted to her.*

And why not? asked a hitherto unheard part of her mind. *She's intelligent, compassionate, courageous, modest . . . and she's got one hell of a body.* The previous memory was brought out for study. Tall, thin, not particularly muscular, but not skeletal either. Rather small firm breasts and enough flesh to be round

chapter ten

in just the right places. Looked at objectively, she would never be a supermodel, but Evelynne's thoughts were anything but objective.

She's gorgeous, the princess admitted. *But she's a woman. A woman. Does that mean that I like—that I'm—*

With an effort, Evelynne pulled her scattered thoughts together. *Okay, first things first. In a few minutes Ally is going to come out—* A stray thought about coming out tried to distract her, but she firmly pushed it aside. *She's going to come out of that room and she's going to be mortified. Now unless she says something, I am going to act like nothing happened. At least until I figure out what's going on with me. I need time to do that, which I don't have right now.*

With that decision made, Evelynne sat up straight and prepared to call on all her years' experience in diplomacy to put on the necessary mask for the upcoming events.

❦ ❦ ❦ ❦ ❦

The cane tumbled unheeded to the floor as the door shut and Ally followed it at a slower pace, coming to rest cross-legged on the thick carpet. The feel of the slightly rough material under her bare buttocks jolted her rational mind back into operation, reminding her that she was completely naked—even though a less rational part had been excruciatingly aware of that fact the whole time.

The young woman reached out a hand towards her clothing lying on the bed. It was still well over two metres from her outstretched fingers and she instinctively tried to pull the clothes towards her.

Nothing happened.

Of course, Ally thought with the small part of herself that was still capable of doing so clearly. *I probably couldn't concentrate enough to move a penny right now.* She was vaguely aware that she was focusing on irrelevant topics to avoid dealing with the reality of her situation. As soon as that awareness impinged on her consciousness, the delicate balance shattered.

Oh my God, she saw me. All of me. She looked down at her body in disgust and shock. It was too thin, too long, too bony; it was not full enough, not voluptuous enough. The shocking white scar over her right breast marred what small amount of beauty was present. In the back of Ally's mind she could hear the memories of the cruel laughter, see the pointing fingers, the piercing stares, and feel the dark hilarity and amused contempt that drove directly into her thoughts. Remembered tears ran down her cheeks and it was only when she felt the salty taste on her lips that she realised they were real.

The tears gave Ally's mind enough of a hold on reality to banish the phantom jeers and allow it to start working regularly once more. *You are* not *ugly,* a familiar voice said, sounding like her mother. *You are beautiful, intelligent and brave. No, you are not like a supermodel. But models are things people use as props, as smaller versions of the real thing. You, Alleandre, are the real thing.* Gradually, Ally's heartbeat slowed. *You are the most beautiful girl in the world,* a memory of her father said. *I know all dads think so, but I happen to be right.*

"Thanks, Mom," Ally whispered. "Thanks, Dad." She let the memories of love and reassurance wash over her as the panic attack faded, leaving a shivering reaction in its wake. She suddenly realised again that she was sitting naked on the floor and had been for some time.

Just then, there was a tentative knock on the door. An equally hesitant voice called out, "Ally, are you all right? You've been in there for a while and I just want to make sure you haven't fallen down or something."

Clearing her throat, Ally called back, "Um, yeah, I'll be just a moment." Taking a deep, fortifying breath, she got to her feet and proceeded to get dressed as rapidly as her back would allow. Once clothed, she moved to the door and opened it to reveal a concerned Evelynne.

Before Ally could say anything, the princess blurted, "I just want to say that I'm sorry for bursting in on you like that. I was just excited and I didn't think that–well, I just didn't think. From now on I'll make sure to–" She broke off suddenly, taking in Ally's appearance. "You're crying," she said, surprised.

Ally reached up and touched her own cheeks, where her fingers encountered the dry, gritty remnants of her tears. She immediately scrubbed them away with her hands. "No, I'm not."

"Well, you were," Evelynne said. As bad as she had felt before, she now felt ten times worse. She reached out to grasp Ally's hands in her own. "I'm so sorry. I never meant to do anything to–"

"No, it's not that," Ally interrupted. "I–it's–can we sit down?" she asked abruptly.

"Of course." Evelynne quickly led her friend to the nearby chairs and they both sat down.

"First off, I want to say that it wasn't you. Actually, it was you, but it wasn't because of anything you did. Although it was what you did, but not–I'm not making any sense, am I?"

"No, not really." Despite the situation, there was something endearing about a flustered Alleandre. *Endearing? Isis, you do have it bad,* Evelynne thought. *Later, deal with it later.*

"Okay," Ally said, taking one last breath for courage. "When I was in elementary school–grade six–I was not the most popular person around. I was very tall for my age, really gawky, awkward, clumsy. I was also, either fortunately or unfortunately, very intelligent." This was said factually, without a trace of boasting, in fact with an almost resentment of that intelligence. "I

chapter ten

was younger than everybody else in my class, had no friends and was generally considered a freak. Well, you know just how tolerant children are of people who are 'different'."

"Not really," the princess murmured.

Ally didn't seem to have heard. Her eyes were fixed on an event taking place over nine years ago. "One day a group of the 'popular' girls decided that it would be *fun*–" she spat the word with deadly venom. "–to show the rest of the school just what a freak I was." Evelynne noted with alarm that Ally was paler now, still fixed on the memory she was reliving. "So during lunch period, they grabbed me–" sweating now "–stripped me–" breathing faster "–and shoved me into the hallway. Right at the end of lunch as all the students were going back to class." Fresh tears were streaming down her face now, and the princess gripped her hands firmly, willing Ally to pull back from the memory. "And everyone was staring at me and pointing and laughing; and I could only stand there, the freak, the ugly freak, and I could *feel* everything they were thinking."

All of a sudden the dam broke, and Ally leaned forward into Evelynne's arms, desperately seeking the comfort and succour that she sensed were being offered. The princess was surprised, but instinctively wrapped her arms around the woman pressed against her, holding Ally as she cried silently into Evelynne's shoulder.

They stayed like that for several minutes, until Evelynne felt Ally start to pull away. She opened her arms to let her friend go, though not without a sense of loss.

"Sorry," Ally said, roughly wiping her eyes with the backs of her hands. "I didn't mean to do that. It's kind of stupid. I mean, it's not like I was abused or beaten up or anything."

"But you were," Evelynne objected. She reached up to tap Ally's temple. "Right here." She lowered her hand to touch Ally's chest. "And here. Just because they didn't punch you or beat you with a stick doesn't mean you weren't hurt."

The other woman nodded. "That's what my therapist said. I don't think he really understood what it was like for me though." *And it's not like I could tell him how I absolutely knew what those kids were thinking. If I had, I'd still be in therapy. As it was, it was over six years before I recovered even a shred of telepathic ability.* "So now you know why I can't stand anyone seeing me . . . you know. If I have time to rationalise it, prepare for it, like going to the doctor, then I'm usually okay, but when it happens suddenly, like just now . . . It's like a panic attack." She waved a hand in the general direction of the bedroom.

"Well, I'll definitely remember to knock from now on." *Darn it.* Sensing that Ally had reached her limit in discussing the matter, Evelynne changed the subject. Giving her friend's hands a final squeeze, she stood and said, "I was originally coming to bring you to breakfast."

"Sure. Just let me go and wash my face, okay?" Ally started towards her bedroom once more.

"I'll wait for you. And Ally?" the princess called softly, causing the taller woman to stop and turn around. "Just for the record, you are anything but an ugly freak. You're beautiful." As Ally blushed, more normally this time, and started to speak, Evelynne held up a hand. "Don't argue. I'm a princess. I'm authorised to make these determinations."

❧ ❧ ❧ ❧ ❧

A refreshed Ally walked with Evelynne down the stairs to breakfast. Their conversation had been stiff and stilted at first, but by the time they arrived they had almost returned to their previous level of comfort. When they arrived at the dining room, the two women saw that Chorus was already there, as well as a person they had not been expecting.

"Uncle Arthur!" Evelynne exclaimed, hurrying around the table to hug him. "I didn't know you were coming back so soon. When did you get in?"

"Your Highness," the bodyguard said formally. At his charge's disapproving look, he relaxed minutely. "Evelynne," he conceded, "officially I am not back as the Master of your Guard yet. However, I have been given permission to say that I will be reclaiming my position once the investigation is officially complete."

The princess smiled triumphantly. "I knew they wouldn't blame you."

"Indeed. While my team and I will not be receiving any medals for our actions, we have been cleared of all culpability."

Evelynne was still smiling. "Excellent. So when did you get in?" she repeated her earlier question.

"I arrived in Kilim yesterday evening, in fact. However, I stayed in the town to help the local authorities deal with an incident."

Everyone sat, and the newcomers started to help themselves to the food that had been laid out.

"An incident?" Evelynne paled slightly. "It wasn't the HBLA, was it?" Hearing the stress in the princess' voice, Ally couldn't help putting a hand on her shoulder in comfort.

"Oh, no," Sir Arthur rushed to reassure her. Evelynne sighed in relief and Ally gave her shoulder a squeeze before removing her hand. "It was a simple missing person case and the local police were asking for help in the

chapter ten

search. A four year old boy wandered away from his parents in the woods of the Sekamat Park Reserve."

Nobody at the table noticed Ally's start or vaguely guilty expression.

"Oh dear," Evelynne said. "Did you find him safely?"

"Well, yes and no," Sir Arthur replied with a wry smile. "It was actually quite odd. It was just after midnight and the searchers were considering calling off the search until morning, when young James Terris suddenly showed up outside the Kilim Hospital with nothing worse than a few scrapes and bruises and a mild case of hypothermia."

"Isis, that's quite a way from the Reserve," the princess said. "Especially for a child that young. Did he manage to walk the whole way?"

"According to the child, he was actually rescued from the forest by a *zhaniyye*."

Chorus interrupted, "Pardon, a *zhaniyye*?"

"A . . . spirit," Evelynne explained. "You might call it an elf or a fairy. A being with magical powers. Specifically, a female one."

"Really," Chorus said slowly, casting a questioning glance at Ally. The young woman appeared to be fully absorbed in her breakfast. "An elf, huh?"

"James said that a beautiful dark *zhaniyye* wrapped him in her magical cloak and used her magic wand to transport him to the hospital. He said that she did not speak a word the entire time. Because of the curse, you see," Sir Arthur said conspiratorially.

"The curse?" Ally asked, startled.

"Indeed. Young Mr. Terris believes that his *zhaniyye* is cursed never to speak until she discovers and marries her true love. He is equally convinced that *he* is that true love and is looking forward to marrying her when he grows up."

"You don't say," Chorus murmured with an amused twinkle in his eye. "That is really very romantic, isn't it, Ally? Do you think that the magical fairy will marry the boy when he grows up?"

Ally was flushing lightly, though Evelynne could not see why. "You never know," Ally said defiantly. "So what do you think really happened to him?" she asked the bodyguard.

"Well, supernatural intervention aside, it seems likely that he was picked up by someone, possibly a woman driving a car," Sir Arthur speculated. "She could have wrapped him in a blanket–hence the magical cloak –and dropped him off at the hospital." He shook his head. "The police don't know why she didn't stay around, though."

"Isis, a real magical mystery," Evelynne mused. "I'd like to visit . . . James, was it? What do you think, Chorus? Do you think he might choose to settle for a princess instead of an elf?"

"Oh, I think that *anything* is possible, Evelynne," he replied, with a very subtle wink at Ally.

☙ ☙ ☙ ☙ ☙

"Hello, Ally."

"Oh, hi Evelynne." Ally looked up. She had been reading quietly in one of the downstairs sitting rooms, enjoying the warm sunshine that was streaming through the large open window. She saw that the princess wasn't alone, but was accompanied by an older man, who wore the largest moustache she had ever seen, and an attractive young woman with long hair so black it seemed to glow and small bead-bound braids over each ear. Ally smiled hesitantly and used her cane to push herself awkwardly to her feet.

"Ally, this is Doctor Alfonso Marens, the director of the local *sa-kima* breeding program. And Ms. Mila'a Porse, his assistant."

"Hello," Ally said, holding out her hand. She realised that these were the people Evelynne had been closeted with this afternoon.

"*Ishta* Tretiak," Dr. Marens greeted, taking her hand and bowing over it. "I'm very honoured to meet you. I wish to thank you for what you have done to serve our nation and Her Highness. We are in your debt."

Ally blushed, but the last few weeks had taught her to accept such thanks with dignity. "Thank you," she said. "I'm, um, glad I was able to . . . do something." It was hardly the most eloquent of speeches, but the Doctor smiled.

"And my assistant this afternoon, Mila'a Porse." He made room for the young woman.

"I am honoured, *Ishta* Tretiak," Mila'a said carefully, her strong Atlantlan accent obvious.

"Er, likewise," Ally replied, shaking the young woman's deeply tanned hand. "So . . . *sa-kima*. I don't think I know what they are."

"Oh, they're—what do they call them in English? Unicorns," Evelynne explained. "Of course, that's a bit of a misnomer. They actually have two horns, but as they mature the horns twist around each other and grow together. In nature they're used in sparring for mates–it looks like a fencing match, actually–but they're used as an aphrodisiac in many places. The *sa-kima* were almost extinct a few decades ago, but with the breeding programs we have in place and the rather harsh penalties imposed on hunters and smugglers, we're up into the thousands again." She saw her audience looking

chapter ten

at her bemusedly and blushed. "Sorry, I get a little carried away, since I'm the Royal sponsor of the program on Avalon."

"Actually Ally, we were hoping you would do us a favour," Evelynne continued. "We've managed to get all of the 'fun stuff' out of the way, but now Doctor Marens and I have to go over a whole lot of boring financial details."

"Not boring, Your Highness," Dr. Marens murmured. "I prefer to think of them as . . . necessary."

"Of course. Anyway, I'm sure Ms. Porse really does not wish to involve herself in this necessary boredom, so I was hoping you could keep her company for a while."

"Um, sure," Ally said, casting a glance at Mila'a Porse's smiling face. "I'd be happy to."

The pleased acceptance in her voice caused the princess to look at Ally quickly, frown and then look away. Ally was just able to keep her own puzzlement off her face. Evelynne had been acting oddly all morning after the "incident". Ally had caught her looking quizzically at various servants and Guards—mostly female ones, she had noticed—and then at Ally with a speculative expression, as though comparing them. The princess inevitably looked away as soon as she saw that Ally had noticed, but by now Ally was quite confused.

"All right, then," Evelynne said brusquely, "I'll leave you two to it. Remember to call if there's anything you need."

"Sure," Ally agreed as, with a final smile and nod, Evelynne and Dr. Marens left the room.

☙ ☙ ☙ ☙ ☙

"And this is called the Re'tac Garden," Ally said, walking slowly with her cane. She paused. "I think. I'm not really an expert on gardens."

Mila'a smiled and shrugged. "I also am not. Re'tac Garden is good. We not . . . we will not tell people and then they do not tell us we are wrong."

Ally laughed. "Works for me." She stumbled slightly on the uneven path and the other woman caught her arm and steadied her. "Thanks," Ally said. As she straightened, Ally realised to her surprise that Mila'a was only a few centimetres shorter than she was.

"You are welcome, *Ishta* Tretiak," Mila'a said. Her accent was musical. She made sure that Ally had regained her balance before removing her supporting hand.

Ally winced. "Please, just Ally," she protested. "I'm not really comfortable with this *Ishta* stuff."

"Of course, Ally. I wished only to show you the respect that is your due."

Ally blushed slightly. "Well, thanks," she said, "but I've been just plain 'Ally' for a lot longer than I've been '*Ishta* Tretiak'. I'm still getting used to it."

"*Y'vis*. I see. However, I do not believe that you were ever–what what did you say–'just plain Ally.'"

Startled, Ally darted a look at her companion. It took a moment, but then she saw what she had been half expecting to see: carefully hidden speculation. While she had seen the look before, only on very rare occasions had it been directed at her. The thoughtful look was very well concealed, as was the inviting expression accompanying it, but revealed just enough to be seen by someone looking for it.

"Um, thanks," Ally said again, knowing that her answering blush would be interpreted–correctly–as acknowledgement of the subtle interaction. Anxious to change the subject, she asked, "So, have you been working for Doctor Marens long?"

Mila'a shook her head. "I have only worked here for two weeks. I am writing my honours thesis on repopulation programs for endangered species. Now it is–what is the word in English? The *sa-kima*, the . . . unicorns? Yes, the unicorns. In December I go to Lyonesse to study *medo'nta*: the elephants. In March I come back to Avalon to study *sekema*: the mountain lions."

"Are you enjoying it so far?"

"Oh, yes. It is very . . . exciting work. Very much after three years in the classroom. It was becoming very . . . stuffy? I think that is the word."

Ally grinned. "Oh, I know about that. 'Ivy covered professors in ivy covered halls.' I remember my last year at university and working on my thesis. Although mine was theoretical rather than experimental, so I spent most of my time inside. Not out in the fresh air like this." She used her free hand to gesture at the beautiful surrounding countryside.

"You did a thesis? On which subject?"

"Physics. 'Using the Schröedinger Wave Equation to Speculate on the Nature of Quantum Gravitation.'"

"*Y'vis*." The other woman was silent for a moment. "And you understand this?"

"Yes. Well, as much as anyone does, I suppose."

"*Y'vis*." A pause. "You were a–what is the word? A 'nord', yes?"

"A what? Oh, a nerd. Of course I am. I even have a membership in 'Nerds Incorporated'. Aren't you a nerd?"

chapter ten

Mila'a made a sad face. "No. I applied, but I was rejected." She tapped the side of her face. "I do not wear spectacles."

"Oh, darn, I can't teach you the secret handshake, then."

"Perhaps I will reapply. When I am accepted, you can visit and teach me this 'secret handshake'."

Ally drew in a sharp breath at the blatant invitation. "Maybe." *Maybe by then Evy will have moved on with her life. Maybe then I'll have to move on with mine.* She cast a shy glance at the woman beside her. *I could definitely do worse.*

❦ ❦ ❦ ❦ ❦

Evelynne gave a final wave as Dr. Marens' vehicle drove out of sight and then looked up at her companion beside her. "So, did you have a good time? Ms. Porse seemed quite pleasant."

"She was," Ally said, still bemusedly looking where the car had gone. "We, um . . . have a date."

Evelynne froze. "A date?" she asked in a tight voice.

Ally didn't notice her tone, still too caught up in the fact that someone as beautiful as Mila'a Porse found her attractive. "Well, not quite a date. More like the opportunity to talk about going on a date. Maybe in a few weeks or so when she isn't so busy."

"Really? You'd like to go out with her, then?"

"Yeah." Ally nodded, then looked worried. "Why, you don't think she really meant it?"

"No, no," Evelynne said quickly. No matter how confused she was feeling at that moment, there was no way she was going to undermine Ally's already fragile self-confidence. "Look at you. Who wouldn't want to date you?" Ally looked at her and blushed. "Honestly."

Now I just have to figure out why I don't want anyone else to . . . and why I would.

chapter eleven

Sitting in his office, reading through yet another boring report, Lord Thomas gratefully received the call from his secretary who informed him that a prestigious visitor was waiting. Immediately granting admittance, he spent a few moments looking out the large windows of his fortieth floor office at the Avaloni capital city of Outremer.

Less than a minute later, the door opened and the Heir to the Atlantlan Throne entered. Her Guard took up position just outside the door.

"Evelynne! How wonderful to see you again, my dear," said Lord Thomas, standing to greet the princess. He made his way around his large desk to embrace her. "I wasn't expecting to see you again for a while. Not that I'm complaining, of course."

"Hello, Domdom. How have you been?"

Taking Evelynne's arm, he led her to the comfortable chairs at the side of his office. As they sat, he answered, "Oh, just like always. Paperwork, endless meetings, having to be polite to people I can't stand. You know how it is. I really wish you would find a young man whom I could make my Heir so that I could finally get a bit of rest." He missed the uncomfortable expression that crossed his guest's face. "So where are young Alleandre and her friend? She promised to visit and discuss Tolkien with me." This time the Duke did notice Evelynne's slight flinch. "Oh dear, is everything all right? Alleandre, is she well?"

"Ally's fine," the princess reassured him. "She and Chorus are visiting the Templar Museum right now. I have a meeting with First Justicar Farrell in a couple of hours, so I decided to come and visit you for a while." Her uncomfortable expression was back. "Actually, Ally was kind of what I wanted to talk to you about." Evelynne fell silent.

"Yes?" the Duke prompted. "Has she done something? Are you worried about her?"

"Noooo . . ." Evelynne drew out the word. "Not really done anything as such. It's just . . ." She was silent for a moment. "This discussion has to remain between you and me, all right? You can't tell anyone."

"Of course, Evelynne. My lips are sealed."

"Good." Another moment of silence. "The thing is . . ." *Now I know why Ally said this is so hard. It is.* "I think I'm attracted to Ally," Evelynne finally blurted.

Lord Thomas' white eyebrows rose. "Really."

The princess didn't seem to have heard him. Now that the dam had burst, the words came flooding out. "No, that's not quite right. I *know* I'm attracted to Ally. And it's not just her. I was also kind of attracted to Mila'a–she works at the *sa-kima* farm, you don't know her–and just now I was looking at your secretary and I thought she was really pretty. But not just 'oh she has nice earrings' pretty, but 'I wonder what it would be like to kiss her' pretty. Although I don't feel for them anything like what I feel for Ally. I mean, Ally's also smart and funny and warm . . . and she does this cute little thing with her lips when she's concentrating really hard. And I keep wanting to hug her, and protect her, and . . ." Realising she was running on, she forced herself to a halt. *All right, here goes.* "Anyway, I think I'm a lesbian."

The Duke's brows remained near his hairline. "I see." Now they dropped into a light frown.

Her heart somewhere around her knees, Evelynne waited for a few moments. "Please say something. I needed to talk to someone and I thought of you, because you always seemed . . . supportive of gay rights and all that. Although Ally said that you can't always tell, so if coming to you was wrong—"

Grabbing the princess' hands, Lord Thomas brought her new babble to a stop. "No, my dear, not at all. I'm glad you did come to me. I was only surprised. But rest assured I am not going to tell you that you should be ashamed. That would be rather hypocritical of me."

Evelynne's jaw dropped. "Hypocritical? But–You mean . . ."

Smiling at her reassuringly, the Duke said, "I mean that I also have an alternative view on what constitutes the fairer sex. I always have."

"But–You were married! To Lady Ariannes! Did you . . .? Did she . . . know?" Thoughts of her own issues disappeared in the face of this revelation.

"Yes, my dear, I was married to Ariannes. And I loved her quite dearly. She was my best friend. She knew whom I preferred, but that was fine, because I also knew whom she preferred. It was something of a marriage of convenience. I had a few young men and she had her young women, and we were both as happy as we could be with the arrangement."

"But . . . why? Didn't anybody know?"

"A few people knew. Your grandfather knew. He was not very happy about it, as he was quite conservative, but he was also my friend. Several

chapter eleven

others suspected, but nothing could ever be proven. We were very discreet. You must remember that this was over sixty years ago and our society was not nearly as tolerant as it is now. Of course, we still have a way to go."

"Isis," Evelynne breathed. "So is that why you never had children?"

"In part. We did try several times to provide an Heir. However, Ariannes died before we were successful. After that I felt it unlikely that I would ever find another woman who would be able to accept a similar arrangement

"Isis," the princess said again. She sat quietly, digesting this information.

"So now you know my secret," the Duke said. "However, you came here to talk about your situation. You believe that you are a lesbian?"

"And that I'm attracted to Ally," she added.

"Let us deal with the first part for now," Lord Thomas suggested. "What makes you think you are gay?"

Evelynne stared at him incredulously. "You mean besides wondering what it would be like to kiss your secretary?"

"Of course. Simple sexual curiosity does not make you homosexual. Over the course of my own life there have been a few women about whom I have been . . . curious. It most certainly does not make me heterosexual."

"This has been more than a few women," Evelynne mumbled.

"I beg your pardon?"

"I said, for me it's been more than a few women," she said more loudly, blushing to the tips of her ears. "I spent most of yesterday looking at every woman around and imagining what it would be like to kiss them. And it felt . . . good." At her host's encouraging expression, Evelynne continued, "So then I tried imagining what it would be like to kiss the men. And while it wasn't really repulsive to imagine–except for a few–" She shuddered. "–there was just . . . nothing there."

The Duke smiled. "Well, that is certainly a good indication. However, it does not tell you for sure."

"So what can?" Evelynne asked plaintively. "How do I *know*?"

In reply, Lord Thomas reached forward to touch Evelynne's chest just above her heart. "Right here. This knows. Listen to it. It will tell you."

Frowning, the princess closed her eyes and searched within herself. *What am I?* she asked. *Who am I?*

The answer came back: *I am Evelynne.* And then she knew.

Evelynne's eyes snapped open. "I'm *me*," she said wonderingly. "I'm sexually attracted to women, but I'm still *me*."

Lord Thomas smiled at her proudly. "Good, Evelynne. Now remember that. No matter what happens, no matter what anyone says, remember who you are. You are a good person. You always have been. A woman who just happens to prefer other women. It is a part of you, and only a part, and in our society that brings the label of 'lesbian'. But that label does not define you."

Evelynne had tears in her eyes, and the Duke fished in a pocket for a handkerchief. "Thank you, Domdom," she said, wiping them away. It felt like a great weight had been lifted and she could breathe easier.

"You are very welcome, my dear." He attempted to inject some lightness into the discussion. "Now on to the more juicy–I mean specific details. Tell me about Alleandre."

"Well, first off, I suppose you should know that Ally's also gay."

"Is she now? I must say that I suspected as much." At the princess' questioning look, he explained, "One of the supposed stereotypes of homosexuals is that they are able automatically to recognise each other. In English I believe it is quite cleverly termed 'gaydar'. Like most stereotypes, it is generally less accurate and more exaggerated than should be believed. However, being part of a fairly small group, we tend to learn to recognise the characteristics of other members of our club, if only subconsciously. It does save embarrassment when asking someone to dance. In fact, 'gaydar' is a quite accurate term, since it involves sending out minute, subtle signals and interpreting the resulting reaction. At least, that is how Jason explained the concept to me."

Evelynne looked slightly bewildered. "Please tell me there's some kind of manual for all this."

The Duke barked a laugh. "I'd imagine there is one somewhere on the Internet. Unfortunately, or fortunately, the rest of us must learn through practice." The princess' cheeks reddened again, and Lord Thomas noticed. "Evelynne Sophia, get your mind out of the gutter."

Though her cheeks were still flaming, she managed to pout, "Don't want to. I have company down here." Becoming serious once more, Evelynne said, "Well, a few weeks ago Ally got a phone call from her ex-girlfriend, and that's when she told me that she was . . . gay." Lord Thomas nodded in understanding. "I guess I was attracted to her even then, because I remember, only in retrospect, that I felt kind of . . . relieved when she said they weren't getting back together. I didn't realise it at the time, though. But then things really came together two mornings ago." The princess cleared her throat uncomfortably. "I, um, went to see Ally in the morning, and I suppose she was just getting out of the bath. Um, I went into her room without knocking and she was . . . well . . . um . . . you know . . . without clothing."

"Oh dear."

chapter eleven

"That's what I thought. So anyway, she was really embarrassed, but we talked for a while afterwards and things seemed to be turning out all right. But all I could think about that day–and yesterday–was that she was–or is–absolutely gorgeous."

"I see. And does Alleandre know how you feel?" the Duke asked.

Evelynne paled. "Isis, no! Definitely not! I think. I've been looking at her quite a bit and I think she might have noticed that something is going on, but she hasn't said anything."

"I see," he repeated. "And what is it exactly that you feel? Is it simply a physical reaction, brought about by your emerging sexuality? Do you have a more romantic interest? Or is your response being enhanced by the knowledge that she did save your life and you're feeling somehow obligated?"

The princess started to respond angrily to the last option, but then stopped and looked thoughtful. "No, I suppose that is a reasonable suggestion. And the answer is, I don't know. I'm . . . pretty sure it's more than just physical, though." She hesitated and her companion motioned for her to continue. "A few days ago I met with Doctor Marens from the *sa-kima* breeding program and he brought along a student he's working with, Mila'a Porse–I mentioned her to you. She and Ally spent some time together and she asked Ally out. Now, I certainly can't blame Mila'a for being interested–" Evelynne indicated herself. "–look who's talking, after all. But I felt . . . jealous when Ally told me. And when she said she was considering it, I felt . . . hurt. It physically hurt, right here." She pressed a hand to the centre of her chest.

"Ah, my dear," Lord Thomas said comfortingly. "I agree that what you feel is more than simply physical. As much as I would like to be able to assure you that what you are feeling towards Alleandre is either infatuation or great friendship or even love, I'm afraid emotions are not so easy." When Evelynne sighed in resignation, he smiled. "Be patient, my dear. These feelings are new and you are dealing with a huge number of issues right now: your injuries, the upcoming assumption of your duties, new friends and most recently your own sexuality. All I can advise is to be aware of your emotions. Do not try to pick them apart. Just let your mind work them out in its own time." He looked directly into her eyes. "And also know that whatever happens, I will always support you. Will you be telling your father about this?"

Evelynne frowned. "Not just yet. I think I want to have things a bit clearer in my own mind before . . ."

The Duke nodded in understanding. "There is one other thing on a more professional level. While I do not believe that your sexuality, whatever it may be, would interfere with you assuming your duties, either as Heir or as Queen, there are enough old laws that someone may be able to raise an objection, no matter how spurious. With your permission, I would like Jason to investigate the matter on your behalf."

"Would you be able to keep my name out of it?" the princess asked plaintively. "At the moment, I'd like as few people to know as possible."

Lord Thomas' eyebrows rose. "Evelynne, my dear, you are the only Heir Atlantl has right now. I think he will be able to guess who I am talking about. However, you can trust him. After all, he has kept my secret for years."

"I guess you're right."

"Of course I am." The Duke rose to his feet. "However, unless I am mistaken, you have an appointment to keep with First Justicar Farrell." He helped Evelynne to rise. "And I have another pile of boring paperwork to do. Since apparently you will not be finding me a young man to be my heir," he teased, "I suppose I must do it myself. Remember Evelynne, if you ever need to talk to me, you are welcome at any time."

"Thank you, Domdom. Who knows? Maybe I'll find you a nice young woman to become your heir instead."

                      ත ත ත ත ත

"Well, Justicar Farrell just wanted me to make some decisions regarding the election of my Advisors. But then, since I have to remain removed from the elections I'm going to be on 'vacation' for a while longer and you have me all to yourselves for the next couple of months." Suddenly realising what she had said, Evelynne winced. "That one's too easy," she declared to Chorus.

Chorus grinned again and picked up the easy points. Turning to Ally who was sitting beside him in the limo, he said, "All to ourselves, eh, Ally? For a couple of months, even. I'm sure we could corrupt her easily, with your feminine wiles and my masculine charm." He flashed his brilliant teeth at Evelynne. "We could rock your world, Princess."

Ally looked blank for a moment before the message clicked. Reddening, she stuttered something incomprehensible. She cast a sidelong glance at the princess and blushed even more furiously.

Evelynne watched the exchange and especially Ally's reaction, with great attention. She had accurately predicted Chorus' response, but the other woman's actions were examined with a new degree of interest. *She looks uncomfortable,* Evelynne thought. *But then she looks uncomfortable whenever sex is mentioned, or even hinted at, for that matter. So her blushing is not really a definite sign of interest. On the other hand, it's not a sign of disinterest either.* Recalling Lord Thomas' recommendation of patience, she filed the reaction away for later

chapter eleven

corroboration. With a new sense of peace, she allowed herself to be drawn back into the conversation. "Sorry, Ally, I went away for a moment there. What were you saying?"

"I was asking if you did anything else while we were at the Museum."

"Oh. Well, I saw Domdom also. We talked for a while."

Ally perked up at the mention of the man who was quickly becoming one of her favourite Atlantlans. "Oh yes, how is he doing?"

"Just fine. As busy as ever, but he's not going to stop until we actually cremate him. He'll probably still be working at his own funeral. Anyway, we had a nice long conversation. He helped me with some . . . personal issues."

"Oh." Ally looked concerned. "Are you okay? Is it something I can help with?"

If only you knew. "No, I'll be fine. It was just some things I had to work out and Domdom helped me talk them out. I feel much better. Don't worry, when I need to, you'll definitely be the first person I talk to about them." *I hope. If you aren't with someone else . . . like Mila'a.* The princess briefly toyed with the idea of arranging to have the student transferred to study polar bear conservation at the North Pole. *No, I can't do that. No matter how I feel, there's no guarantee that Ally will ever feel the same. And she does like Mila'a, so they could be happy together.* She sighed mentally. *So no North Pole. Darn it.*

Ally studied Evelynne. The princess had a quirky smile on her face, as if she was enjoying a private joke. Evelynne's entire bearing was subtly different from earlier in the day. That morning—the whole two days before, actually—the princess had been somewhat stiff, hesitant, almost frightened. Now, though, she was more relaxed and confident, nearly the same woman she had met in the hospital in Marseilles. Although something was different. Nothing Ally could put her finger on, but—

Evelynne suddenly thought of something. "Oh yes, I also ran into Omar ibn Larak, *za*'s Foreign Affairs Advisor. You remember him?" At Ally's nod, she continued, "He asked me to ask you respectfully if you had given any more thought to giving an interview with a media agency. Apparently everyone wants to know about you and the websites just aren't enough."

"Websites?" Chorus asked.

Evelynne nodded, then grinned. "Advisor Larak showed some of them to me. You're quite the hot commodity in certain circles, Ally. In addition to the basic 'who is Alleandre Tretiak' sites, there are a several where men—and more than a few women, I might add—have . . . speculated, shall we say, about what you're like in bed."

"Me?" Ally squeaked. "They—it—they—in *bed?*"

Chorus looked on with intense interest.

"Oh yes," Evelynne said solemnly. "In fact, some are speculating that the reason you haven't really been seen since France is because I'm keeping you locked up as my love slave."

"Locked . . . l-love slave? What?" Ally knew that she was going to spontaneously combust any moment now. Or implode from lack of oxygen.

"Yes. They go into quite a bit of detail, actually. I made some copies here if you want to see." Evelynne started to reach for her bag.

Ally's hand shot out to grab Evelynne's wrist. "No! No! Nonono." Suddenly, without warning, she couldn't breathe. Her vision dimmed and a dull roaring filled her ears. The roaring quickly re-formed into laughter and the darkness sprouted mocking eyes and pointing fingers. Ally froze, locked into the memory, waiting helplessly for the contempt and denigration to sear themselves directly into her brain. Nothing came, but still she waited. *Please let it stop. I don't want to hear them. Please let it stop. I don't want to hear them. Please let it stop . . .* Some small part of her mind, hopelessly trying to inject reason, was dimly aware that she was saying the words aloud. And still she waited for the dreadful emotions to come.

"Ally! Ally, it's okay. You're not at school. Nobody is laughing at you. It's just Evelynne and Chorus here. Please, Ally, let it go . . ." From far away, Ally heard a familiar voice. There were emotions associated with that voice and they were not the cold, hard ones she was expecting. Hesitantly she opened herself to the emotions, like a turtle emerging from its shell, ready to pull back at the first sign of danger. She only sampled the surface, though, reading *guilt/friendship-love/concern/fear/anger-directed-elsewhere*. Reassured, Ally seized the emotions like a lifeline and slowly pulled herself up and out of the pit.

Evelynne shook her head violently as a wave of dizziness crashed over her. She put it out of her mind, though, when she saw Ally's eyes—which had been terrifyingly blank—clear and the intelligence behind them emerge once more. She was kneeling before Ally in the cramped space between the fore- and back-facing seats, but she ignored the discomfort. Chorus was sitting beside the stricken young woman with his hand resting carefully on her shoulder. The car rocked slightly as it came to a halt on the side of the road, stopped by Evelynne's panicked command.

With the clarity returned to Ally's eyes, Evelynne raised a hand to rest against her cheek. "Oh Isis, Ally, I'm so sorry. I didn't realise—I didn't think—I'm sorry."

Ally dredged up a ghost of a smile. Her voice was hoarse, as though she had been screaming, as she said, "It's okay. I didn't think either. Sometimes it just hits me." She laughed bitterly. "I guess I'm not as over it as I thought. Maybe I should sue my shrink, eh?"

chapter eleven

The door to the limo opened suddenly to reveal the concerned faces of a couple of Evelynne's Guards. "Your Highness, what's wrong?" one asked.

Hoping to spare Ally any further embarrassment, Evelynne ad libbed, "*Ishta* Tretiak is just feeling carsick, that's all. I think she needs a bit of fresh air."

The Guard nodded in sympathy and offered a hand to the still pale young woman. His companion pulled back and spoke quietly into his mike. "I understand, *Ishta* Tretiak. We are well out of the city right now, so stopping for a few minutes should pose little risk."

Ally shot a grateful look at Evelynne before accepting the Guard's assistance out of the vehicle.

Once the young woman was outside and taking deep breaths of air, Chorus moved closer and whispered, "What just happened here?"

The princess was torn. "Has Ally told you about her panic attacks?" she hedged.

Chorus was surprised. "No, she hasn't said anything like that to me. What happened?"

Evelynne hesitated. "Well, she gets attacks. I can't tell you why. You have to ask her and if she wants you to know she'll tell you. Just be aware that it's really hard for her to talk about, so be careful, all right?"

Though dissatisfied, the young man nodded acquiescence.

A moment later Ally re-entered the car. She was still pale and pinched around the eyes and lips, but looked much better. "Sorry about that," she said, obviously wanting to put the incident behind her.

Her companions quickly reassured her and after several awkward minutes, the conversation picked up once more. However, it wasn't long before Ally's newly battered psyche succumbed to sleep, and she dozed for the rest of the journey.

ॐ ॐ ॐ ॐ ॐ

In a large room in the Common Guard Headquarters, a low murmur of speech, computers and radio signals filled the air. Throughout the intelligence-gathering area, analysts sought out any possible threats to the Atlantlan Realm.

Lieutenant Alfred Toburn, a young analyst who had recently arrived in the Guard, exclaimed in triumph as he recorded one particular piece of data. The exclamation attracted the attention of General D'vaya Danun, Marshal of the Common Guard.

"You have something, Alfred?" she asked brusquely.

The young technician looked up. "Yes, Ma'am," he replied. "We have another transmission from Unknown Beta-43 to the HBLA."

As usual, the General's unsmiling face remained unchanged. "Is it encrypted like the others?"

Alfred's face fell. "Unfortunately yes, Ma'am."

General Danun sighed. "Well, send it off to Decryption, Alfred. Maybe we'll get lucky."

"Already done, Ma'am." Greatly daring, he asked, "If I may, Ma'am, why is this code so hard to break?"

The General sighed again. "Because it's very, very good, Lieutenant. Oh, we break encryption every day here. Everything from the American CIA to Moroccan drug smugglers. But this is absolutely top of the line encryption. Only the very highest levels of any nation's intelligence and military use anything like it. And we *know* that it's not one of ours. Which means it's an external agency. And *that* is what scares me." She smiled humourlessly at the young man's disbelieving expression. "Yes, Alfred, some things scare even me. The fact that a very powerful unknown foreign agency is communicating with those lunatics in the Hy Braseal Liberation Army is one of them. I'll add to that the fact that we still have absolutely no idea what the messages say." She looked carefully at the now very sober analyst. "Good. *Now* I think you are paranoid and frightened enough to work here."

chapter twelve

"Yes?" King Jad looked up from the work on his desk to see Mohammed al-Shan, his personal secretary, standing in the doorway.

"Grand Dame Greta McMurray to see you, Sire," the secretary announced.

"Ah yes, of course, of course," the King rumbled, rising to his feet and smoothing his tunic. "Thank you, Mohammed. Please show her in."

"Yes, Sire," Mohammed said, standing back to usher the older woman into the King's personal study.

The King smiled broadly at the woman, genuinely pleased to see her. Dame Greta had that effect on people. In her youth she had been one of Atlantl's greatest screen actresses before she had left show business to become Grand Mistress of the Order of Saint Mary the Virgin. It had been a shock to many when she had been inducted into the Order, since that particular group accepted only virgins. It was, therefore, possibly the smallest Order in the Realm.

"Greta, welcome back," the King said, embracing his friend. The two of them had known each other for decades and there had once even been a rumour that they were lovers, but that had quickly withered when Greta's true status became known. "Please, sit, sit."

"Thank you, Jad," Dame Greta replied. "It's wonderful to be back."

The King took his own seat, then looked at an ornate clock hanging on the wall, and sighed. "I'm afraid I can't spend very long with you," he said. "I must catch a flight in about twenty minutes."

"I understand," Greta said. "I believe I have what you need anyway."

"Oh yes? So how much screaming was there?" The King's brows rose in amusement.

"Surprisingly little, considering the personalities involved. Apparently you were not even the first to consider the idea. Mbala and Eileen were actually about to approach you with the proposal to knight *Ishta* Tretiak. Sir Arthur Ramirez is one of Eileen's, you know, and he's already volunteered as a Nominator."

"Really? I'm impressed. I imagine it wasn't all smooth sailing, though."

"Alas, no. Massey has flatly refused to let the girl into his Order. He says it's because she's not a Christian, but he's really just pleased that he doesn't have to admit it's because she has the poor taste to be a lesbian."

Dame Greta frowned. "He does have the core of a solid point though," she admitted grudgingly. "Each of us *do* have certain requirements. For instance, much as I'd like to, I don't know if *I* could offer her the Spur, since we're still debating whether a woman who has had relations only with other women is technically still a virgin." She shrugged apologetically. "In the same way, while Eileen would love to induct young Alleandre into the Templars, she also requires Christianity as a prerequisite, or at least a degree of adherence to Templar-Christian values."

"I see," the King said thoughtfully. "Still, none of you are about to Ban her from the Spur outright?"

Greta shook her head firmly. "No. And those Orders for which she might qualify are downright eager to snatch her up." She snorted a laugh. "Mbala and Khwaja from the Dragons practically challenged each other to a duel over her."

King Jad laughed outright. "Well, that's good, I suppose," he said, still chuckling. "Well, my trip this afternoon is actually to go and visit with my daughter and Alleandre, and I plan to broach the subject with them both. Hopefully I will be able to find out which Order she might actually qualify for."

ॐ ॐ ॐ ॐ ॐ

"What's up with you?" Chorus asked Ally, as they stood with Evelynne in the bright morning sun and watched the helicopter make its final approach. "You've been jumpy all morning."

"Nothing," Ally declared. "I'm fine." Chorus and Evelynne shared a disbelieving glance behind Ally's back. The taller woman saw it. "Okay, I'm a little nervous."

"Why?" Evelynne asked. "They're your parents. I would have thought you would be happy to see them."

"Oh, I am," Ally declared. "It's just that . . . I haven't seen them in over six months. On top of that, they just found out that I've been shot. That sort of thing tends to make parents a little, well, crazy. You should know."

"Ah yes," the princess murmured, recalling several instances since her return when she had witnessed her father's reactions in private. Publicly he had been strong and stoic, but when they were alone he had completely broken down. Evelynne had rarely seen her father cry and the experience was still unreal. "You know it's only because they love you, though."

"I know. And believe me, it helps. A little."

The trio, along with a small contingent of Guards and servants, braced themselves against the wind as the helicopter touched down on the landing

chapter twelve

pad. A fine spray was kicked up from the pad, damp from the morning's light rain.

As the aircraft's motor slowed, the waiting ground crew moved forward to place the blocks under the wheels and place a step for the occupants. The ramp came down and a uniformed Guard positioned himself to assist the passengers in disembarking.

Unfortunately for the Guard, he was violently pushed aside as a small dark-haired woman rushed down the ramp, ran a short distance away from the vehicle, leaned over and vomited heavily onto the pavement. A moment later, a much taller balding man with a small moustache exited the aircraft much more carefully and hurried over to hand the stricken woman a cloth.

The onlookers at the side of the pad watched the scene in surprise, except for Ally, who only sighed heavily. When Evelynne looked questioningly, she muttered, "Ladies and gentlemen, my mother."

As the enthralled audience looked on, the easily recognisable form of King Jad disembarked. He walked over and addressed the small woman, who was still bent over, though no longer retching. The woman Ally had identified as her mother shook her head and the balding man said something in response. After wiping her mouth a final time with the handkerchief, Mrs. Tretiak looked for a place to put it. The King waved over one of the waiting servants, who took the offensive item with admirable aplomb.

The most urgent matter now taken care of, Mrs. Tretiak finally looked around at her surroundings, leaning on her husband's arm. The King said something else and pointed towards the welcoming party standing patiently about twenty metres away. The couple caught sight of their daughter nervously leaning on her cane and suddenly they were both rushing towards Ally.

Ally saw her parents coming towards her and moved awkwardly forward to meet them. Time seemed to stretch and then she was buried in her mother's arms, her cane falling to the ground, as she was joined a moment later by her father, who wrapped his own strong arms around them both. Ally felt her mother's face buried in her chest, felt all the arms around her tighten even stronger and had no qualms about opening her mind completely to them, feeling her mother's relief and overwhelming love pour into her soul. Her father's emotional output remained a stubborn blank and she felt a momentary pang that she had never been able to share this part of her gifts with him. As if he could tell what she was feeling, the tall man's embrace strengthened once more, as he strove to show his love and support through purely physical means.

They remained that way for several long minutes. Evelynne looked on with a sense of envy, but this time it was directed at Ally for having two parents to love her. She smiled at her father, who was avoiding intruding on the private moment and somehow knew that his thoughts were travelling along similar lines. He saw her smile and shared a smile of his own as they both paid silent tribute to a woman who Evelynne, at least, could barely remember.

Finally the reunited family broke apart, with much sniffling on the part of Mrs. Tretiak and Ally's father produced yet another handkerchief, which she used to wipe her eyes. Once she had, Mr. Tretiak reclaimed the article and used it to wipe away his own tears.

Looking down at her diminutive mother, Ally gave a watery smile of her own and said, "Hi, Mom. Hi, Dad. So how's life been treating you?"

The question startled a laugh out of her mother and her father gave a chuckle of his own. "Oh, pretty well, you obnoxious imp," Mrs. Tretiak replied. "Of course, you have been scaring the pants off both of us. What have you been getting yourself up to this time, young lady?"

Ally looked away, suddenly shy. "Well . . . I—"

"Never mind that now," her father interrupted. "We can talk about that later. Right now all I want to know is how you're doing."

"I'm doing . . . well. I was in kind of bad shape for a while," she admitted, then hurried on as her mother's face, still pale from her recent flight, whitened even more, "but now I'm almost healed." It was only a small exaggeration.

"Good," Mrs. Tretiak said. She wrapped her arms around her daughter once more and whispered, "We both love you, Ally. Don't you ever do anything like this to us again. We want you to be well."

"I love you too, Mom," Ally whispered back. In a louder voice she continued, "I'm actually doing pretty well. They're treating me quite decently here."

"I'd imagine so," her father said wryly, a twinkle in his eye. "You have helicopters and limousines to take you everywhere, servants to cater to your every whim. . ."

"It's not like that," Ally protested before seeing the joking grin. "Of course, how silly of me. I have slaves waiting on me hand and foot, bringing me caviar, wine and jewels. I do nothing but lounge on pillows all day and have my free choice of w—men from the Royal Harem." She cast a quick glance at King Jad, but he appeared to have missed her near slip.

"Harem?" Chorus stage-whispered to Evelynne. "You have a harem? Why wasn't I told about this?"

chapter twelve

Everyone, except for the perpetually dour Nancu Ylan, laughed.

Any potential ice broken, Ally turned to the waiting people, still leaning on her mother's arm. She saw Evelynne holding her fallen cane and reclaimed it with a mouthed "Thank you."

With her balance regained, but with her mother still holding tightly to her arm, Ally introduced, "Your Majesty, I know you've already met them, but I'd like to formally introduce my parents, Catherine and William Tretiak. Mom, Dad, His Majesty King Jad of Atlantl."

The King smiled. "Indeed we have met, but we were unable to speak much. I was somewhat busy on the trip over." Given her mother's actions upon landing, Ally suspected that the excuse was a polite fiction to cover up Mrs. Tretiak's inevitable airsickness. "However, I hope to rectify the missed opportunity."

Turning to the next ranking member of the entourage, Ally said, "And this is Her Highness Princess Evelynne Sophia al-Heru DeMolay, Heir to the Throne. Your Highness, my parents."

Now that she had a clear view of Ally's parents, Evelynne could see where her friend's looks came from. Except for being slightly thinner and at least twenty years younger, Ally's face was an almost exact replica of her mother's, right down to the small mole just below her left ear. Her hair was also the same colour, though the older Tretiak's was significantly longer, reaching almost to her shoulders. However, Mrs. Tretiak was even shorter than the princess, leaving her husband and daughter to tower over her. Ally's height and build were obvious genetic gifts from her father, who topped a few inches over six feet. That was the only resemblance between them, as his balding head and sandy hair were very different from Ally's own. The only way in which Ally resembled neither of her parents was the shade of her eyes. Mr. Tretiak's were a rich brown and his wife's were a deep blue; both were totally unlike Ally's striking grey eyes.

Evelynne chuckled delightedly. "Oh, Ally, that's very good. Very formal." Turning to the two older Tretiaks, she said, "What Ally *actually* meant to say is, 'This is my friend Evelynne.'" To emphasise the informality, she moved forward and caught Ally's parents in a strong embrace. "Thank you so much," she whispered, pitching her words for their ears alone. "If it wasn't for your daughter, I wouldn't be here right now." After a final squeeze she pulled back.

Taken aback by the princess' actions, Mrs. Tretiak said, "You are quite welcome, Your H–Evelynne." She changed the title at Evelynne's admonitory finger. More confident, she continued, "We're quite proud of our Alleandre."

Flushing at the praise, Ally next introduced, "And this is Keitumetsemosimaniwapula Tladi. Also known as Chorus."

Now out of the unfamiliar heights of nobility, Ally's parents confidently shook the young man's hand. "Of course, Chorus. Ally has told us about you in her letters."

"Don't believe a word of it," Chorus said promptly. "It's lies, all lies. Lies and slander. Completely untrue. Whatever she's told you, I didn't do it."

Mr. Tretiak's eyebrows rose. "So when she says that you're a very pleasant, intelligent, well educated young man, we shouldn't believe her?"

The young man turned to look Ally square in the eye. "Ally, you said that? I think you must like me." After receiving a blush as reward, he turned his attention back to the Tretiaks. "Okay then, that part is true. But anything bad you've heard is false and I have the pictures to prove it."

"And we really don't want to see those pictures," Ally declared. "Trust me." She shot a thankful smile to Chorus for successfully getting her parents to relax.

"Shall we go inside?" Evelynne asked. "Not that it isn't very pleasant out here, but Latifa has made us a late lunch and I, for one, am starving."

"What about our luggage?" William Tretiak asked.

"It has already been taken up to the Palace," King Jad answered. "By now I'd imagine it is being unpacked, knowing Nancu Ylan as I do." The party began to make its way up the path leading to the Palace. "Tell me, Mr Tretiak, what is it exactly that you teach?"

"Geography and history, er . . . Your Majesty."

"Please, I owe your daughter, and you by extension, a great debt. To you I am Jad, at least in private. Now, what level do you teach?"

"High school . . . Jad."

"Ah, very important subjects and a very important age. Do you enjoy it?"

The two men's voices faded as they moved ahead of Ally and her mother.

As they started up the pathway in pairs, Evelynne and Chorus leading, Ally and her mother were left to take up the rear. Holding her daughter's right arm, Mrs. Tretiak said, "Ally, it's so good to see you again."

"I'm glad to see both of you too, Mom. It's been a while."

"Indeed it has." They were silent for a few moments, simply reaffirming the bond between them. Looking up, Catherine Tretiak saw her husband and the King engaged in spirited conversation. "It looks like your father has made a new friend."

"I know." Ally laughed. "It gets a little surreal when you suddenly realise that these people are in charge of running an entire country. And here's the

chapter twelve

ruler of one of the most powerful nations on Earth talking to Dad about teaching in Canada."

"You seem to be settling in just fine," Ally's mother remarked.

"Well, I have had nearly two months to get used to them. It helps that they're such likeable people. Especially Evy and her father."

"I see." The shorter woman looked sidelong at her daughter and Ally wondered if she had given too much away. "I have a question to ask you."

"Shoot." Ally braced herself.

"You wouldn't happen to have a breath mint, would you? I'm afraid I am a little rank."

Alleandre felt like she had dodged a bullet. "Actually, I do." She reached into her right hand pocket and pulled out a large handful of small hard candies. "I know how you get when you fly, so I came prepared."

"Smart-aleck," her mother muttered.

ও ও ও ও ও

More guests meant moving lunch from their more familiar informal dining room to the main hall. The room was much longer, panelled in rich, dark wood and hosted a huge table. King Jad sat at the head of the table, with Princess Evelynne to his right and Ally next to her. The older Tretiaks and Chorus took up the other side of the table. Over a dozen places remained unfilled.

"That was absolutely delicious," William Tretiak said, pushing his chair back from the table. "Your chef is a genius. I'm just sorry you weren't able to eat any of this, dear." The last sentence was directed at his wife, who was still slowly finishing her bowl of plain yoghurt.

The yoghurt had been served at exactly the same time as the rest of the meal. Through some mysterious means Latifa had heard of Ally's mother's illness during flight and had automatically arranged something bland and comforting for the unfortunate woman.

"Thank you, honey, but at the moment I am quite happy with the yoghurt. I'm sure I will be able to try some of–Latifa, was it? Some of Latifa's cooking soon." She suddenly looked uncertain. "Although I'm not sure how long we are going to be staying. We came rather suddenly and I don't know how long we're welcome."

"Oh, you are more than welcome to stay for as long as you wish," Evelynne declared immediately.

"Absolutely," confirmed King Jad. "In fact, now that you're here, we're counting on you to be here at least until after the banquet that's scheduled for next weekend."

"Banquet?" Ally asked, startled.

"We only confirmed it this morning," the princess explained. "It's been sort of a last minute thing. I'm sorry I haven't had a chance to tell you about it." She mouthed another "Sorry" to Ally with an entreating expression on her face.

Completely unable to not forgive Evelynne, Ally said as much with her expression. Aloud, she said, "Okay. Well, I'm sure you'll have fun at the party."

Evelynne shared a wry glance at her father, who explained, "No, I'm afraid you don't understand, Alleandre. The banquet is in honour of my daughter's safe return and recovery. Considering the part you played in that return, I was–we were hoping that you would join us as one of the guests of honour."

Ally paled. "Me?" she squeaked. "Guest of honour?"

Her mother recognised the signs of Ally's nascent anxiety and reached over the table to comfort her, but was surprised when Evelynne grasped her daughter's hand first.

"Yes, you." The princess' tone was gentle. "You need to realise that you didn't just save my life. You also saved the life of the next Queen of Atlantl and there are a lot of people who want to acknowledge that. And around here, one of the traditional ways to do so is to present you to them. Now, if you honestly believe that you can't handle that much attention, you do not have to go. Nobody is going to force you." Evelynne smiled at her friend encouragingly. "But *I'd* love it if you would come."

Damnit, Ally thought. *How am I supposed to resist that? I can't disappoint her. Crap. It's almost as if she knows I'm half in love with her.* She made a decision. Some inner voice was raising issue with use of the word "half", but she ignored it. "Okay, I'll go." Ally put on a theatrical frown. "But I refuse to enjoy myself."

"Awww." Evelynne's face formed an equally dramatic pout, complete with a trembling lower lip. "Pleeeeease? Please say you'll have fun. I'll hold my breath until you do," she threatened. She even looked ready to do so.

Even though she knew it was only in jest, Ally melted internally. "Okay, okay," she mock-grumbled. "I'll have fun. I wouldn't want you to pass out and have to save your life again."

Catherine Tretiak watched in amazement as she watched her shy, reserved daughter and the Crown Princess of Atlantl . . . *flirting* with each other. It was the only word she could think of to describe what they were doing. She looked to her husband, but he had missed it. A glance to her other side showed that Chorus had noticed something going on and was watching the exchange with avid curiosity.

chapter twelve

She wanted confirmation, however, and knew only one way to get it. Lidding her eyelids slightly, Catherine sank into herself, shutting out external distractions. Just as her daughter had taught her, she sought the correct mental frame to extend her perceptions. The process had nowhere near the skill and finesse with which Ally did it, but Catherine's mind slowly, haltingly, began to receive the emotional currents in the room.

Sharing Ally's moral distaste for eavesdropping on unsuspecting people, the woman quickly shut out any but the emotions leaking from her daughter. And they were certainly leaking. Ally's mind was more open, more free and more relaxed than her mother could ever remember it being before. And prominent among the emotions were those Catherine had been half afraid–and half hoping–to find.

She withdrew her perceptions back into herself to find the table's other occupants looking at her with concern. "Pardon?"

"I was asking if you were all right, Mrs. T," Chorus repeated.

"Oh." She looked across the table at her daughter and saw that Evelynne still had not released her hand, though neither seemed aware of it. Catherine's slightly strained smile wasn't faked. "I think that blasted helicopter is still bouncing my stomach around a little. Would you all mind if I had a little lie down?" She awkwardly directed the question to King Jad.

"Of course, Catherine," the King said, nothing but concern on his red face. "In fact," he continued, rising to his feet, "I must speak with Alleandre for a little while. Alone." His expression halted Evelynne's automatic objection. "Evy, perhaps you could show Mr. and Mrs. Tretiak to their rooms."

❧ ❧ ❧ ❧ ❧

"I hope that you will agree to stay for a while," Evelynne commented as she walked Ally's parents to the suite of rooms that had been set aside for them. "I know that she's been missing you a lot."

Catherine Tretiak was leaning heavily on her husband's arm. Now that she knew that her offspring was safe–physically, at least–the adrenaline that had been supporting her during the long flight to Atlantl was rapidly dissipating. "We would love to stay for a while and we will for as long as we can." She squeezed her husband's arm. "The school board was more than willing to extend William a leave of absence, but he is going to have to get back before the school year is too far advanced. As for myself, while I can, in theory, take as long as I like, I have several research projects that are going to require my attention. But I'm sure that we can stay for at least a few weeks." Catherine looked to William for confirmation.

"Absolutely. Some things are more important than work."

More hesitantly, Catherine asked, "Er . . . Evelynne, has Ally said anything about what she intends to do? What her plans are?"

Evelynne's voice betrayed her own uncertainty. "Well, we haven't really talked about it much. So far we've just been concentrating on getting her well again. Once she's fully functional. . ." She shrugged, unable to completely keep the distress from showing. "Personally, I'd like Ally to stay around, but that might not fit in with her plans for the future. Still, she is more than welcome to stay for as long as she wishes."

"You sound like you two are very . . . close."

"Oh, I like to think that we've become really good friends," Evelynne affirmed. *For now,* a hopeful voice whispered in her mind. She felt herself redden and noticed Mrs. Tretiak watching her curiously.

The princess' flush confirmed Catherine's uneasy suspicions. *Oh dear,* she thought. *I really must speak with Ally about this.*

As they talked, they had passed several doors along the hallway. "This is my room," Evelynne said, pointing to a doorway on the right. "And just up here next door is Ally's room." The princess stopped them at a door in the opposite wall. "And this is where you will be staying." She opened the door and waved the couple inside.

"Oh my," Catherine said as she and William took in the room's beautiful décor. Like Evelynne's and Ally's rooms, this one featured a motif based on a mythological creature; in this case Phoenixes appeared to set the walls and furniture ablaze. "Oh my," Catherine repeated. "I think we may have to stay a while after all."

ಶ ಶ ಶ ಶ ಶ

Alleandre nervously followed King Jad into the study. The King lowered his large frame into a comfortable armchair and waved his guest into another. Ally silently did as she was bidden, leaning her cane against the arm of the chair and sitting stiffly upright. Sir Adun, the King's vigilant bodyguard, took up an inconspicuous position near the door.

"Oh, this is nice," the King said, sighing heavily. "You have no idea how few opportunities I get to simply sit back and talk with someone on non-life-threatening matters."

Uncertain how to reply, Ally just smiled nervously.

The King must have made some hidden signal, because suddenly Nancu Ylan was standing near the King's chair. "Your Majesty?" the Seneschal asked.

"Ah, Ylan, would you please bring me a glass of . . . oh, make it port. Something mellow."

"Of course, Sire." He paused and appeared to be waiting.

chapter twelve

The King also seemed to be waiting, looking at Ally, who stared back blankly. Finally, after several moments, he said, "Alleandre, would you care for anything?"

Ally blushed bright red. "Oh, right. Um, sorry. Uh . . . ginger ale, please?" she asked the Seneschal meekly.

Nancu Ylan nodded solemnly and Ally knew his expression would have been the same if she had requested a glass of warm goat's milk. "Of course, *Ishta*. Your Majesty." He bowed and left the room.

"So, Alleandre, how have you been doing lately?"

"Um . . . much better, thank you, er . . . Sire," Ally stammered. "I still get tired easily, but, um, that should pass."

King Jad smiled encouragingly. "Actually, you do not need to call me 'Sire', Alleandre. Since you are not one of my subjects, I am not the symbolic head of your family."

"Oh. Uh, okay, then . . . Sir."

He smiled in approval. "Well, I am very happy to hear that you are recovering well. It helps me with some considerations that I must, well, consider."

Conversation was temporarily halted as Nancu Ylan returned, served drinks and left again.

The King took a large mouthful and sighed in satisfaction. Ally sipped her own ginger ale more slowly.

"Ah, now we can get down to business," King Jad declared. Leaning forward, he placed his glass on a nearby table and looked up at an obviously nervous Ally. "Alleandre, relax," he commanded gently. "I'm not about to order you beheaded. I just wanted to talk to you, get to know you a bit better."

Ally strove to relax and managed to produce a reasonable facsimile of ease. She found that she had no desire to try to read the King's intentions and put it down to his obvious authority. "Yes, Sir."

They discussed Alleandre's activities over the last few weeks. " . . . and the Templar Museum was absolutely fascinating," Ally concluded finally.

King Jad nodded. "Oh, I agree. Did you happen to visit the Grand Mosque while you were in Outremer?"

"No, Sir. I saw it as we drove past and it looks beautiful, but we didn't go in. I'm afraid religion really isn't a priority for me."

"Now, I'm curious, although I realise that religion is not usually a politely discussed topic, but I was wondering how you describe yourself spiritually."

"Oh. Well . . . I guess I'd call myself a . . . scientific emergent spiritualist, Sir."

"I see. And what exactly is a scientific emergent spiritualist?"

"Well, Sir, in a sense, I believe that the entire universe is alive in some manner, but not necessarily sentient and at the same time ruled by invariable physical laws–hence the science. On a local level, I believe that groups of sentient beings who all believe in the same thing cause the object of their belief to form as an emergent property. So if a lot of people all believe in a particular god, that god coalesces out of their collective will. Not as a physical being, but as a kind of . . . group consciousness. And if enough people concentrate on their belief and endow it with certain 'powers', who knows what it can accomplish?"

"Fascinating," King Jad murmured. "So, for example, the Israelites escaping Egypt reach the Red Sea, which blocks their path. They pray to their 'God', in reality focusing their wills on removing the barrier and their combined willpower actually parts the waters."

"Exactly, Sir." Ally was surprised that the King had grasped the concept so readily.

The reason for his perspicacity was revealed when he said, "Hector Cortez, one of my Advisors, has a similar theory, although it is slightly more classically religious in nature. I'm sure he would enjoy speaking with you."

"I'd like that as well, Sir," Ally confirmed.

"Actually, Alleandre, I must admit that I have an ulterior motive in talking with you right now." He smiled. "Don't worry, it's nothing bad. Quite the opposite, in fact. Because of your actions, there has been some discussion on the best way to reward you." He held up a hand to forestall Ally's objection. "Hear me out. My Office, along with several others, has been flooded with suggestions. Some of them are quite frankly impractical, however well meaning. One suggestion was that I marry you, for example, and make you Queen." He laughed when Ally choked on her ginger ale. "As I said, well meaning, but unfortunately impractical."

"I quite agree, Sir," Ally choked out, red from both her coughing fit and embarrassment.

"On the other hand, some of the ideas hold merit. A significant number of both Nobles and commoners would like to see you knighted, for example."

"They want to *what*?" Ally exclaimed, her eyes wide. "Sir?" she added belatedly.

"We would like to knight you," the King repeated calmly. "Assuming you accept, you would be Dame Alleandre Tretiak."

"You want to do this *now*?" Ally asked incredulously.

"Oh, goodness, no," the King said, shaking his head. "We must first determine which Order of Knighthood you would be raised to. Then the actual knighting is a quite involved ceremony lasting two days. Fortunately, you no longer have to duel anybody."

Ally ignored the attempt at levity. "But why me, Sir? Aren't knights supposed to be, like, celebrities or heroes or . . . something . . ."

King Jad saw the comprehension spreading across Ally's face. "Exactly, Alleandre. Whether you like it or not, you are a celebrity—at least for the moment—and you are also most definitely a hero. Or heroine, as the case may be. This is merely an attempt to acknowledge that fact."

She sat for a moment in silence, trying to wrap her mind around this concept. The King waited patiently. Finally, Ally said slowly, "Sir, let's assume that I agree to . . . this. What exactly would happen next?"

King Jad carefully hid his delight. "Well, the first thing is to determine exactly which Orders you are eligible for. Each one has certain specific criteria that potential neonates must fit. The Templars, for example, accept only Christians, just as the Order of Mohammed only accepts Muslims. You would, therefore, be unable to join either. However, even if you are eligible for a particular Order, you may not wish to join. The Order of the Illuminated Word, for example, accepts nearly anyone, but they are a cloistered monastic Order, devoted to debating and writing religious commentaries.

"Now, if an appropriate Order is found, you would then be formally nominated by a member of that Order. If no Order is satisfactory, you could still be knighted as a Knight Errant, answerable to a particular Noble Sponsor. And given the response in the Hall of Nobles to your actions so far, there will be no shortage of candidates eager to Sponsor you.

"Then would come the knighthood ceremony itself, which is really too involved to go into detail right now, but involves investing you with your new coat of arms and you would become Dame Alleandre."

"Oh." Ally voice was small. "After that, what do I do, Sir? Do I ride around on a horse and fight for honour?"

The King was relieved that Ally seemed to be taking the suggestion more in stride. Either that or she was in shock. "Well, a few things change. For one, you would be a citizen of Atlantl, with all the privileges and responsibilities thereof. You would be required to pay taxes, contribute to the Realm, vote for the Advisory Councils and so on, but you would also be protected by all Atlantlan laws and the Ithikan Compact. Because you are a Canadian citizen, you are also a subject of Queen Elizabeth and the British Crown, which could potentially cause some complications. However, since I do not anticipate a war with England any time soon, they should be fairly easy to iron out. Other than that, your life would be much the same as it was before." He smiled again, large white teeth gleaming through his red beard. "Riding horses is entirely optional."

"Okay." Ally seemed to have regained some equilibrium. "Um, do I have to decide right now, Sir?"

"Not at all. Although I was hoping to make the announcement this weekend at the banquet."

"Oh. Well . . . I'll think about it tonight and let you know tomorrow, Sir."

The King waved away the statement. "Please, Alleandre, there's no rush and it is a momentous decision. Take your time. If you could let me know a day or two in advance, though, I would appreciate it." He leaned forward and looked at the woman in front of him, who looked impossibly young at the moment, although there was a certain ancient wisdom in her grey eyes. "I also want you to know that even if you decide not to accept this honour, for any reason of your own, many people greatly respect you anyway, including myself. For saving my daughter, you will always be welcome in my company."

Though uncomfortable with the blatant praise, Ally chose to accept it gracefully. "Thank you, Sir. Evelynne has come to mean a lot to me. I have no regrets about my actions."

"Excellent." The King leaned back comfortably in his chair and Ally relaxed more into hers. "Now, how about if I tell you a little about the various Orders of Knighthood. Purely for educational purposes, of course."

He was rewarded with the first genuine smile Ally had bestowed on him all afternoon. "Of course, Sir. I'd like that."

chapter thirteen

"Thank you, Rifa," Evelynne said to the servant as he cleared the remnants of the morning's breakfast from the table. "Please be sure to compliment Latifa for me."

"Tell her thanks from me too," Ally added. "I think I'm getting fat, much to my mother's delight." The princess watched sceptically as the other woman patted her stomach, which was still flat as a board.

"Of course, Your Highness, *Ishta*," Rifa said. Smiling and bowing, effortlessly balancing an arm full of plates, he left the room.

Sitting back, Evelynne smiled at her breakfast companion. "So what were your plans for the day? I suppose you'll be catching up with your parents."

"A little later I will," Ally admitted. "This morning I think they'll be sleeping in. Jet lag and all. Right now I wouldn't mind going for a walk with you, though, if you have the time."

Evelynne grinned happily. "Absolutely. I'm pretty free these days. *Za* is the one who's being run off his feet."

In fact, the King had barely had a chance to sit down to breakfast before he had been pulled away by some emergency. Murmuring an apology to his guest and daughter, he had hurried off to deal with it.

Chorus was also absent from the table. When Maïda, appalled by the scheduling of an official banquet on such short notice, had announced her intention to travel into Kilim to obtain some "absolutely vital" supplies, the young man had attached himself to her entourage. He had claimed a desire to immerse himself more in Atlantlan language and culture, but Ally suspected from the gleam in his eye that he had some secret mission.

So the two young women were alone as they left the small breakfast room and made their way into the outer gardens. The day had dawned bright and clear, and despite the early hour it was promising to be a warm one.

Ally and Evelynne wandered along the pathways, enjoying the bright colours of the flowerbeds. When Evelynne naturally took Ally's right arm, the taller woman accepted the familiarity without flinching. Instead, she relaxed, leaning more of her weight into Evelynne's body and less on her cane, and enjoyed the warmth of the contact.

An internal part of her winced, however, as the action brought up the memory of her mother's visit the night before.

The knock on her bedroom door came just as she was preparing for bed. The unforgotten "nudity incident" made Ally quickly check to make sure that she was, in fact, dressed in her red silk pyjamas before calling, "Come in."

Catherine Tretiak cautiously opened the door. She took in the bedroom's décor, impressed. Seeing her daughter standing by the huge bed, she commented, "I should have known you would manage to get yourself a room with lots of dragons in it. Of course, it's a bit bigger than your old room at home, isn't it?"

Ally quickly crossed the floor to hug her mother with one arm. Releasing her, she said, "It is a little large, huh? I think we could fit half the house in here. Although you're right, I do like the motif."

"It's quite impressive. Your father and I are in a room with those—you know, those fiery birds. What do you call them?"

"Oh, the Phoenix room. That one's gorgeous."

"That it is. However, I'm a little worried about my reaction if I wake up suddenly in the middle of the night. I'll probably think the room's on fire."

Ally laughed. She led her mother over to the bed, where she eased herself down cross-legged. Catherine perched on the edge. "Of course, Dad will sleep through it. I'm assuming he's asleep now."

Her mother nodded. "You know your father. I'll be joining him soon, but first I wanted to talk with you a little."

Ally swallowed the trepidation that was slowly growing inside her. "Sure."

"First of all, Ally, are you sure you're okay? We've been out of touch with the news for the last six weeks, but I saw a few of the reports when we were flying out here. Now tell me, what exactly happened?"

"Well..." Ally paused. This was one of the questions she had been dreading. Seeing her mother's expectant eyes, she finally decided to go with the truth. "When Evelynne was visiting Marseilles someone tried to shoot her. I, um . . . I saw them and knocked her down. They kept shooting, though, and they—I was hit twice. Three times, actually, but only two did anything."

As she had been expecting, Ally's mother's face was pale. Her voice was remarkably steady, however, as she asked, "Can I see?"

The young woman didn't say anything, just pulled down the collar of her pyjama jacket to show the still shiny scar on her right shoulder, then turned and pulled up the back to display the one in the middle of her back. She flinched as Catherine's cool fingers gently touched the scar. Feeling suddenly exposed, she let the hem fall.

chapter thirteen

Her mother's pallor had increased, but her voice was still eerily calm as she said, "Oh my. What happened?"

Deciding that the straight truth would be appreciated, Ally explained, "I was actually really lucky. The shoulder bullet went right through with only a flesh wound. It actually hit Evelynne in her left shoulder too. The one in my back missed the spine and all of my organs. I was paralysed for a couple of days because of the swelling, but that passed quickly. Since then I've mostly been repairing the damage to the muscles and rebuilding strength. The doctors say my prognosis is good. It still hurts a lot of the time, but it's not too bad." She spared a glance at her mother, who was still looking at her levelly. "You seem to be taking this rather well," she said tentatively.

Mrs. Tretiak rubbed a hand over her eyes. "Right now I'm extremely tired and in shock," she admitted. "I've scheduled my breakdown for tomorrow." She sat in silence for a moment, then said carefully, "Exactly how did you do all this? Am I correct in assuming that it was . . . with special assistance?"

"Yes," Ally confirmed. "I just knew when they were going to shoot and I managed to push the gun enough with my mind to make the first shot miss." She paused.

"But you said you were hit three times but only two 'did anything'. How did that happen? I don't think you could do that before. Are you bullet-proof now?"

"Not quite. You remember that Taoist monastery I visited in Thailand?" Catherine nodded. "There was a monk there who was a Kung Fu Master and he could direct his chi to minimise blows. So he showed me how. I didn't tell him," Ally hastened to add. "He just knew I had the potential. I would have liked to stay longer, but the other monks didn't like the idea of a woman staying for an extended period of time and Lung Shou Wei wasn't willing to leave. I promised to visit again, though."

"I see. And does anyone here know? About you?" This time the anxiety was clearly evident.

"Chorus knows," Ally admitted. "Don't worry, he won't tell. He's special himself."

"Oh? How so?"

"He's a Savant. You know, kind of like Uncle Philip is with math. Chorus picks up languages incredibly fast. He spoke Thai fluently after three weeks. He speaks twenty-three languages. The last time I checked, anyway."

"That's incredible." Ally waited as her mother processed this information. "So does anyone else know? Does Princess Evelynne know?"

Ally felt her cheeks heating and cursed herself for being unable to control her reaction. "No, nobody else does. No one's said anything, anyway, and I think they would, if only in disbelief. Not even Evelynne."

Catherine watched the blush pass over her daughter's features and sighed as more evidence was added to her suspicions. "Ally, what is going on between you and Princess Evelynne?"

Ally felt herself heating more. "What do you mean?" The question came out more defensively than she had intended. "We've become friends."

"Is that all?"

"Of course it is! What are you trying to say?"

Catherine sighed. "Ally, when we were downstairs at lunch I read you. I know."

"You what?" Ally exclaimed indignantly. "Mom, how could you? We have rules, remember?"

"Ally, as your mother there are times when the rules do not apply. I didn't read anyone else, just you."

"But still, Mom, that's . . ."

Her mother interrupted. "Ally, we can argue about that later. Right now I want to know what you're planning to do." Seeing her daughter about to object again, Catherine overrode her. "You're not listening, Ally. I know that you like her. That's fine. I know you're attracted to her. That's also fine; she's a beautiful girl. However, I know that you're also in love with her. And that's what I'm worried about."

Ally couldn't find the words to respond.

Catherine's tone lightened in sympathy. "I'm only saying this because I don't want to see you hurt. She is not just your friend Evelynne. She is Crown Princess Evelynne, future ruler of this country. Even if she were to reciprocate your interest—" which I suspect she might, she added to herself. "—princesses simply do not date women. Even if you were to somehow begin a relationship, eventually she would be forced to leave you."

"Annie said the same thing," Ally murmured softly.

"She did?" asked her mother, startled. "When was this?"

"A few weeks ago. I talked to her on the phone." Ally took a deep breath. "And I'll tell you what I told her. Right now Evelynne and I are just good friends." She no longer bothered trying to deny her emotions. "Nothing more is going to happen and when I finally have to leave, or she does, I'll be depressed for a while, then move on." She took her mother's hand and strove to inject some humour into the discussion. "I expect you to be there to get me ice cream while I'm moping. Annie's offered to supply the consolation sex."

"Alleandre Tiffany Tretiak! I do not need to hear about that!" Though she wanted to maintain the light tone, Catherine knew she had to make her next words serious. "You know I love you and I only want what's best for you. I don't want to see you hurt."

"I know, Mom, and I really do appreciate it, but remember that it's my life, hurt or no hurt. And you know how one makes a sword . . ." Her mother nodded in understanding. Ally leaned forward, ignoring the warning twinge in her back, to wrap her mother in a tight hug. "It's okay, Mom. I have things under control."

ಌ ಌ ಌ ಌ ಌ

chapter thirteen

"I have things under control."

The words rang through Ally's head mockingly as she tried to control her body's reaction to Evelynne's proximity and casual intimacy. She could feel her emotions expanding and knew that she was less in charge of herself than she had confidently informed her mother. *Damnit, this is going to be hard.*

Ally realised that her companion was speaking and attempted to focus her attention on the words, rather than the body the words were issuing from. "Pardon?"

"Are you all right? You seem a bit . . . spacey. I was asking what you were talking about with *za* yesterday afternoon. You were alone for quite a while." *Two hours and seventeen minutes, to be exact. Not that I was timing it or waiting or anything,* the princess told herself. *No, I really wasn't.* An internal voice was laughing hysterically.

"Oh, yeah. We talked for a while. That's actually kind of what I wanted to talk to you about. I, um . . . I have a favour to ask you." Spotting a stone bench, intricately carved with startlingly lifelike flowers, Ally delayed by asking, "Do you mind if we sit down?"

"Not at all."

Arranging herself comfortably on the seat, Ally sighed in relief. Most days her back was relatively pain-free, but today it was bothering her more than usual.

"I love the view here," Ally commented as she took in the scenery. They had walked up the hill behind the Palace and could now see all the way to the distant ocean. The land in between glowed in the morning sunshine. "Especially on days like today. It feels like you could almost see Spain from here."

Evelynne laughed. "Not quite, unfortunately. But if you went out there–" She pointed out across the distant water. "–about thirty kilometres, you're able to see Portugal on a clear day. However, from here you can see . . ." She twisted around to look at the mountain rising behind them. She searched for a moment and then pointed triumphantly. "Right there, see? What looks like a faint cloud near that cliff?"

Ally squinted through her glasses. "I think so. Right where that split is?"

"That's it. That cloud is actually steam from a series of hot springs on the side of Mount Sekemat. Most of them are completely inaccessible, and the only way they can be seen is by the steam escaping from the pools."

"Cool," Ally said. *Completely inaccessible, eh? Methinks not.*

Looking back towards the ocean, Evelynne prompted, "You said you wanted to ask me something?"

"Yeah," Ally said, suddenly more nervous. "Um . . . Your father was talking to me because he wants to reward me for . . . you know, what I did. I told him I didn't need anything, but he was quite insistent."

Evelynne grinned. "Good for him. You deserve everything you're offered."

"It's still very weird to be receiving gifts from the King of Atlantl. Actually, there was one thing he wanted to do, and that was—well . . . he wants to . . . to knight me."

The princess looked blank for a moment, then a huge grin spread across her face. "Isis, Ally, why didn't you tell me? Why didn't he tell me?" she gushed. "Oh, this is perfect! Dame Alleandre Tretiak! I can't think of anything more appropriate." She hesitated when Ally failed to match her enthusiasm. "Wait, you did accept, didn't you?"

"Well, I actually told him I'd think about it. It was a bit of a shock, you know? I never in my wildest dreams imagined that anything like this would happen to me. Well, maybe in my *wildest* dreams, but . . ."

"Okay, I can understand that," Evelynne sympathised. "I think you should accept. Of course, I am a little biased. So did you want my help in deciding?"

"No. It was—your father explained to me about being nominated to an Order, and all of their entrance requirements. Some I don't meet, of course. I'm not really of any established faith, so that knocks out six Orders right there. Out of the ones remaining, a few just don't match my lifestyle." She reddened slightly, remembering the discussion about the Order of Saint Mary the Virgin. "I think I qualify for about four Orders. In fact, the one that seems to fit me the most is the Order of Sir George and the Dragon." Ally took a deep breath. "To make a long story short, even with the Orders I could be raised to, I'm not really comfortable with having an organisation, even a benevolent one, control my allegiance. So the other option is apparently getting a Noble to Sponsor me. I don't really know many of the Nobles, so my choices have been basically narrowed to Duke Thomas and, well, you." She stole a glance at Evelynne, who was watching her with an unreadable expression. Steeling herself, Ally finished, "So, um . . . I was hoping you would Sponsor me. I trust you."

Evelynne sat staring at her friend for a moment, leaving Ally to wonder if she had done the wrong thing, before exploding forward to envelop the taller woman in a fierce embrace. The princess pulled Ally tightly to her, striving to put across the emotions she was feeling.

Ally returned the embrace, tentatively at first, but then with more strength. She felt Evelynne's upper body pressed to her own and the princess'

chapter thirteen

chin was resting on her shoulder. Despite her resolution to avoid any intense emotional entanglement, for several moments she just enjoyed Evelynne's warmth and the sensations her proximity generated.

Finally they pulled apart, with a great deal of hidden reluctance on both sides.

"So, um, is that a 'yes'?" Ally asked.

The question startled a laugh out of Evelynne. "Of course it's a yes." She reached down to take both of Ally's hands in her own and looked her friend directly in the eyes. "Alleandre Tretiak, I would be honoured to Sponsor you for elevation to knighthood." She laughed again, and dashed a hand across her eyes. "Now look what you've done. You've made me cry."

"Um, sorry?"

"Oh, stop," Evelynne chided. She gave Ally another shorter hug before sitting back. "So did *za* say when this was going to happen?"

"Well, he suggested some time around Christmas for the actual ceremony itself. Not on Christmas Day, since I'm not a Christian, but maybe on the Solstice. It would allow my parents to come without my Dad having to miss school and my Mom has less work in winter. It's also exactly six months from my birthday, so that might have some symbolic significance."

"Christmas, hmm? That's just over three months from now. Well, that should give me just enough time to get everything ready."

"It'll take that long?" Ally asked, surprised. "I'm obviously no expert on knighthood ceremonies, but what do you have to do?"

"Oh my. Well, I have to file the paperwork, construct the ritual, design your blazon, actually arrange for the necessary components, commission your weapon, et cetera. And then review and edit everything, rehearse and so on and so forth."

"Oh." Ally looked uncertain. "I didn't mean to make this so hard on you. I don't—"

Evelynne interrupted with a finger to Ally's lips. She firmly suppressed the shiver that shot through her. "Hush," she instructed. "Don't worry, I'll have help. Besides," she continued softly, moving her hand to the side of Ally's face, "you're worth it."

chapter fourteen

"No! There is no way I'm coming out dressed like–like this!"

Those words–strongly spoken but muffled by the closed door to Ally's bedroom–were the first thing Evelynne heard as she walked into the sitting room. Chorus and Mr. and Mrs. Tretiak looked around as she entered and the young man barely suppressed a low whistle of appreciation as the princess moved closer to where they were clustered around Ally's bedroom door.

"Good evening, Evelynne," Chorus said quietly. "*O'derenn mai-lata presh ala-at.*"

Evelynne was wearing a deep blue dress similar to the one she had been wearing on the fateful day in Marseilles. This one was quite form fitting in the upper body, leaving her right shoulder bare and then billowing out at the waist to trail down to the floor. A simple coronet held the princess' flaming hair in place, although this time it had been allowed to trail partway down her back. Small gold earrings in the shape of some great cat were the remaining extent of her jewellery and a small purse, in a shade matching the dress, completed the ensemble.

"Thank you," the princess said. "You don't look so bad yourself. Any of you."

It was true. Chorus was wearing a dark green overcoat with gold buttons, left open in the front, allowing the shirt beneath to show. The bright white of the ruffled shirt was an extreme contrast to his dark skin, and also to the lighter green of his trousers. The red cummerbund around the young man's waist and gold clasp at his throat gave him a decidedly piratical look.

Mr. Tretiak looked downright plain in comparison. He was wearing a much more conventional tuxedo. However, elegant stitching in silver thread created patterns that chased each other around his arms and shoulders. When he moved his arms, the reflected light was mesmerising.

Catherine Tretiak outdid them all in terms of colour. The top of her outfit was a Middle-Eastern style kaftan that hung to her knees. The elaborate dye-work and embroidery created a riot of colour: blues, greens, reds, yellows and purples, which were continued on her baggy pants.

"We scrub up pretty good, Princess," Chorus replied with a roguish smile. Or perhaps it was merely his ensemble that made it seem roguish. "I'd just like to say that I appreciate going to a party without having to wear a tuxedo. They are just so boring."

Evelynne shook her head. "If there's one thing Atlantlans know about men, it's that they love to dress up just as much as women. So why make them all wear the same clothes?" She looked at Mrs. Tretiak, who was vainly trying to convince her daughter of something through the still closed door. "What's going on?"

William Tretiak sighed and answered, "Alleandre does not wish to come out. She is concerned about her outfit."

"That's not quite true," Catherine objected. "She thinks the dress is beautiful, but doesn't think that she is good enough to wear it."

"Come on, Ally," Chorus called through the door. "I'm sure you look fine. Come out and we'll tell you so."

"No! I can't wear this thing out there!" Even muffled, Evelynne could hear genuine panic in Ally's voice.

"Ally," Chorus coaxed, "come on. I picked out that dress myself."

"I know! And you're the person I'm going to strangle with it!"

The dress was the real purpose of Chorus' early morning expedition with Maïda almost a week earlier. Upon hearing that there was going to be a party, he had assigned himself the mission of making Ally "drop dead sexy" for the event. With the lady-in-waiting's collusion, he had chosen a magnificent dress.

Apparently, he had only been partially successful.

"Alleandre Tiffany Tretiak, get out here right now!" Catherine resorted to her greatest weapon, the dreaded Triple-Name Mom Voice and everyone waited with bated breath for several seconds for the response.

Finally it came. "No!" The people waiting exhaled in disappointment. "I told you, I can't wear this! I'm just not the right kind of person. People like me don't wear these. You *know* that Evelynne's going to be there in some gorgeous gown," she continued, unaware that the princess was present, "and looking absolutely perfect, and everyone is just going to fall in love with her like they always do and then they'll look at me and think, 'What is *she* doing here?'" There was a pause as the emotional voice seemed to swallow back tears. "And I *can't* take that! So tell them I'm sick or something, and go without me. Please."

Evelynne listened to the plea from behind the closed door and held back her own emotions. Chief among them was sympathy for her friend's obvious distress, but a smaller part was pure fury directed towards those who had made Ally so insecure about herself in the first place. That part longed to

chapter fourteen

track down the perpetrators and pummel them with her bare hands. *Maybe I can persuade Sir Arthur to arrange a little "visit" from the Guard . . .*

Yet another part was concentrating on and revelling in Ally's declaration of Evelynne's "perfection."

For now, the princess carefully kept those parts from revealing themselves as she called softly, "Ally, this is Evelynne. Nobody is going to be doing anything like that to you. Listen, do you trust me?"

A muffled, "Yes," was the response.

"Okay, then *please* come out here and let us see you. I promise that we'll tell you the truth. Okay?"

There was another long pause. "Okay," came the reluctant answer. "But if anyone laughs, I'll kill them." Despite the levity forced into the words, the tone was still apprehensive.

There was a brief rustle on the other side of the door before it swung open slowly to reveal Ally leaning on her cane and nervously twisting a length of black cloth in her free right hand.

The onlookers were absolutely silent. Evelynne's mouth dropped open and she had to put a hand on the back of a nearby chair to keep from falling over. Any lingering doubts she might have had about her attraction to Ally or her sexuality in general rapidly withered away.

Ally endured the stares and silence for a long moment before saying suddenly, "See? I told you. I can't do this." She turned and made to re-enter her bedroom.

Without quite knowing how she had crossed the intervening distance, Evelynne found herself grasping Ally's arm. "No, wait!" she blurted. "That was just shock. Not bad shock. More like . . . 'wow' shock." She looked around at her companions for confirmation.

"Oh yeah," Chorus said, still staring. "Definitely 'wow' shock. I mean—damn, Ally, if you weren't gay and I weren't a gentleman, I'd do you right here. Ow!" He was suddenly snapped out of his daze by the impact of Mrs. Tretiak's hand on the back of his head. Looking in that direction, he saw the threatening glares from both of Ally's parents. Immediately cowed, he stammered, "I mean—that is—" Despite twenty-four languages worth of vocabulary, words failed him and he finally just waved his hand to indicate Ally's body and said, "Wow."

"Despite your friend's language," Ally's mother said, with another glare at the offender, "he is right. You look absolutely wonderful." She took Ally's other arm and gently tugged her forward. "Come into the light so we can see you better."

As they moved to the centre of the room, the full effect of Ally's outfit and makeup could be seen.

The gown was a sheer black sheath, shot through with silver threads that glittered in the light. The dress conformed to her body, hugging her from just above her breasts to her ankles. Two straps ostensibly held the dress in place, but Ally suspected that sheer willpower was the major factor. Nearly skin-tight, the dress stretched with each movement, creating a fit that she had to admit was very comfortable, if a little disconcerting. It felt oddly like wearing a strong wind.

In addition to the dress, Maïda had also spent some time that evening taming Ally's tousled hair into a more elegant style. Through some mystical process she had managed to straighten it and because it had grown in the months since the shooting, had been able to brush it all to one side, so that it framed the right half of Ally's face like a dark brown shield.

As everyone admired the dress, their eyes inevitably fell on one of the main reasons Ally had been so reluctant to venture into public. In the middle of her right shoulder, just below the collarbone, the shiny white scar of her bullet wound was clearly visible. When she saw Evelynne staring at the scar, Ally instinctively tried to cover it up with her hand, but since her left was occupied with holding her cane, the right could only do the job with much awkward fidgeting.

"I don't–I can't–it's–" Unable to give voice to her embarrassment, Ally finally shrugged and hung her head, hiding her face behind her newly styled hair.

"It's impressive," Evelynne said firmly, raising her friend's face again. "Wear your scars proudly. They are a mark of honour."

Catherine and William stood back, looking on with surprise as the princess managed to skilfully draw their daughter out of her shell.

"Um . . . I know," Ally said softly. "But I don't–"

"That's okay," Evelynne said in sympathy. "I didn't either. But that's why you have this." She reached down and plucked the cloth out of Ally's hand. Shaking it out, she proceeded to fold it in half diagonally and then drape the shawl over Ally's shoulders. "And this." Reaching into her purse, she pulled out a small brooch bearing a single large emerald to fasten the scarf in place.

Ally relaxed visibly as the scar–and, incidentally, her upper chest–was covered. She even managed a weak smile down at Evelynne. "Thank you."

The princess reached up and gave her friend's shoulder a final pat. "You're welcome." Then she stepped back and eyed Ally's form, considering. "Now, what are we missing here?" she asked the room in general.

"A trench coat?" Ally said hopefully.

Ignoring her, Evelynne said, "Earrings. Or one earring anyway." Ally's mother nodded.

chapter fourteen

"Um, I don't wear earrings," Ally objected. "My ears aren't even pierced."

The princess shared a glance with her co-conspirators. "And that," she said triumphantly, "is why I had these modified to clip-ons." Reaching back into her purse, she produced a pair of dangling silver earrings in the form of an ankh. Looking carefully, Ally could see that each was inscribed with tiny Egyptian hieroglyphics.

Giving in to the inevitable, Ally bent down so that Evelynne could affix one earring to her left ear.

"There," the princess said once she was finished. She tried to ignore the subtle floral scent that clung to Ally's body. "These are yours. I'll save this one for when you need it." Stepping back, she cast appreciative eyes over her friend's tall form, trying not to drool too obviously. "You look gorgeous."

Ally blushed predictably, and said, "Okay, let's get going before I go insane."

"Of course, dear," Mrs. Tretiak said. She put her arms out and pulled her daughter into a strong hug. "You look beautiful, Ally," she whispered. "We all think so."

She stepped back and William took her place. "Your mother is right," he said in an equally low voice. "You're wonderful."

"Thanks, Mom. Thanks, Dad."

"All right, why don't you three go ahead. Your father and I will join you in a moment," Catherine suggested.

"Sure thing, *Mma* T," Chorus said. "Shall we?" Turning, he offered Ally his arm before noticing that Evelynne had extended hers as well.

Ally solved the dilemma by handing her cane to Chorus and then linking arms with both of them.

As the trio exited the suite, Catherine turned to her husband and asked in a low voice, "So? What do you think?"

"About what?"

"You saw how they were acting."

He sighed. "You mean that our Ally seems quite taken with young Evelynne? Who, if I'm not mistaken, returns the interest?"

Catherine looked surprised. "You mean you noticed?"

"Hon, just because I don't have yours or Ally's gifts does not mean that I'm blind. Of course I noticed."

"And it doesn't bother you?"

"Of course it bothers me, but not for the reasons you might think. Evelynne lives in a world where many powerful people would do anything to exploit Ally's abilities. I worry because of that. As for a possible relationship between them, I am concerned, yes. But I can't say that I actively disapprove."

"You don't? Why not?" The surprise was still evident in Catherine's voice.

"Because Ally needs to be with someone who is her equal. That was my chief concern over her relationship with Anabel. Once I got over the whole lesbian thing, of course." He smiled wryly. "While I truly liked Anabel, she was simply not Ally's equal in power or potential. She was much too . . . common. Evelynne, however, is anything but common. She is a person who one day will control an entire nation and influence many others. I can't think of a better mate for Ally."

By now Catherine's surprise had changed to shock. "But what about public reaction? The world does not tend to find homosexual leaders acceptable. In Evelynne's position that is going to have a strong effect."

"Dear, what the public finds acceptable changes every day. Twenty years ago, the mere idea of gay marriage would have been unthinkable. Today, it is legal in several countries including Atlantis and is being debated in many more. Who knows what society will find acceptable in five years? Ten years?"

Catherine looked up at her husband with an adoring expression. "You know, at times like these I remember why I married you."

William looked hurt. "You mean it wasn't my dashing good looks?"

"Well, that too," she admitted with mock reluctance. She sighed, becoming serious once again. "So you're telling me to just back off and leave things alone."

William gently embraced his wife. "Honey, we are here to help her, to support her when she needs it. We cannot control her life for her. It is her life to live, her mistakes to make. Her rewards to win."

Catherine rested her head on his chest. "I suppose so. But they're our worries to fret about."

"Naturally. However, right now," William said, looking at his watch, "it is time for us to go and see our wonderful daughter rewarded."

"Then let us do that," Catherine decided, allowing her husband to escort her out of the room.

ಹಿ ಹಿ ಹಿ ಹಿ ಹಿ

"So how are you holding up?" Evelynne asked. When there was no answer she turned in the car's seat to look at Ally sitting beside her. "Ally?"

The young woman was sitting silently with her eyes closed and breathing deeply and for a moment Evelynne thought she had fallen asleep. She looked at Chorus, who was sitting across from her, facing the rear of the

chapter fourteen

car and arched her eyebrows in question. His answering shrug displayed his own ignorance, so she turned back to Ally. Calling her friend's name again finally brought a response.

With a deep exhalation, Ally's eyes opened and she relaxed into a more natural position. She looked out the window at the darkening city outside the window then saw Evelynne's concerned gaze.

"Sorry," she apologised. "I just needed to calm myself down a bit."

"You were meditating?" Evelynne asked.

"Yeah, just some breathing meditation," Ally explained. "I learned it from Mrs. Chen, a Chinese friend in Vancouver." *Among other things.*

Now that she knew what her friend had been doing, Evelynne could see that Ally appeared visibly more relaxed and her complexion had returned to normal from its previous paleness. "Did it work?" she queried needlessly.

"Oh, yes. Of course, what I'll be like when I actually have to talk to people . . . who knows?" Ally managed a wry smile.

"Well," Chorus said, looking out the window, "you're about to find out. I think we've arrived."

The limousine pulled smoothly to a stop outside the brightly lit entrance to an impressively large building, the Royal Banquet Hall of Outremer. Ally was puzzled by occasional bright flashes of light until she realised that there was a large gathering of reporters and photographers lined up some distance away. The thought of all the press almost broke through Ally's newly acquired calm, but she carefully suppressed the panic.

"You ready?" Evelynne asked, bestowing an encouraging smile.

"Too late to back out now," Ally replied, steeling herself as the door to the limousine was opened by a smartly uniformed Guard.

As befitted her rank, Evelynne exited first, allowing the Guard to help her out of the car and then standing aside as Ally followed. Ally's parents came next, while Chorus took up the rear.

Ally blinked in the sudden barrage of flashbulbs as she exited into the warm evening air. She fought the instinctive urge to hide her face. Instead, she took her cue from the princess beside her and waited calmly while her parents got out of the car.

Evelynne noticed her companion's aborted attempt to hide and smiled when Ally visibly drew herself together. She was struck by the beauty and projected confidence of the woman beside her and her smile turned feral as she thought of some of the people who might see the pictures. *Take that, you bastards,* the princess directed the thought at all the people who had made her friend so insecure over the years.

At the top of the steps, the King and Queen were waiting to personally welcome their guests. The King looked fiercely handsome. His blue and purple tabard brought out the fire of his hair and beard, while the cut of his suit seemed to add even more mass to his already impressive bulk. A large crown adorned his head. He looked like some refined war god, just off Mount Olympus and Ally half expected to see flames shoot from his mouth as he spoke.

In comparison, Queen Cleo el-Kareen appeared much more refined and delicate, although she was wearing a tabard very similar to the King's in both colour and style. The apparent fragility was immediately dispelled by her strong, determined eyes, which were nearly identical of Evelynne's own. It was also immediately apparent from which side of her family the princess got her figure. Although the years had added a small amount of thickening to the Queen's body, she was still a strikingly attractive woman.

Despite the similarities, Queen Cleo was not Evelynne's mother, but her aunt. As the princess had explained to Ally, the Atlantlan Constitution required both a King and Queen who split power between them. While each Diarch was fairly autonomous, certain decisions—such as a declaration of war—required unanimity of purpose. When Evelynne's mother, the previous Queen, had died before her Heirs were old enough to assume her Throne, the Hall of Nobles had elected her sister to succeed her until either Evelynne or Patrick came of age. Since then, the current Queen had served in an exemplary manner, displaying a distinct diplomatic ability that offset the King's more volatile temperament.

All of this sped through Ally's mind as she and her companions approached the Diarchs. Used to the exuberant way in which members of Evelynne's family greeted each other, she was surprised when they met with a formal handclasp and brief kiss on the cheek. Then she remembered the cameras and realised that on this occasion more reserve was in order.

Evelynne finished her murmured greetings to her father and aunt and then it was Ally's turn. She offered her hand to the King and was briefly surprised when he grasped it and then pulled her forward to kiss both her cheeks.

"*Ishta* Tretiak," King Jad said, "it's good to see you again. You are looking well."

"Thank you, Your Majesty," the young woman replied. "I'm feeling well, except for a bit of nervousness."

The King laughed. "Well, we shall see what we can do to alleviate your fears." He turned to his sister-in-law. "I believe you have already met Queen Cleo?"

"Yes, Sir, briefly, just after I arrived. Your Majesty," Ally said, offering her hand once again.

chapter fourteen

"*Ishta* Tretiak," Queen Cleo said, clasping her hand and smiling in friendly greeting. "I am happy to see you walking again. The last time you were still in your wheelchair."

"Yes, Ma'am. I managed to leave it behind a few days after you visited." She was desperately trying to remember all of the protocol that Evelynne had spent the last few days trying to teach her.

"Excellent. I am glad to see it."

With her own greetings out of the way, Ally's next task was the introduction of her parents and Chorus. She avoided sweating her way through them with sheer willpower and felt that her grasp of protocol must have been adequate, if Evelynne's approving smile was anything to go by.

The introductions complete, the group moved off the steps and into the foyer of the Hall. Ally breathed a sigh of relief once out of the glare of the cameras and noticed that her father, never a hugely social person himself, likewise relaxed.

"I'm afraid Patrick was unable to join us this evening," the King said. "Apparently he is fighting a rather nasty cold."

"I know," the princess said. "I talked to him earlier. We're going to meet up as soon as he feels better."

The party moved into the foyer where a man dressed in a spotless white uniform adorned with gold braid and carrying a heavy looking sceptre was waiting for their arrival. As soon as they were through the door, he hurried over.

"Your Majesties," he said in a high voice, bowing deeply.

"Donald," King Jad replied to the Seneschal. "I believe that unless there are any objections—" He looked around, but none were forthcoming. "—We are ready to enter."

"Of course, Sire." Bowing again, the man turned and marched to the large gilded and elaborately carved doors at the other end of the room. He paused while the rest of the group formed up behind him. The King and Queen took their places at the head of the line. Ally, uncertain of her place, was startled when Evelynne firmly took her arm as she had done on the walk through the garden several days ago. Casting a helpless glance at her parents, she allowed herself to be manoeuvred into position at the princess' side right behind the Diarchs. The elder Tretiaks took up the rear, Catherine bracketed by her husband and Chorus, who each took one of her arms.

Satisfied that everyone was in order, the uniformed man raised his sceptre and struck the double doors solidly. Everyone except Evelynne and her father and aunt jumped at the booming sound that erupted. As if by magic, the doors swung slowly inward revealing the huge chamber beyond and the crowd of people within. The party started forward. A deep, respectful silence had fallen when the doors opened, which was broken as soon as the Seneschal crossed the doorway.

"Hear ye, hear ye!" he bellowed in a strong, carrying voice strangely at odds with his normal, almost effeminate tone. "My Lords and Ladies, Citizens, Ambassadors and Guests! Entering are His Royal Majesty King Jad Richard ibn Jad deMolay! Her Royal Majesty Queen Cleo Janet el-Kareen! Her Royal Highness Evelynne Sophia al-Heru deMolay! *Ishta* Alleandre Tiffany Tretiak! Mrs. Catherine Rachelle Tretiak! Mr William Oliver Tretiak! Mr Keitumetsemosimaniwapula Tladi!" Ally was highly impressed that the Seneschal had managed to speak Chorus' full name without even a stutter. "All hail Their Majesties! All hail Her Highness!"

"*Salé!*" the gathered people shouted.

Then the quiet was broken only by the shuffling of feet, rustling of clothing and murmured greetings of the people who had moved aside to form a long aisle to a small platform at the back of the room. As the Royal party passed, each person either bowed or curtseyed deeply to the King and Queen, then did so again as Ally and Evelynne went by.

The Reception Room of the Royal Banquet Hall was impressive. Unlike many of the buildings in Atlantl, this one was decorated along Classical European lines. A veined marble floor was interspersed with tall white columns that in turn supported a high arched ceiling. The ceiling sported brightly painted frescoes of scenes from the old myths. Chairs and couches lined the walls and many green plants added colour.

Ally was painfully aware of her cane and slow, limping pace, along with the form-fitting nature of her gown, as she tried to shut out the hundreds of eyes upon her and fight back rising panic. Evelynne seemed to sense her growing unease and tightened her hold on the taller woman's arm in silent support. Ally relaxed slightly when, towards the end of the seemingly endless walk, she saw the stooped and aged figure of Lord Thomas, who gave her a smile and bow.

Evelynne, able to read the expressions of the man she had known all her life, could see the impish grin behind his apparently innocuous smile. In case she was mistaken, the subtle wink he gave her, as if he was a little boy with a secret, confirmed it. The princess felt herself flushing uncontrollably under his knowing gaze. She had not spoken with him about her feelings since seeing him in his office and was sure that now he was looking at the two of them with satisfaction.

Of course, with the way I'm practically draped over Ally right now he probably thinks we're already lovers, Evelynne thought. *Not that she seems to be complaining at all . . .* Glancing at Ally out of the corner of her eye, she took in the faintly

chapter fourteen

glassy eyes and stiff smile and decided that perhaps the only person getting a bit of a thrill out of the contact was herself.

She happened to be wrong. Ally was also deriving a certain sensual pleasure from having Evelynne pressed against her. She recalled the discussion she had had with her mother, though and reluctantly pushed the sensations to the back of her mind.

The group reached the low podium at the other side of the room. Those members of the Royal party not used to such occasions arranged themselves in front and to the side of the dais. Leaving his companions after a last kiss to Evelynne's cheek, King Jad mounted the platform and turned to address his guests.

"My Lords and Ladies," he began, speaking in English for the benefit of the foreigners present, "fellow Citizens, honourable Ambassadors and respected guests. A little over two months ago assassins attempted to take the life of Her Highness, Princess Evelynne. They were thankfully unsuccessful, but did succeed in wounding her." He paused. "As a King, I was shocked and dismayed. As a King, I have dedicated significant resources towards finding those responsible. As her father I was devastated, as any parent would be when his child was injured in such a brutal way. And it is as a father that I welcome you all here tonight, to celebrate Evelynne's survival and recovery from her injuries.

"However, I have another reason to celebrate. If it had not been for the quick actions of a certain young woman, we would be mourning instead of celebrating. At great risk to herself, *Ishta* Alleandre Tretiak used her own body as a shield, placing herself between my daughter and the assassins' bullets. She was sorely wounded through her courageous actions and it is only through the Universal's grace that we are not now mourning her death. Instead, *Ishta* Tretiak is also here with us tonight, so that we may thank her appropriately for her selfless actions.

"Also present are Catherine and William Tretiak, the people responsible for raising such a fine, courageous and generous young woman." He turned to address them directly. "I have had several chances to speak with *Ishta* Tretiak and must also lay the credit for her intelligence and grace at your feet as well."

William beamed proudly and Catherine mouthed a "Thank you" to the King before smiling at Ally, who was by now beet red.

King Jad continued, "This is supposed to be an informal occasion, so I will keep this brief. I am sure there will be plenty of boring flowery speeches after dinner." There was a general chuckle from the audience. "For now, just let me repeat my thankfulness for the return of my daughter safe, if not necessarily sound, and my gratitude to *Ishta* Tretiak for allowing her to do so. Ladies and Gentlemen, Princess Evelynne and *Ishta* Tretiak!"

He stepped off the dais applauding and the assembled crowd joined in. They held back while King Jad embraced his daughter and Alleandre again before moving forward to give their own greetings.

The faces passed in a blur as it seemed as though half the population of Atlantl shook Ally's hand. She quickly lost track of the names and ranks of the numerous Barons, Baronesses, Counts, Countesses, Ambassadors and Citizens. Still, she tried to maintain a pleasant demeanour, and return their salutations and comments with appropriate words of her own, even as the constant pressure of so much attention wore on the young woman's natural reserve.

After what seemed like hours, but was really only fifteen minutes, the last of the well-wishers stepped back after a handshake. Ally breathed a surreptitious sigh of relief as the guests began to break up into small groups and the hum of conversations filled the air. "Whew," she said softly. Looking to Evelynne, who smiled back at her, she asked, "So what happens now?"

The princess reached out once more and pulled Ally's hand to rest on her arm. "Now we mingle. We have to show you off, you know."

"Mingle?" Ally's expression was doubtful. Looking around, she saw that her mother was already dominating a conversation with a group of elegantly dressed Nobles. Chorus was flirting with a group of women whose ages ranged from eighteen to eighty. She couldn't see her father, but assumed he was off somewhere discussing politics. "I'm not really the mingling type. Now the wallflower thing–*that* I can do."

"Nonsense," Evelynne objected. "My father has already attested to your 'intelligence and grace'. You don't want to call him a liar, do you? He *is* the King, you know." She began gently guiding Ally towards one of the smaller knots of people. "Come on, I know the Canadian Ambassador is just dying to meet you."

Ally sighed in relief as she sank into one of the chairs lining the walls of the room. The last three-quarters of an hour had been stressful; she had been standing for the entire time and her back was beginning to ache with a vengeance. Also, in the intervening forty-five minutes she had been separated from Evelynne somewhere in the press, whether by accident or design she wasn't sure.

The social pressure had not been as bad as she had expected, but Ally had found that much of the conversation revolved around the political and social events in Atlantl, topics in which the young woman had little

chapter fourteen

experience. So, after enduring the last conversation with a false expression of interest plastered on her face long enough to appear polite, she had excused herself and found her way to a large, comfortable chair by the wall.

Now Ally sat sipping a glass of wine and watched the social dance unfolding in front of her. Observing the guests, she amused herself with imagining what might happen if she reached out and tripped some of them. She was chuckling internally at the image of the entire roomful of people collapsing like so many dominoes when she became aware that another person had taken a seat on the couch to her right.

Turning, she saw a very handsome young man, probably in his mid-twenties, with wavy golden hair and wearing a deep red tabard. Seeing that he had attracted her attention, the young man said, "Are you sure you ought to be sitting out here on the sidelines? You are one of the guests of honour." He smiled winningly, revealing perfect teeth.

Ally flushed. "Actually, my back—I was getting a bit tired. So I decided to sit down and have a rest from . . ."

"From all the bluster and pompous self-importance out there?" the man finished for her, waving a hand to indicate the ballroom. When Ally started to stutter a denial, he said, "Relax, it's why I'm out here as well. If I had to listen to Lord Graham say one more thing about 'the natural historic rights of the aristocracy' or 'the required respect from the lower classes', well . . ." He shuddered theatrically. He stuck out his hand. "I'm Larrel, by the way."

More at ease, Ally placed her hand in his, flushing as he raised it to brush his lips across the back. "I'm Ally . . . er, Alleandre Tretiak."

"Pleased to meet you again, Ally. Weren't you at this party earlier?" Larrel teased, not letting go of her hand.

"Um, well, yeah," Ally muttered. "Wait a minute. Larrel? Evelynne's Lech—um , cousin Larrel?" She lowered her eyes in embarrassment at her slip.

Far from taking offence, Larrel grinned delightedly. "That would be me," he confirmed brightly. "Larrel Peren, Count Alsatz, at your service, milady." He executed an intricate bow from his chair. "As for all those rumours about me . . ." He leaned closer and spoke in a conspiratorial whisper. "They're all true." He leaned back as Ally blushed. "However, I don't believe you have anything to fear. From what I hear, I'm not exactly your type. But if you're ever in the mood to try . . ." He waggled his eyebrows suggestively.

"Thanks, I'll keep that in mind," Ally said wryly. She could tell that the Count was putting on an act to set her at ease, but found herself relaxing anyway.

"Actually, I was on my way to the kitchen to see if any of the waitresses were amenable to some company later this evening. I could try to find one for you if you'd like."

Ally choked on her drink. "No, no, that's quite all right. Um, I'm sure I can find, uh, companionship on my own, thank you." Of their own volition, her eyes sought out Evelynne in the crowd, finding her engaged in conversation with another tall, handsome man.

Larrel noticed the direction of Ally's gaze and his eyes narrowed in speculation. Making a decision, he leaned in closer and spoke in a low whisper. "Ally, while I can find no fault in your taste, I feel I must warn you. My cousin Evelynne is not the most available person. As much as I would wish it otherwise, she does not have the greatest freedom in choosing her partners. The man she is speaking with right now, for example, is the heir to Count Jazeer and has been widely rumoured for several years to be a likely candidate for Her Highness' spouse. While I personally do not believe that the affection between them is so great—on either side—it may not be up to them. Politics has ended more than one relationship."

"I'm not in a relationship with Evelynne," Ally replied quietly, feeling an urge for complete candour. "And I know that I'll never be in a relationship with her. That doesn't mean I can't look, does it?"

"Of course not!" Larrel exclaimed, brightening. "In fact, a healthy fantasy life is absolutely vital. The only thing more vital is turning those fantasies into reality, which I try to do on a regular basis. And if I can't actually slip someone into your bed, you can't stop me from turning a few in your direction. So tell me, besides red hair, what are you looking for in a woman?"

Ally laughed.

       howl   howl   howl   howl   howl

" . . . and so if the entire universe can be considered to be a single complex particle, then all of its associated phenomena can be described as being peaks in the Schrödinger Wave Equation of that particle. All of the matter and energy of the universe actually arises where the probability wave collapses into reality."

"Very well, I can see that, but how is this useful? I think the universe is too big to calculate on a computer."

"True, but even with the lack of specific or precise calculations, certain physical laws and even the general shape of the universe itself can be posited simply by looking at the behaviour of the wave. It would also give us an

chapter fourteen

opportunity to test various physical theories by applying them to the wave as a model and comparing the results to reality . . ."

Evelynne hung back for several minutes and listened bemusedly to the conversation a few feet away. Finally, she interrupted. "May I break in, or do you two want to get a room?" she asked with amusement.

Startled, Ally and Larrel looked up at the interloper. Larrel recovered first and stood to kiss the princess' cheek. "Evelynne, we didn't hear you come up."

"Obviously," Evelynne said wryly.

"We were just talking and I remembered that Ally has a degree in physics, so I asked her to explain something from special relativity for me. Before we knew it we were solving the Grand Unified Theory of the universe. We didn't even see you standing there."

"Of course, because we didn't observe her, there's some question as to whether Evelynne was actually present, or whether she existed only as a probability waveform until we saw her," Ally added, rising to her feet. She was relieved to see that the princess' potential husband-to-be was nowhere to be seen.

"Really," Evelynne said, looking at her friend strangely. "Well, I can say that dinner actually exists, whether you can see it or not and I've come to take you to it, just to make sure."

"Excellent," Larrel said, offering an arm to each young woman. "I'm starving."

"Understanding the universe will do that to you," Ally commented sagely.

ॐ ॐ ॐ ॐ ॐ

Dinner was a lavish affair.

The guests were seated at an immense table. It was the kind of table where one needed an outside phone line to ask another person at the far end to pass the salt. The King and Queen sat at the head of the table and the other diners were seated in descending rank. Evelynne sat at her father's right hand and Ally was by now only mildly surprised to find herself in a place right next to the princess. Lord Thomas, whose city was hosting the event, was across the table at the Queen's left. To Ally's right sat Hassan el-Shahir, the Duke of Lyonesse and his wife. The third Duke of Atlantl, Marsden Hallack, Duke of Hy Braseal, had sent his regrets at being unable to attend, but he was busy dealing with the fallout of several more HBLA attacks. Ally's parents were a short way down the table and Chorus was near the end, though he had shown no particular regret at the situation.

The attractive Holly Bualo, attending with her father, Arris Bualo, Baron ty-Koatl, may have been a factor.

Ally had engaged in a spirited conversation with Lord Hassan during the meal–it was too polite to be called an argument. Though the Duke had obviously disagreed with several of Ally's personal qualities, he had been exquisitely polite and by the end of the meal the two had reached an unspoken agreement that while they would never be great friends, they could at least respect each other.

The seventh and final course was being cleared away; Ally had been stuffed after the first four. With the last plates removed from the table by the efficient servants, the King stood and cleared his throat to call for silence.

"My Lords and Ladies," he said, his voice carrying easily throughout the room. "As I promised earlier, we have arrived at the flowery speeches part of the evening." Laughter rolled around the table. "I have decided to exercise my Royal privilege and speak first, though I will be brief."

"Thank Isis," Evelynne said in a stage whisper, and everyone laughed again.

"Earlier this evening I said most of what I wanted to say," King Jad continued. "All I can do is reiterate my sentiments: I am more grateful than I can express that my daughter has come home alive. I am especially thankful to *Ishta* Tretiak for saving her life. I was actually searching for an appropriate way to reward this wonderful young woman and was unable to think of anything, when one of my close friends, Lord Thomas, suggested a reward that I found particularly apt." Evelynne and Ally both shot surprised looks at the elderly Duke. This was the first they had heard of his involvement. "I am therefore honoured and pleased to announce that, with the blessing of both the Canadian and British governments and Her Majesty Queen Elizabeth the Second, in several months Alleandre Tretiak will be knighted to become Dame Alleandre Tretiak, Sponsored by Her Highness Princess Evelynne deMolay." The dinner guests erupted in a buzz of conversation. Most reacted with surprise and a few were obviously delighted, though they were balanced by the few who were clearly disapproving. King Jad continued over the din, "I am certain that Princess Evelynne's first Sponsorship will create a positive precedent for her future." The King raised his glass. "To Princess Evelynne and *Ishta* Tretiak!"

The assembled guests echoed the salutation as Ally grinned sheepishly and her parents, Evelynne and Chorus smiled in pride.

Lord Thomas was the next to rise. "I have had the privilege of being able to speak with young Alleandre several times since she honoured our nation with her presence," he began, "and I have been struck by the

chapter fourteen

grace, intelligence and insight she displays. I think that even if I had met her in some manner other than as a result of the unfortunate events that forced her here, I would still have been honoured to call her a friend. I am therefore truly honoured to be able to present to her a reward for bringing home our princess, whom I consider to be my own granddaughter. The Hall of Nobles has created a fund in *Ishta* Tretiak's name and each member has donated a sum from his or her own Privy Purse. At last count, the sum total of the fund was—let me check to make sure . . ." He reached into a pocket and pulled out a small piece of paper. "Ah, yes. Two million, four hundred sixteen thousand, eight hundred and fifty seven *tali*." Ally became aware that she was staring dumbfounded, her mouth hanging open. Lord Thomas saw her and shook a finger at her. "My dear, did you think that we just passed a hat around the office?"

A chuckle arose around the table as Lord Thomas sat down again, leaving Ally to attempt to regain her composure. Evelynne rested a comforting hand on her arm.

Two million tali! Ally thought. *That's, like, four million dollars! Oh my God.*

A number of other people stood up to make speeches. Most followed the King's lead and kept them relatively short, although a couple rambled on for several minutes before making their point. The Canadian Ambassador spoke of Canada's pride in producing such a distinguished "Native Daughter" and made it sound as if he personally were responsible for her exploits. The Ambassador of France expressed her country's regret that such a terrible event had occurred on its soil and concluded by stating a hope that it would not affect future visits. The Italian and Swiss Ambassadors, representing countries that the princess would have visited had her tour not been cut short, issued open invitations for future visits.

Ally had absolutely no desire to speak, and thankfully it appeared that nobody expected her to. She suspected that her discomfort with public speaking, well known by now to both the King and Evelynne, had been taken into account.

Evelynne had planned on making a speech of her own, but seeing the tension and growing tiredness on her friend's face she opted against drawing more attention. Instead, once the other speeches had ended, she sent her father a prearranged signal with a tilt of her head and a raised eyebrow.

Receiving the message, King Jad stood once more. "Ladies and Gentlemen," he announced, "I am afraid we must bid goodnight to our guests of honour. *Ishta* Tretiak has yet to recover fully from her injuries and I have been told that she has a therapy session early tomorrow morning." It wasn't completely true. Her therapy wasn't until the afternoon, but the fiction allowed her to save face.

The other guests rose to bid farewell to Ally and Evelynne, and Ally didn't have to feign fatigue as she was helped to her feet. After a final round of farewells, they left the dining room, accompanied by Ally's parents and Chorus, as well as the King and Queen.

"You don't have to leave with us," Ally protested to her parents and friend. "If you want to stay you can. I'm just totally wiped right now."

Catherine hesitated and looked at her husband. "I wouldn't mind staying a while longer," she admitted. "I was having a fascinating discussion with Lord Thomas about aquaculture."

"Certainly," Evelynne said. "When you're ready to go just tell one of the servants and they'll get the Seneschal to arrange transportation. I assume you'd like to stay as well." This last was directed, with a twinkle in her eye, at Chorus, who grinned unashamedly.

"Oh, I think I'll be able to suffer through a bit longer," he confirmed.

"Then that's settled," the King said. He hugged Evelynne, holding her for several long moments. Then he did the same for Ally. "Sleep well, both of you," he instructed.

"Thank you, Sir," Ally said. She received a warm hug and kiss from her father and mother, who echoed the King's sentiments. "Good night."

Ally's tired mind, stressed from the evening's events, barely registered the short walk out of the Hall to the limousine. Once inside she leaned her head back just for a moment, to rest her eyes, and then knew nothing more.

chapter fifteen

"Evelynne, do you mind if I talk to you for a few minutes?" Ally asked as she walked into the main study of the Summer Palace.

Evelynne looked up from the old, leather-bound book she was reading and smiled in greeting. "Of course you can. You know you don't need to ask." She took a moment to assess Ally's demeanour and was pleased with what she saw. The day after the banquet she had been pale, drawn and obviously stressed, even though she had slept until nearly noon. Now, a few days later, her friend was much more relaxed and rested, and radiated a confident poise that made her extremely attractive. *Not that I'm biased or anything,* Evelynne thought with an internal smile.

The taller woman came closer and sat down in a chair opposite the princess. "Well, I wasn't sure if you were busy, or . . ."

Her companion made a face. "No, not really. I'm just brushing up on my heraldry." She held up the book she had been reading. Ally looked at the title, but it was written in Lantlan and she couldn't translate it. "This is one of the classics on heraldic symbolism. It's very complete and very interesting, but it was written in 1872 and the author was somewhat long-winded."

"So why are you reading it?"

"For you, silly. You can't very well be a knight without a coat of arms and as your Sponsor it is my responsibility to provide you with one."

Ally blushed. "Oh. Don't you just put some animals or something on a shield?"

"Oh, Isis, no!" Evelynne exclaimed. "Every part of the blazon has meaning. The type of animal, the various bars that cross the shield—those are called *ordinaries*, by the way—their positions. Even the colours used are symbolic. For example, red symbolises 'military fortitude' or 'magnanimity,' silver is 'peace and sincerity' and so on."

"Oh," Ally repeated. "So you have to try to describe, well, me, using those symbols?"

"You, your actions and achievements, part of your history if I can. Of course, this will just be your initial blazon. As time goes on you'll gain more achievements and your arms could change. And then if you ever have children, and one of them is knighted, they'll inherit it."

"Well, I don't know about the 'having kids' part," Ally said wryly, "but I suppose stranger things have happened."

"Indeed they have," Evelynne agreed, trying to imagine Ally as a mother. It was surprisingly easy. She shook off the image. "Speaking of parenthood, where are yours? Your parents, I mean."

"Well, Dad is talking planting times and cultivation techniques in the grounds with the gardener and Mom went into Kilim for the afternoon. Lord Thomas apparently promised to introduce her to one of the local cetacean biologists, so she's going to be in her own little world for a while. Chorus went with her. He mumbled something about 'Baron Bumbbmbmbbl's *cough* daughter'." Ally managed to mimic Chorus' voice perfectly.

"Well, good for him," Evelynne said, grinning delightedly. "So you mean I've got you all to myself?" *Oo, bad princess!*

"I'm all yours," Ally confirmed, then seemed to realise what she had said. She flushed predictably. "Um, that is—I'm—yes, yes, you have me," she finally said, deciding to simply let the slip go and hopefully die a quiet death.

"Good," the princess said. *Oooh, Ally, you have no idea what you do to me, do you?* She quickly drew her mind back from that line of thought. "So what did you want to talk to me about?"

"Oh, right." Ally also seemed to have to bring her thoughts back on track. "Well, you know how some people have been talking to me about giving an interview?"

"Nobody's been pressuring you?" Evelynne asked, suddenly protective.

"No, no," Ally said. "I mean, they obviously want me to but they haven't been insisting or anything. And I suppose that since I haven't said, 'No,' outright that they're justified in asking. Anyway, I was thinking of just giving an interview and getting it over with." She paused. "Plus, I've seen some of the articles and things that have been written already, and they haven't all been . . . totally accurate. So I thought I'd just kind of set the record straight."

"That makes sense," Evelynne said. "What do your parents say?"

"Well, they both know just how much I hate being the centre of attention but they also think I'll keep getting hounded until I do. Also, I've been talking to Annie and some other relatives and they've been getting questions too, but they didn't want to say anything until I'd said something. I'm hoping if I do this they'll finally be left alone."

"It sounds as if you've already made up your mind."

"I guess so," Ally admitted. "But I wanted to run it by you first. You have more experience than I do in this kind of thing, anyway."

"That I do. So how exactly did you want to do it?"

chapter fifteen

"Well, I was wanting to talk to a Canadian reporter, probably someone from CBC. I always thought they had a good reputation. But I also thought I should talk to someone from your main network–LANTA, is it? After all, this is where I am at the moment and in a while I'll be a citizen, so it only seemed polite."

Evelynne nodded approvingly. "Very diplomatic. I'll make a Lady out of you yet. And you said you weren't a people person," she said chidingly.

"I have to say there's another reason for wanting to do this. The interviews, I mean. A kind of ulterior motive." Ally flushed.

"Oh?"

"Well, I was thinking about it last night and thought that it would be . . . fun to shove all this into the faces of all the people who used to call me a freak. Kind of a 'kiss my ass' statement." She chuckled sheepishly.

Evelynne, though, broke into peals of laughter. "Oh, that's perfect," she said after several moments, still giggling. "You know, it's good to know you're not always as noble as you usually seem." The princess grinned again. "Besides, I dare you to say that during the interview."

ಲೆ ಲೆ ಲೆ ಲೆ ಲೆ

"Thank God that's over," Ally breathed with a sigh. She let herself collapse backwards into a large armchair.

Around her, the study showed no signs of the equipment that had recently filled it–lights, cameras, microphones, and seemingly enough cable to run from Atlantl to Canada–and Evelynne smiled as she lowered herself into a chair opposite in a more dignified manner. "It didn't seem to go too badly," she said. "So you're talking to–who was it, Mr. Tyler? Your old teacher? The one that works for the newspaper? You're talking to him this evening?"

Ally nodded. "I offered to fly him out here, but he broke his leg a few weeks ago and really didn't want to fly. So instead, we'll be talking on the phone. That should be good."

"Well, it'll definitely be less exciting."

"Oh, yeah," Ally said. She hesitated. "On another note," she continued, "there was something else I wanted to talk to you about." She paused, uncertain of how to proceed.

"Yes?" Evelynne asked.

"Um, I'm not sure how to put this, but . . . I think I need a break," Ally said.

"A break? From what? The interviews are almost over."

"No, it's–please don't take this the wrong way, but I need a break from . . . all this." Ally's expansive gesture took in the whole room. "All of the people, the banquets, the interviews, everything."

"Oh." Evelynne thought she understood now. "You mean a vacation? We could do that. We could go and visit one of the retreats that–" She trailed off upon seeing Ally's uncomfortable expression. "What's wrong?"

Ally felt terrible. "That isn't quite what I meant. If you and I went somewhere, we'd still take along a bunch of servants, bodyguards and so on, and that's part of what I want to get away from." She sighed. "You know I'm naturally a very private person, and having people around all the time is . . . draining. Don't get me wrong, I've been having a really good time, but being around people constantly is just really exhausting for me. You seem to actually gain energy from personal interaction, but for someone like me, each person I talk to wears off a bit of my armour and eventually I start feeling . . . raw."

"Oh." The princess was surprised. She knew that her friend often got tired easily in social situations, but had not realised that it was an ongoing process. "So you want to leave?" She carefully hid the pain she felt.

"I don't *want* to, really, but I think I *need* to," Ally said. "I can feel it right now." She placed a hand in the centre of her chest. "Right around here. It's almost a physical sensation. Like someone's rubbing my soul with sandpaper."

"Ouch." Evelynne managed a half smile. "So were you thinking about going back to Canada with your parents?"

Ally shook her head. "No, I think that would be worse. If I go back it'll just start all over again. I'll be a celebrity again and I'll have to deal with more reporters, people wanting to meet me, talk with me. And I won't even have the insulation that you've been able to provide here with all the security. I know I'll have to go back eventually, but right now I don't think I can."

"Okay, I can understand that." Now that she knew what to look for, Evelynne could see some of the more permanent effects of the strain Ally had been under and kicked herself for not noticing sooner the toll her friend was paying. "So if you're not going back there, where did you want to go?" Though her tone was calm, inside her heart was breaking.

"Well, I was thinking of maybe buying or renting a house or apartment somewhere here in Atlantl, since I am apparently a wealthy woman now." Ally smiled self-deprecatingly. "I'd do it quietly, so that there's no big fanfare and just become a hermit for a couple of weeks. After that?" She shrugged. "I don't know. I was also thinking of maybe applying to a university to start my Master's degree."

chapter fifteen

"Are you going to be able to live on your own? You know, with your back and all? What about your physiotherapy?"

"I thought I'd use my new-found wealth to hire someone to come in and clean every few days. I've never been a big fan of cleaning anyway. As for my back, I can basically do my exercises on my own now. I'd still go in for check-ups, but that's easy to set up."

"It sounds like you have everything worked out." Despite her best efforts, Evelynne couldn't entirely keep the mildly petulant tone out of her voice. "You've been thinking about this for a while."

"Yeah." Ally looked embarrassed. *I can't tell you the other reason for doing this,* she thought. *I'm getting in too deep with you. It's all very well to put on a brave face with Annie or Mom about what I'll do when you finally do get together with Count Whatsisname's son, or some other suitably heterosexual male, but I know it'll be hell. So I need to start some kind of separation now, so that you can move on with your life without me holding you back.*

"Can I come and visit, at least?" Evelynne asked.

"Of course! You're still my friend, Evelynne." *Although I wish you could be more.* "Not only that, but soon you'll also be my Liege Lady, so it's not as if I can say, 'No,' can I?" Ally managed a genuine smile.

"Darned right," Evelynne said firmly, returning the grin.

☙ ☙ ☙ ☙ ☙

"So what do you think, Mom?" Ally asked. She waited nervously for her mother's reply.

"I like it," Mrs. Tretiak answered as she walked back into the room. "I especially like this living room. It's very bright and open." She looked around the large sitting room, taking in the white walls, made brilliant by the afternoon sun pouring through the large westward facing windows.

"It'll get a bit smaller once I get some furniture in here," Ally commented. "I thought I'd go into town the day after tomorrow, once I move in, to find some."

"Something in a nice beige would be good. But that's up to you. It is your house, after all." Catherine laughed. "Your house. I never thought I'd see the day." She moved to wrap an arm around her daughter.

Ally shrugged. "I figured that since I'd be here until at least the new year I might as well get something good. At least the bedrooms are bigger than my one at home."

"They certainly are." Her mother paused, uncertain of how to bring up the next topic. "So you think you'll stay here until then? You're not going to be staying with Evelynne?"

"Subtle as usual, Mom. No, I told her I need some 'alone time,' which is true. I also figure that she's going to be more and more busy, and I really don't want her to have to keep on taking care of me." Ally saw her mother's penetrating stare and folded. "I also think that if I can create a little distance now it'll make it easier when she moves on," she said quietly. "And it'll give me a chance to get on with my life. I hope we stay friends, though."

Catherine wrapped her daughter in a gentle hug. "Of course you will. Trust me, nobody forgets you easily. And don't worry, some day you'll have a princess all your own."

Ally squeezed her mother tightly, and then pulled back. "Thanks, Mom." She looked around the room once more. "So where did Dad get to?"

"Right here," the man in question answered as he walked into the living room. "I was checking out your back yard. You have a very nice swimming pool back there. It almost makes me wish we weren't flying home tomorrow." He looked at Ally sternly. "You just be careful about swimming there by yourself, especially with your back."

"Relax, Dad," Ally chuckled. "You know me. Do you honestly think *I'm* really in danger of drowning?"

"Maybe not," William admitted. "But you be careful anyway. I also noticed that the trees and hedge in the back yard block any view from your neighbours, even though they are half a kilometre away."

"Really?" Ally said innocently. "I hadn't noticed." She saw her father's disapproving stare. "Okay, okay. I thought they might be useful in case I went . . . out at night."

"As odd as this may sound, I wish that only meant that you were going skinny dipping."

"Dad! Please!"

"I know." This time it was William's turn to embrace his child. "You just make sure you're careful, all right?"

"Aren't I always?"

"Ha!" Catherine barked. She tapped Ally's cane. "Look at what happened the last time you were 'careful'."

Ally ostentatiously cast her eyes around the luxurious room. "And this turned out badly how, exactly?"

�� �� �� �� ��

"So what do you think, Evy?" Ally asked. She waited nervously for her friend's reply.

"It's nice," the princess said. "It's not as big as the Summer Palace, of course, but . . ."

chapter fifteen

"Evelynne, I hate to break it to you, but there are sports arenas which aren't as big as the Summer Palace."

Evelynne smiled wryly. "True." Turning serious, she asked, "Are you sure you're going to be okay here on your own?"

"I'll be fine," Ally assured her. "I'll be going into Outremer tomorrow to pick out some furniture. My Mom has left me detailed instructions on suitable colours and styles." Both Ally and Evelynne grinned. "Someone will be coming in to clean the place every few days."

"Good," Evelynne said. "And you have the number to call in an emergency?"

"It's right up here." Ally tapped her head. She rattled it off.

"Good," the princess said again. For some reason she couldn't think of more to say. Awkwardly, she said, "Well . . . then I guess I'll leave you to get settled in." She hesitantly held out her arms in Ally's direction.

Ally willing moved into them, and the two women spent several moments holding each other.

"I'll come and visit you," Evelynne promised, "I'll call beforehand."

"Excellent. You don't need to call; you're more than welcome anytime."

"Thank you," Evelynne whispered and it wasn't clear just what she was thankful for.

Ally still seemed to understand. "You're welcome."

Evelynne looked up into Ally's face until, greatly daring, she stretched upwards and brushed her lips across Ally's. Then she turned and hurried out the front door into the darkness.

Ally stood stunned, hearing the sound of the princess' motorcade starting off down the road back to the Summer Palace. She lifted her fingers to her mouth briefly, feeling oddly both exhilarated and depressed.

"I've got to get out of here," she said aloud, turning and heading to the door leading to the back yard.

A few minutes later, the recently purchased property was vacant.

chapter sixteen

Evelynne sat in her large, warm bed in the early morning twilight and simply relaxed, letting her mind contemplate any topic that cared to cross it. Right at the moment it was idly wondering just how Seneschal Nancu Ylan managed always to have hot coffee waiting even before his mistress awoke—no matter when that happened to be. Regardless of whether she slept in—a rare occurrence these days—or if she woke before the sun had fully lit the sky—like today—the coffee was always there, hot and fresh. Eventually she decided that the Seneschal had implanted some kind of device directly into her brain, which informed him when she was about to wake up.

Sighing, Evelynne let the lighter, idle thoughts go and reluctantly focused her attention on the events of the past month. Although she had yet to assume her full duties, the princess' days had been filled by a steadily increasing number of things which required her attention: a formal meeting with her Advisory candidates; preliminary discussions on setting up her office; meetings with various government officials and Nobles; a seemingly endless pile of papers which needed reviewing and signing and the usual appearances at public events. There had been fewer of the last than there would normally have been. The Guard was still nervous nearly three months after the shooting and refused to allow their charge into any situation that they could not tightly control. It had become even worse now that Sir Arthur had been reinstated as Master of the Heir's Guard and Evelynne had once snapped that she felt lucky to go to the toilet alone. She hadn't liked the speculative expression that had appeared on her bodyguard's face.

With everything that had been happening, Evelynne had almost had no time to miss Ally. The princess had visited two weeks after her friend had moved into her new house, wanting to give her the requested time alone and she had seemed to be settling in well. Evelynne had noticed that Ally was more relaxed and happy than previously and had felt guilty about not noticing her friend's stress earlier. They had also spent several evenings in long conversations on the phone, something that Evelynne had looked forward to with great anticipation.

Now she realised that it had been seventeen days since her last visit—she didn't really want to admit that she had been counting—and almost a week since the last phone call. The princess momentarily contemplated calling Ally right now, but remembered that her friend had a tendency to sleep late and probably wouldn't appreciate a call at–she peered at her bedside clock–six thirty in the morning. The last time she had called Ally early, she had been greeted by a sleepy, "'Lo?" which she had found absolutely adorable.

It was time, the princess decided, to stop by and visit again. She had an early meeting in Outremer this morning to go over some details of Ally's knighthood ceremony and then wanted to visit with Lord Thomas. By that time even her late-rising friend should be awake and she would drop by the house outside the city.

That decided, Evelynne finished her coffee, climbed out of bed and prepared herself to convince Sir Arthur to accept the diversion.

❧   ❧   ❧   ❧   ❧

"Evelynne, my dear, it's wonderful to see you again," Lord Thomas enthused, escorting the princess into his office. "Would you like some tea?" He indicated the drinks already set out.

"Yes, please," Evelynne said, as they sat down.

"So, my dear, I have not seen you much lately. You've been busy, I suspect."

"Nobody's seen me much lately," Evelynne said. "Wait, that's not quite true. Actually, *everybody's* been seeing me lately, just not many of the people I really care about." She hesitated. "That doesn't sound quite right either. I mean, I do care about these people–they're going to be my subjects, after all–but I don't care–oh, you know what I mean," she finished.

"Indeed I do," the Duke replied. "I understand completely. They are just not your close personal friends and family."

"Exactly. See, my brain has turned to total mush."

"Oh dear." The Duke's eyes were twinkling.

"I was just in the city talking to one of the Heralds about Ally's blazon," she said conversationally. "Since I was in the area I decided to come and visit you as well."

Evelynne smiled wryly as she remembered the meeting. She and Master Herald Cahir had settled on the form of the coat of arms, but then the princess had added one final change to the finished design. In and of itself the change was minor, but the implications were huge and Evelynne almost chuckled as she remembered the way the elderly Herald had nearly swallowed his teeth–quite a prospect, as they weren't even dentures–at her proposal. The fallout would likely be significant, but she had extracted his

chapter sixteen

promise to keep the matter secret until the knighting and to get the same promise from those actually embroidering and inscribing the final seal.

"Well, I'm glad you did. Even though it is only nine thirty I've had about as much frustration as I can take today. I'm dealing with a possible drug seizure."

The princess frowned. "Isn't that part of the police's job? Or maybe Customs?"

As the hub for practically all seagoing traffic throughout the Atlantic Ocean and the Mediterranean, Atlantl saw an enormous number of ships going through its waters and transferring cargo at its ports. Along with the hundreds of billions of *tali* worth of legitimate cargo there was inevitably a proportionally large amount of smuggling. Not all of it–in fact a quite small amount–was actually intended for Atlantl, but the country was still responsible for ships passing through its waters. While they could stop a lot of it, not even a department as large and well-funded as the Atlantlan Customs Control could intercept all the contraband.

"Normally, yes. However, the Outremer Police recently received a detailed anonymous tip about several large shipments being smuggled through Atlantlan ports, giving names and also the locations of several stockpiles of hard drugs: cocaine and heroin from the Americas, opium from North Africa and Europe. Normally we would catch a lot of them, but whoever sent the police the tip has apparently provided dates for what seems to be every illegal drug shipment for the next month. So many, in fact, that even working at full manpower, the local police and Customs agents would not be able to handle them all. So my office is trying to co-ordinate support in the form of military Special Forces attached to the regular officers. We also want to try to seize all the shipments simultaneously if possible."

"Wow. That must be a lot of drugs."

"If our informant is correct, the street value is estimated at over fourteen billion *tali*."

"Isis," Evelynne breathed. "Well, if you need someone to help you cut through red tape, let me know. I may not be official yet, but I can still browbeat obstinate peons."

"I'll certainly keep that in mind." Changing the subject, the Duke asked, "How is young Alleandre these days? I'm afraid I have not had the chance to speak with her recently."

Evelynne flushed, a reaction the Duke noticed with interest. "The last I spoke to her she's been doing well. Unfortunately, I've been so busy that was a week ago." She paused. "That was actually one of the reasons I came to see you today."

"Oh my, an ulterior motive! You mean it wasn't for my wit, charm and roguish good looks?"

The princess laughed. "Actually, in a sense those were what I wanted to see you for. Your wit and charm, anyway. I'm sorry to say that your roguish good looks really don't do anything for me."

The Duke's brows rose. "Ah. You are referring to our last conversation? You have become more sure of yourself?"

Evelynne shrugged more casually than she actually felt. "Well, I'm sure I'm gay." The words were surprisingly easy to say. "I'm also . . . more sure about other things." She decided not to hide her thoughts. "I'm sure that I'm attracted to Ally. I *think* I'm in love with her. I mean, I've never been in love before, so I don't know exactly what it's like, but . . ." She trailed off, remembering. "I'm pretty sure that kiss clinched it, though."

"Kiss?" The Duke looked shocked.

Evelynne flushed again. "It was just one and it was really quick. It happened at her new house."

"What happened after?"

"I, um . . . left."

Duke Thomas blinked. "I see." A pause. "So what, exactly, did you want to talk to me about?"

"Well . . . I was thinking that, um, I'd like to . . . try to . . . move forward with Ally," Evelynne said hesitantly. "And please don't just give me reasons for why it's a bad idea. I'm pretty sure I've already thought of all of them."

"And you still wish to try this."

"I do." Her tone was firm, belying her hidden nervousness.

"Very well. There is one thing that I believe I must ask first, though. It is all very well for you to decide this is what you want, but do you know if it is what Alleandre wants? You and I are both aware of what a shy and private person she is. Is she willing to embark on this course, knowing the scrutiny she will be under when–not if–it becomes public knowledge?" Lord Thomas smiled sympathetically. "You know I will support you, Evelynne, but Alleandre is my friend also and I feel I must protect her, especially when she has shown herself to be less than willing to protect herself at times."

"I know, Domdom," Evelynne said, "and I love you for it." She sighed and then continued in a quiet voice. "The truth is that I don't know what she wants. I don't know if the idea has ever even crossed her mind. That's why I want to go very slowly and carefully. I want to find out if she's interested in the first place. I want to make sure she knows the possible repercussions. Then, if she's willing . . . I want *her*." She reddened again. "I just have one problem."

chapter sixteen

"Yes?" the Duke asked when she didn't elaborate. "That is?"

"I have no idea how to do it," she said plaintively. "Don't laugh! I've never been interested in anybody before. And before you say anything–" Evelynne held up an admonitory finger. "–your nephew does *not* count. I was five at the time."

"I wasn't going to say a word," Lord Thomas said, although his eyes betrayed his true thoughts.

"Well, good. Anyway, I suppose ordinary people learn how to do these things somehow, but I never have."

"So you want me to help you . . . What? Date Alleandre Tretiak?"

"Well . . . yes."

"I see." Lord Thomas was silent for several minutes. "I suppose the first thing that you should do is find out if she is indeed interested. The simplest way to do that is to reveal your own interest."

"But what if she isn't? Then she knows I like her, but she doesn't like me that way, and it would get . . . awkward." The princess looked on the edge of panic.

"Then you act more subtly. You casually touch her. Listen to her, talk to her, spend time with her."

"Wait a minute, you mean flirt with her!"

"Ah yes, I knew there was a word for it." The Duke beamed triumphantly. He turned serious again. "Listen, from what I have observed, I believe that Alleandre is, deep down, a very romantic person. She does not have a very high opinion of herself and she wants to be flattered, to have attention paid to her and most importantly to feel loved. She wishes to be courted, in fact."

"Courted . . ." Evelynne mused. "I remember she was talking about her previous lover and how Annie courted her. She used that exact word, in fact. Annie was–is a dancer, so a lot of it had to do with dancing and music." She looked up at her host. "I'm–well, I'm a princess. What do I do?"

"No, Annie did not use dance simply because she is a dancer. She just used what she had, something that was special to her. You have to find something that you have and use it. It might or might not have anything to do with being the Heir."

"Okay," Evelynne said.

"And most importantly . . ." Lord Thomas waited until he was sure of her attention. "Do not rush things! Be sure before you take each new step. Ordinarily I would give this advice to anybody, but for you it is particularly important, given your unique circumstances. Because of who you are, any mistakes you make–possibly even any correct moves–could have far-reaching consequences, not just for you, but for Alleandre as well. I am not saying this to try to frighten you off, but only to be sure you are thinking about all the possibilities."

"I know," the princess said soberly. "But I have to try. I can feel it. Right here." She touched her chest.

Evelynne sat back in the seat, her stomach roiling with a combination of exhilaration and nervousness, as her car drove up the long road leading to Ally's house. She thought back to the last few pieces of advice Lord Thomas had given her before she left. *Okay, just be myself. Only don't hold myself back so much. Don't be outrageously blatant, but don't dissemble either. I want her to fall in love with me, not some person I pretend to be to impress her. Don't be surprised if she doesn't pick up on what I'm doing right away. As Domdom said, she probably has not had much experience being pursued. And also give both her and myself time to adjust. Don't rush anything.* The princess thought for a moment more. *I think that's it. Am I forgetting anything? Probably. Oh Isis, what if I do something wrong? What if I'm too obvious and it scares her off? What if—*

Her growing panic was interrupted by a low mutter next to her, and she looked across at Sir Arthur who was driving the vehicle. She was momentarily confused, but understood when she saw that the bodyguard had not in fact spoken to her, but had said something into his collar-clipped mike. He listened for a moment to the inaudible reply and then turned to address his charge.

"That was the unit keeping an eye on *Ishta* Tretiak's house," he explained. "Apparently she has a guest." He frowned. "Her guest's background has been cleared but I still wish you had allowed me to prepare this visit more carefully."

Evelynne shook her head, even as she restrained her impulse to ask who her friend's guest was. Ally had the right to entertain whomever she wished without having nosy princesses keeping track of her every move. A Guard unit had been assigned to discreetly protect the young woman, but that amounted to observation only, with no interference unless absolutely necessary.

Instead, she turned her attention to Sir Arthur's other concerns. The princess had not wanted to visit Ally with the full motorcade, lights flashing and sirens blaring. That had left only an incognito visit. Sir Arthur had flatly refused to let her go without protection and a compromise had finally been reached. Evelynne had borrowed a uniform from one of her female bodyguards and was now disguised as a member of her own Guard. The uniform was a decent fit, but she was aware that Sergeant Christine Himmerman was

chapter sixteen

both larger around the limbs and smaller around the chest, so it alternately constricted and ballooned around various portions of her anatomy. The dark glasses and simple hairstyle completing the disguise made her look far removed from the Heir to the Diarchy.

"It'll be fine," she assured the Guard. "This is Ally we're talking about. I'm pretty sure she isn't hanging around with criminals and assassins. Besides, we're already here."

Sir Arthur looked disgruntled–not an uncommon expression–but refrained from arguing further, knowing the discussion was pointless.

The car pulled to a stop in Ally's empty driveway, and Evelynne spent a moment getting the butterflies in her stomach under control. *Stop it!* she commanded herself sternly. *This is just Ally. Just be yourself . . . only more so.*

With that thought she got out of the car and walked up the path to the front door, Sir Arthur close on her heels. The princess knew that it would be pointless to try to get him to stay in the car. With a civilian of unconfirmed motivations nearby, there was no way he was going to let his charge out of his sight.

Reaching the front door, Evelynne rang the doorbell and then stood waiting. It was an odd sensation. She was not accustomed to needing to wait for someone to open the door. There was silence for a moment, then the sound of soft feet on the floor beyond. The door swung open partway to reveal Ally, dressed in a pair of baggy blue track pants and a grey tee-shirt, her hair–slightly longer than the last time Evelynne had seen her–uncombed.

Evelynne couldn't believe how good she looked.

"Hello?" Ally said questioningly, her gaze puzzled. The look cleared suddenly when she recognised the princess. "Evelynne?"

"Hi, Ally," the princess said. She was a little surprised at how steady her voice was. "How are you doing?"

"Great," Ally replied. She took a moment to look over Evelynne's uniform-clad form. "You look different."

Evelynne lowered her voice and stage whispered, "I'm incognito." She made a show of searching the vicinity for eavesdroppers. "Don't tell anyone." Ally laughed and Sir Arthur made a suspicious snorting sound. "Can we come in?"

Ally started. "Yeah, of course." She opened the door wider and beckoned her new guests in. "Duh. I don't think my brain's working yet."

Entering the house, Evelynne looked through into the living room. Ally had obviously been furniture shopping, as a new plush couch and several comfy looking chairs now occupied the room, along with a few small tables. Interesting paintings hung on the walls and a large flat-screen television and enough electronics to launch a small satellite dominated the far wall. All of the furniture except for the couch had been pushed aside and several blankets, pillows and the remnants of snack foods lay in the middle of the floor. A small pile of videotapes lay nearby. The princess raised an eyebrow at the sight.

"Up late last night?"

"Kind of, yeah," Ally replied and Evelynne watched as she blushed.

The butterflies in Evelynne's stomach were beginning to turn into something more unpleasant as her mind began to put together various clues. She didn't like the picture it was building. Ally had apparently had a guest the previous night; a guest whom her Guard detail said was still in the house. Add to that Ally's embarrassed expression...

Evelynne was sure that everyone present could hear the thud her heart made as it joined her stomach in her shoes when the distinctive form of Mila'a Porse exited a room further up the hall.

The attractive young woman was fully dressed, but was towelling her still-wet hair as she spoke. "Ally, I think I will be having to leave now. I did not think it was so late and I must be back at the university by this evening. I–" She suddenly cut off as she noticed the new visitors. "I am sorry, I did not hear you come in. You–*Ur-mata*?" she asked hesitantly, her eyes wide as she recognised the Heir. "*Eta-o?*"

"Hello, Ms. Porse," Evelynne greeted, holding out her hand. Somehow she managed to keep her voice level and calm. "I should actually be the one to apologise. I didn't realise Ally had company."

"No, no, er, Your Highness. It is . . . *ekani'is* . . . fine. I must leave now anyway. I must return to university and it is a long journey."

"All right, then. It was good to see you again," Evelynne lied.

"*Ca'era, Ur-mata*," Mila'a said, bowing. "An honour."

"I'll see you out," said Ally, who had been silent until now.

Evelynne stood deceptively calmly a ways down the hall and tried not to look as Ally walked her guest to the door. She still caught them speaking softly out of the corner of her eye and had to suppress a fresh stab of jealousy when Mila'a hugged Ally and gave her a quick but thorough kiss. The two women exchanged a few more quiet words and then Ally opened the front door and let the other woman out. Ally stood for a moment, then ran a hand through her unkempt hair in an attempt to straighten it and walked back to where Evelynne and Sir Arthur were waiting.

"As you can see, the lounge is a bit messy," she explained. "Come on into the kitchen instead."

chapter sixteen

The princess and her bodyguard were escorted into the large, modern kitchen. Unlike the living room, this room looked nearly untouched, and Evelynne felt a mild amusement as she remembered her friend's culinary abilities—or lack thereof. An unopened packet of potato chips sat on the counter, along with an almost empty bottle of soft drink and a couple of used glasses. Ally hurried to place the glasses in the sink while her guests took seats at the kitchen table.

"Would you like tea or . . . well, tea?" Ally asked. "Sorry, but I don't have any coffee. Oh, and I also have whatever this green fruit drink is, and milk."

"What kind of drink?" Evelynne asked, stalling for time to put her emotions in order.

"Um, I think it's called *ilasi* fruit. Now, I don't know exactly what *ilasi* fruit is, but I've found that I like it."

"Oh, that's kind of like a pineapple, I suppose. But with a tinge of vanilla, and an . . . indescribable undertaste. I must say I'm a little surprised you like it. Not many people do."

"Well, it is definitely an acquired taste, but I tried it when I was in town a while back and I've found that I like it. Would you like some?"

Evelynne shuddered. "No, thank you. It is one taste I have never acquired. I'll just have milk."

"Sure," Ally said, opening a cupboard to pull out a clean glass. "Would you like anything, Sir Arthur?"

"Thank you, *Ishta*, but no. In fact, with your permission, I will go and inspect the grounds. I do not wish to intrude on your visit," the Guard replied.

"Oh, okay." Ally almost suggested sending him out with some tea for the Guard detail watching her house, but then remembered that she wasn't supposed to be aware of their presence.

The bodyguard left while Ally filled two glasses with milk, placing one in front of Evelynne as she took her own seat at the table.

"I should apologise," Evelynne said after an awkward moment of silence. "I didn't think that you might have other company. I hope I didn't chase her away."

Ally shook her head. "No, Mila'a had to leave to drive back to the university by this evening. She was actually just visiting her father for a few days in Outremer. I bumped into her a few days ago in the city."

"I see. So are you two . . . dating?"

Ally looked slightly uncomfortable. "Well, actually–" She was cut off by a knock at the front door, immediately followed by the sound of it opening.

Evelynne was briefly concerned, then realised that with Sir Arthur and another Guard detail outside, the only people who would be allowed into the house were those deemed acceptable by both. Her thoughts were confirmed a few moments later when a grizzled, elderly man arrived in the kitchen doorway.

"Apologies, *Ishta*," the man said with a heavy accent. "I see car outside and know you have visitor. If you wish I come later."

"No, that's quite all right, Vilet," Ally said. "*N'amassa*. No problem. In fact, this is—"

"Sophia," Evelynne interrupted, standing to shake the man's hand. "I'm a friend of Ally's."

"Good to meet you, Sophia. I am Vilet. I am cleaner for *Ishta* Ally."

"And I'm afraid I've given you a bit of work today, Vilet," Ally said apologetically. "As you probably saw, the living room . . . er, *va'wer* is pretty messy."

"*N'amassa*. Is no problem." He turned to address Evelynne conspiratorially. "I say to *Ishta* Ally, she need husband and children. They make house messy so I have work. But she does not listen." He sighed theatrically. "No husband. No children. House is clean. I have no work." He brightened. "Sophia, you will help, yes? You will find *Ishta* Ally a husband?"

His expression was so earnest that Evelynne couldn't help but smile. "Well, I'll see what I can do."

"*Bona*. Good," Vilet said, nodding in satisfaction. "Now I go clean."

"Oh, Vilet," Ally called before he left the room, "you'll also have to set up the guest bedroom again. I had company last night."

"In guest bedroom?" The elderly cleaner tsked. "You do not get husband if they sleep in guest bedroom, *Ishta* Ally." Still muttering, he started off down the hall to the stairs leading to the second floor.

Evelynne looked at Ally, who blushed. "So that was your cleaner, huh?" She was carefully protecting the flame of hope that had ignited upon hearing that the guest bedroom had been used.

"Yep, that's Vilet," Ally replied. "He's determined to find me a husband."

"Does he know you're gay?"

"Oh yes. It's just that in his mind, if I marry *anyone*, because I'm a woman I'll automatically be a wife. Ergo, my spouse must be my husband, regardless of actual gender. In Vilet's world there are no such things as 'wife and wife' or 'husband and husband'. Only a husband and wife are actually married."

chapter sixteen

"I see. I must admit it makes sense . . . in a weird sort of way." The princess paused. "So how close is Mila'a to becoming your 'husband'? No, never mind, it's none of my business."

"That's okay. The answer is: not very close."

"So you're not seeing each other? Romantically, I mean."

"Well, we've gone out a couple of times. And, of course, she stayed here last night. In her own room," Ally hastened to add. "But there isn't really a . . . spark, if you know what I mean. I mean, I like her and I think she likes me, but at the moment there isn't really anything more. Part of it is probably because we both know that it would be really hard to start something right now, since she's really busy with her school. We'd probably only be able to see each other every few weeks. And I know I'm certainly not the kind of person to engage in casual sex." She blushed furiously again. "I'm pretty sure she would have liked to . . . you know, last night, but she knew not to push."

"Well, that's good," Evelynne commented. Inside she was jumping for joy.

"Yeah. We've sort of agreed that when she's finished her university and if we're both still single we'll see what happens. Knowing me, I'll probably still be single, but as for her . . ." She shrugged.

"Oh, you never know," Evelynne protested. "Someone could just be waiting to sweep you off your feet."

chapter seventeen

Major Lantree, of the Royal Atlantlan Army (Covert Operations), raised a clenched fist suddenly. The rest of his highly drilled team instantly halted behind him in near-perfect silence. They remained still, alert and wary, with weapons at the ready, while their team leader scanned the nearby area trying to determine if the faint sound was a waiting ambush or just one of the many rats which made the warehouse their home. But apart from the distant but clear sounds of several workers in a different area of the building, there was only silence.

However, the sensation of unseen eyes watching his every move persisted, as it had since the Major had entered the warehouse. If it had only been himself, Major Lantree would have dismissed the feeling as nerves, despite his fifteen years' military experience, but many other soldiers, as well as Customs agents and police officers engaged in the anti-drug operations, had mentioned a similar sensation of being watched. It had never been officially reported, of course, as there was no real evidence, and the Major had scoffed at the rumours–until tonight.

Now he was remembering that a very few agents and police had claimed to have seen a dark flitting shadow out of the corners of their eyes. It had been dubbed "The Angel" by several of the more superstitious officers.

Certainly *something* appeared to be assisting the authorities while they executed a string of the largest drug seizures in Atlantlan history. The smugglers were organised and well-armed, but seemed to be afflicted by a widespread case of terrible luck. Shots fired at agents would miss, doors would stick as they tried to escape and several criminals had apparently knocked themselves out by running into crates, boards, tables and–in one memorable case–each other.

It had not been a flawless operation but then nobody had expected it to be. Two Customs agents, three police officers and a soldier had been killed, and several others had been wounded. Still, the raids had netted over a hundred and fifty suspects. The drugs seized had exceeded even the highest estimates and no less than four cargo ships had been raided and impounded. Even before the operations were complete, they were obviously putting a pinch on somebody's pocketbook, if the number of voluble protests coming from "respectable and legitimate" businessmen and companies in Europe, the Americas and Asia was anything to go by. Many of the suspects already captured were providing a wealth of information that would likely see the downfall of a number of prominent figures.

Major Lantree had absolutely no compassion for such businessmen. The raid he was currently engaged in was on the final target provided by "The Informant" and the smugglers had been getting progressively more desperate as the operations proceeded. Right now the Major's only goals were to keep his squad alive and to capture or kill as many Bad Guys as possible. In that order. Other teams had also penetrated the warehouse–which normally stored a variety of legal goods–and a full platoon of Royal Army troops was backing up the Customs agents who surrounded the building.

This location had been saved till last, partly because it was the largest suspected cache. The co-ordinating officials had speculated that after the initial raids, the smugglers would be desperate enough to try to remove all the drugs at the same time, at which point most of them could be captured. It seemed to have worked. Infrared imaging had located the bulk of the smugglers near the centre of the warehouse, loading the drugs into trucks.

It was towards that concentration of criminals that Major Lantree's squad was slowly moving. There was always the threat of wandering lookouts, hence the need for stealth.

Finally deciding that the noise was not a threat, Major Lantree signalled his team forward, and they continued their slow creep through the tall stacks of crates. They stopped several more times to scan for ambushes before moving on at a careful, patient pace.

At last the squad reached the place where the crates gave way to a cavernous, well-lit open area. Within the open space the Major could see a number of men, some engaged in loading large, obviously heavy boxes into the backs of five trucks and the others standing guard. The guards were armed with an assortment of deadly weapons, from automatic pistols to assault rifles and Major Lantree cursed silently as he saw the arsenal.

He keyed his mike and spoke softly, knowing the throat-mounted pickup would transmit his words clearly. "Command, this is Charlie. Over."

"Charlie, Command. Over."

"Charlie in position. Be advised Target is well armed. Estimate threat level Eight. Over." To qualify for threat level Nine, the Target would have had to have a hand-held rocket launcher.

There was a pause as Command considered this information. "Understood, Charlie. Query: Proceed. Over."

chapter seventeen

Major Lantree thought. As the first squad leader to reach the scene, he had the authority to continue with the current plan or fall back and bring in the Big Guns. "Charlie says Proceed. Over."

"Understood, Charlie. Stand by for unit confirmation. Over."

The Major turned and nodded to Sergeant Ykindes, who responded by unlimbering the big tear gas launcher from his back. Seeing this, the rest of the squad took turns donning their gas masks. They had just finished when another voice came over the radio.

"Alpha in position. Over." The transmission was repeated three more times as Bravo, Delta and Echo squads took up position around the open area.

"All squads, this is Command. Charlie is point. Proceed. Over and out."

Major Lantree checked his squad once more, and then said, "All squads, Charlie. Give Go, No Go."

"Alpha, Go."

"Bravo, Go."

"Delta, Go."

"Echo, Go."

Major Lantree nodded decisively. Sergeant Ykindes readied his gas gun. "On my mark. Three . . . Two . . . One . . . Mark!"

With a heavy "phut," the tear gas canister launched from the gun and arched gracefully towards the middle of the workers. More canisters flew from four other locations. Tear gas was not generally recommended for use in enclosed spaces, and could be very dangerous—even lethal—in high concentrations, but the government soldiers were taking no chances with the weaponry arrayed against them.

The five canisters hit the ground nearly simultaneously in a ring around the smugglers and immediately began spewing thick, choking fumes. The workers and guards all reacted with varying speeds. Some, obviously confused, just stood and looked, not comprehending what was happening. Several whirled about and tried to detect from where the canisters had been fired. And some took off towards the doors and surrounding crates in a bid to escape.

They ran into various members of Alpha, Bravo, Charlie, Delta and Echo squads, who moved forward in near silence. Only Major Lantree bellowed, "Crown agents! Get down, now!" Having been officially identified, per regulations, the rest of the assault team didn't pull any punches. Fists and rifle butts flashed out with precise efficiency and men who had been struck did not get up. Outnumbered, at least inside the warehouse, by two to one, the soldiers were taking no chances. A number of smugglers did drop to the ground and cower, their hands behind their heads.

But other smugglers reacted by opening fire, though their aim was thrown off by their surprise and the effects of the growing clouds of tear gas. Still, Major Lantree saw two of his men go down, one with a bullet through the leg, the other struck in the chest. His body armour had probably stopped the projectile from penetrating, but the force of the blow was enough to wind him. The shooter, however, had no such protection and his torso sprouted red patches in three places as three soldiers took him down.

The air was filled with cries and gunfire, but Major Lantree observed that his troops were rapidly gaining the upper hand. The smugglers were too surprised, disorganised and increasingly incapacitated by the choking gas to put up an effective resistance. He saw a man crouched behind a crate, firing wildly at some nearby soldiers and took him out with a shot through the shoulder. Orders were to take as many prisoners as possible.

Suddenly the scene was much quieter. Most of the criminals were either dead or unconscious. Three members of Bravo squad were subduing a screaming gunman by sitting on him, literally, while another bound his hands and feet, and other smugglers were being restrained as well.

The Major keyed his mike. "Command, move–" His request for reinforcements and mop-up was cut short when he saw, standing on a catwalk above him, a lone gunman. The man's eyes were wide and his face white with panic as he brought up his assault rifle. Major Lantree cursed inside his own head for not checking the gantries and yelled a warning to the rest of his troops, even as he tried to bring his own weapon to bear. Time seemed to slow and he knew he was too late.

Suddenly, the crazed shooter's eyes widened even more as his feet slipped out from under him. That was the only way the Major could describe it. The gunman's feet shot out from under him as if he was in an old movie and had stepped on a banana peel. His finger tightened reflexively on the trigger, but the shots flew harmlessly towards the roof of the warehouse. Falling backward, the gunman's head cracked into the catwalk's rail and he slumped to the gantry floor.

Major Lantree suppressed a disbelieving sigh of relief as he barked an order to his soldiers to keep an eye on the catwalks for further shooters. He felt a sudden desire to offer up a prayer of thanks to The Angel or whoever had saved his ass just now. He put that on hold for a few moments while he completed his earlier aborted transmission. "Command, move in."

A minute later, more gas-masked troops were pouring in through the doors, assisting in subduing the prisoners and providing medical aid to

chapter seventeen

soldiers and criminals alike. The Major finally breathed a sigh of relief when he saw that all of his soldiers appeared to have made it through the operation alive, if not quite unscathed. He was still tense and alert, though, adrenaline quickening his reactions, when a scratching sound behind him amongst the crates sent him whirling around, gun automatically aiming.

He relaxed slightly when he saw that it was only a small grey cat, obviously a stray from its bedraggled fur, sneezing and coughing from the slowly dissipating tear gas. Though he was not a cat person, the Major felt sympathy for the poor creature. A shout from a group of Customs agents near the trucks distracted him momentarily and when he looked back, the cat was gone.

Shrugging, Major Lantree turned and jogged over to the trucks, where the agents had opened one of the boxes the smugglers had been loading. Though their expressions were hard to read through the gas masks, their body language screamed surprise.

When he got close enough to see into the box, the Major understood.

There were no drugs inside the crate. Instead, neatly packed inside were ten 7.62 mm light machine guns. Major Lantree's gaze roved over the dozens of other boxes that had been in the process of being loaded and despite–or perhaps because of–his years of military experience, felt fear ice his stomach.

&ə; &ə; &ə; &ə; &ə;

Evelynne rang the doorbell again and mused on just how domestic it felt. Prior to Ally's purchase of her house, the princess had never rung a doorbell in her life and this was the second time she had done so at this same house. It made her feel . . . normal.

There was still no answer and Evelynne frowned. Turning to her companion, she asked, "I did schedule this visit, right? This is the right day?"

Her brother, Patrick, was not wearing his monk's robe but instead a simple, casual outfit. The only marks of his calling were the rosary beads and cross around his neck. "I don't know, Evy. You're the one who arranged everything. I just came along for the ride."

Evelynne shifted the bouquet of flowers in her arms and frowned at the door again. "Well, it is Friday and I'm sure I arranged this visit for today. I–"

The front door suddenly opened to reveal the house's owner. As before, Ally was dressed very casually, but this time she seemed to have taken it to even further extremes. Again she was wearing track pants and a tee shirt, but these were liberally soaked with water. Ally's hair was also damp and a smudge of soap marked her cheek.

"Hi, Evelynne," she said. "Sorry about that. I was just dealing with something." She rubbed her arm, where the princess could see a long scratch. Noticing Evelynne's brother, Ally exclaimed, "Patrick! I wasn't expecting to see you. Please, come on in."

"Thank you."

Now that she was closer, Evelynne could see that, in addition to her dishevelled appearance, Ally's eyes were red and puffy and she kept sniffling. "Ally, are you all right?"

"What? Oh, yeah, I'm fine. This just started last night. I think I ran into something," the other woman replied vaguely. "I must be allergic to something. I also haven't got a lot of sleep the last few nights." Changing the subject, she asked, "What, no bodyguards?"

"Not inside," Evelynne answered. "Actually, Uncle Arthur and Maïda are enjoying a little quality time on their own." She giggled. "I think they're cute. Anyway, this is a purely social call and I guess they trust you with us."

"Actually, they trust you with *me*," Patrick interrupted, "since I am a man of the cloth, after all, and therefore incorruptible. They're likely hoping I'll be able to keep you away from Evelynne." He grinned widely as both women blushed furiously.

"Riiight," Ally said, recovering her composure. "Well, come on into the living room."

This time the lounge was clean and tidy. The princess and her brother took seats on the couch and Evelynne held out the flowers to their hostess. "Here you go," she said. "These are for you."

"Thank you," Ally said. "You know, *someone* has been sending me flowers every few days for the last two weeks." She cast her gaze meaningfully around the room to the blossoms that seemed to take up every available space, before returning it to Evelynne. "They've all been sent anonymously. You wouldn't happen to know anything about this, would you?"

"Me?" Evelynne asked innocently. "Now how would I know anything about that?"

"Well, come to think of it," Patrick said, "James the Groundskeeper has been complaining lately about the thief who seems to be making off with his favourite blooms. Maybe Evmmph–"

Evelynne clapped a hand over his mouth. "What Patrick means to say is that he knows nothing about it. Right, Patrick?" She used her hand to force his head up and down. "See? I thought so."

Ally laughed as she observed her friends playing and wondered for a moment what it would have been like to have a sibling. Then she remembered that while Evelynne had a brother, she had lost a parent and decided that she would be happy with what she had.

chapter seventeen

"Well, while you two sleuths study this mystery," Ally said, "I'll go and put these into some water. Then I'll just go and get–" She was abruptly cut off by a mournful howl coming from somewhere upstairs. Her guests started. "Oh, hell, Cassie! I'll be right back." She hurried out of the lounge towards the stairs.

Evelynne and Patrick looked at each other. "Cassie? Does Ally usually have other women in her house?" Patrick asked.

His sister shrugged. "Not that I know of. I mean, last time I visited there was Mila'a, but Ally really isn't the type." Now that she knew there was nothing serious between the other two women, Evelynne was able to speak her rival's name without jealousy. Much jealousy, anyway.

"Well, whoever it is," Patrick said, wincing as another yell echoed through the house, "she is not happy."

Well, I wouldn't be happy if Ally was ignoring me, Evelynne thought. *I don't think I'd shout like that, though. Although it's certainly attention getting.*

Fortunately for her guests' curiosity, Ally re-entered a few minutes later, carrying a small object wrapped in a towel. Walking closer to her guests, Ally said, "Evelynne, Patrick, I'd like you to meet Cassie. Cassie, these are Evelynne and Patrick."

For a brief, completely irrational moment, Evelynne thought that Ally was carrying a baby, but then reason returned and informed her that, among other things, the bundle was too small to be even a newborn. This conclusion was reinforced when the princess managed to peek into the towel and saw a tiny, triangular and above all fur covered face. The cat was obviously little more than a kitten and currently a very unhappy one at that. Wide yellow eyes set beneath a pair of enormous ears looked out indignantly from a grey face. The cat's fur was wet and sticking out in clumps, giving it a thoroughly pathetic appearance.

Predictably, Evelynne cooed, "Awwww. She's so adorable! I didn't know you got a cat."

"I, uh, found her yesterday," Ally replied. "Be careful, I don't know how she'll react to strangers."

The warning was unnecessary, as Cassie, obviously deciding that she had had enough of being wrapped in a cold, wet towel, squirmed free and launched herself at Evelynne's shoulders. The princess yelped as tiny claws dug in for purchase, but the kitten possessed excellent balance and was soon sniffing her hair and ears.

Evelynne giggled. "Well, hello, Cassie." She turned her eyes back to Ally. "Is that her full name?"

"Actually, I decided on Cassiopeia," Ally replied, "but that's a bit of a mouthful, so 'Cassie' for short."

Patrick was leaning forward to examine the cat, which was still finding Evelynne's hair fascinating and he sniffed gently. "Ally, I don't mean to insult your friend, but she smells rather strongly." In fact, his eyes were beginning to water from the odour.

"I know," Ally said wryly. "I think she must have, um, come into contact with something. I think that might be what's got me all stuffy. I've been bathing her all morning."

As if she could understand, Cassie shot Ally a baleful look and proceeded to determinedly make a nest for herself on Evelynne's shoulders.

"Well, we're just going to have to buy some air freshener then, aren't we?" Evelynne asked, addressing her new occupant. Speaking to Ally again, she said, "In this case, how about if we stay around here today? I know we were supposed to go to the beach, but with that pool you have in your back yard, this could be just as good."

"If you don't mind," Ally agreed diffidently. "I really wasn't looking forward to leaving a new cat here on its own."

"No problem at all," Patrick said. "In that case, I'll go and tell the Guards outside and bring in our swimsuits and equipment."

Ally and Evelynne suddenly pictured each other in a bathing suit.

"Swimsuits?" Ally asked weakly.

༄ ༄ ༄ ༄ ༄

Ally stood in front of the full-length mirror set in her closet door and eyed herself critically. The simple green one-piece swimming suit hugged her body revealingly and she was painfully aware of just how little there was to reveal. She didn't exactly fill the suit in any kind of sexy or alluring way. The knowledge that Evelynne was changing into her own suit in the bathroom down the hall brought with it the image of her friend's much more voluptuous figure, emphasising Ally's own perceived inadequacies. She wondered why she was so bothered by her own appearance.

Because despite everything I've tried to do, a part of me still hopes she'll find me attractive, Ally answered herself.

Ally had in fact tried to put her own attraction to the princess behind her and had partially succeeded, especially when they had been largely out of contact for two weeks. The diversion with Mila'a had helped and Ally had found herself thinking of a possible future relationship—one that might actually work—with cautious optimism. Then Evelynne had come back and she found all of her carefully constructed emotional distance evaporating like mist, as the princess insinuated herself relentlessly back into her life.

chapter seventeen

Though Evelynne had been too busy to visit Ally's house since that morning two weeks ago, she had called at least every couple of days just to talk and catch up. Due to her own "extracurricular activities" Ally had missed a few of those calls and had returned home one afternoon to find a brand new answering machine waiting for her. That had not been the only gift. Several new pieces of art now hung from her walls and a signed first edition of *The Lord of the Rings* rested on her bookshelf. It had all become a little overwhelming and when she had hesitantly spoken to Evelynne about it, the princess had apologised and promised to restrain herself. In spite of which, the flowers had kept on coming.

While Evelynne had not had a chance to come to Ally's house, the taller woman had been invited to the Summer Palace several times. During those visits, they had found themselves slipping easily back into their old friendship. There was something else added to the equation, though, some quirk or distraction in Evelynne's manner that had not been there before. Ally had firmly suppressed the impulse to find out what was behind it more directly and had settled for simply enjoying her friend's solicitous company.

The thought of company reminded Ally that she was supposed to be the hostess today. She looked in the mirror once more, trying to see what Evelynne would see, when, without warning, the attack hit her.

Several minutes later, Ally found herself huddled on the floor, the soundless taunts and jeers fading from her mind. She fought to get her breathing back under control and realised that her already irritated eyes were streaming with fresh tears.

"Shit," Ally cursed softly. She was beginning to get worried. This had been the third panic attack in as many months; before coming to Atlantl she had suffered perhaps as many in a year. She had thought that she had dealt with and buried the incident and wondered what had changed to bring it back to the surface.

She still had guests to attend to, so she got back to her feet. Wrapping a large towel about her waist, the young woman scrubbed the tears from her face. Hopefully, Evelynne and Patrick would think that her redder eyes were simply a continuation of her "allergic reaction" and not the result of several minutes spent huddled, crying, on the floor.

& & & & &

Ally lounged in a comfortable deck chair, enjoying soaking up the warmth of the sun's rays. Despite being early November, some quirk of climate caused this area of Avalon to stay much warmer than the rest of the island. Even in late fall there were occasional days of twenty-five degree weather. Today was such a day.

With a sigh, the young woman shifted slightly to maximise her exposure to the sunshine. She always felt as though she had more energy after a day in the sun and didn't know if the solar radiation was actually feeding her abilities or whether the effect was purely psychological. Right now, though, she had no desire to experiment to find out and simply let herself relax even more bonelessly.

Splashing from the pool drew Ally's attention and she looked in that direction to see Evelynne in the pool splashing water at her new cat. The kitten would dodge away from the spray, then turn and bound back to the pool's edge and meow until the princess splashed once more. Finally Cassie miscalculated a dodge and caught a steam of water full in the face. With a yowl of protest, the cat leapt back and glared accusingly at her playmate before sitting down to wash herself.

Evelynne laughed and Ally thought again just how appealing her friend was, especially dressed in a blue two piece swimming suit. Ally had been noticing the suit–and the body beneath it–all afternoon and sometimes, if she hadn't known better, she could have sworn princess was deliberately flaunting her body to attract Ally's attention.

Whether it was intentional or not, it was working and Ally turned away as she caught herself staring. Turning her head to look at her other companion, she laughed at the sight of Patrick, wearing baggy swimming trunks, lounging in the chair next to her, his nose coloured bright yellow with sunscreen.

Patrick turned his head in Ally's direction at her laugh. "What?"

"Oh, I was just thinking of how you looked. No offence, but you really don't look like a monk right now."

"Oh? And what should a monk look like?"

"Oh, you know. Robes, staff, one of those big hoods. In a church somewhere mumbling and communing with God."

"Ah, I see. In my case, I think it is just as effective to commune with God where I am right now. If I was, as you put it, mumbling in a church somewhere, I would have lost this opportunity to enjoy God's beautiful creation on this day." He swept an arm to encompass the entire world.

"Well, good for you," Ally said. She paused a moment. "You know, there was something I've been wanting to ask you but I'm not sure how to say it."

"As the Good Book says, 'Be swift to hear, slow to speak, slow to wrath: For the wrath of man worketh not the righteousness of God.' So speak and I will be swift to hear."

chapter seventeen

Ally hesitated. "In a way, that was what I wanted to ask you about. You're a monk–a Christian–and . . . I was wondering what you thought of me . . . liking women."

Patrick smiled benignly. "Before I answer, could I ask why you want to know?"

"Well, if it was just you, I probably wouldn't care," Ally replied honestly. "But you are Evelynne's brother and she is my friend. You're obviously important to her and I guess I just wanted to know if me being friends with her was going to come between you. The last thing I want is to push you apart."

"A good answer. And I can put your mind at ease, at least in that respect. I personally have no problem with your homosexuality. I cannot speak for every member of my Order, of course, but I believe most of my Brothers feel similarly. I belong to the religious arm of the Order of the Illuminated Word. We have an attached Knightly Order." Ally nodded, remembering her discussion on the Orders with the King. "The Order's Charter is to translate the Word of God, whether that Word be written in the Bible, the Quran, the Hindu *Devas* or anywhere else, so that His children may understand Him more clearly. I am personally taking part in a project dedicated to translating the Bible into the modern languages from its earliest original form, usually Hebrew or Greek. We wish to provide the most accurate possible translation from the Words that God spoke through His prophets. However, we are also aware of the fact that much of His Word may only be understood in its historical context, so we are also writing a commentary based on the known history of the area and how it relates to the Bible. For example, is the prohibition against homosexuality–or the one against shellfish, for that matter–based in a more earthly plane, such as perhaps some outbreak of disease?"

"That sounds fascinating."

"Oh, it is. Even just going through the various editions of the Bible and examining their differences is interesting. Not to mention sometimes very amusing. For example, one edition printed in 1631 had to be recalled, as a single word had been omitted as a typographical error. That Bible unfortunately had a Seventh Commandment which read, 'Thou shalt commit adultery.'"

Ally burst into laughter. "Oh, no! You're kidding!"

"Unfortunately, no. But that example alone justifies the work my Order is doing. What if that typo had been missed? How many other mistakes, deliberate or accidental, have occurred throughout the centuries? How much has God's Word been distorted?"

"I understand and wish you good luck. When you're done, be sure to put a copy aside for me-eeek!" Ally squealed and jumped as something cold and wet dripped onto the exposed part of her chest. She looked up in shock to see Evelynne standing next to her, a bemused expression on her face and holding a dripping arm over Ally's body.

Satisfied that she had gained Ally's attention, Evelynne dropped her arm. "You two were talking so seriously I had to see what was going on," she explained. "So what were you talking about?"

"Oh, Ally was just concerned that I was going to try her for heresy and burn her at the stake," Patrick said airily. "I told her I was still considering it."

"Sure, Patrick," Ally shot back. "Right." Shifting her attention, she looked around the poolside. "Do you happen to know where my cat went?"

Before anyone could reply, Cassie jumped up onto the end of Ally's deck chair and sat down, looking about with a curious gaze. Ally looked down at the cat between her legs and blushed. She shot a look up at Evelynne and saw that the princess was red also.

Patrick cleared his throat, and Ally needed no telepathic ability to know what he was about to say. Before he could speak, she whipped a finger in his direction. "Don't say it," she ordered. "Don't even think it."

The young monk grinned insolently. "What?" he asked innocently. "All I was going to say was that your pussy . . . cat is right there." He pointed between Ally's legs and laughed uproariously as both Ally and Evelynne turned the colour of ripe tomatoes.

chapter eighteen

Evelynne walked down the hallway of the Royal Palace in Jamaz with a deep scowl on her face. "*K'kela'i*," she swore. "Bastards."

A passing servant looked up in surprise, saw the princess' bad mood, and hurried away before her displeasure could spill over onto an innocent bystander. Her Highness had a reputation for an even temper and was friendly towards even the lowest servant, but she was still the Heir and it behoved lesser mortals to treat her with care.

The princess frowned again, looking once more at the newspaper–as if the rag could claim that title–in her hands. Its headline had not changed since the last time she had glared at it and the words "DYKE KNIGHT" screamed at her in large font across the top of the front page. What followed was a story–an apt word, as it was largely a work of fiction–digging into Ally's past with a complete lack of decorum or relation to reality. If anyone were to take the article seriously, the young woman in question was the greatest sexual deviant since Caligula. The writer had been careful to put things in terms of innuendo, with no statements which could be defined as libellous, but a few actual quotes from Annie–the only actual lover Ally had ever had–taken obviously out of context gave the story a false sense of authenticity. Ally's supposed relationship with the princess was also spared no scrutiny–if only of a highly imaginative kind.

Evelynne swore again, then sighed and tried to relax. Fortunately, the paper was one of Britain's more sensational publications, with little solid reputation amongst serious journalists, but it was only one symptom of the larger problem. A number of more reputable journals worldwide had taken Ally's sexuality as a central focus of their stories, if slightly less sensationally. Instead of concentrating more fully on her actual achievements and personality, they had taken this one topic and discussed it to exhaustion. It had not helped that numerous gay rights groups had seized on her as a kind of symbol.

When Ally had learned of the articles, she had shrugged and tried to ignore it, but Evelynne knew she was hurt and embarrassed by the attention being paid to something she considered one of the most private and intimate aspects of her life. Since then Evelynne had avoided bringing the more offensive stories to her friend's attention. Fortunately, there were enough articles that mentioned Ally's orientation only in passing, if at all, to lend some balance. It had become worse in the last week leading up to Ally's knighting. With the ceremony taking place tomorrow, the Canadian and Atlantlan newspapers were speaking of little else.

Evelynne sighed again. *Oh, well. There's nothing I can do about it now anyway,* she thought. In a few days things would hopefully calm down a bit and she would speak to her newly elected Advisors about obtaining some subtle revenge over the worst of the offenders. So far Mary Ogden, her Public Relations Advisor, had displayed a wicked deviousness in dealing with members of the press and seemed to enjoy putting one over on them. It boded well for the future working relationship between the princess and her Advisor.

Evelynne stopped, realising that her musings had led her to the door to Ally's room. Noticing that she was still carrying the offending newspaper, she looked around for a place to put it and finally slipped it behind a large potted plant nearby. There was nothing to be done about it now and the last thing Ally needed was another detail to make her more nervous.

Smoothing her hands over her formal blue tunic and trousers, Evelynne knocked.

"Come in!"

The princess opened the door to reveal Ally sitting in a chair before a mirror, while Maïda put the finishing touches on her hair. It was much simpler than the elegant style she had worn to the banquet, but since she would have no chance to fix it for the next twelve hours, the lady-in-waiting had insisted on doing something to at least keep it in place.

"Your Highness," Maïda greeted, not stopping in her task. "You are just in time. I will be done just about . . . now." With a final brush, she stepped back, satisfied.

Ally turned her head back and forth in the mirror, examining the result. It was a fairly simple style, dropping straight down the sides of her face, her hair's natural slight wave giving it volume. The back of her neck was clear and Maïda had promised she would be glad of the exposure before the night was over. Nodding to herself, Ally stood and grinned at Evelynne. "Hey, Evelynne," she said. "I didn't think I'd see you before we got started. Are you sure you're allowed to see me?"

Evelynne smiled back. "I'm knighting you, Ally, not marrying you." She laughed when Ally flushed and then looked her friend up and down. "You look good," the princess declared.

Ally laughed self-deprecatingly. "I'm dressed in grey pyjamas," she protested mildly. "It's not exactly the height of fashion."

chapter eighteen

"They're not pyjamas, they're penitent's clothes. Besides, you make anything look good."

Ally flushed again. Evelynne had been doing that a lot lately; compliments, gifts and casual touches came frequently. At first she had almost panicked, thinking that her friend might be flirting with her, but had then firmly squashed the hope that arose and decided that it was simply part of Evelynne's outgoing personality. So she had relaxed, and had begun to hesitantly return the favours.

"No, I'm wearing grey pyjamas," Ally insisted playfully. "You're the one who looks . . . elegant."

"You both look beautiful," Maïda interjected firmly. "And I am older than both of you put together, so don't argue."

"Yes, Maïda," both young women said meekly.

The ensuing laughter was cut off by another knock on the door. Maïda moved to open it and blushed when Sir Arthur appeared on the other side. The budding relationship between Evelynne's lady-in-waiting and her Guard had been great fun to watch, especially when the couple were trying to remain discreet. The Guard controlled himself better and said formally, "Milady." He turned his attention to the avidly watching young women. "Your Highness. *Ishta* Tretiak. It is time to go."

Ally took in a deep breath and let it out shakily. Evelynne took her hands and looked up into her friend's eyes. "You'll be fine," she said confidently.

"I will. Although you don't suppose we could just go back to the Summer Palace and play *Vei'Chel* in front of a warm fire, do you? I'd let you win."

The princess laughed. "I always win anyway. Now go. Later we can play to our hearts' content." She gave Ally a little push in Sir Arthur's direction. "I'll come by and see you later on."

"You don't have to," Ally protested. "It's going to be late."

"I know I don't have to. I want to." Evelynne hesitated and then wrapped Ally in a fierce hug before pulling her down for a lingering kiss on the cheek. "You'll be fine," she whispered again. "I believe in you."

☙ ☙ ☙ ☙ ☙

Ally looked around the chapel to which Sir Arthur had led her. It was an ecumenical place of worship and in their attempt to make the hall into a place of reflection, meditation and prayer acceptable to people from all religions, its decorators had abstained from recognisable religious images and stuck to geometrical shapes and designs. The chapel was covered from top to bottom in both simple and complex patterns. Incredibly intricate multi-coloured mandala-like drawings shared space with the most basic geometric shapes: squares, circles and triangles. In contrast, the entire back wall was painted a pure and brilliant white, with the result that even amongst the riot of form and colour there remained an area of calm; a place to rest the mind.

Finishing her inspection, Ally turned back to Sir Arthur. "It's an interesting room," she said.

"Indeed." The Guard smiled. "There is a bathroom through there if you need it," he continued, pointing to an almost invisible door in the wall. "You may select any area of the room and move about freely. The only injunction is that you remain reasonably silent. If you meditate by chanting, singing or dancing, please keep it within a reasonable volume."

"Not a problem. Anything else?"

"Not at this time. I will check in on you from time to time." Sir Arthur bowed. "*Ishta* Alleandre Tiffany Tretiak, may your musings be enlightening," he pronounced formally.

Ally bowed back awkwardly, and he turned to take up his appointed position by the door. As her Nominator, the experienced knight was supposed to guard Ally while she meditated on her own soul and worthiness to become a knight herself. The vigil would last no less than twelve hours, until dawn the next morning, and theoretically the candidate was forbidden from sleeping, though Ally had been assured that unless she actually started snoring nobody would object.

Ignoring Sir Arthur's presence, the young woman moved farther into the room. A large cushion was set in front of the altar at the far end and she decided it was as good a place as any to sit for the time being. Carefully lowering herself to the ground, Ally crossed her legs and set her cane within reach. She let out a heavy sigh and tried to calm herself and lessen the tension over what was going to happen the next day. *Well, I have all night to rest and relax,* she thought. *On the other hand, I have all night to fret and worry! Hmm. Kind of a toss-up.*

With a mental chuckle, she decided to just make the most of the time alone. She was supposed to be meditating, so she thought that might be a good place to start. Taking a deep breath, Ally closed her eyes and consciously focussed on relaxing her tense muscles. Her back ached mildly, but she concentrated on managing the pain and it quickly vanished from her conscious mind.

As relaxed as she could be for now, Ally took stock of herself and nodded, pleased by the results. Even with this shallow introspection, she could tell that much of the tension and near claustrophobia she had been feeling two months ago was gone. The retreat from public scrutiny had been the

chapter eighteen

best thing she could have done. Though she had missed Evelynne, the rest had done her a world of good.

Putting thoughts of the princess and their attendant worries from her mind for the moment, Ally next focused her will, extending her perceptions outward, the exercise relatively easy in the calm and quiet of the room. She did not try for full vision of the area, settling for reading the subtle fluxes of energy that permeated the room. Sir Arthur was the most prominent and as Ally watched, his mind settled into a light meditative state of its own. She wasn't surprised. If he was going to stay up with her all night, he would need all the help he could get. With the knight's presence burning brightly in her mind, Ally didn't extend her mind any farther outward, but focused more closely on the immediate vicinity. Slowly the less intense life forms were brought into focus. In various corners, spiders that had escaped the cleaners pulsed softly with life. A small colony of ants bustled within a wall, and the floor under the altar was home to at least six mice. Actually—no, one of those was a group of baby mice, bundled together so closely that their bright life forces seemed to merge. Pushing for a bit more resolution, Ally could feel the strain building in her mental workings. She was actually very pleased. She was rarely able to attain this level of clarity. As she worked, she slipped down another level and the world became truly alive. The bright auras of the animals seemed to grow, Sir Arthur becoming a brilliant beacon. On a lower level, the very air was teeming with the tiny lives of uncounted bacteria and the solid objects were coated with minute insects and mites. The two potted plants in the room were subtly but distinctly different, their vegetative life forces no less alive, but unquestionably alien to the animal lives in the room. Ally could even see a fungal infection afflicting one of them and marvelled that although it was a disease, the fungus was as alive as anything else.

She spent several long minutes revelling in the interplay of forces around her. Then, with a mental sigh of resignation, she slowly released the strain that was building and regretfully allowed her perceptions to contract back into their more normal range. There were a few moments of confusion as her mind readjusted to its regular parametres. *I have never gone that far before. I have to try that again. But not right now,* Ally concluded, registering the protests of her normal senses. *I need to get used to it first.*

Sitting back comfortably, she spent some time allowing her mind to drift, letting it process the experience. After a while, when she had regained her mental equilibrium, Ally reigned it back in with practised ease. *I'm supposed to be examining my soul tonight. That's something else I haven't done in . . . too long.*

Ally concentrated on the flow of energy through her body and her breath came slower and slower as she slipped into a deep meditative state.

☙ ☙ ☙ ☙ ☙

Evelynne opened the door as quietly as possible and slipped silently into the chapel. Sir Arthur turned, identified the intruder and smiled in greeting.

The princess looked around the room and saw her friend sitting cross-legged on the floor near the altar. It was after midnight and Ally was well into the fifth hour of her vigil. The young woman was sitting facing away from the door. Were it not for her upright posture, the princess might have thought she was sleeping. Still, she didn't stir as Evelynne came into the room.

On near silent feet, Evelynne moved closer to her bodyguard and whispered, "How is it going? Is she doing all right?"

"I believe so," Sir Arthur whispered back. "Although she has been like that for almost four hours. I checked and she does not seem to be asleep. She hasn't responded, though. You're welcome to try if you wish."

Nodding at him, Evelynne walked quietly to where Ally was seated on the floor. Coming around in front, the princess saw that Ally's eyes were closed and her breath was coming slowly and evenly.

"Ally?" she whispered softly. If her friend was indeed meditating or even if she was asleep, she did not want to disturb her. There was no response, not even a twitch, and Evelynne nodded before silently sitting down on the floor next to her friend. Encouraged by Ally's apparent obliviousness to the external world, she took the opportunity to study the calm features.

Ally's eyes were not moving under her eyelids. Whatever state she was in, it was not REM sleep. Evelynne's gaze moved to the rest of Ally's face, completely calm and relaxed. The princess had only seen such a lack of expression before when she managed to catch her friend asleep. Unlike the cliché, Ally did not really look younger when she was sleeping. Instead, her face took on an ageless quality, as though she was a marble statue carved by some ancient Greek master. It wasn't cold like stone, however, but possessed an incredible vitality, as if a sun was hidden just under the shield of her skin.

While the other woman almost always looked calm and collected, Evelynne had learned to read the subtle changes in her face and posture. Prior to Ally's retreat from the Palace she had been strained and pale, as if the pressure had been eating her away from within. *Which it was,* Evelynne mused guiltily. *I can't believe I didn't see it then. Actually, I did see it, but I just didn't want her to leave. If she hadn't insisted, she'd probably still be there, putting a brave face on everything like she always does.* The princess had to admit that the time in seclusion had done wonders for Ally's state of mind. Now there was almost no trace of her earlier strain. Earlier in the evening she had been understandably nervous, but she had obviously used the time to replenish her reserves.

chapter eighteen

Relaxed, Ally was beautiful, Evelynne thought. There was a softness to her features that often turned to wariness in the presence of strangers. Right now, like this, she looked appealingly vulnerable. Evelynne slowly became aware as she watched, however, that in spite of her friend's relaxed and open posture, there was still an undercurrent of strength and power running through her. With sudden certainty, Evelynne knew that if any danger threatened, Ally would be up and reacting before it was even though the door.

It was an unsettling dichotomy and the princess became a little uncomfortable, not sure of just how conscious Ally was of her staring. Standing, she hesitated and then bent down to whisper in Ally's ear. "I believe in you." It wasn't exactly what she wanted to say, but in the circumstances she thought it was enough.

There was no reaction to her statement, and Evelynne spent another moment watching her friend, then turned and quietly left the room.

       ҩ ҩ ҩ ҩ ҩ

Ally floated deep within her own mind, almost completely unaware of her physical surroundings. She was vaguely conscious of a presence nearby, someone very important, but there was no urgency or danger coming from the source. Rather, it was warm and friendly and loving. It did not stay long, moving away after a few minutes and Ally was aware of a muted pang as she felt it go. Still, it seemed to leave behind some kind of echo, as though part of it had stayed.

Once she was sure the presence had left, Ally turned her attention inward again. She looked out over the landscape of her own mind, perceiving it in ways for which there were simply no words. She knew that once she arose from her trance, the specific memories of her experiences here would fade like dreams, possibly converted into a more symbolic form by a consciousness lacking the facility to completely comprehend what was happening. For now, though, her perceptions were clear and understandable, as simple and natural as seeing.

As she inspected her mind, Ally became aware that it had changed since she had last gone this far into a meditative state. That had been over a year ago. *I really should have done this sooner.* The basic structure had changed little. A year's worth of memories and experiences had been added and a few had vanished, victims of time. The thought-forms of her special abilities were easily found and responded with varying degrees of alacrity when she stimulated them softly, not enough to activate them. A couple had apparently merged with the more mundane sections of her mind. *Hmm. I wonder if that means they're more natural now, like walking and talking. I know that some things I hardly even have to concentrate on any more.*

Satisfied that those parts were healthy and even thriving, she moved on to others. Not all of the experiences of the last year had been good ones. She saw the mental and emotional wound of her break up with Annie. It was well healed, however. Linked with it now were memories of happy times and love, and also a feeling of genuine friendship and affection. Ally was pleased. *I love you, Annie.*

Moving back, Ally's awareness impinged on another emotional scar. Disturbed, she examined it closer. It was deep within memories of the past and she recognised the traumatic experience that spawned her panic attacks. It had previously been buried under shields of logic and willpower, carefully protected from exposure. Those shields had not always held in the past, but the ones Ally examined now were somehow weaker, more brittle.

Not quite sure how she was doing it, Ally reached out and touched the unhealed wound.

Suddenly she was back in that grade six body, watching the taunts and laughter, feeling the cruel amusement and contempt. With a wrench, she pulled herself out of the memory, nearly losing the trance. For an unknown length of time she worked on slowing her breathing and heart rate and smoothing the now-restless surface of her mind. Finally she was calm once more.

What the hell happened there? I've never been able to do that deliberately before. Tentatively, Ally reached for another area of memory and she was suddenly listening and seeing with perfect clarity as Evelynne explained the rules of *Vei'Chel* to her. She reflexively tried to speak to her friend, but found herself unable to move. *Of course, it's only a memory.* Removing herself, she marvelled at the new ability.

Then she paused. Though impressive in itself, this development didn't seem to have anything to do with why or how the shield over the trauma had been breached. Examining more closely, she became aware that other areas were affected too, as though a virus had spread within her mind. It did not seem malignant, though. On the contrary, it was strong and bright and familiar somehow.

Then she saw it. Ally was surprised that she hadn't seen it before, but even in the unconventional dimensions of her mind it was almost on another plane. A link, ethereal and strong as spider's silk, ran through all her protections to anchor itself deep in some primordial realm of thought. And it was coming from outside.

chapter eighteen

Hesitantly, reverently, Ally reached out and touched the link and instantly knew its source.

Evelynne.

For a brief instant, Ally nearly panicked, thinking that somehow the princess had deliberately entered her mind. It was possible, she knew, for a suitably gifted person to do so, though doing it without the subject's knowledge and consent was hellishly difficult. Immediately, though, the suspicion faded. Evelynne would never do such a thing, even if she could and besides, the link was recognisably an unintentional creation.

And it went two ways. Now that she knew what to look for, Ally could see part of her own mind pushing outward in the fathomless direction of Evelynne's mind. Ally was tempted to follow, to see what she found at the other end, but restrained herself. *Not now. I need to figure out what's going on first. I also don't know how long it will take. Or what time it is right now, for that matter.* Perceptions of time were different in this internal realm. Minutes could seem like hours and vice versa.

As she reluctantly began the journey up to a more conventional state of consciousness, Ally knew that she would definitely have to re-evaluate her relationship with Evelynne as soon as possible.

☙ ☙ ☙ ☙ ☙

Evelynne watched the great doors of the Royal Throne Room swing open majestically. She was sitting on her throne on the stepped dais at the head of the chamber, just below and to the right of the other two thrones, which were occupied by King Jad and Queen Cleo. Both rulers were dressed in their full formal attire, as was the Heir, crowns of state upon their brows. This huge chamber had been the official ceremonial site of the al-Heru/de-Molay Diarchy for over five hundred years and it fairly reeked of decorum. Large stone pillars supported the arched roof and the walls were hung with knightly blazons. Not every knight in the Realm was represented, as the blazons of most were hung in the Hall of their Sponsoring Noble or Order. In this room were only the shields of those personally sworn to the Kings and Queens of Atlantl.

Today another would be added here. This one, though, would share a certain characteristic with only two others out of the dozens lining the walls and the princess suppressed a surge of nervousness at the thought of the controversy which would certainly erupt from it. She was surprised that it had not leaked out sooner, but those who had actually constructed, engraved and embroidered the new blazon had obviously taken their oaths of secrecy very seriously. *Too late now,* Evelynne thought. Although she would not have changed it if she could have. Words spoken five months ago in absolute privacy would finally be revealed to the world.

The princess was shaken out of her musings by the murmur that arose from the crowd of Nobles and guests who had assembled at this hour just after dawn to witness the proceedings. Discreetly placed television cameras would record the events for posterity.

The young woman they were all waiting for walked slowly and solemnly through the doors. She was trailed by her Nominator in full regalia, his immaculate tabard proudly displaying the red cross on white background of the Order of the Temple of Jerusalem. Sir Arthur's sheathed sword was held stiffly across his wide body. He kept in perfect step with his Candidate.

Ally was still dressed in the simple loose grey tunic and trousers of a suitably humble Candidate. Her feet were bare. A virgin Candidate would have worn white but Ally had blushingly but firmly declined. In her own opinion, she was hardly a virgin and though Evelynne had felt a pang of jealousy, the princess had acquiesced without demur.

As Ally walked slowly closer, the princess wondered how her friend was bearing up under the intense scrutiny of the onlookers. Looking at her more closely, Evelynne almost gasped aloud.

The hesitant, awkward Ally was gone. Here walked a woman of immense grace and poise. Dignity and power seemed to roll off her in waves and her feet hardly seemed to be touching the ground. Even her glasses gave her a wise and powerful look. Evelynne could only stare as the proud form of her friend came closer. *Isis, Ally,* she thought. *What in the Duat did you do last night?*

For her part, Ally felt like a changed woman. She experienced no discomfort from the watching crowd. Instead she thought, *Okay, you want to see me? Here I am. I am as good as any of you.* She could feel a thread of power running through her and could not truly tell if she was controlling it or if it was controlling her. Either way, it seemed to be having some effect, as every face in the crowd appeared impressed. She had no idea how long it would last and knew she would revert to her old self eventually, but while it lasted she was going to enjoy it.

Ally looked up and saw Evelynne seated on her throne at the other end of the chamber. Now that she knew it was there, she could feel the connection between them clearly. *Even if you never love me, Evelynne, we will always be connected.*

As Evelynne watched Ally come towards her, she felt an odd sensation of dizziness. It was similar to a feeling she had experienced the night before when Evelynne could have sworn she heard Ally say something to her

chapter eighteen

and had found herself going back to the chapel to see if she was all right. However, the other woman didn't appear to have moved. The Princess shook her head slightly as the dizziness faded.

Finally, the long walk ended and Ally stopped before the dais, catching a glimpse of her parents, Chorus and a few other family members nearby. Dropping to one knee, she bowed her head.

King Jad and Queen Cleo both rose. "Good Knight, whom do you bring before us?" the King asked, his voice carrying clearly across the room.

"Your Majesty, I bring before you Alleandre Tiffany Tretiak, daughter of Catherine and William Tretiak of the Dominion of Canada."

"And for what purpose do you bring this woman before us?" Queen Cleo asked.

"Your Majesty, so that she might be considered by your august selves to be raised to the spur of Knighthood."

"And what deeds has she performed that she might be worthy of this honour?" asked the King.

"Your Majesty, when the Heir to our Realm was set upon by cruel and cowardly foes who did seek to end her life unjustly, Alleandre Tretiak did set her own self betwixt the Heir and her attackers. Alleandre Tretiak was sorely wounded, and spent days near unto death. She was no subject of yours, yet she did act as a great and noble warrior in your service."

The Diarchs nodded gravely. "Is there a Noble of the Realm who will vouch for the honour of Alleandre Tretiak and Sponsor her and be as Lord or Lady unto her?"

Evelynne stood. "Your Majesties, I, Evelynne Sophia al-Heru deMolay, Crown Princess and Heir to the Throne of Atlantl, a Noble of the Realm, gladly Sponsor Alleandre Tretiak. For it was mine own life she saved and I can well vouch for her honour and courage."

King Jad spoke to Ally. "Alleandre Tiffany Tretiak, you have been Nominated to the spur by the goodly Knight Sir Arthur Ramirez. Her Royal Highness Evelynne Sophia al-Heru deMolay has Sponsored you. Are these goodly persons acceptable in your eyes?"

Ally's voice was clear. "Your Majesty, I would be honoured to be Nominated by Sir Arthur and Sponsored by Her Highness Evelynne deMolay."

"Is there any goodly man or woman of the Land who does know some reason why Alleandre Tretiak should not receive this honour?" This time the King addressed the assembled crowd. There was no response.

"Then we hereby find you worthy of the spur of knighthood, Alleandre Tiffany Tretiak." At a gesture from the King, a servant stepped forward bearing a sheathed sword, which the King took. Together the King and Queen descended the steps of the dais, gathering the princess as they went. Sir Arthur bowed and stepped back, leaving Ally alone before them. King Jad turned and formally presented the sword to Evelynne.

The sword resembled a Japanese *katana*, curved and sharp along one edge. Unlike a *katana*, the blade flared out, so that it was wider at the tip than the base. The pommel and scabbard were decorated in a style reminiscent of both Mayan and ancient Egyptian art. It was, fittingly, a new weapon, crafted by Reen K'Martis, one of only two Master Swordsmiths still remaining in Atlantl and one of perhaps a dozen worldwide. She had laboured over the blade for more than a year, since long before anyone in Atlantl had ever heard of Alleandre Tretiak and the weapon was a masterpiece of both artistry and functionality. Ally could attest to that, having seen it demonstrated by K'Martis—who was also one of the few Master Swordswomen in the world—at the blade's ritual blessing a few days earlier. The sword was the King's gift to Alleandre.

Now Evelynne unsheathed the sword and stood with both the blade and scabbard resting on her open palms. Ally reached up to touch them, accepting the princess' authority and mercy.

"Alleandre Tretiak, do you swear to obey and uphold the Laws of the Realm of Atlantl and the Ithikan Compact?"

"I do."

"Do you pledge allegiance and loyalty to the lawful Rulers of the Realm of Atlantl?"

"Insofar as my allegiance and loyalty to the Dominion of Canada and the leaders and rulers thereof allow, I do."

There was some muttering from the audience at the response, but it was generally accepted, since it came as no surprise.

"Do you accept me, Evelynne Sophia al-Heru deMolay, as your overlord and swear to obey my lawful commands and submit to my justice?"

This time Ally swallowed before she replied, but still spoke clearly, "I do."

"Do you swear to uphold the good, to protect the innocent, to be charitable and to work for the good of Atlantl and her people?"

"I do."

"Then I, Evelynne deMolay, do take you as my subject. I swear to abide by the Laws of the Realm and the Ithikan Compact in my dealings with you. I offer my shield and my justice in your defence against your enemies. Should you be hungry, I will feed you. Should you need shelter, I will provide it.

chapter eighteen

"I find you worthy of the spur of knighthood." Evelynne touched Ally on one shoulder with the sword and on the other with the scabbard. "Therefore, rise, Dame Alleandre Tiffany Tretiak and receive the honours that are your due."

Smiling, Ally rose to her feet. Evelynne grinned back and took her new subject's face in her hands to press a kiss on both cheeks. If they were slightly more lingering than was customary, nobody else noticed.

More servants came forward. They were carrying what looked like a very heavy white robe. The robe was actually covering a long tabard, which hung nearly to the floor. Special seams made it very easy to slip on, though it was utterly impractical for anything but this ceremony. It would be modified later for more general use. Soft shoes, complete with spurs, were brought forth and Evelynne herself placed them on Ally's feet. Then she stood once more and, with Ally, turned to face the hall.

"My Lords and Ladies, Dame Alleandre Tretiak!" Evelynne shouted.

As the assembly cheered—and Ally's parents cried—the princess slipped the white robe off Ally's shoulders, displaying her blazon for the first time. Simultaneously, a banner bearing her new coat of arms was unfurled above their heads.

The crowd cheered and applauded as the banner was revealed but as they took in its detail, the acclaim was replaced by a near unanimous indrawn breath and then a silence broken only by urgent mutters. For the first time since the ceremony began, Ally felt her composure begin to crack, as shock, confusion and disapproval flowed off the gathering in waves. She felt Evelynne stiffen beside her and a quick glance showed that the princess had drawn herself up proudly and defiantly. She wished she could ask what was happening, but settled for examining her new coat of arms out of the corner of her eye.

Ally was no expert on heraldry, but what she saw was a field of green at the top, while the bottom wedge-shaped area was a rich purple. Two silver triangles projected from the right and left sides toward the middle. Facing each other on the green background were two black catlike beasts supporting a golden ankh between them. In the middle of the purple field rested a red maple leaf. It was all probably very symbolic and meaningful, but Ally had only read a single, albeit large, book on the subject and so the bulk of the meaning passed her by.

The only symbols that were immediately obvious were the two animals flanking the shield: a rearing unicorn, native to Atlantl, faced a leaping orca, a common sight along the west coast of Canada. Together they spoke of homelands, new and old, and the support that both offered to her. The rest of the shield was a mystery.

Even as she thought that, it was as if she had the book in front of her mind's eye, waiting to be referenced. Startled, Ally "paged" through the volume, almost able to see the pages. She "stopped" when she saw a picture of the two black beasts, accompanied by a caption:

Panther: While the lion does represent a man of great courage and valour, so does a panther a brave woman, who, while tender and kind to her young, defends it fiercely, even to the hazard of her life.

Ally felt dazed. *I've never been able to do that before,* she thought. *Did someone stick a computer in my head when I wasn't looking?*

Shaking herself back to the present, she realised that the crowd's muttered conversations had not ceased and looked back at the coat of arms to try to detect the source of their consternation. Despite the knowledge that seemed lodged in her head, Ally could not see what was so unusual. Except that the base of the shield rested on a crown that was an almost exact replica of the princess' and as she looked around, Ally could see that all of the other blazons around the room–the ones she could see, at any rate–had crowns placed above the shield. She had no time to consult the new encyclopaedia in her head as to its meaning and instead whispered to Evelynne, "What's going on?"

The princess smiled an apology and then raised her hands for silence. Slowly the assembled Nobles quieted and now Ally could see that even the King and Queen looked shocked.

Once she was sure of the people's attention, Evelynne spoke. "Your Majesties, my Lords and Ladies, I understand your surprise. It has been two hundred years since this circumstance was last existent among us. However, it is neither a mistake, nor a hasty decision. Five months ago, while in the French hospital, I realised that this admirable young woman had saved my life, nearly losing her own in the process. In that realisation, I felt the urge to declare Viamadi and so I spoke the Words with intent in my heart." There was dead silence now. "Do not blame Dame Alleandre. Had I not revealed it now, she would still have no knowledge and I could have ignored the Debt indefinitely. However, my own honour would not allow me to do so and I therefore chose to reveal the Life Debt, so that all may know." She indicated the blazon. "None can now deny that my crown supports Dame Alleandre in all things, even to the extent of my life." Evelynne turned and addressed Ally and her voice, though quieter, still rang clearly throughout the Throne Room. "I am bound to Dame Alleandre Tretiak by Life Debt. She saved my

chapter eighteen

life and it now belongs to her to do with as she pleases." The princess sunk down on one knee and bowed her head.

Ally looked down in complete shock. "What are you doing?" she hissed.

"My life is yours," Evelynne said quietly.

Ally shot a glance at the assembled Nobles, who were watching with their collective breaths held. She looked to her parents, but they appeared as confused as she was. "What am I supposed to do?"

"Whatever you like," the princess replied, still bowed. "Right now you could cut off my head and nobody would raise a hand against you." She paused. "I hope you don't. I'm rather attached to it."

Ally missed the attempt at humour. She thought furiously. *Damnit, I'm not good at this kind of thing!* she wailed internally. *I'm not supposed to have my friends offering to let me kill them!* She hesitated. *My friends . . .*

Reaching down, Ally took Evelynne's hands and helped her back to her feet. "My friends don't kneel in front of me," she said, making sure her voice carried. "Especially not you."

A collective sigh emanated from the people in the hall and they started to clap, as Evelynne allowed herself to be helped up. The princess' eyes were suspiciously bright. She reached out and gathered Ally into a strong hug and despite the watching eyes, Ally let her.

"Don't you *ever* do that to me again," Ally whispered.

Evelynne just smiled, and turned to escort her friend to the masses waiting to congratulate her. Her parents were the first.

ઇ ઇ ઇ ઇ ઇ

Much later in the evening, Evelynne escorted the new knight back to her quarters. Ally had changed from the oversized tabard into a more comfortable, but still formal, set of pants and tunic. She kept reaching up to touch the blazon embroidered on the front, still unable to believe it was there. Evelynne just smiled in contentment.

They reached Ally's suite and sank down on the couch in the sitting room. Ally sighed with relief. "Remind me not to do this again, huh?"

"I thought you were having a good time at the reception," Evelynne replied.

"Oh, I was. It helps when you have people there that you know. I haven't seen my grandmother in ages."

"Well, Chorus was certainly happy to see you again. Did he tell you he's taking a job with Domdom? You should see him more now."

"He told me. Gee, Chorus actually working. Will wonders never cease?"

Evelynne laughed. "And of course your parents were very proud. You know, I've never been able to picture 'button-bursting pride' before, but I think your Dad nearly took out Count Yul'tec's eye!" When their laughter died down, Evelynne said, "I had an interesting conversation with your grandmother. I don't think she likes me."

"Don't take it personally. She doesn't really know you. But don't worry, she told me she'll pray for your entire family. She already prays for me. I'm going to hell, you see."

Evelynne was startled. "Why, because you're gay?" She couldn't believe that the elderly, acerbic woman she had met could be so callous, especially to her own granddaughter.

"Surprisingly no, although it doesn't help. I'm already damned because I haven't taken the Lord Jesus Christ as my Saviour. Until I rectify that little oversight Grandma isn't going to bother with minor things like homosexuality."

"Oh." Evelynne watched as Ally yawned widely. "You look tired."

"Ugh, I'm really not looking forward to this visit to Canada next week."

"I know, but you really need to be seen there. So just go, sit back, relax and let everyone make a fuss over you."

Ally sighed. "I guess so. I just don't want there to be any more surprises." She cast a pointed glance at her companion. "Like what happened today. Why didn't you tell me about that Life Debt thing?"

"I wanted to," Evelynne admitted, not looking her friend in the eye. "But I could never find the right time. It really isn't something you bring up in casual conversation. Have you ever had something you wanted to say, but were too afraid to say it?"

That brought Ally up short. *You have no idea.* "Yes." Cursing herself for her cowardice, she hurried on. "So what does this Life Debt entail, exactly?"

"Well, it basically allows you to request anything of me. Theoretically, if you were to abuse me or the Debt, I could at some point declare the Debt fulfilled. But I know you wouldn't do anything like that."

"No, I wouldn't." Ally thought for a moment. "So, for example, if I wanted you to wear a French maid's outfit and bring me wine and grapes, you would?" Her eyes twinkled.

Evelynne flushed severely. *You don't need a Life Debt to get me to do that,* she thought. Aloud, she said, "Well, um . . . yes. If you really wanted me to." She hesitated. "You . . . don't really want me to, do you?"

chapter eighteen

Yes. "No." *Damn it.* "What I would like, though, is a bit of help getting out of this get-up." Ally indicated her formal attire. "Part of it's fastened at the back and right now I'm too stiff to reach it. After that I need to get some sleep." She could have used her talents to undress herself, of course, but at this point her mind was as tired as her body and besides, she wanted to spend a few more minutes with Evelynne.

Evelynne nodded and stood. She held out a hand to her friend. "Come on, then. Let's do this in the bedroom, so you don't have as far to go."

Ally took the proffered hand and gratefully let herself be helped to her feet. The princess didn't drop her hand as they walked to the bedroom. Once there, Evelynne made her turn around and worked on unfastening the tabard. When it was lifted off Ally's shoulders, she sighed in relief.

"God, that thing is heavy." She rotated her shoulders, pleased when the right one didn't protest with more than a mild twinge.

"Oh?" Evelynne asked, draping the tabard over a nearby chair. "I think you're getting soft." She poked Ally in the side and was fascinated by the squeak that emerged. "Or maybe you're ticklish."

"No, I'm not," Ally said firmly, moving away from the offending finger. "I'm just tired."

"Really? So you get ticklish when you're tired?" Another poke, another squeak.

"Yes."

"So you *are* ticklish." Poke, squeak.

"No, I'm—" Ally saw Evelynne's flexing fingers and the evil grin on her lips. "You wouldn't."

"No?"

"No."

"Wrong!" Evelynne pounced on the other woman, sending them both tumbling onto the bed. The princess' agile fingers, well trained from years of practice with her brother, quickly found their way to each and every one of Ally's ticklish spots.

Ally tried to fend off the seeking hands, but her reactions were delayed by the suddenness of the attack. A reflexive part of her wanted to push the princess away with her abilities, but even if Ally's conscious mind had wanted to, it was unlikely she would have been able to concentrate enough.

Finally, Evelynne gave in to Ally's pleas for mercy and stilled her fingers. The taller woman lay sprawled bonelessly on the bed, her head propped up on the pillows, completely exhausted. Evelynne lay quietly next to her, her head resting on Ally's shoulder.

It was peaceful and each woman simply enjoyed the other's proximity.

"I love you," Evelynne said softly and then clamped her mouth shut. She hadn't meant to say anything, especially not that, but the words had bubbled up and escaped before she could stop them. The body beside her tensed and her own tightened, uncertain of the response.

After several long seconds–hours, Evelynne's mind insisted–the tension in Ally's body lessened slightly. "I love you too."

Nothing more was said and the two women just lay there, letting themselves come to terms with this new development. As they relaxed more, Evelynne realised that Ally's arm had wrapped itself around her shoulders and a tentative hand was softly stroking her back.

Responding to the touch, Evelynne shifted closer, then hesitantly lifted her head to look into Ally's face. There was nervousness in Ally's eyes behind her glasses and a vulnerability that tugged at Evelynne's emotions. Slowly raising herself on her elbow, the princess carefully shifted upward, ready to retreat at any sign that this was too much. There was no such sign and as she got closer, Evelynne could see the love and longing behind the nervousness.

Slowly, she kept moving and was aware of Ally slowly lifting her head to meet her and then their lips softly brushed. It was a brief, hesitant contact and Evelynne pulled back slightly to see that Ally's fear had nearly dissipated, leaving behind love and a slow burning desire that sent a shiver down her spine. She reached out with her free hand and carefully removed Ally's glasses, setting them at arm's length away on the bed. Then she brought their lips back together in a more solid kiss.

They remained that way for several minutes and Evelynne felt one of Ally's hands pressed against her back, while the other gently cupped the back of her head, encouraging her responses. Her own hand had found Ally's waist and was pulling them closer together. The princess was hardly an experienced kisser, but Ally certainly knew what she was doing and responded ardently to her experiments. When she felt the soft touch of a tongue against her lips, Evelynne's entire universe narrowed to the woman beneath her.

Finally, they broke apart and with a few more brief pecks, Evelynne reclaimed her position with her head resting on Ally's shoulder. They lay in silence for several minutes.

"This is going to be hard, isn't it?" Ally whispered, her words resounding through her chest to Evelynne's ear.

"Yes," the princess whispered back. She raised her head again. "But I think it's worth it."

chapter eighteen

In response, Ally brought her down for another kiss. When she was done, she said softly, "I think you should go now. If you don't, you might not have another chance before morning."

Evelynne thrilled at the implications of that statement. She was aware that it was far too early in their fledgling relationship to be taking such steps. "Okay."

It was still many minutes before she actually left for her own bed.

PART TWO

"The ancient adepts were subtle, mysterious, profound, comprehensive.
Their thoughts were deep and unfathomable.
Because they were unfathomable,
We can describe them only vaguely:
Hesitant, as a man crossing a stream in winter;
Timid, as a man afraid of his neighbours;
Courteous, as a man who is a guest;
Yielding, as ice near melting;
Simple, as an uncarved block of wood;
Hollow, as a cave;
Clouded, as a muddy pool.

Yet who can evolve with quietness and slowness until the mud has cleared?
Yet who can move with slowness and stillness from the unalive to the alive?
He who is one with the Tao does not seek to be fulfilled.
Because he is unfulfilled,
He can remain hidden, as a new shoot,
And never hurry to premature growth."

~Tao Teh Ching 15

chapter nineteen

"*Earlier this evening, Dame Alleandre Tretiak, recently knighted by Her Royal Highness Princess Evelynne deMolay of Atlantis, attended a gathering in her honour at the National Arts Centre in Ottawa.*" The reporter's voice faded out as the television news show cut to footage of an older man, the Canadian Prime Minister, speaking from the stage. Thankfully, the news program showed only a few excerpts from the speech, which had probably been extremely long-winded, as such things tended to be.

Evelynne watched the television intensely, her eyes drawn to Ally's image on the screen. She was glad that she had the study to herself at this late hour, because if anyone else had been present, they would have easily seen her soft and affectionate expression. While Ally started rather stiffly into her own prepared speech, Evelynne concentrated on her friend's more hidden communication.

It was immediately obvious—at least to Evelynne's eyes—that speaking in front of several hundred people was the last thing Ally wanted to be doing. Still, she managed to keep her voice clear and steady. Evelynne could easily see the strain the other woman had been, and was still, under. The newly raised knight had deteriorated slowly but steadily over the week, as she played the Canadian media circuit. Initially she had not even needed to use her cane, but as the days went by she depended on it more and more. Ally and Evelynne had spoken on the phone several times. Each time the fatigue in Ally's voice had become more evident and part of the princess hated the Canadian and international media for what it was doing to her friend.

Ally had finished her own short speech and the news program cut back to the anchor. He spoke some more on the story, but Evelynne stopped listening.

That decides it, she thought. *She needs a break.* Ally would be returning to Atlantl in three days and the princess had already arranged to have her friend taken directly to the Summer Palace. She had made plans to move herself and her Advisors to the Government Offices in Kilim. That way, Evelynne would be able to continue her administrative duties and still spend time with Ally.

Hopefully they would be able to take things up again where they left off.

Absently turning off the television, Evelynne thought back to where their relationship had been before Ally had left. Seeing each other the morning after the ceremony had been awkward at first. Throughout breakfast Evelynne had been almost physically unable to tear her eyes away from her–*What is she? My friend? My girlfriend? Not my lover . . . yet.* However, mindful of the additional company, in the form of both sets of parents plus Patrick, Maïda, Sir Arthur and a number of other relatives, the princess had been able to remain relatively discreet. Seeing Ally's shy, uncertain glances in return had made it nearly impossible, though.

Afterward, they had managed to steal some time alone, under the pretext of Evelynne helping Ally change for the short press conference.

Evelynne knocked on the door to Ally's bedroom, entering when she heard her call, "Come in."

Ally stood by the bed, laying out the clothing she was going to wear. She was already dressed in deep blue trousers and a simple white dress shirt. "Um, hi," she said softly.

"Hi," Evelynne replied.

The two women spent several uncomfortable moments just standing and looking at each other, uncertain of how to proceed from the night before.

"Um, do you think you could help me with this tabard?" Ally finally asked hesitantly. She grimaced. "They want to show me off for the cameras again." She indicated the heavy shirt, a near duplicate of the one she had worn the previous day, which was draped across the bed.

"And so they should," Evelynne declared. "You need to look good, you know. Your grandmother would never forgive you otherwise."

That evoked a laugh. "You're right. Grandma is always more concerned about my appearance than I am."

Evelynne clucked reprovingly. "You know she loves you. Even if you are going to Hell." This was better; this relaxed banter put them both on more familiar ground. Moving to the bed, the princess picked up the heavy material. "Go sit on the bench there," she ordered, "so I don't have to reach up your gargantuan frame."

Ally smiled wryly and obediently sat down on the cushioned bench with her back to the princess. She heard Evelynne behind her and felt her presence coming closer. There was a pause and the sound of the princess fiddling with something on the tabard, then silence for several seconds. Ally could feel Evelynne standing right behind her and could feel her heart rate speed up at the proximity, but sternly told herself to calm down.

The silence stretched on for several more seconds and Ally was about to turn around to see what was happening, when she suddenly felt the soft brush of lips against the back of her neck. She could not contain the quick gasp that escaped. Her head reflexively fell

chapter nineteen

forward, inviting further contact. Evelynne complied by placing more feather-soft kisses along the arch of Ally's neck and the tabard fell unheeded to the floor.

Reaching up, Evelynne gently tilted Ally's head to the side and bestowed the same favours along the side of her throat. She had no clear idea of what she was doing, acting only on instinct. So she was gratified when she brushed over a sensitive spot just behind Ally's left ear and heard the other woman's breathing hitch again.

Ally slowly turned her head, allowing Evelynne to softly nuzzle the side of her face and then their lips met once more, letting them start again where they had left off the night before.

Long minutes passed as lips teased and nibbled, and then, by mutual consent, the two women pulled back slightly. Ally looked over her left shoulder into the deep blue eyes of the woman who was pressed up against her back. Ally smiled. "Hi," she said again.

"Hi," Evelynne replied, her eyes dancing. She darted in for another quick kiss. "I've been wanting to do that all morning."

Ally flushed in pleasure. "I've wanted you to do that all morning," she admitted, ducking her head shyly.

The princess used a finger to raise her chin again. "I love you," she said seriously.

"I love you too." Ally's eyes met Evelynne's once more, allowing both women to see the truth of their statements.

When they became mildly disconcerted by the intensity of the moment, Ally turned her head forward again and Evelynne let her. It was enough for now for them to know that what had been confessed the night before was still true in the light of morning.

ʃ ʃ ʃ ʃ ʃ

And how true it was, Evelynne mused. Similar scenes had played out in the days leading up to Ally's return to Canada. They had been very careful to avoid what Ally termed "Public Displays of Affection;" Ally because of her natural shyness and Evelynne because she was still uncertain of the public response if their relationship became known. Until she was surer of what the popular reaction would be, she was not going to expose either of them to possible public scrutiny or censure.

Despite their best efforts, Evelynne felt sure that Catherine Tretiak suspected that something was going on. She wasn't sure, but based on some of the looks she and Ally had received . . . the princess shrugged. If she knew anything about Ally's mother, it was that she would do nothing to cause her daughter undue distress. She might say something privately and if she did, Evelynne would deal with it. Until then there was little the princess could do.

Suddenly realising what time it was, Evelynne winced. She had wanted to stay up to see the Canadian news program's coverage of Ally's last formal appearance. Given the time difference that had meant staying up far later than was probably wise. The princess was going to be busy tomorrow–or today actually–to get matters arranged to move back to the Summer Palace by the weekend.

Standing and stretching, Evelynne made her way out of the study towards her bedroom.

Once in bed, she sent a thought into the night. *I love you.*

Just before she dropped off to sleep, she thought she heard an answer. *I love you too.*

Ally knocked on the door of the apartment in front of her.

She was alone in the tenement's corridor, but if she extended her perceptions just slightly, she could detect the presence of at least two people nearby with their attention focused on her. The first time she had felt them, she had been alarmed. A quick scan of their surface intentions had told her that they meant no harm; on the contrary, both were undercover agents of the Atlantlan Guard with specific orders to protect her–as discreetly as possible, of course. She smiled wryly and wondered if she should compliment Sir Arthur on the quality of his fellow Guards when she saw him again. *Maybe not.*

The door swung open. Ally had already announced herself when she buzzed at the building entrance, so her appearance was hardly a surprise. Still, the green eyes of the tall blonde widened when she saw Ally standing at her door.

"Ally!" she exclaimed and rushed into the hallway to envelop her in a strong embrace.

Ally returned the hug awkwardly, her cane dangling from one hand. "Hey, Annie," she said into the nearby ear. She felt her body react involuntarily to the familiar form pressed against her, even through the winter jacket she was wearing, and felt a pang of guilt. Annie broke off before she could become truly uncomfortable and stood back to look at her ex-lover.

"You look good, Ally," Annie said. "Please, come on in."

Ally entered, looking around the apartment. It was smaller than the one she and Annie had shared a year before, but then, Annie wasn't sharing it with two other people either. "Nice place."

Annie shrugged, first taking Ally's jacket and hat–whose concealing bulk had disguised her enough to slip past the still-present reporters–and then guiding her guest into the living room. "It's okay," she admitted. "I miss the balcony we, uh, had. You know, in our apartment," she finished as Ally settled on the couch.

chapter nineteen

"Nothing will beat that balcony," Ally admitted. Changing the subject, she asked, "Have you seen Phil recently? I've tried to get in touch with him, but I don't know where he is." Phil had been the third person sharing their university apartment.

"Oh, didn't you know? Phil's in New Zealand. He got a job at one of their thermal power plants."

Ally's eyebrows rose. "Really? I thought he was going to Brazil."

"He was," Annie confirmed. "But then six months ago he met a New Zealander who was attending a conference here and the rest, as they say, is history. They're engaged now."

Ally almost choked. "*Phil?* Engaged? You're kidding." Annie shook her head. "My God, old Phil-anderer getting hitched. Wow. This has been quite the year, hasn't it?"

"Yeah, I guess it has." Annie's voice was quiet and her eyes strayed involuntarily to Ally's cane. She jumped up suddenly and asked, "Do you want something to drink?"

"Sure, whatever you're having."

"Ally, please, this is me." Annie's face had a sad tinge to it. "You say, 'Whatever you're having' to strangers. I'm still your friend. I hope."

"You are." Ally paused and then smiled. "Bring me a beer, woman!"

Annie laughed. "Better. Much better." She left and returned a moment later with two bottles and glasses. "I have *Keith's,*" she announced.

"Oh, bless you," Ally said. "Say whatever you want about Atlantlans, but their beer is crap." She shuddered. "It should be poured back into the horse."

Annie chuckled. "That bad, huh?" Ally's only reply was a deep sigh as she took a long sip of her beer. "So . . . I saw you on TV when you were knighted. And the reception in Ottawa. And your interview on *The National*. My mother has practically been claiming you as her own. She's getting a lot of mileage out of the fact that she was almost your mother-in-law." Ally rolled her eyes at the thought of the tiny Spanish woman who was Annie's mother. It was a far cry from the reception she had originally received from Mrs. Bourne. Annie made her eyes comically round. "Dame Alleandre," she said breathily, "can I have your autograph?" She mimed passing over a pen and paper.

Ally stuck her nose in the air and took the imaginary items. "Jeeves," she sniffed, holding them out to the equally imaginary servant, "sign these for me, will you? Then remove this peon." She waved dismissively in Annie's direction.

The "peon" snorted. "Oh, that's good. Did your princess teach you how to do that?"

"She's not my . . . princess . . ." Ally trailed off. *Is she? Oh God, if we're involved . . .* She looked up to see Annie staring at her intently. "What?" she asked, flushing deeply.

"*Madre de dios,*" Annie said softly. "I've seen that look before. Of course, the last time it was directed at me." Ally averted her eyes and blushed even deeper, but couldn't find the words to refute her ex-lover's observation. "Ally, you're in love with her, aren't you?"

Ally was silent for several moments, still not looking at her hostess. "Yes," she mumbled.

"Oh, Ally, I warned you about this. Does . . . she know?"

"Yes." This time the word was even quieter.

Annie inhaled quickly. "Is she okay with that?" She watched, fascinated, as Ally reddened further.

"Um, yes." Ally took a deep breath. "You might say she's . . . happy about it."

Annie's jaw hung open in shock. She made a couple of attempts at speech before finally saying, "You mean you're–she's–are you a couple?"

"Um, I'm not really sure," Ally said quietly. She looked up finally, and the other woman could see the naked uncertainty in her eyes. "I mean . . . I love her. And I know she loves me. And we've kissed." *Oh my, how we've kissed.* "But nobody else knows and it's not exactly as if we can go out on a date. So I guess we're involved, but does that make us a couple?" She shrugged helplessly.

"*Madre de dios,*" Annie repeated, slumping back in her chair. She had been prepared to hear that her ex-girlfriend had resolved her feelings towards the princess or even that she was still "admiring from afar", but to think that she was–that she had . . . The dancer shook her head in an attempt to order her thoughts. "You know for sure that she feels the same way?"

Ally nodded emphatically. "Oh, trust me, I know."

"I hate to suggest this, but do you think she might just be reacting to the fact that you saved her life?"

Ally shrugged again unhappily. "It's possible." She paused. "There is something else, though." She hesitated again.

"Yes?" Annie prompted.

"We're . . . linked," Ally said finally.

"Linked?"

"Linked. Joined. Bonded. Soulmates. I don't know what to call it. All I know is that there is some kind of incredibly strong psychic connection between us." Ally tapped the side of her head. "I have no idea how it got there, but I'm pretty sure it can't be broken without some serious psychological damage, at least on my side." When Annie looked sceptical, she closed her eyes and concentrated. "Evelynne is right *there*." She pointed, her arm to the east, but also downward, through the earth, at a fairly steep angle. "She's... annoyed with... somebody. Arguing, I think. She's... hungry." Ally opened her eyes to meet Annie's shocked gaze.

"Jesus, Ally, she's practically on the other side of the planet! You could never read anyone that far away before."

"I still can't. I can only do it with her."

Annie shook her head. "Ally, I'm not the person to be talking to about this. Have you talked to Mrs. Chen? She helped you before."

Ally smiled ruefully. "Mrs. Chen's visiting her family in China. Believe me, I wish I could ask her."

"Damn. So does Evelynne know about this? About you?"

"No. Not yet." When Annie looked concerned, Ally quickly added, "Believe me, I want to tell her!" She sighed. "I have to tell her. Especially now that we're... involved." She laughed harshly. "You know, half of me wants to tell her so badly because I love her so much and the other half is scared to death. She's exactly the kind of person I've been afraid would find out about what I can do. You know, a powerful government type, with the resources to bring a lot of pressure to bear if I don't do what she wants. Oh, I don't think she would do that," she said quickly, "but the people she associates with... what if one of them found out?"

Annie forced a smile. "Well, if any of them try, let me know and I'll turn your mother and Mrs. Chen loose on them. And that Kung Fu master you met in Thailand. Trust me, they won't know what hit them."

Ally laughed and the germ of an idea took root in her mind. It disappeared before she could focus on it and she let it go for the moment. "Thanks, Annie."

"And as for your relationship with Evelynne... I can't believe I'm going to say this." Annie drew a breath. "Go for it." When Ally looked up in surprise, she continued, "You're special, Ally. You should be with someone else who is special and I'm not it. No, don't argue. I'm not on your level and I know it. I'm not necessarily any *less* than you are, but... anyway, like I said, you need someone special to complete your life and if the Crown Princess of Atlantis isn't special, I don't know who is. But–" She held up a warning finger. "–you need to tell her. About you, about this bond, everything. I know it won't be easy. Heck, I know how *I* reacted! But unless you're going to break this off she deserves to know. She *needs* to know." Ally opened her mouth to speak, but Annie forestalled her. "Now you're going to ask, 'What if this whole thing is only because of this link? What if she only loves me because we're bonded somehow?' See, I'm telepathic sometimes too. The answer is that it doesn't matter. If she loves you, she loves you. Are you in love with her only because of this bond?" Ally shook her head. "Good. Don't assume that she is, either." She reached forward to take Ally's hands. "Whether you believe it or not, you are a very attractive person, Alleandre Tretiak. Believe that she can love you just for who you are."

Ally squeezed the hands in hers. "Thanks, Annie," she said, her voice husky. "I'll try."

"Good. As for what might happen . . . No matter what, I'll always support you. If you need help, any sort of help, just get word to me. Your parents, Mrs. Chen, Kung Fu man, Phil, myself. Heck, a whole bunch of Australian mothers and fathers. We'll be the Marines if you need us. Just remember that you have powerful friends."

Ally couldn't speak and got up to wrap her friend in a warm hug. Annie held her until she moved back and brushed her hand across her eyes. Annie gave her several minutes to regain her composure. Finally Ally had herself back under control.

"So," Ally said, "enough about my life. What's yours like? Did anything happen with Ms. Cello Player?"

Annie let her friend change the subject. "Alas, no. It turned out she was just curious and I'm long past my experimental stage. However, on a non-romantic subject, there is a dancer in my troupe by the name of Aaron who I think you might be interested in talking to when you're back this way again."

"Really? You think he's special?"

"Well, I'm not positive, but he seems to stay up in the air during jumps just a *mite* longer than he really should. As I said, I'm not sure, but something just seems a little . . . off."

"It would be interesting if he was. I always thought some of those really good ballet dancers could levitate just a little."

"Ally, you're back," Evelynne breathed as the woman approached after disembarking the helicopter. She held out her arms in invitation.

Ally hesitated for just a moment before allowing the welcoming arms to wrap around her. She revelled in Evelynne's closeness for several long minutes, feeling much of the stress of the past two weeks ebb out of her body. "Hi, Evelynne. I'm home," she whispered, marvelling at her use of the word. *Home. I'm home.*

chapter nineteen

"Yes, you are."

The two women held each other for longer than was strictly appropriate, considering the Guards and servants nearby. Finally they broke apart when Ally shivered in the cold winter air.

"Come on," Evelynne urged, offering her arm in support. Ally accepted the help gratefully.

"It's so good to see you again," Evelynne said as they carefully made their way up the pathway to the Palace. The morning's rain had made the way treacherous and a chill breeze threatened snow. "I really missed you." She cast a surreptitious glance at her companion.

A tired smile played at the corner of Ally's mouth. "I missed you too," she admitted. "I thought about you all the time."

Evelynne smiled in pleasure. "So did I." Looking up at Ally again, she noted, "You look tired."

Ally sighed. "I am tired. Very tired. I thought that would never end. I need to rest. Please." Her voice was more plaintive than humorous.

"I know," the princess soothed. "I know you probably would have liked to go back ho–to your house, but I thought if you stayed here for now you wouldn't have to worry about anything like cooking or cleaning. And I've told everyone to leave you alone as much as possible. Besides, I wanted you nearby." Evelynne flushed at the admission.

Ally smiled. "I'm glad. Are you going to be here for long?"

Evelynne scowled. "Yes and no. I was supposed to have everything set up to work from here. Unfortunately, I have to go back to Jamaz tomorrow for a few days to figure out some unfinished details. After that I'll be back here full time." She paused. "I was thinking that when I get back we could go and see the excavations at Aztlan. It would be completely low-key," she hastened to add. "No official meetings or press affairs. More like a museum tour, with really good tour guides." She waited apprehensively for Ally to respond.

Ally thought for a moment. "That sounds okay," she admitted. "I think I'll be rested in a week or so. And I am really interested in seeing the site. As long as it's no problem for you."

"No, no problem for me," Evelynne said as they walked up the front steps to the Palace. "Now that my administration has been set up, I actually don't have a huge amount to do. Right now I mostly just catch things that my father's and aunt's offices are too busy to deal with. Formal protocol stuff, mostly."

As the two women approached the door, it swung open smoothly to reveal Nancu Ylan just inside. He bowed formally and stood back. "Your Highness. Dame Alleandre," he intoned.

"Hello, Ylan," Evelynne said. "As you can see, she got here safe and sound."

"I am gratified to see that, Your Highness," the Seneschal said, though his even, dry tone displayed no real satisfaction. Ally knew better than to take offence; he rarely showed emotion of any sort. "It is an honour to see you again, Dame Alleandre."

"Thank you, Seneschal Ylan," Ally replied.

As the Seneschal went to take charge of Ally's luggage, the women moved further into the warmth of the Palace, shedding coats and boots as they went.

Ally chuckled suddenly.

"What?" Evelynne asked.

The taller woman shook her head. "I'm still not used to being 'Dame Alleandre'. I keep looking around for some old woman with my name. It's a little disconcerting."

"Ah. Well, if it's any consolation, I *am* a princess. Mere knighthood doesn't impress me." Evelynne affected a supercilious air.

"Oh really? Well, I was president once, you know. It was of the high school physics club and there were only four members that year, but still . . ."

"Well now you're talking." Her hand on the doorknob, Evelynne said, "There is one other person here who won't be impressed by your new titles. She's been missing you too."

"Who?"

In answer, the princess opened the study door and waved her companion in. Ally walked in, immediately appreciating the warmth from the blazing fire. She was not the only appreciative party, as the noise of the door opening caused a small grey cat to perk up from where it was lying before the fireplace.

"Cassie!" Ally exclaimed excitedly.

Cassiopeia appeared less thrilled at the interruption and slowly stood up, taking the time to stretch thoroughly before walking over to her human, complaining loudly at the intrusion. Ally scooped up the cat, who deigned to forgive her when Ally began to scratch the feline behind the ears. Cassie was soon purring loudly.

"Hey, Cassie, did you miss me?"

The cat did not answer, but Evelynne came close after carefully closing the study door. "She did, you know," she whispered. "We both did."

Ally looked down into the other woman's eyes and Evelynne's hand slowly came up to gently stroke her cheek. Ally sighed and leaned into the light pressure, turning her head to press a kiss to the princess' wrist. Evelynne

chapter nineteen

tugged her down softly to bring their lips together. Ally willingly followed the urging, mindful of the cat still in her arms. Soon, though, she lost track of her burden, instead concentrating fully on the lips and body against hers. A plaintive cry finally interrupted them and the two young women reluctantly broke apart to look down at the source of the sound.

Evelynne started to laugh, and Ally was not far behind. "Oh dear. Are we neglecting you?" the princess asked. She reached out to rub Cassie's head and the cat closed her eyes in satisfaction. "Too much mushy stuff? You're getting to be spoiled, you know? At least you'll get to sleep with Ally at night." Suddenly realising what she had said, Evelynne blushed and looked up quickly to see Ally's equally red face. "Um . . . well, yeah. She *is* lucky."

Ally sat down on a nearby sofa. Cassie promptly curled up in her lap and went to sleep. Evelynne hesitated and then deliberately sat down next to her. She tentatively placed an arm around Ally and rested her head on the taller woman's shoulder. Ally paused and then took the princess' other hand in her own. They both smiled.

"This is nice," Evelynne said softly. "It's so good to have you here." She turned to place a kiss on the cheek by her head. "I love you."

A part of Ally relaxed. "I love you too."

Evelynne felt the subtle release of tension. "Were you worried that I'd change my mind?" she asked quietly.

"No. Well, a little. I mean, when I left we hadn't really talked about . . . this. I thought that maybe in two weeks you had reconsidered. Maybe you had realised that you weren't interested in women after all. Maybe you had decided you could do better than me. Maybe you were–I don't know." Ally avoided her companion's gaze. "I'm sorry."

Evelynne squeezed her a bit more tightly. "Don't be sorry. I've been scared of the same things. Although I didn't think you would decide you weren't gay." That earned a slight laugh. "But I did think that maybe you had decided that a relationship between us was going to be too hard, because of who I am. Maybe you'd meet up with Annie again and realise you still wanted to be with her. Um, you don't, do you?"

Ally chuckled again. "No. I did go and see her, but . . . that ship has sailed. We're still friends–good friends, I think–but that's all we are. That's all we need to be."

"Good." Evelynne sighed. "I suppose we never did talk about . . . us before you left, did we?"

"No. And we have to."

"I know."

"But not right now. I'm too tired and this is too serious. There are things I want to tell you. Need to tell you. Things that you need to know. Nothing bad!" she said when she felt Evelynne stiffen in mild alarm. "At least I hope not. I don't have a disease or anything, but there are some . . . psychological things that need to be exposed."

"I suppose we also have to talk about what this might mean if it gets found out." Evelynne grimaced. "I don't really want to keep it a secret, but . . ."

"I understand." There was silence for several minutes. "For now, can we just sit here?" Ally shifted to a more comfortable position, eliciting sleepy protests from both females.

"I'd like that," Evelynne said. She listened quietly while the breaths beneath her ear became slower and deeper, until they evened out into sleep.

❧ ❧ ❧ ❧ ❧

Far out in the middle of Haperu Bay, on the west coast of Lyonesse, a boat of the Royal Atlantlan Coastal Service drew closer to the bulk of what appeared to be a medium sized fishing boat. The other craft was running without lights, a flagrantly illegal practice, especially on a night as dark as this. Ensign Cal Pratt swung the powerful spotlight mounted on his boat to shine on the dark trawler. Next to him Ensign Alice Rawlings manned the small craft's single machine gun.

Below him, on the bridge, Captain Emilio Reeves, RACSS *Siren*, spoke into the microphone of his amplifier. "Unknown vessel, this is the Royal Atlantlan Coastal Service. You are running without proper lights or identification, in contradiction of Marine Regulations. Heave to and prepare to be boarded." The Captain spoke to his second in command. "Well, Janet, it looks like we've got another poacher. You up for some excitement?"

"I suppose so, Skipper. Personally, though, I like boredom better."

Reeves tsked. "You're getting soft, Janet." Speaking into the microphone once more, he ordered, "Unidentified vessel, I say again, heave to and prepare to be boarded. You are in violation of Atlantlan Marine Law. If you do not halt I will fire a cautionary shot. That will be your final warning. Further refusal on your part will force me to open fire."

Illegal fishing was an irregular, if persistent, problem in this area. It was serious enough to be a nuisance, but not serious enough for intense military policing of the region. Which left the matter in the hands of patrol boats like the *Siren*. And frankly, that was how Captain Reeves preferred it. The last thing he wanted was a bunch of stuck-up Navy types telling him how to patrol his bay.

chapter nineteen

As it was, illegal boats would be intercepted regularly and the owners would be fined or indentured, depending on the size of their catch. The serious ones would be back as soon as they had finished paying off their debt and the cycle would begin again. The most regular offenders were always careful of just how much they caught and not just because of the possible repercussions when they were captured. They were also aware that if they did over-fish the area, there would be no more to poach later and therefore saved their "extracurricular activities" for times when there was an abundant supply.

Most of them also surrendered when they were caught, which was why the Captain was getting annoyed with this particular customer. Just as he was about to repeat his order to heave to—he had never yet had to actually fire a warning shot, much less sink a boat—the other craft suddenly cut its engines. Reducing speed, the patrol boat came alongside, keeping the other boat firmly in its spotlight beam. The Captain chuckled to himself. His two Ensigns were so new they squeaked, and were obviously being as precise as possible.

"Okay, Janet, it's your show."

"Yes, Sir." Lieutenant Janet Devereaux settled her firearm snugly in its holster. In all her years as a Coastal Service agent she had never had to draw the weapon, let alone fire it, but regulations forced her to carry it on any search. She made her way to where the *Siren* nestled against the larger trawler and called out over the side, "Ahoy! I am a member of the Royal Atlantan Coastal Service. I am going to board your vessel and search it under Marine Regulations. I am armed. Please assemble your entire crew on deck immediately."

There was no reply and Devereaux frowned at the empty deck of the boat. She was about to repeat her challenge when an answer came, but not in the form of words.

There was a rapid, heavy "phut, phut, phut," which she had no opportunity to identify before a barrage of bullets streamed from the trawler and impacted in the centre of her body, sending her flying backward. She was dead before she hit the deck. Captain Reeves only had time to gape, stunned, before a second stream of shots shattered the cabin window and blew him backwards. Simultaneously, separate sustained bursts of gunfire killed Ensigns Pratt and Rawlings before they could even begin to react. A bullet took out the spotlight, throwing the entire area into darkness.

Then there was silence, broken only by the slap of water against the sides of both boats.

Several dark figures emerged from where they had been crouched on board the trawler and quickly boarded and secured the patrol boat. A few minutes later one approached a tall man still on the fishing boat's deck.

"They're all dead, sir," he said in English.

"Shit," the other man swore. "Do we know if they radioed for help?"

"No, sir, they didn't. Davy was monitoring their transmissions the whole time. Their last was that they had intercepted a suspected fish poacher and were about to search."

"Shit. So their base knows they met someone. Any chance we could fake a message? Make them think their boat was mistaken?"

"Unlikely, sir. The Captain sounded pretty chummy with the guy on the other end."

"God damn it. Okay, get someone to fire up that boat. We'll take it as far from here as we can and sink it. We'll have to send a message back to Control that this route will be cut off for a while. They'll have to find some other way to get our people in."

"Yes, sir. Our contacts on this side will probably do that anyway, though."

"Maybe so, but I'm not trusting a bunch of Anties." The tall man swore again loudly. "Okay, fuck it. Get that boat and let's get out of here."

A short time later the fish had the area to themselves again.

chapter twenty

"Are you ready to go?" Evelynne asked from the doorway to Ally's suite.

"One moment," Ally requested. She was sitting in a chair tugging on a pair of sturdy boots. Once done, she grabbed her cane and stood up. "All righty then, good to go."

Evelynne came over to where Ally was standing and reached up, tugging her down for a kiss. After a quick check to make sure that nobody was looking in the open doorway, Ally complied.

Breaking away, the princess hummed. "I like doing that," she said half-cheekily and half-seriously.

"I like you doing that," Ally admitted quietly. "You have to stop going away so that we can do it more often."

"I know, and I'm sorry my trip took longer than I thought it would. Besides, before that you were the one who left."

"Yeah, I know. How about if we try to stick around each other for a while?"

"Deal." Evelynne linked their arms, escorting her companion out the door and down to the foyer. "I'm also sorry we haven't had a chance to have our talk. I would have postponed this trip today, but the weather is good all the way down the coast, and who knows how long it will last?"

"That's okay," Ally reassured her. "Depending on when we get back. This talk could take a while." She seemed nervous every time the subject was raised.

"Maybe then," the princess agreed. She wondered why Ally was so apprehensive about whatever she had to reveal. *It's not as if she's going to come out of the closet to me. I know about her panic attacks. I'm positive she isn't into drugs or dying of some disease. She isn't married and I'm certain she doesn't have any children. Heck, maybe she is into bondage and S and M and doesn't know how I'll react. Although I don't know how I would react in that case. Not that something like that is bad, necessarily, but I don't think it's my thing. Of course, I can't really say what my 'thing' is . . . except her.* She cast a sidelong glance at Ally. *Oh well, whatever it is, I'm pretty sure I can handle it.*

Sir Arthur was waiting for them in the foyer. As Master of Evelynne's Guard detail, he had been up for hours arranging the last minute details of this trip to the Aztlan excavations. "Your Highness," he greeted. "Dame Alleandre. Good morning."

"Hello, Uncle Arthur," Evelynne said cheerily.

The Guard sighed. So that was how today was going to be. When his charge was in a particularly good mood—as she had *not* been for the week she had been away from the Summer Palace—she tended to become almost defiantly friendly and informal. Under normal circumstances that was not a problem, but for a visit to a location as large and difficult to secure as Aztlan it could be disconcerting. At least he had managed to train her to not attempt to escape her Guards . . . usually. Given how she had been staying close to Alleandre and the latter's difficulties in moving quickly, Sir Arthur had hopes that she would remain relatively sedate for the duration of the tour.

"Your Highness, must you be so informal today? We are going—"

"Oh, hush," Evelynne chided. "You're almost family now. Or am I reading your intentions towards my lady-in-waiting incorrectly? I noticed that you two spent quite a while in the garden last night. Hmm?"

To the princess' disappointment, Sir Arthur's expression did not change. "I'm afraid, Your Highness, that I can neither confirm nor deny any of my personal relationships. To do so could compromise my position."

"You know," Ally said in a stage whisper, "Maïda doesn't seem to be awake yet. Do you think she got—ahem—tired last night?"

That suggestion put a wicked twinkle back into Evelynne's eye. "You're right. Well, Uncle Arthur? Did you keep Maïda 'busy' last night?"

To someone who knew him less well, the bodyguard's expression would have appeared as set in stone as ever. However, Evelynne recognised the amusement lurking behind his impassive façade. "Your Highness, I can neither confirm nor deny my—"

"Blah, blah, blah," the princess interrupted. "Damnit, Uncle Arthur, I want to be an aunt, or a reasonable facsimile thereof! How is that supposed to happen unless you get busy? Huh? You know Patrick won't be producing any offspring any time soon."

The barest hint of a smirk showed on the Guard's face. He tilted his head slightly to listen to his earbud. "Your Highness, we are ready to leave now. At your leisure." He indicated the front door.

"Hmph," Evelynne pouted. "Obstructionist bodyguards. They think they can get away with that 'confirm or deny' stuff. I should have them . . ." Her mumbling faded as she passed through the doorway.

Behind her Sir Arthur and Dame Alleandre traded grins.

chapter twenty

The man who hurried out to meet the Royal party as they disembarked the helicopter at the outskirts of Aztlan was a personification of the absent-minded professor. His wispy white hair was blown in all directions by the wind from the slowing rotors, although it was likely that there would have been little difference had the air been dead calm. Large, thick-lensed spectacles rested on his nose and threatened to slide off every time he nodded his head. Which was often.

"*Bon'gier'a, Ur-Mata*," he greeted, hurriedly touching his fingers to his forehead, lips and chest. "*Et hura'i o si arra'at. A mak pro'phes* Dusan Collins."

"Good morning, Dr. Collins," the princess replied in English for Ally's benefit. Though her friend had begun learning Lantlan, she was still at a very basic level. "I'm happy to be able to visit." She turned to Ally. "Dr. Collins, may I present my friend, Dame Alleandre Tretiak. Ally, Dr. Collins runs the excavations here."

The academic blinked owlishly. "Er, yes, good morning, Dame Alleandre. Welcome to Aztlan. Although I hesitate to contradict Her Highness, it is my secretary who actually, er, runs the show here. I am too often distracted by new discoveries." Dr. Collins waved a stout middle-aged woman forward. "This is Ms. Alice Bennett, my secretary."

"Your Highness, Dame Alleandre," the woman said with a thick Scottish accent. She bowed. "Ah'm pleased to meet ye."

"Ms. Bennett," Evelynne said. "It's always good when the people nominally in charge understand who really runs things, isn't it?"

Alice smiled. "Aye, Your Highness." She looked up at the much taller Doctor. "Ah'm glad Dusan kens that, as weel."

"Finally, Your Highness, this is Reanne Poloi, the foreman of the heavy excavation crews."

The huge bear of a woman who stepped forward threatened to eclipse the sun. She look to be at least seven feet tall, and moved surprisingly softly for a woman of her size. "Yer Highness," she rumbled. "Dame Alleandre."

"Pleased to meet you all," Evelynne said, and Ally murmured similar sentiments. "Now, I believe we have a tour, don't we?"

"Of course, Your Highness," the Doctor said. "In fact, you are in luck, visiting today. A few days ago we finally completed the restoration of the Maze Chamber of the Grand Temple and you will be the first official visitors. We were just waiting for your arrival. If you would care to enter one of the cars?"

Obediently Evelynne and Ally climbed into the back seat of one of the golf-cart-sized "cars". As they drove along a dirt road towards the centre of the city, Ally saw several trucks and pieces of earth-moving equipment working in the distance. Occasionally the tops of buildings could be seen poking up through the dirt. "Whereabouts does Aztlan start?" she asked, leaning forward so that Doctor Collins could hear her. "I mean, where's the city boundary?"

"Back that way." Collins pointed back the way they had come. "We have used ground penetrating sonar to roughly map the entire city. It's approximately twenty-four kilometres across. We are actually driving on top of the city right now." Ally looked down, but could only see dirt. "The entire city was buried under between, oh, ten and fifty metres of soil. Silt, actually. It preserved the buildings wonderfully. Of course, we have only just begun to uncover it all. Almost four per cent has been excavated. Still, that's about fifty-five square kilometres. Only seventeen hundred to go!"

Ally whistled. "That's huge."

"Indeed it is. It is, in fact, slightly larger than New York City."

"That's impressive."

"Yes," Collins agreed. "However, even more impressive are the canals that once banded and divided the city. The narrowest is just under four hundred metres across, and all are over two hundred metres deep. The work required to construct such 'Circle Seas', as they have been called, is almost incalculable."

"So how did the ancient Atlantlans do it?"

"We have no idea," the Doctor admitted. "Oh, there are all sorts of theories, of course, but they all have one or more fatal flaws. They had no heavy lifting equipment—at least, none that we can recognise as such—and they were inconsiderate enough not to write down how they did it." He made it seem like a personal affront. "Not that we'd be able to read it if they did. To date, nobody has been able to decipher their language."

Tired of having to shout, Ally sat back and watched as their car sped on. She could not see much in the way of obvious excavation in the direction they were travelling and wondered where the centre of the city was. All of a sudden, the ground in front seemed to open up like a crater and the centre of the city was spread out before them.

Of course, Ally thought. *The whole place is buried. They have to dig* down *to get to it.*

The Doctor brought the vehicle to a stop, allowing his guests a chance to see the uncovered part of the city from a vantage point about fifty metres above the level of Aztlan's roads. Ally could instantly see that almost the

chapter twenty

whole central "island", a perfect circle, had been excavated. Several large buildings, still elegant and majestic despite their obvious age, dominated the core. The style of architecture was somehow both familiar and different, a blend of styles found elsewhere around the world and Ally could see why many people thought that Atlantl had been the birthplace of civilisation. Unlike the fanciful spindles and minarets that some fantasy authors had pictured the ancient city having, Aztlan's palaces, temples and houses were heavy, solid constructions, which still managed to be beautiful and graceful at the same time. Middle-Eastern style domes joined with Grecian columns and South American stepped pyramids. The result was a milieu that was both eclectic and disconcertingly beautiful to modern eyes. What the city's original inhabitants had thought was anyone's guess.

The road leading down into the city had been carefully placed so that as it descended it eventually merged with one of the original thoroughfares. As the vehicle drove down the slope, Ally was even more impressed as the size of the ancient roadway became apparent: it was at least as wide as a modern four-lane highway. Large stone buildings loomed on either side. They rarely exceeded three stories, but their gaping empty windows and doorways and the palpable feeling of age they radiated made them appear more imposing.

Despite the apparent desolation of the ruins—though most were still, amazingly, in excellent condition—they seemed to lack the mournful loneliness of many other ancient sites. Perhaps it was because their obvious age suggested that any imagined ghosts had long departed. Maybe it was the fact that the intricate and beautiful carvings and murals that graced the buildings still seemed as vibrant as when they were first carved. Ally suggested as much to Dr. Collins.

"Yes, the inscribed carvings are impressive and the fact they have survived so long is also a wonderful testament to the artists. Of course, part of that is due to the stone: it is a very hard form of granite. From remnants we have discovered on various murals, it seems that the ancient Aztlani were also very fond of covering their murals and statues in coloured enamels, copper, silver and even gold leaf. Because oricalcum is not as malleable, it was used mainly as an inlay to highlight certain works. It's fairly obvious that the ancients regarded gold and silver as primarily decorative elements, but not as possessing more abstract value, like money. In fact, our archaeologists have yet to find any recognisable forms of currency. Some think that the Aztlani used some form of money that simply hasn't survived to the present day—perhaps wooden tokens or foodstuffs of some kind, much like the

Mayans used cocoa beans—while others believe that a barter system was exclusively used. A few have suggested that the population simply shared its produce, rather like antediluvian Marxists."

"How old is the city?" Ally asked as they passed a house where a work crew was busy digging soil from its interior. Other workers were using brushes to clean dirt from its fronting carving, a fanciful representation of some kind of cat, which reminded Ally of a cross between Egyptian and Mayan hieroglyphics.

"Well, we have carbon-dated certain artefacts to about 9,000 BC, which corresponds with geological estimates of the date of the Deluge. Naturally, Aztlan was in existence well before then, although how old it was at the time of the Flood is uncertain. Given its size, one or two thousand years has been considered a reasonable guess and certain other sites found throughout Atlantl seem to support that number."

Ally whistled soundlessly. For a metropolis over eleven thousand years old, it really was in magnificent condition. Even the oldest ruins found in Iraq and Iran only dated to about 5,000 BC. To think that these ruins were at least four millennia older . . . "So the debate over whether Atlantl really is the cradle of civilisation is pretty much moot, isn't it?"

"Largely, yes," Malloy agreed. "At least western civilisation. After the Deluge we know for a fact that refugees fleeing Atlantl got as far as Egypt and South America. They likely introduced such things as farming and architecture to the locals, which then spread to other regions. After that, they probably interbred with the native populations. Given the low numbers of survivors, they effectively disappeared into the gene pool. The South American legends in particular speak of wise and learned 'bearded white men' who appeared and taught them civilisation, then disappeared. Still, there are enough archaeological mysteries around the world to intrigue us for generations to come. The giant stone heads of Easter Island, for example, have little similarity to any Atlantlan artefacts. There is speculation that another technologically advanced island nation, similar to Atlantl, existed in the Pacific, and experienced a similar demise. It is generally referred to as 'Mu' or 'Lemuria', although it is extremely unlikely that its natives would have called it as such. Just as the ancient Atlantlans almost certainly called their island something other than 'Atlantis'. Even the name of this city, Aztlan, is a guess based on certain old documents."

They were approaching the largest buildings they had seen so far, located at the centre of the city, as Ally asked, "So how did Atlantl sink, anyway? What caused the Deluge?"

chapter twenty

"Well, assuming that it was not actually the wrath of God who made the rain fall for forty days and forty nights, the most likely culprit was a massive tectonic shift. A mega-earthquake, if you will, right along the fault line that Atlantl straddles. Today, the southern part of the fault is the Mid-South Atlantic Ridge. Eleven thousand years ago, a large enough earthquake could have caused sufficient upheaval in the surrounding ocean to create a massive, globe-encircling tsunami. The mass of flood-related legends that can be found world-wide support the hypothesis."

ಉ ಉ ಉ ಉ ಉ

"And this, Your Highness, is the Maze Chamber of the Grand Temple." With a flourish that made him look slightly ridiculous, Dr. Collins ushered his guests through the huge porticoes and into the vast, echoing chamber beyond.

Ally and Evelynne gaped at the massive empty space of the room they had just entered. "*E'met*," Evelynne murmured. "Amazing. They hadn't restored it nearly this much the last time I was here."

The circular Chamber looked nearly new, as though it had been abandoned for mere days, rather than millennia. It was at least a hundred metres across and the floor was covered entirely in blue-veined marble, the slabs set so closely that the seams were nearly invisible. At the east and west walls, huge statues of a man and woman, respectively, supported the roof on their shoulders, nearly fifty metres overhead. The woman had long flowing hair and the man wore a thick beard. Both statues were completely nude. The detail of each sculpture was intricate and Ally felt her face growing red involuntarily as she look at them. It didn't help that both giant faces were angled so that they seemed to be looking down over the occupants of the Chamber with knowing, wise and slightly amused expressions. The only decoration on either statue was the eight-pointed star that graced each of their foreheads.

"She looks kind of like you," Evelynne whispered to Ally, pointing up at the woman above them. "That is, if you had long hair."

"Yeah and wore a thirty-four D bra," Ally muttered back.

The roof that the man and woman were supporting was a perfect half-spherical dome, plain and unadorned. In the exact centre, a twenty-metre wide hole let sunlight in to illuminate the Chamber.

As Ally started to make her way across the gleaming floor with her companions, she felt that her booted feet, though carefully cleaned before entering the building, were somehow sullying the perfection of the floor. As she walked, she noticed that the marble was not actually seamless, but was inlaid with veins of oricalcum and some other metal that looked like white gold. The metal looked as though it had been poured into intricately carved grooves in the stone to form complex and visually disconcerting designs. Intrigued, she asked the archaeologist about them.

"Ah, yes. Those make up what we call the Maze," Collins replied. "The metals are oricalcum and a gold-silver alloy called electrum. They cover the entire floor of this chamber. We have managed to reconstruct a picture of the pattern in its entirety and it seems to be a quite intricate fractal pattern. That in itself is causing quite a stir in the scientific community, I can tell you. Supposedly, fractals were first discovered a few decades ago, but here we have a pattern going back to prehistory. It's another example of just how much we don't know about the ancient Atlantlans. Take the roof, for example." He pointed upwards. "That entire dome is composed of only eight pieces of stone, each carved into a perfect eighth of a half-sphere. Not only that, but the only things holding up each section are its two neighbours." He shook his head. "The technical expertise required to construct the thing, let alone construct it well enough to survive eleven thousand years intact, is incredible."

"You have no idea how it was done?"

"Not for certain, no. We have found a rather symbolic mural in a building that we think was a construction office. It depicts six men lifting each block into place using only their hands." The Doctor smiled wryly. "Considering that each slab weighs over six tons, I think we can safely assume that the drawing is purely metaphorical. Unless one wants to believe that the Aztlani could each lift two thousand pounds with their bare hands."

Collins and Evelynne laughed, and Ally joined in, but she was thinking, *Two thousand pounds, huh? Well, I can't quite do that, but...*

Looking down at the floor again, Ally realised something that had been troubling the back of her mind since she entered. "The floor is concave," she said in surprise.

"Yes, it is," Collins said. "You have a good eye, Dame Alleandre. It is, in fact, the bottom of a perfect sphere with a radius of exactly 824.253 metres. In other words, Your Highness," he explained to Evelynne, "if you were to continue the curve of the floor all the way, it would form a sphere with the centre almost a kilometre above our heads. A most amazing example of mathematical engineering."

"I'll take your word for it," Evelynne said. "My own math skills are less than stellar."

"There's one other thing, Doctor Collins," Ally added. "You say these lines on the floor are electrum and oricalcum?" The Doctor nodded. "Well,

chApteR twenty

that means they conduct electricity. The only reason I mention it is that this—" she pointed to a section of pattern. "—looks like it would make a simple parallel plate capacitor. And unless I'm wrong, *this* would probably make a simple inductor." She pointed again. "To me, this looks like one huge circuit board." She shrugged. "Of course, I'm a physics major, not an archaeologist, but . . ."

"No, no, no," Collins interrupted. He was staring at the floor with unalloyed shock. "You're right, I never considered the similarity. Oh, it may be a coincidence, of course, but it certainly bears examination." He looked up. "Dame Alleandre, it seems I may be hiring some electronic engineers soon. Are you interested?"

"Me? Oh, I'm certainly interested, but I don't think I'm the best person for the job. I specialised in astrophysics, not electronics. I only recognised the floor because I had to take a few courses in electrical engineering. Although if you want another wild theory . . ." Dr. Collins nodded frantically, sending his glasses to perch perilously close to the tip of his nose. "Well, the curvature of the floor and that aperture above remind me of parts of a huge reflecting telescope. I don't know how it would work, exactly, especially with the focal point over eight hundred metres overhead, and I don't think the floor is reflective enough, but it might be something to check out. Of course if there was originally a lens of some sort in that aperture, things would be much different." She shrugged. "As I said, it's only a wild theory . . ."

"*Pole'can war esse tolu'a mens*," Collins murmured. "*Del mek si'aerat on pellk.* I beg your pardon." He was looking around the room as though he had never seen it before. "Dame Alleandre, all new theories are considered wild when they are first advanced. Even if these ideas of yours are not in fact correct, they have still shown me that we seem to have become too narrow in our focus here at the excavations. We are concentrating too much on the purely archaeological side of affairs. To be fair, we *are* archaeologists. I believe I will have to see about hiring some researchers of other scientific disciplines after all. I'm sure I could find you a job here if you wanted it. You appear to have a knack for thinking of possibilities that nobody else has considered. I would love to hire you for that ability, if for nothing else, and the fact that you have no preconceptions is actually an asset." He looked at Ally earnestly. "It will take some time to come up with the proper funding, but I would appreciate you keeping my offer in mind."

"Um, sure," Ally replied. "I'll certainly think about it."

"So you think you might enjoy working here?" Evelynne asked quietly.

She and Ally were trailing Dr. Collins as they walked towards the last stop on their tour. Darkness was slowly approaching and Sir Arthur had flatly refused to allow the tour to continue after nightfall.

"Hmm, pardon?" Ally asked abstractedly. She had been watching the bodyguard out of the corner of her eye. He had seemed distracted for the past half-hour. It was so subtle that Ally guessed that anybody without her heightened sensitivities would be oblivious. However, she could see his eyes darting back and forth, seeking threats even more rapidly than usual and also the faint sense of confusion or puzzlement, as though he kept seeing things out of the corner of his eye that disappeared as soon as he focused on them. Knowing that the bodyguard was drawing upon decades of experience, Ally had tried a quick scan herself, but had detected nothing out of the ordinary.

I guess he's just jumpy about something, she thought. Suddenly she became aware that Evelynne was talking to her again. "Sorry, I went away for a minute. What were you saying?"

"I was asking if you were seriously considering Doctor Collins' offer. You know, the job?"

"It's tempting," Ally admitted. "I think it would be a lot of fun. Although I really wouldn't want to be away from you." She shrugged sheepishly.

"I wouldn't want you to go, either. But I also don't want to hold you back. No matter what happens with . . . us, you still have a life of your own to consider. Somehow I don't think you're the type to become a pampered Lady."

"Probably not. I wouldn't mind trying it out for a while, though." She grinned. "Seriously, though, I don't–"

"No, you don't have to decide now. Besides, Dusan said it would take him a while to get funding. Even if I help him speed things along it will take at least a month or two to obtain. That's just how government bureaucracies work." She squeezed Ally's arm. "If you did, I'd expect you to visit regularly. Daily, even. Just think about it, all right?"

"Okay," Ally agreed.

A short distance ahead, the sound level was noticeably higher, the noise of engines echoing across the ancient city. Cranes were lifting objects into and out of a large hole in the ground. Trucks piled high with dirt passed regularly on their way out of the city. The cranes hung out over the edge of the pit and were operated from small aluminum cabins some distance above the ground.

"In terms of sheer scale, this is probably the most impressive project under way in Aztlan right now, Your Highness," Dr. Collins said, raising

chapter twenty

his voice above the noise. As the group moved closer, the size of the pit became much more readily apparent. They stopped several metres from the edge. "Aztlan is ringed by a series of concentric circular canals, the Circle Seas. This is the innermost. We have begun dredging it. As you can guess, the entire project is likely to take a while. Since this particular canal is about four hundred metres across, and two hundred deep, we must remove a little over six hundred million cubic metres of dirt. That corresponds to well over a billion tons."

"Holy cow," Ally murmured. She could see trucks and earthmovers busily digging away at the soil filling the canal. The workers had dug a huge trench all the way to the other side of the canal and were now concentrating on digging it deeper. The set-up struck her as inefficient. "Wouldn't it be easier to just start at the top and kind of spiral your way around as you dig? I think it would be easier than having to haul everything directly up and out."

"Yes, it would, but at this stage we unfortunately have other considerations as well. While the Crown supplies the lion's share of the funds for excavation, Their Majesties' purse is not bottomless. In a few months there are plans to open the site up to tourists to raise additional capital and we wish to present the most spectacular sights possible." Collins seemed personally offended at having to allow gawking tourists—other than the ones he was currently guiding—tramping all over *his* site. Collecting himself, he said, "I think *that* must certainly be one of the most stupendous sights anywhere."

He pointed to the far wall of the canal, where diggers had exposed over a hundred and fifty vertical metres of stone. Each massive block in the wall was at least ten metres across and carved to fit perfectly with its surrounding stones, like a gigantic jigsaw puzzle.

"No kidding," Ally said. "You know, I'd challenge any modern nation to construct anything half that big."

"Oh, I agree, despite our technology I believe even something half as large would be utterly impossible." Collins waved at the distant canal wall. "It's not bad for a civilisation without heavy construction equipment."

The group remained, looking over the excavations, until a loud whistle split the air.

"Ah, it is time to quit for the evening," Collins said. "The lifts will now bring the workers down below back up to this level."

"Your Highness, we should move away now," Sir Arthur said in a low voice. "None of these people have been adequately investigated."

"Very well," Evelynne said, taking a last look at the work site. She held out an arm for Ally, who had begun to lean on her cane more as the day progressed. "Shall we?"

They started back towards the centre of the city, Evelynne and Ally asking a few more questions of the Doctor as they walked. They were about fifty metres from the edge of the canal when Ally saw Sir Arthur's head shoot up suddenly and he stared intently at the nearest crane. Startled by his sudden movement, Ally stopped, dragging her companion to a halt as well.

Nothing happened for several seconds, then the screeching sound of bending metal filled the air. Everyone's eyes immediately snapped to the cranes overhead. Despite the deepening twilight, it was easy to see the length of the crane's arm as, seemingly in slow motion, it began to buckle. Slowly it folded in upon itself, shedding steel spars as it came crashing down. The cries of workers could be heard, as the first group to begin its ascent suddenly found itself uncontrollably returning to the bottom of the pit.

Sir Arthur and the rest of the Guards reacted instantly, even though the collapsing crane was fifty metres distant. Evelynne found herself squeezed between the bodies of four solid bodyguards, each of them instantly alert and ready to respond further if needed. For her part, Ally was surprised when two more Guards were suddenly bracketing her with their own bodies.

The entire collapse seemed to take hours, but it could only have been seconds before the vibration of buckling machinery ceased, leaving the cries of wounded workers, the creaking of swaying metal and the sputter of cut electrical cables. Dr. Collins was already gone, running towards the accident site. He looked faintly ridiculous, his long, lanky frame all pumping arms and legs, but the turn of speed he had produced was impressive.

Even with the immediate threat over, the princess' bodyguards had not relaxed in the slightest and Evelynne had to physically force a small opening to see the aftermath. "Isis," she breathed. Making a decision, she ordered, "Sir Arthur, send some people over there to help." She knew that even suggesting that she go herself would be pointless and an easy way to get herself bundled off to the helicopter as quickly as her Guard could move.

Sir Arthur looked stubborn. "Highness, we can't–"

"Damnit, I'm fine! Nobody is going to be coming after me. They need you more than I do." She pointed to where workers were gathering from all over the site to peer down the wall of the canal. The huge figure of Reanne Poloi, the foreman, could be seen barking orders.

chapter twenty

Sir Arthur hesitated a moment more, then nodded abruptly. "Major Nixon and I will stay with the princess. Rawson, al-Rashan, take up a perimetre. Everyone else, go and help. Move!"

Obediently, the Guards scattered, though they were obviously unhappy about leaving their primary charge.

Evelynne clutched Ally's arm as they watched. Ally looked on while feeling particularly useless. *Damnit, there's nothing I can do! There are too many people.* She breathed a sigh of relief as she saw emergency medics converge on the location. *At least they seem to have things fairly well in hand.*

Several minutes passed and then Sir Arthur cocked his head and listened to the report coming through his earbud. He relaxed minutely. "The lift was only about twenty metres up when it fell," he reported. "Most of the injuries appear non-life threatening. However, several workers are in serious condition." He paused a moment. "Evacuation helicopters are en route."

"Good," gritted Evelynne. "At least–" She broke off when Ally stiffened.

Ally had been watching anxiously, and was beginning to hope that things would turn out well, when she hissed as a sudden blast of pure psychic energy slammed into her mind. There were no words to the silent scream, but the meaning came through clearly.

HELP! 'can't breath, tightness' ANYBODY! 'dying, fear' HELP ME! 'painpainpain' 'loneliness, cold, warmth trickling' NO!

Without even realising what she was doing, Ally found herself running, with no conscious thought of direction, ignoring the pain in her back. She angled to the side of the crashed lift and realised that she was heading towards the cabin of the crane, which had toppled over so that it was some distance from the edge and away from where all the rescuers were gathered. *The operator!* Ally realised. *He's still alive!*

The cabin of the crane had survived relatively intact, rather than shattering as it hit the ground. It had, however, been crushed by the impact and a heavy length of girder had broken loose and slammed into the side of the cabin, compressing it even more. Reaching the cabin, Ally saw that nobody was nearby. All of the rescuers had congregated at the edge of the canal over thirty metres away and were busy helping the workers trapped there.

Moving closer, Ally looked in through the crain's shattered windows. Inside, the operator was trapped, slowly being crushed by his wrecked cabin and the girder that lay across it. Despite the obvious pain and panic he was experiencing, the young man, his face pasty white, visibly brightened when he saw Ally looking down at him, and another burst of thought hit her.

ANGEL! 'crushed, no air' HELP ME! 'terror, hope' DYING! NO!

Evelynne hurried up behind Ally. She had been startled by her friend's sudden decision to bolt and had reflexively followed. It had surprised Sir Arthur and Major Nixon as well, and they arrived a bare moment later. "Ally what's–oh, Isis," the princess said, seeing the trapped man. She whirled to face her bodyguard. "We have to get him out of there!"

The Guard had been about to chastise his charge for running off, but stopped when he assessed the situation. "We need to get that beam off, but we need equipment to do it with. It's too–" He broke off when he saw what Ally was doing.

The young woman had managed to get among the wreckage of the crane so that she had a good grip on the steel beam resting across the side of the cabin.

"Ally, what are you doing?" Evelynne shouted. "You can't–"

Ally narrowed her perceptions, concentrating solely on the metal in her hands. *They're going to see,* a part of her warned. *I know,* she told herself. *But I can't help that. There's no time! I can't let this guy die. Damnit, he's like me!*

Setting the thoughts aside, Ally focused, reaching deep into her strength and channelled power, lifting with the entire force of her will. Ally's purely physical muscles could lift, under normal circumstances, perhaps fifty kilograms at most. However, she was not using only physical strength. Power surged through her mind, focussed by her will and guided by the physical act of lifting.

At first nothing happened and Ally threw even more power into her efforts, feeling a sudden stab of pain as her brain protested. Then, impossibly, the steel beam began to shift. Ever so slowly, creaking and groaning in protest, the metal began to lift up, away from the crane's cabin.

Evelynne stared, completely amazed by what she was seeing. Then she heard a groan and realised that it was not coming from the slowly bending metal, but from the woman lifting it with her bare hands, her face absolutely white from strain. The princess was frozen until she noticed the thin trickle of blood emerge from Ally's nose. Then she somehow found herself at Ally's side, lending her own meagre strength to the effort. A moment later Sir Arthur and the Major joined them.

Finally, the beam had been bent back far enough to reach the cab of the crane. Power still thrumming through her body, Ally curled her fingers around the sides of the crumpled door and proceeded to rip it completely off its hinges, while her audience looked on, beyond amazement. She almost despaired when she saw that the young operator was no longer conscious, but when she jumped into the cabin and pressed her fingers to his neck, she was relieved to feel a steady, if weak, pulse.

chapter twenty

Climbing out of the wreckage of the cab, feeling more tired than she could ever remember feeling before, she looked down into Evelynne's face. "He's alive," she said dully. Then the power seemed to drain out of her like water, her knees collapsed and she would have fallen if Evelynne hadn't caught her and eased her down to the ground. "Oh shit," she whispered through the pain of her stunning headache.

Evelynne gently wiped away the blood from Ally's face with her sleeve. "Ally, what just happened here?" she asked, her voice trembling.

"Had t'get to 'im," Ally mumbled. "Called me." She closed her eyes. "Please, not now. Later. Promise. Hurts now. Can't think."

"Okay," Evelynne said softly, stroking Ally's face with a shaking hand. "Later. You just rest now."

As much as she wanted to, Ally could not fall asleep, and had to bear the pain for what seemed like days.

chapter twenty one

Ally sat in the most comfortable chair in her suite and rested her face in her hands, massaging her forehead with her fingers. The brain-imploding headache had thankfully subsided to a dull throb, but remained ready to return the instant she overextended herself again.

That was close, she thought. *If I had pushed any more I think my brain might have begun oozing out my nose . . . literally. I should be thankful it was only a nosebleed.* She sighed. *And now Evelynne knows. And Sir Arthur and Major Nixon. They might not know exactly what happened, but they know it was something out of the ordinary. Damnit, it wasn't supposed to happen like this! I was supposed to go with Evelynne somewhere private and secluded and carefully and calmly explain how I was . . . different. There would be plenty of opportunities for escape and things to hide behind if she got really mad. But no. Instead, I had to go and start bending steel bars with my hands like goddamn Superman. And any moment now she's going to be coming in here demanding explanations and there's no way I can avoid it. Well, actually, there is a way, but somehow I think she'd still track me down. Between her and Sir Arthur, they could too.*

In the aftermath of the accident at Aztlan, Ally, Evelynne, and her Guards had remained to help for several hours, until long after it was dark. One worker had died, caught under the lift as it fell, and half a dozen others had received fairly serious injuries but by some great stroke of fortune, the casualties had mostly been minor. The young man that Ally had saved was currently in hospital with at least four broken ribs, a broken arm and a cracked humerus. He had not regained consciousness, so Ally had not had an opportunity to speak with him about his mental screams, which had initially caught her attention.

Finally, the Royal party had boarded the helicopter for the flight back to Kilim. The journey had been mostly silent. Ally had feigned unconsciousness in an attempt to delay the inevitable discussion—although after a while it had been unnecessary to fake. She had awoken to find herself lying across several seats, her head pillowed in Evelynne's lap. Ally had revelled in the closeness, while at the same time wondering how long it would last. She had adamantly refused to see a doctor about her condition, claiming that with time she would be fine.

Upon returning to the Palace, Ally had been sent immediately to her suite with orders to have a shower and wait for the princess. The order had not seemed angry. Evelynne appeared more dazed than upset. Ally held onto a faint hope that at least their friendship would survive the upcoming revelations.

That had been half an hour ago and nervousness was steadily eating away at that hope. Ally looked wistfully out the doors to the balcony. *I could still escape,* she thought. *Not even the Guard could stop me. But they'd still know where my friends and family live . . . Shit, my friends and family.*

Ally picked up the telephone on a nearby table and dialled.

"Dumela?" a sleepy voice answered.

"Chorus? This is Ally."

"Ally? What's going on? Why are you calling me at the ungodly hour of . . . one in the morning?"

"Chorus, something happened. There was an incident."

All traces of sleep vanished from Chorus' voice. "An incident? Are you okay? Is Evelynne–"

"No, we're both okay, physically, at least. There was an accident at the excavations at Aztlan. A crane collapsed. It happened right in front of us. But what I'm calling about is that I saved a man there this evening."

"Saved a–oh shit, Ally, you mean you used . . ."

" . . . unconventional means, yes."

"Did anyone see you?"

"Evelynne, Sir Arthur and Sir Arthur's second in command, Major Nixon. They were right there. I don't think anyone else saw, but I'm not sure."

"Damn, Ally. What's happening now?"

"Now I get to explain everything to Evelynne. But what I need from you right now is a favour."

"Name it."

"I need you to call my parents and let them know what's happened. If you can't reach them, call Annie. They'll know what to do. I'd call myself, but I don't know how much time I have. You should also be prepared just in case someone comes for you. I know you can't do what I can, but . . . hopefully I'm being paranoid, but just in case, you need to know." There was a hesitant knock at the door to the room. "I have to go. My interrogator is here. Chorus . . ."

"Don't worry, Ally, I'll take care of it. And remember, this is Evelynne. She loves you." Even though he meant it in a purely platonic sense, still being unaware of their changed relationship, Ally still held onto the thought.

"I hope so. Look, I really have to go."

"Go. And good luck."

"Thanks."

chapter twenty one

Ally hung up as the knock came again. Taking a deep breath, trying to calm her roiling stomach, she called, "Come in." She felt absurdly proud of the fact that her voice did not waver.

Slowly the door opened. The first person into the room was small and grey, and immediately walked over to Ally's feet and loudly demanded to be picked up. Ally reached down and complied, bringing the cat up to bury her face in its soft fur. "Hey, Cassie." Ally looked up to see Evelynne standing in the doorway. There was an awkward silence, which Ally finally broke. "Hey, Evelynne. Please, come in."

The princess did so slowly, closing the door behind her, and Ally's heart broke as she saw just how uncertain the woman she loved was. Evelynne took a seat and silence reigned once more.

"You're looking better," Evelynne said finally. "You're not as pale."

"Thanks. I managed to meditate a bit. That always helps."

"It always—do you mean this kind of thing happens regularly?" Evelynne asked quietly.

"No, not really regularly, but it does happen. This evening was the worst it's ever been, the hardest I've ever pushed myself."

"Tonight . . . Ally, what happened tonight?" The princess' voice was raw with confusion. "I saw you move that metal bar. And it wasn't like it was aluminum either. It was steel and must have weighed four hundred kilograms. And you *bent* it. With your bare hands. Ally, *what happened?*"

Ally sighed, leaning back in her chair and looking up at the ceiling. "When I was growing up," she began, "I found out that there were things I could do that nobody else could do. I would know things that nobody else knew. It was sporadic and difficult at first, and sometimes months would go by and I would be as normal as the next kid. But as I got older, I began to experiment, to see what my limits were. To be honest, I still haven't found them."

"By 'things', you mean, like bending steel beams?"

"Not quite. I didn't learn how to do that until much later, when I was in university, actually. And before you ask, no, I'm not an alien and I wasn't found in a spaceship like Superman. My parents are Catherine and William Tretiak, and while they can be a little weird at times, they are as human as anyone. No, one of the first things I realised was that if I tried hard enough, sometimes I could tell what people were feeling. Not thinking, but whether they were happy, sad, angry, confused . . . over time, I learned to expand that ability and *then* I was able to read people's thoughts. Needless to say, it didn't make me particularly popular. Still, it was something that stayed with me until grade six. Then it . . . didn't vanish, exactly, but it got buried."

"Grade six," Evelynne murmured. "What happened in–" She broke off as realisation dawned. "When they–when you got . . ."

"When I got shoved naked into a school hallway," Ally finished bluntly. "You have literally no idea what it's like not only to have that happen, which is humiliating enough, but to *know*, for a *fact*, exactly what the people laughing at you are thinking and feeling. The scorn, the derision, the petty spitefulness. All of the words they were thinking but couldn't bring themselves to say in a school –not to spare my feelings, but for fear of getting caught. Anyone who tells you that 'sticks and stones can break my bones, but words can never hurt me' is talking absolute bullshit." She hung her head. "Needless to say, that put an end to my mind-reading experiments for a while. It took me six years to discover how to use those abilities again." Ally laughed humourlessly. "I went to a therapist for a while, but he couldn't understand why I was so traumatised and it wasn't as if I could tell him."

"Isis, Ally. You mean those panic attacks . . .?"

"A nice little down payment on all these 'gifts' I've been blessed with." Ally sighed explosively, consciously forcing herself to relax. "It's not all bad, of course. In addition to the ESP, I found out that if I concentrated in the right way, I could make things move without physically touching them. Discovering that was the high point of my childhood. My parents were, naturally enough, mildly surprised." She chuckled honestly for the first time at the obvious understatement. "I remember my Dad coming out into the back yard to find me hitting a baseball thrown by a pitcher who wasn't actually there. It would have been a home run too, but the pop fly was caught by an invisible outfielder who threw me out at first."

Evelynne laughed as well, although her laughter was more strained. Just when she thought there was nothing more to shock her, Ally threw something more in her face. "So, uh, you just concentrate hard enough and things move?"

Ally sighed. "It's not about how hard I concentrate, but just *how* I concentrate. Think of it this way: no matter how strong you are, there's no way you can pick up a ball using the back of your hand." She tapped hers for emphasis, and then wiggled her fingers. "You have to grasp it with the front. In the same way, if you don't use the right mental 'muscles', nothing is going to happen. But when you do . . ." Ally took brief stock of herself. *I can do this, as long as I don't try anything too intricate.* She reached for the right frame of mind. Looking towards the bookshelves along the walls of the room, she raised a hand and held it out in a reaching motion.

There was a moment as she focused and channelled, and then a small leather-bound book eased out of its place and impacted an instant later in

chapter twenty one

the palm of her outstretched right hand. *Hmm,* The Tempest. *How appropriate to see you, Prospero.*

Evelynne jumped at the slap it made. Ally hadn't moved an inch from her chair and Cassie slumbered peacefully in Ally's lap, blissfully unaware of the events around her.

"Oh, Isis, Osiris and the Duat," Evelynne gasped.

Ally ignored the outburst. "And, like anything else, with practice I became better at controlling it." Holding the book resting on her upheld palm, she dropped her hand. The book remained floating in the air, bobbing slightly, held up by nothing more than Ally's will. She made a small twirling gesture with her fingers and the tome started to move, slowly at first, then faster, until it was rapidly orbiting Ally's head. "And better." Another hand movement brought another book from the shelf into a different orbit. "And better." A third joined the other two. By now Ally looked like the nucleus of a very literary atom.

Ally sat in the centre of her shell of books and watched them, easily controlling the flows of thought that regulated their movements. The difficult part was getting things started. After that it became a simple matter of maintaining the flow, rather like juggling tennis balls. Eventually, after several moments, she stopped the motion. Another thought sent the books across to where Evelynne was sitting, and one by one they gently dropped into her lap.

Evelynne stroked the covers of the books, hesitantly at first, then more steadily as her fingers assured her that the leather-bound volumes were real. She looked up at Ally. "You can really do this," she said in awe. She paused. "That's how you saved me, isn't it? In Marseilles. You stopped the bullets."

"Almost." Ally rubbed her shoulder. "I basically created a—an aura, I suppose, that absorbed the bullets' kinetic energy. I wasn't in as much danger as everyone thought I was, which was why I was so uncomfortable when everyone thought I was a hero. I managed to stop one completely, but I wasn't so lucky with the other two. Believe it or not, I don't regularly go around stepping in front of bullets. The most I'd stopped before was an arrow, when Lung Shou was teaching me how to do it."

"You mean you didn't know it would work."

"No."

"But you did it anyway, even knowing you might be killed." Evelynne's voice was intense.

"Well, actually, I didn't really think about it. I just reacted," Ally said uncomfortably.

"You see?" Evelynne said. "You *are* a hero. Even though you had . . . certain advantages, you didn't know if you could do it, but you tried anyway."

She smiled genuinely, despite her roiling thoughts. "No matter what, I'll always consider you a hero."

Ally squirmed in her chair, eliciting a sleepy protest from Cassiopeia.

Evelynne thought for a moment. "You said your mind reading abilities went away for six years. Does that mean that they're back? Can you just hear what people are thinking?"

Ally shook her head. "It doesn't work quite like that. I have to concentrate on it, usually, and then all I get are impressions of what the person is thinking at that particular time. Emotions and concepts, mostly. It isn't like in the movies where the telepath can delve into your most secret memories while you're unaware. It's only what you're thinking right now. Of course, if you happen to be remembering something, I can read that, but I can't bring it up on my own. It's usually really confusing too. Different people think in different ways, in different languages, using different symbols. And their thoughts are chaotic too; they jump from one topic to the next and back almost at random. So I usually settle for just getting a surface scan of the concepts."

"Have you ever read my mind?" Evelynne asked haltingly.

"Once," Ally admitted, hanging her head again. She looked up at Evelynne's gasp, and saw the hurt expression on her face. "I don't go around reading people's thoughts at will! I actually have a personal code against it. I only do it when absolutely necessary, in an emergency or with the person's permission." She faltered. "Sometimes I can't help doing it, though. I'm sorry."

"So when . . .?"

"Do you remember that day, just after we got here, when I talked to Annie on the phone?"

Evelynne cast her mind back. "You mean that morning you told me you were gay?"

"Yeah, that's it. You told me you were all right with it, and I–I had to know for sure that you were. I've had experience with people who say they're okay out loud, but really think I'm an abomination. I didn't want you to be one of them. You were already my friend and I *needed* to know you weren't like those other people." Ally swallowed. "I shouldn't have done it and I'm sorry."

"That time . . . you were sitting in front of me . . . I was holding your hands and you looked into my eyes. I said, 'Can you see that I'm telling the truth?' That was it, wasn't it?"

Ally nodded. "Yes." She was a little surprised that Evelynne could recall the exact circumstances so well.

"I felt you doing it," Evelynne whispered.

chapter twenty one

Ally head snapped up. "What?"

"I felt you doing it," the princess repeated. "You looked into my eyes and I suddenly felt dizzy. Like I was off balance. Does that usually happen?"

"Never," Ally said. "As far as I know it's undetectable. At least, nobody I've ever read before has said anything."

"Can you do it now?"

"Now?" Ally asked, startled. "You mean you want me to . . ." Evelynne nodded. "Um, okay. You're sure?"

The princess nodded, looking more certain than she was. "I'm sure. I just want to know if it was what I felt."

"Oh. Okay."

Feeling very uncomfortable, Ally slowly and carefully stretched out with her mind, opening it to the thoughts of the woman in front of her. It seemed to happen incredibly easily and she found herself following the link that she had discovered weeks before. Then Evelynne's mind opened up within her. Ally was careful to remain mostly detached, sampling her friend's thoughts and emotions with a feather light touch.

Those thoughts were a confused jumble of amazement, curiosity, hurt, uncertainty, love and embarrassment. Too many to distinguish. Ally just left her mind open, trying to intrude as little as possible. Across from her, she saw Evelynne shake her head.

"You're doing it right now, aren't you?" Evelynne asked in a whisper. "I can feel . . . something. Like . . . someone else is looking out of my eyes. But that's not quite right. I don't have any words for it." Experimentally, Ally withdrew her mind from the link. Evelynne's eyes widened. "And now you're gone, right?"

"Yes." Ally was shocked. Nobody but Mrs. Chen had ever been able to feel her before and the Chinese woman was a special case.

"Do it again," the princess requested.

Ally complied, easily re-establishing the link. Suddenly the jumble of thoughts cleared slightly and words appeared, as clearly as if Evelynne were speaking aloud. *'Ally, can you hear me?'*

She nodded. "Yes. I can hear you."

'What number am I thinking of? 43, 43, 43, 43 . . .'

"The number is forty-three."

"Isis," Evelynne said aloud. "You really can do it."

"Yeah. Of course, what you were doing is a special case. You were basically going through the entire mental aspect of speaking out loud, but without sending any signals to your actual vocal cords. Normally, people are just a big muddle."

"Wow," the princess said. "So if you can do all this, why have you kept it such a big secret? I mean, you could be the biggest celebrity in history and even if you didn't want that, I know of literally hundreds or thousands of scientists who would love to study what you can do."

Ally laughed mirthlessly. "Yeah, because society in general has always treated 'special' people really well, hasn't it? Evelynne, the last person to publicly display abilities anything like mine got himself nailed to a cross. And while I'm certainly making no claims of being any kind of Divine Messenger, do you think anyone would listen? I would be either the next Messiah, or more likely the Antichrist, and either way my life would be over. Besides, what about my friends and family? What would happen to them? They don't even have my abilities to protect themselves. And what about the other people like me around the world who just want to be left alone? When faced with things they can't explain or control, people panic. The more people, the lower their collective intelligence."

"Wait a minute. People like you? You mean you're not the only one who can do this?"

"Not really. I have the most diverse set of talents of anybody I've personally met, but there are a few people out there who can do similar things. With all of the stories of witches, magicians and miracle workers out there, I'd imagine there must be more. Not all of them can do the same things, of course. In my mind, I've classified people according to their psychogenic abilities into three . . . no, make that four categories."

"So what are those four categories?"

"Well, first there are the people who have little to no ability at all. Obviously, they make up the bulk of humanity. Oh, occasionally someone will get a 'hunch' or be really 'lucky', but it's usually not something they can control.

"Then there are what I call the Savants. They're those people who can perform one skill at a—I hate to use the term, but—superhuman level of ability. Those people who can play symphonies when they've only heard them once, paint excruciatingly exact replicas of works of art, figure out the cube root of three million, four hundred eighty seven thousand, two hundred and five in their heads. You know. For some reason the ability seems to emerge in autistic people a lot, but not always. Chorus is a savant." Evelynne looked surprised. "He has this absolutely incredible ability to learn languages. I think the longest it's ever taken him to learn one fluently is about a month. And not just grammar and vocabulary, either. Also colloquialisms, speech patterns, social rules to some extent. It's really quite awesome to watch."

"You're right," the princess murmured. "He's learned Lantlan a lot faster than I realised. I just never thought about how strange it was."

"He doesn't exactly broadcast it. And even if someone gets surprised, so what? He's just a guy with a 'gift for languages'."

"I guess so. So that's two. What's the third?"

"I guess the third category are those people who possess one, or rarely two, abilities that could be considered 'paranormal'. I call them Talents, because they have one, well, talent. Yuri Geller can bend spoons and some of those psychic hotline people might actually be precognitive. There are a whole lot of examples in movies. They can all do one thing, albeit sometimes extremely well. I've met exactly four people who could be called Talents. My Mom is Talented," Ally added. "She can pick up on a person's emotions, kind of like I can. Actually, I was the one who taught her how to do it. But if she hadn't had the potential to begin with, she'd never have been able to learn."

"Your mother is like that? What about your father?"

"Ah, Dad is a very special case. The only term I've been able to come up with is 'anti-psychic'. It is literally impossible for a telepath to read his thoughts. It's like he's not even there. I have absolutely no idea why. It sucked when I was a kid, because he was *always* able to sneak up on me. On the other hand, I could play hide and seek with him without even being tempted to cheat by scanning for his thoughts." Ally shook her head, smiling slightly at the memory. "Other than that, he has no psychogenic abilities whatsoever. The downside is that whenever I'm with my Mom, I always *know* for a fact that she loves me. With my Dad, I have to do what everyone else does and listen to his actual spoken words. Oh, I'm not complaining. I know my Dad loves me too, but just once I'd like to be able to *feel* it."

There were several moments of silence, as they both contemplated those ideas. "So who are in the fourth category?" Evelynne asked finally.

"As far as I know, the fourth category is, well, me." Ally pointed to herself. "I've never met anyone who could do all the things I can. Through whatever random mutation or developmental accident, I'm kind of a mixture between a Talent and a Savant. I have the Talent potential to do these things and the Savant ability to actually learn from other people how to do them. Like I said, Talents normally have only one ability and no matter how hard they try, they can never learn another. I guess it's the same kind of thing with Savants; they tend to be incredibly specialised. Chorus can learn languages, but he's absolutely hopeless at art. And his singing . . ." Ally shuddered theatrically.

"So people have taught you how to do things?"

"Yeah. A woman in Vancouver taught me how to better control my telepathic abilities and a Kung Fu master in Thailand showed me how to use my psychokinetic ability to deflect bullets. Actually, he taught me how to deflect punches, but I improvised. I'm not going to tell you exactly who they are," she said. "They don't deserve to have people bugging them about what they can do. It's not that I don't trust you," Ally hastened to add, "but, well, it's their secret and their privacy."

"That's okay," Evelynne said. "I understand." She paused. "So what made you expose yourself tonight? I mean, you could have stood back and just let things happen."

Ally sighed. "I know. And I really wanted to help out with the rescue at the main lift, but I also didn't want to reveal myself in front of all those people. I do have some experience with using my abilities surreptitiously, but they seemed to have things under control. But then that man . . ." She trailed off, remembering.

"What about him?" Evelynne prompted gently. "How did you even know he was still alive?"

"He . . . screamed," Ally said quietly.

"He did? I didn't hear anything."

"No, with his mind. He couldn't speak, so he projected his thoughts. As for why he didn't project them to everybody around, I don't know. Maybe he recognised my own mental abilities. Maybe we're like magnets and telepaths' thoughts are naturally drawn to one another. I think he's at least a Talent, although it could have been a fluke. A one-time thing where the brain does whatever it can to survive."

"Isis," Evelynne said. "How do you think he learned?"

Ally shrugged. "Like I said, maybe he didn't. From the few cases I've seen, Talents sometimes emerge during a traumatic event, so this might be the first time he's used his abilities. I'd like to talk to him and find out."

"You might be able to do that in a few days. In the meantime," Evelynne said, "I'll see about keeping the authorities away from him." She looked Ally in the eye. "Regardless of what else you've said, I agree with you that he doesn't deserve to be poked and prodded just because he's different." She smiled crookedly. "You've taught me that too much publicity is not always a good thing." She sighed and rubbed her face. "I think that it would be the understatement of the century to say that you've given me a lot to think about."

"There's something else." Ally spoke so quietly she was almost inaudible. This was the part she'd been dreading most. She had considered avoiding it altogether, but her conscience had vetoed the idea.

"What is it, Ally?" For the first time, Evelynne thought that Ally looked frightened. Before she had been cautious, nervous, but still relatively calm and confident. Now she looked as though she was expecting someone to drive a knife between her shoulders.

chapteR twenty one

Ally struggled with the words for several seconds. "We're . . . linked," she said finally.

Evelynne frowned. "Linked?"

"Our minds," Ally explained. She pointed to her own head, then Evelynne's. "There's a–a psychic connection. I discovered it the night before–the night before you knighted me, when I was meditating. It's like a string, or a wire between my mind and yours. I don't know why it's there."

"You mean you didn't create it?" Evelynne still wasn't sure exactly what Ally was talking about.

Ally winced and said in a very quiet voice, "No, I'd never do that, not without your knowledge and permission, even if I knew how. It was just . . . there. And it's been there ever since. For all I know, it's been there since we first met."

"Oh." Evelynne digested this new piece of amazing information. She was surprised that she could still find it amazing, after all the revelations of this evening. "So what is it doing?"

Ally shrugged again miserably. "I don't know. Nothing active that I can tell. All I know is that it makes you the easiest person to read that I've ever met. And, if I concentrate, I always know exactly where you are and what your general emotional state is. Nothing specific," she said quickly, "just whether you're content or angry, or hurt or anything."

"Always?"

Ally nodded, still not looking up. "Even when I was back in Canada I could tell. Usually I need to be at least in the general vicinity to do something like that. I was afraid . . ." She broke off.

"You were afraid of what, Ally?" Evelynne asked softly.

"I was afraid that this link was what was drawing you to me. That it was what made you think you loved me." Ally hunched her shoulders as if expecting a blow.

Evelynne was shocked. *A bond drawing me to Ally? How could she do that to me? But she didn't, did she? She said she didn't know why it was there. And she wouldn't lie, not now when she's been revealing everything else. She said she knew what I was feeling. I wonder . . .*

The princess closed her eyes, not quite sure what she was doing, and fumbled in her mind for some kind of "string" or "wire" connecting her to Ally. She could feel her love for Ally still present, if a little shaken, when she thought of the other woman, but other than that, no pull, no drawing together that seemed out of place. *Of course, I don't really know what I'm "looking" for,* she admitted. *But what if . . . ?* Drawing a picture of the other woman in her mind, she concentrated on it. *Where are you?* she asked the image. *What are you feeling?*

"Holy Isis!" Evelynne gasped. Ally's head shot up. "I saw you. I *felt* you. And you were–oh, Ally." In an instant she was out of her chair and wrapping her arms around Ally's startled body. "Oh, love," she whispered.

Cassie was knocked from Ally's lap to the floor, where she complained loudly once, then sat down to wash herself. She was ignored by the two humans.

For a brief moment, Evelynne had felt Ally's emotions as if they were her own. The other woman was awash in misery; sure their relationship would never survive this particular bit of knowledge. A hopeless longing was entwined with deep sadness and guilt over her imagined transgression. Worst of all, a bone deep loneliness at the thought that this person, this other piece of her soul, would soon be gone. Then the connection had broken, but it had been enough to catapult Evelynne out of her chair.

Now the princess felt Ally's arms hesitantly come around her own body as she knelt on the floor and kept up her tight embrace, stroking Ally's back. Ever so slowly Ally relaxed, fearful that this support would be snatched away, until she suddenly collapsed into Evelynne's arms. Rare tears streamed down her cheeks as she buried her face in the side of Evelynne's neck and she let loose all her fear and anxiety in helpless sobs.

Evelynne rode out the storm, keeping up a continuous stream of soothing words and not relaxing her hold in the slightest. "Oh, love, it's all right," she murmured. "It's all right."

Eventually the tears passed and Ally slowly loosened her frantic clutch. Raising her head, she displayed tear-reddened eyes. She sniffled. The princess smiled and pulled a handkerchief out of a pocket. "Here," she said.

"Thanks," Ally whispered hoarsely, wiping away the remnants of her tears. "Sorry."

"Don't be sorry," Evelynne said. She paused. "You know, I thought of something."

"Oh?" Ally asked in a small voice.

"Well, you were thinking that maybe I was in love with you because of this bond, right?" Ally nodded. "Well, what if you got it backwards? What if the bond exists because we love each other?"

Ally looked surprised, then speculative. "I never thought of that," she murmured.

"That's why, even with all your abilities, I'll always be considered the brains of this fa–relationship," Evelynne joked. She was rewarded with a quiet but genuine laugh. The princess sighed. "Ally, I'll be honest with you. You've given me a lot to think about. Which is certainly an understatement." She felt Ally stiffen again, but continued. "You've just turned many of my views of the world on their heads. I can't say it won't have an impact on me

chapter twenty one

or on our relationship. But I promise you that no matter what, I will talk to you about how I feel and what I'm thinking."

"Okay," Ally said softly. "And I promise that whenever you want to ask questions, I'll answer you as best I can. Even though I myself don't know everything there is to know about what I can do, I'll always be honest with you."

"That's good." Evelynne laughed suddenly.

"What?"

"Oh, I just thought that I made a mistake in knighting you." She grinned. "I should have made you my court wizard instead."

Ally smiled back. "Believe me, the irony has not gone unnoticed on my part."

Evelynne's chuckle was interrupted by a yawn. "I need to sleep," she said, "although I don't know how much I'll actually get." She hesitated. "Before I go, though . . ." She turned to pick up the books that had scattered from her lap when she had left her chair so quickly. Holding them out in Ally's direction, she sheepishly asked, "Um, could you do that spinning book thing again?"

chapter twenty two

Ally heard the whispered argument as she approached the open door of the study. She couldn't hear the exact words, but they seemed to be very emphatic. Peering around the doorframe, she saw Evelynne talking with the Master of her Guard. Sir Arthur's back was to the door, but Ally could see the princess' expression and it was stormy, to say the least.

Not wanting to intrude, especially when she was still uncertain of her relationship with Evelynne after the previous day's events—not to mention the evening's revelations—she tried to back away unnoticed. Unfortunately, Evelynne spied her as she was attempting to make her escape.

"Ally!" the princess called. She glared at her bodyguard as she hurried around him towards the door. "Wait!"

Ally reluctantly made her way back, halting just inside the doorway. "Hi," she said softly. She took in Evelynne's flushed face, which made her red hair seem even more so, a visible sign of the princess' anger and passion. Despite her trepidation over Evelynne's temper, Ally thought the other woman looked beautiful. She was relieved when Evelynne's expression softened as she came closer.

"Good morning," the princess replied. Her tone was admirably level. "Did you sleep well last night?"

"Actually, yes," Ally admitted. "I was completely out of it. I usually am after I've . . . you know. Especially when I, uh, overexert myself."

"Oh. That makes sense, I suppose." Evelynne hesitated. "How are you feeling this morning?" She hated this forced politeness, but the events of the previous day—which had spilled into the early hours of this morning—had left her still feeling uncertain.

Ally lowered her eyes. "Um, okay, I guess. Physically, anyway. Mentally and emotionally?" She shrugged, the vulnerable expression on her face pulling at Evelynne's heart.

"Oh. Well, I managed to get maybe two hours of sleep last night. You could say I had a lot on my mind." The princess smiled wryly at the double meaning of her last statement, but Ally remained solemn. "And then I came down and found that my bodyguard had made certain arrangements without discussing them with me." She shot a disapproving glance at the Guard, and

Ally was glad that Evelynne was not the one who possessed psychokinetic abilities. If she had, the unfortunate Sir Arthur would have been a large flat spot on the wall.

Overhearing, the Guard in question sighed and said, "Your Highness, I had no choice. My duty as you protector requires me—"

"—requires you to inform your superiors of the possible ramifications of yesterday's events," Evelynne completed. It was obvious that she had been discussing the matter at some length and had heard the phrase several times before. "Okay, fair enough, you had your duty. What you *could* have done was wait until you had talked to me first!"

Ally had felt a cold ball of fear settle in her stomach at the words "inform your superiors," and couldn't help but ask in a tight voice, "Who exactly did you tell and what exactly did you tell them?"

Sir Arthur turned to the young woman and was briefly concerned that she might faint. Her face was deathly pale, with the expression of someone watching a bullet come towards her. "As per regulations, I reported to my immediate superior, General Danun of the Common Guard, and informed her of my direct, personal observations. I also submitted the reports of the Guards under my command, who had previously submitted them to me. At the General's request, I also speculated on the nature of my observations. She was . . . concerned. Your Highness, this is my job. I am bound by honour and duty, and also by personal choice, to protect you from any and all threats to your person." He cast another glance at Ally, obviously uncertain of the risk she might now pose. All he saw, though, was the same attractive young woman he had begun to know and even like over the past months. "If necessary, I can and will call upon any and all resources necessary to carry out that task. That may include seeking advice from other experienced personnel."

Evelynne had not missed the covert glance. "Ally is *not* a threat!" she exploded. "She is my *friend*!"

"Frankly, Your Highness, because she is your friend, she automatically compromises your objectivity. Personally, I also consider Dame Tretiak a friend." Ally was startled. "However, I do not have the privilege of allowing *any* sort of personal relationship to interfere with my job. Which is one reason I am required to report to an unbiased superior."

Evelynne looked about ready to explode again, but Ally forestalled her by saying, "So what is going to happen?"

"The General wishes me to escort you to the Guard Headquarters for an interview. The results of that interview will be taken into account for her next decision. I will not speculate on what that decision might be."

chapteR twenty two

Ally nodded, and wished she didn't feel like she was going to throw up. The morning was turning into something from out of her worst nightmares. First there was Evelynne's obvious discomfort, which seemed to have seriously shaken any chance of rekindling their relationship. Now she was about to be interrogated by a member of a formidable government security agency, who probably had the power to completely destroy any chance she had for a normal life. And not just Ally's, but her family's and friends' as well. *I should have followed my original decision and just stayed away,* she thought dully. *Now my secret is out and the person that I risked it for can't even bear to touch me.* Ally wallowed in her misery for a moment and then gave herself a kick. *Okay then, the only thing I can do is deal with it. It isn't going to be easy and it's going to hurt like hell, but there's nothing else to do. I know how to make a sword . . .* The beginnings of an idea, which she had occasionally considered for an occasion like this, began to take shape in her mind. "So when do we go?" she heard herself ask.

Evelynne looked shocked and even Sir Arthur appeared mildly surprised at her sudden capitulation without a struggle. "Er, immediately after breakfast," the bodyguard said.

"Ally, you can't—you don't—" Evelynne stuttered.

"Yes, I do," Ally said softly. "Even you wouldn't be able to shield me forever, which means that sooner or later I'd be up before the firing squad. Figuratively speaking, of course. I hope." She sighed. "Right now I'd prefer it to be sooner." She looked into the princess' eyes. "Remember, I'm not totally without resources of my own." Ally managed a crooked smile.

"Very well, Dame Tretiak," Sir Arthur said. "I will go and make the final preparations for our journey." Saluting briskly, he left the room, leaving the tension that resonated between the two women.

Refusing to meet Evelynne's eyes, Ally made her way to a chair and sat down, the stress of the morning already making her back ache. The princess closed the door and, after a moment's hesitation, sat back on her heels on the floor in front of Ally and folded her hands in her lap. She seemed to be searching for words and Ally let the silence stretch, her gaze locked on her own hands.

"I spent a long time last night . . . thinking," Evelynne started haltingly. "I won't lie to you and say that I've worked everything out, but I came to a few conclusions."

"Oh?" Ally asked, when the other woman didn't seem about to continue.

"Yes. I think the biggest thing was, well . . ." In a quick, surprising move, Evelynne rose to her knees and ducked her head under Ally's, bringing their lips together in a hard kiss. At the same time, her hands shot out to grasp Ally's shoulders lightly.

At first, Ally was too shocked to react, but then instinctively relaxed into Evelynne's embrace, the kiss softening, becoming less fierce and more passionate and loving. Her arms snaked automatically around the princess' body, drawing it in between her legs. For several long minutes they stayed like that, lips moving against each other, until Evelynne drew back with a soft gasp. Ally reluctantly let her go.

Evelynne felt the heat in her own flushed cheeks and saw that Ally's face was equally red. Both of them were panting slightly. Evelynne rested her hand against Ally's cheek. "I love you," she whispered. "That's the first thing I wanted to tell you."

With a soft sob, Ally buried her face in Evelynne's neck and the princess felt tears dampen her skin.

"I love you too," Ally murmured. "So much."

Evelynne held Ally as the storm passed and mused on the contradictions in the woman she loved. Despite her discomfort with crowds and social situations, and her preference for solitary pursuits, Ally was still desperately lonely and craved the support and approval of those around her. Despite her obvious intelligence and poise, not to mention her beauty, she still had serious doubts about her own worth. She was usually genuinely surprised when someone praised her. Now, with this latest revelation and despite all her extraordinary abilities, she was just as fragile and vulnerable as anyone else. Evelynne thought back to the previous evening, to the image of Ally lying in her arms, blood pouring from her nose and nearly unconscious from pain after bending the metal beam and saving the life of a complete stranger. Again. Now Ally had opened herself up completely, revealing her greatest secret, willing to accept whatever decision Evelynne made concerning their future. *Not only her own future,* Evelynne thought, *but those of her parents and friends. I could utterly destroy her with what I know now and I know she wouldn't lift a hand against me. She might run, she might hide, but she would never strike back.* She turned to press a kiss to the head beside hers. *Thank you for this gift, Ally. I won't throw it away.*

Finally, Ally pulled back, sniffling. Evelynne took out another handkerchief, the way the action mirrored events of the previous night not going unnoticed. "Thanks," Ally murmured.

Once she was done wiping away her own tears, she gently removed those that had stained Evelynne's neck. The princess closed her eyes and leaned into the soft stroking, disappointed when the cloth was taken away. "No matter what, I'll always be here for that," she said. "I don't pretend to

chapter twenty two

know what's going to happen with us, or even what today is going to bring. But I love you. I don't know exactly what to think about your abilities, or how they relate to me. I'm not sure what to think about this bond between us. One night isn't really enough time to work all that out."

"I understand," Ally said in a more normal voice. "Believe me, I understand."

"I suppose you do. You had to do this with Annie, didn't you? I mean, did she . . .?"

"She knew," Ally confirmed. "I told her after we'd been going out for about six months. Believe me when I say you're reacting better than she did. She didn't even talk to me for two weeks. But she accepted it eventually. Although apparently not as fully as I thought at the time."

"Isis. That's why she broke up with you, isn't it?"

Ally shrugged nonchalantly, but her expression gave away her feelings about the painful memory. "I don't really blame her. She was brought up Catholic and they're not exactly known for their liberal views on paranormal phenomena. Of course, she did go against her faith by admitting she was a lesbian. Sometimes I wonder if she didn't accept me because of a similar rebellious impulse."

Evelynne couldn't stop the surge of jealousy, but it was quickly eclipsed by the anger she felt at the almost offhand manner in which Ally put herself down. "I don't think so," she said. "I think she just realised what she knew all along, that you're smart, funny, beautiful, charming. And she would be an idiot to let you get away. Whatever happened afterward, you never stopped being those things."

Ally blushed. "Well, when I talked to her a while after we broke up, she admitted that she wouldn't have been able to deal with it even if I was just a cop. She wanted 'someone she could be sure would be there at the end of the day'."

"There you are, you see? And as harsh as that is, it is a valid concern. Some people can't handle things like that. Why do you think that police officers have one of the highest divorce rates around? So it was never any fault of yours." Evelynne smiled. "Selfish as I may be, I happen to be glad that Annie let you back into the market. It gave *me* a chance to snap you up."

Ally smiled sheepishly, embarrassed by Evelynne's enthusiastic defence. "I'm glad too."

"Now, one of the perks of being your girlfriend–" Evelynne broke off. "That sounds strange. Girlfriend. Hm. Strange but nice." She shook her head to clear it. "Anyway, one of the perks is that I get to stick to you like glue. So I'll be there today when you have your 'interview'."

"Evelynne, you don't have to—"

"Ah, what did I say? It is my prerogative to go anywhere you do. Besides, you wouldn't be trying to argue with the Crown Princess of Atlantl, would you?"

"What about the Life Debt thing?"

"Hm. Good point. However, on consideration, I think that the Girlfriend thing overrules the Life Debt thing. So there."

Ally chuckled. "I can see who's going to wear the pants in this relationship."

Evelynne looked puzzled. "What do you mean? What does wearing pants have to do with it?"

"It's—never mind, I'll explain it to you later."

❦ ❦ ❦ ❦ ❦

General Danun stood as the group came into her office. Alleandre entered first, followed by Major Nixon, Evelynne and Sir Arthur. The General observed the first person intently, but saw only a perfectly composed face, with no emotions showing at all. The young woman's cane and slight limp gave the impression that she was particularly harmless, an appearance at odds with her reported actions of the previous day—or at least their potential.

"Dame Alleandre," she greeted, successfully keeping the suspicion out of her voice. "Your Highness." This time faint but clear disapproval could be heard. "Please, take a seat."

Ally and Evelynne did so. Major Nixon stood alertly by the right wall of the office, while Sir Arthur took a post near Evelynne's right shoulder.

"Your Highness, it was not necessary for you to come yourself. The purpose of this meeting was to have a short interview with Dame Alleandre." The General's eyes flicked briefly to Sir Arthur, a subtle chastisement for allowing the princess to come along.

"I'm sure it was, General," Evelynne replied calmly. "However, every Atlantlan citizen being interviewed by any government representative is entitled to legal counsel, should they desire it. As Dame Alleandre's immediate liege lady and her Lady of Justice, I may act as her counsel under any circumstances I choose. I am simply exercising that privilege. In fact, under the terms of our treaty with Canada, a Canadian citizen is also entitled to have a representative of the Canadian government present as well. Dame Alleandre has chosen to waive the latter right."

"I see." Another quick glance at the Master of the Heir's Guard got a subtle shrug in reply. Apparently his charge had used that argument on him and he had had no choice but to comply. "Very well, Your Highness," General Danun conceded. "As you were also a party to the recent events, perhaps your presence is appropriate as well."

Evelynne noticed the General's attempt to regain control over the proceedings and chose to let it go. It would not do Ally any good to antagonise the commander of Atlantl's primary security agency. "Certainly, General."

The General turned her attention to Alleandre, who was still sitting impassively. "Dame Alleandre, first of all I wish to inform you that this is an informal discussion. Even so, you are forbidden from discussing what occurs here with anyone other than your legal counsel." She looked at the princess. "Revealing what occurs here or what you see in this building, will subject you to prosecution for espionage, with a sentence up to and including the death penalty. Do you understand?"

"I do." Ally spoke for the first time since entering.

"Good." General Danun was silent for a moment. "We are here because Sir Arthur's report of yesterday evening's extraordinary events has raised some questions that I simply cannot ignore." She looked at a file on her desk. "What I would like is for you to describe those events yourself."

"Before I do that," Ally said, "I have two questions of my own. Who else is aware of these . . . 'extraordinary events'? How many people have seen that report?"

The General looked at her intently and then shrugged her wide shoulders. "Sir Arthur, of course, as the author of the report. Major Nixon's observations are also included." She indicated the thin bodyguard. "The report was submitted directly to my office and I can guarantee that I am the only person to have read it. So, barring a witness who has not made himself known, only those of us present in this room suspect that something unusual occurred." She noticed that Ally had been staring at her with a penetrating gaze while she spoke.

"Okay," Ally said. The other woman was telling the truth or at least believed she was. A very light scan had revealed none of the emotions associated with someone knowingly telling a lie. Of course, that could mean that the General was simply very good at lying or controlling her emotions somehow, but Ally couldn't see why she would. It wasn't as if the older woman was physically hooked up to a lie detector. "My second question is whether this conversation is being recorded. If it is, then I have nothing to say."

General Danun considered briefly. "No, there are no electronic recording devices in this room. The work I do is too sensitive to allow anything of the sort. And my office is also swept for bugs at least twice a day."

Ally nodded. "All right. So what do you want to know?"

"Start from the beginning. From when you first arrived at the site."

Ally related the events of the previous day until she got to the accident. Then she seemed to hesitate. "The rescue workers had things under control," she said. "They were busy trying to help the people who had fallen in the lift. Sir Arthur had sent most of the Guards to help. He and Major Nixon stayed behind." She paused uncertainly. "That's when I . . . became aware that the crane operator was still alive, although he was in trouble. The rescuers had overlooked him. They were concentrating on the bulk of the workers and even if they thought of him, they might have assumed that he had already been killed in the fall. Anyway, I ran over to the crane's cab, which was about thirty metres away from everyone else. The cab was partially crushed by the fall and a piece of metal from the crane had fallen across it and trapped him inside. With the help of Sir Arthur, Major Nixon and Ev–Princess Evelynne, we managed to move the bar and get him out of there. I, um, overexerted myself and kind of passed out for a while, so I'm not sure what happened next."

The General nodded. "I see." She consulted the report on her desk. "What you have described generally confirms the bulk of the Guards' observations. Except for the last part of it. According to Sir Arthur, the piece of metal you described was in fact a beam of solid steel almost three metres long and ten centimetres thick. Yet, he also reports that you grasped it and proceeded to bend it with nothing more than your bare hands. This, obviously, is the fact that has piqued my interest. How do you explain what has been reported?"

Ally sighed. "I don't suppose you'd accept an adrenaline spurt, would you?"

Evelynne coughed to cover a laugh and even the General evinced a ghost of a smile. "No, I wouldn't."

"I didn't think so. Adrenaline couldn't do it anyway, despite all the stories of mothers lifting cars off their babies. The muscles and tendons of the average human body are simply physically incapable of withstanding that kind of stress without tearing, with or without adrenaline. That's a physical and biological fact." Ally was aware that she was avoiding answering the question. Years of hiding her abilities had made it second nature. "What those women actually do is activate a latent ability that exponentially increases their lifting power while bypassing the conventional muscular action. It's a form of psychokinetic ability. And what they can only do automatically and uncontrollably, I can call upon at will."

"I see." All traces of amusement had vanished from General Danun's face, leaving her regular stern, unsmiling mask. "And how much exactly can you lift with this ability?"

chapter twenty two

"The most that I know of for sure is about three hundred and fifty kilograms," Ally replied. "Possibly more, but that is the amount I know of from my own experiments. Actually, that beam was certainly more."

"Isis," Evelynne murmured. "That's well above the world record for weightlifting for someone of your weight." She looked at Ally again, once again taking in her slim build and lack of obvious muscles. "Isis."

"And I'm assuming that simply lifting incredible amounts is not the only thing you can do."

"No, I can do other things that would be considered . . . superhuman." This time Ally didn't elaborate.

"And I assume they are also equally impressive."

"I suppose so."

"I see," the General said again. She sat in thought for several moments. "I will be blunt. The fact that you can do these things would concern me under any circumstances. They make you difficult or impossible to control should you decide to use them against this country. As well, you have a close relationship with both Princess Evelynne and the rest of the Royal Family. Frankly, all of these factors make you a clear and present threat to security. Tell me, why should I allow you to remain at large and not eliminate you altogether?"

Evelynne opened her mouth to object, but Ally was already acting. She had caught a hint of the General's intentions and while the older woman was speaking, Ally had been mentally preparing for her next move.

Concentrating on the most likely threats, she had begun to create the right thought-forms, spinning them deftly into her consciousness, but not activating them yet, like a juggler preparing to toss her batons into the air. *One.* The thought slid into place. *Two.* Another lay waiting and ready. *Three.* A mental 'hand' reached out. *Four.* Another was poised to act. It was difficult, like trying to think of the lyrics of four songs simultaneously, but not impossible. The moment the General stopped speaking, Ally channelled energy into her foci, feeling the exhilarating thrill as her mind obeyed her commands.

She noticed with interest that a full second before she moved, Sir Arthur did, grabbing Evelynne and shoving the princess behind him, guarding her with his wide body. A part of Ally nodded at the confirmation of a theory.

Rising swiftly from her chair, Ally thrust out both arms, fingers spread, as though pushing against some obstacle–which she was, even though her hands touched nothing. Her left arm pushed forward, towards where General Danun sat behind her desk, while the other pointed to the side, where Major Nixon had begun to move an instant after Ally had. Ally's first and second thoughts responded instantly. With one part of her mind she pushed forward and the General's heavy desk moved backward with a loud shrieking and scraping, catching the surprised woman behind it in her chair and continuing until it had pinned her, still sitting, against the far wall. The second thought reached out like a giant invisible hand, grasping Major Nixon before she could move more than a few centimetres and pushed the Guard back until she was pressed, spread-eagled, against the wall. The bodyguard hung a foot off the floor.

A moment after those two women had been incapacitated, Ally's fingers, on both hands, twitched and she released her third and fourth foci. These required far less energy, as they reached into General Danun's jacket and the holster at Major Nixon's side and sent the guns that were there flying across the room to land in Ally's outstretched hands with audible slaps.

There was silence for several long seconds, broken only by the sounds of General Danun gasping for breath against the edge of the desk pressing into her chest and the faint struggles of the Major as she attempted to free herself from her invisible bonds.

Looking at Ally with stunned eyes, General Danun whispered, *"Adeptus!"*

Then Ally became aware out of the corner of her eye of Sir Arthur, his weapon drawn and pointing directly at her. When she turned her head, Ally could see Evelynne behind the bodyguard, gaping at her with a shocked expression on her face.

"Alleandre, put the guns down now." Sir Arthur's voice was calm but firm, with only the very slightest hint that its owner was at all shaken by the events that had just taken place.

Ally looked at him for another few moments before slowly and calmly bending down to place the two guns on the floor. Rising, she turned to the still trapped Major Nixon and released her hold, gently lowering the bodyguard to the floor. She quirked a brief smile of apology at the Guard, who stood tense and uncertain near the wall, before walking over to the General's desk. Channelling once more, she grasped the edge of the desk with one hand and proceeded to drag the heavy piece of furniture back to its proper place.

Ally's audience spent the next few minutes regaining their composure. Eventually they resumed their previous positions, although Major Nixon was now visibly tense and Sir Arthur had positioned himself so that he stood between Ally and the princess. Ally simply sat, outwardly calm, but inwardly frightened, examining her hands in her lap.

chapteR twenty two

"Well," General Danun said, breaking the uneasy silence, "I think you've made your point with that demonstration. However, you have also shown just how dangerous you could be."

"Maybe," Ally said. "But I actually had two points to make. One was, quite obviously, that I would not be easy to 'eliminate', should you decide to try. On the other point, I'd like you to notice that I only . . . restrained you and Major Nixon."

"So you did," the General noted. "Why did you not restrain Sir Arthur as well?"

"Because I knew what his reaction would be and I was going to do nothing to interfere with it. His very first thought was to protect Evelynne. You and the Major would have tried to confront me. He would have done everything he could to protect her. I will do absolutely nothing to threaten Evelynne's safety. *That* is the second point I was trying to make. I want you to know that I will do nothing to act against Her Highness, her family or the Atlantlan government."

"I see. However, despite this demonstration, we must still take your word on that matter. You are obviously a very dangerous woman, even more so than I originally suspected. How do I know that you can be trusted?"

Ally shrugged. "For now, you don't know. And before you even consider it, don't even think about threatening my family or friends to try to control me. Oh, don't worry, I'm not reading your mind." *Right now.* "I'm just aware of how vulnerable they could be. It would be logical for you to consider using them to control me. Not smart, but logical. Let me be honest and put my cards on the table." She leaned forward. "If anything happens to anybody I care about and I find out you or anyone in your organisation is responsible, I can and will take this entire building apart." Ally smiled coldly. "If my parents happen to die in a car accident or my Dad has a heart attack, so be it. Accidents happen and even I can't stop them all. But I will investigate the matter *very* thoroughly and if it was done on purpose, the person or persons responsible will end up being *very* sorry. As will their superiors. And just in case you think you could get away with hiding it . . ." Ally paused, staring at the General. "Who did you sleep with last night?" she asked abruptly.

"What?" General Danun asked, surprised, but Ally was already nodding in satisfaction.

"Interesting," she said. "And not your husband either." Everyone gaped at her. "Don't worry, I'm not going to tell anybody who it is and I'm sure nobody else here will discuss it either." Ally sighed, suddenly exhausted and rubbed her eyes. "It may seem like I'm threatening you and I guess I am. But I want you to know that I really don't want to cause any problems. Not only is Evelynne my friend and I don't want to compromise her or her eventual reign, but I also like this country. I'm an Atlantlan citizen now and I'd like to protect it. So basically the way I'd like it to work is this: assuming that nobody threatens my parents or my friends, the worst that will happen is that I will remain neutral. I will not do anything to threaten the Guard or the Atlantlan government. I will neither aid nor hinder their operations. On the other hand, the best that might happen is that I might offer my services to help you in some way. I might not do everything you ask of me, but I will at least consider it. As my Sponsor and Liege Lady, Evelynne can order me to accept any assignment and I will if she does so. If not, as I said, at worst I will maintain a non-interference policy." Ally sighed again. "So that's my offer. The only other option is to order me to leave the country, which I will do if Evelynne tells me to."

"You are *not* leaving the country," Evelynne said immediately. "Until and unless you choose to do so."

General Danun nodded distractedly, obviously thinking about Ally's statement. The possibilities raised by Dame Alleandre's demonstrated talents were intriguing, even in the limited offer available. And if she could be persuaded to use them more actively . . . It certainly justified the time to investigate more thoroughly. "You put forward a persuasive argument," she said cautiously. "What kind of aid can you provide?"

"I have certain . . . abilities in both a support and information gathering role. In fact, I have already helped Atlantl in both ways, although nobody has suspected it yet. A few months ago there was the small matter of several large drug shipments that somehow came to the attention of the Customs agency."

"That was you?" Evelynne asked. "You're the one who provided all the times and locations?"

Ally nodded. "I was staying in Outremer at the time," Ally said. "Once, when I was in town, I noticed a dealer selling to kids outside one of the high schools. I considered just reporting it to the police, but then decided to try to find out who the supplier was. So I followed him. I have . . . ways of not being noticed. When I found the supplier, I thought that I might be able to work my way back at least as far as the source on Atlantl. It took a while, but finally I did. With a bit of special, er, eavesdropping when they were discussing incoming shipments, I was able to compile a list of dates, places and names. Then I just sent the list anonymously to the proper authorities. They took it from there."

"I see. And what about the 'support' you mentioned?"

Chapter Twenty Two

Ally shrugged, embarrassed. "Because I knew where and when the busts would take place, I stuck around to see what I could do to help. It was still the police and soldiers who did the real work. I just tried to provide a little . . . luck."

"The Angel," Major Nixon breathed. When everyone looked at her in question, she explained. "I have a friend who was part of the operation and he told me that all sorts of bad luck seemed to be hitting the smugglers. Their guns would jam, they would trip and fall, things would fall on them, that kind of thing. The squads figured there was an Angel watching over them."

Ally blushed. "Well, I don't know about the Angel part, but yeah, that was me."

"Isis," Evelynne said. Suddenly something seemed to strike her. "Oh gods, the bounty!"

General Danun, Sir Arthur and Major Nixon appeared startled, then speculative, while Ally remained baffled. "The what?" she asked.

"The bounty," the princess explained. "By Atlantlan law, anyone who reports a criminal act which leads to a conviction receives a reward. It's proven to be an incredibly powerful incentive. In the case of smuggling, it amounts to two hundred fifty *tali*, or one per cent of the total value of the seized goods, whichever is higher. Most of the time it gets paid out to lesser criminals who decide to sell out their bosses, but this time . . . The last I heard, the Justicars overseeing these investigations estimated the street value of the drugs seized at approximately eight billion *tali*." She looked to the General for confirmation.

"I believe that is correct." The older woman nodded. "However, they have also confiscated and impounded five of the cargo ships that were involved, and seized the assets of at least two companies fronting for the smugglers in this country. According to a report I just read, they have chosen to add those assets to the bounty calculation. Of course, nobody has come forward to claim it yet. At least, nobody who can back up their claim."

"I guess one per cent doesn't seem like a lot, but . . ." Ally made a quick mental calculation. "Jesus, on eight billion, that's eighty million! That's almost a hundred and sixty million dollars!"

"It is," the General confirmed. "And with the cargo vessels and company assets added in, the value would increase even more." She looked at Ally, who seemed dazed by the information. The young woman's reaction actually helped alleviate some of the General's mistrust. *She does not seem the sort to do things only for money,* she thought. *And she did provide the information without knowing about the reward she would receive.* General Danun found herself grudgingly beginning to respect the young woman. Thinking of something about the drug seizures, she asked, "Exactly how much did you know about the drug shipments?"

"Well, basically just the time, place and approximate amount. Pretty much all the information I provided to Customs."

"So you didn't know anything about other shipments?"

Ally looked confused. "Um, no. I don't think so. Why?"

The General considered for a moment. "One of the shipments–the last one we seized, in fact–did not actually contain drugs. Instead, it consisted of a very large consignment of weapons, bound, we suspect, for the Hy Braseal Liberation Army. You did not hear anything about it?"

Evelynne gasped audibly and Ally looked startled. "No, nothing like that. None of the people I . . . overheard thought it was anything other than drugs."

"*Paka,*" the General swore softly. "That fits with what we've learned through our interrogations. Apparently someone is funnelling weapons to the HBLA and using our domestic organised crime to do it. And without them being aware of it, either." She swore again. "I have all these bits and pieces that tell me the HBLA is planning something big, but I have no idea what it is. Weapons smuggling, assassination attempts, unbreakable codes . . ."

"Codes?" Ally asked.

"Yes." The General considered how much to reveal, then decided that the basics wouldn't hurt. *Besides, if she really wants to know, I'm sure she can find out,* she thought sourly. "We have been intercepting messages from an unknown source directed to the HBLA. Unfortunately, we have been completely unable to break the encryption. Finding out what they're saying would be invaluable. You don't happen to have a gift for code breaking, do you?"

"Nooo . . ." Ally thought briefly. "But I might know someone who does." She cast a glance at Evelynne.

"Oh," the princess said, "you mean . . ."

"Yeah." Turning back to the woman behind the desk, Ally said, "If I do suggest this person, I would consider him or her to be under my protection. That means all of the same things we talked about earlier. No coercion, no threats. It will be up to him or her to accept or decline any offer you make."

"Agreed."

"I have a friend who has . . . call it a gift for languages. This friend's abilities also extend to a very impressive aptitude for such things as word puzzles and translation. In my opinion, there's no reason why they can't be extended to code breaking. After all, when you encode something, all you're

chapter twenty two

basically doing is taking a statement and writing it in another way: another language, in effect. What you need is a translator. My friend has displayed an ability to learn new languages literally from scratch and regardless of prior knowledge, in weeks."

"Really?" General Danun's tone was speculative. "How do you know your friend can break this code?"

Ally shrugged. "I don't, not for sure. But it seems to make sense to me. If you want, give me a sample of one of your own codes and I'll see how my friend does. Nothing critical, obviously. Heck, encode a bunch of Shakespeare's plays. That way you have absolutely nothing to lose."

"Very well. Suppose I do that and suppose your friend does show this ability. How will I know he is willing to work for us?"

"My friend will tell me, I'll tell Sir Arthur and he'll tell you. From there you can arrange to meet."

"I see." The General smiled crookedly. "You know, Dame Alleandre, you have a knack for espionage. You seem to understand code breaking, chains of contact, covert operations . . . blackmail. Are you sure there's no chance I could hire you myself? I could certainly use someone of your talents."

"Nope." Ally shook her head vehemently. "I would absolutely hate it. While it may seem selfish of me to avoid helping this country like that, I do have some more philosophical objections. While I believe that you, and most of the people working for you, are honourable and decent, what happens if someone with less admirable qualities takes over? What would they do with someone with my abilities? Today I showed you that I could take out every person in this room without touching a soul. If someone found the right leverage to force me to work for them–" She carefully did not look at Evelynne. "–would you want me unleashed on the world? So, no. Instead I will be guided by my own set of ethics, which I believe are fairly decent, if not stellar. I will help you from time to time, should I think it appropriate, but I won't do it full time."

"Fair enough," General Danun said. "I thought you would say that."

"Do you mind if I ask a question now?"

"Of course, go ahead."

"Earlier, when I was–you know–you said something. *Adeptus*, I think it was. What did you mean by that?"

"Ah. I am a knight of the Order of the Eye. There are certain legends in the Order of members who had the ability to move things with their minds, read thoughts, summon spirits, create fires and so on. Magicians, in fact. Of course, my Order is hardly unique in this. The Templars were persecuted and driven from Europe because they were accused of practising magic."

She indicated Sir Arthur. "That was the official reason, anyway. In reality, of course, both the Church and various monarchs at the time wanted to get their hands on the Templars' vast wealth. In any case, the word used in my Order to refer to people with your gifts is Adept. Or in Latin, *Adeptus*. They are further divided into the *Adepti Major*–those possessing greater power– and the *Adepti Minor*–those with only limited ability."

"Oh, okay. I never did come up with a name I liked for what I could do. For a while I thought of myself as a Mage or Wizard, but that just didn't sound right."

"You did not have a teacher or peers?" When Ally seemed disinclined to answer, the General said, "No, that is all right. You don't trust me. I can understand that. To be blunt, I don't completely trust *you*. However, I believe you when you say your primary goal is to protect your family and friends. Fair enough. My primary goal is to protect my country from any and all threats to its security. We are both very powerful people. I hope that as long as our goals do not contradict each other, we can at least share a respect."

Ally smiled genuinely for the first time since entering the room, and a small portion of her anxiety fell away. "I think we can do that."

chapter twenty three

"So, what do you think, Mr. Tladi?" the young cryptographer of the Guard Communications Department asked.

"Hmm," Chorus said noncommittally. He didn't look up from the screen where the encrypted message was displayed. "Interesting."

"Oh. Er, is that good or bad?" the young man asked.

"What?" Chorus shook himself. "Oh. At the moment I don't know. It's certainly more complex than the one you tested me with, Gerry."

"And may I say again just how impressed I am that it only took you a week to break it?"

Chorus shrugged. "The fact that you sent me so much made it easier, actually. It made it easier to find patterns. And nobody ever said *War and Peace* was lacking in detail." He pointed to the screen. "That's why this particular code could be difficult. There just isn't much to work with. I assume that's normal procedure when sending messages."

"It is," Gerry confirmed. "The idea is to send all the relevant information as economically as possible. It makes the message harder to intercept and also, as you said, more difficult to break. Does that mean you don't have enough to work with?"

"I don't know," Chorus admitted. "I'm used to more conventional languages. If you're immersed in a culture, the amount of data available to help with translation is huge. Context, different methods of syntax, colloquialisms, contractions, accent, emphasis. Simply being able to guess that someone is saying 'tree' when they point to one. Here, you're asking me to learn a language that is effectively being spoken by two people. That isn't a very large 'culture'. On the other hand, the fact that it is an inevitably mathematical 'language' cuts out a lot of confusion."

"So you think you can do it, then." Gerry looked hopeful.

"Given enough time . . . yes. Just by looking at this I can pick up on at least some pattern to the code."

Intrigued, the cryptographer asked, "Oh? Where?"

"It's not like I can actually point it out. It's more like a–a sense. A hunch. You know, it's ironic. Here I am talking about the structure of a language and I don't have the language to do so." He laughed. "Think of it this way. You know those three-D pictures where you have to look at them a certain way and then suddenly a boat or a horse appears?" Gerry nodded. "Well, before you see the actual picture, you can still see a certain pattern in the seemingly random lines. That's what I'm doing here. I need to figure out how to look at this 'picture' so that the underlying image jumps out at me."

"I understand." Gerry nodded again. "So what do you need to do that?"

"Information," Chorus said promptly. "As much context as possible in which to place the messages. Time and place of sending, destination, method of transmission, known couriers . . . If you're right and they are going to the HBLA, what were they doing before and after each message was received? Basically everything you've got."

The cryptographer nodded. "I'll see what I can do." He hesitated. "Do you know how long this is going to take?"

Chorus shook his head. "Not a clue. I haven't done anything quite like this before. It could be a week, two weeks, a month, a year. Maybe I'll never get it. Still, I'll try my damnedest. I owe All–Dame Alleandre a lot."

"As do we all," Gerry replied.

As he headed off to start collecting the requested data, the young man wondered at that. The meeting between the Director of the Common Guard, Princess Evelynne and Dame Alleandre a week ago had become the talk of the building. Nobody knew what had happened and General Danun was putting over forty years of intelligence expertise to good use in obfuscating the truth of the matter, but there were still rumours of the odd noises that had escaped the General's office. For a few days afterwards, the General could be seen rubbing her chest, as if it pained her and a hesitant rumour had spread that perhaps Dame Alleandre had assaulted her. The rumour had died quickly, since all anyone had to do was look at General Danun's stocky build and Dame Alleandre's thin frame, not to mention her limp, to realise that it was ridiculous. Besides, Sir Arthur Ramirez and Major Theodora Nixon, both epitomes of Guard training, had also been present and there was no way they would have allowed anyone to assault their superior.

Still, whatever had happened had created quite a response. Another rumour had spread that no less than twelve covert agents had been assigned to Code Seven Surveillance on some of Dame Alleandre's friends and family. Code Seven mandated agents to remain undetected by the subject, but also to protect the subject's well-being at all cost. Gerry wasn't sure exactly what Dame Alleandre had offered in exchange for such protection–assuming the rumour was true –but apparently Chorus Tladi's code-breaking skills were a part of it. After months of trying to break the same code with no success,

chapter twenty three

Gerry and his team were more than happy for the assistance, no matter how unconventional.

❧ ❧ ❧ ❧ ❧

Ally walked along the corridor in the Summer Palace, the unfamiliar weight cradled in the crook of her arm the focus of her self-appointed mission. It was her hope that this mission would take her mind off her current troubles for a time. Ahead she saw the wide form of her quarry and sped up to intercept him. "Sir Arthur!" she called out.

The bodyguard stopped at her call and turned to face the young woman. He was dressed in plain grey workout clothes and he noticed that Ally was wearing a similar outfit, though hers was blue. His eyebrow twitched in surprise as he saw the sword she carried.

"Dame Alleandre," the Guard greeted. "How are you this morning? I notice you are without your cane."

"Yeah, I'm feeling pretty good," Ally replied. *Physically, anyway.* "My back's just feeling a bit stiff." She grimaced. "According to my therapist, this is probably about as good as it's going to get. Especially with this weather." A torrential rain had been falling for the past four days. "Still, considering the alternative, I'm happy I can still walk."

"Indeed. A very pragmatic view."

Ally shrugged. "I guess so. Anyway, I was wondering, if you're not too busy, if you could do me a favour."

"Certainly, Dame Alleandre. Currently I am about to have a training session. However, I can postpone that if you wish."

"No, no, that's okay. Actually, that's what I was going to ask you about." She held up the sheathed sword. "I was doing some research and I found out that as a knight I'm technically supposed to be able to use this thing to defend my Sponsor if necessary."

"Technically, yes. But that requirement has not been enforced for decades."

"Yeah, I know, but I thought that I'd like to learn anyway and I was hoping you'd be willing to teach me."

Sir Arthur's brows rose. "Indeed. I must admit that I am surprised. I believe you have successfully demonstrated that you possess other methods, shall we say, of self-defence."

Ally nodded, instinctively looking around to see if anyone was listening. "Yeah, I do, but there are times when doing things . . . that way isn't really an option. For obvious reasons. Besides, it's something I've wanted to learn for a while, but I've never had the chance. Even if you don't want to teach me swordplay, I'd still like to learn some more martial arts. It'll give me something to do while Evelynne's away."

She said the last part nonchalantly, but Sir Arthur picked up the hurt and sadness in her voice, and he felt a surge of sympathy for the young woman. Of all the people present at the meeting the previous week, Evelynne had appeared to be the most shaken by the experience. Sir Arthur himself, after the initial shock, had accepted the abilities Ally had revealed almost as a matter of course. The Templars had a long tradition of esoteric practices and while they no longer had any true magicians, at least as far as he knew, the existing legends had left him open to the idea. He was still assimilating the information fully, but while he did so he treated Ally in much the same way as always.

Major Nixon's reaction was more confused. She vacillated between a kind of awe over how easily Ally had subdued her, a wary alertness to the young woman's power and a big-sister complex over Ally's actual physical appearance and personality. Sir Arthur was sure that the Major would work out her feelings in time, but for now she seemed uncertain whether to worship Alleandre, eliminate her as a threat or hug her.

General Danun had reacted to the revelations with the same solid pragmatism that had served her so well for her entire career. She had cautiously accepted Ally's offer of aid and had taken the young woman's threats to heart. Unbeknownst to Ally, she had assigned covert agents to protect Ally's parents and several of the young woman's closest friends. Currently those agents had orders to observe and protect only if necessary. Ally's parents would be very safe from muggings and robberies for a while. However, also unknown to Ally, the General was willing to change those orders if she felt it was necessary.

"She is a very powerful wild card," the General had explained to Sir Arthur. "And while at the moment I trust her not to threaten this country, I can't afford to take it for granted. If, for whatever reason, she does become a threat, I need to be ready, willing and able to take her out, by whatever means necessary. I believe her concern for her family and friends is genuine. If I have to, I am prepared to use them against her. And if she never does anything untoward, she'll never know."

Sir Arthur personally didn't think that Ally would ever do anything to harm Atlantl, but he recognised that his superior could not take the matter on faith.

It was Evelynne, though, whose reaction had been the most out of character. Sir Arthur knew that Ally had explained things to her the night before the meeting and the next morning she had seemed accepting, if shaken.

chapter twenty three

He remembered the argument he'd had with her and how she had emphatically protected her friend. Since returning from the Guard Headquarters, however, she had retreated, and while she was still polite, she had held Ally at arm's length. Two days after returning, the princess had gone to Outremer on the pretext of government business. What was supposed to have been a one-night stay had turned into two, then three and now she had been there for a week. In all fairness, Evelynne had been quite busy with administrative work but Sir Arthur knew that most of the work could have been done from the Palace. He suspected that Ally knew it too.

While Ally had apparently accepted the princess' distance at first, allowing Evelynne time to adjust, she had become more and more depressed at her friend's constant polite rebuffs of her offers to talk. Sir Arthur suspected that Ally had quite a crush on Evelynne and while he wasn't sure that the princess returned the affection, it was obvious how Ally treasured their friendship.

Which brought Ally here, seeking some diversion from her loneliness.

"Certainly, Dame Alleandre," Sir Arthur replied, pulling himself from his musings. "I was not planning to practice swordcraft today, but I would be happy to instruct you in some martial arts. Have you learned any styles before?"

"Um, can you call me Ally? I'm still not used to being 'Dame Alleandre'. I keep looking around for someone else."

"Certainly . . . Ally."

☙ ☙ ☙ ☙ ☙

Princess Evelynne was sitting behind her desk in her office in Outremer, looking out the window into the pouring rain. Maïda stood, unnoticed, just inside the door to the office, watching her with concern. She could easily see reflected in the window the princess' uncertain, abstracted expression, tinged with confusion and unhappiness. Evelynne had been like this for a week, ever since the day of the mysterious meeting in Jamaz, and the lady-in-waiting was worried. She knew that Evelynne was wrestling with some problem. Actually, the princess was avoiding dealing with whatever had her so depressed. Instead, she threw herself into work, and while Maïda was proud of how effective the princess was becoming at her duties, she also knew her charge was desperately unhappy. At first the lady's hope had been that Evelynne's new friend would be able to pull her out of her depression, but it had quickly become evident that whatever the problem was, it involved Alleandre directly.

Well, it's time to get to the bottom of this, Maïda thought. She also knew that Alleandre was equally hurt by the princess' distance.

Maïda walked briskly into the room and placed the tray holding a pot of Evelynne's favourite tea on the desk. Startled, the princess spun her chair to face her and then smiled in greeting. "Hello, Maïda," she said. "Sorry about that. I was just—" She waved a hand vaguely at the window. "—thinking."

Maïda made sure the door was closed and set about pouring two cups of tea. "Quite all right, Highness," she replied, purposefully keeping her tone light. "And what were you thinking about that had you so concerned?" She passed a cup to Evelynne, and then took one for herself before easing her frame into a large comfortable chair.

"Oh, um, I was just . . . trying to figure out how to let Count el-Rahan keep his best doctors and still maintain his budget," Evelynne temporised.

Maïda shot her a severe glare and clucked disapprovingly. "Highness, it wasn't too many years ago that I tanned your hide for lying," she said, "and I'm not afraid of doing it again. So now you have a choice. You can tell me the truth about what is bothering you or you can say nothing at all. If you tell me nothing, then I will go back to Kilim tonight, because I know there is someone there who could use my comfort instead."

Evelynne had been about to respond belligerently, but the last statement hit her like a punch to the belly and she suddenly deflated. She sighed heavily, staring at her cup of tea.

The silence stretched uncomfortably, until Maïda put down her tea, ready to follow through on her ultimatum. She was stopped by Evelynne's low murmur.

"Have you ever thought you knew someone, then one day found out that they weren't who you thought at all?"

"Of course, Highness," the lady replied. "Every day. Every time I learn something about a person that I didn't before, it changes who they are in my mind. Just today I learned that young Sergeant Mason in your Guard is married. It had honestly never crossed my mind before and now I find myself thinking of him in terms of a wife and child in his life."

"Oh. Will you . . . treat him differently now that you know?" Evelynne was circling the subject and Maïda let her for the moment.

"Of course I will. I will be sure to give him some small gift on his anniversary. I will also be keeping my eye out to see that none of the servants becomes too 'friendly' with him."

That coaxed a giggle out of Evelynne. "I'm sure he'll appreciate that."

"It is part of my job, Highness. I am required to poke my nose in where others may not wish me to. As I am doing now." She examined the princess carefully as Evelynne stiffened again. "I do not like to see people hurting, Highness and if I can somehow help them when they are, I will do

chapter twenty three

so without hesitation. Right now I see that you are hurting. Not only you, but young Ally as well."

"I know," the princess whispered. "I–I learned something about Ally last week. When I first found out, I thought I could handle it. Oh, it was a shock and I knew it would take a bit of time to fully come to grips with it, but I didn't think it would affect our relationship. Then something else happened and it just . . . freaked me and I couldn't handle it anymore. And then combined with . . ." She trailed off.

"I see." Maïda had suspected as much, though she had no idea exactly what it was that had upset Evelynne. "And this new information, it was unexpected?"

"Completely," Evelynne said promptly. "I had never even considered the possibility that she had–that she was–"

"You can tell me, Highness. Or is it too great a secret?"

The princess almost blew hot tea out her nose. Choking and coughing, she replied, "Secret! Yes . . . you could . . . say that!" She laughed, and the sound had a hysterical edge. "The world's biggest secret!"

Maïda frowned. "I don't understand, Highness."

Evelynne finally got herself back under control and breathed deeply. "No, you wouldn't. Not many people would." She sat quietly, thoughts racing through her head.

Her lady-in-waiting saw the struggle and let her think it out.

I'm sorry, Ally, Evelynne thought finally. *I have to talk to someone, and I can't talk to your parents, or Annie, or anyone else who already knows. No matter how good and kind they are, and no matter how impartial they would try to be, their first priority would be you. Right now I need someone whose first priority is me.*

"Ally is . . . different," the princess said quietly. "She has certain abilities that are, if not unique, then certainly incredibly rare. These days, not many people seriously believe that what she can do is even possible." She saw Maïda's blank but attentive expression and sighed. "Ally can . . . move things without actually touching them. She can just look at something and then, bam! It's in her hand. Or circling around her head. When that accident happened at Aztlan, a man was trapped in the cab of a crane. There was this metal bar bent across, pinning him inside. There was no way anybody should have been able to move it without at least a blowtorch. But Ally, she got in there and actually *bent* the metal back using nothing but her bare hands and her thoughts." The older woman was looking at her incredulously. "I'm not crazy. It really happened. Uncle Arthur was there and he saw it all. Anyway, later that night, I went to Ally's room and she explained it all to me, told me what she could do and how she learned to do it. She can read minds too, you know, if she tries hard enough. Apparently she can't send thoughts, but she can pick them up. At the time, I was still in shock, obviously, but I really thought I could handle it. I also knew that Ally was really scared that I'd go and turn her over to the Guard, or a research facility or something." Evelynne did not want to share the knowledge of the Link with Maïda; it was too personal, too intimate for another person to know about.

"Then the next day we had to go to the Guard Headquarters in Jamaz. Uncle Arthur had reported everything to his superior and she was . . . concerned. I went along, because I wanted to protect Ally and make sure she was okay. But then . . ."

"Then?" Maïda prompted.

"At one point I suppose Ally thought she was threatened and felt that she had to make some kind of demonstration. It was impressive. You know Major Nixon?" The other woman nodded. "Well, Ally picked her up and pinned her to the wall. I mean literally pinned to the wall, about a foot off the floor. She pushed the General's desk halfway across the room. All this without even touching either of them. She just kind of waved her hands and bang! They were out. She didn't do anything to Uncle Arthur and later she said it was because she knew he would protect me. I guess that was when I realised just what she was capable of."

Maïda was silent for several minutes, thinking about the story she had just been told. This was about as far from what she had expected as it was possible to be. Finally, though, she asked, "So how did you feel after that?"

"I was . . . scared," Evelynne said. "I mean, it was one thing to see her do things in her room. It was actually really neat; she made these books go around her head. Even when she was twisting that beam she was still defending someone. But this . . ." She shook her head. "This was raw power, *aggressive* raw power and she used it to incapacitate two professional soldiers. She could have done the same to Uncle Arthur as well. And it was just scary, that she could do it so easily. And she was so–so cold when she did it too."

"Did you talk with Alleandre about it afterwards?"

"I tried to, but every time I saw her I kept seeing General Danun and Major Nixon being thrown across the room and I just couldn't. I know I hurt her, even though she never said anything. Now I just wish I could get over this, and get things back to the way they were, because I–" Evelynne broke off abruptly.

"What, Evelynne?" Maïda asked softly. "Because you what?"

"Because I love her so much," the princess said quietly. She looked up briefly and the older woman could see tears pooling in her eyes. "Surprise. Remember when I asked you if you ever thought you knew someone and

chapter twenty three

it turned out they were someone completely different? Well, here I am." Evelynne laughed brokenly. "I'm in love with Ally. Not just as another person, not just as a friend. This is complete head-over-heels, heart-devouring, romantic love. And there's a part of me that's scared to death of her." Now she broke down into tears.

Maïda had acted as Evelynne's surrogate mother for most of the princess' life and her reaction was swift and instinctive. In a heartbeat, she had crossed to Evelynne and scooped her up in her arms, cradling her like a child. She murmured soothing nonsense words into the young woman's hair, gently stroking her back as she rode out the storm.

Eventually, Evelynne's tears subsided. "Sorry," she mumbled. She tried to back out of Maïda's embrace, but the older woman's surprisingly strong arms wouldn't let her. "I never wanted to disappoint you."

"Oh, dear, you have never disappointed me," Maïda objected. "I have never been disappointed in the past and I am not disappointed now. Shocked, yes, but certainly not disappointed."

"Thank you," Evelynne murmured.

"So, does young Ally know of your affection?"

The lady-in-waiting could feel the heat of Evelynne's blush. "Um, yes. She, uh—we, um . . . we're—"

"Evelynne!" Maïda exclaimed, and the princess pulled back to see her scandalised expression.

"Oh no, not—we haven't done *that*. But we've—we're . . . involved."

"Oh. Well, good." Maïda's face shifted to a worried frown. "Have you thought about—"

"Oh, I don't think there are any possible complications about a relationship with Ally that I haven't already dreamed of myself. And if I've missed them, I'm sure Domdom hasn't."

"His Grace knows?"

"About me and Ally, yes. About Ally's special abilities, no."

"I see." Maïda was quiet for a moment and then looked down to stare into Evelynne's face. "Are you sure about this?" she asked. "Do you really love this woman?"

"I do," Evelynne replied, and then looked away. "But there's this part of me that's afraid of her and what she can do."

"I see." A pause. "You will have to give me some time to get used to this, I'm afraid. To me you are still my little Evelynne and the idea of you in an adult relationship is odd. And with a woman, no less. A woman who is also a—what do you call her?"

"What? Oh, you mean . . . Well, General Danun called her an Adept. I suppose she could also be a witch, wizard, mage, sorceress. I don't think she likes those words, though."

"I see. I can understand why you might be intimidated. After all, I am more than a little shaken and I am not even the person directly involved. So I believe your apprehension or even fear is understandable."

"Really? You mean I'm not just being a coward?"

"Certainly not! You are simply trying to work your way through multiple stressful situations. Of course, that does not make it any easier on you. Or on Ally, for that matter. While you are understandably apprehensive, she is certainly hurt by the situation and for an equally valid reason. She seems to be a remarkably perceptive and clear-headed person, but she is undoubtedly carrying her own fears and insecurities, which your actions are not helping. I am not blaming you; all I am saying is that you both have issues to resolve and I believe it would be better for you to deal with them together."

"Oh. Does this mean you approve? Of Ally and me, I mean." Evelynne's voice was small, but hopeful.

"Well . . . Looking at her personality, I would have to say yes. She is courageous, intelligent, caring and kind. With the benefit of hindsight, it is also obvious she worships the ground you walk on. She is not a member of the Nobility, but, considering the personalities of some of those who are, that could be a good thing. Of course, I will deny saying that last if you repeat it." Evelynne giggled. "So all in all, if she were a man, I would be the first to encourage your relationship. However," she continued when the princess stiffened, "I will still completely support your relationship. All I ask is that you give me a little time to get used to the idea."

"Deal," Evelynne said softly.

"In fact, to begin with, I would like to help you resolve your current situation. Now, from what you have told me, young Ally has entrusted you with her greatest secret and that takes great courage. What *you* need to do is learn to trust *her*. And if, for any reason, you cannot bring yourself to trust her, you must let her go. Because I also know that she will not leave until you tell her to and it would be cruel to leave her hanging onto the hope that you might someday decide to accept her."

Evelynne was quiet for a long time and Maïda was as well, allowing the princess to process what she had said, while at the same time assimilating her own recently acquired knowledge. The tea was long cold by the time Evelynne stirred in Maïda's arms. The lady-in-waiting looked down to see that Evelynne's expression was much calmer, though still tinged with apprehension.

chapter twenty three

"Well," the princess said, "I think we need to be getting back to the Palace. You have a man to see and I–I have to go and trust a woman. If she'll let me."

❧   ❧   ❧   ❧   ❧

"Whew," Ally said, wiping sweat from her brow. She winced, kneading at her back. "The muscles aren't as strong as they used to be and I'm feeling a little sore. Do you mind if we sit down for a while?"

"Certainly," Sir Arthur agreed.

They sat on a bench and Ally looked out over the deserted gym. It was a well-equipped area, with numerous weight machines, stationary bikes, treadmills, barbells and practice mats. All of the equipment necessary to tone the human body to the peak of physical perfection or reduce it to a quivering mass of exhausted muscle. There was even a set of parallel and uneven bars, and a pair of rings suspended from the ceiling.

The two exercisers, who had just been practising some low-speed sparring techniques, sat in silence for several minutes before Ally broached a subject she had been dying to ask about for some time. "Um, do you mind if I ask you a question?"

"Not at all."

"Well, you know about my abilities," Ally said and Sir Arthur nodded. "Well, I was wondering about your unusual talents."

The Guard looked perplexed. "I am not sure I understand what you mean. Are you referring to my skills as a Guard?"

"No, not that. At least, not directly. I meant your . . . you know." Ally gestured vaguely to her own head and then to her companion's, but his expression remained blank. "You really don't know what I'm talking about, do you?"

"I am afraid not."

"Okay. Well, do you ever know that things are going to happen before they actually take place? Do you ever see things in your head that turn out to be true later on?"

Sir Arthur still looked uncertain. "No, I do not believe so."

"How about hunches? Do you ever have a–a gut feeling about certain situations?"

"Occasionally, yes. But I am a Guard. We are all trained to respond to possible threats and subconsciously notice information. Anyone who cannot learn to do so simply does not become a Guard." He looked at Ally quizzically. "Why do you ask?"

"It's just that I've noticed a few things that have given me some suspicions and since you now know about me, I wanted to try to explore them. For example, that accident at Aztlan. You were jumpy and anxious all afternoon. Why?"

Sir Arthur tried to remember. "It was a very exposed location and I was concerned about possible uncontained risks."

"I guess that makes sense. Although I've seen you in other situations and you haven't acted like that."

"Possibly," Sir Arthur conceded. "What is your point?"

"Okay, you were concerned about security all afternoon. Fair enough. But what really caught my attention was your reaction when the crane collapsed. *Before* the crane collapsed, actually. You see, you were doing your normal 'Search for Assassins' routine, but then you suddenly turned around and stared at the crane for a full ten seconds. And *then* it collapsed. It was like you knew it was going to fall before it actually did."

The Guard looked sceptical. "Are you certain? Perhaps I simply heard some of the girders begin to bend."

Ally shook her head. "No, there was no sound until it actually began to fall. Trust me, I remember." *Oh yeah, I remember. This new eidetic memory is handy at times.* "That wasn't the only time. The next day, when we were in the General's office and I . . . you know, did my thing? You were moving to protect Evelynne before I had even twitched. Way back in Marseilles, you were moving and shouting orders *before* any of the snipers' shots were fired. Now, the last two examples could mean that you are a low-level empath and you're subconsciously picking up on peoples' motivations before they act. But with the crane nobody knew anything was wrong until the thing actually began to collapse, which means that the other possibility is that you're having precognitive flashes of some sort."

Sir Arthur still looked highly uncertain, but given Ally's revealed abilities, he was unwilling to dismiss the suggestion out of hand. He spent a few minutes trying to remember what he had been thinking during those named occasions. "When Evelynne was shot," he began slowly, "I remember that I just knew that someone was going to shoot at her. And I knew that the two men on the roof were dead." He shook his head, clearing his thoughts. "I did not think of it at the time, or afterwards, but I knew too much that nobody had told me. I knew one of the shooters was a woman, although we did not learn that officially until days later. I suppose I simply dismissed it as speculation . . ."

"Like a hunch that just happened to come true?" Ally suggested.

chapter twenty three

"Exactly. At the accident I knew *something* was going to fall and a lot of people were going to be injured. Again I dismissed it." He looked up at Ally and the dazed expression on his normally impassive face would have been amusing if he hadn't been so shocked.

"From what you've said, I'm leaning more toward the true precognitive ability," Ally said, "rather than the subconscious empathy."

"But I was under the impression that reading the future is impossible."

"Maybe," Ally said, bringing her water bottle to her lips for a drink. "But then, psychokinetically levitating inanimate objects is also 'impossible'." She held out her hand and released the bottle. Rather than falling to the floor, it hung in place, unsupported. Tapping it with her finger, Ally sent it tumbling slowly towards her companion, who caught it reflexively. "Although I personally believe that true visions of the future are impossible. I think that what we call precognition is really caused by the mind bringing together immense amounts of data, observed consciously, subconsciously and unconsciously, and then extrapolating the most likely outcome. Rather like a weather prediction computer, only much more powerful and accurate, since the human mind is billions of times more complex than any computer. Of course, that would only allow predictions based on things observed in one's immediate vicinity. Possibly people with more far-reaching abilities also have remote sensing gifts or subconsciously tap into the universal unconscious. Someone who could use not only their own mind, but the collective minds of the entire species, would have incredible predictive abilities."

"Indeed." Sir Arthur seemed to be taking the suggestion very well, but Ally had not expected anything else from the unflappable Guard. After a few moments, he asked, "What should I do with this ability?"

"Oh, I don't know," Ally said. "I'd imagine that in your line of work it would come in extremely useful, especially if you can find some way to develop it. I've had a few precognitive hunches in the past, but never anything in the least spectacular, and I've never been able to improve the ability. Maybe I don't have the potential or maybe I just haven't figured out the right way to activate it. I guess my best advice would be to do what you'd normally do to develop a skill: practice. Start listening to your hunches all the time and see just how accurate they are. The nice thing about that ability is that it has a very obvious feedback mechanism; if you're doing it right, you'll sure know it. Also don't totally dismiss the empathic possibility. Try getting a feel for what people around you are feeling or thinking. If you *do* find that you can read people's emotions or thoughts, I *can* help you develop that."

Sir Arthur was quiet for several more minutes. "Well, Alleandre," he said finally, "while you haven't completely convinced me that I possess this gift, I cannot afford to ignore the possibility. I will do as you suggest and . . . experiment."

"Well, good." Ally stood and stretched, pleased that her back did not protest. "In that case, would you like to try some sparring? I'll try to be unpredictable. Just try not to hurt me too badly."

Sir Arthur humphed as he joined her on the mat. "Alleandre, I believe that anybody who tried to hurt you would soon find themselves incapacitated." *At least if they hurt you physically. Your emotions, however, are particularly vulnerable—especially to a certain Heir, who should be here right now. Hopefully Maïda is having some success on that front.*

chapter twenty four

The limousine pulled up to the impressive front doors of the Summer Palace and Evelynne drew in a deep breath to calm her stomach. A Guard opened the door and held out a hand to help her out of the car; she managed to grace him with a thankful smile.

The rain had stopped, but the dark clouds overhead threatened to spill at any moment, so the princess and her lady-in-waiting wasted no time hurrying up the steps to the doors where the Seneschal was waiting to greet them. "Good afternoon, Your Highness," he said, reaching out to remove Evelynne's coat. "I trust your trip went well."

"Quite well, thank you," Evelynne half-lied. "We managed to get a lot of work done." That much at least was true. Looking around, the princess was half-relieved and half-disappointed that Ally had not arrived to meet her. "Where is Ally, Ylan? Do you know?"

"I believe Dame Alleandre is in the gymnasium, Your Highness," Nancu Ylan said. "We were uncertain of the exact time of your arrival."

"The gym?" Evelynne's brow furrowed. "Does she have physical therapy today?"

"No, Your Highness. Dame Alleandre has begun to exercise with Sir Arthur."

"Really? When did this start?"

"I believe their first session was yesterday, Your Highness. I am afraid they become quite focused on their activities. It is possible they did not receive the message of your arrival."

Either that or Ally is so mad she doesn't want to see me, Evelynne thought guiltily. *Although even if she is, Uncle Arthur would still come and meet me. So maybe they are just busy. But I didn't think Ally worked out a lot.* Turning to Maïda who was standing nearby, Evelynne said, "Maï-ma, do you want to come with me?" Evelynne's question was casual, but Maïda could easily see the anxiety behind her words.

"Of course, Highness."

❧ ❧ ❧ ❧ ❧

"Shall we try again, a bit faster this time?" Sir Arthur asked, having just finished watching Ally and "Dicky" Nixon demonstrate a technique in exaggerated slow motion.

"Sure."

Ally retook her position, waiting for Sir Arthur to strike. This time he was much quicker, but Ally knew he was still pulling his punch. Ally took it in stride, however, catching his strike in the deceptively open Butterfly block and continuing in one smooth movement, first drawing him towards her, then pushing him back several paces.

Sir Arthur shook his head bemusedly at how easily this thin, decidedly unmuscular woman was able to knock him back. The day's exercise had shown him that she was by no means an expert at fighting, but she seemed to have an intuitive knowledge of the most efficient ways to move and he knew that given time he could turn her into a magnificent fighter.

Major Nixon had been watching with intense concentration. "I think I've got it," she said. "Let me see if I've got it right."

Nixon stood, relaxed, until Ally's fist lashed out towards her chest. When they had begun training together that morning, Ally had instinctively tempered her speed, but had quickly found it unnecessary. What Dicky lacked in strength she more than made up for in quickness. Her hands instantly flashed out in a perfect block. Before Ally could blink, she felt those hands resting on her ribs. She knew that if Dicky had not pulled her strike at the last possible moment, she would likely have several broken bones.

"Not bad," Ally said with exaggerated nonchalance.

Nixon giggled, an incongruous sound that made her sound like a six year old. "Almost, but something didn't quite flow right. Let me try again."

The next time was worse.

Ally had just begun her strike when the door to the gym opened and Evelynne entered. Ally had just enough time to recognise the princess when she felt her wrist trapped by Nixon's crossed hands. While the technique was intended to pull the attacker off-balance, Ally was so distracted that she fell completely forward. Major Nixon, startled, could not react in time to maintain her balance and both women collapsed to the floor in a tangle of limbs.

Through a red embarrassed haze, Ally felt herself being carefully helped up off the prone body of Major Nixon, who appeared equally uncomfortable, if her bright cheeks were anything to go by. Sir Arthur was supporting her and Ally looked up, mortified, to see that Evelynne had somehow teleported across the floor and was now looking at her with a worried look on her face.

chapter twenty four

She was also saying something and it took a moment for Ally to make it out over the roar of blood rushing in her ears. "Oh Isis, Ally, are you all right?"

"Um, yeah, I'm okay," Ally found herself saying. Unable to look at Evelynne's concerned face any more, she looked down and saw that Major Nixon was in the process of lifting herself up off the floor. "Oh geez, I'm sorry," she said, bending down to help the other woman up. Once they were both upright once more, she grimaced. "So, some great *sensei* I am, eh?"

"Oh, I don't know, Ally," Sir Arthur said. "It was certainly effective in knocking your opponent to the ground." Now certain that Ally was indeed all right, he turned to face the princess. "Good afternoon, Your Highness. Welcome back. I was not aware you had arrived."

"Oh, that's okay," Evelynne said, her eyes never leaving Ally. "We only just got in."

"Indeed. Well, Ally, I believe we can quit for today. I must go and speak with Sergeant Y-Ellani so that she can make her report." At the princess' request, Sergeant Y-Ellani had temporarily taken over as head of the Heir's Guard while she was in Outremer. Officially the Sergeant had been assigned as part of her training, but unofficially Evelynne had found Sir Arthur's constant presence a distraction and a reminder of what she was trying to avoid.

"Certainly," Evelynne said. She felt a sinking sensation in her stomach as Ally seemed engrossed in brushing non-existent dust off the knees of her workout pants, still refusing to look in her direction. "Maïda is also right outside. I'm sure she'd like to see you."

"Indeed, Your Highness," Sir Arthur said. "In that case I will speak with you later." He saluted. "Your Highness, Dame Alleandre." He left the gym, Major Nixon trailing behind him.

Evelynne still seemed to be in a kind of trance, until the bang of the gymnasium door closing broke her reverie. "Um . . . hi," she said softly.

Ally's eyes briefly flicked to Evelynne's face before darting away again. "Hi," she replied.

"So . . . how was your week?" The princess wanted to suck the words back in again instantly at the expression of pain that flitted across Ally's face. She hurried on. "I, um, I think we need to talk."

"No, really?" Ally said, unable to keep the bitterness out of her voice. She instantly moderated her tone. "I'm sorry. I'm just feeling a little . . . I don't know." She folded her arms across her chest and bent her head in an unconsciously defensive gesture.

"No, that's okay," Evelynne said, feeling her guilt begin to gnaw at her once more. Looking around, she seemed surprised that they were still in the gymnasium. "Um, would you like to go someplace else?"

Ally was startled as well. "Yeah." She looked down at her own sweat-stained attire. "I think I need a shower too."

"Well, I wasn't going to say anything, but . . ." Evelynne teased lightly, and was rewarded by a slight, if fleeting, smile. "How about if you go and have a shower and I'll bring some food up to your room?" She wanted the discussion to take place in a relatively private setting, but also thought that Ally might be more comfortable in a place that she identified as her own.

Ally thought for a moment. "Okay, that sounds good. I'll, um, see you up there, then."

      ಶ   ಶ   ಶ   ಶ   ಶ

When Ally stepped out of the shower, she walked into her bedroom and spent several moments considering what to wear. She didn't know what Evelynne was going to say, having ruthlessly shut down any hint of empathic awareness and therefore wasn't sure what kind of clothing was appropriate. *Is there any kind of clothes one wears when possibly breaking up with one's royal girlfriend, even though one's never technically dated? Ah, to hell with it.*

Deciding that, whatever the outcome, she might as well be physically comfortable, Ally grabbed a pair of black silk pyjama pants, then threw on a baggy, red button-down silk shirt.

Decently attired, she drew in a deep breath for courage, held it for a moment and then exhaled explosively. Thus fortified, Ally entered the sitting room.

She saw that Evelynne had taken the opportunity to change into more comfortable clothing also; in her case a pair of baggy blue trousers and a rich purple sweater with the Royal Seal above the left breast. True to her word, the princess had brought up a tray of sandwiches and fruit, which rested on a nearby table. Evelynne had taken one end of a long couch and was sitting so that she was partially facing the unoccupied end. The implied invitation for Ally to join her on the couch was obvious, but she was also sitting so that she was facing several single seats across from her, leaving the choice of seating arrangements in Ally's hands. *That's Evelynne,* Ally thought. *Always the diplomat. What's that saying about diplomacy? Ah yes. "The art of telling people to go to hell in such a way that they're looking forward to the trip."*

Evelynne was also entertaining another guest, who looked up with interest as Ally entered. The new guest quickly jumped down from Evelynne's lap and bounded across the floor to Ally's feet, loudly greeting her at the same time. Cassie made an abortive attempt to climb Ally's leg. Ally hurriedly bent

chapter twenty four

over and picked her up before the cat could pull her pants all the way down to the floor.

Evelynne watched the two females with a wry smile. "Well, that shows me who's really important around here, doesn't it?"

Ally looked up from the bundle of grey fur buzzing happily in her arms. "Oh, don't kid yourself. This beast has taken over this place completely. I'm afraid there was a coup. Not a bloodless one, as a few of the servants can attest, but it was over really fast. It seems you've been replaced. *This* is the actual ruler of Atlantl now."

Ally had walked forward and sat down in a chair across from the princess. Evelynne winced internally at her choice, but carefully kept the reaction from her face. "Really? Well, in that case I suppose I must pay tribute. Although what I have is more for Her Majesty's Regent." She reached over the arm of the chair and picked up a cloth bag that had been lying on the floor. Evelynne hesitated. "I wanted to get you something to say 'I'm sorry' but I wasn't quite sure what. I thought about maybe a private jet, a diamond necklace or perhaps a small Caribbean island, but I decided that might give the wrong impression. I really don't want to buy your forgiveness. Not that I think you even would forgive me if I tried like that. So instead I, um, got you something that a, uh, normal person would get." She handed the bag across. "I don't have much experience with apologising for things like this, so I'm hoping that the thought will count for something."

Ally automatically took the bag. Hesitantly she reached inside and found that there were actually two objects inside. She sat looking at them dumbly for a moment, unable to quite believe what she was seeing. Finally she looked up at Evelynne. "*Ghostbusters?*" she said incredulously. "You got me *Ghostbusters* on DVD? And *Ghostbusters II?*"

The princess shrugged uncomfortably. "Like I said, I wanted to get you something . . . normal and I remembered that you liked those movies. I also figured that it was kind of appropriate. You know, because things have been kind of weird lately."

Ally looked down at the DVD's again, then back at Evelynne. "Um, thank you," she said. "This is really cool." Despite Ally's sparse words, the princess could tell that she was truly pleased and the tight band around Evelynne's chest loosened slightly.

"Well, I wanted to get you some physical gift to show you that I was sorry. But that isn't the apology. To truly apologise, I have to say . . ." She took a deep breath. "I'm so sorry," Evelynne said earnestly. "I'm sorry for hurting you. I'm sorry for not trusting you. I'm sorry for leaving like I did."

"But why did you?" Ally asked, her voice hoarse with a week's worth of repressed emotion. "I told you I was there if you wanted to talk. I would have answered anything you asked. Even if you needed time to yourself, all you had to do was say, 'Ally, I need some time to think.' I wouldn't have liked it, but I would have left you alone until you did want to talk. But you didn't. You just took off, and you didn't say a word, and I didn't know what was going on, after you promised me you'd talk to me. I mean, I know you were mad at me—"

"Mad at you?" Evelynne's head shot up. "I wasn't mad at you!"

"What?" Ally asked, confused.

"I wasn't mad at you," Evelynne repeated. "I'm still not mad at you."

"But I thought—"

"No, Ally. I was never angry with you. Well, maybe briefly, but I got over it quickly. I understand why you never told me about any of your abilities before. I really do. I believe you when you say you were planning on telling me soon anyway."

"Then why did you go?" Ally's tone was bewildered.

"Because I was . . . afraid of you," Evelynne admitted softly, looking down at her hands clasped in her lap. She looked up at a sharp gasp to see that Ally had paled alarmingly.

"Afraid of me? But I–it–you seemed okay with it before. That night when I showed you . . . you know." She waved a hand near her head. "You seemed to find it . . . fun."

"Oh, I did," Evelynne protested. "And I was okay. But then later . . ." She sighed at Ally's confused expression. "You remember the meeting with General Danun? What am I saying, of course you do. Well, you were sitting there and I could tell you were a little nervous, but you were answering questions and everything was going okay. I was looking at you and thinking, 'That's my Ally' and I was ready to back you up in any way I could. But then you were bargaining with her and frankly threatening her. Then suddenly you stood up and threw them around and you weren't 'my Ally' any more. You were this demigoddess and I could practically *see* the power coming off you. You did it so easily and you were so–so cold, so impassive, so focused. I felt like I didn't know you any more and it scared me." By now tears were streaming down Evelynne's face, and Ally looked like she wanted to throw up.

"Oh God, Evy," Ally said, shaken. "I didn't–I wasn't–I didn't realise. That day I wasn't 'a little nervous'. I was terrified. I was going to meet people who could end my life if they wanted to, both literally and figuratively. I was *frightened*, Evy. But I also knew that if I wanted to stay in control and protect myself, I couldn't let them see how scared I was." She laughed bitterly. "That apparently worked, if you couldn't tell. I also didn't know what they were

chapter twenty four

like. It's not like I hang around with national security agencies on a regular basis. So I thought I'd just be up front with what I wanted. I wasn't bluffing. If *anyone* tries to hurt the people I love, I *will* strike back in any way I can. But I also know that I'm not particularly imposing, so I had to show them that I could back up my threats if I had to, so I gave my demonstration. That took a lot of concentration, so I wasn't impassive, Evy. I was just so involved that I guess my emotions kind of shut down." Ally hung her head. "I didn't realise I was so frightening. I'm so sorry."

Evelynne was surprised. She had assumed that Ally had been nervous, perhaps even a little frightened, in spite of the confident mask she had worn that afternoon. Learning that Ally had actually been terrified came as a shock. Although now that she thought about it, Evelynne couldn't see why she should be surprised. *She doesn't like being around people she doesn't know in the best of circumstances, which those certainly weren't. Her greatest secret had been revealed to people she didn't know and didn't trust, people who could, as she said, destroy not only her life, but also those of her friends and family. I think I'd be more worried if she wasn't scared. Then I just sat there, letting her take the heat and did nothing. It doesn't matter that she seemed so much in control; I should have done something.*

The princess saw that Ally hadn't moved. Her head still hung, and her arms were wrapped around her chest in a vain attempt to protect her already battered psyche. She didn't even seem to notice that Cassie was rubbing her head against the crossed arms, trying to provide some comfort of her own.

Evelynne stood and, moving slowly as if she was approaching some skittish animal, crossed the short distance between them to kneel in front of Ally's chair. *This seems to be becoming a habit,* an irreverent part of her thought.

She carefully placed a hand on Ally's knee, but the only reaction was a small wince, so Evelynne reached up and gently pried one of Ally's hands from where it was locked around her other arm. Drawing it down, she held it in her own left hand, softly stroking the palm with her right. "I'm sorry," she apologised again. "I didn't know and I should have. I really messed up this time. I don't know why you should put up with me."

There was silence for a moment and then Ally asked in a very small voice, "Are you breaking up with me?"

Evelynne paused in her stroking as the question shot like an arrow through her belly. "Do you want me to?"

There was another endless silence before Ally whispered, "No."

The princess couldn't hold back a sigh of relief. "Good," she whispered back. "I don't want to either."

Ally hesitantly raised her eyes at the answer to search Evelynne's face. The other woman responded by spreading her arms wide in invitation. Cassie wisely jumped down from Ally's lap before she was crushed between the two women.

There were no tears this time, just a gradual release of tension as pent-up anxieties slowly vented themselves, banished by the safety of that embrace. They remained locked together for long minutes. Evelynne ignored the growing protests from her knees, concentrating instead on stroking Ally's back, feeling the muscles there slowly relax. Suddenly realising that Ally's neck was in tantalising proximity to her lips, Evelynne couldn't help turning her head slightly to place a feather-soft kiss there. Ally emitted a tiny surprised but pleased squeak at the touch, instinctively tilting her head slightly to encourage the contact. Evelynne complied by placing a series of kisses along the arch of Ally's neck, beginning near the shoulder and slowly working her way up, lingering at the point just behind Ally's left ear, enjoying the hitch that developed in her partner's breathing. Then she made her way along the jaw-line, culminating in a soft but passionate shared kiss that seemed to last for hours.

Finally they broke apart. "Is my apology accepted?" Evelynne asked, her eyes sparkling.

"Of course," Ally replied, her tone a mixture of mirth and seriousness. "Maybe we should have more misunderstandings if that's your usual method of apology."

Evelynne's eyes darkened. "No, I don't want that. I'd prefer to never have any more misunderstandings between us."

"As nice as that would be, love, it's not going to happen. We will have misunderstandings, arguments and even fights. They're inevitable. But they can be used to make us stronger. You know how one makes a sword . . ."

The princess looked at her curiously and then winced. "Ouch, my knees are killing me. Sorry, love, but I've got to move."

"Okay, here." Ally helped the other woman up and then drew her into her lap. "Is this okay?"

Cassie looked at the usurper who had stolen her position and then stalked off to another chair with a dismissive flick of her tail.

Evelynne slowly relaxed into Ally's warm embrace. It had been a long time since anyone had held her like this. "This is perfect," she murmured. "I'm not crushing you, am I?"

"A little," Ally admitted. "But I like it. I was never able to do this with An–anyone else."

"Okay," Evelynne said, snuggling in. "What were you saying about a sword?"

chapter twenty four

"What? Oh, that. Well, whenever bad things happen, either to me or anyone else, I always try to remember how a sword is made. You start out with a lump of iron, which is of strictly limited usefulness. If you leave it and do nothing with it, maybe keep it warm and safe, it does nothing. If you cool it with water when it gets hot, it will rust. In order to make anything useful out of it, first you have to take that iron and stick it in a fire until it gets red hot. Even then if you leave it, it goes back to the way it was before. To make a sword—or a plow, or anything else—you have to take that red-hot iron and start beating the crap out of it with a hammer. Then you cool the iron in water, and then heat it and hammer it again and again, until it forms the shape you want. It is only after a lot of stress and activity that you end up with a sword."

Evelynne looked at her curiously. "So that's your metaphor for life? You're making a sword?"

"Oh no, I'm not *making* the sword, I *am* the sword. Whenever you have conflict in your life, you get beaten a little more into a useful shape. You have to have stress so that you can be receptive to the change. In between, you have to be 'cooled off'. Of course, there's a balancing act going on. Too much heat and the metal becomes brittle and breaks easily. Too many blows with the hammer and the shape is deformed. Keep the iron in the water too long and it rusts. But if you do it right, the result is a beautiful tool. Of course, you can extend the metaphor. Good swords require impurities: carbon to turn the iron to steel, other metals to make stronger alloys."

Evelynne was gazing into Ally's eyes with an impressed look. "Wow," she said. "You're quite the philosopher, aren't you, love?"

Ally blushed. "No, I just think a lot. I've had my share of conflict and I was looking for some way to justify it. Then I realised that everything I have done and everything that has happened to me has had a part in making me who I am today. I'm quite content with who I am. Changing anything about my past would make me a different person and there's no way of knowing if I'd be better or worse. So even if I had the chance, I would never change a thing."

"Like I said, you are a philosopher. For the record, I'm quite content with who you are too." Evelynne reached up and placed a kiss on Ally's lips, then settled back down, resting her head on Ally's shoulder.

They sat in silence for a few minutes more, just enjoying each other's company, until Ally's stomach growled. "Hmm, someone's hungry," she said. "What time is it?" She peered at a dragon-adorned clock. "It's almost six! No wonder I'm hungry. I haven't even had lunch yet."

"Well, then," Evelynne said, rising to her feet after a last kiss, "I suppose we'd better feed you." She held out a hand to help Ally out of her chair. "Over supper you can tell me just what you were doing beating up my bodyguards."

≫ ≫ ≫ ≫ ≫

"So, you got everything fixed up, Sir?" Corporal Driscoll asked the two men in work fatigues coming out of the Main Armoury of the Ru'en Army Base just outside Jamaz.

"I think so, Corporal," the older of the two replied. His insignia marked him as Sergeant Olles with the Royal Atlantlan Army, Logistics Division. "Of course, you probably won't need that air conditioner until summer."

"Probably not, Sir," the young Corporal agreed. "I'm not quite sure why it had to be fixed now."

"Don't ask," the Sergeant said. He continued with a conspiratorial air. "This is the military, Corporal. You'll soon learn that orders coming from anyone above the rank of Sergeant-Major aren't supposed to make sense."

Driscoll laughed. "If you say so, Sir. We'll still be glad to have a brand new air conditioner when June comes around anyway."

"That you will, Corporal," Olles said. Heaving a put-upon sigh, he hefted his toolbox. "Well, I suppose I'd better get back to keeping this place running. As you were, Corporal. Let's go, Ivan."

"Aye, Sir." The on-duty soldier behind the counter saluted.

Sergeant Olles and his work mate walked quickly out of the armoury, bound for another task.

Behind them in the armoury, a piece of electronics in no way related to the proper functioning of the air conditioner lay dormant within its innocuous shell, awaiting the signal to activate. Built directly into the machinery of the cooler, not even Sergeant Olles knew it was there.

chapter twenty five

Evelynne hung up the phone with a sigh of relief. *That does it for this morning,* she thought with satisfaction. The morning had been a long, tedious affair of trying to track down Count Driscoll and his Economics Advisor, whose permission was required to allow several companies based in Orland County to expand into new areas. Finally, though, the Princess had managed to get the Count to at least consider the proposal and she deemed the time well spent. Now she had nothing pressing for several hours and she was determined to find Ally and spend some quality personal time with her friend.

Leaving her office, Evelynne was lucky to run into Seneschal Ylan almost immediately. "Hello, Ylan," she greeted. "Do you happen to know where Ally is?"

"Your Highness." The Seneschal bowed his head in greeting. "I believe Dame Alleandre is currently secluded in the Meditation Garden."

Evelynne's face fell. As much as she wanted to see Ally, the princess was not about to interrupt her if the other woman wanted to be alone. "Oh."

"However," Ylan continued, "she asked me to inform you that you are welcome to join her if you wish."

"Oh!" Evelynne brightened. "Thank you, Ylan."

As she made her way to the door closest to the gardens, Evelynne thought back about the past week. While she herself had been unusually busy with routine administrative details, Ally had spent more time training. Even after only a week of working out with Sir Arthur, Ally was already beginning to put on more muscle mass. Her build and metabolism seemed sure to prevent her from ever being "buff", but the Guard had taken that into account and appeared determined to develop Ally's speed, grace and dexterity instead. It appeared to be working too. Evelynne found the more confident way Ally was beginning to move extremely attractive. At times, especially when she "just happened" to be passing by the gymnasium while Sir Arthur, Major Nixon and Ally were training, the princess had to drag herself out of the enticing mental scenarios that taunted her with increasing frequency.

It would likely be a while longer before those scenarios came any closer to reality, unfortunately. While Ally had forgiven Evelynne for her actions, the other woman was still clearly hesitant about moving any further in their relationship. Evelynne knew that it would take time for the emotional hurts to heal. *And it's not like I know how to move forward,* Evelynne thought. *I'm not sure that I even know how to, well, do . . . that.* She chuckled internally. *If I can't even think it, I know I shouldn't do it.*

Her musings had taken her to the nearly hidden entrance of the Palace's Meditation Garden and she paused to knock lightly on the wooden gate. She heard "Come in!" and entered the small walled area.

It had been built as a retreat from the rest of the Gardens, surrounded on four sides by high stone walls to ensure privacy. The plants inside were less ordered than in the formal Gardens and had been allowed to create a wild beauty presided over by a small spreading oak that overhung a fishpond.

Ally was sitting by the pond, her back to the gate, staring intently at a pebble that was hanging unsupported in the air in front of her face. Evelynne shook her head bemusedly at the demonstration of Ally's talents. "You should be careful, you know," she chided. "Anyone could have come in."

Ally finally looked at her and blushed, and the stone dropped to land in the pond with a small "plop". "Oh, um, actually, I knew it was you. I, uh, felt you." She gestured vaguely between her head and Evelynne's. "Sorry."

"Don't be," Evelynne said, sitting down on the stone bench next to Ally and kissing her lightly. Ally looked ready to argue, so the princess cut her off with another kiss. "I don't mind. You weren't intruding in any way. So what were you doing? Practicing?"

Ally nodded sheepishly. "Actually, yeah." She looked down at the now-submerged pebble. "I was, uh, trying to remove the water from that wet rock."

Evelynne blinked. "All right," she said, drawing out the words. "Why?"

"Um . . . to see if I can?" Ally made the statement a question.

"All right," the princess said again. "So were you having any luck?"

"Not really," Ally admitted. "I just can't seem to feel the water when it's that–that fine."

"You mean you can normally move water?"

"In larger amounts. Like . . ." Ally reached out towards the surface of the pond and made a pulling motion with her fingers. A small hump appeared and grew until it abruptly separated from the larger mass to form a small liquid ball about the size of a marble. Without physically touching it,

chapter twenty five

Ally drew it upwards to rest on the surface of her palm. Evelynne watched, fascinated. "Like that. Here." Taking the princess' hand, Ally gently tipped the ball into it.

"Isis." Evelynne hesitantly touched the shimmering globe with her fingertip.

"I can also . . ." With an expression of utter concentration, she stared at the ball and it abruptly broke and flowed up Evelynne's finger to the base, where it recoalesced into a fat ring encircling the digit.

"Oh my," Evelynne breathed, turning her hand around to inspect the ring from every angle. "How long will it last?"

"Only as long as I concentrate on it," Ally said and the strain in her voice caused Evelynne to look up. Ally's face was a mask of complete focus, her eyes on the fluid ring and, despite the cool air around them, a sheen of sweat could be seen on her brow. "Keeping it that shape is pretty easy, but I also have to make sure it moves where your hand does, since it won't do that on its own."

"Oh." With a final admiring look, Evelynne held her hand out over the pond. She looked up at Ally and nodded. As her friend's face relaxed, the ring dissolved, its liquid running over Evelynne's hand to splash back into the pool. Wiping her hand on her trousers, the princess said, "That was amazing. Thank you."

Ally's face flushed with pleasure. "You're welcome. Actually, I was, uh, showing off a bit," she admitted sheepishly. "I haven't had someone I could show off with in a while."

"You don't have to, you know. You don't have to try to impress me. Of course, if you really *want* to I won't object," Evelynne teased. "So how do you do that, anyway?"

"Well . . . okay." This time Ally reached both hands towards the water, and the ball that coalesced was much larger, about the size of a person's head. With the ball hanging in the air, Ally frowned thoughtfully. "Hmm, let's see . . ."

She reached out with a finger and Evelynne watched in delight as she ran it over areas of the rippling mass. Where Ally's fingertip passed, ridges or furrows formed. Slowly Evelynne realised that a face was taking shape on the surface of the water. As she worked, Ally spoke. "What I do is take whatever it is that I want to move and sort of take it and make it a part of myself. I kind of take the whole shape and . . . store it in a bit of my mind. Then, once it's there it's as easy to move as any other part of me, like my arm or hand. Moving my arm is easy; I've been doing it my whole life. So I just visualise the result, flex the right mental muscles and . . ." Pausing to look at her work critically, Ally continued, "That's why removing the moisture from the rock was hard. It's just like . . . trying to pick up single grains of sand with your fingers. I mean, I can *do* it, but it takes a *lot* of concentration." She paused again to indicate the face she was working on. "This is actually relatively easy. Holding it as a ball is pretty simple. I'm also using my fingers as a kind of focus for what I want to do, which makes the–the sculpting easier. I suppose I could do it all at once, but that would be exhausting." The end of Ally's speech coincided with the culmination of her work, and she leaned back, satisfied.

"That's–that's me!" Evelynne exclaimed, and indeed the rough water sculpture bore a certain resemblance to the princess' face. It was inexpertly done, but considering both the medium and the sculptor, Evelynne was not about to complain in any way. Except . . . "My nose is not that big!"

"No?" Ally looked at the translucent mask critically. "Well then . . ." She reached out and grasped the offending feature and pulled. "How about that?" she asked innocently, as Evelynne gaped at the six-inch spike now protruding from "her" face.

ॐ ॐ ॐ ॐ ॐ

Evelynne looked down from the book she was reading to the tousled head resting in her lap and couldn't help but smile. Ally was out cold, her mouth slightly open and for some reason her nose was twitching.

Following on from the amazing water sculpture, Ally had happily demonstrated a few more of her talents. After Evelynne had extracted appropriate compensation for the indignities done to her likeness, of course. As the afternoon wore on, though, the temperature had dropped and the pair had gladly retreated indoors to Ally's suite and settled down on the long couch in front of the fire, which a servant had thoughtfully lit against the chill.

Taking up positions at either end of the couch, Evelynne was reading a thick book on international law, while Ally had chosen a lighter work of fiction. After a period of prolonged silence, Evelynne had looked up to see the other woman fast asleep, her head resting awkwardly on the arm of the couch, her book lying abandoned in her lap. It hadn't taken much coaxing to get Ally to stretch out along the length of the couch and the princess had carefully covered her with a handy blanket.

Ally's nose stopped twitching and her features tensed in a slight frown. The creases in her brow quickly disappeared as Evelynne's light touch brushed them away. Then Ally's entire body tensed in one of her peculiar full-body stretches and her grey eyes opened to look up at her companion.

chapter twenty five

"Mmm, hi," she said sleepily.

"Hi," Evelynne replied, still grinning. "Sleep well?"

"Mmmhmm," Ally hummed, stretching once more. "How long was I out?"

"Only about half an hour."

"Oh. Um, sorry about that."

"Don't be. You obviously needed it."

"Mm, I usually do after I do, you know, stuff like this afternoon."

Evelynne thought back to Ally's unconsciousness after her intervention at Aztlan and frowned. "I thought you might. You didn't have to do all that for me, you realise."

"That's okay. I wanted to. Besides, I can always tell when I really start overexerting myself and I wasn't near it today." This time Ally looked concerned. "I seem to keep pushing my limits, though, so that really isn't as sure as I'd like it to be."

"Well, growing and learning is a good thing, isn't it?"

"Usually, yes," Ally admitted. "But I'm going into unknown territory. There aren't exactly a lot of concrete examples of what people like me become as they grow. Supposedly we only use about ten per cent of our brains. If this is me at ten per cent, what will I become at fifteen? Twenty? Fifty?"

Ally sat up, her expression troubled. She would have moved away, but Evelynne automatically wrapped her in an embrace. Ally slowly relaxed into it, resting her head on the Princess' chest.

This was an aspect of Ally's abilities that Evelynne had never considered. The afternoon's events had shown that Ally took such a delight in the use of her talents that the princess had never considered she might be afraid of them. "So do you ever think about stopping? Not using your talents any more?"

"Occasionally, but never really seriously. I mean, whatever makes me different is probably genetic or at least hard-wired into my brain by now, so it'll likely never go away. The only thing I can do is try to understand as fully as possible. That's why I constantly practice at control. I have the equivalent of a large bomb in my head and I don't even know what the trigger is." Ally sighed. "Even in the last few months I've learned things. I have an eidetic memory now, you know. I didn't before Christmas."

"Really? You mean it just appeared?"

"Pretty much. Of course, maybe I had it all along and just didn't know how to use it. If you need to know the address or phone number of anyone in Kilim, just ask. I tested it by memorising the phone book." Ally smiled wryly. Then the smile disappeared and she looked worried. "I'm not completely freaking you out, am I? An–other people have got really uncomfortable when I talked about it."

"Not at all," Evelynne assured her, then proved it by dipping her head and capturing Ally's lips in a thorough kiss. Coming up for air, she smiled down at her equally flushed companion and tried to get her libido under control. *Too soon to go too far,* she thought reluctantly. *But soon . . .* "I'm curious," she said, returning to the subject. "You said maybe you could do it all along and just found out how." Ally nodded. "Would that work with other people? That they can do things but not know it?"

"Possibly," Ally agreed. "Probably. For all I know, everyone is a potential Adept but they've just never thought the right way."

"Hmm. What about me? Do you think I could learn?"

Ally looked surprised. "You'd want to?"

"Of course! It wouldn't be fair if you were the only superhero, would it?" Evelynne grinned. "Seriously, though, maybe you teaching me will even help you understand your own abilities."

"That's true," Ally said, her mind obviously racing with possibilities. "When would you want to start?"

"What's wrong with right now? Let's make some magic!"

chapter twenty six

Ally sat on the edge of her bed and unhurriedly pulled on her pants, then looked at the fuzzy set of blobs that comprised her bedroom. Sighing resignedly, she reached out and with a flick of her mind she brought her glasses to her hand. Pleased with the ease with which she had accomplished the feat, she slipped them on and peered at the glowing red numbers of the clock by her bed.

Hmm, quarter past eight. I slept in. After indulging in a long, sinuous stretch that left her entire body humming, Ally completed dressing. *Could get used to this. Ha! What am I saying? I am used to this! I suppose I'd better enjoy it while I can,* she thought. *I won't be able to do it when I start work in a couple of weeks.*

True to his promise, Doctor Collins, the chief administrator of the Aztlan excavation, had managed to create the "Alternative Theory Department" for the project and had offered its supervisory position to Ally. The position came with a staff and Ally had been given an almost free hand in hiring her own people, something she would have to take care of as soon as she took up the post. She was impressed and surprised by the speed with which the Doctor had cut through the red tape and obtained funding, since less than a month had passed since they had met. Ally suspected that he had Royal assistance; Evelynne's protestations of innocence were somewhat less than convincing.

Thinking of the princess, Ally felt a stab of guilt, as she often did when she awoke particularly late. Evelynne regularly rose at dawn to begin her own work helping various Nobles with their own legislative tasks. The work was intended to prepare her for her eventual rise to the Throne and Ally had to admit that as a training technique it was very effective, but it left the princess without much free time. The free time that she did get tended to be used for intensive relaxation, as she tried to make up in quality what she often lacked in quantity.

Fully dressed, Ally walked to the large glass doors leading to her balcony and threw the curtains wide. Normally she could see both the distant sea and the Palace courtyard from this position, but today the view was obscured by a blanket of thick white fog. *Ugh,* Ally grimaced, *what a nasty day. I was hoping to get Evelynne out for a walk, but it looks like we'll have to stay inside today.* She was about to turn away when a thought struck her. She almost dismissed it out of hand, but then considered it more seriously. *I wonder...*

Opening the door, Ally stepped out onto the cold, damp balcony. Ignoring the wetness, she stood still and closed her eyes. Loosing her mind, she spent several minutes scanning her environment. Coming back to herself, she shook off the usual disorientation and considered for a few more moments. *Why not?* she thought finally. *Evelynne could use a break and this is something I think would be really special.* A moment of doubt assailed her briefly, but then she shrugged it off. *Oh well, if this doesn't freak her out, nothing will. Now, what do I need?*

Thinking hard, Ally re-entered the Palace, carefully planning the day.

It took a few hours for Ally to assemble the supplies she needed and transport them to the appropriate location, which meant that it was late morning before she knocked on the door to the study that Evelynne had set up as her office and stuck her head in the room.

As expected, the princess was reading some official document, but given her pained expression and the speed at which she looked up at Ally's knock, she was not enjoying the experience. Her face brightened perceptibly and she grinned, running a hand through her red hair.

"Ally!" she said happily, quickly getting up and walking over. As she came closer, Ally could see that she was carrying Cassie, who had previously been sleeping on her lap and was now less than thrilled by the unnecessary movement. Coming to a stop, Evelynne surreptitiously checked the door for observers and then freed one of her hands to pull Ally's head down for a morning kiss.

"Good morning," Ally said when they parted. She reached out to scratch Cassie under the chin, thereby earning the cat's forgiveness–this time. "How are you doing?"

Evelynne made a face. "Bleah. Let's just say that when I become Queen I'm going to pass a law banning unnecessary language in all official reports."

"Ah, you plan and intend to remove, cut out and eliminate unnecessary, superfluous and redundant verbiage, language and phrases, huh?"

"Exactly." Evelynne leaned back, taking in Ally's appearance. "So what have you been up to this morning?" She reached up to pat Ally's hair. "You're damp. Have you been outside? It's nasty out there."

"Yeah, I have," Ally said. "Actually, I was, uh, arranging something. I was, um, wondering if you wanted to take the day off. I've been putting together something that I think might be fun."

chapter twenty six

Evelynne was surprised at how nervous Ally seemed. "That sounds wonderful. I just have couple of things to finish up here, which should take me about half an hour. I can postpone the rest. I don't know why I'm working on a Sunday anyway. Where are we going?"

"It's a surprise," Ally said. "Um, come on up to my room when you're ready. Dress warmly." With a final light kiss, Ally turned to leave, then paused at the doorway. "Oh yeah, bring a swimming suit too."

"A swimming suit?" Evelynne asked, but Ally was already gone. "I really hope she isn't planning on going swimming in the pool in this weather."

As promised, Evelynne arrived at Ally's room thirty minutes later. She had taken some time to dress herself in a pair of warm woollen pants and a thick sweater, and carried a waterproof jacket under one arm. Uncertain of Ally's exact plans, she had decided to simply wear her swimming suit under her other clothes. *The nearest indoor pool is in Kilim. And there's no way I'm going in the ocean at this time of year, no matter what she says. Besides, for a trip we'd need to bring Guards and I know she doesn't like taking them everywhere.*

She arrived at the open door to Ally's room and looked in to see her friend standing in the middle of the room, inspecting a white sheet at arm's length. Knocking on the doorframe, the princess called, "I'm here. So what's the plan?"

Ally looked up at the words and smiled in greeting. "Come on in," she instructed, draping the cloth over the back of a chair. Walking past Evelynne, she closed the door. "I told people not to bother us today."

"Ooo, privacy," Evelynne teased, her eyes twinkling. "Are you afraid I might try to escape when you have your way with me?"

Ally blushed predictably. "No, if I was afraid you'd run I'd just handcuff you to the bed," she rallied.

"Hmm, kinky. I always knew this shy girl routine was just an act." Evelynne laughed again as Ally reddened further and looked away. Taking pity on her, the princess asked, "So, if you're not going to ravish me, what are we doing in here, dressed in our warm clothes, with the door closed?"

"Strip poker," Ally said with an admirably straight face, which quickly crumbled at Evelynne's gape. "Just kidding. Actually, we won't be here long." Picking up the white sheet again, she suddenly looked nervous. "I want you to know that if you get too freaked out and want me to stop, just say the word. Okay?"

"Okay," Evelynne said, puzzled. "But what are we doing, exactly?"

"Come on." Instead of answering, Ally took the other woman's hand and led her to the balcony doors. Outside, the chill made Evelynne start to shiver and she slipped on her jacket.

Ally spent several moments peering through the fog, but it was so thick that she could barely see a couple of metres in front of her. Nodding in satisfaction, she moved close to Evelynne and wrapped the sheet around them both. "Camouflage," she said enigmatically when Evelynne looked up at her quizzically.

Before the princess could ask any more questions, Ally closed her eyes and centred herself, easily slipping into a light trance. What she was about to do she had rarely done before with another person and there was no way she was going to take any chances, especially with this person. She focussed her mind, letting the thought-form wrap both of them, rather than just herself. It was, as she expected, more complex, but still not terribly difficult. When she had the form firmly in her mind, Ally opened her eyes and looked down at Evelynne, seeing both curiosity and trust there.

"Hold on," she instructed, wrapping her own arms firmly around her companion. "And remember: if you want me to stop, just say so."

"All right," Evelynne said. She still had no idea what Ally intended, but there was no way she was going to pass up a chance to hold the woman she loved tightly. She knew it would be something related to Ally's psychogenic abilities, having recognised the signs of focussing and now she saw Ally's gaze go slightly vacant as she channelled.

The result still took her completely by surprise as she felt her stomach drop away suddenly, as if she were falling. Unable to contain a startled yelp, she reflexively clutched Ally tighter, who held her closer in return. Moving her legs, Evelynne was clearly aware that her feet were no longer touching the ground. She spent a moment wondering why Ally had lifted her up, then realised that she was no higher on Ally's body than she had been before. Feeling cautiously with her feet, Evelynne confirmed that Ally's legs were also dangling freely. Then a few other clues forced their way into her consciousness. She became aware of a wind on her face, and though it was hard to see, the fog around them was definitely moving — downwards.

All of this information crashed into Evelynne's mind, bringing her to one inescapable conclusion. "Isis, we're flying!" she gasped. A moment later the conclusion was confirmed when they suddenly broke through the upper layer of fog into clear sunlight. The princess looked around with wide eyes, instinctively clutching Ally hard enough to bruise. The ground-hugging fog stretched for kilometres, looking just like the tops of clouds that Evelynne regularly saw from airplanes. This time, though, there was no roar of engines,

chApteR twenty six

no reassuring seat under her, no tiny window to look out. Instead, there was only pure sensation. Evelynne was silent for several minutes as she tried to process the experience.

"Are you okay?" Ally's worried voice broke through her daze, and she looked up to see a concerned face.

"Uh, I, um, you, uh . . ." Words seemed to have been left on the ground some unknown distance below.

"Do you want me to go down?" Ally asked, worried.

"No!" Evelynne blurted. "I just–I don't–" She took a deep breath, and felt that the air seemed somehow cleaner up here. "No words," she said simply, and felt Ally relax slightly. With the subtle release of tension, she noticed that she was still grabbing Ally's arms in what must have been a painful grip and consciously loosened her hold slightly.

Ally smiled reassuringly. "That's okay. Take your time."

Now slightly more confident that she was not about to crash to earth at any moment, Evelynne gazed around once more. The fog only a few metres below them looked pristine, like new-fallen snow. Overhead, the sky was completely clear. The sun, though bright, did little to warm them, but it did lend a brilliant, crisp light to the scene. Casting her eyes further afield, Evelynne could see the occasional tree poking up from the whiteness and in the distance she could see where the fog dissipated, revealing the blue of the ocean. In the other direction, the bulk of Mount Sekamat loomed like an island in the middle of a vast white sea.

"Oh, Isis," Evelynne breathed, feeling more than a little overwhelmed.

"Are you okay?" Ally asked again softly.

"Am I okay?" Evelynne repeated dazedly. "I–this–it–I'm–stunned. This is just–" She closed her eyes tightly and opened them again. "Um, could you pinch me? This *has* to be a dream."

Ally raised her eyebrows, grinning when Evelynne jerked in her arms.

"Ow! All right, not a dream." The princess looked up at Ally wonderingly. "How are you doing this?"

"It's the same as when I use my psychokinetic abilities," Ally said. "I can pick up other objects with my mind, so why not my own body? It's just a matter of looking at it the right way. It's more tiring for some reason, but . . ." She nodded her head to indicate their surroundings. "It's worth it."

"Oh, it's worth it," Evelynne agreed fervently, looking around again. She still wasn't totally convinced that this wasn't some incredible dream. "This is so wonderful. I can't believe you showed me this."

"I love you," Ally murmured. "I wanted to share something with you that I enjoy more than anything in the world. If you were to take away all but one of my powers, this is the one I'd keep."

Evelynne stared up at her, then shifted so that she could bring their lips together. After a moment, though, she felt her stomach give a little lurch and Ally quickly pulled away.

"Sorry," Ally said. "I need to maintain a bit of concentration to do this, and, well, you tend to break it when you do things like that. Now if we were only a little way up, I'd be happy to experiment, but up here I think I should keep my wits about me."

"Darn." Looking around again, Evelynne asked, "Do we have to go down now?"

"Not unless you want to. I did have something else planned, though, if you want."

Evelynne's eyes were wide. "You mean there's more?"

"Um, yeah. I'll show you." Turning in the air, Ally began to propel them both towards the mountain.

ଛ ଛ ଛ ଛ ଛ

As they flew–Evelynne had to keep pinching herself to make sure she wasn't dreaming–the princess tried to take in every sensation. As well as the lack of engine noise or confining metal, there was another aspect that made this very different from flying in an airplane or helicopter: the feeling of total weightlessness. It reminded her of the few occasions when the aircraft she had been flying in had hit an air pocket and dropped suddenly, leaving her stomach behind. This sensation was both more intense and, unsurprisingly, sustained. Evelynne was thankful that she did not get airsick. It made her wonder if this was what astronauts felt while in orbit.

They were horizontal to the ground, still wrapped in the sheet. Evelynne was pressed against Ally's right side, her arms wrapped around the other woman, while Ally's right arm held her securely. The air rushing at them from ahead made the princess' eyes water, so she settled for gazing down and to the side. Ally was looking straight ahead, her glasses protecting her vision.

The only sound was the rushing of wind past her ears, making her realise suddenly that they were moving at quite a high speed. The nearly unchanging cloud below and the slowness with which the mountain came closer made their velocity appear deceptively low.

"How fast are we going?" Evelynne asked, hoping as she did so that she wasn't breaking Ally's concentration. She had to raise her voice to be heard.

Ally considered for a moment. "I'd say about, oh, a hundred kilometres per hour."

Evelynne blinked. "Wow. How fast can you go, anyway?"

chapter twenty six

"I'm not sure. It's all acceleration, really. I can accelerate about as quickly as a medium-sized car easily. Faster accelerations are way more tiring. Once I'm at 'cruising speed' it's actually fairly easy, but I can still only go for about an hour at a time. I guess theoretically, if I didn't get tired, I could probably reach escape velocity."

The princess almost choked. "What, you mean get into space?"

Ally managed to shrug, despite the awkward position. "Possibly. I've never tried that. Going too high means there's no air and I still need to breathe. Until I get myself a spacesuit—and a really good parachute—I'm not going to be going *too* high." Though her tone was joking, there was still a slightly serious undertone.

"Well, I hope not! I'd prefer for you to stay close to Earth, love. Relatively close, that is." Evelynne looked around again. "This height is just fine."

Ally's lips twitched. "Yes, Mom. And I'll be sure to wear a sweater."

Evelynne mock-scowled at her. "You be sure you do." Risking a glance ahead, she saw that the mountain was significantly closer and they seemed to be heading for a cliff face. Clouds of steam emerged from the rock in places and Evelynne recognised the area of Mount Sekamat that contained the hot springs, though she had never seen it from this close before.

The wind was lessening, and the princess realised that they were slowing down. Ally was scanning the cliff face, looking for something.

"So where are we going, exactly?" Evelynne asked.

"Ummm . . . right . . . Ah, there it is!" Ally found what she was looking for and their course changed towards one of the steam clouds.

For a brief moment Evelynne was afraid that they were going to run into the mountain, but they slowed further. Ally was aiming for the base of one of the pillars of steam and they were briefly surrounded by warm, wet air. Then they were through and emerged into a tiny slice of Paradise.

Evelynne could only stare. Even if the previous miraculous events could somehow be true, *this* must surely be a hallucination. It was only after blinking several times and pinching her already bruised arm again that she slowly began to accept the reality of what she was seeing.

As Ally drew them closer, she reoriented them so that they were vertical once more, before coming in to land on a soft grassy surface. Evelynne hardly noticed when her stomach and inner ear reported the apparent return of gravity. In fact, she would have fallen if Ally had not been holding her in a firm embrace.

The place was amazing. Thousands of years of erosion had carved a niche in the cliff face. The notch in the mountain measured only about ten metres across at its opening. It opened up inside, widening to about thirty metres across at its widest point, until it tapered to a narrow point forty metres into the cliff, creating a space like a rough teardrop. The rear third of the grotto was covered by a pool of water—warm water, if the steam and heat in the air were any indication. There was a faint but noticeable smell of sulphur, confirming the pool's status as a volcanic spring. Somehow, soil had been transported into the niche over the years and its shelter had allowed rich green grass to grow, creating a verdant carpet that covered nearly the entire area. The grass was the only plant life growing there, except for two small, stunted coniferous trees that clung tenaciously to the side of the grotto a few metres up. Several large, smooth rocks dotted the area, one of them poking up a couple of feet in the middle of the pool.

Evelynne couldn't bring herself to speak, or even think as she took in the view and it took her a few seconds to realise that Ally was speaking to her. Reluctantly, she turned dazed eyes on her companion, who was looking down at her with a gentle smile. "Uhhh . . . what?" she asked eloquently.

"I asked what you thought," Ally repeated softly. "Do you like it?"

"Do I like it?" Evelynne asked bemusedly. "There are two possible explanations for this. One: I've gone insane and this is my mind's attempt to create the most perfect place imaginable. Or two: I'm dead and the Gods have created this for me because it's the most perfect place imaginable. Either way, it's the most perfect place imaginable."

"Well," Ally said, "If you're crazy, then I am too, because I can see the same thing. And if you're dead, then so am I. Either way, we're here together."

"We are," Evelynne said, looking deep into Ally's grey eyes. Suddenly she pulled the other woman's head down and kissed her with more passion than she had ever expressed before. Even when Ally lost her balance and toppled backward to land with a muffled grunt she did not stop, instead following Ally down so that they were both half-reclining on the grass.

Eventually Evelynne pulled away, and it was Ally's turn to look dazed. "I love you," the princess whispered.

"I love you too," Ally whispered back, her hand softly stroking a smooth cheek.

"I can't believe you brought me here," Evelynne said, looking around the grotto once more.

"I knew you were under a bit of stress," Ally explained, "and I wanted to show you something to take your mind off it."

"I still can't believe we're in this place." Evelynne shook her head. "I can't believe we flew here." She turned her head to look towards the entrance to the niche. From inside, she was surprised to see that she had a good view

chapter twenty six

of the land at the mountain's base—or would have if the fog had not been obscuring the countryside below. As it was, she could still see the distant ocean, its surface sparking in the morning sunlight.

"Do you want me to show you around?" Ally asked when Evelynne had been silent for several minutes.

"Pardon? Oh, yes, of course," the princess said. "Sorry, I'm a little overwhelmed."

"That's okay," Ally said. "I wanted to overwhelm you a little. You've been dealing with so much mundane stuff the last week that I wanted to bring some magic back to your life."

"Well, it worked." Evelynne slowly got up from Ally's body. She held out a hand to help the other woman rise, expressing concern when Ally winced. "Are you all right?"

"Yeah," Ally said, twisting her shoulders slightly. "I just jarred my back a little when we fell down."

"Oh, Ally, I'm sorry." The mention of Ally's injury brought Evelynne back to reality, reminding her that regardless of Ally's psychic and mental powers, her body was just as frail and injury-prone as anybody else's. "Will you be all right?"

"I'll be fine," Ally assured her. "Fortunately, we have a hot tub right here." She pointed towards the hot spring.

Evelynne's eyes widened. "You mean you can swim in that?"

"Yes. It's only about five feet deep, but it's at the perfect temperature. Actually, if you go to the back, the water gets warmer."

"Oh wow. How did you find this place? Or do I want to know?"

Ally laughed sheepishly. "Do you remember a few months ago, we went for a walk in the Palace gardens and you pointed out the steam coming off the mountain?"

Evelynne thought. "That was . . . September, right? Your parents had just arrived. We went to the gardens and you asked me to be your Sponsor."

"That's it. You said that nobody was able to reach any of these springs. Well, I kind of took that as a bit of a challenge and a few nights later I, um, went exploring."

"You mean you . . ." Evelynne made a flying motion with her hand.

"Yeah. I didn't find this place right away, but I kept coming back and then one day I just stumbled across it." Ally waved at the rock nearly surrounding them. "There are a couple of other places that are similar, but this one is the most beautiful of the lot." She looked shyly down at Evelynne, who had not released her hand. "Especially now that you're here."

"Oh, Ally." This time the kiss was gentle, a promise of love and affection. When they separated, Evelynne looked around again, unable to restrain her curiosity. "So is this where you were when you went 'outside' this morning?"

Ally blushed. "Yes, I came once to make sure I could still find it and then came back with some supplies." Releasing Evelynne's hand, Ally walked toward a large rock near the side of the grotto, shedding the sheet as she went. Reaching behind the stone, she brought out a large wicker basket. "Latifa is a little confused about why I wanted to have a picnic with you in my room."

"Oh my," Evelynne said, her eyes wide.

Crossing back to a flat area of grass, Ally put down the basket, spread out the sheet and started to unpack a number of pottery and bamboo containers, followed by plates, glasses and a bottle of red wine, as Evelynne watched in growing delight.

"Ally, this is the most incredible thing anyone's done for me," she said sincerely. "This even exceeds when you saved my life." Ally looked surprised. "Then, you gave me my life," Evelynne explained. "This–this is . . . more."

Ally smiled bashfully. "Would you like to eat?" she asked, changing the subject.

"I would," Evelynne said, but she cast another glance at the pool. "But first I'd like to check out that water." She looked back at Ally. "Now I know why you told me to bring a swimming suit."

"Now you know. Um, you can go behind that rock over there if you want to change."

"No need." Evelynne was already eagerly stripping off her outer layers of clothing. "I *really* came prepared," she said as her blue two-piece was revealed. She looked up to catch Ally's wide-eyed stare at her nearly nude body and the growing flush in her cheeks. "Did you bring yours?" she teased.

"Uh, yeah." Ally shook herself out of her pleasant trance. She reached down and pulled a small bag out of the basket. "I'm just not as prepared as you are. I'll just go and . . ." She gestured towards the large boulder.

"You don't have to," Evelynne teased, a wicked glint in her eye. "I have seen you naked before, remember?" Ally's blush deepened until the princess took pity on her. "Ally, it's all right. I'm just teasing you. You change. I won't peek, I promise."

A few minutes later, Ally emerged from her semi-private changing area attaching a short piece of rubber material to her glasses to secure them to her head. She was dressed in a form-hugging black one-piece suit, to Evelynne's mingled delight and disappointment. Disappointment that a large portion of Ally's skin was still covered, but delight that the suit still

chapter twenty six

fit like a second skin. Managing, with difficulty, to restrain her hormones, Evelynne was soon splashing and playing with Ally in the warm water, taking great pleasure in "accidentally" brushing herself against the other woman's body as she swam. The bottom of the pool consisted of small pebbles, worn smooth by the action of the water, thankfully sparing their feet.

A particularly energetic burst of horseplay resulted in Ally being dunked, and she retaliated by initiating a devastating splashing war. Despite her smaller hands, Evelynne had a technique that allowed her to propel a huge amount of water and Ally found herself retreating to the edge of the pool. During a brief respite, the two women eyed each other warily.

"Come on, Ally," Evelynne taunted. "You have those big hands of yours and I'm still beating you. What are you, a wimp?"

Ally slowly cupped her hands in the water. She stared at Evelynne in a piercing and distinctly predatory manner as she replied, "A wimp, huh? You think I'm a wimp? You'd better watch out, Princess. You don't know who you're dealing with."

"Oh yeah? And who am I dealing with? I think you're all talk." Evelynne loved to see Ally like this: playful, confident, all shyness gone, overcome by what Evelynne believed was Ally's true spirit.

Ally stared at her a moment longer. "Look up," she said, twitching her eyes to a point above Evelynne's head.

The princess did so. She had a brief moment to see the huge ball of water almost a metre across hanging in the air above her before it abruptly came crashing down, knocking her down and pushing her under in the process. Evelynne came up, coughing and spluttering, and glared at Ally. "No fair!" she shouted, wiping strands of fiery hair from her face. "That's cheating!"

Ally smirked. "Oh? I didn't know there were rules."

"Well there are!" Evelynne cried, unable to stop her grin. "Rule number eighty seven states that the use of super powers is strictly prohibited."

"Really? Well, those must Atlantlan rules, because the Canadian rules say no such thing. And because I happen to be a dual citizen, I can choose which rules to use. I pick Canadian."

"Oh yeah? We'll see about that!" Evelynne challenged and the battle was rejoined.

⁂

Some time later, a truce was called and both exhausted combatants left the pool to refuel. It was well past noon and the sun had shifted so that it no longer shone into the grotto, leaving it in shadow. Still, the hot spring kept the air inside at a very comfortable temperature and neither woman had any urge to put on more clothing as they ate. They were sitting side-by-side, most of Latifa's food demolished.

Ally was sitting with her arms wrapped around her knees, watching the pool with a contemplative but slightly sad look on her face.

"What's wrong?" Evelynne asked quietly. She was seated in a similar position, occasionally leaning to rest her head on Ally's shoulder. "You look troubled."

"Hmm? Oh, no, not really. I was just thinking that in all probability, nobody has ever been here before, walked on this grass, swum in this pool . . . And now it'll never be like that again. It just makes me a little sad, like it's lost something."

"Are you sorry you brought me here?" Evelynne asked.

"God, no!" Ally blurted. "Not at all. I'm really happy that I showed you this and that we've had fun here. It's just that any time something beautiful changes and can never go back to the way it was, I always feel a little . . . depressed. Even if it's still just as beautiful afterwards, like this–" She waved an arm to encompass the peaceful grotto. "–It'll still never be the same." She shrugged one shoulder. "That might not make a lot of sense, but it's the way I feel."

Evelynne reached up with her hand to gently turn Ally's face towards her. "It makes perfect sense, love. I think it's normal to mourn the loss of something unique, something irreplaceable. But nothing can stay the same forever."

"I know," Ally whispered, her grey eyes caught and held by Evelynne's blue ones. Slowly, with infinite gentleness, she felt herself drawn forward by Evelynne's hand, their bodies turning towards one another, her eyes closing as she felt Evelynne's soft lips beneath her own.

They kissed softly, gently, for what seemed like hours, until Evelynne's hand drifted down slowly from Ally's cheek, trailing along her neck, across her shoulder, until it came to rest against the side of her left breast. With a soft gasp, Ally pulled away, her breathing ragged and her pulse pounding rapidly in her throat. She had to swallow several times before she could speak. "Evy," she murmured, her voice ragged, "I–I didn't bring you here to seduce you. I just wanted to show you something beautiful; something that means a lot to me. I never intended–"

Evelynne silenced her with another kiss. "I know, love." Her hand remained where it was, the thumb softly brushing Ally's breast through her swimming suit, as she listened to the hitches in Ally's breathing. "I know you

chapter twenty six

would never try to seduce me. But that is why I want–why I *have* to seduce you. But only if you want to be seduced. I love you Ally and I want to show you just how much. But if you don't want to, you just have to say the word and we'll stop." Although Ally was the one with previous sexual experience, Evelynne felt that she was the experienced one, confronted by Ally's lack of confidence. At the same time she clearly felt a delicious anticipation and frisson of nervousness that ran through her body.

Ally closed her eyes and Evelynne let her think, stilling the motion of her thumb, though she kept her hand in place. Finally Ally opened her eyes and locked them with Evelynne's. The princess could almost see something opening up within her would-be lover's gaze, something deep and powerful and terribly intimate. Momentarily, she was confused. But suddenly she understood. *Isis, she's opened her mind to me. She knows everything I'm thinking and feeling . . . and she wants me to know that she knows. I'll never have a secret from her when we're like this.* Fast on the heels of this revelation came another. *This is part of what Annie was afraid of; what she couldn't handle. Opening oneself to a lover like this requires total trust and Ally needs to know she has mine. She needs to know I won't run from this. That I won't break her heart again.*

All these thoughts ran through Evelynne's mind in an instant and then she was leaning back, pulling Ally with her, as she proceeded to demonstrate her answer.

    ❧   ❧   ❧   ❧   ❧

The sun had long since hidden itself behind the mountain, leaving the lands below in shadow. Within the grotto, the darkness was even greater, mimicking that of the approaching night. Outside, the air was quickly turning chillier, but within, the steaming pool lent its warmth to the interior–and its inhabitants.

Evelynne lay on the sheet, her bare body wrapped around the equally bare torso of her lover. Her head rested on Ally's breast and one arm and leg were thrown over the body next to her. Her hand was idly stroking the soft skin under her fingers as she lay languidly, enjoying as well the sensations of her own body. There was a certain slight soreness in some places, including places where she hadn't even known she had places before, but that was more than overcome by the lingering feeling of pleasure that infused her limbs and body. She turned her head to place a soft kiss on the breast near her face and shivered as she felt Ally's fingernails continue their light scratching on her back.

The princess smiled lazily and then frowned as the ear pressed against Ally's chest registered an odd sound. It was brief, but when Evelynne ran her fingers across Ally's belly once more, the sound was repeated and she couldn't stifle a giggle.

Ally's fingers paused. "What?" she asked.

"Oh, nothing," Evelynne replied lightly. "It's just that you're . . . purring."

Ally's brows climbed her forehead and she craned her neck to peer down at the head on her chest. "I'm what?"

"Purring," her lover repeated.

"I do not purr," Ally stated firmly.

"Yes, you do," Evelynne refuted. She rubbed Ally's stomach once more, proving her point. "It's cute."

"It can't be cute, because I don't do it. I don't–" Ally stopped when she saw Evelynne lift her head to look her in the eyes and raise her own eyebrow. "Okay, fine, I do purr. Annie used to say I did, but I never–" She trailed off when she saw Evelynne's expression turn into a frown. "I'm sorry," she said softly. "I didn't mean to–I wasn't–" She sighed. "I've never had a new lover that I had to avoid talking about my old lover with. I'm not sure–I'm sorry."

Evelynne's face softened. "It's all right, love. I know that you loved her and I know she loved you too. I certainly can't blame her for that." She giggled. "I've never had a lover who had an old lover that I should be jealous of, either," she said. She looked at Ally seriously. "I don't mind if you talk about her, love. Please, don't talk about her when we're . . . like this. I want this to be just us."

"I promise," Ally said.

"Thank you." Evelynne stretched up to kiss Ally thoroughly before returning to her previous position. After a while, she spoke. "I was just thinking . . . You said that when you picked things up with your mind, you kind of made them a–a part of yourself."

"Yes," Ally agreed. "In a sense."

"Well, this morning, when you picked me up and we flew, was I a part of you then?"

"Sort of," Ally said. "It's like I take your entire being and put it in my mind and it does become a part of me. Like I know every thing about your body, but not–not *specifically*." She struggled for words. "It's like you know your own hand, but you know nothing about the individual cells that make it up. But that's still not exactly right. It's–" Ally sighed. "I'm sorry. I can't really describe it properly."

"That's all right." Evelynne smiled. "I just like the thought that I was a part of you, literally, even for a short time."

chapter twenty six

"You are a part of me, Evy. You have been since I first saw you," Ally declared, hugging Evelynne closely to her, revelling in her warmth.

"We should get going," she added reluctantly. "It's getting late. I don't want Sir Arthur getting worried because he hasn't seen you all day."

"Oh!" Evelynne said, reality intruding into her dream world. "We didn't go for dinner!"

"That's okay," Ally reassured her. "I told Latifa and Maïda that we might have supper in my room." She grinned wryly. "They think I'm getting you to rest, because you've been working too hard."

Evelynne laughed out loud. "Well, they're wrong about the rest. Physically, anyway." She smiled seductively at her new lover. "However, emotionally and mentally this has been the most restful day I've ever had." She shivered again, the pool's warmth unable to completely fight the oncoming cold. "I suppose we should go."

After a final passionate kiss that threatened to delay them still further, Ally and Evelynne got to their feet, quickly dressing in their warmer clothing.

The next few minutes were spent clearing up the remnants of their visit. Once they were done, Ally looked at the basket and said, "I'll come and pick this up later." She glanced up to see Evelynne gazing around the grotto, a contemplative and slightly sad expression on her face. "Hey, are you okay?"

"Yes, I am. You're right. It is sad when things change." She stared at Ally with an expression of total love. "But I'm glad they did." She looked around again. "Can we come back?"

"Of course, Evy, whenever you want."

"Good," Evelynne said, taking a deep breath. "Then let's go home."

A minute later the grotto was deserted once again.

    ❧   ❧   ❧   ❧   ❧

As Ally lightly touched down on the balcony outside her room, she could hear a clock somewhere in the Palace striking midnight. Evelynne had been silent throughout the flight and now she turned in Ally's arms and gripped her tightly, showing no signs of letting go. They remained for several minutes, until Ally spoke.

"Evy, I think you have to go. You need to sleep."

Evelynne raised her head, her expression vulnerable. "Can I stay with you tonight?" she whispered.

Ally hesitated, though every part of her urged her to agree. "What about everyone else?" she asked. "Do you want everyone to know about . . . us?"

"Please, Ally? I'll go back to my room before anyone notices. I just need to be with you for a while."

Ally hesitated a moment, then released Evelynne to take her hand. "Come on," she said, leading her lover inside.

chapter twenty seven

Ally drifted towards consciousness, in no hurry to allow the outside world to encroach on her cocoon of blissful comfort. Her sleepy mind was not quite sure *why* it was so blissful, but it seemed like too much effort to find out.

Nonetheless, it was impossible to keep her waking mind quiescent for long and rational thought slowly emerged. Rather than bringing a dash of cold reality, her waking senses confirmed that things were just as blissful.

There was a delightful warmth pressed against Ally's back and a now-familiar link carried its own emotional warmth from the person behind her. A soft arm was thrown around Ally's body, one that she was hugging to her breast. The hand attached to the arm was tantalisingly close to her lips and she couldn't resist placing a loving kiss on the fingertips. The body behind her reacted to the sensation with a soft mewling sound, but didn't wake. The residual thoughts coming over the link reflected their owner's sleeping contentment, reminding Ally of the time she had tried to scan Cassie's thoughts while the cat was still asleep.

Hmm, she thought muzzily. *And she was trying to say that I purr. If only she could hear herself now.*

The thought served to recall the memories of just how Ally and her bedmate had ended up in this position. Ally had led Evelynne through the doors of her balcony and into her bedroom. Once inside, there had been a moment of embarrassed self-consciousness, which had evaporated quickly when, moving nearly as one, they had gravitated to each others' arms and into a passionate kiss. Self-control left quickly after that, though Ally had retained just enough concentration to reach out and close the balcony door before they collapsed onto the bed.

No words other than intently whispered "I love you's" had emerged after that, though the clearly felt emotions were more eloquent than mere sounds could ever be. Now fully conscious of Evelynne's inexperience, Ally had tried to restrain herself. Evelynne would have none of it. Intensely passionate lovemaking had been followed by incredibly gentle loving for a long time afterwards.

Ally smiled to herself over the memories of their encounter. After their slightly awkward first time, Evelynne had proven to be a surprisingly talented and intuitive lover–not that Ally had much to compare it with.

There was some thought struggling to make itself known, something that she somehow knew would disrupt this pleasant haze. The suppressed thoughts were becoming more insistent and Ally realized that there were actually several things clamouring for her attention. The first was enough to make her eyes spring wide open, suddenly fully awake.

Oh God, she thought, *she was just supposed to stay for a little while and then go back to her own room.* A quick glance at the light leaking around the closed curtains confirmed that considerably more than a little while had passed, though Ally could not tell the exact time. The light still had an early-morning quality to it, but the intensity indicated that it was well past dawn. *Well, maybe nobody's noticed yet.*

That optimistic thought was shattered by the second revelation of the day, as Ally's mind finally processed the signals her sense of smell had been sending. A deeper sniff had her squinting blurrily at the nearby night table and thoughts sped through her head.

Coffee! But I don't drink coffee! Maybe Evy got up and got some. But I would have woken up if she did. Someone else came in . . . and saw us! Ally remembered Evelynne talking about her ritual morning cup of coffee and how Seneschal Ylan brought it, without fail, every morning. *Oh God, he saw us like this! Ally sat bolt upright.*

The sudden movement was more than enough to wake the woman who had been slumbering peacefully against her back. "What? Huh?" Evelynne said, confused by the circumstances of her rude awakening. She rubbed her eyes, propping herself on one elbow. It took her a moment to become fully conscious, but then she looked up to see her lover's bare back, stiff with tension, as Ally sat on the edge of the bed, staring at nothing. "Ally? Are you okay?" Evelynne asked hesitantly, reaching out to place a hand on the expanse of skin, pulling back, hurt, when Ally flinched at the contact. *Isis, please don't let her be regretting what we did. I don't want to lose her.*

Ally said something, her words too low to be made out.

"What did you say?" Evelynne asked.

"I said somebody was in here," Ally repeated in a louder voice. "They brought coffee." Her voice cracked slightly. "And they must have seen us."

Evelynne recognized this tone of voice. This was the incredibly shy and private Ally, struggling with the knowledge that someone had seen her so exposed and a hair's breadth away from a panic attack. Fortunately, the princess had also learned how to deal with a situation like this: very gently.

chapter twenty seven

Sitting up slowly, acting as though Ally was a frightened animal ready to bolt, Evelynne carefully knelt behind her lover and rested her hands high on Ally's back. The right covered the small round scar of Ally's shoulder wound and Evelynne stroked the shiny skin with her thumb before pressing a kiss between Ally's shoulder blades. Ally tensed briefly, then slowly relaxed into the caress. Evelynne took advantage of the more compliant form to wrap her arms around the other woman, transferring her lips to a smooth neck.

"Ally, love," she whispered between soft kisses, "it's all right. Everything will be okay."

"O-okay?" Ally said, her voice hitching in response. "But someone *saw* us. In bed. Naked. Together. Do you really want this to come out now?"

Evelynne sighed and rested her chin on Ally's shoulder, maintaining the embrace and revelling in the sensation of skin on skin. She forced herself to focus on the issue at hand. "Love, the only person who probably saw us is Nancu Ylan. He always brings my coffee. And–" a glance at the side table "–he also brought you some hot chocolate. Somehow I don't think he would do that if he thought I was in danger. Also, that man is the very epitome of discretion. He will never tell anyone about what he saw. So don't worry; our secret's safe." The last phrase caused a sliver of resentment to enter Evelynne's tone.

Ally relaxed further. "I'm sorry," she said, hanging her head. "I just–I'm not good with . . . exposure." She turned her head to face Evelynne. "Does it bother you that I don't want anyone knowing about . . . us?"

"No, not really. There is a part of me that wants the entire world to know that we love each other. But the larger part is not ready for anything like that."

"That's how I feel," Ally admitted. "Of course, in our case, it would *literally* be a case of having the world know, and I'm nowhere near being ready for that."

"That's all right." Evelynne smiled and placed a wet kiss on a handy expanse of neck. "Now," she said in a seductive tone, "do you want to drink your hot chocolate, or . . ."

Ally looked hesitantly towards the closed door to the bedroom, as if expecting someone to come bursting through at any moment. "Um, I don't know . . ." She was rapidly becoming distracted by her lover's attentions.

"It's all right," Evelynne coaxed, urging Ally back towards the middle of the bed. "Neither Ylan nor anyone else is going to come in here. It's early still. We have plenty of time . . ."

Now on her back, with Evelynne draped atop her body, Ally looked up. "Okay," she said, her hands beginning to move across the other woman's back. "Hot chocolate's better cold, anyway."

Sir Arthur and Maïda were in the breakfast room eating when Evelynne finally entered looking for food. The princess paused in the doorway, self-consciously smoothing her black silk blouse and gray trousers. While she didn't think either of them knew what she had been doing for the last few hours, a part of her was convinced that it was written across her forehead.

"Good morning, Highness," Maïda said. She looked to the door but didn't see who she was expecting. "Is Alleandre joining us?"

Evelynne blushed. "Um, no. She's . . . still in bed right now." A servant came out and she spent a moment placing her order and then faced her bodyguard. "How are you two this morning?"

"Quite well, Your Highness," Sir Arthur replied. "And yourself? Are you feeling better?"

"Better?" Evelynne asked blankly.

"Yes." The Guard looked puzzled. "Seneschal Ylan informed us that you were indisposed this morning."

"Oh. Right. Yes." Both Maïda and Sir Arthur were puzzled by the blush that deepened even further. "I was . . . indisposed. Actually, it's Ally who's, uh, indisposed right now. Uh, that's why she's still in bed. It was probably something she . . . ate." *Or someone.*

It appeared as though Evelynne's face was threatening to catch fire.

"You still look very flushed, Highness," Maïda observed. "Have you spoken with Latifa about what it might have been?"

"No!" the princess blurted. "That is–I know it wasn't anything Latifa provided. It was, uh, something that *I* gave Ally." *Several times, in fact.*

"I see. But you are all right?"

"Absolutely." *Couldn't be better.*

"You should probably avoid giving Alleandre whatever it was from now on."

"I'll, uh, keep that in mind." *Not likely.*

There was something about Evelynne's behaviour that Maïda could not put a finger on, some vibe that was clamouring for attention. It wasn't until the princess absently rubbed a red mark on the side of her neck that it clicked. The bite mark was unmistakable. "Oh my." The fork dropped from Maïda's hand.

chapter twenty seven

"Are you all right?" Sir Arthur asked. There was something nudging his subconscious as well, but he couldn't figure out what it was.

"Oh, yes. I only just realized something, that's all." A second glance at Evelynne's neck and face showed that the princess was smiling as she rubbed her skin, apparently distracted by some memory. The lady-in-waiting tried to bestow a reassuring smile on Sir Arthur, while her maternal instincts were screaming at her to do... something. "Really. There is just something I must take care of after breakfast."

"Of course," the bodyguard said. He returned his attention to his charge. "Are you going to have Latifa send up something to eat?"

"Um, no. I thought I'd take something up for her myself. You know how she hates having people she doesn't know around when she's not feeling well." It wasn't quite a lie. Evelynne knew that Ally really did hate intruders when she was ill. "In fact, I thought I'd take the day off and ... tend to her. There aren't any really pressing issues to deal with today anyway. Could you let my secretary know?"

"Certainly, Your Highness," Sir Arthur said. "I hope Alleandre is feeling better soon."

Evelynne flushed. "Oh, I'm sure she will." *If I have anything to do with it.*

ಞ ಞ ಞ ಞ ಞ

Evelynne finally tracked down Nancu Ylan in his office, where he had been reviewing the Palace's accounts. It took her longer than usual because she didn't want to draw attention to the fact that she was seeking him out. In retrospect, it would probably have been more inconspicuous to simply ask a Guard, but it was too late now.

The princess was feeling a little rushed, since it had been a while since she had left Ally, hopefully still asleep, but this conversation was potentially life-changing—one of many life-changing experiences Evelynne had gone through lately. The Seneschal had the power to either keep both women's lives private or complicate them immeasurably by revealing what he had witnessed that morning. Evelynne could only pray that her earlier reassurances to Ally about Ylan's discretion were accurate.

The Seneschal looked up as the princess knocked on the door. There was no surprise on his face, suggesting that he had been expecting Evelynne's visit. But then it could have simply been his normal impassive expression. He rose instantly as she entered. "Your Highness," he greeted solemnly.

"Seneschal," Evelynne replied, taking refuge in the formality of the greeting. Her stomach was in knots and she seriously considered leaving and avoiding this discussion, but steeled herself and faced Ylan regally. Then she realised that she was still dressed in her casual silk outfit, which was hardly the most regal attire and almost laughed. The princess held back the hysterical reaction carefully and managed to say, "How are you this morning, Ylan?"

Nancu Ylan's white brow rose. "Quite well, thank you, Your Highness. And yourself?"

"I'm doing . . . extremely well this morning." Evelynne closed the door, ensuring them some privacy, and sank down into a chair. "I suppose we need to have a talk," she said quietly, looking down at her hands clasped in her lap.

"I suppose so, Your Highness," Ylan replied, taking a seat of his own across from her and waiting patiently.

A tense silence stretched for several minutes before Evelynne finally said, "I assume that it was you who came into–into Ally's room this morning and left the coffee and chocolate."

"It was, Your Highness," the Seneschal confirmed.

"And you saw us."

"I did, Your Highness."

Evelynne waited for him to continue, but he did not speak further. She began to feel irrationally angry with him for making her spell out the situation. "Damnit, Ylan, I want to know what you–" She deflated suddenly, hugging her arms to her body in a protective gesture. "I want to know what you're going to do about it," the princess finished in a small voice.

"Do, Your Highness? I intend to do nothing."

Evelynne looked at the Seneschal carefully. His tone had been as unassumingly bland as it usually was, but it seemed as though she could detect a faint note of . . . "You don't approve, do you?" she asked softly. "Of Ally and me."

"Your Highness, it is not my place to–"

"Ylan," Evelynne interrupted, "please. I consider you a friend. I need to know what you really think."

The Seneschal frowned, but appeared to relent by a minute amount. "Very well, Your Highness. I do not believe that Dame Alleandre is the best choice for a . . . liaison."

"You don't like her," Evelynne stated. "Or is it because she's a woman?"

"Not like her, Your Highness? Not at all. I have great respect for Dame Alleandre. I find her to be a most remarkable individual. However, the fact that she is a woman does concern me. Not for the reasons you are probably expecting," he continued, volunteering information for the first time. "I am concerned about your position, Your Highness. If you were a commoner, I would completely support your decision to engage in a relationship with another woman, especially one as admirable as Dame Alleandre. I have no objections on an emotional level to homosexual relationships. As you may recall, my son has been living with a man whom he loves very much and they are planning to marry some time this year. However, he is not in your position. You are the Heir, and as such, any alliances you may make must protect your authority and the respect due your title. With all deference to Dame Alleandre, she is not only a commoner, albeit an admirable one, but also a recent Citizen. As such, her loyalties could be called into question. Your political opponents could use that as a weapon to attack your authority. That does not even consider the fact that she is a woman. These factors lead me to believe that Dame Alleandre is unsuitable as your consort." The Seneschal cocked his head, a gesture that was the equivalent of a shrug. "I apologise if I have upset you, Your Highness, but I am sworn to protect your interests and I believe that they are best served by the truth. That said, you need not worry that I will reveal what I discovered this morning."

Evelynne wiped away the tears that had formed in her eyes. Ylan's words had brought the unwelcome reality of the situation crashing down on her. The Seneschal could be considered to be a fair representative of the Atlantlan citizenry, which lent credit to his opinions and raised serious concerns over the future of her nascent relationship. Still, the thought of ending this wonderful new experience so soon was even more painful.

"Well, thank you for being honest with me, at least," she said, her voice cracking. The princess cleared her throat. "I appreciate it. But this isn't just a liaison for me. I love her. I've never loved anyone like I love her and I don't want to let her go."

Ylan nodded. "Would you consider abdicating for her, Your Highness?" He knew that he was crossing out of what would be considered the proper territory of a mere Seneschal, but he felt that the Heir must consider all the options.

Evelynne opened her mouth to reply, then hesitated. She wasn't sure what the answer was. "Isis, I don't know," she whispered. "I love her and part of me would give up everything to be with her. But I've been training to rule my whole life, first as Princess and then as Queen, ever since Patrick abdicated. There has been nothing else. Until now. So, I don't know."

"I did not mean to suggest that you should, Your Highness," the Seneschal said. "In fact, in my personal opinion, if I may be so bold, you will make an excellent Queen when you ascend the Throne. However, I believe you must be aware of all the options."

"I know, Ylan. Thank you." The princess smiled sadly, but with some genuine humour. "Damnit, I want to have my cake and, uh, eat it too," she said, blushing. She sighed. "For now I'm grateful that you aren't going to say anything to anyone."

"Of course not, Your Highness." Ylan paused. What he was contemplating saying could be considered a breach of confidence, but under the circumstances . . . "You may not believe me, Your Highness, but this morning was not the first time that I have intruded on a similar situation involving a Royal couple. In this Palace as well, as a matter of fact."

"What are you talking about? Did you find Patrick . . . But no, I'm pretty sure he's never done anything like that. Or was it–" Evelynne broke off, as a horrible possibility filled her mind. "Oh no. It was . . . *za*? Who was he with?"

"He was with your Royal mother, of course, Your Highness. Before she was your mother, however."

Evelynne relaxed slightly. "Oh, all right. At least they were married–" She saw the merest hint of change in Ylan's expression. "They . . . *were* married . . . right?"

"Not at the time, Your Highness. This occurred several months prior to the wed–"

"No, no, no," Evelynne said, covering her ears with her hands and screwing her eyes shut. "I do *not* want to hear this." She opened one eye a crack to glare at Nancu Ylan. "Thank you *so* much for that image, Ylan. And today of all days." She shuddered.

"I apologise, Your Highness," he replied. The twinkle in his eyes was very well hidden. Those who claimed that the Seneschal had no sense of humour really didn't know him at all.

�� �� �� �� ��

Evelynne quietly entered Ally's rooms, a tray piled high with food balanced carefully in her hands. Latifa had offered to send breakfast up with a servant, but the princess had declined, claiming that Ally felt uncomfortable having other people around when she was sick. In reality, Evelynne felt that Ally would be even more uncomfortable to have someone walk in when she was naked and asleep, but she hadn't said that to the cook, of course.

Closing the door behind her, Evelynne walked across the living room and peeked into the bedroom. The unruly mop of mussed brown hair poking up from above the blanket on the bed showed that Ally was still sound asleep. Evelynne silently placed the tray on the bedside table, then snuck closer to look at her lover's face.

Ally was resting mostly on her stomach, her head turned towards the outside of the bed. The blanket was pulled up high, leaving only a small portion of her shoulders and neck visible. Her face was completely relaxed

chapter twenty seven

and Evelynne realised that all the clichés about people having a childlike innocence when they were sleeping were true. This Ally before her was not the incredibly powerful Adept, nor the intelligent scientist, nor even the kind, shy woman she had come to love. This was just Ally. She remembered watching Ally as she had slept once before and how that woman had seemed somehow still alert, with a subtle tension running through her body, and wondered at the difference. *Trust*, she realised. *This Ally trusts me completely, even after this morning and so she's relaxed completely.* She looked at the open face. *I did that. Ally, I pray I never betray that trust.*

Evelynne spent several moments crouched by the side of the bed, just watching her lover sleep. *She's so beautiful*, the princess thought. *She doesn't believe that she is, but it's there for anyone to see. And I'm so grateful that I've seen more than most.* Unable to stop herself, Evelynne reached out and began to run her fingers through Ally's short hair, lightly scratching the scalp. This, she had learned last night, was one of Ally's favourite sensations, capable of reducing her to a puddle of jelly. It seemed to be working now too. Still deeply asleep, Ally let out a contented sigh and snuggled further into the blanket. Evelynne listened carefully for a moment and then grinned. Ally was purring again, the soft, pleased humming just barely audible, but she still didn't wake. *I wore her out last night. And this morning*, Evelynne thought, absurdly pleased with herself. *The poor thing. Of course, she wasn't exactly complaining . . .*

Feeling her libido waking once again at the memories, Evelynne instinctively leaned forward to brush her lips over Ally's. The sudden slight gasp and mild tension that resulted informed her that Ally was now awake. The knowledge was confirmed when her lover snaked an arm out of the blankets and around her neck, drawing her closer for a proper "Good Morning" kiss.

Several minutes later they both came up for air. Evelynne pulled back, sitting back on her heels by the side of the bed. Ally's left hand remained loosely cupped around the princess' face, lightly stroking her cheek with the thumb.

"Good morning," Ally said lazily, her voice still rough from a mixture of sleep and emotion. She cleared her throat, then her eyes widened as she realised their position. "You're dressed," she blurted.

"I am. But you're not," Evelynne replied, sneaking a hand under the blankets to stroke bare, soft skin. She grinned cheekily. "I like your way better."

Ally blushed, and then her breathing hitched as Evelynne brushed against some very sensitive skin. "So do I," she whispered hoarsely. "However—"

she reached in to capture the wandering hand "–right now, I really need to go to the bathroom."

"Okay," Evelynne agreed, pressing a kiss to Ally's forehead. She stood, holding out a hand.

Ally looked at the hand for a moment and then reached out to take it, sitting up as she did so. She tried to keep the sheet wrapped around her body, but couldn't quite manage it. She fumbled for a few seconds before Evelynne took her other hand.

"Ally," the princess said, "what are you doing?"

"I'm–um. Well . . ."

"Love, I've seen it all before." Evelynne voice was gently teasing.

Predictably, Ally blushed again. "Sorry," she said, casting her gaze downwards. "It's just force of habit. I really don't like anyone seeing me, well, you know . . ."

"It's all right, love. I know." Evelynne reached out to bring Ally's eyes level with her own and then placed both hands on her lover's shoulders. Not breaking eye contact, she said, "Stop me if you want to, all right?" Ever so slowly she brought her hands down, taking the sheet with them and baring Ally's upper body. Ally tensed, but made no move to stop her. When her lover was bare from the waist up, the blanket still covering her lower body, Evelynne stopped. She didn't look away from Ally's eyes. "Ally, you're beautiful. You don't have to hide yourself from me." She raised her right hand to cup Ally's breast, smiling inwardly at the sharp gasp the move brought. "I love looking at you." Giving the breast a final caress, Evelynne pulled her hand away. "But I also want you to be comfortable. If you don't want to show yourself, that's all right also. I never want to make you unhappy, love. Do you understand?"

Ally nodded shakily, her emotions–love, fear, embarrassment, happiness–plainly visible on her face. "I understand. Thank you. I love you." She suddenly chuckled embarrassedly. "But right now I *really* need to go to the bathroom."

Evelynne laughed. "All right," she said, standing up. "Go ahead."

Ally hesitated a moment longer, then pushed back the blanket and stood up in front of her lover, not bothering to cover herself. Evelynne eyed her with a frankly appreciative gaze and Ally managed not to hide herself with her hands, allowing the princess the opportunity. The only signs of her discomfort were a constant flush and her twitching hands, which tried to automatically cover her most private areas. *Damnit, this is Evelynne,* she thought. *And she was right; she has seen everything I'm displaying now. More, in fact.* Her flush deepened at the thought.

chapter twenty seven

Evelynne finished her perusal, fighting the urge to throw Ally back onto the bed again. *I don't think that would be a good idea right now. But when she gets back from the bathroom . . . watch out.* Ally refused to look at her. She gently but firmly reached out and forced the blushing woman to meet her gaze. Pulling her lover down, Evelynne kissed her passionately, and then broke away. "Go," she ordered, pointing to the bathroom.

A suspicion of tears in her eyes, Ally smiled tremulously. Turning away, she walked towards the bathroom, consciously forcing down her instinct to hide as quickly as possible. Evelynne watched her retreating form, eyes hot on her back. And lower regions. Reaching the bathroom, Ally smiled apologetically before closing the door.

Evelynne shook her head and turned back to the breakfast tray, extending its short legs and placing it in the centre of the bed. It was odd, she mused as she worked. Despite the fact that Ally was the one who had the experience in these matters, so far it was the princess who felt that she was the experienced one, at least in some areas. *Still, I suppose it makes sense in a way,* she thought. *I've been raised and trained my whole life to both be confident and to instill confidence in other people. It's a necessary part of my life. But Ally has apparently had several hard knocks, and it's shaken her. I know that her parents, her friends, and even . . . Annie–* she managed to think the name with only a moderate twinge of jealousy *–have done their best to reassure her and bolster her self-confidence, but for whatever reason it hasn't been enough. Of course, carrying around the secrets she does and not being sure exactly what she's capable of becoming, would be enough to shake anyone's self-image. It's not as though she's had hundreds of lovers who could have helped her gain that confidence, thank Isis! So I suppose that task must fall to me.* Evelynne grinned wickedly. *Oh dear, however will I manage it?* But in spite of her bravado, there was an unacknowledged thread of insecurity in her ruminations.

Hearing the toilet flush, the princess snatched up a pair of Ally's green silk pajamas. It was enough that Ally had managed to expose herself–both physically and emotionally–once this morning. Evelynne didn't think that her lover would be able to eat breakfast while naked.

The door to the bathroom opened then and Ally stepped out, still in all her glory. She had taken the time to splash water on her face and Evelynne watched, mesmerised, as a drop of water that had escaped the towel slowly wound down Ally's neck. The brief respite also seemed to have restored Ally's confidence somewhat, because much of her earlier tension appeared to be gone.

Realising she was staring again, Evelynne held out Ally's pajamas in one hand and her glasses in the other. She was considerably surprised–though pleased–when her lover simply brushed them aside, wrapped the smaller woman in her arms and bent down to kiss her deeply and passionately. Evelynne eagerly returned the embrace, dropping what she was holding. Without quite understanding how it had happened, the princess found herself back on the bed, pressing Ally into its surface, her wandering hands mapping bare skin.

Finally breaking away, Evelynne looked down to find Ally's intense grey eyes looking deeply into her own. "Hello," Ally said hoarsely, her own hands rubbing up and down Evelynne's back through her shirt.

"Hello yourself," Evelynne murmured back. Her mouth quirked into a smile. "That's a very nice way to say good morning."

"Mmm," Ally agreed. "Maybe when you're Queen you should enact a law making that the official greeting in the Realm. 'Thou shalt passionately kiss the first person thine eyes lay upon each day.'"

"I like it," Evelynne said, giggling.

"I'm pretty sure it would boost morale. Maybe you should add on a bit about kissing the first person you see at work."

"Now *that* would increase workplace satisfaction. Of course, it might also hamper productivity. People might find themselves 'greeting' their co-workers more than actually working."

"That's true. So I suppose we should just keep this to ourselves, huh?"

"I suppose we should," Evelynne whispered, ducking her head back down to kiss Ally with definite intent.

Ally kissed her back for a few moments and then managed to pull back slightly. "I hate to keep breaking the mood," she said, punctuating her words with kisses to Evelynne's jaw, "but I am absolutely starving."

"Mmm, eat later," Evelynne hummed. She paused. "Or you could eat now . . ." She raised an eyebrow wickedly.

"As tempting as that is," Ally said, "right now I really need food. Although later we could have . . . dessert."

"Mnm, mnm," Evelynne murmured, burying her face in Ally's neck. Her voice was muffled. "Dessert now, food later."

Ally sighed and called on all her self-control. Rolling to the side, she managed to put several centimetres between them. "Trust me, love," she said. "Anticipation makes the best dessert even better."

"To the Duat with anticipation," Evelynne pouted. "I've been anticipating for months now."

"And didn't it make last night . . . really good?" There was just a hint of insecurity in the question.

"Really good? Try absolutely amazing. Mind-blowing. Incredible." Evelynne's voice dropped and took on an earnest quality. "Loving."

Ally's gaze softened. "Good," she whispered.

chapter twenty seven

Holding her lover's eyes for a few moments longer, Evelynne sighed. "All right," she said. "We'll eat now. Breakfast, that is. Afterwards, though . . ."

"Afterwards," Ally promised.

"All right." Sitting up on the bed, Evelynne reached to the floor and picked up the carelessly discarded pajamas and glasses. "Here," she said, holding them out.

"Thank you," Ally said. Slipping on her glasses, she looked around. "Ah, that's better." She quickly pulled on her pajama pants and slung the shirt over her shoulders. She was about to button it up when Evelynne stopped her.

"Let me," the other woman said, her fingers already at work. Ally raised her eyebrows but said nothing. The only sounds she made were the soft hitches in her breathing when Evelynne's fingers "accidentally" brushed against her skin.

"You're quite the seductress, you know," she said when the task was complete. "Are you sure you've never done this before?"

"Positive," Evelynne replied, smirking. "I'm just inspired." The look she gave Ally almost made the other woman discard her resolve.

"Okay, let's eat—that is, let's have breakfast," Ally said hurriedly.

The next few minutes were silent, as both women ate. After several minutes, Evelynne began feeding Ally morsels of food. Ally blushed, but returned the favour. "This is good," Ally commented. She paused. "So . . . what did they say when you asked for breakfast in bed?" Her tone was again anxious, though less so than earlier that morning.

"Well," Evelynne replied, finishing off a strawberry, "everyone thinks you're sick. 'Indisposed' was the word Nancu Ylan used. I—well, I didn't say anything to disabuse them of the idea." The princess' eyes twinkled. "In fact, they now think that you're in bed because of something you ate last night."

Ally choked on her apple juice, coughing and hacking until her face was bright red. "Oh no," she rasped. "Please tell me you're joking."

"I'm not. The reason that *I'm* not 'indisposed' is because I didn't eat exactly the same thing that you did. So you see, everything I said was completely true, from a certain point of view." Evelynne let her eyes drift down Ally's body.

"Oh no," Ally repeated, burying her face in her hands. "I'll never be able to look at them again." She sighed and looked up, and her tone and expression were serious now. "So, what did Ylan say about us? Does anyone else know?"

"No. He's not going to say anything. As far as he's concerned, this falls under the heading of 'Personal Secrets,' and unless it becomes a threat to the stability of the Diarchy and Realm, he won't say a word."

"Oh. Okay." Ally's voice was relieved. "Did he say anything to you personally?"

Evelynne hesitated, considering how much to tell her lover. *Honesty, Evy,* she thought. *This affects both of you, so you have to be honest.* "He's–he doesn't approve of you," she said finally. Ally winced and Evelynne reached out to take her hand.

"Damn," Ally whispered. "It's because I'm a woman, isn't it?"

"Yes. But not quite in the way you probably think." Evelynne took in Ally's tight, shuttered expression, wishing, not for the first time, that she had the Adept's thought-sensing ability. "He doesn't have anything against you on a personal level. Actually, he thinks you're quite 'admirable.' However, he is concerned about the effect our relationship will have on my legitimacy and authority to rule. Some of the Nobles could cause quite a few problems. He also has issues with the fact that you aren't part of the aristocracy. Traditionally, Royal Spouses and Consorts have come from the various Noble houses or from foreign royalty, although there have been exceptions to that rule."

"Oh. Okay," Ally said after a moment. She forced a smile. "At least now I–we know. So, how do you feel about that?" she asked hesitantly.

"I'm . . . all right for the most part," Evelynne admitted. "Naturally, I would have liked complete acceptance and support, but I truly believe that his concerns are professionally motivated."

"Okay," Ally said. "As long as you're okay with it."

"I will be."

They were silent for a few more minutes. At one point Ally looked up to see Evelynne looking at her with a questioning expression on her face. "What?" she asked.

"What?" Evelynne echoed, startled. "Oh. I was just wondering something. Can I ask you a question?"

"Evy, you can always ask me any question," Ally said. "Of course, I may not always want to answer, but never be afraid to ask."

"All right. I was just wondering. This morning, when you were, you know, trying to hold up the sheet with one hand . . ."

"Um, yeah?" Ally blushed at the memory.

"Well, why didn't you use your mind to hold it up? I mean, I assume you could, right?"

"Oh." Ally looked a little startled. "Well, yeah, I could, I guess. To be honest, I just never thought of it. Even though sometimes I can and do use

chapter twenty seven

my abilities automatically, usually I have to consciously decide to do something. And, well, this morning I just didn't even think of it." She shrugged. "Sorry, but that's the best answer I can come up with."

"Oh, that's all right. I was just curious, that's all. I suppose I was wondering just how natural your abilities are to you."

"Well, for the most part, it hardly ever feels *unnatural* any more. It's just not automatic. Who knows, maybe one day I'll be able to pick things up psychokinetically without even thinking of it, as though it was my arm or hand. Maybe it will be like having ten hands. I don't know."

"Hmm," Evelynne mused. "Ten hands, eh? You know, that could be very useful in . . . some situations." She stared at Ally hungrily.

"Oh?" Ally said.

Her eyes narrowed and suddenly Evelynne gasped, her right hand flying to her inner thigh. The princess gasped again when another phantom touch brushed the curve of her breast. It was a nearly indescribable sensation. The touch lacked any sort of friction or heat, being composed solely of a kind of moving pressure, almost as if she was being very gently caressed with a small, rubbery ceramic rolling ball. It was somehow incredibly erotic. "Oh, Isis," Evelynne groaned.

"Are you okay?" Ally asked. "Is that okay?" She was truthfully a little worried. While she was fairly certain that the feeling wasn't pain, she wasn't certain how Evelynne would react to being touched in such an unconventional way. "Are you—" She was cut off by the impact of a leaping redhead, who proceeded to smother her in kisses and caresses. She managed to keep control of her awareness just long enough to rescue the breakfast tray, lifting it off the bed and onto the floor before it could spill its contents all over them.

   ∾ ∾ ∾ ∾ ∾

Ally lay staring up at the multicoloured blob that was the ceiling, lazily running her fingers through the flame-red hair that lay spread out across her stomach. Evelynne was humming happily at the attention, turning her head every now and then to press a kiss to the soft surface she was lying on. Her hand also rested near her face, softly stroking the skin beneath it and occasionally inching lower to tease short, wiry hairs.

Ally was content simply to lie back and revel in the sensation of pleasure recently and energetically achieved, along with the constant, low-level arousal that Evelynne was keeping alive. Her contemplation was interrupted by Evelynne's low murmur.

"Ally, love," the princess began.

"I know, I know," Ally interrupted languidly. "I'm purring."

Evelynne giggled, causing delightful sensations to ripple over Ally's lower abdomen. "Actually," the princess murmured, "I was going to say something else. But you're right. You *are* purring."

"Hmph," Ally pouted. "Okay, then, what were you going to say?"

"Well. . ." Evelynne hesitated before turning her head so that she could look up at her lover. "I kind of had a question." She trailed off.

"Remember, I told you that you can ask me any question you want." Ally peered down at Evelynne's face, cursing her eyes for turning such a beautiful visage into a near-shapeless blob.

Moving her hand south more deliberately, Evelynne slid upwards until her head was level with Ally's and they were pressed against each other for almost their entire lengths. Shifting, she began to place tiny nibbles along one flushed ear. She was hoping that by concentrating on this, she would be able to ask the question that actually had her very nervous.

"Uh, yes?" Ally breathed. She was trying to use a meditation technique that she usually used to control pain to maintain her concentration, but it wasn't working very well. The thing about pain was that it was generally unwelcome to begin with, whereas this . . .

"I want to know . . ." Evelynne paused and swallowed, stilling her hand. "I need to know . . ." She trailed off again, causing Ally to focus on her.

Seeing the uncertainty in her lover's face, so close to her own, Ally whispered, "What, love? What do you need to know?"

Evelynne swallowed again. "I need to know . . . Do I satisfy you? Do I do . . . things that you like?"

Ally would have laughed if Evelynne's face hadn't been so serious. "You're here, doing this–" She reached down to rest her own hand over Evelynne's. "–and I'm almost passed out from it and you're worried that you don't satisfy me? Trust me," she gasped, "you have nothing to worry about."

Evelynne smiled a little tremulously. "It's just that I've never done this before yesterday and you have, so I want to be sure that I'm doing all the things that satisfy you."

"Evy," Ally said seriously, "you haven't done *all* the things I enjoy. It's not possible anyway. We've been lovers for a day, so there is an absolute limit to what we could've done. Trust me when I say that there's time. Besides, some things that I enjoy, you might not and vice versa. For that matter, there may be things that I like that I don't even know that I like yet. And the same goes for you." Giving Evelynne's hand–and herself, by extension–a squeeze, Ally smiled. "Believe me, we have time."

"Good," Evelynne said, truly smiling again, as she began to move her hand once more. "I just didn't know whether you were comparing me to Annie, or—"

"To Annie...?" The words cut through the haze of Ally's mounting pleasure and she stilled Evelynne's hand with her own. Though flushed and panting slightly, Ally looked at her lover with a deadly serious expression. "I will *never* compare you with Annie. It isn't fair, either to you or her. Or me. You are two different people and they are two different relationships. I will not cheapen either one by comparing it to the other. If you have specific questions, I will answer them as objectively as possible. But do not ask me to put a value judgment on any part of either relationship, because I won't." Ally's face softened, and she reached up to stroke Evelynne's face. "When I'm with you, I'm with *you*. I'm not imagining or wishing you're anyone else. Except maybe Angelina Jolie." The weak joke drew an equally weak smile from Evelynne. "When I was with Annie, I was with her and she was with me. None of her previous lovers were there. Right here, right now, like this—" Ally covered Evelynne's hand again. "—there's just you and me." Raising her head, Ally kissed Evelynne hard.

"And Angelina," Evelynne murmured, smiling. She began moving with purpose.

"And Angelina," Ally gasped.

"Well, she can wait her turn. Right now you're mine." Evelynne gazed down into Ally's face; flushed, eyes closed tightly, pulse beating rapidly in her neck. "I love you," she whispered, although she didn't know whether her lover was hearing her or not. "I love the way you smell, the way you feel against me. And I especially love the way you look . . . right . . . about . . . now," she finished, holding Ally as she convulsed.

chapter twenty eight

"Hello, Alleandre," Dr. Collins shouted over the roar of the helicopter. "I'm glad to see you arrived safe and sound. Alice tells me you nearly missed your flight." His secretary was standing some distance away, having chosen not to chance the wind kicked up by the rotors.

"Hi, Dr. Collins," Ally replied, shaking his hand. They quickly moved away from the aircraft while a uniformed worker collected Ally's baggage. Out of range of the blades, they were able to speak normally. "Um, yeah. I got delayed at the Palace. Thankfully Sir Arthur was able to get me to the airport just in time." The memory of the reason for her tardiness, unexpected but very pleasant, brought a high blush to her cheeks and she hoped that the Director wouldn't notice.

Realising that her lover would be gone for at least a week, Evelynne had spent much of the early morning making sure that Ally wouldn't forget her. After the morning's demonstration it was downright impossible, even had they not been habitually sharing a bed. Each night they would retire to Ally's rooms with the stated intention of Evelynne returning to her own bed after making love. Somehow that had never happened and now Evelynne hadn't slept in her own bed in a week.

Ally had expressed her concern over what the servants might think, but Evelynne had reassured her that Seneschal Nancu Ylan was committed to preserving their privacy and even if a servant suspected, he would carefully control the access. However the Seneschal had done it, apparently it had worked, because nobody had given them odd looks, or knowing winks or any sign of knowledge of their new relationship.

The week had also been marked by a steady discovery of each others' bodies. With no previous experience to draw on, but a very fertile imagination, Evelynne had begun by mainly following Ally's lead, until she gained enough confidence to begin experimenting. She had discovered little that she didn't like and there were some things that were incredibly enjoyable for both parties. Taking charge had been inspired, as Ally had revealed a preference for being somewhat submissive while making love, leaving the more dominant role to her partner–a role that Evelynne took to with great relish. It was by no means the "whips and chains" fetish that Evelynne had once speculated about and Ally had shown a distinct aversion to actual pain.

Still, it had been an incredible turn-on when Evelynne had realised that this massively powerful person was willing–eager, even–to have her take charge.

Once Evelynne had realised the amount of pleasure she was getting from her dominance, she had spoken to Ally, worried that she might be getting too much enjoyment. Ally had laughed heartily, leapt on her lover and reversed their roles in a love-making session that had Evelynne completely at the other woman's mercy for several hours.

Dr. Collins remained oblivious to his new employee's reaction, as he nodded distractedly. "And how is Her Highness? Well, I hope."

"Oh, yes, she's fine." *Better than fine, actually, if the way she was reacting this morning was any indication.*

"I'm glad to hear it," the Doctor said as they approached two other people standing nearby. "Alleandre, I believe you remember Alice Bennett, my secretary?"

"Ah, yes," Ally said, smiling and shaking the other woman's hand. "The one who actually runs things around here."

Ms. Bennett smiled broadly. "Aye. Ye do remember, then. Shows ye have a good head on yer shoulders."

"Indeed it does," Collins said, grinning. "Don't worry if you forget; Alice will be sure to remind you who's in charge. This is Ms. Laura Garrity, your own secretary." Ally looked shocked. "Believe me, you will be thankful you have one once the paperwork starts piling up." He scowled.

Everyone laughed and Ally shook her new secretary's hand. The other woman, a blonde, extremely fit woman in her mid-thirties, had a firm, no-nonsense grip that Ally immediately appreciated. "Ms. Garrity," she greeted. "I'm not quite sure what to do here. I've never had a secretary before."

"No problem, Ms. Tretiak," Laura said, smiling politely. "I'll be sure to let you know what to let me know to do."

While Ally worked out that sentence, Alice Bennett laughed. "I think she's the best kind, Laura. You can start training her right away."

Introductions complete, Dr. Collins escorted them all to the waiting cars. He showed Ally and Laura Garrity to one car and helped them in. "I hate to leave you so quickly," he said, "but I have a telephone conference with several of our university contacts in about fifteen minutes. So, I will leave you in Ms. Garrity's capable hands. She'll show you to your office and new quarters, and give you a tour of our residence area. She also knows how to contact me if necessary." He smiled at both women. "Alleandre, welcome to Aztlan."

෴ ෴ ෴ ෴ ෴

chApteR twenty eight

"And here's your office, Ms. . . . . er, Dame Alleandre," Laura Garrity said, opening the door and allowing Ally to enter.

"Please, call me Ally," the other woman said, looking around curiously. She smiled wryly. "To be honest, I'm still not comfortable with all the Dame Alleandre stuff."

"Of course, Ally," Laura said. "I'm not used to using all these titles yet."

"Oh? I thought all Atlantlans learned all that etiquette."

"I'm sure they do. However, I'm not Atlantean. Um, Atlantlan."

"Really? Where are you from?" Ally asked curiously.

"Texas," Laura replied. "I'm here on a work exchange program."

"Really?" Ally said, surprised. "I didn't realise."

"What, you didn't recognise the accent?" Laura teased, smiling.

"Oh, I noticed it. It's just that I've heard so many different accents since I've come here that it didn't really click. I'm just a little surprised that you're from America. I didn't think Atlantl and the U.S. were that friendly."

"Oh, it's not that bad," the secretary explained. "Heck, even during the Cold War, Russia and the States had similar exchange programs. They were usually simply covers for espionage operations on both sides, but some good did come of them. The politicians have to play up the tension for their own reasons, but those of us who are actually working can usually ignore it for the most part." She paused. "It doesn't bother you, does it? That I'm American?"

"Oh, no. Not at all. I just don't know many Americans. My uncle became an American citizen a couple of years ago, but I don't see him much." Ally shrugged. "You know how they describe Canadians, don't you?"

"No, I don't think so."

Ally smiled. "Canadians are just unarmed Americans with health care."

Laura laughed. "I see," she said. "Is that all?"

Ally shrugged again. "Pretty much. Actually, we tend to make a big deal out of how we're different and in some ways we really are. Canadians are one of the only nationalities that define their cultural identity by what they're not. Ask any Canadian and the first thing they'll say is, 'We're not Americans.'" Laura laughed again. "No, really, it's true."

"Okay," Laura said. "Well, if you don't have a problem with me being a gun-toting American . . ."

" . . . I hope you don't have a problem with me being a pansy-assed Canadian."

"No problem here."

"Good," Ally said, relieved. She hesitated, and then continued in a more serious voice. "Speaking of problems . . . You might know—hell, the whole world knows that I'm a lesbian." Laura nodded. "Well, some people I've worked with in the past have had a problem with it. And this job is really important to me . . ." She trailed off.

"I have absolutely no problem with your sexual orientation," Laura assured her. "As long as you're breaking no laws, I really couldn't care less. I happen to be happily straight, but I assume it doesn't bother you. Does it?"

"Of course not."

"Then there you go. Subject closed." Laura smiled. "Now, back to business." She waved a hand to indicate the office. "Before we got off track, I was going to give you the nickel tour." She looked around the small space and was silent for a moment. "Well, this is it. It's not much, but then this post is brand new. Apparently nobody's quite sure what exactly you'll be doing, so we're starting small. We can get more office space and equipment as we need it."

Ally looked around the small room. It was some six metres square, constructed of pre-fabricated panels that could probably be deconstructed in less than an hour. Small windows were set in two of the walls, while the door to the outside was in the middle of another. A second door was in one corner. A skylight let light into the room, enhancing the fluorescent bulbs that were the primary source of illumination.

Those would have to be the first things to go, Ally decided. For some unknown reason, fluorescent lights—either the frequency of their light, their subliminal sounds or something else—had a dulling effect on her telempathic and clairsentient abilities. Something more conducive to concentration would have to be installed.

Two simple desks occupied the lion's share of the floor space. One, already sported an impressive collection of papers and files. Ally assumed it to be her secretary's. A few framed pictures, their faces away from the door, lent a more personal feel to the workspace. The other desk was nearly pristine, with neatly arranged office supplies bracketing a sleek-looking LCD computer monitor, keyboard and mouse. Other than that, the only furniture consisted of a few desk chairs—Ally could see that those would be the next things to be replaced—a small table at the side of the room and a couple of file cabinets.

Finishing her scrutiny, Ally faced her new secretary again. "Well, once we add a bit of colour, this'll be a pretty good place to work." Pointing to the second door, she asked, "What's through there?"

"Bathroom," Laura replied, confirming Ally's guess. "I've been assured that we can expand with additional storerooms or lab spaces as needed,

chapter twenty eight

within reason, of course. If you want a scanning-tunnelling electron microscope in a sterile lab, that might take a bit of work."

"I'll keep that in mind," Ally said wryly. "I *think* it would probably be easier to send things to Jamaz University in that case."

"I'd imagine so," Laura agreed. Taking a seat at her desk and snatching up a PDA, the secretary waved Ally into another chair. "Now, I don't mean to rush you into anything, but I was wondering what you were intending to do."

"Oh. Okay then. Well, what's been done so far?"

"Not much. The basic summaries of the excavations so far have been uploaded to your computer and Doctor Collins said to let you know that if you have any questions to feel free to call him. All the computers on site are video linked. Now, I imagine you want to spend a few days getting caught up on things, but I was wondering if you had any ideas for your first project."

"Okay." Ally had actually been able to read and memorise—thanks to her newfound speed-reading and eidetic memory—much more than the summaries of the excavations. Practically a whole library of information had been "uploaded" directly into her brain. She couldn't access it automatically, instead having to read it behind her eyes, but she thought it would still come in very useful. "Well, I know we're going to need more people. So if you could maybe get together some information on what we have to do to hire some people. Procedures, budgets, that sort of thing." She smiled crookedly. "I've never done anything like this before. I'm a little out of my depth."

"No problem," Laura said. She was making notes on the tiny screen of her PDA. She looked up. "So who were you looking to hire?"

ช ช ช ช ช

"Well, Mr. Islin, welcome to the team," Ally said, rising and holding out her hand. "I think you'll fit in quite nicely."

Taldas Islin, a handsome young man studying electronics at X'Han University on Lyonesse, grinned as he accepted the handshake. When Ally had posted the job opportunities she was offering throughout the country's universities, calling for "unconventional thinkers", Taldas had been one of the first to apply. His reputation for new and innovative ideas was near legendary amongst the faculty and had therefore obviously annoyed a great many older, established professors. Now he had the chance to explore new concepts without formal restrictions among a few more like-minded researchers and was greatly looking forward to the opportunity.

"Thank you, Ally," he said. "So I'll be starting on Tuesday?"

"That sounds fine," Ally replied. "Oh, and remember to call Laura to—"

She was interrupted as the door opened suddenly and a heavy-set, bespectacled young woman entered, blinking owlishly on entering the relative dark of the office. The newcomer's expression cleared as her eyesight did and she saw Ally sitting with Taldas. "I am sorry," she said with a thick Arabic accent. "I do not know you have . . . visitor."

"That's okay, Rena," Ally said, waving the young woman over. She and Islin stood. "Mr. Islin here is going to be joining our merry band of misfits. Taldas Islin, Rena bel'Oman. Rena's our resident material sciences expert."

"Ah, greetings, fellow misfit," Islin said, grinning as he shook Rena's hand.

The other woman looked confused. "I am sorry. What is . . . 'misfit'?"

"*Y'ek'sal*," Islin translated into Lantlan and Rena's face cleared and she smiled broadly.

"Ah, yes," she said. "I am also misfit."

"Rena here got in trouble with her faculty because she was trying to show that the ancient Egyptians must have had something resembling ultrasonic drill bit technology," Ally explained. "Plus trying to show that whatever it was must have been about a hundred times more efficient than anything we have today."

"But, of course 'everyone knows' that all ancient cultures are too primitive to have developed that kind of technology," Islin concluded. He shook his head ruefully. "Even with Aztlan here and all the incredible things around, they still insist that the canals were made using slave labour and elephant power. Personally, I think some kind of levitation device is much more likely."

Ally smiled internally. She had her own theories about how such huge projects could have been completed, even by some society with no technology, and Islin wasn't that far off. "Mr. Islin," she said, "I think you'll fit in pretty well here."

chapter twenty nine

Jennifer Armston shivered, for several reasons.

The first was simple cold, caused by a combination of driving wind and the knife-like slivers of freezing rain and spray cutting into her skin. The wind-blown ocean spray was completely undeterred by her light shirt and pants, which were now thoroughly soaked. Her life jacket, while providing adequate protection from drowning, did nothing to separate her from the cold. With the frightening condition of the sea around her tiny life raft—two metre waves threatening to capsize it at any moment—even the protection offered by the life jacket was significantly degraded. Although, given the events of the last hour, Jennifer's estimate of the danger she was in was thoroughly confused.

Another reason she was shivering was in reaction to at least two kinds of shock. The first was most certainly bad shock and Jennifer felt—in the eerie calmness of her traumatised mind—that she was justified in her reaction. After all, it wasn't every day that her airplane, en route from Kilim to Ekion Bel, crashed into Refuge Bay and certainly not every day that she survived to tell about it.

Somehow, though, she felt that her survival was more assured than it rightfully ought to be. *Something* was looking out for her and the other occupants of the life raft, although neither she nor any of the others were sure about exactly what that *something* might be.

The proof of their guardian sat huddled within the near-crushing circle of Jennifer's arms and was the source of her more happy shock. As if sensing her thoughts, that source squirmed and looked up into his mother's face, barely visible in the near-total darkness. "Mama, you're squishing me," he complained.

"I know, dear," Jennifer said, but she didn't let up her grip in the slightest. The life raft was still rocking alarmingly with the swells and there was no way she was going to lose her son to the turbulent ocean again. She had miraculously recovered him once, and she didn't want to tempt fate—or her son's unknown protector—by lowering her guard.

When the plane had first gone down, Jennifer had been sure that she, along with everyone else on board, was about to die, if not in the impact itself, then drowned in the ocean. In the first of what was about to be several miracles, both Jennifer and her son, Lemar, had survived. The businessman seated across the aisle from them had been less lucky, his neck snapping instantly when the aircraft hit the surface of the sea. The flight crew of the small plane had been exceptionally professional, successfully evacuating most of the passengers from the rapidly sinking craft to the emergency rafts. Disaster had struck–again–just as Jennifer was scrambling onto the tiny rubber boat, when a sudden breaking wave nearly capsized it and tore Lemar from her arms, despite her frantic efforts.

She vaguely remembered screaming, and trying to dive into the frigid water, and being held back by those passengers and crew who had already boarded the raft. After a time, she had come back to herself, shivering with cold and grief, certain that her son had been lost forever. The raft and its huddled inhabitants–eight passengers and a flight attendant–had already been blown away from the wreckage of the downed aircraft and were alone on the dark ocean.

Then the second miracle had occurred.

Before anyone realised it was happening, Lemar had appeared by the side of the boat, not quite fully submerged in the water, but more as if he was being held up by something *outside*. A stunned stewardess had reacted instinctively to reach out and grab the silent, shivering boy. Realising that her son was alive, Jennifer had scrambled to get to him and a fortuitous flash of lightning had revealed to her a dark figure moving away from the raft. She was still uncertain of what she had seen, if it had in fact been anything at all and not a trick of the light and waves, but catching the stewardess' eye had left both of them oddly certain that *something* had been out there.

The miracle had been repeated twice, once with an elderly gentleman, who was now praying quietly but fervently in Arabic, and a second time with the co-pilot of the plane. The co-pilot was unconscious, blood dripping sluggishly from a blow to the head. Both times the casualties had suddenly appeared beside the boat–which was becoming overcrowded–supported by some outside force that kept them from the worst of the storm's effects.

The rain was lessening, although thunder kept rolling and lightning continued to pierce the darkness intermittently. Jennifer was on the verge of drowsing off, exhaustion overcoming adrenaline, when a shout from one of the raft's other occupants startled her back to alertness. In what was becoming a near-routine action, two of the stronger men hurried to help the latest person rescued from the sea onto the raft. This time it was a middle-aged woman, stunned and groggy. Jennifer could sympathise.

chapter twenty nine

One of the men, who seemed to have some medical training, quickly checked their newest companion's pulse and breathing. "She'll be okay!" he shouted over the roar of the waves and wind. "Shock and hypothermia, but she should be fine." He didn't need to add that the continued survival of all of them rested on being rescued, soon.

Jennifer just nodded, unable to muster the energy for more of a response. The rest of the passengers were similarly exhausted.

Suddenly, the young woman was aware of a presence next to her where she sat huddled at the side of the boat. She looked over the edge, seeing a dark man-sized shape holding onto the raft's rubber rail mere centimetres away. Before Jennifer could cry out and alert the others, a low voice came to her ears over the whistling wind.

"Don't say anything," the figure said in English. There was a pause. "And hang on."

Jennifer instinctively responded to the order by tightening her grip on Lemar, ignoring his small cry of protest. Then, even over the constant irregular movement of the raft in the sea, she felt the small craft begin to accelerate, this time in a particular direction, although she couldn't see what made this vector any different from the others, except that it was at near right angles to the wind. None of the other passengers appeared to notice the movement, small as it was compared to the violent swells of the waves and Jennifer restrained herself from saying anything, still unsure if what she was experiencing was real.

Unable to stop herself, she turned her head to look at the dark figure, attempting to piece together details in the gloom. It was definitely man-sized and shaped, although the majority of its form was obscured by a bulky black garment that looked almost like huge leathery bat wings. Looking closer in the intermittent flashes of lightning Jennifer was able to spot legs trailing behind the figure as it appeared to stretch out on the water and hands gripping the rubber rails along the side of the raft near her.

Hesitantly, Jennifer reached out with one hand and touched the pale hand nearest to her. She felt the hand give an involuntary jerk at the contact, which only made her reflexively grasp it more firmly. The hand felt incredibly ordinary, if cold and clammy, unsurprising since its owner had obviously been in the rain and spray for some time. It was most certainly not the immaculate appendage of an angelic being that Jennifer had been half expecting to encounter. The hand appeared startlingly white against the surrounding darkness, which also made the smear of blood running on its back more readily apparent. The hand was unpleasantly cold and wet, but also unmistakably human.

Jennifer said nothing, just kept one hand in contact with the stranger's, and the other wrapped around her son, and was gratified that their shared body heat seemed to be warming the skin under hers. She resolutely refused to consider what she guessed might be happening.

Finally, after what seemed like hours in the cold and dark, but couldn't have been more than ten minutes, one of the men shouted and pointed ahead of the raft. At first the rest of the passengers saw nothing, but then the boat cleared a swell and the lights of some larger vessel could be seen no more than a hundred metres away. Someone scrabbled to load a flare from the raft's emergency box and after a moment it was fired into the air.

In the light of the flare, Jennifer was able to see the figure she assumed was their rescuer for the first time.

It was swathed in what appeared to be a hooded cloak of some sort. In the flare's brief light, Jennifer could see under the hood, to the shockingly pale face beneath and she sucked in a gasp as its appearance registered. At first it looked spectral, but then she realised that what looked like empty eye sockets were in fact simply grey eyes, surprisingly behind silver-framed glasses and surrounded by skin so dark and bruised that it appeared black. The nearly demonic visage was accentuated by three streams of dark red blood; one running from each nostril and a third from the corner of the figure's right eye. Then the stranger looked directly into Jennifer's eyes and the young mother was shocked at the incredible pain and weariness etched there. It was an image that remained with her for years. As the flare's light slowly faded, the face was thrown into shadow again.

The rest of the raft's occupants were completely focussed on the distant ship and so missed what Jennifer had seen.

With the flare launched, Jennifer felt the figure release the boat, but she refused to likewise release the stranger's hand. Instead, she held on for a moment, forcing the dark form to hesitate. Somehow she knew that once she let go, she would never see her saviour again.

"Are you . . . all right?" she asked over the sound of the wind and surf, struck by the surrealism of the situation.

In some way she sensed the figure smile tiredly. "I will be," it replied.

"Is there someone who can help you?"

This time Jennifer got the feeling that the smile was genuine. "There is."

"Good." After a last silent exchange, she released the hand.

A moment later, the being was gone, as if it had never been there. Jennifer wondered if it ever had been.

chapter twenty nine

Then she turned back to the approaching vessel, which she vaguely recognised as an Atlantlan Navy Patrol boat and prepared to board it to safety.

Evelynne winced as another crash of thunder shook the Summer Palace. "Isis, that sounded close," she murmured to Maïda, who was sitting and reading in a chair opposite.

"Indeed," the older woman agreed. "Thankfully, I believe the worst of the rain has stopped."

"I think you're right," the princess said. "Still, I wish Ally wasn't flying home in this."

While the mid-spring storm had not caught the region by surprise, its severity had. Torrential downpours occurred quite often at that time of year, although it had been decades since the last storm of such magnitude.

"Oh, I'm sure Alleandre will be fine," the lady-in-waiting assured her charge. She didn't even blink at Evelynne's use of the word "home". In the four weeks since Ally had left to assume her work, the princess' lover had managed to return every weekend and Maïda was slowly becoming used to the young knight's role in Evelynne's life. She remained concerned over the possible repercussions of the blooming relationship, but had to admit that the princess had never appeared happier–and the same was true of Ally.

In an unofficial alliance with Seneschal Nancu Ylan, the lady-in-waiting had successfully managed to conceal Evelynne's and Ally's true relationship from both the public and the majority of the Palace staff. She did not believe that they had fooled everyone, since at least three of the servants had displayed a remarkable creativity in inventing excuses to distract others when the two lovers were "indisposed" in various parts of the Palace. Nobody had said anything, but the knowing smiles and veiled remarks spoke volumes to those who knew to look. Maïda and Ylan had discreetly rewarded those involved for their discretion.

"I'm sure you're right," Evelynne said, though a hint of strain in her voice showed her insecurity. She set aside the book on Atlantlan High Justice she was reading and stretched, looking at the clock. She frowned. "Shouldn't Uncle Arthur have called by now? Her flight was supposed to land at five and it's almost six thirty now. Even in this weather it shouldn't take them that long to get back."

The princess' bodyguard had offered that evening to go and fetch Ally from the airport in Kilim. Evelynne had desperately wanted to go herself, but had acknowledged that showing too much enthusiasm to meet her "friend" would certainly spark the curiosity of the press. While the Atlantlan media was far less intrusive than their American or European counterparts, there were certainly limits to their discretion.

As if on cue, the ornate telephone on the end table by the princess' chair rang. Evelynne instantly snatched it up. "Yes?"

"Sir Arthur is on the line, Your Highness," the Seneschal's voice proclaimed.

"Oh, good. Put him through, please," Evelynne requested, relief plain in her voice.

There was a click and then Sir Arthur's voice could be heard. "Your Highness," he said.

The strain in his voice instantly brought Evelynne's anxiety back. "Oh Isis, what's wrong?" she asked sharply, dread lacing her tone. Maïda looked up quickly, a concerned frown on her face.

"There has been an accident," the bodyguard said without preamble. "A plane crashed this evening. Not," he added quickly, "Dame Alleandre's aircraft. We heard about it just as she was arriving. We were on our way back to the car when Major Nixon picked it up on her radio. I immediately called the local control tower to offer my assistance. When I was finished, Dame Alleandre was gone."

"Gone? What do you mean, gone?" the princess barked.

"When I returned to the car, she was not present, You Highness," Sir Arthur explained. "Neither I nor Major Nixon saw where she went. I–" He broke off. "One moment, please, Your Highness." Evelynne waited impatiently as muffled voices came over the line. She was aware that Maïda had risen and was now standing behind her, warm fingers massaging her shoulders. "Apologies, Your Highness, but I just received some new information. It seems that a Navy vessel picked up two of the aircraft's life rafts a few minutes ago. Twenty one of the plane's thirty passengers and crew were on board."

"Thank Isis," Evelynne breathed, instantly guilty over forgetting the occupants of the downed aircraft in favour of more personal concerns. "Are they all right?"

"Most of them, yes. Most are suffering from hypothermia and shock. Three have been listed as 'serious', and one is 'critical'." There was a pause on the line. "The boats were recovered nearly four kilometres from the crash site in a direction not consistent with the prevailing winds. They were directly in the path of the nearest rescue ship. In addition, several of those rescued were thrown into the ocean following the crash and report being helped back to the rafts by 'something'. One man claims it was 'one of

chapter twenty nine

Allah's messengers', while another insists it was a 'mermaid' or 'selkie'." He paused to let the implication sink in.

Evelynne immediately had a memory of the "Angel" of the drug raids and reached the same conclusions. "Isis," she gasped, "Ally."

"It is . . . a possibility," Sir Arthur said cautiously. "However, she was not among the individuals picked up by the Naval vessel. It is possible that she will return to the car once she has done whatever it is she is doing."

"All right. Wait there for her. Also, help the rescue effort with whatever they need. Call in whomever you have to. And call me as soon as Ally–" Evelynne broke off suddenly, a distant look on her face. Without realising it, her gaze turned upwards, towards the upper floors of the Palace. "She's here," she breathed.

"I beg your pardon, Your Highness?"

Shaking her head, Evelynne spoke to her bodyguard again, though her tone remained distracted. "She's here," she repeated. She was looking at something nobody else could see. "I need to go."

Without waiting for a reply, Evelynne hung up. Standing quickly, she brushed past Maïda as though she wasn't even there and rushed out the door. The lady-in-waiting looked after her ward in surprise and then hurried after. She exited the study in time to see Evelynne run up the stairs, nearly bowling over a pair of startled servants before disappearing.

Maïda followed as quickly as possible, cursing her ageing knees as the stairs punished them. At the top she caught up with the princess just outside the Royal bedrooms. Evelynne had halted and appeared uncertain of which door to enter. "Highness," the older woman said, puffing and panting, "what is happening?"

"Ally's here," Evelynne replied, still distracted. "And she's hurt."

Maïda's eyebrows rose. "How do you know?"

Evelynne shook her head. "I just do," she said. "And she's over . . . there." Choosing the door to Ally's suite–although Evelynne had been using it just as much recently–she quickly opened it and hurried through, Maïda on her heels. Taking a cursory glance around the sitting room, which was empty, her step didn't pause as she moved to the bedroom.

Once there, she immediately turned on the light and looked around, obviously disappointed not to find the object of her search there. The imperative that had been driving her disappeared, taking with it the sure knowledge of Ally's location. "She's not–" Evelynne began, but was interrupted by Maïda.

"What was that?" the lady-in-waiting asked, looking at the door to the balcony. "I heard something."

Before she could finish, her younger companion had hurried to the glass doors, threw them open and peered outside into the cold and wet. Suddenly, she rushed out onto the balcony, heedless of the rain, and dropped to her knees before a still figure sitting propped up against the railing.

Not completely still, however. Even in the dim light, Evelynne could see that Ally was shivering, although the movement was almost lost in the random spasms that seemed to be affecting all of her muscles. Ally's gaze was glassy and unfocussed, her eyes wide in her deathly white face and she appeared unaware of her lover's presence. Bloodstains were smeared across her face from her nose and the corner of one eye.

"Ally," Evelynne whispered, slowly reaching out with her own shaking hand, as though afraid her lover would break if she moved too quickly.

She was immediately heartened at the way Ally's eyes focussed on her, though still alarmed at the slowness with which they did. "E-E-Evy," Ally managed to stutter. She smiled shakily, the muscles of her soaked and pale face twitching spasmodically. "H-h-h-ho-home." Then she closed her eyes, the effort of keeping them open obviously too much of a strain.

With a choked sob, Evelynne hurled herself at her lover, wrapping the other woman in a strong, tender embrace and burying her face in Ally's chilled neck. "Home," she assured her lover, her tears mixing with the rain pouring down her face.

Ally managed a single shaky nod before going completely limp, sagging into Evelynne's cradling arms. Both reassured and alarmed by Ally's quick breathing, the princess looked up for aid from Maïda. Seeing the naked fear in Evelynne's eyes, the older woman immediately took charge. "Let's get her inside," she ordered. Together they were able to lift Ally's limp, twitching body and manoeuvre it inside. Fortunately, the bed was nearby and Ally was soon lying on top of the blankets, her wet clothing instantly soaking the spread.

"We need to get her out of this," Evelynne said. "Help me lift her." She whipped off the stricken woman's glasses, held in place by a cord and, with Maïda's help, she was able to lift Ally and strip her of the black cloak she wore. Sniffing, Evelynne could detect a slight odour of the sea clinging to the clothing. Shaking her head at having her suspicions confirmed, she murmured, "Love, when you wake up we're going to have a long talk about this." The thought that Ally might not come around was too frightening to contemplate. Refocusing on the matter immediately at hand, she turned to Maïda. "Maï-ma, go and get Doctor Rayssom. Quickly! And try not to alert the staff." *I'm sorry, love, that I have to let yet another person in on your secret. Your private world has become very exposed recently, hasn't it? Still, maybe . . .*

chapter twenty nine

Realising that Maïda had already left to fetch the Royal doctor, who was always present in the Palace in case of an emergency, Evelynne set about wrestling Ally's remaining wet clothes off her still shaking body. Suddenly realising that fresh blood had begun to leak from her lover's nose, Evelynne cursed and used the wet shirt to stanch the bleeding, silently praying for the doctor to arrive soon.

This is what Annie was afraid of, she thought, feeling a sudden sympathy towards Ally's ex-girlfriend. *I wonder how many times she had to deal with something like this. I only hope that I can.*

❧ ❧ ❧ ❧ ❧

Evelynne sighed, trying to focus on the book resting on her left leg. Giving up, she looked down and began to stroke the dark head pillowed on her right leg. She was heartened when Ally shifted slightly and tightened her hold briefly on Evelynne's leg before relaxing back into sleep again. Curled up against Ally's back, Cassie didn't even twitch at the movement. Evelynne sighed and leaned back against the headboard, closing her eyes and thinking back on the events of the last three days.

Dr. Rayssom had arrived promptly upon Maïda's urgent summons. He had been surprised to find that it was not Evelynne who was injured and even more so at both the identity and condition of his real patient. Thankfully, he had refrained from asking unnecessary questions until Ally's condition had been stabilised. It had been a difficult task, given the lack of information that Evelynne had been able to provide. He had finally diagnosed Ally's symptoms as being somewhere between a seizure and a mild stroke, but had confessed complete bafflement as to the cause.

Evelynne had successfully managed to deflect the doctor's questions about exactly how Ally had contracted her condition. However, the doctor had been able to convince Evelynne to allow Ally to be taken to the hospital for extensive testing. He had performed so many scans of Ally's brain that Evelynne was surprised it wasn't glowing.

Actually, in a sense it was. The CAT scans had shown that parts of Ally's brain—parts normally unused in ordinary people—were incredibly hyperactive, but erratically so. The damage appeared to be healing itself, amazingly quickly according to Dr. Rayssom, but he had speculated that the erratically firing neurons had been the cause of Ally's apparent seizure.

After assuring himself that there was nothing more he could do at the hospital, Dr. Rayssom had reluctantly agreed to transfer Ally back to the Summer Palace. Since then he had been constantly monitoring her condition and was cautiously optimistic when it appeared that she had slipped into a more normal healing sleep. She had been sleeping that way for the last thirty-six hours straight.

Evelynne had spent much of that time nearby, if she wasn't actually in the bed with her lover. Ally seemed to respond to her presence, instinctively seeking out her lover whenever she was close, as she was now. Currently the princess was sitting with her legs stretched out in front of her. Ally was sleeping next to her on her side, one arm wrapped around Evelynne's leg and her head resting on a silk-clad thigh. Evelynne smiled and looked back down at the woman sleeping beside her, reaching down to run her thumb across a smooth brow. After the unnatural pallor of that first night, she was pleased to see a return to Ally's normal healthy colouring. Ally twitched her nose at the touch, but didn't move otherwise.

Evelynne had personally called Dr. Collins at the Aztlan excavation to explain Ally's absence from her new job and the Doctor had agreed that Ally should do everything possible to recover quickly from her "bout with the flu". He had sent his wishes for a speedy recovery and all of the people Ally had been working with closely had called at some point to express their own good wishes.

Ally was worried about people not liking her, Evelynne thought with a wry smile. *She really has no idea how charismatic she can be, and how people respond to her honesty. She's so completely non-judgemental and a lot of people really like that. She seems to collect all these protectors . . . and she doesn't even know she does it!*

The thought of two of those protectors in particular brought another crooked smile to Evelynne's face. The morning after Ally had appeared, the princess had called the elder Tretiaks and explained the situation to them. Evelynne had immediately arranged for them to catch the next available flight out. They had arrived, exhausted and completely distraught, several hours later, in time for Dr. Rayssom to present his prognosis for recovery.

After realising that their daughter would be all right and getting a good night's sleep, Catherine Tretiak had had a long conversation with her daughter's new lover. Evelynne, averse to lying to someone so important to Ally–and uncertain of her ability to get away with obscuring the truth to an empath–had been completely honest. It had been uncomfortable and embarrassing, especially when Catherine had asked point blank about the possibility of either of them contracting a sexually transmitted disease. Evelynne had confessed that Ally was her first lover, something that Mrs. Tretiak had found surprising but gratifying. However, ultimately it had been a rewarding and liberating discussion, even with Catherine Tretiak's final warning:

chapter twenty nine

"Now, I know this is a first for you, and you think these feelings are going to last forever and I hope they do. But I also know that if, for whatever reason, the two of you don't work out, Ally is going to be devastated. If there's one thing I know about my daughter, it's that she will always give her whole heart to someone she's in love with. Fortunately, her heart is infinite, so she will be able to give it again eventually. But no matter what, you'll always have it. That is what makes her so vulnerable. What I'm trying to say is that if you ever hurt my girl intentionally or callously, or out of neglect, I will find you and confront you. It won't matter if you're Queen of the entire Atlantic Ocean. I will hold you accountable."

Evelynne, unsurprised at the message, if a little shocked by the vehemence with which it was delivered, had immediately assured Mrs. Tretiak that she would never do anything to intentionally hurt her lover. Catherine had taken her at her word and the remainder of the conversation had passed in a much more pleasant manner.

Looking at the clock, the princess decided that she would get no more done tonight and leaned over to set her book on the bedside table. Then she stretched, feeling stiff back muscles strain in protest, careful not to disturb the sleeping woman who was using her as a pillow. She would get up and retire to her own bedroom in a few minutes. She felt too self-conscious to spend the night in the same bed with her lover, knowing that said lover's parents were sleeping just down the hall, despite the fact that she knew that they knew exactly where she had been sleeping recently.

The catalyst for all of these events, the crash of the Atlantlan Air shuttle from Kilim to Ekion Bel, had dominated the news for the last few days. Twenty-four out of the thirty-one passengers and crew had survived, a miraculously high number, given the conditions of the crash. In fact, the "Miracle of Flight 663" was already being touted as one of the first great mysteries of the twenty first century among some of the public. Rumours of a strange being–variously described as a "dark angel," "alien" or "*ney'rad*," a kind of sea nymph–had been floating around ever since the first of the survivors had been interviewed by emergency personnel. Since then, however, there had been a distinct lack of information coming from those who had supposedly had the most "direct contact" with the mysterious figure. It was as though, Evelynne considered, those particular passengers and crew had collectively decided to avoid speculation on the matter.

Naturally, most of the media was reporting it as a kind of "mass hallucination" or a form of "traumatic stress". Knowing at least some of the facts of the matter, Evelynne couldn't help but speculate on how many other "mass illusions" reported in history had some basis in reality. It made her appreciate just how much her horizons had expanded since learning Ally's secret.

Thought of her lover made Evelynne look down at the tousled brown hair resting on her leg and she couldn't hold back a smile. Sleeping like this, Ally hardly looked like the "Dark Angel" that had single-handedly saved seven people from drowning and helped rescue over a dozen more. *Well, maybe an angel,* Evelynne thought, *but not a dark one.* Her hand drifted down to lightly brush Ally's cheek. *Isis, I love you.*

As if she had heard, Ally shifted and sighed. Then Evelynne heard Ally mumble, quietly but clearly, "Love you too."

Startled and unsure if she had actually heard anything, Evelynne paused in her stroking of Ally's cheek. The sleeping woman frowned slightly, as if in protest. "Ally? Are you awake?"

There was no response, and the princess had just about given up, putting the words she had heard down to either wishful thinking or a dream on the part of her lover—which pleased her—when another thought stole into her mind. Although their attempts to develop her psychogenic abilities had been unsuccessful, Ally had never given up hope. "Hell, I don't know how *my* talents work," she had said. "I have no idea if yours—assuming you have any—work the same way. For all we know, you could be the most powerful telepath or psychokinetic in the world, and you've just never 'thought' the right way yet."

Remembering how she had simply *known* that Ally was both nearby and hurt three nights previously, Evelynne hesitantly tried to "think" in Ally's direction, while at the same time attempting to recapture the mental frame she had been in at the time. *'Um . . . Ally? Can you hear me?'* Feeling slightly foolish, she was actually relieved when there was no reply. Putting the incident down to coincidence, Evelynne yawned. *I love you anyway.*

This time the response was unmistakable, as Evelynne heard clearly inside her own head, *'I love you too.'*

Startled, the princess looked down at the head in her lap with wide eyes. *'Ally, is that you? If you can hear me, please wake up.'*

The reply came in a combination of words and feelings. *Warm. Happy. 'Don't want to wake up.' Safe. 'Love you.' Sleepy.*

'Ally, please,' Evelynne pleaded mentally. *'I need you to wake up. I need to know I'm not imagining this. Please. I have to know you're all right.'*

Ally frowned in her sleep, and then her features softened as her eyes slowly opened. She looked confused for a moment and then smiled as she focused on the blurry face above her. "Heard you," she murmured fuzzily. Then her voice and gaze both sharpened. "I love you."

chapter twenty nine

Before Evelynne could answer, one long arm snaked up and wrapped around her head, pulling her down into a kiss that was a gesture of love, passion, affirmation and desire. When she could finally think again, she found herself on her side, held firmly in Ally's arms. "Ally . . ." she began, only to be interrupted by her lover's lips on her own again.

"Later," Ally whispered hoarsely, placing a row of kisses along Evelynne's jawline to a point just behind her ear. "Be with you now." She pulled back to look into the princess' eyes and Evelynne was struck by the combination of love, lust and fear etched on her lover's face. "Please."

Evelynne responded by unbuttoning Ally's light silk shirt. "I need you too," she said, brushing her lips against newly uncovered skin.

☙ ☙ ☙ ☙ ☙

The sun was already well on its way across the sky when Evelynne woke up. She was briefly confused by her nakedness, until the sensation of an equally naked body in her arms jogged her memory and she couldn't help but blush. Ally had never been as aggressive as she had been the night before, a fact that several sensitive areas of the princess' body were happily reminding her of. It was almost completely against her lover's normal submissive demeanour and she wondered just how much was due to what Ally had gone through.

Suddenly concerned, Evelynne listened carefully to the breathing of her lover in her arms. The princess was lying on her right side and Ally was curled in a loose foetal position facing her, her head nestled under Evelynne's chin and partially covered by red hair. The taller woman's arms were resting in the warm space between their bodies, and one knee was comfortably ensconced between Evelynne's legs; almost too comfortably, the princess' awakening body was telling her.

Pushing that aside–for the moment–Evelynne listened to the sound of Ally's breathing and realised that, while it was slow and even, it was not the sound of sleep. "Ally? Are you awake?" she whispered, just in case she was mistaken.

The response was a low, gentle chuckle, followed by a kiss placed between her breasts. "I am," Ally replied in a low voice. "There's a part of me that doesn't want to be, but it's being soundly drowned out by the part that's happy to be exactly where I am and conscious to appreciate it." One hand briefly stroked the underside of one breast to demonstrate.

"Oh!" Evelynne gasped. She battled with the desire to simply allow Ally to continue with what she was doing, but finally her concern won out. She managed to capture Ally's distracting hand and pull back far enough to look her lover in the face. The sight of her lover's calm, relaxed visage, free of pain, allowed her to relax a little more. "Ally, are you all right?"

Ally sighed. "I think so," she said, deciding not even to try to avoid the coming discussion. "I haven't tried anything . . . extraordinary yet, but I feel pretty much okay. Very okay in some places." She blushed and lowered her eyes, an action that Evelynne found endearing, even if it was completely incongruous with her actions last night.

"Good. Then you won't get hurt when I yell at you for scaring the soul out of me the other night." Evelynne's tone was only slightly joking.

"I'd appreciate it if you didn't," Ally said, her eyes still downcast, although now not out of embarrassment and Evelynne could detect a return of the fear that had been there the night before.

The princess used one finger to force her lover's face up and look at her. "Ally," she murmured, "what are you afraid of?"

Ally seemed to want to look anywhere but at her lover, but Evelynne wouldn't let her. "I'm afraid–I'm afraid that you won't want to be with me now that you know . . . what sometimes happens," she whispered. "I *know* how badly I was hurt. I *know* there was a chance I might not have come back. Now *you* know it too. Some people can't deal with that."

Some people like Annie, Evelynne thought. "Ally, I'm not 'some people'. Do you remember when you said that you wouldn't compare me and Annie when it came to making love?" Ally nodded. "Well, now I'm going to ask you to do the same thing with this. I'm not her and I won't act the same way she did. Please try to realise that."

"I try," Ally admitted. "I know it intellectually, but emotionally . . . Well, it's harder."

"I know it is. I'm glad you know it too. Now, as for me leaving you because you might get hurt." Evelynne laughed, though there was a touch of bitterness to it. "Ally, you got shot saving my life and I was still willing–eager even–to be in a relationship with you. And this was before I knew about your talents and all the unique ways you have to protect yourself. So, am I concerned about you getting hurt? Of course, how could I not? Am I going to leave you because I'm afraid I might get hurt in the process? Of course not." She paused. "Because you're with me, you stand a very good chance of being the target of any political attack that happens to be launched my way. Anyone could dig up your past relationships, your sexuality–because you're openly 'out' and I'm not–every embarrassing moment in your life and throw it out into the public eye for everyone to see. Despite that risk, do you want to be with me?"

chapter twenty nine

"Of course," Ally said instantly. She hesitated. "I see what you mean." She sighed. "I'm sorry. Like I said, I know this intellectually, but emotionally . . ."

"Emotionally, someone you loved ultimately rejected you–through no fault of her own–and you're afraid it will happen again. I understand. And I know that kind of trust will take time."

"Yeah," Ally said. She blinked and when she looked in Evelynne's eyes again her own were misty. "Be patient, please."

"Oh, I will be," Evelynne assured her, drawing the other woman into a tender hug. She pressed a kiss to the side of Ally's head. "I'm not going anywhere."

"I'm glad," Ally whispered into Evelynne's neck.

"Good. Now," Evelynne said, pulling back slightly, "what exactly happened the other night?"

Ally frowned. "The other night? How long was I out?"

"Love, you've been asleep for three days."

Ally looked startled. "Three days? Holy cow. Oh my god, my parents! What are they–"

"Your parents are fine," Evelynne reassured her. "In fact, they're here." She smiled wryly. "Your mother had a long discussion with me about how I'm never supposed to break your heart. She was quite vehement on the subject."

"They're here?" Ally repeated. She paled. "You mean I–we–we–we did–in the same *house?*"

Evelynne chuckled. "We certainly did. Why? It's not like they would have walked in unannounced."

"Don't be so sure," Ally muttered. At Evelynne's questioning glance she explained. "It's happened before. Only once, but still . . ." She shuddered. "It was at exactly the wrong moment too. You know . . . that moment." She glared at her lover, who was suppressing laughter. "Go ahead, laugh. I still have nightmares. Talk about ruining the moment."

"Sorry," Evelynne said, although she sounded anything but. "In any case, they're fine. They're going to be really happy to see you awake. Now, enough stalling. Tell me what happened."

Ally sighed. "Well, I got into Kilim just fine, although the weather was sure shaking us around a lot. Now, I'm not afraid of flying–obviously–but I've become less of a fan of airplanes ever since I discovered I didn't need them. Anyway, we landed, no problem and I met up with Sir Arthur. We were just heading out to the car when he got the emergency dispatch on his radio." She shrugged with one shoulder. "I couldn't just do nothing. I heard that the plane had gone down only a few kilometres out to sea and I knew I could make it that far. I also knew that the more conventional rescue teams would be having a hell of a time in that weather. Now, you know that I don't usually go out looking for people to save, but when something like that happens and I'm right there . . . well, it's almost like the universe, or God, or the collective unconscious, or something, *wants* me to be there so that I can do something. Like when I saved you. Of all the days to be in Marseilles, to hear about your visit to the museum, to find a place near enough that when everything went down I could do something . . . I don't really *like* the idea of something or someone else controlling my actions as if I have no choice in the matter, but sometimes I can't help but feel that way."

"I get that feeling too sometimes," Evelynne said. "I think everyone does."

"Maybe. Anyway, I didn't really think, I just reacted. I, uh, ditched Sir Arthur and just, er, took off."

"Literally."

"Uh, yeah. Anyway, once I was away from the town, I was able to sense where the survivors were and went to see what I could do. I knew it was a small plane, so I wasn't expecting it to take long, one way or the other." She shook her head. "They were really lucky. Most of them had managed to get on board a couple of life rafts, so they were relatively safe, but I could feel some others in the water. Some of them hadn't survived. So once again I just reacted and I started picking up the ones who were alive and taking them to the rafts. I think I managed to keep out of sight for the most part. But I hadn't counted on the cold, and the wind and the ocean. I was getting really tired and thinking about heading back to land. After all, the passengers were relatively safe and I knew the rescue boats would come along soon. But then . . ." Ally's eyes were distant as she remembered the sensation. "Then one of the survivors—I don't know who—started having a heart attack or something and it was almost like what happened that time at Aztlan. Whoever it was just reached out and somehow latched onto my mind and I couldn't get free. They weren't making me do anything, but . . . Now, I've been in contact with a person as they're dying before. A very old friend of the family. She was old, and just . . . dying. It wasn't a bad thing, and she wasn't in any pain and in the end she just slipped . . . away. Not really gone, just . . . somewhere else." She shook her head. "I simply can't describe it. But the dying person in the raft wasn't like that. They were afraid and in pain, and instead of just *going*, it was as if they were being ripped away. And I *had* to get them to help. It may sound self-serving, but I don't think I could handle living with that experience in my head. So I went back and pushed the life raft closer to the rescue boats." Ally laughed harshly. "By then I was fried and I knew it. The ironic thing is that whoever it was that was having the heart attack basically recovered as I was doing it. I don't remember much after that. I just remember trying to get to this bright, warm beacon, where I knew I'd be safe." Ally's eyes refocused on Evelynne's. "And then someone was calling to me, telling me they loved me and that I should wake up. And I did. And you were there."

"I was," Evelynne whispered, her eyes shining. "I still am." She moved forward to kiss Ally intently. Ally returned the kiss, slightly hesitantly at first, then with equal passion.

"So how did you do that?" Ally asked when they finally parted.

"Do what?"

"Talk to me with your mind like that. I know you heard me, like I heard you."

Evelynne frowned. "I thought that was you. I thought you were just, I don't know, receptive."

"I don't think so. I've never done that in my sleep before. At least, not that I can remember." Ally paused, and seemed to be concentrating intently. "Well?"

Evelynne was puzzled. "Well, what?"

Ally shook her head. "I was trying to project my thoughts to you. Apparently it didn't work. You try."

"Um, okay." Feeling a little self-conscious, Evelynne tried to focus as she had before, concentrating on her link with Ally and the emotion invested in it. *'All right, can you hear this?'*

Ally's eyes widened. *'I can. And I know I'm not trying to read your thoughts. Can you understand me?'*

"Isis," Evelynne breathed. *'Isis. It's like you're a ventriloquist. Your mouth isn't moving, but I can hear you as though you're speaking out loud.'*

'Exactly,' Ally said. *'And that's how I know it's not me doing it. Whenever I scan someone else it's usually just a jumble of thought, concept and emotion. This is like actual mental telepathy. I can't pick up anything except what you're sending. Just words.'*

"Oh," said Evelynne aloud. "Wow." She was stunned. "And you're sure you can't do it yourself?"

"Well, stop trying to 'talk' to me or 'listen' to me for a moment." Ally concentrated again. A moment later she said, "Nope, I think it's just you. I don't even know what 'muscles' to use."

'Really. So what does this make me? Am I an Adept, like you?' It was certainly going to take some time for the novelty of this experience to wear off.

'I don't know. Obviously a Talent at the very least. Just be sure to let me know if you start levitating or teleporting, huh?'

'One superpower at a time, thank you,' Evelynne sent back. *'Still, this opens up a whole range of possibilities.'*

"Well, yeah. I'm sure Sir Arthur will be thrilled that you have a method of communication with him that can't be intercepted or traced. Assuming that you can do this with other people, that is."

"Oh. Well, yes. But I was actually thinking . . ." Evelynne's smile was seductive. *'You're always so quiet when we make love. Now maybe I can hear what you're really thinking. Especially when you . . .'*

Further experimentation took some time.

chapter thirty

"Tell me again how you talked me into this," Ally complained from behind her bathroom door.

Evelynne couldn't help smiling as she perched on the edge of the bed. "If I recall correctly, all I had to do was flash a bit of leg and you were only too eager to accede to my every desire." She twitched the shawl around her shoulders into a more comfortable position. The shawl was a rich emerald green colour, only slightly darker than the ankle-length green dress she was wearing. The shade of the dress, matched by the real emeralds in her ears, made the princess' hair gleam like fire as it tumbled across her shoulders. Amazingly, the entire outfit had taken only an hour to get into.

Ally snorted, the sound muffled by the door. "If *I* recall correctly, you flashed a whole lot more than 'a bit of leg' and the blood wasn't really flowing to my brain at the time. That's psychological warfare, you know. I'm sure it's outlawed by the Geneva Convention."

Evelynne lifted an eyebrow, even though Ally couldn't see her. Although perhaps she could. "You weren't complaining at the time," she pointed out. "In fact, 'eager' was probably too mild a word. 'Slavishly devoted' is probably more accurate. Besides, all's fair—"

"—in love and war," Ally finished. There was a put-upon sigh from the bathroom. "Okay, I'm coming out now. Remember, if you laugh you're going to this thing by yourself. And sleeping alone tonight."

"Come on, Ally," Evelynne coaxed. "You know I'd never laugh at you." She was well aware that, no matter how confident and comfortable Ally appeared around her, there was still a core of shyness and insecurity that ran deep within her lover. "And those Pink Panther boxer shorts you had on the other night don't count. You were trying to make me laugh."

"Okay, just remember that I'm not wearing them now."

The door to the bathroom opened and Ally emerged, freshly brushed and showered. Flatly refusing to wear another evening gown, the taller woman had consented to wear a loose blue silk shirt and a pair of baggy silk trousers, along with a darker blue jacket. She had also refused an elaborate hairstyle. Her hair, much longer than it had been when they first met, was still damp from her shower and curled slightly around her face. The light brown locks now reached nearly to the nape of her neck.

She stepped out into the bedroom and held her arms out at her sides. "So? What do you think?" She threw in a quick pirouette for good measure.

Evelynne smiled and stood, unable to contain herself. "I think you look gorgeous," she said, walking over to her lover. She saw that Ally was wearing the earrings she had given her before the last formal outing. "I think everyone's going to be jealous that I have such a beautiful date." She faltered. "Even if . . ."

"Even if I can't really be your date," Ally said. She shrugged dismissively, but Evelynne could see the hurt in her eyes.

"I'm sorry," Evelynne said. "I know I've said it before, but . . ."

"I know," Ally replied. "The world isn't ready yet for the Atlantlan Heir–the *female* Atlantlan Heir–to be involved with a woman. I understand."

"I'm glad," Evelynne said, although she wished there was some way to take the pain out of her lover's eyes. While Ally had been intensely private in her past relationship, she had never actively had to hide it. The princess knew that having to do so now weighed on her sometimes. "Still, at least I'll be able to dance with you tonight."

Ally shook her head violently. "Dance? Oh no, no dancing. Dancing, me . . . not good. Bad, even. Pain ensues."

"Oh, you're not that bad. Just think of it as one of your Kung Fu forms and you'll have no problems."

Ally looked at her strangely. "You want me to beat the crap out of you?"

Evelynne rolled her eyes. "That wasn't what I meant and you know it. Besides, you lived with a professional dancer for a year. I'm sure you must have learned something."

"Well, I'll try," Ally said uncertainly. "But I didn't know that we could dance together. Won't that, you know, let the cat out?"

"Well, we can't dance together as a couple," Evelynne said, bracing herself for the disappointment on Ally's face, "but there's nothing stopping me from dancing with one of my knights. In fact, with the Debt I owe you, you could get away with ordering me to dance with you. It would be considered very bad form, but nobody would stop you."

"Okay, I can live with that. Not the Debt thing, but the other part. Still, I'll have to see about the dancing. There'll be a lot of people there . . ."

"All right," Evelynne said, already knowing that nothing was going to stop her from convincing Ally into at least one turn around the floor. "You could always start with my cousin Larrel. He's an incredible dancer and he seems to be able to pass on some of his grace to others for a time."

chapter thirty

"I'll think about it," Ally said. She looked up the clock. "Are we ready to go yet? I'd like to get going before I completely lose my nerve."

"Almost," Evelynne said. "There's just one thing." With that, she reached up and pulled Ally down into a searing kiss. After several moments they finally separated. "Okay, now we're ready."

ॐ ॐ ॐ ॐ ॐ

"Evelynne, my dear, you are looking particularly lovely tonight," Lord Thomas said as a Guard helped the Heir from the limousine. He bent to kiss her hand. A moment later, his eyebrows rose as Ally similarly exited the vehicle. "And Alleandre, you are quite stunning. I feel that I must insist on a dance later this evening. I will be the envy of all the men present as well as a fair number of the women, I'm thinking." Ally blushed and looked away, and the Duke took the opportunity to wink surreptitiously at the princess.

Evelynne grinned back. Step one of her plan was complete. She knew that Ally would be unable to turn down a dance from the grandfatherly Lord Thomas. In the middle of it, the Duke would be "called away" to speak with some other guests and Evelynne would be conveniently nearby to take his place. After all, it would be impolite to leave a woman dancing alone, wouldn't it? It was unlikely that Ally would be fooled for long by the deception, even without using her talents, but by that time it would be too late.

"I'd be honoured," Ally said. She looked up at the wide glass front doors of the Ducal Residence of Outremer and could easily hear strains of music coming from inside. The music was the typical style of Atlantl, a combination of European classical and Arabic traditional music. It took some getting used to, but captured the islands' melding of cultures perfectly. "So, how often do you throw one of these shindigs?"

Lord Thomas laughed as he began leading his guests up the stairs, one on each arm. "I plan a shindig, as you say, once a year. It may not be as lavish as the Royal Galas in Jamaz, but we muddle through."

Evelynne snorted, a very unprincesslike reaction that earned her a startled look from a nearby Guard. "Muddle through, indeed. The truth is that everyone attends the Royal Galas because they have to. They are usually extremely boring events, where only those with a deep interest in political manoeuvring have a good time. Domdom's parties, however, are the place to just—what's the term? Hang out. Yes, hang out and have a good time. Which isn't to say that politics and making sure you're seen in the right company isn't done, but at least the people have fun doing it."

"Oh, good," Ally said. "Just as long as I'm not expected to talk politics all night. I'm just not cut out for that sort of thing, I think."

In her other relations with various members of the aristocracy and government, the young woman was taking events largely in stride, although she often sported a slightly puzzled look, as if she couldn't quite believe that she was actually socialising in such circles. For someone whose most prominent interaction prior to coming to Atlantl was bumping into a movie star in a mall in Vancouver, she was handling things very well.

The trio navigated their way up the stairs to the main doors, which were opened by two servants in Ducal livery. As they walked out of the warm evening and into the coolness of the marble foyer, Ally and Evelynne found another person waiting to greet them.

"Chorus!" Ally exclaimed, releasing the Duke's arm so that she could hug her friend, who was dressed in a smart tuxedo bearing the Ducal crest on its left breast. "I thought you were still busy dealing with that, er, language job."

"I am," Chorus replied. "But the details of the job are such that I can work on it just about anywhere, so I've been helping out His Grace's Economic Advisor in the meantime."

"Doing a fine job of it too," the Duke declared, smiling at the stocky young man. "He's been extremely helpful in setting up some new diamond imports from Botswana that should be bearing fruit–so to speak–in a few months."

Chorus shrugged. "My uncle works in the Ministry and he certainly knows a good deal when he sees one. Of course, the efficiency, or lack thereof, of the Botswana bureaucracy is legendary, otherwise we'd be seeing results a lot sooner." Turning to the princess, he bowed. "Your Highness, it seems that our friend Ally still hasn't learned proper etiquette." He mock-scowled at the woman in question, who blushed. "I'm happy to see you again. Have you been successful in keeping our boorish friend out of trouble?"

Evelynne laughed at Ally's indignant splutter. "It's Evelynne, remember? And yes, she has been staying out of trouble . . . for the most part."

"Mmm, I saw the news reports. I admit I had my suspicions." He frowned at Ally, who looked away. "How bad was it?" he murmured.

"It was . . . bad," Evelynne admitted. "Fortunately I was in a position to . . . take care of her afterwards."

The way in which she said it made both Chorus and Lord Thomas, who had appeared slightly puzzled by this exchange, look at her closely. Nearly simultaneously, they arrived at the same conclusion.

"Jesus, Ally, you're–"

"Oh my, Evelynne, you–"

chapter thirty

Their immediate responses ran over and through each other, while the two young women made desperate shushing motions.

"Yes," Evelynne said, "we are." She appeared more than a little apprehensive over her friends' reactions, as did Ally.

Chorus looked shell-shocked and Lord Thomas recovered first. "Are you happy, Evy?" he asked softly. "Both of you?"

"I am," the princess replied in a low but firm voice. She shared a look with her lover. "We are. Very."

"Good," the Duke said. "Then I am happy for you."

"Jesus, Ally," Chorus said again, still stunned. "How . . . when?"

"'When' was about six weeks ago," Ally replied quietly. "The 'how' is none of your business."

"Oh, Ally, do you know what you're getting into?"

"No," Ally admitted. She looked at Evelynne again. "But I'm learning." Both the good and bad connotations of that statement weren't lost on the princess. "Nobody said love was ever going to be easy."

"Indeed they didn't," the Duke murmured. He looked up to where another servant, this one more formally attired, was trying to get his attention. "Unfortunately, it seems that my Major Domo feels our presence is required inside."

☙ ☙ ☙ ☙ ☙

"Ally, darling, you look absolutely ravishing tonight!"

Ally started at the loud, friendly voice that suddenly intruded into her incredibly boring conversation with Lady Tar'he, Countess Keranna–although "conversation" implied a two-way exchange–and turned, grateful for the interruption. She smiled. "Larrel, it's good to see you." Her eyes telegraphed her genuine feelings. "Lord Larrel, I'm sure you know Lady Tar'he," she introduced.

"Of course," Larrel said, smiling broadly. "How are you, My Lady? And how is your lovely daughter?"

The Countess scowled, but quickly, if inexpertly, smoothed her expression. "I am quite well, My Lord. As is Janessa, as I am sure you know."

"Alas, I have been unable to keep in touch with her quite as much as I had hoped," the smiling young man bemoaned with mock sorrow. "However, I remember her fondly. I understand that she has recently been confirmed as your Heir. You must be quite gratified."

"I am," Lady Tar'he said, her bland but still disapproving expression still firmly in place.

"Well, I look forward to working closely with her when she takes her office, though hopefully not for some time to come, of course," Larrel said, his eyes twinkling. "Our two Counties would benefit from, ah, closer contact." Sighing dramatically, he gestured towards Ally. "Unfortunately, I fear I must steal this young Knight from you for a time. One of Lord Thomas' Advisors has requested her presence."

"Of course, My Lord," Lady Tar'he conceded. She bowed her head in Ally's direction. "Dame Alleandre, I enjoyed our discussion. I hope we can repeat it in the future."

"As do I, My Lady," Ally said respectfully, before allowing Larrel to take her arm and lead her away.

"Thank you," she said quietly but fervently as soon as they were safely out of earshot.

"My pleasure," Larrel said in a matching voice. "Her Highness happened to see you get shanghaied by the esteemed Countess, but was unable to extricate herself from her own discussion. So she sent me instead."

"Well, thank you both, then. If I had to hear one more thing about stock trading with Russia . . ." Ally shook her head to clear it of the horrific memories. She glanced sidelong at the Count. "So what was all that about her daughter? There was something going on under the surface."

"Ah yes, Janessa. Several months ago, I engaged in some quite pleasant, ah, social interaction with the good Countess' daughter. It was highly . . . rewarding for both parties. Unfortunately, Lady Tar'he did not appreciate our attempts at increasing contact between our two realms of influence."

"Really." Ally's tone was uninflected. "So does that sort of thing happen often? Irate parents objecting to your, uh, social interactions?"

"Oh, occasionally," Larrel said, waving his hand as if to brush away an annoying insect. "However, quite often I am able to relieve their concerns. I'd say about half of the time, actually."

Ally shook her head. "I'm not even going to bother asking which half." Changing the subject, she asked, "So did one of Lord Thomas' Advisors really want to talk to me?"

"Oh dear, did I say Advisor?" Larrel's eyes were twinkling. "I meant to say one of his Aides. I really hope I didn't inflate your reputation too much by suggesting that the *Duke's Advisors* inquire after your opinion on various matters. That would simply gain you too much respect."

Ally's eyes narrowed as she scowled at him. "You're way too devious, you know that?"

"Me? But who did I say sent me to rescue you in the first place? I think *she* may have mentioned something about enhancing your reputation. Of course, I *may* have misheard."

chapter thirty

"Sure you did," Ally muttered, just as an opening in the crowd revealed Chorus' stocky form waiting near the side of the hall. "Chorus! So you're the 'Duke's Aide' who wanted to see me. I should have known."

"Well," he said innocently, "I do work for that worthy personage in an advisory role. Besides, Evelynne thought her cousin might need backup."

"Somehow I don't think he does," Ally said, while Larrel chuckled. "So where is Evy–Evelynne anyway?"

"Hobnobbing," Chorus replied. "You know, shake-shake, kiss-kiss, talk about nothing."

"He's not quite right," Larrel protested. "Well, he is about the 'shake-shake, kiss-kiss' part. But Her Highness rarely talks about 'nothing' at these gatherings."

"I know," Ally said. "For some reason she actually likes these things." She looked puzzled, as though contemplating a completely alien concept.

"She is going to be the next Ruler of the Islands," Larrel stated. "Enjoying this is practically a job requirement. We only hope that her husband will be equally competent."

"Right," Ally said, her voice going flat. "Her . . . husband."

Chorus looked at Ally sharply and Larrel looked a little puzzled at her tone, but something caught his eye before he could comment. Ally and Chorus could see an attractive dark-skinned woman in her thirties beckoning in their direction.

"Ah, apparently Lady Alice, Baroness Holden, wishes to speak to me," the Count said. He smiled. "I honestly enjoy hearing her perspective on a number of issues, so I believe I would like to talk with her." He hesitated. "Would you like to join me? I can guarantee that she speaks about far more interesting things than Russian stock trading."

"Is this going to be one of your attempts to 'increase contact between your two realms of influence'?" Ally asked wryly. "Because you know I don't want to cramp your style."

Larrel laughed. "Alas, no. Despite my efforts, Alice remains out of my sphere. In this particular case, I believe that you, my dear Dame Alleandre, would have more success in that area. She has, in fact, made several, ah, discreet enquiries about you. This could be an occasion for you to discuss the matter, if you wish."

"Oh." Ally was startled, but managed a hesitant smile at the Baroness, who smiled back. "Uh, well, tell her that I'm, uh, flattered, but right now I have . . . other engagements."

"Oh? Serious engagements?" Larrel looked surprised but pleased.

"Very serious."

"Permanent?"

Ally hesitated and steadfastly refused to look in the princess' direction. "I don't know."

"I see. Well, I shall pass on your regrets."

"Thank you."

"In that case . . . Dame Alleandre." The Count bowed to her. "Mr. Tladi."

With that he was off through the crowd again and Ally was both impressed and envious over the ease with which he interacted with people. In contrast, the young woman usually felt as though she was forcing herself into a particularly tight-fitting dress, no matter how pleasant the company. The constant pressure of so many strong-willed minds was draining, even when she steadfastly avoided opening herself to their thoughts. It was a little like being forced to carry a moderately heavy backpack all evening; easy enough at first, but after a while, the constant weight was exhausting.

"So, Ally," Chorus said after several moments' awkward silence. "How are . . . things . . . going between you and Her Highness?"

Ally looked at him sharply, then around herself, but nobody appeared to be taking much notice of the pair at the side of the hall. The rest of the guests were too engaged in socialising and Alleandre's presence had lost much of its novelty after so many months.

Still, she was careful to keep her voice pitched low as she said, "Pretty well." A smile broke free as she thought of her lover. "Amazing, actually." She saw Chorus looking at her with a combination of amusement and concern, and frowned again. "Not all smooth sailing, of course, but . . ." She shrugged. "Incredibly well, considering."

The amusement won out on Chorus' face. "What, does she hog the covers?"

Ally barked a low laugh. "Hardly. She hogs *me*, actually. Trying to get her to let go is a real challenge, especially when I need to go to the bathroom." She paused, a bemused expression on her face. "I can't believe I just told you that."

Chorus laughed. "Neither can I, actually. It seems you're loosening up." Turning serious once more, he asked, "Are you sure you know what you're doing? Considering who she is, this has the potential for a disaster that will make your break-up with Annie look like a disagreement over who takes out the garbage. You could get seriously hurt here, Ally."

His companion sighed. "I know," she said, "and all I can say is that I'm taking it one day at a time. I don't know what will happen when we get found out by the press–and we will, it's just a matter of time. Too many people know about us already for it *not* to leak: Maïda, Seneschal Nancu, Sir Arthur,

chapter thirty

several of the Palace servants, and now you and Duke Thomas." She sighed again, her voice concerned. "But it's not me that I'm most worried about. Sure, I'll be hounded by reporters, have my picture taken way more than I'd like, but eventually they'll move on to the next flavour of the week and forget about me. Evelynne, though . . . This will follow her for the rest of her life and make her job as Queen of Atlantl that much harder. Assuming someone doesn't find some way to get her to abdicate because of it. *That's* what worries me the most, because she was *born* to do it. I mean, just look at her." Ally had caught sight of the princess through a break in the crowd and could see the red-haired young woman speaking earnestly with a group of Nobles who were all giving her their undivided attention. "And not just the balls and parties, either. You should see her when she's working, trying to help some Baron find a way to finance low-income housing while maintaining his budget margin. It's indescribable. And the trouble is that if–when–it comes down to it, I don't know who she'll choose. A part of me obviously wants her to choose me and to hell with ruling the country. But another part of me recognises just how magnificent she'll be when she does take the Throne and I feel it's selfish of me to prevent her from doing that." Ally shook her head sadly. "A bit of a quandary, as you can see."

"I can see that," Chorus murmured. "In any case, you know that whatever happens I'm behind *you.*"

Ally looked at Chorus. Eventually, she reached out and squeezed his arm tightly, the most physical gesture she was comfortable with in the circumstances. "Thank you," she said, and her voice had a husky tone. "I appreciate that." The pair was silent again for a few minutes, as Ally recovered her composure. Finally, wishing to dispel the overly emotional atmosphere, she asked, "So, speaking of translations . . . how's that job coming along?"

"Frustratingly," Chorus replied, accepting the subject change and the reason behind it. "Whoever it is changes their, er, language on some schedule I haven't been able to figure out." He was careful to remain vague in the midst of this crowd. "Every time I think I have it, I get a new . . . letter that changes everything." He scowled. "Still, there *is* some pattern there, I can *feel* it. And I *know* that I'm close. Any time I need incentive to keep going, I just have to turn on the news."

Ally nodded, her face grim. The Hy Braseal Liberation Army had been increasing the frequency of their attacks against Atlantlan government and civilian targets. Now a week didn't go by without some new bombing or shooting. The government, as well as all of the major news agencies, had expressed bafflement at the motives behind the attacks, since they were rarely targeted at any installation that was at all related to Hy Braseal's "liberation".

The attacks were confined to the island of Hy Braseal. Ally had tried several times to find and stop any attack she could, but despite her powers, she was still just a single person, and by the time she reached the site of an attack, it was always too late.

"Well, you know you can ask me for help whenever you need it," she said. "And if you want, talk to General Danun about involving the people I work with. They may not have your particular talents, but they're still a scarily intelligent group of people when you get them together."

"I know," Chorus replied. "It's what I'd expect, with you as their leader. I will bring it up with the General." After this, the young man felt the need to change the subject to something more pleasant. "So, tell me what your group of 'scarily intelligent people' has come up with recently. I heard about the 'circuit board' theory of the Maze you were working on."

"Ah yes," Ally said, warming to a topic she was enthusiastic about. "Actually, it's a bit more than a theory now. We think. Taldas—he's our computer scientist—has managed to map and model the entire thing on computer, and he's been running simulations for a while now. So far we know that *something* definitely happens when we run electricity through it. Unfortunately, we don't know exactly where to hook up the battery or what current or voltage we should be using or whether we should be doing it at night or in the rain. Or only when the moon is six days past full and there's an 'R' in the month, for that matter. I've actually managed to borrow a grad student from Thanelli University who's researching ancient Atlantlan mythology and ritual and she's busy looking for references in Atlantlan legend that might give us a clue. *That* ruffled some feathers, let me tell you. Getting a *mythology* expert to help solve a scientific problem? Blasphemy!"

Ally continued, never quite noticing the way that people would come closer to listen to her speak and become drawn into the discussion. When the Duke's Major Domo announced that dinner was served, Ally was startled to finally realise that over fifteen people had been listening and speaking with her for the past half-hour and all without a single instance of shyness or uncertainty on her part.

෴ ෴ ෴ ෴ ෴

"Oh my, that was good," Ally said, as she and Chorus made their way from the Dining Hall to the Ballroom. She patted her full stomach carefully with the hand that wasn't holding Chorus' arm.

"It was," Chorus agreed. "However, there are times when all I want is a big steak, rather than all this fancy stuff."

chapter thirty

"A steak!" Ally scoffed. "Here we are, having just eaten . . ." She hesitated. "Well, whatever it was that we ate and you want a steak." She shook her head. "Savage."

"Sorry, I'm a Motswana," her companion said, shrugging. "We live for our steak. Not to mention our sausage, ribs and roast. But mostly our steak. Heck, it's our second highest export, we have so much of it."

"Yeah, and heart attacks are your highest non-accidental cause of death."

Chorus shrugged again and grinned. "Yes, but at least we die happy. Fat, but happy." As the pair entered the Ballroom, he looked around at the other guests who were slowly filling the large open space. "So what happens now?"

"I'm not sure," Ally admitted. "I didn't get a chance to ask Evelynne exactly what the game plan is." The princess had been called away temporarily to speak with Lord Thomas on some matter.

"Oh?" Chorus asked, smirking. "Too busy getting dressed this evening to talk, huh?"

Ally shot him a withering glare that just bounced right off, so she changed tactics. "Yes, frankly. In fact, due to . . . circumstances, we had to get dressed several times." She mock frowned. "A number of dresses were ruined by our enthusiasm, actually."

Chorus froze, his gaze fixed on some internal vision. Shaking himself, he said plaintively, "Ally, you just can't do that to a healthy, heterosexual male. Now do you know what I'm going to be thinking of for the rest of the evening?"

"Oh, believe me, I know," Ally replied, smirking. "Intimately. But you'll just have to suffer, you pervert."

"That's not fair, Ally," Chorus protested. "You're the one who explained how guys' fascination with lesbians is genetic."

"I did and it is," Ally agreed. "You're still a pervert."

"Well, in that case, would you care to dance with this pervert?" Chorus said, offering her his hand as music began to play and brightly dressed guests began to fill the dance floor. "I promise to keep my hands to myself. Mostly."

"Dance?" Ally said, freezing and then shaking her head vehemently. "No, no, no. I can't dance–"

"–with you, my dear Mr. Tladi, because she has already promised me the first dance," Lord Thomas' voice interrupted her. The Duke came closer, a wryly grinning Evelynne on his arm. "Well, my dear, shall we dance? I should inform you that it is considered bad manners to refuse the host of the Gala such a request." Without waiting for a reply, he bowed to the princess and took the stunned Ally's hand, leading her out onto the floor. As they moved off, Evelynne and Chorus could hear him saying, "Now, please remember that I *am* quite old, my dear, so no wild stunts, please. I'm afraid that 'dirty dancing' is a wee bit out of my range at the moment. Have you seen the film?"

As their voices were lost in the surrounding hum of music and conversation, Evelynne turned to Chorus. "Well, that went exactly according to plan," she said calmly. "Stage two should be ready any moment now."

Chorus shook his head. "Somehow, Your Highness, I don't think I want to know. However, if you would care to dance . . . ?"

"I would," Evelynne replied, smiling, "but I promised someone else first. Now, if I can only find him . . ."

As if on cue, the flamboyant form of Lord Larrel appeared at Evelynne's elbow. "My apologies, Cousin," he said, sweeping an extravagant bow. "I was just engaging in some planning for a small, ah, get-together later on tonight. It took somewhat longer than I had anticipated."

Evelynne cocked an eyebrow. "Oh? Was she *that* resistant to your charms?"

"Not at all," Larrel replied, without a hint of embarrassment. "She was simply inquiring into the possibility of Dame Alleandre joining our, ah, discussion, since she saw us conversing earlier. Alas, I had to inform her that not only would Dame Alleandre find my presence at such a meeting off-putting, but our honourable Knight is already involved with her own affairs." He frowned. "Unfortunately, my efforts to elicit the identity of Dame Alleandre's paramour have met with failure." He looked at the two people in front of him. "I don't suppose she's mentioned the matter to either of you?"

Evelynne blushed, but Chorus managed to take the question in stride. "She has, actually," he said. "However, it's a delicate matter, not to mention very personal, so . . ."

"Say no more," Larrel said. "I, of all people, understand the necessity for discretion in delicate, personal matters. I will enquire no further. However, I believe I promised the first dance to my beautiful cousin." He held out a hand, which Evelynne took. "Shall we?"

ನಿ ನಿ ನಿ ನಿ ನಿ

"So, how are you enjoying the 'shindig', my dear?" Lord Thomas asked as they moved slowly but gracefully across the dance floor.

"I'm having fun," Ally admitted honestly. She was finding that the simple dance moves Annie had taught her were coming back and she was

chapter thirty

moving with more confidence. "I got trapped by Lady Tar'he earlier, but other than that, I've been having a good time." *Of course, I'd be happier if it was just Evelynne and me, and dinner in front of the fireplace,* she thought. She caught sight of her lover dancing with Lord Larrel and laughing heartily at something her partner was saying.

Lord Thomas chuckled. "Ah yes, dear Tar'he. A more dedicated, selfless Countess you will not find, but unfortunately, she is in love with her own voice."

"Tell me about it," Ally agreed.

Ally's eyes fixed on the princess, who was slowly making her way, with Lord Larrel's assistance, in their direction. Lord Thomas carefully hid his smile, simultaneously catching the eye of his Major Domo, who was watching from nearby for just this moment. A faint head nod signified that the signal had been received and understood. The Duke was fairly certain that his servant was unsure exactly why this subterfuge was taking place, but, like all good personal assistants, the Major Domo would not ask questions. On cue, when the princess and her dance partner were conveniently close by, Lord Thomas "noticed" his manservant apparently giving him a signal and paused in the dance. "Alleandre, my dear, it seems my presence is required elsewhere," he said with unfeigned regret. "I am sorry to leave you hanging like this, as it were. I should think you will have no problem finding willing– no, eager–dance partners."

"Really, Domdom?" Evelynne asked. She had "just happened" to overhear their conversation. She looked up at her own dance partner. "Larrel, would you mind if I cut in with Alleandre? I would like to dance with my Knight. I'm sure you'll have no problems finding another partner."

"I'm sure I'll manage," Larrel said with a twinkle in his eye. "Who knows, I may even dance with one of them." He bowed, in turn, to Evelynne, the Duke and Ally. "Your Highness. Your Grace. Dame Alleandre." Then he was off into the crowd.

"Your Highness," Lord Thomas echoed and suddenly Evelynne and Ally were alone in the middle of the crowd.

"Okay then, Ally," Evelynne said, taking charge since the other woman had frozen and looked ready to bolt at any second. The princess stepped forward and arranged their arms appropriately. "And . . . we're off."

Neither of them moved.

"Er, Ally, one of us is going to have to lead," Evelynne said wryly.

Ally blushed deeply, mortified. "Um, okay. Who?"

"Well, I thought that since you were taller, you'd lead."

"Okay," Ally said uncertainly. "It's just that I don't have a lot of experience with leading."

"Really? You mean when you and Annie danced, she'd lead?"

"Um, yeah. I'm more comfortable letting someone else take charge," the taller woman admitted. Her heightened blush reminded Evelynne that the dance floor wasn't the only place that Ally preferred a more submissive role.

"All right, then. I haven't done this a lot, but part of my dance lessons included how to lead." Reversing the positions of their arms, Evelynne smiled up at her partner. "And *now* we're off. I hope."

Ally couldn't help but chuckle slightly, but she responded much more readily to Evelynne's control and soon they were moving across the dance floor in a relatively graceful fashion. At first Ally was incredibly self-conscious, but after several minutes, where nobody had commented adversely on seeing the Heir dancing respectfully with another woman, she began to relax.

"This isn't so bad," she murmured reluctantly.

'See? I told you so,' Evelynne replied and there was a distinct flavour of satisfaction in her mental voice.

Ally looked at her askance. *'Why do I get the feeling that I was set up?'* she asked. *'This all seems just a little too . . . convenient.'*

'Oh, I don't know. Maybe you're psychic.'

Ally laughed mentally. *'Maybe I am. Still, I'm glad you did it,'* she admitted.

Evelynne smiled. *'Good. So, have you been having a good time so far?'*

'Why does everyone keep asking me that? Yes, I have, actually.'

'Good,' Evelynne repeated. She deftly steered them around another couple who were obviously even less skilled than they were. They were silent, both inside and out, enjoying their dance for a few more minutes before the princess noticed a young man approaching them. *'Well, I'm afraid I must go and be sociable again,'* she sighed. *'I wish we could have had longer.'*

Ally noted the same handsome young Noble, and forced down the surge of jealousy that threatened to erupt. The young man paused nearby and asked respectfully, "Your Highness, may I have the honour of this dance? With your permission, Dame Alleandre?"

"Of course," the princess replied and Ally gracefully handed her off to her new partner. "Alleandre." Ally winced internally at the formal tone.

A number of people requested the young woman's company for a dance, but Ally begged off, claiming a strained back muscle and soon she was back on the sidelines, alongside the others who chose relaxing over dancing. Ally found herself a seat at a small table with a pair of older Nobles, a Countess and Baroness, with whom Ally had spoken earlier. Lady Shoroi, Baroness Orken, the younger at sixty-eight years of age, smiled at her warmly. "Alleandre, 'ow are ye?" she asked, her accent a thick mixture of

chapter thirty

Portuguese and Irish brogue common among the inhabitants of the northernmost region of Lyonesse.

"I'm doing well, thank you, My Lady," Ally replied. "Getting a bit tired, though."

Lady Grace, Countess Milles, a more reserved but nevertheless friendly woman, clucked her tongue. "Now, none of that. You're too young to be getting tired this early. Why, when I was your age–"

"–she'd'a be dancin' an' partyin' 'till the nex' risin' o' the sun," Lady Shoroi finished, laughing. "Ignore 'er, lass. She didna' any such thing. 'Er pa woulda tanned 'er 'ide. She's jus' tryin' to live agin through ye, ol' bat tha' she be." Lady Grace glowered at her companion, who just laughed again. It was obvious that such volleys were a common occurrence.

"Ignore her, girl," Lady Grace stage whispered to Ally. "The poor thing's senile. We've tried and tried to get her to step down, but . . ." She trailed off, shaking her head sorrowfully.

This time Ally joined in their laughter, comfortable enough to relax in their friendly presence. Snagging a drink of juice from a passing servant, she sat back and watched the couples on the floor. As the princess swept by at one point, in the arms of yet another handsome young man, Lady Grace murmured something to Lady Shoroi in Lantlan. Ally, who had been focussed on her lover, thought that she was being addressed, and asked distractedly, "Huh? Pardon?"

"Oh, I'm sorry, Alleandre," Lady Grace said. "I was just asking Shoroi whether she thought Lord Alistair's young heir–" She pointed to the man dancing with Evelynne. "–was going to announce his status as a suitor at the Conclave in two weeks."

Ally felt a chill stab through her chest. "What do you mean? A suitor as in . . ."

"Marriage, yes," the Countess said. "Now that Her Highness has been confirmed as Heir, it is traditional for all those interested in seeking her hand in marriage to announce their interest each year at the first Nobles' Conclave. It is not binding and she is not obligated to choose now or even for several years. She could even marry someone who has never announced his interest formally. Still, it is customary for the Heir to at least acknowledge her suitors. Of course, it also allows those with political agendas–and we all have them–a chance to see who might be the next King of Atlantl."

"Oh," Ally said, her heart somewhere in the pit of her stomach. "But she'll have to marry eventually, right?"

"Well," Lady Grace said slowly, "not technically. However, the last bachelor Diarch we had was . . ." She paused, thinking.

"King Ursan bel-Heru d'Molay," Lady Shoroi murmured.

The Countess nodded to her companion. "Thank you. Yes, King Ursan. And he was King . . ."

"1722 ta 1727," the Baroness said. "Didna rule fer long. Abd'cated ta join the Church, 'e did. Rumours 'bout 'is preference fer other lads. Ne'er confirmed yet."

"Ah yes," Lady Grace said, "I remember now. Good ruler, by all accounts, but he was forced out by the combined Nobility. Officially, of course, he had been called to the cloth by God."

"I see," Ally said, striving to keep her tone level and not reveal the shock and despair that were rising within her. She knew she should have been thinking of this issue long before, but the happiness she had found with Evelynne had left her instinctively avoiding the subject.

"Aye," the Baroness said. "'Tis only ta be hoped tha' 'Er 'Ighness chooses so well as 'er father did when it was 'is time ta pick a bride. Queen Isarin, now she was tha ver' soul o' nobility, Osiris keep 'er."

Ally tuned out the two older women who began a nostalgic discussion of Evelynne's late mother and concentrated instead on breathing deeply and forestalling a panic attack. It actually wasn't that hard; the sensation in her middle left her feeling as though her stomach had been removed entirely, along with her heart and lungs. What was left was a kind of blank stunned feeling.

Suddenly, she realised that the music had stopped and Duke Thomas was mounting a small dais at one side of the hall. He lifted his hands and cleared his throat to get everyone's attention, and the room swiftly grew silent. "My Lords and Ladies," he announced in a voice surprisingly energetic for someone his age. "I tender my apologies for interrupting your evening, but several of my guests must leave shortly and I wished to make an announcement before they did so. What I am about to say you would most likely have learned very soon in any case, but I was not about to pass up an occasion to be the one to pass on some welcome news. Having scores of people hanging on one's every word is a rare privilege for gentlemen of my age. And since I outrank nearly everyone present, nobody can stop me now." There was good-natured laughter from the assembled guests. "However, I also know better than to push my luck, so I will not keep you waiting. I find it amazing that Count Larrel has lasted this long without flirting with any of my servants."

"Don't be so sure, Your Grace," Larrel's voice called out. "A number of them are quite receptive to sign language."

The laughter returned and this time Duke Thomas joined in. "I will keep that in mind. However, on to my news, although I claim no part in its making. Earlier this evening, negotiators reached an agreement with the

chapter thirty

American government for a state visit by their own Secretary of State. This will be the first visit by an American official in thirty-two years. He will be arriving in time to take part in the Conclave of Nobles in two weeks. I am sure we are all pleased at what this might mean in terms of lessening tensions between ourselves and the United States. I have a feeling this Conclave will be memorable."

༷ ༷ ༷ ༷ ༷

"Ally, are you feeling all right?" Evelynne asked her lover. The other woman's face was strained and pensive, obvious even in the dim light of the limo. "You look worried."

Ally seemed to come back to herself with a start and looked away from the window she had been staring out of. She glanced at the princess, then away again quickly, unable to meet her eyes. "Yeah, kind of. I just . . . Could we talk about it back at the Palace? I need to think for a bit."

Evelynne nodded, worried by Ally's mood. It had appeared that Ally had been having a good time, in spite of her generally reclusive nature, and the princess didn't know what had happened to change that so suddenly. She wondered whether someone had said something or done something to hurt her lover and instantly felt her protective instincts kick into high gear. *If someone was rude or insulting they're about to be reminded that I protect my friends. Especially ones I happen to be in love with.*

The remainder of the ride back to the Summer Palace was silent. The atmosphere remained strained, despite Evelynne's attempts to gently coax Ally into conversation. The other woman would reply absently and briefly to each question, then fall quiet again. The princess' attempts to contact Ally mentally also met with failure. The Adept had closed her mind against any intrusion. All Evelynne could detect through their link was a vague sense of emotional pain, with vague flashes of what might have been jealousy and resentment.

When they finally arrived at the Palace, before splitting up temporarily to maintain the illusion that they were actually going to spend the night in separate rooms, Ally turned to Evelynne and said, "I'll . . . see you soon." She looked away again. "We . . . have to talk." The way she said it sent a chill through the princess' stomach, but before she could respond, Ally had disappeared.

༷ ༷ ༷ ༷ ༷

A quarter-hour later, Evelynne quietly slipped inside Ally's suite. Ally was not waiting in the bedroom, as had become normal, but instead was sitting slouched in an armchair, gazing pensively into the empty fireplace. Cassie was curled up in her lap, stroked absently by Ally's long fingers. She didn't appear to notice Evelynne's entrance until the princess murmured a soft, "Ally? Love?"

Startled, Ally looked up at the woman who was standing a few feet away and quickly got to her feet, placing the cat on the floor at the same time. "Evy," she whispered and made as if to embrace her, before halting herself suddenly.

Evelynne, in contrast, had no problem in wrapping her arms around her lover and resting her head on Ally's breast. "Ally," she breathed, pleased but worried when Ally's arms slowly–too slowly–came up to return the embrace. Lifting her head, Evelynne drew Ally down into a kiss and almost panicked when Ally refused to escalate it into something more passionate. Breaking off, Evelynne asked, "Ally, what's wrong?"

Ally sighed. "I have to talk to you about something," she said finally. She released her hold on Evelynne and started to sit down again, but the princess refused to let her return to her chair, drawing her so that they could sit side by side on the couch instead.

"Well, I think you've made that clear," Evelynne replied with a lightness she didn't feel. "Was it something that happened this evening? Did someone say or do something?"

Ally sighed again, and looked down at her hands. "In a way, yes. It's actually kind of an . . . ongoing thing, but tonight someone–several someones, actually–said something to bring it to a head." She took a deep breath. "I think I need to go away for a while." The way she said it made it clear that she was miserable about the prospect.

The princess felt the bottom drop out of her stomach. "Away? What do you mean? Away from the Palace? Away from Atlantl? Away from . . . us?"

Ally laughed humourlessly. "Yes. Maybe. I need some space to think."

"To think? For how long?"

Ally shrugged. "Until I can come up with an answer."

Evelynne swallowed. "What's the question?"

"The question? That's part of the question. If I knew for sure what the question was, maybe the answer would be easier." One side of Ally's mouth quirked up in a half smile. "I'm being cryptic, I know." She sighed again. "Tonight it became painfully clear that I don't know if we'll ever really be able to be together. At the next Conclave young men are allowed to begin announcing themselves as suitors for your hand in marriage. Now, you may not know them, you may not love them, but I've read enough and heard enough to know that sooner or later you'll *have* to marry one of them, to provide an Heir, if nothing else. And then you'll have a *husband*. And where will *I* be?" Ally laughed harshly. "You know, for a while I actually had this

chapter thirty

fantasy that even when you were married and became Queen, that I would be your hidden mistress? Every night you'd sneak away from your husband to come and meet me, because we were so much in love. And for a while I actually thought I could do something like that. After all, if we love each other enough, we should be able to work around a little thing like a husband, right? But I don't know if I can. I mean, let's take a best-case scenario, where your husband knows about us and has no problems with it. Maybe he has a mistress of his own. That still means that even though we can be together in secret, I'll never be able to hold your hand in public or kiss you without worrying who might see us. Damnit, I *like* kissing you and holding your hand! But to have to hide *all* the time . . . Or what about the flip side, where your husband doesn't know and wouldn't approve and you have to go to his bed each night so that he won't get suspicious?" Ally shook her head. "I couldn't stand the thought of someone touching you like that." She shrugged again, the set of her shoulders signifying exhaustion. "Who knows, maybe if you truly loved him and he truly loved you things would be different. After all, how could I begrudge someone who loved you as much as I do? But even then, where does that leave me? On the outside, at least, I'd be alone. I wouldn't have a partner or a family of my own. I . . ." She trailed off. "That pretty much covers it, I think."

"So you're leaving?" Evelynne asked, her tone dull.

Ally nodded reluctantly. "For a while. I just need some time to work some things out in the privacy of my own head. I don't know, maybe I'll come to the conclusion that I can live with being your secret lover. Right now I'm just really confused." She tried to smile. "Don't worry, you'll know what I learn . . . one way or the other."

Evelynne couldn't muster an answering smile. She was feeling too much like this was some particularly bad dream. "When—when will you go?"

"Tomorrow morning," Ally replied soberly. She leaned in to kiss Evelynne, although the princess' lips were unresponsive, then stood. "Tonight, though, I think I'm going to go . . . out." She waved a hand towards the glass doors leading to the balcony. "I need . . . I don't know what I need, but I know I can't stay here." She hesitated and then walked purposefully towards the balcony doors. Just before going through, she stopped and turned around. "I love you," she said, her voice catching. Then she was out the door into the night, leaving a silently sobbing Evelynne behind her.

chapter thirty one

Evelynne stood as Seneschal Nancu Ylan ushered Jason McKendrick, Lord Thomas' Legal Advisor, into her office at the Summer Palace. She managed to smile at him in a friendly greeting, an action that felt odd and unnatural. For the past week–since Ally's departure from the Palace, although not from Atlantl–she had found little to smile about. However, she was hoping that the results of this meeting might give her spirits a boost. It would not be the final solution to her problems, but hopefully it would at least provide a pathway.

"Hello, Jason," the princess said, extending a hand for her guest to take. The Seneschal discreetly bowed his way out, closing the door behind him. He had orders that this meeting was to go uninterrupted for anything less than the rising of Atlantl from the sea.

"Your Highness," Jason said, bowing over her hand extravagantly, as Evelynne rolled her eyes. If there was one person who absolutely loved playing the whole formal etiquette game, it was Jason McKendrick. It was extremely fortunate that he did consider it a game, to be played by the proper rules to be sure, but ultimately for fun. Otherwise he would be absolutely insufferable. It also helped that under the right circumstances he could be persuaded to drop the act.

"Really, Jason," Evelynne teased, "you'd think I was, oh, the Crown Princess or something with the way you carry on."

"You must admit, Your Highness, that the likeness is remarkable," he replied seriously, although the twinkle in his blue eyes showed that he was enjoying the banter.

"I'll be sure to tell the actor playing Ylan that," Evelynne said wryly. "He'll be gratified that his practice has paid off." She waved her guest into a chair. "Please, have a seat. Would you care for some refreshments?"

Jason shook his head, placing his black briefcase by the side of his seat and running a hand through his thick, wavy chestnut hair. "No, thank you, Your Highness," he declined. "If it is Latifa's customary exquisite work, I fear that I will be too distracted to remain focussed on business." He hesitated. "I assume that this is a business meeting, Your Highness?"

Evelynne didn't say anything for a moment. "It is," she admitted finally, "although it involves a personal matter..." She trailed off, uncertain of how to continue.

"Your Highness, would this 'personal matter' happen to involve a certain Dame Alleandre Tretiak?" Jason asked delicately.

"Yes," the princess blurted, surprised. "But how did—"

"Your Highness, several months ago Lord Thomas approached me with a certain 'theoretical' legal issue that he wished me to investigate. Last week I was informed that I should expedite my research, as the theoretical issue had the potential of turning into a practical one. He also provided me with certain, er, parameters so that I could focus my efforts. Dame Alleandre's name was one of those parameters."

"Oh," Evelynne said, stunned that this was going to be less difficult than she thought.

"Before I continue, however, Your Highness, I would like to ask why you have not involved your own Legal Advisor in this matter. While I am, of course, happy to help you in any way that I can, I must also inform you that my primary allegiance is to His Grace. Under the right circumstances, he *could* compel me to reveal the facts of our discussion here today. I'm afraid I cannot guarantee my confidentiality in that case."

"That's simple," Evelynne said. "The fact is that I trust you more than I trust my own Legal Advisor. While Tran ibn Tellah is very competent, and I'm probably doing him a disservice, the fact remains that I've only been working with him since December. On the other hand, I've known you for several years now. And the overriding factor is that Lord Thomas trusts you. As for telling him, I'm explicitly stating that you're free to do so. I'm pretty sure that he knows all the pertinent details anyway, and what he doesn't he's probably guessed." She shrugged.

"In that case, Your Highness, and having already looked into the matters I presume you will wish to discuss, I can already give you some good news. There are only three major sticking points and all of them are largely out of your direct control. None, however, are insurmountable. Before that, though, I'd like to lay out the groundwork that I've already prepared."

Evelynne walked across the courtyard, somehow extremely conscious of the fact that the men working around her were not paying her much attention. As princess, she was used to being the centre of public attention wherever she went. However, occasionally she would go to some place where the inhabitants either didn't know or didn't care that she was the Heir

chapter thirty one

to the Throne of Atlantl and it was always a welcome relief. This was one of the latter, since the brown-garbed monks assiduously working in the gardens answered to an even higher authority. There was respect, even friendliness in their eyes, but none of the deference the princess was used to receiving, whether she wanted it or not.

At the moment, though, most of her thoughts were focussed on the one monk she had specifically come to the monastery to see, and a gut-churning apprehension over the topic of their imminent conversation.

That particular monk appeared suddenly from a door at the other end of the courtyard, beaming at his sister, and Evelynne couldn't help but smile back. She felt herself choking up as he grabbed her up in a bear hug and she buried her face in the coarse wool covering his shoulder. The other monks looked on with some amusement at the spectacle.

"Evelynne," Patrick murmured into her ear. "It's so good to see you."

His sister squeezed him tighter. "It's good to see you too."

Patrick loosened his grip so that he could hold Evelynne at arms' length. He scrutinised her face carefully, and frowned when she wouldn't meet his eyes. "You look tired, Evy," he said. "Stressed. Are you doing all right?"

Evelynne shrugged half-heartedly. "There's a lot happening right now," she replied. "Actually, that's one of the things I came to talk to you about." She looked around at the nearby monks. "Is there somewhere private we can go?"

"Of course," Patrick said. He began leading her towards the door he had exited from. "The Chapel should be nearly deserted right now."

A few minutes later, Evelynne sat down with relief, not caring about the hardness of the wooden pew. The Chapel was simply furnished, with a cross, altar and several *prie-dieux* at one end, and the rest of the space filled with pews. The only real decoration was a small but beautiful stained glass window above the altar. As Patrick had predicted, there was no one else there.

The princess' brother sat down a moment later, after briefly dropping to one knee and saying a quick prayer. He looked at Evelynne who had wearily closed her eyes and leaned her head back.

"So, Evy, what's wrong?" Patrick asked. "You aren't looking good."

Evelynne opened her eyes and rubbed them wearily. "I've been having some . . . personal problems," she admitted finally. "And I've been really busy with some official projects." She sighed. "But it's the personal things I wanted to talk to you about, before I talk to *za*." She swallowed, uncertain of where to begin.

"You know you can talk to me any time," Patrick said gently. "I am a monk, you know. We're supposed to help people with their problems."

His sister laughed wryly. "Actually, you being a monk has the potential to make things worse in this case," she said.

Patrick frowned. "I don't understand."

Evelynne took a deep breath in a vain attempt to steady her roiling stomach. "I suppose I should start at the beginning," she said. "You know how Ally and I have become really good friends?"

"Of course. I consider her a friend as well."

"Yes, well, shortly after she was knighted we became . . . *more* than good friends. Much more."

"I don't . . ." Patrick's frown suddenly reversed as his brows rose dramatically. "Oh. *Oh!* I see." He appeared stunned. "I don't–I never thought–I mean, I knew that she was–but I never thought that you–"

Evelynne took pity on him. "It was a bit of a shock to me too. However, I finally came to terms with it and told her how I felt. She felt the same way too . . ." She shrugged uncomfortably and stared at her hands. "Are you disappointed?"

"Disappointed? No, of course not." Her brother hesitated. "To be honest, a little. But that's just shock talking," he hastened to add. "I think I would feel the same no matter who you were in an intimate relationship with. After all, this is my little sister we're talking about. Er, this is an intimate relationship, isn't it?"

Evelynne blushed. "Um, yes. Very."

"I see. Please spare me the details. Not only are you my sister, but I am a monk, after all." The attempt at humour was successful in lightening the mood.

Evelynne finally managed to look at her brother out of the corner of her eye. "So you're not mad?" she asked hesitantly.

"Mad? Of course not, Evelynne. I'm not mad. Shocked, yes. Concerned, yes. Mad? Definitely not." He shook his head. "Just give me a bit of time to get used to the idea, all right? Are you happy?"

"Yes," Evelynne replied instantly, then paused. "At least . . . I was."

Patrick curled an arm around her shoulders and drew her close. "What happened?" he asked gently.

"She, um, left," the princess replied, her voice hitching.

"Left? Why?"

"A pretty good reason, actually. She knew that I'd never be able to acknowledge our relationship and that I'd also eventually have to get married, 'to provide an Heir, if nothing else,' as she put it. She didn't know if she

Chapter Thirty One

could handle that. So while technically she hasn't left me permanently, I don't hold out much hope of getting her to come back as things stand. Even if she did, a life of hiding like that isn't what she deserves."

"All right, I can understand that," Patrick said, stroking her hair. "So what did you do?"

"Well..." Evelynne sniffed and moved out of her brother's embrace, dabbing at her nose and eyes with a hand. "The night that she told me she was leaving–that was the night of Lord Thomas' Gala–I was too shocked to do anything. I love her so much, Patrick, and the thought of her leaving for good was..." She looked up at him with expressive eyes, begging him to understand, and grateful to find gentle acceptance there. "The next morning, though, I begged her to stay. I told her that we could work it out together." She sighed. "Eventually I stopped, though."

"She wasn't going to give in?"

"No, actually I stopped because I realised that she was *about* to give in and I realised that doing so would be unfair to her. Whatever *I* may feel, *she* feels the need to get away and think about it. But I also know that if I had convinced her to stay when she needed to be alone, she wouldn't feel that she had resolved things in her own mind. I also know that I have enough power over her to make her do what she really doesn't want to and it's wrong of me to exploit that power."

"I understand," Patrick said. "And I think that what you did–or didn't do–showed a lot of maturity. God gave us all free will, and taking away someone else's, even with the best of intentions, is a great sin."

Evelynne smiled crookedly. "I don't know about sin, but I do know that it just felt wrong."

"So what have you been doing since then?" Patrick asked. His sister looked at him quizzically. "I know you, Evy. You never were one to let things rest when there was something you wanted. You're going to try to do the right thing. So what is it?"

"Well, I have been getting some advice," Evelynne admitted, "and I know what I want to do. Unfortunately, it depends on the agreement of a number of people. *Za* is one. The Hall of Nobles is another. Ally, of course, is the key figure. And you are another." She took a deep, fortifying breath and looked directly into her brother's eyes. "Patrick, I have a *really* big favour to ask."

ം ം ം ം ം

Evelynne walked into the gardens and looked around, catching sight of her father standing under a tree with his eyes closed, enjoying a brief respite from his duties. "Hello, *za*," she said, touching his arm lightly.

"Evelynne," King Jad boomed, sweeping his daughter into a hug strong enough to lift her feet off the ground. "How are you, my little fireball?" Placing her back on the ground again, he looked at her quizzically. "The Conclave isn't due to start for another two days. I wasn't expecting you until tomorrow at the earliest. Don't you have a meeting with the Avaloni Education Council this afternoon?"

The princess shook her head ruefully. She was used to her father knowing every aspect of her professional life. He never interfered, but she also knew that compared to his decades of rule she was very much a green recruit and it was comforting at times to know that he was discreetly looking over her shoulder—even if it was from two islands away.

"I postponed it," she explained, hugging his arm as they started on a slow walk through the gardens. "All they were going to do was try to convince me to support their less important proposals at the Conclave. I already know what I'm going to endorse and I'm not about to change my mind at the last minute."

"Ah," Jad said. "You know that Lord Bransen is on that Council, don't you?" King Jad said casually. "He was most put out by you backing out. It seems that you are maybe . . . let's see, how did he put it? 'Taking your duties to your loyal future vassals somewhat frivolously.' Something to that effect, anyway." There was no censure in the King's tone.

Evelynne laughed. "Lord Bransen is a useless, incompetent, egotistical fool," she said scathingly. "The only reason he hasn't been stripped of his title by the rest of the Nobility is that he's blessed with a truly spectacular Advisory Council and he's lazy enough to let them do all the work. He really wanted me there so that he could leer at my breasts and make oh-so-subtle insinuations as to his qualifications as my future husband and, incidentally, the next King of Atlantl."

"I suspected as much," King Jad remarked calmly. Then his face darkened. "Although not about the leering." His tone was dangerous.

"It's all right, *za*," Evelynne said. "He's harmless. Creepy, as Ally says, but harmless."

"If you say so," Jad said. "I trust you can fight your own battles. And know to call for assistance when you need it." He stopped to pick an orchid and handed it to his daughter, who smiled and smelled it appreciatively. "Speaking of young Dame Alleandre, how is she? She is scheduled to present a report on her current work at Aztlan during the Conclave, is she not?"

chapter thirty one

"She is," Evelynne confirmed, suddenly showing the nervousness that had been hiding just under the surface. She twisted the stem of the orchid anxiously. "Actually, she's what I'm here to talk to you about. Um . . . I need to get something from you."

ये ये ये ये ये

Ally swallowed, already feeling a sense of apprehension, even though she was nowhere near its source yet. She had arrived in Jamaz early that morning and the opening ceremonies of the Conclave of Nobles were not due to begin until after lunch. She was scheduled to present a preliminary report to the Conclave Science Council on the research her team was conducting at Aztlan but not until later in the evening. The thought of standing in front of so many people already had her stomach tied up in knots. Although there was really only one person she was truly nervous about meeting.

All of her staff–it still felt strange to have a staff–had accompanied her on this trip and were currently eating breakfast at a small café near the port. She was glad for their supportive presence, even if she couldn't tell them the true reason behind her apprehension.

"Boss, are you okay?" Taldas asked from across the table. "You're looking a little green around the gills."

"Yeah, are you feeling all right?" Laura Garrity asked.

"I'll be okay," Ally said, less than convincingly. "I was just trying to psyche myself up for this presentation thing this evening."

"Psyche . . . up?" Rina asked. "What is this, Boss?"

"I'm trying to prepare myself," Ally explained. "I get . . . scared when I have to speak in front of a lot of people. And stop calling me 'Boss.'"

A chuckle swept around the table at the familiar complaint. Taldas Islin had been the first to give her the title, snapping to attention with a crisp "Yes, Boss" when she had asked him to get some food from the commissary one evening and for some reason it had stuck, much to the "Boss'" annoyance.

In reality, though, Ally was more than pleased with her team. She got on well with all of them, although she and Marjorie Melan, the linguist, didn't click as well as she'd have liked. They weren't hostile or unfriendly, but incompatible personalities kept them polite but distant. Fortunately, the linguist got on very well with Taldas, letting him act as an intermediary between them. Ally suspected that Marjorie would like to be more than friends with the handsome man, but he was already taken, if Ally was reading the signals between him and Rina correctly.

"What do you mean?" Taldas asked. "You never have any problem speaking with us."

"Yeah, but you're not actually people," Ally teased. "You're my slaves."

"So do the same thing at the presentation," Laura suggested. "Pretend they're all your slaves."

Ally's brows rose. "You're kidding, right? Somehow I don't think *any* of the Nobles could be anyone's slaves. Certainly not King Jad or Princess Evelynne."

Laura shrugged. "Well, it might be better than picturing them in their underwear."

Ally began to speak, then stopped. There was no way she was going to say that she had already seen Evelynne in her underwear. In far less, in fact. She shook her head to clear it. Despite two weeks of trying, she had yet to come to a conclusion regarding her erstwhile lover and now was probably not the time to be distracted with such thoughts. Her nearly overwhelming desire to simply jump into Evelynne's arms and never let go, regardless of other circumstances, constantly conflicted with her sense of independence and wish for a more open life; a life where she could show the person that she loved exactly how much she loved her, no matter where they were or who else was around.

Realising she had been silent for several seconds, Ally said, "Please, have you *seen* some of those Nobles? Lord Victus comes to mind." She shuddered dramatically and everyone laughed.

"Okay, okay, point made," Laura said, still chuckling. "Well, then, just pretend that it's only us there. Everyone else is just like those robot things at Disney World. What are they called? Oh yes, animatronics."

"Now there's a plan," Ally said. "Have I mentioned how glad I am that you're my assistant?"

"Not in the last hour," Laura replied, smiling. "Marjorie came up with it, actually." Ally looked at the blonde linguist, who just shrugged and smiled. "And remember, you can reward us by arranging for us to meet King Jad, Queen Cleo and Princess Evelynne." There was a general murmur of agreement from the rest of the table. They had been subtly hinting–although sometimes the subtle hints were tied to a two-by-four–that Ally use her personal connections to allow them to at least meet the country's rulers, for some time now. They were never too demanding or obnoxious, but Ally understood that they would consider it a great honour to do so.

"I'll see what I can do," Ally conceded. "They'll probably be way too busy to do anything today, but tomorrow might be a bit easier. Just remember, I'm not promising anything."

A pleased response came from her friends around the table and Ally suppressed a sigh. She wasn't entirely sure her "connections" with the

chapter thirty one

Atlantlan Royalty were still in good standing. She hadn't heard from or spoken to Evelynne in almost two weeks and while part of her was gratified that the princess was allowing her to work things out on her own, another part was worried that the same lack of contact signalled a more permanent break on Evelynne's part. Regardless, Ally was both dreading and looking forward to their next meeting.

"Sure thing, Boss," Taldas said. He glanced down at his watch. "Should we get going? We still need to get changed into our monkey suits and then it'll probably take forever to get through security. Believe me, you really don't want to miss the opening ceremonies."

Everyone agreed and after settling the bill, they started off down the street, Rina asking Taldas to explain just what a "monkey suit" was.

"Man, this place is nuts." Ally had to raise her voice over the din of hundreds of voices. "And we're not even inside yet."

She and her crew had cleaned up and changed, and were now in line to pass through security and enter the actual Hall of Nobles itself. The large courtyard was packed with people, all of whom simply had to be there, at least in their own minds. The close quarters, coupled with the late May sun directly overhead, were making Ally sweat and she tugged at the uncomfortable high collar of her formal attire. The tunic and pants were purple, trimmed with silver, the official colours of her blazon, which was prominently displayed on her chest.

"It's the security," the man in front of her commented as the line moved forward slowly. He wasn't quite able to turn around in the press. "Godsdamned HBLA is making everyone nervous."

That much was true. The Hy Braseal Liberation Army had been suspiciously quiet for the last week, leaving the entire population wondering what they would do next. The Conclave was the most obvious target for their next attack. That, plus the fact that the American Secretary of State had arrived for the first official visit in thirty years, meant that security had been tightened to unbelievable proportions.

"I know," Ally said earnestly. "I know they make *me* nervous."

The man nodded. "No way we're going to let the *teki'a* force us to postpone the Conclave, though. Too many interesting things going on at this one. The States' visit, for one. Princess Evelynne's suitors may begin announcing themselves. Plus, there's a rumour that Her Highness has a big announcement to make. Nobody seems to know for sure what it's about, though."

"I heard that she was going to announce that she was giving up all claim to the Throne," another man nearby said. "Apparently she had a meeting with King Jad that left His Majesty in quite a state. I heard that later that day he punched his Legal Advisor."

"Rubbish," Ally's original speaker scoffed. "Although it would be a great loss if she did decide to abdicate. Unless her brother agreed to take the Throne again, the succession would pass to her cousin, Lord Argyle. A decent enough man, but not a candle to Princess Evelynne." He awkwardly managed to extend his right hand behind himself without turning around. "Roald Myrfield, Economic Advisor to Baron Hutana."

Ally gripped his hand. "Alle–I mean, Dame Alleandre Tretiak."

Roald twisted around to look at the young woman incredulously. He quickly took in her formal attire and his eyes widened. "Dame Alleandre!" he exclaimed. "What are you doing here?"

Ally looked confused and sneaked a glance at Laura. The secretary shrugged. "I'm here to give a presentation to the Science Council this evening," Ally said.

"No, no," Myrfield said, shaking his head. "I meant, what are you doing standing in line with the rest of us? Peers of the Realm have their own entrance."

"Oh," Ally said, surprised. "I didn't know. I thought I just lined up with everyone else. I've never been to anything like this before."

"Very well," Myrfield said. He peered around, noting that the way back out of the crowd was just as packed as the way forward. "You'll never get around to the Nobles' Entrance in time. In that case . . ." He took a deep breath and bellowed, "Peer of the Realm! Dame Alleandre Tretiak coming through! Make way! Peer of the Realm!"

There was an impression of surprise, but the word soon spread, and a relatively clear pathway began to open up as more voices added to the cry.

"There you are, Dame Alleandre," Roald said, sweeping his arm forward. "We can at least get you to the front of the line. An honour to have met you."

Red-faced, Ally murmured her thanks and moved forward, her small retinue trailing behind her. She couldn't help but feel embarrassed at the bows and salutes that were directed her way as the people parted to let her through.

"Breathe, Boss," Taldas murmured in her ear. "And smile." Ally managed a rather frozen grin. "Needs work."

It took only a few minutes to finally arrive at the first of the security checks, prior to entering the Hall of Nobles. The Guards on duty appeared

chapter thirty one

startled by Ally's sudden appearance, but quickly recovered and waved her forward.

"Dame Alleandre," a tall Guardswoman manning a metal detector greeted. "Please, step through."

Naturally, the metal incorporated in Ally's uniform set off the detector and the Guard smiled apologetically and waved a wand over her body from head to toe. Satisfied that the Knight was bearing nothing more threatening than a pocketful of loose change and the steel clasps on her tunic, she saluted, touching forehead, lips and breast. "Dame Alleandre, welcome to the Hall of Nobles. I am Major Tyran," the Guard said, as Ally awkwardly returned the salute. Other Guards were performing similar searches of Ally's companions. "You could have entered through the Nobles' Entrance."

"So I was just told," Ally replied wryly. "Neither I nor my secretary have been to one of these before and I suppose nobody thought to give us instructions."

"I see," Major Tyran said, nodding in sympathy. "If you will wait a moment, one–" She broke off suddenly, her hand cupping her ear as she listened to her earbud. Nodding, she spoke briefly into her wrist-mounted mike and then refocused her attention on Ally. "Dame Alleandre, Her Highness Princess Evelynne would like to speak with you before the Conclave begins. If that's all right, I will have someone escort you to Her Highness."

"Um, sure," Ally said, the butterflies in her stomach suddenly growing teeth.

"Excellent," the Guard said. "Your companions will be shown to their seats in the meantime." She nodded to a younger Guard nearby. "Please escort Dame Alleandre to Her Highness in section eight C."

"Yes, Major. If you'll come this way, Dame Alleandre," the young man said politely.

"Thank you," Ally said. She turned to face her crew. "I'll see you in a bit, okay?"

ఎ ఎ ఎ ఎ ఎ

Ally felt her stomach begin to settle as she walked beside the Guard through the gorgeously accoutred hallways. The combination of smooth cool stone and large, bright windows gave the Hall a calming effect. Marble pillars and exquisite paintings, tapestries and sculpture from five thousand years of Atlantlan history looked down on Ally and she couldn't help but feel impressed. Vases, statues and weapons both ancient and modern all had their own stories to tell and Ally wished she had the time to hear them.

There didn't appear to be any rhyme or reason to the decorations, but they still seemed to complement each other nicely. After descending a stairway, Ally realised that the windows overlooked a large garden, on the other side of which was an imposing building she recognised as the Royal Palace. *The Heru Gardens*, she thought, *named after the first King of the al-Heru Dynasty, who planted them and built both the Hall of Nobles and the Royal Palace over eight hundred years ago.* The information scrolled in front of her mental eye as her eidetic memory brought it up.

Ally was so busy admiring the lush gardens as she passed that she didn't notice the figures waiting for her until she was practically upon them. Her stomach lurched and she stumbled and almost tripped as she recognised Sir Arthur and Maïda standing there in formal dress. But most of her attention was fixed on the pale-faced, redheaded young woman standing stiffly, holding a box under one arm.

Evelynne was fully and formally attired as Heir to the Throne. Her gown, heavy with decoration and coloured in purple and gold, nevertheless looked light and comfortable as it was blown slightly by a soft breeze coming through an open door leading to the gardens. Her shoulder-length hair was styled surprisingly simply and was held back from her face by the formal coronet resting on her brow. Kohl designs had been applied around her eyes and her lips shone with gloss, but that appeared to be the extent of her makeup. She looked so incredibly attractive that Ally was torn between dropping to her knees in awe and fainting.

Focused on Evelynne, Ally was only vaguely aware of her escort formally announcing her to the princess and then withdrawing. She was pulled from her reverie when Maïda reached to clasp her hand. "Huh? Pardon?" she said.

"I said, you look very good today, Alleandre," Maïda repeated. "Dignified."

"Oh. Thank you," Ally said, taking in the lady-in-waiting's own modest formal dress. "You look good yourself."

"Alleandre," Sir Arthur rumbled, taking her hand in his own bone-crushing grip. "How are you?"

"Um, okay, I guess," Ally replied. She laughed shakily. "A little nervous."

"You'll be fine," Maïda reassured her and Ally thought she could detect a hidden meaning in her words. "You both will." Before Ally could ask what she meant, the older woman patted her on the arm. "We'll leave you two alone now. Just remember, Highness, the Conclave begins in half an hour."

chapter thirty one

Gathering up Sir Arthur by his sturdy arm, she walked off, leaving Ally and Evelynne alone.

"Hey, Ally," Evelynne whispered, looking up at the other woman with an expression Ally couldn't decipher.

"Hey, Evy," Ally replied. "Um, so how are you?"

Evelynne choked out a strangled laugh. "That is a far more interesting question than you realise at the moment. Isis, it's more than *I* know right now."

"Oh, okay," Ally said, confused. She had been expecting a declaration of anger, of hurt, of sadness, even one of love or resignation. This uncertainty was quite unlike her lover's normal confidence. "So what–"

"Let's go outside," Evelynne interrupted, already moving towards the double doors to the garden, tightening her grip on the box under her arm.

"Uh, sure." Ally hurried to catch up.

Once outside, a strained silence fell, as Evelynne led them both deeper into the gardens. "I–I like your hair," the princess said finally, glancing at the locks in question out of the corner of her eye.

Ally reflexively brought her hand to her head. "Um, thanks. It was getting a bit long, and I wanted it out of my face. Mila'a did it for me, actually." Her hair now reached to just below her chin, and its natural wave was broken by a single small braid just in front of each ear.

"Oh, have you been seeing her?" Evelynne asked with forced casualness.

"She came out to the site about a week ago. I'd promised her a tour." Ally paused. "I wasn't, uh, seeing her in that sense. You know, like going out."

"I didn't think so. I . . . trust you." It was mostly true, although there was a small kernel of doubt that she ruthlessly ignored. *After all, Mila'a is beautiful, intelligent, friendly . . . and isn't carrying the baggage that I am. Ally might be better off with her anyway.* "Besides, your mother reassured me on that point."

Ally's brows rose. "You talked to my mother?"

"Um, yes." Evelynne blushed. "They're here, actually."

Ally blinked. "Here? You mean my Mom and Dad came?"

"Yes. I hope you're not angry. It's just that if things work out well today, I think they'll want to be here."

"Okay." Ally paused. "What did you mean by things?"

"Here, let's sit down," Evelynne evaded, stopping at an intricately carved stone bench, its inscriptions almost vanished with age. An ancient oak tree provided shade. They sat down some distance apart and the princess asked, "So, have you had a chance to reach any . . . conclusions? About us?"

Ally sighed, leaning forward with her elbows on her knees and looking down at the ground. "No, not really. Believe me, not for lack of trying. It's like I'm caught between the classic immovable object and irresistible force. You're the force; you pull me towards you like nothing I've ever experienced. But then I hit the immovable object, which is that I can't live in hiding about something like that." She laughed hollowly. "I know, I've been living in hiding my whole life. You'd think I was used to it by now."

"That's different," Evelynne said gently. "You hide what you can do for your own safety and the safety of those you're close to. I understand why hiding who you love is so much harder."

"Yeah," Ally said, still contemplating her clasped hands. "It's still damned frustrating not to know what I have to do, though." The vehemence of her tone betrayed her inner conflict.

"Well . . ." Evelynne began, fidgeting with the box on her knees. She swallowed hard. "I think I might have a solution. One that I pray to Isis you'll accept. I've been thinking a lot and I've decided that I've been letting convention limit my options."

With a final fortifying breath, she stood briefly before kneeling in front of Ally, who jerked back at the unexpected move. Holding the beautifully engraved box in both hands and looking directly into Ally's eyes, she said, *'Alleandre Tiffany Tretiak, will you marry me?'* She opened the lid of the box, revealing a shining silver coronet inside. It was only slightly less ornate than the princess' own circlet, the silver inlaid with oricalcum and studded discreetly with a number of precious stones.

Ally froze both physically and mentally, in complete shock, unable to believe the words that had appeared in her mind. Frantically trying to respond, she managed to stammer, "Wha–but–it–uh . . . that," before falling silent.

"I know this wasn't the kind of solution you were expecting," Evelynne said hurriedly, worried by the other woman's silence, "but I know I want to be with you. Always. Although I don't know that this is the life you want. I don't know if you've ever thought about staying with me permanently or if you want to now. I don't know if you want the obligations and responsibilities of being married to me. It won't be easy, and a lot of people won't approve, but . . ."

The main part of Ally's mind tuned out Evelynne's voice, instinctively falling into a meditative state she occasionally used when working out problems. No words crossed her mind, only a rush of pure concepts, almost too fast for her consciousness to follow, as her subconscious and unconscious examined her feelings and thoughts with a speed only another Adept would

chapter thirty one

be able to match. Time seemed to slow around her as her enhanced mental processes kicked into high gear. Logic and emotion battled with each other, complemented each other. Love, fear, doubt, trust, uncertainty, certainty, intellect and animal instinct were all considered and applied to the final equation.

In the end, the final answer was a single word.

Time sped up again and Ally realised that Evelynne was still babbling, her apprehension and fear over Ally's continued silence clearly discernible to the Adept's increased perception.

"Yes."

Evelynne's speech jerked to a halt. "Pardon?"

Ally smiled fully for the first time in weeks. "I said, 'Yes.'"

"Yes?" An answering grin slowly grew on Evelynne's face. "You mean . . . Yes . . .?"

"I'll marry you," Ally said. Reaching down, she cupped Evelynne's face and drew her up slightly into a long kiss that the princess settled into with a satisfied sigh.

When they finally broke apart, they both looked dazed. Evelynne sat back on her heels and noticed the open box on her knees. "Oh," she said. Placing the box on the ground, she reverently lifted out the coronet. "Then you need this."

"Is that . . .?" Ally asked.

"This is the *Tyl'kas e'Moru e'Ur-Matan*, the Coronet of the Heir Consort," Evelynne said. "At least, the one worn by brides." The word felt strange on her tongue. "The men's one is much uglier." Neither could stop the slightly hysterical giggles that erupted, releasing some of the tension. "As a member of the Nobility, I don't have a ring to exchange. The *Tyl'kas* serves the same purpose."

"Oh," Ally said, still stunned. She held still as Evelynne carefully lowered the "engagement crown" onto her head. *I'm engaged,* she thought dazedly. *I'm going to get married!* Then she stopped thinking as her new fiancée leaned in to kiss her once more.

Several minutes later, they parted. Ally's mind kept repeating, *I'm engaged!* not quite believing it, until finally the reality of the situation kicked in. "Evy," she said seriously, "can you do this? I mean, I'm not–I'm–"

"I can," Evelynne said, smiling. "I've talked to quite a few Legal Advisors about it and technically, there are only three things that could stop me. As the Diarchs, my father and aunt could overrule my choice of Consort. They didn't. If two of the three Dukes of Atlantl agree, they could overrule me also." A worried expression crossed her face for the first time since Ally had accepted her proposal. "We'll see today whether they do or not." She trailed off, apprehensive.

"Evy, you said three? What's the third?"

Evelynne broke into a broad grin. "You, of course. You could have said no."

"Oh. Well, it's a good thing I didn't, isn't it?" Ally frowned. "Are you *sure* you want to do this? I can't even imagine the problems you'll face."

"That *we'll* face," Evelynne corrected. "No, it won't be easy. But if I'm not willing to fight for us, then I wouldn't love you like I do." She smiled again. Her cheeks were beginning to ache, but she didn't care. "There are a few things you do need to know, though. I–" She was cut off abruptly by the sonorous tolling of a bell from the direction of the Hall of Nobles. "Damn," she cursed. She looked at Ally apologetically. "That means the Conclave is about to Open. I–*we* really need to be there." She pulled Ally to her feet, and then kissed her hard. "I promise I'll explain everything."

"Okay. I trust you," Ally said seriously.

"And I love you," Evelynne replied, taking her fiancée's hand as they headed back through the garden.

Reaching the doors leading into the outer Hall, Evelynne paused, taking a deep breath. "All right. Here we go," she said, grinning up at Ally nervously.

Pushing through the doors, they saw the Master of Evelynne's Guard and her lady-in-waiting quietly talking. They looked up as the door opened and Maïda's face creased into a wide smile as she took in the coronet on Ally's brow. Sir Arthur's response was more reserved, but even his pleasure was obvious. The older woman immediately crushed her charge in a wide hug. "Congratulations," she whispered into Evelynne's ear. "I'm happy for you."

Sir Arthur just smiled wryly at Ally. "So you said yes."

Ally blushed. "Uh, I guess I did," she said. She returned his smile. "You think I had a choice?"

"You always have a choice," Maïda said seriously, turning her attention to Ally. Despite her serious tone, her eyes were sparkling. "I want you both to know that we will stand by your choice in any way we can."

Sir Arthur nodded solemnly. "Right now, though, Your Highness, My Lady," he said, acknowledging Ally's change in status with the new title, "we must hurry. You are already a little late for the Opening of the Conclave. Their Majesties are about to be announced."

"Then we had better hurry," Evelynne announced. She squeezed Ally's hand in reassurance. "Everything will be fine."

Chapter Thirty One

They set off along the corridor towards the Conclave Hall, magically acquiring a full Guard escort along the way. More than a few of the soldiers had barely concealed grins as they took in Ally's new status, leaving her wondering just how many of them had been aware of the lovers' relationship before now. Major Nixon was smirking openly, but Ally's stomach was roiling too much for her to do more than glare weakly at Sir Arthur's second.

Before long–far too soon, in Ally's opinion–the grandly carved doors of the Diarchs' Entrance to the Conclave Hall appeared ahead and Ally could recognise the red-haired form of King Jad waiting with the smaller Queen Cleo. When they were still some distance away, the King looked up and saw his daughter and her party approaching. When he saw who was accompanying her, he smiled tightly, then turned to the Warden, a uniformed man bearing a large gong on the end of a pole in one hand and a large staff in the other. Speaking in a low voice, he gave the Warden some instructions that clearly startled the man. Still, this was the Diarch giving the order and there was no way the Warden was going to disobey his order, no matter how much it went against protocol and tradition.

Turning to face the doors, the Warden struck them three times with his staff, paused, then a fourth time. In response, the large double doors swung ponderously open. The Warden strode through purposefully, halting just inside the Conclave Hall. Raising the gong, he struck it once, the echoes of the sound carrying to every corner of the vast Hall. The room quickly grew silent. "My Lords and Ladies," the Warden bellowed in Lantlan, his clear voice surprisingly loud, "His Royal Majesty King Jad Richard ibn Jad deMolay, Bearer of the Four Crowns, Lord Protector of the Isles, Keeper of the Laws, Provider of the People, Sovereign of Atlantl! Her Royal Majesty Queen Cleo Janet el-Kareen Sarin, Keeper of the Four Crowns, Lady Protectress of the Isles, Provider of the People, Sovereign Regnant of Atlantl!" The slight differences in their titles showed that while King Jad was the permanent ruler, until such time as he died or formally abdicated, Queen Cleo was effectively holding her Crown in trust against the time that Jad took another wife or regular succession replaced her. Even so, while she held the Throne she was the King's equal in every way. "All Loyal Subjects Hail Their Majesties!"

There was a loud roar of approval as the assembled Nobles and other dignitaries showed their heart-felt approval, but there was a tinge of surprise and confusion as well.

That surprise was echoed in Evelynne's expression. She had come to an abrupt halt a good ten metres from the doors. The surprise and shock on her face slowly turned to a tremulous smile and tears welled up in her eyes.

"Evy, what's wrong?" Ally asked worriedly, painfully aware of the tight grip the other woman had on her hand.

"Wrong? Nothing's wrong," the princess replied looking up with bright eyes at the woman she loved. She took a deep breath and explained. "The Nobility enters the Hall in strict order of rank, from lowest to highest. Naturally, the Diarchs enter last." Another breath. "By entering before us, *za* and Aunt Cleo have just not-so-subtly told everyone that whoever follows takes precedence over even them, at least in this particular circumstance." She smiled even more widely. "They've just told everyone, although the rest of the world doesn't know it yet, in the strongest possible terms that they fully support our union and that, today at least, it ranks even above their own positions as King and Queen."

"Oh," Ally said, slightly stunned. "So he's not going to kill me for, you know, corrupting his daughter?" Her tone showed that there had been a core of true fear behind the seemingly joking words.

"He might," Evelynne replied teasingly. "But it will only be as a father, not as the King of Atlantl."

"Oh, that makes me feel better," Ally said sarcastically. Events seemed to be spinning out of Ally's control, but there was also a sense of rightness to them that was making her just allow things to unfold as they would.

As they were talking, the Warden marched back into the corridor. He had held his post for thirty years and never before had the Diarchs deferred to anyone living. On rare occasions, some hero would be honoured posthumously when his or her casket or colours were the last to enter the Hall, but no living person had ever been so privileged. Those were the Warden's thoughts as he exited the Hall and they were brought to an abrupt halt when his mind finally processed the appearance of the two people Their Majesties had deferred to. Her Highness was easy to recognise and even the young knight by her side was familiar, but what that knight was wearing... The last time he had seen the Crown of the Heir Consort had been near the beginning of his career, when a much younger *Prince* Jad had escorted his own bride-to-be into this same Conclave Hall. He gaped, all sense of propriety fleeing and his gaze darted back to the face under the Coronet, half expecting to see the son of some Count or Duke, thus proving that he had been mistaken.

No mistake. That face, pale, strained and obviously nervous, was definitely Dame Alleandre Tretiak, Knight Errant to Princess Evelynne deMolay. And now Consort to the Heir to the Throne of Atlantl.

The Warden saw, out of the corner of his eye, the princess' lady-in-waiting looking at him with a cocked eyebrow and disapproving expression.

chapter thirty one

He closed his mouth with a snap. He was a professional, he reasoned, and regardless of his own feelings over the appropriateness of this occasion, he would discharge his responsibility. While there were obviously no protocols dealing with exactly this situation, it would be a simple matter to adapt one of the existing ones.

Squaring his shoulders and falling back into his role, the Warden turned once more to face the still open doors. He was aware of the people behind him falling into place, Dame–*Lady* Dame Alleandre slightly reluctantly, Her Highness with more assurance. When he was sure they were ready, he strode through the great doors once again. He paused just inside and struck his gong with the staff.

"My Lords and Ladies, Her Royal Highness Princess Evelynne Sophia al-Heru deMolay, Heir Apparent to the Throne of Atlantl, Duchess Itinerant!" The Warden took a deep breath and spoke again, his voice clear and unmistakable. "And Her Ladyship Dame Alleandre Tiffany Tretiak, Knight Errant to Her Highness Princess Evelynne . . . and Consort to the Princess Heir!" The assembled people broke into loud, confused and excited murmuring, almost drowning out the Warden's final words. "All Loyal Subjects Hail Her Highness and Her Ladyship!" His job thankfully completed, the Warden stepped back and to the side, bowing to allow the Heir and her Consort entrance into the Conclave Hall.

Ally and Evelynne walked slowly through the doors, hand in hand. The princess winced slightly at the crushing grip on her hand. A glance at Ally out of the corner of her eye revealed a glazed look and clenched jaw muscles. Evelynne could tell that the other woman was fighting the urge to bolt. Without resorting to speech, she sent a message of love and support through their link. She was gratified when the grip eased ever so slightly and there was a subtle lessening of tension in Ally's face. She managed a tight smile in Evelynne's direction.

Then they were through the doors and Ally saw the Conclave Hall at its maximum capacity for the first time.

The semi-circular Hall was constructed like a vast auditorium and reminded Ally of some of the university lecture halls she had been in. The curved half-circle sloped up steeply, its seats placed so that every occupant would have a clear view of the bottom of the Hall. This was where the Nobles sat, each with his or her own desk. The lowest rank, the Barons, occupied the highest tiers as representatives of their own small territories, usually comprising only a few towns or cities. Below them sat their immediate superiors, the Counts and Countesses, each counting several Barons and Baronies as their vassals. Finally, at the bottom of the slope sat the Dukes, each representing one of the islands of Atlantl: Hy Braseal, Avalon and Lyonesse. Naturally, there wasn't enough room to fit all members of the same rank on exactly the same level, which meant that for each Conclave the Nobles were randomly assigned to seats within their own particular section, thus preventing any one Noble–a Count, for example–from claiming superiority simply because he was seated one step below his peers. Wide stairs separated the amphitheatre into three sections, one for each island and its ruling Duke.

At the very bottom, in the centre of the "stage," were placed the Twin Thrones of Atlantl, neither one above or behind the other and identical in appearance. Behind and to the sides sat the Thrones of the Heirs: a total of eight, although for the last six years only one had ever been occupied. Today, two would be. It was no accident that every King and Queen of Atlantl for the past eight hundred years had been forced to look up in order to see the men and women who supported their rule. In fact, above the topmost row of Nobles were the galleries, where any citizen was allowed by law to view the proceedings, assuming they could find the room. Today, given what the people knew–or thought they knew–about the issues that would be discussed, the Galleries were packed.

Off to the side, to both the left and right of the Thrones, were two smaller seating areas, specially designated for visiting ambassadors, dignitaries and other VIP's. Today, one was occupied by the American Secretary of State and assorted members of his staff and Secret Service detail. The other contained a number of other guests of the Crown, including Evelynne's brother Patrick and, Ally noted with a slight shock, Catherine and William Tretiak. Ally's mother had her hands over her mouth and was unsuccessfully holding back tears, her eyes shining, and William appeared surprised and uncertain whether to be pleased and proud, or worried and disapproving.

Stepping further into the Hall, Ally allowed Evelynne to guide her towards one of the Heirs' Thrones, as the sound of discussion and speculation grew to a dull roar. She saw Lord Thomas wink at her and give her a discreet thumbs up, and she smiled back crookedly. In contrast, Lord Marsden appeared uncertain, frowning as he listened to an Aide whisper in his ear. Lord Hassan looked downright disapproving, scowling thunderously at her. Ally was unsure of the overall response of the rest of the Nobles, as they disappeared into a vast blur of faces and voices and there was no way she was about to open her mind more directly in this kind of atmosphere.

Once Ally and Evelynne had taken their seats to the right of the King and Queen, the Warden appeared once more. Despite the extraordinary events that had just occurred, certain formalities still remained before

chapter thirty one

the Conclave could officially open. Walking briskly in front of the seated Diarchs, he struck his gong several times, calling for silence. It took much longer than usual, unsurprisingly, but finally a modicum of quiet settled over the Hall. Turning to the King and Queen, he bowed deeply and intoned, "Your Majesties, it is, by law, the time for the Conclave to commence. Do you acknowledge the law, that your actions and those of your vassals, may be examined and judged; that your subjects may have their Voice; that the laws may be made, modified or repealed according to custom and the highest law?"

"We do," the King and Queen replied formally.

The Warden bowed deeply and stepped back.

King Jad and Queen Cleo looked up at the three Dukes arrayed before them and repeated, in unison, the question that the Warden had asked. When the Dukes replied with an affirmative, they each turned to their own immediate vassals, thus continuing the question up the Hall. Finally, the Barons and Baronesses turned and faced the assembled citizens and commoners in the Galleries. "Loyal citizens," they proclaimed, their voices blending together surprisingly well for such a large group, "your Lords sit before you in Conclave. Will you abide by their decisions and accept their decrees made under the law?"

The response was much less coherent, but still unmistakably affirmative, if the sheer volume was anything to go by.

"Then I declare the Conclave open," the Warden declared. "May your deliberations be guided by the Universal and the law!"

Cheering arose, which quickly subsided as the Atlantlan National Anthem began to play.

With the Conclave officially open, there followed a very long period as each and every Noble in the Hall came forward individually to pledge their allegiance to the Realm and Diarchy. The Dukes began the process and it continued down to the very newest Baroness, a young woman who was obviously nervous at representing her Barony for the first time. With all one hundred and twenty three Nobles coming up one by one, the entire process took over three hours. By the time it was over, Ally's rear was nearly asleep. On the plus side, the novelty of the situation wore off after the first few Declarations of Allegiance and she had found herself relaxing enough to calm her roiling stomach. Evelynne, as Heir, had stood with her father and aunt to accept her vassals' pledges of loyalty.

The "allegiance phase" of the ceremony completed, the princess cast a meaningful glance at her father, receiving a nod in reply. As the King and Queen took their seats, Evelynne remained standing, looking up at the assembled people. Taking a deep breath, she spoke, her voice carrying clearly over the waiting Nobles and commoners, who were completely silent. While the formalities previous had taken place in Lantlan, she now spoke English, in deference to the woman who would be the focus of her speech. "My Ladies and Lords, loyal citizens," she said, "I know that it is traditional for the Diarchs to make the first speech of the Conclave. However, as you may have noticed, we seem to be breaking away from tradition this year." A low chuckle rolled through the chamber, although it was offset by the number of disapproving glares. "Earlier today–just before the Conclave opened, in fact–I sought out Dame Alleandre Tretiak and asked her to marry me." Another rush of whispered conversation erupted at this final confirmation. Evelynne ignored it, instead turning and walking to where Ally was still sitting, nervously twining her fingers in her lap. The princess held out a hand to her fiancée, who hesitantly took it and allowed herself to be raised to her feet. Still looking at Ally, Evelynne continued, a broad smile breaking across her face. "As you can see, she agreed."

More murmuring broke out, but this time it was more speculative than uncomfortable.

Keeping Ally's hand in her own, Evelynne moved back to the centre of the Hall, drawing her lover with her. Addressing her audience once again, she said, "Needless to say, I am expecting a great deal of controversy surrounding my decision. I am also not so naïve as to believe it will not be the central focus for most, if not all, of this Conclave. So let me announce some things, so that they can be aired, rather than allowing them to fester among rumour and speculation." She paused for a moment and the entire Hall held its collective breath. "I am a lesbian." The words were spoken clearly and slowly, without room for misunderstanding. "I desire the companionship of other women–specifically this one–and have no desire for a relationship with a man greater than friendship. So regardless of whether you disagree with my choice, I will not be seeking a husband. Should you somehow prevent me from marrying whom I choose, you can rest assured that I will not marry whomever you choose." She smiled thinly. "In such a case, I will become the first bachelor Diarch in three hundred years." She looked up at Ally again, her facing softening noticeably. "I am, of course, hopeful that you will not overrule my choice."

There was near silence for several seconds, broken only by intense whispering. Finally, Lord Hassan, widely known as the most conservative of the Dukes, stood slowly. His strong, handsome face was solemn. "Your Majesties. Your Highness. I think it will come as little surprise that I am very . . . disturbed by Her Highness' decision. I obviously have strong per-

chapter thirty one

sonal and moral objections to Her Highness' apparent . . . choice of lifestyle. However, I am also aware that my personal feelings are not sufficient grounds for objection on this matter. I must, like all of us, remain bound by the law. And my apologies, Your Highness, but I cannot help but doubt whether your decision is, in fact, lawful."

'Here it comes,' Evelynne told Ally. *'Time to see whether my preparation will pay off. Please, just follow my lead. And remember that I love you. And . . . trust me.'*

Ally swallowed. She closed her eyes briefly. *Trust her? Can I really do that right now? Can I really jump and trust her to catch me?* a part of her asked uncertainly. Another part replied, *I've been trusting her since I met her. She's been capable of destroying me so many times. Yet she not only hasn't, she now wants to spend the rest of her life with me . . . openly. So much so that she's defying her entire country to do so.* Just like her decision to accept Evelynne's proposal, the answer to this question was simple. She took a deep mental breath and leapt.

'I trust you.'

Evelynne smiled at Lord Hassan. "I was expecting your objections, Your Grace. I hope it comes as little surprise that I am prepared to meet them."

"Of course, Your Highness. I'd expect nothing less from the Heir, particularly one with such potential." They nodded to each other, like gladiators squaring off for combat. They might disagree, even dislike each other, but there was a degree of respect and an acknowledgement that each was being honest to their own beliefs.

"My first concern, Your Highness, is that any marriage between you and Dame Alleandre–or any other . . . woman–may not be legal. There are certainly no precedents for such an act."

"On the contrary, Your Grace. There were, the last time I checked, at least four hundred forty eight precedents that pertain directly and another four hundred fifty two that are one step removed. The first number is the number of confirmed marriages between women that have taken place since the Marriage Equality Decision was handed down. The second is the number of marriages between men in the same time frame."

"Very well, Your Highness. I will take your word on those numbers. However, that particular Decision is now being appealed before the Justicars."

"Irrelevant," Evelynne dismissed. "Until and unless the Decision *is* revoked, it remains as law and the appeals process has no bearing on its implementation."

Lord Hassan nodded reluctantly. "True, Your Highness. Even so, I am not certain that the Decision applies in your particular case."

"Why not?" the princess asked. "That Decision is classless and applies equally to all citizens of Atlantl. By virtue of her Knighthood and sworn

Oath of Allegiance to me, Dame Alleandre is a citizen of Atlantl. I am most certainly a citizen as well. And by the Fifth Order of the Ithikan Compact, 'all laws criminal or civil duly passed shall apply to all citizens, commoner or noble, unless specifically and lawfully exempted.' The Marriage Equality Decision makes no such specific exemption. So unless you are suggesting that as a Noble I am not bound by the laws of the realm . . ." She trailed off, an eyebrow raised.

Realising the danger of such a suggestion, Lord Hassan quickly backed down. Nobles who attempted to prove themselves or their peers above the law—or in this case, below it—were usually swiftly and decisively removed from their positions. In some cases in the past, about a foot—or head, depending on how one measured—shorter than they were when they first took their inheritance.

"Not at all, Your Highness," Hassan said. "I am merely investigating possibilities." He paused for a moment to regroup. "I will concede, for the moment, that the common law does not oppose you in this, pending further study, of course. However, there is also, in your case, royal law to consider. Such law does pertain to the Nobility in particular. One specific law comes to mind. Whomever you do marry, Your Highness, must be able to provide you with an Heir of your body. And forgive me for being blunt, but barring significant medical advances, it seems to me that neither yourself nor Dame Alleandre is able to perform such a feat." A shocked gasp echoed through the Hall at this statement, but neither Lord Hassan nor, most significantly, Princess Evelynne appeared ruffled.

"I'm afraid I must correct you, Your Grace," Evelynne said calmly. "The Law of Succession does not, in fact, require that I produce an Heir of my own body. It is commonly believed to, and in the past has acted as such, but the actual wording is somewhat different. In reality, the law requires only that the Royal Consort be able to provide 'an Heir of the Blood Royal.'"

"I don't see the difference, Your Highness."

"It is fairly simple, Your Grace. In order to be eligible as my Consort, Dame Alleandre must only be capable of bearing a child of the Royal Bloodline. I, personally, am aware of no medical impediment to her doing so. Nowhere does the law specifically state that *I* must be the parent of the child." Evelynne smiled wryly. "In the past, of course, it has always worked out that way, for obvious reasons. The Kings and Queens of the al-Heru deMolay line have been only too happy to produce as many Heirs as were needed all by themselves. However, this is a new situation. Legally, all I must do is find a willing male of my own bloodline to, ah, donate the required material." Lord Hassan's eyes were widening in slow realisation and he glanced

chapter thirty one

to his left. Evelynne nodded in confirmation. "As of this morning, Brother Patrick has informed me that he has obtained special permission from the Superior of his Order to so assist, should it be required." She smiled broadly at her brother, who grinned back at her.

Ally had thought that she had exceeded her capacity for shock for the day. She had been wrong. *A baby? Me? I'm supposed to . . .? With Patrick? Okay, maybe not the traditional way; he's got that vow of celibacy, after all. But—*

'I'm sorry,' she heard in her mind. *'I know I should have talked to you about this. I know you've talked about having kids before and a family, so I hope you're not too angry. But I knew they'd bring this up at some point, so I had to be prepared.'*

'Angry? No, I'm not angry. I'm just . . . Well, I mean, yeah, I've considered having children, but not . . . I didn't think it would be an issue so soon. I've always sort of assumed that my . . . partner would do it. Although I've thought about having one myself, but not for a long time to come. And Patrick? He's—well, he's—he's Patrick. And he's a monk! Are you sure he's okay with this?'

'He is,' Evelynne assured her lover. *'He was understandably surprised when I told him about us and asked him this favour, but he was actually very supportive. Once he had got used to the idea, his specific words were, 'Tell Ally, anytime.' Apparently he thinks you're good breeding stock.'* The mental smirk was clear.

'Oh. Really. Sorry, I'm still a little . . . zoned. I thought that becoming a future wife would be the extent of my shocks for today. Now I've just learned that at some point I'm going to be a mother. Just give me a while to get used to it, will you? I'm not upset, just . . .' She shrugged mentally, bewildered.

'I understand. I promise that as soon as we can we'll have a long talk about all this.'

For the first time, Lord Hassan looked shaken. Visibly gathering himself, he bowed his head to the princess. "It seems that I am out of legal arguments for the moment, Your Highness," he said. "However, I trust *you* recognise that I, and many of the people I represent, still have grave misgivings. We will speak again, I'm sure, once I have had the opportunity to consult with my Advisors."

Evelynne nodded back. "Of course, Your Grace. Opposition is what keeps the Nobility honest. I trust you recognise that I cannot and will not wish you success." She looked up into Ally's face again and her own softened from its previous businesslike mask. "I am in love, Your Grace, and all I ask is the chance to remain so publicly and without reservation."

Lord Hassan cleared his throat, obviously uncomfortable with the sentiments being expressed. "Before we can examine that issue, there is one other matter that should be revealed."

The princess looked back at him, slipping back instantly into her role as Heir. "Yes, Your Grace?"

"It is the matter of Succession. Not yours, Your Highness, barring a full Deposing by the Nobility thus removing your right to Succeed." His tone reflected his torn feelings between his loyalty to the Heir and his new reservations over her suitability. "However, our Realm *must* be ruled by a Queen *and* a King. This is spelled out quite specifically in the Constitution. Assuming, for the sake of argument, Dame Alleandre *does* become your . . . wife—" The Duke's aversion to the idea was obvious. "—she will, obviously, be ineligible for the Throne. In such a case, who will occupy the second Throne?" He smiled thinly. "I assume, Your Highness, that you have prepared for this eventuality with your customary efficiency."

Evelynne smiled back, unruffled. "I have, Your Grace. Again I am forced to point out that you are mistaken. While it is true that the Constitution does require both a King and Queen, nowhere in any of the Laws of Succession is there any specification as to the *gender* of the Diarchs." This was a tricky point–in a whole field of tricky points–but technically it was accurate. "We must have a King and Queen. However, there is nothing specifically preventing a male Queen, or, more pertinent to this discussion, a female King."

This time the uproar was truly spectacular. Ally didn't hear any of it and she nearly broke Evelynne's hand in her shock.

chapter thirty two

Ally walked into the room where her parents were talking quietly while looking out the large windows overlooking the city of Jamaz. Occasionally they cast glances towards the muted television in the corner. Ally couldn't see what was on the screen and at that moment didn't really care. There were more important things on her mind.

"Hey, Mom. Hey Dad," she said softly.

William and Catherine whirled around to face her and then were embracing their daughter tightly. Ally held them just as tightly, closing her eyes and leaning into the embrace, feeling a small part of the tension wound around her insides dissipate.

When they finally broke apart, Ally gave a strained chuckle. "I hope this means you're not upset."

Catherine couldn't help but laugh as well and William's mouth quirked into a smile. "Of course not," he said. "Surprised, of course. Rather worried, yes. But upset? Not at all."

Ally looked at her father and then quickly glanced away. "I know this wasn't quite what you wanted, you know, with me being with a woman–"

"Ally," William interrupted, "all I've ever wanted was for you to be happy. Now I'll admit that when you first told us that you were a–a lesbian, I wasn't as supportive as I could have been. I was raised in a very different world and to be honest the possibility never crossed my mind that you would–or even could–be like that. But now I know it's a part of who you are, and nothing I or anyone else can do will change that–nor should it. So with that in mind, all I want to know is: Do you love her?"

"Completely," Ally replied without hesitation. "Absolutely. Without reservation." She paused. "Well, actually, with some reservation. If she had actually married someone else I might not have been able to any more, but I suppose that's not going to happen now."

The bewildered look on her face made her mother laugh. "I should say not. When she arranged to have us come out here I thought it was another award you were going to be receiving. Maybe they'd make you a Baroness or something. I never even considered she was going to propose."

"Neither did I. I never even thought it was a possibility. But apparently . . ." Ally shrugged.

"Yes, she did make quite a case, didn't she?" William commented. "She'll make a remarkable Queen. And you know how I normally feel about centralised authority." He pointed to the television in the corner. "The networks have been showing nothing but this afternoon's events."

"Well, it's not every day that the future female ruler of a country proposes to . . . another . . . woman . . . and . . ." Ally trailed off, her eyes glued to the screen. With the sound muted, she could only see the images, but that was enough to render her speechless.

The tape being played was of Evelynne engaged in her debate with Duke Hassan. The princess was the very picture of poise and confidence, her eyes flashing as she made some point that the Duke had to concede with a nod of his head. That in itself would have been enough to seize Ally's attention, but the woman standing next to Evelynne on the screen ... Intellectually she had to acknowledge that it was herself, but that woman appeared cool and confident, if a little stiff, standing upright as she held the princess' hand. In fact, she seemed almost bored, as though the outcome was assured and the entire debate was merely formality. *That's me?* Ally asked herself incredulously. *I was seriously ready to pass out at that point. I was just hoping that Evelynne would catch me.*

She became aware that her mother was calling her name. "What?"

"Are you okay, Ally?" Catherine repeated. "You're looking a little pale."

"Okay?" Ally asked in a strangled voice. "I–I'm–I need to sit down."

"Well, here." Her parents quickly helped her onto the long couch.

Ally closed her eyes. "Can you turn that off?" she asked.

"Of course," her father said. "There's a remote around here somewhere." He began searching around the couch and nearby coffee table.

"Never mind," Ally said. With a wave of her hand she switched the TV off, pleased when the electrical whine ceased.

"Now, Ally," Catherine said, stroking her daughter's hair. She paused when her hand encountered the coronet resting on Ally's brow and she took a moment to admire the piece. "That's really beautiful." Her voice was low murmur.

"What? Oh, yeah, it is." Ally reached up to gingerly touch the cool metal. "It's the Coronet of the Heir Consort: Female Edition. Think of it as my engagement crown. Instead of a ring, you know? Royalty apparently doesn't use rings."

"Oh? So what will Evelynne be wearing to show that she's engaged?" William asked.

chapter thirty two

Ally froze. "I have no idea. Am I supposed to give her something? She never said–she didn't ask–" She was heading quickly towards irrational panic, her mind seizing on a minor issue in an attempt to release some of her tension.

"Ally. Ally? Ally!" Her mother finally forced her to look into her eyes. "Calm down! If it was absolutely necessary for you to give her something I'm sure she would have told you. So you can think of something to give her later, if she wants it." She smiled reassuringly. "Besides, I think Evelynne already has what she really wants."

"Oh? What's that?"

Catherine sighed. "You, hon. Why else would she have proposed to you?"

"Oh, right." Ally blushed. "I'm sorry. I'm just–I'm a little overwhelmed," Ally admitted, and then laughed. "And the Understatement of the Year Award goes to . . ." She sighed and rubbed her eyes. "Seriously, though, it's all just a bit too much for me to really take in. A part of me keeps thinking that any moment now I'm going to wake up."

"Do you want to talk about it?"

"I do, but I can't, just now. I need to process first. I have this presentation to give in about an hour. If I start talking now, I'm never going to stop. I just need to keep in control until . . ."

"All right," her mother agreed. "Are you seeing Evelynne this evening?"

"I will be seeing her, but I don't know if I'll be . . . staying with her tonight. Monarchies tend to take a dim view of people sleeping with their Royal Heirs out of wedlock. And considering that it's us, I don't know if we should be giving the media any more ammunition." She waved towards the now-dark television screen. "I think they have enough as it is. So for now, please just talk to me about anything else. Anything. Dad, tell me about school. Mom, what happened to that whale you were tracking up by Alert Bay? Just please distract me for the next hour."

ও ও ও ও ও

"My Lords and Ladies, good evening," Ally said, her voice carrying to every part of the lecture hall over the speakers.

A lot of people were listening. This room had been prepared well in advance for this evening's presentation, in anticipation of a modest but respectable turnout by those most interested in the Aztlan excavation, and the theories and discoveries Ally's team was advancing. That, of course, had been well before a certain very public acceptance of an offer of marriage by the main speaker. Now the room was filled to capacity—and beyond—with what seemed like the entire population of Jamaz and its outlying regions. So many people had wanted to attend that the Conclave's organisers had broached the possibility of moving the venue to a larger location, possibly the Conclave Hall itself. Ally had vetoed the idea and when the planners had objected, Evelynne had given them a look that clearly said, "Are you planning on arguing with the possible future Diarch of this country?"

That meant that the room was now packed to the rafters and Ally took a deep breath, pretending to look down at her non-existent notes to stall for time. Real notes were unnecessary, since everything she needed was at hand in her eidetic memory. As fortified as she could be under the circumstances, Ally looked up at her audience once again.

"Thank you for coming to this presentation. There are certainly more people than I was expecting. I never realised that ancient archaeology was such a crowd-drawing subject." The light sarcasm in her voice evoked a ripple of laughter. Not many of those present were under any illusions as to the real subject of interest. Ally smiled slightly, then turned serious once more. "Actually, while I'd like to believe that the work my team and I have been doing at Aztlan is sufficient reason to attract such attention, I know that many of you, especially from the media, are here for a very different reason. So I'd like to say, right off, that you will be getting no comment on the subject of my engagement to Princess Evelynne. I was planning for this lecture long before Her Highness proposed to me and I will not throw away the hard work of either my team or myself. Therefore, I will give my presentation as intended. During and afterwards, there will be breaks for questions. I will state right now that I have spoken to Lord Townsend, our Moderator, and he has agreed that any questions not related to the work I have been doing will not be tolerated. I have his express permission to have the Guards expel any member of the press or public who goes . . . off topic, at my sole discretion." Her gaze was stern, although inside she was wondering where this assertiveness was coming from.

There was a general murmur of disappointment from the assembled journalists, accompanied by furtive glances at the Guardsmen stationed prominently around the hall. Ally didn't have to look behind her to see that her own Personal Guard—something she had apparently automatically inherited when she became the Heir Consort—were looking particularly forbidding. It was still disconcerting to know that she had her own cadre of personal protectors shadowing her every move.

Lord Townsend nodded in agreement from his place among the other Nobles comprising the Science Council at the foot of the stage. He had actually been the one to suggest removing any overzealous reporters who

chapter thirty two

stepped over the boundaries, something that Ally had not even thought of. He had made it clear that, while he was still undecided over her engagement, he hated most of the press with a passion and would be more than happy to play the bully in order to allow her to speak freely. "Besides," he'd said gruffly, "I've been reading your preliminary reports on your theories and I'm very interested in learning more. And I hate people talking while I'm watching a movie."

"This will be your only warning," Ally continued. "We are here to discuss science and history. I am quite sure that there will be ample opportunities later to investigate other topics. On the up side, many of you may go home to your editors with a fascinating science story. At least, I hope so."

She paused, but nobody seemed ready to challenge her yet. "Very well, then," she said, calling up her first slide on the screen behind her, "I will begin by giving an overview of what has hitherto been named the 'Great Maze', located in the Great Temple of Aztlan. Following that, my associate, Mister Taldas Islin, will present some possible theories on the function of the Great Maze. This will be followed by a series of computer simulations . . ."

ॐ ॐ ॐ ॐ ॐ

"Thank you, Abdullah," King Jad said absently as the servant finished pouring the *cer'ant* into the fine crystal glasses.

Abdullah smiled in return and exited the room. With a glance and flick of his eyes the King soundlessly instructed Sir Adun, his Guard, that he wanted to be alone. Knowing that the King's current guest was no threat, Sir Adun bowed and complied, taking up a post just outside the door.

Taking a hefty swallow of the *cer'ant*, feeling the fiery liquor burn a path down his throat, the King turned and looked at his guest, seated opposite in another of the room's exquisite chairs. Quirking an eyebrow, he said, "Quite a day, eh, Thomas?"

"That it was, Jad. That it most certainly was," Lord Thomas replied with a wry grin, swirling his own glass of liquor thoughtfully. He looked carefully at his Diarch and friend. "How are you taking Evelynne's revelations?"

The King barked a laugh. "Exceedingly well, if I may say so myself." He shook his head ruefully. "I thought I was ready for anything she might do, you know? Given her potential, her intelligence. She exceeds me in so many ways." He saw Thomas about to say something and waved away the imminent objections. "Oh, I know I'm a good King," he said without conceit, "maybe even a very good one. But Evelynne . . . She's going to be a *great* Queen. When the history books write about us, I will simply be 'King Jad Richard ibn Jad deMolay', with maybe a few paragraphs on my accomplishments. *She* will be 'Queen Evelynne the Great', or 'the Lawmaker', or 'the Inclusionist', or some such thing, and entire volumes will be devoted to her life."

"Assuming the Nobles allow her to take the Throne," Thomas commented quietly.

Jad snorted dismissively. "That's one thing I'm not too worried about," he said. "It'll take a lot more than a bunch of weak Nobles to stop her. No offence."

Thomas chuckled. "None taken. I agree, actually. None of us is strong enough to take her on alone and we're too fractious a bunch to be very dangerous as a group."

"Exactly. And now that she has . . . Alleandre–" he only stumbled slightly over the name "–with her I don't think *anything* is going to stop her."

"Oh?" the Duke asked, knowing they had come to the crux of the discussion. "So how do you really feel about that? I know you're showing full support publicly–that was a brilliant move with the Order of Precedence, by the way –but I'd like to know how you feel on a personal level."

The King sighed, staring into his glass, watching the light reflect off the greenish liquid within. "I'm conflicted," he said finally. "On the one hand, I like Alleandre. She's brave, intelligent, honest, fair-minded and refreshingly non-self-absorbed. Once she finally gets some confidence she'll be a force to be reckoned with." He looked up and saw Thomas' raised eyebrow. "Don't look so surprised. I've spoken with her several times and I've also talked to others who have done so. Not to mention that I have my own sources. Sources that have had some very interesting things to report." He frowned, and then waved away Thomas' questioning expression. "They are a matter of some . . . not concern, exactly. Well, yes, concern, but also with huge implications. I'm afraid I can't speak more clearly." Jad sighed. "In any case, if Alleandre were a man I'd think she was the perfect match for my daughter." He sighed again. "On the other hand, she's *not* a man. That bothers me, as much as I try not to let it."

"Do you really object to homosexual partnerships?" the Duke asked.

"Not at all. As you know, I've thrown my support completely behind such things as the Marriage Equality Decision. That said, however, it's different when it's your own child. Yes, I know it's not rational, or fair or just, but that doesn't change how I feel."

"It will," Thomas reassured him. "Because you *do* know that what you're feeling isn't rational, or fair or just. That will help you come to terms with it over time."

chapter thirty two

"I hope so. It makes me wonder how Alleandre's parents came to deal with her sexuality." It was obvious that the young woman's sexuality and how it related to his daughter, still made him extremely uncomfortable.

"Ask them. I'm sure they'd be happy to talk with you."

"That's a good idea. I don't even know why I didn't think of it."

"You're just not used to thinking in such terms. I know it's not truly possible for you to access the support groups that are available to those in less exalted positions. I can also, if you wish, introduce you to certain other members of the Nobility who are in a—a similar situation. It is highly informal and unofficial, for obvious reasons, but some of us in the Nobility have seen the need to create our own support group."

The King looked startled. "Oh?"

"As you might know, Jad, I happen to prefer the company of men myself. Or I did when I was younger."

Jad nodded. "My father knew and he told me a long time ago. I just didn't know there were enough . . . people like you in the Nobility to create a group."

"Oh, there are more than you might think and it only takes two to create a support group. Not all are 'people like me'. Many are simply parents who are having to deal with their children's sexuality, just as you are."

"Well, you will certainly have to introduce them to me," the King said firmly. "If I am going to be standing behind my daughter, it will be nice to know that there are others standing behind *me*."

They were both silent for several minutes, each contemplating their own thoughts.

"What do you think the ultimate reaction will be politically?" the King asked suddenly. "I know I said I didn't think anyone could stop Evelynne from taking the Throne, but how do you think this will affect her standing?"

Thomas considered for a moment. "Right now it is very hard to say," he said finally. "The Nobles are too confused for anyone to predict what they will ultimately do. Prior to today, Evelynne was immensely popular amongst the Nobility, not to mention the commoners and Advisors. I have kept an informal poll of her supporters, as I'm sure you have, and I placed her popularity at seventy-four percent among the Nobility and eighty-five percent among the commoners."

The King nodded thoughtfully. "My figures are a little different, but not by much."

"Indeed. Now, it remains to be seen just how much Evelynne's decision today affects that support base. It *will* take a hit. Just how much I don't know.

Despite how much we like to pride ourselves on being an open and tolerant nation, alternative sexualities are still a very contentious issue. I'd predict a larger drop among the Nobility. We've always been much more conservative than the general populace. What that ultimately means in absolute terms is unknown." Thomas sighed. "If she had to Assume the Throne today, I'd give her a reasonable chance. Over time, I think her chances get higher. We'll know more tomorrow."

"Mmm," the King mused. "What about Alleandre? Assuming that Evelynne's right and having a female King really is technically legal, what are the chances of the Nobility allowing her to assume her own Throne, do you think?"

"My personal opinion is that when Evelynne is able to take the Crown, Alleandre will not be far behind. Let's assume that the Nobles eventually do allow your daughter to claim her position. By that time, I think the overriding consideration will be practicality. Let's face it, Alleandre is simply too intelligent and capable to waste in anything other than a central role. As long as she continues gaining support in the Nobility and Advisory Councils through her actions she's going to create a truly impressive base of allies."

"Indeed," rumbled King Jad, a smirk visible through his thick beard. "You heard that she nearly single-handedly solved Lord Urubi's employment problem through that chance remark about recycling? Well, now Urubi is convinced she can walk on water and Lady Ressick isn't far behind." He was distracted by a momentary thought, but shook it off. "Doctor Collins' reports on her work at Aztlan have been glowing and he has the ears of a lot of the Nobles on the Royal Science Councils, not to mention the College of Advisors." He shook his head ruefully. "You know, until Evelynne told me she wanted to marry the girl I was hoping she'd eventually go into the Advisory College herself." Jad frowned again. "If her . . . other talents didn't take her down a very different course."

Thomas was becoming very curious about these mysterious references, but realized his friend was unwilling or unable to discuss them. He smiled and addressed the King's original comment. "I had the same thought myself."

The King frowned. "You realise, of course, that all this is mere conjecture if they aren't allowed to marry in the first place."

Lord Thomas nodded seriously. "At the moment, there are two powers that could prevent that. You are one and from the way you've been speaking, I presume you and Cleo have chosen not to veto Evelynne's choice."

Jad sighed. "To be honest, there have been more than a few moments when I've been tempted. When Evelynne first came to me three days ago

chapter thirty two

and told me they'd been lovers for a while now and that she wanted to propose, I was a tad shocked."

"Understandably," Thomas said. "Rumour has it that you broke your Legal Advisor's jaw."

"Nonsense," the King scoffed. "It was his nose. And that was in response to certain unflattering remarks directed towards a certain minority that I'd recently learned my daughter is a part of." He waved away the Duke's surprised look. "In any case, at first I was completely against it and dead set on having Alleandre transferred to a scientific platform in the middle of the Antarctic Ocean. But then Evelynne started talking about her and . . ." His face softened and his gaze stared into memory. "I realised that my daughter truly did love her. I have seen that amount of devotion exactly twice before in my life. Once was when Cleo married Jeremiah. The second was when Evelynne's mother looked at me." He shook his head slowly. "No matter how I feel about it, Alleandre apparently makes my daughter happier than I've ever seen her before and I refuse to stand in the way of that."

The King shook his head more briskly, bringing himself back to the present. "In any case, that leaves only the second power capable of vetoing her decision. And that's the Dukes. Two of you together can successfully ban the marriage. I presume that you will vote in favour of the union and I think we can assume that Hassan will oppose it. That leaves Marsden as the deciding vote. Do you have any idea which way he will swing?"

"I wish I did, Jad. He's always been a balancing force between Hassan and myself. In some matters he supports me, in some he supports Hassan. He is more conservative than I am, although not as much so as Hassan." Thomas exhaled a long breath. "I think in the end it will come down to what he perceives as the most beneficial outcome for the Kingdom as a whole. Both Hassan and I have a lot of personal beliefs and personal morality involved in our politics. Marsden is much more objective. Now, whether he finally concludes that the advantages of Alleandre's support of Evelynne and her possible future rule, outweigh the inevitable political dissension that will arise over it, that I can't tell you. Until he does decide, the issue will remain unresolved, barring a miraculous display of open-mindedness on Hassan's part." They both smiled ruefully. "I think we can safely wager on that not happening. So, this may not be decided tomorrow, or the next day, or this month or even this year."

"Well, I hope, for the sakes of both my daughter and possible future daughter-in-law, that the answer is both swift and positive."

"I'll drink to that," Thomas said, clicking their glasses together. He took a healthy swallow and sighed. A few minutes later he asked, "What about the international community? I would imagine that even by now you've received some interesting phone calls."

"Oh yes. Interesting." Jad rumbled a laugh. "Naturally, it's still early, but I have spoken to a number of foreign leaders. Do you know, Queen Elizabeth actually told me how good it was for me to *finally* have some scandal in my family? Apparently she's been quite—what was the phrase she used? Oh yes, she has been most 'put out' at having to bear the lion's share of familial personal and sexual indiscretions for the past several decades. She thinks it's high time I had a turn." They both shared a chuckle at that. "On a political level, I believe she will stand behind us. She has some personal reservations, naturally, but she respects Evelynne too much to let them get in the way. Even though her Monarchy has nowhere near the power ours does, she still possesses a very large amount of influence."

"That's true."

"As for other nations, I actually don't see much change, at least in the middle term. In the short term, of course, we will see much the same confusion that we can expect locally, but that will settle in a few weeks, once everyone sees that we won't be changing any of our foreign policy over this. After that, all of our closest allies will remain our allies. Cuba relies on us too much for protection against American provocation. We have ties going back far too long with Portugal, Spain and Morocco for them to weaken, even though they are rather conservative socially. The Canadians, of course, are likely to be falling all over themselves to improve relations, once they get over their collective shock. The Middle East won't be too happy, but we haven't traditionally had strong ties with them, so I don't see massive repercussions. I have a feeling we'll be seeing some restrictions on the oil we buy from them, but in that case we'll just import more from South America, which will actually improve our standing there."

"And in the long term?"

"In the long term? I can honestly say I don't have the slightest idea. What will the world be like when Evelynne and Alleandre actually ascend their Thrones? We'll just have to wait and see."

"Your Highness, Her Ladyship is on her way up," Sir Arthur informed his charge.

Evelynne looked up from where she was sitting in an overstuffed armchair. She had been reading a draft proposal for a new set of environmental laws that would be discussed the next day, but had been staring at the same page for fifteen minutes. She brightened perceptibly at her bodyguard's

chapter thirty two

announcement. "Oh good," she said with feeling. "Show her right in. Oh, did the kitchen send up dinner yet?"

"Five minutes ago, Your Highness," Sir Arthur said, casting a meaningful look at the spread set out on a table near the wall.

"Oh, Isis," Evelynne said, flushing. "I was completely . . . gone. I never even heard them come in."

"I understand, Your Highness. You have every reason to be distracted."

"Well, I'm not going to be distracted any more once Ally's here," the princess declared. "How did she do, by the way?"

"According to Captain el-Jahir, very well," the Guard replied. Captain Emil el-Jahir was the brand new commander of Ally's Personal Guard. "She only had to throw out three reporters."

"Really? Well, good for her. Remind me to thank Lord Townsend for suggesting it to her."

Sir Arthur raised an eyebrow. "Are you sure you need to, Your Highness? After all, I believe it was *you* who sent a discreet message to *him* just before the presentation began."

Evelynne shrugged innocently. "So I may have made a few hints. He didn't have to follow them."

"As you say, Your Highness." The bodyguard listened intently to his earbud for several seconds. "Her Ladyship is here."

Evelynne stood quickly, smoothing down her simple green dress. "Thank Isis. Oh, and Uncle Arthur? Could you not call her 'Her Ladyship' for a while? I think she's probably feeling more than a little strange as it is."

"Of course." Sir Arthur nodded, then moved to the door. He opened it to find Ally hesitating outside. "Good evening, Alleandre," he said.

"Hi, Sir Arthur," Ally said with a tight smile. "I just wasn't sure if I was supposed to knock or not."

"A good question," Evelynne said, grinning at her fiancée. "In this case I think you're safe." She beckoned Ally into the room.

Sir Arthur nodded a salute to Captain el-Jahir, who remained outside the room, and shut the door.

Evelynne saw the stress and anxiety etched into Ally's face and instantly wrapped her in a warm embrace, feeling the tension in Ally's tight shoulders and back. "How are you holding up?" she asked.

"I'm . . ." Ally seemed at a loss for words, settling for a shrug and buried her face in Evelynne's shoulder.

"It's all right," Evelynne soothed. "Are you hungry? Do you want to eat something? I had them bring up some food."

Ally pulled back, already feeling slightly more relaxed. "Am I hungry? I'm starving. Do I want to eat something? Not on your life. I just know that whatever I eat I'm going to taste twice: once on the way down, and . . ." She swallowed, resting her cheek on Evelynne's head. "Maybe in a bit, but . . ." She leaned back to look in her lover's eyes, darting a glance at Sir Arthur, who was studiously ignoring them. "How long can I stay?"

Evelynne frowned. "What do you mean?"

"I mean, am I supposed to go back to my own rooms tonight? I don't know what I'm supposed to do here."

The princess smiled. "You can stay for as long as you want. Forever, I hope. Um, that is, assuming you *want* to stay with me tonight."

"God, yes!" Ally blurted and then blushed.

"Good." Evelynne frowned. "Of course, there is the matter of propriety. Fortunately, a Special Agent of the Heir's Guard has just volunteered to stay here this evening."

Ally's face fell. "A Special Agent? Who?"

Evelynne's lips twitched as she beckoned Sir Arthur over.

"Your Ladyship," the Guard said formally, "by virtue of your Oath of Allegiance to Her Highness, Princess Evelynne deMolay, I hereby appoint you Special Protector in the Atlantlan Guard. You are hereby charged with protecting Her Highness' body and soul with every means at your disposal. May God protect you. Congratulations, Your Ladyship Corporal Dame Alleandre Tretiak." Sir Arthur saluted, then smiled, turned and left the room.

"See?" Evelynne said. "I told you. Now I can honestly say that a member of my Guard was with me all night when they ask me tomorrow." There was no response and Ally was still staring fixedly at the closed door. "Ally? Are you all right?" The princess reached out and gently turned her lover's face towards her.

Ally's face had a fixed quality and Evelynne could see the muscles in her jaw clenched tightly. Most striking, though, were her eyes, wild and turbulent and more expressive than Evelynne could remember seeing them for a long time. There was a particular fragility about her, as though Ally was holding herself together so tightly that she would fly apart if she released her control a fraction.

Evelynne reacted on instinct, gathering her lover into her arms, cradling her, letting her feel the love and support. Ally remained stiff for a moment more before melting completely, collapsing into Evelynne's arms almost bonelessly. Fortunately, Evelynne was able to lower them both to the floor, where she sat cradling her lover in her lap, one hand cupping the back of Ally's head, as the other woman sobbed soundlessly into her neck. The

chapter thirty two

princess kept up a constant stream of wordless reassurance, with both her mental and physical voices, wrapping Ally in a supportive cocoon. She felt tears of her own slipping out as all the strain, tension, anxiety and sorrow that had been building over the past two weeks, and culminating in the day's events, poured out of Ally in a stream.

Neither knew how much time passed before Ally's tears slowed and finally stopped. Evelynne found herself sitting on the floor with her back against the couch, her legs stretched out in front of her. Ally was wrapped around her, head resting just under the princess' breasts, body pressed against her right side. Evelynne was stroking her lover's hair, intrigued by the novelty of Ally's two new tiny braids as they slipped through her fingers and revelling in holding the woman she loved close by her once more.

"I'm sorry," Ally whispered finally, her voice hoarse. "I just . . ."

"It's all right, love," Evelynne replied, pressing a kiss to her lover's hair. "You've had a very rough day, I know. As your future wife, this is part of my job. I'm here to pick up the pieces when you fall apart."

"Yeah, but it seems like you're always the one taking care of me," Ally said softly. "What do I do for you?"

"What do you do?" Evelynne asked incredulously. "You *love* me. That alone is worth everything. You're there to listen when I talk, to give me advice or even just a receptive ear. While I may not have broken down on you yet, I'm sure I will some day. And when I do, I know you'll be there to pick up *my* pieces. That will be *your* job, my wife."

"My wife," Ally mused. "I never thought I'd be that, you know. Like the whole legal, full-fledged marriage, equal partners thing. Oh, I'd imagined moving someplace like Holland with my partner or something, at least before Canada recognised equal marriage, but never as a serious thought, you know? Just kind of an idle fantasy. Now, though . . . I'm actually going to get married."

"You are," Evelynne confirmed. "*We* are. If I have to disband the entire Hall of Nobles, we are." She changed her stroking of Ally's head to a light scratching, chuckling softly as she felt her lover become even more boneless and practically melting into her. "You're purring again."

"Mmhmm," Ally agreed wordlessly. She was silent for several more moments before slowly and luxuriously stretching every muscle in her body, looking and sounding even more like a cat as she did so. Once she was done, she looked up into Evelynne's eyes. "Will you make love to me tonight?" she asked, her eyes shy and oddly vulnerable. "Please? I want to be with you so much."

Evelynne bent her head and captured Ally's lips in a searing kiss that quickly escalated beyond the point of no return. *'Isis, I love you,'* she spoke into Ally's mind. It was an extremely erotic sensation, to be able to talk to her lover without needing to free her lips from whatever they were doing–currently, kissing her lover as if her life depended on it.

'*I love you too,*' Ally replied in the same manner and somehow even her mental voice managed to sound breathless. Her lips broke away to begin kissing a trail to the pulse point behind Evelynne's ear.

"Oh, Isis," Evelynne breathed, her eyes closing. Her hands traced aimless paths across Ally's back and sides, gripping more tightly when her lover nipped at a particularly sensitive area. Feeling things heightening further, she struggled to regain control for a moment. As intriguing as making love on the floor of the sitting room might be, she was still very aware that there were any number of Guards posted right outside the door. "Bedroom." She tried to urge Ally to her feet, but the other woman was having none of it.

Instead, Ally tightened her hold on Evelynne's shoulders before stretching out nearly on top of her lover. "Hold on," she whispered in Evelynne's ear. Then she extended her mind, wrapping them both in her mental focus, and channelled. Immediately they started to rise from the floor, still horizontal.

Evelynne felt the telltale, stomach-dropping sensation of levitation and reflexively gripped Ally tighter. She looked up at her lover, stretched out above her, and gasped at the smouldering look in her eyes. Unable–and unwilling–to resist, she pressed her mouth to Ally's, pouring all the love and desire she was feeling into the kiss. After a moment, her stomach lurched slightly and Ally pulled away.

"First the bedroom," Ally gasped. "I can't concentrate when you do that."

Evelynne nodded her understanding and settled for nuzzling her fiancée's ear as Ally propelled them towards the bedroom. The door opened, apparently of its own accord, as they approached and closed again once they were through. Nearing the bed, Ally twisted them so that they were vertical and lowered them slowly to the floor, Evelynne's back to the bed. Ally backed away a little, her hands on Evelynne's shoulders. One hand lifted to stroke a smooth cheek and the princess leaned into the caress.

"Don't move," Ally whispered and her eyes sharpened in concentration.

Almost instantly Evelynne felt invisible hands at the fastenings on the back of her dress. The sensation startled her so much that she instinctively turned her head to see who was behind her, but of course there was nobody there. She turned back to Ally's smiling face and couldn't stop herself from leaning forward to kiss her lover softly. A moment later she felt the last of

chapter thirty two

the clasps release and lifted her arms so that the same unseen hands could lift her dress over her head, leaving her clad only in her underwear.

"Well, I can't do exactly what you can," Evelynne said quietly, reaching her lover's clothing, "but I'm sure I'll manage."

Ally smiled softly and turned her head toward the light switch, intent on removing the already dim lighting, but was stopped by Evelynne's hand on her cheek. Their first time together had been one of the only times that Ally had let Evelynne see her completely nude in full light. Almost every other time had taken place in near darkness, a situation that the princess knew arose from her lover's shyness and poor body image. She also knew that Ally's actions so far had stemmed from a desire to feel some control, after a day where she had found little. However, she didn't want Ally hiding from her in any way during their first night as an engaged couple. "Don't," she said, her eyes entreating. "I want to see you." She reached up and carefully removed Ally's glasses, then gently rubbed the red marks on either side of Ally's nose as the taller woman's eyes closed reflexively. This was another action that often had Ally purring with pleasure.

Ally hesitated and then acceded with a slightly tenuous nod. Evelynne took the gesture as a sign to begin unfastening the large brass buttons down the front of Ally's formal tunic, leaning forward to kiss her lover's throat. Once the heavy garment had fallen to the floor, there was a lighter blouse underneath, and then an undershirt under that.

"You have way too many clothes," Evelynne muttered once the blouse had joined the tunic on the floor.

Ally chuckled, her breath catching as Evelynne's hand not so accidentally brushed against her breast through her undershirt. "You should try standing in the Conclave Courtyard for half an hour in the sun in this."

"No, thanks," Evelynne said. She leaned in for a kiss, then curled her fingers under the edge of Ally's undershirt and pulled it up and over her head. That left only the pants, which were thankfully fastened only with three buttons and were much more quickly defeated, leaving Ally in her sports bra and panties.

Ally had to force herself not to cover herself with her arms, a reaction that Evelynne noted anyway. The princess wrapped her arms around her lover, pleased when Ally returned the gesture. "I've said it before, and I'll say it again, as many times as it takes for you to accept it. You're beautiful. Believe it!"

"I'll try," Ally murmured.

They remained like that for a moment before both became increasingly aware of the heat building between them. To Evelynne's pleased surprise, Ally took the lead, slowly pushing the other woman back until Evelynne climbed onto the bed. Ally followed her until they were in the same position they had been in the air, Ally looking down at Evelynne with eyes full of love and desire. They kissed passionately, for long minutes, hands making short work of the remaining clothing, until Ally began moving down Evelynne's body trailing kisses as she went and they rejoined each other completely, in mind, body and spirit.

મ મ મ મ મ

Much later, Ally mused idly on what time it was. She knew she had a watch in her pants pocket, but at the moment she couldn't quite remember where her pants had ended up, eidetic memory or not. Besides, she was pretty sure that there was no good reason to move from her current position, spooned snugly against Evelynne's back. The hedonistic softness of the bed had allowed her to wrap both arms around her lover, rather than the "third arm" half embrace that was the bane of lovers everywhere. She couldn't move the lower arm, it was true, but her upper hand was idly tracing patterns across Evelynne's abdomen. She knew from her breathing that Evelynne wasn't asleep, even if she hadn't been able to feel the warm, languid thoughts of her lover's mind.

Ally drew breath to speak, then paused and let it out again.

"What?" Evelynne asked lazily, shifting and snuggling back so that she was pressed more tightly against Ally's front.

"What?"

"You were going to say something. What was it?"

Ally hesitated, and then said, "I wanted to say something, but I didn't want it to sound like I was mad, or unhappy or anything. Because I'm not."

"Oh? Well, just say it. Now that I know you're not mad, or unhappy or anything, you don't have to worry." Evelynne's voice was gently teasing.

"Okay. I just wanted to ask you to please not spring any more surprises on me for a while, okay? Don't get me wrong, getting engaged to you was… is the best thing that's happened to me. But on top of that, it happened after we'd been apart for a while, and then I learned that I was going to have to have a baby, and then I found out I might be the next King–or Queen, or whatever–of Atlantl. That sort of thing only happens in dreams or really cheesy fantasy novels. And just when I thought I was out of surprises, I'm suddenly a Corporal in the Guard." She laughed, but there was a slightly hysterical edge to it. "What are all my titles now? Her Ladyship Corporal Dame Alleandre Tretiak? My titles are longer than my name!"

Despite the joking tone, Evelynne could feel the real tension and confusion in her lover's voice. She twisted around so that she could look into Ally's face, close enough to be clearly seen even in the dim light. As she

chapter thirty two

expected, the other woman's eyes were slightly wild and a little lost, so she immediately leaned in to kiss her lovingly and reassuringly, rather than passionately. Pulling back, she asked, "Does it really bother you?"

Ally laughed wryly. "What part?"

Evelynne smiled. "Well, let's take this in the order you brought it up. Does having a baby bother you?"

Ally thought for a moment. "Not really. I mean, obviously I'm not ready to do it right now, but I figure that'll happen some time down the road. Ask me in five years or so. The thought of your brother . . . you know . . . is a little weird, but that's because I've never had any desire to have contact with any sort of, uh, male material."

"Indeed." Evelynne was silent for a few more moments, idly enjoying Ally's hand stroking her bare back. "So, does becoming King also bother you?"

"Hell, yes!" Ally blurted and then blushed, although it was invisible in the darkness. "Sorry. It's just that, like I said, this kind of thing only happens in dreams. I mean, when you asked me to marry you I think I vaguely assumed that I'd be kind of like Prince Phillip, Queen Elizabeth's husband. Sort of in the background, help you out of the car, walk three steps behind kind of thing."

"Well, that is an option," Evelynne said quietly. "Nobody, not even me, can *force* you to Assume the Throne. If you choose not to, someone else in the line of succession would. Probably my cousin. I would still be Queen and Argyle would be King."

"Oh." Ally looked startled. "It's just that the way you were talking in the Hall . . ."

"Love, all I was trying to do was lay all my cards on the table, as it were. This way, if you do decide to take the Crown, nobody can claim we ambushed them. When we get married you will have that right and I wanted to make sure that it was understood. Of course, the Hall of Nobles could revoke your Right of Succession, just as they could mine, but that is an incredibly long, involved process and I have quite a few allies. My father has even more." *And you have more than you realise.* "As for being a Corporal, I am too, technically."

Ally looked at her in surprise. "Really?"

"Yes. You would have been assigned a rank anyway. It's all to get around a tricky issue in the protection protocols. In an emergency Sir Arthur might have to order me to get inside or take cover or any number of other possibilities. By law there's no way he can order Princess Evelynne, but Corporal deMolay is another matter. We have to be low enough in rank to fall under the official chain of command, but it was considered impolitic to make us mere privates. Even my father is just a Corporal, albeit one with a lot of seniority."

"Okay," Ally said. She closed her eyes. "Get back to me in a decade or so when I've processed all this, okay?" Her eyes snapped open suddenly. "Speaking of your father, how is he taking all this?"

Evelynne smiled wickedly. "Well, you'll find out tomorrow. We're going to be meeting him for breakfast."

"Oh God," Ally moaned. "He's going to kill me."

"Well . . ." Evelynne moved, slowly pushing Ally onto her back before stretching out on her lover's body. "I suppose I should make your last night on this planet pleasant then."

Before Ally could reply, Evelynne's mouth covered hers, and then neither of them spoke coherently for a long time.

In a room high in an office tower overlooking the city of Jamaz, a figure sat gazing out across the lights and brooded. The damned Heir's latest actions had thrown the entire country into an uproar and the figure was unsure of how this would affect the plans already set in motion. Trying to predict how the public would react to anything was uncertain at the best of times.

Still, the Atlantlan public's reaction, while important, was less so than that of the rest of the world once the operation had entered its final stages.

I've been thinking about this all wrong. A smile in the darkened office. *I've been thinking too much like an Atlantlan. This actually gives me the perfect excuse. Nobody will think twice about actions taken against a decadent, corrupt government. One that would allow its next ruler to behave in such a morally bankrupt fashion.* The figure nearly laughed. *I don't even need to change the schedule.*

A handheld device was produced from an inner pocket. It looked much like a regular PDA and fulfilled nearly identical functions, but this tiny computer had certain enhancements that would have piqued the interest of any Guard Agent.

A few commands later and three new highly encrypted, nearly untraceable messages had been sent out over the airwaves.

The figure leaned back in a leather chair. *What is it the Americans say? Ah, yes.*

Showtime.

But while the device that had sent the messages was untraceable, the device receiving them was not. By dint of intense espionage, the Atlantlan Guard had managed to insert a tap into the transmitter that relayed the

chapter thirty two

messages. Neither their source nor their ultimate destination had been pinpointed yet, but the messages themselves were instantly picked up by the Guard Cryptography unit, which had yet to break the encryption.

Unfortunately for the Guard, time was about to run out.

chapter thirty three

"Ally, relax!" Evelynne pleaded. "I was kidding when I said he was sharpening his sword last night. He's really not going to have you executed out of hand." The words had little effect on the woman walking stiffly beside her down the hallway.

"Relax? Come on, Evy. The most powerful man in the world has learned that his virginal daughter has been sleeping with another woman, and now they want to get married. And you're trying to tell me he's not upset?"

"I never said he wasn't a little upset," Evelynne said in exasperation. "But he's *not* angry and he's *not* going to do anything mean or malicious. This is just a friendly breakfast between our two families. You don't think your parents are going to stand by and do nothing if things do get bad? When it comes to you, they wouldn't care if he were the Pope, the Prophet Mohammed, Alexander the Great, Vlad the Impaler or Osiris Himself. And do you think *I'll* stand back and do nothing?" She sounded hurt at the idea. "When I proposed to you I made it clear to the world, my father included, that you come first."

Ally stopped and took a deep breath. "I know. I'm sorry," she apologised. "It's just that this will be the first time I've talked to anyone in your family since they learned about us. The whole 'meet the parents' thing is making me a little nervous. Okay, a lot nervous. Let's face it, your Dad can be pretty scary sometimes."

Evelynne's face softened and she grasped Ally's hand, stroking it softly. "I know he can. But he loves me and I know he'll come to love you as well. Just remember that for this breakfast he is *not* the King of Atlantl. He's just my father. After all, your parents didn't kill me when they found out about us."

"True," Ally admitted. "But they'd had a much longer time to get used to the idea. My Mom suspected something the first time she met you."

This was a surprise for Evelynne. "Really? But we weren't together back then."

"No, but you're forgetting that my Mom's an empath. She could sense my feelings for you even way back then." Ally laughed. "She called me on them and I confidently assured her that nothing was ever going to happen between us."

Evelynne laughed as well, and they set off down the hallway once more, arm in arm. "Well, I think that proves your lack of precognitive ability," she said, still chuckling. "Speaking of precognition, do you think Sir Arthur's feelings about today are accurate?"

"Well, it's not like he has much to go on," Ally replied. "All he said was that something seemed 'off' about today. He wanted my opinion on it." She shrugged. "I scanned him like he asked, but I couldn't really sense anything specific. Of course, I don't know what to look for, either. Still, I know he's putting both your Guard detail and mine on higher alert. It could be nothing, though. The brain plays enough tricks on us even without psychogenics complicating things. I mean, take a look at what we go through monthly as women. There have been times when I've been positive that the entire world was about to explode. And others when I actually hoped it would." Ally turned serious. "Still, I'll be keeping my eye out today. He does have a pretty good track record for hunches."

"All right." Evelynne nodded. "So I should be alert, but not worried."

"I think so," Ally agreed. "With the amount of security they have working the city I don't see anything terribly major happening." Stopping in front of a modest-sized set of doors, they both paused and Ally took a deep breath. "Okay, here goes nothing."

Evelynne took both Ally's hands and squeezed. "It'll be all right. And don't worry, Patrick will be there, so if I'm wrong he can administer Last Rites."

"Okay, I'm not going."

A few hours later, Ally was nervous for a similar reason, as she and Evelynne stood outside the Diarchs' Entrance to the Conclave Hall, awaiting the Warden's signal to enter. Having made their point the day before, today the King and Queen would enter last, as befitted their rank, and they were standing and talking quietly several metres away. They saw Ally looking at them. Queen Cleo gave Ally a friendly smile and the King nodded reassuringly in her direction. Ally smiled back nervously.

Breakfast had been nowhere near as terrible as Ally had feared. There had been a few tense and uncomfortable moments at the beginning, but then Ally's father had engaged Queen Cleo in a discussion of Atlantlan political systems and the ice had been broken. Patrick had kept the mood light by telling increasingly bawdy jokes, leaving Ally wondering just how he had become a monk in the first place–when she wasn't bent over in laughter. Ally had finally relaxed enough to dredge up a joke of her own from the depths

Chapter Thirty Three

of her memory, one that had her parents in stitches, and the Atlantlans present looking at each other in confusion. When she had finally managed to explain it to them, Evelynne had smiled sweetly and patted her on the head, reassuring her that, yes, it really was a funny joke, really. Ally had grumbled and sulked in mock anger until Evelynne had unexpectedly chased it away by leaning over and kissing her briefly but fully on the lips. Ally had lost her self-consciousness—and all awareness of her surroundings—long enough to return the kiss with interest, only coming back to herself when someone had cleared their throat loudly.

They had broken apart quickly, red-faced, to see indulgent smiles on the faces around them. King Jad's right eyebrow had been almost lost in his red hair and the set of his beard had suggested that he was torn between discomfort and amusement. A comment from Queen Cleo about "young love" had everyone else laughing while Ally and Evelynne suddenly found the food on their plates extremely interesting.

Coming back to the present, Ally looked down to see that Evelynne was also staring off into space. "What are you thinking about?" she asked.

The princess shook herself out of her thoughts. "Pardon?"

"I was wondering what had you so engrossed."

"Oh, I was just thinking about this morning." She looked up to see Ally's amused smile. "You too?"

"Yup. Heh. Um, I also wanted to thank you again for agreeing to meet with my team this afternoon. They've been bugging me about it for a while and now that things are, uh, different I can't see that changing."

"Of course, Ally, I'm happy to meet them. They're important to you and therefore important to me." Evelynne chuckled. "I can only imagine what they said to you yesterday before your presentation."

"Oh, it was interesting," Ally agreed, remembering.

Ally took a deep breath and stepped into the conference room where the other members of her team were waiting. Two Guards from the detail that had so magically appeared in between her departure from the Conclave Hall and her arrival at this room stepped in behind her and took up prominent positions to either side of the door. Their imposing presence drew the attention of everyone else in the room. Taldas' eyebrows climbed his forehead, and Rina looked startled and a little frightened, her eyes wide. Laura looked at them inscrutably as though she wasn't quite sure what to make of them, and Marjorie was frowning.

Once they were all reassured that neither of the forbidding Guards was about to start blasting away at anyone who simply looked at them strangely, all eyes migrated to the young woman they were guarding. Ally blushed fiercely as everyone looked at the coronet still on her head and she repressed the sudden urge to take it off and hide it somewhere.

No more hiding, *she thought to herself.* The entire world now knows that Evelynne and I love each other. It's a little late to start worrying about the engagement jewellery.

"*Horus in Flight,* Bo—er, Your Ladyship," Taldas said, his tone a little shaky. "You never said you were that close to Her Highness." He looked uncertain whether to salute, bow, or give her a high-five.

"Please, don't start with that 'Your Ladyship' stuff," Ally pleaded. "Call me 'Ally', call me 'Alleandre' . . . hell, call me 'Boss'. I need a little normality right now. Or at least as normal as you guys get."

That earned a slightly strained chuckle from the group, although their eyes cut to the Guards standing impassively by the door, afraid there might be retribution for such lesé majesté. When the two showed no signs of hearing, let alone reacting, the others relaxed a little.

"Okay, then . . . Boss," Taldas said. "You kind of threw us for a loop, you know. We were waiting for you up in the Gallery and we were afraid you'd been held up. Rina thought that maybe Princess Evelynne had offered you a space in the dignitaries' seats, so we weren't too worried. But then . . ."

"Well, let's just say that you were even closer to the Throne—the Thrones than that," Laura finished. "I mean, once I realised what was going on I didn't know whether I should start whistling or not. I'll tell you, it was a bit of a shock. We knew you were friends with her, but now you're . . . you're . . ."

"Engaged," Ally supplied. "And yeah, it was a shock for me too. Still is, actually. But . . ." She took a deep breath. "Right now we still have a presentation to give, so I think we should get ready for that. Okay?"

"Sure thing, Boss," Taldas agreed, happy to see that his friend hadn't, in fact, disappeared. "But now you've got to get us in to meet Her Highness." He grinned cheekily. "We need to make sure she's good enough for you." Enthusiastic murmurs of agreement accompanied this statement.

Ally sighed. "I'll see what I can do."

Ally brought herself back to the present. "Yeah, you could definitely say it was interesting," she repeated.

"Islin sounds like quite a character," Evelynne commented. She broke off as the Warden made a signal that they were ready to proceed. "Well, here we go." She glanced up at her fiancée quickly. "Are you going to be all right?"

chapter thirty three

"I think so," Ally said. She was still obviously tense and nervous, but the near-terrified brittleness that had been present the day before was gone. "You'll catch me if I pass out, won't you?" Her tone was only half joking.

"Of course," Evelynne said with a reassuring smile. "But you'll be fine." A hand squeeze and a quick kiss later, and they were ready to face the Conclave once again.

As she and the princess entered in front of the King and Queen, Ally's more relaxed mental state allowed her to take in more details than she had been able to the day before. She noted that the expressions of the watching Nobles were more of speculation and curiosity than yesterday's shock and surprise. Lord Thomas was openly grinning encouragingly and Lord Hassan was still plainly disapproving, while Lord Marsden's face was bland and neutral.

Evelynne noted the same expressions, paying particular attention to Lord Marsden's. *So, the jury's still out,* she thought. She had considered many of the same things that her father and Lord Thomas had discussed the night before, and independently come to many of the same conclusions.

Everyone present bowed to or saluted the princess and her Consort as they entered and Ally was even able to suppress her flinch when the Warden used her full title again—less her new Guard rank, which was an internal Guard matter. Then King Jad and Queen Cleo strode regally into the Hall and took their Thrones, as their titles were proclaimed. With the formal Opening of the Conclave already complete, there was much less ceremony this time, the idea being that matters of law and governance should take priority over ritual.

I have a feeling that there's going to be one topic dominating today, the princess predicted.

She was right. The closing words of the King's formal speech had barely stopped echoing when Lord Hassan struck the small bell on his desk, calling for attention.

By custom, speakers in the Hall of Nobles were heard in a "first ring, first heard" order, although a lower-ranking Noble would often cede his or her place if a higher Noble wished to be heard.

This time, though, Lord Hassan's Chime of Attention was the first to be heard and nobody was about to break protocol and interrupt him before he had said anything. Instead, the watching Hall waited politely—straining, in fact—for him to speak and he wasted no time in doing so. As soon as the Warden of the Conclave, who acted as moderator for all proceedings, acknowledged his right to speak, he began.

"Your Royal Majesties, Your Highness, fellow Nobles, Citizens, and honoured Dignitaries. I will not presume to insult anyone's intelligence today by assuming that one particular topic has not been the focus of attention over the last twenty four hours." He smiled thinly. "Her Highness', ah, engagement took us all by surprise." There was a general murmur as the Nobles realised that Hassan was going to drive straight for the point. The tone of the whispered conversations sounded more speculative than confrontational, but Evelynne could hear a few pockets of much more hostile discussion. "I myself spent much of last night meditating, praying and speaking with my Advisors on this topic. And I have come to a conclusion." Ally gripped Evelynne's hand more tightly as they sat close to each other on their thrones. "By Law, the Dukes of Atlantl have the right to ban any marriage between the Heir and any candidate if two of the tree agree and they can declare a valid reason. I have given much thought to the topic and find that I must Object to this proposed marriage on the grounds of Moral Questionability."

Evelynne was saddened but unsurprised by either the Objection or the grounds given. Moral Questionability under the law was a valid reason for an Objection such as this. It was primarily used as a means to prevent a criminal from attaining power, but the law was worded vaguely enough to allow this particular use. The key phrase was that the subject must "engage in behaviour deemed morally reprehensible by a significant portion of the citizenry". And that was certainly the case here, unfortunately.

"Under the circumstances, I do not believe that allowing such a marriage to occur is either morally justified or in the best interests of Atlantl. My Objection is therefore hereby published." The Duke looked at Evelynne with a little sympathy. "I believe the Realm would be ill-served by the inevitable mistrust that such a union would inspire, both among the Nobility and international community. Furthermore–"

"Trust, Hell!" a loud voice burst out from amongst the Nobles sitting directly behind the Duke, interrupting him in blatant violation of protocol and good manners. Everyone present was too shocked to respond, including Lord Hassan himself. "There is no way any decent, morally sound person would allow such an–an *abomination* to occur." Evelynne recognised the distinguished features of Lord Bransen, now twisted in anger and disgust. "With all due respect to Her Highness–" There was little respect evident in his tone. "–she has obviously been influenced by the *perversions* of this–this *woman*." He sneered at Ally, who looked icily calm, although the strength with which she was gripping Evelynne's hand betrayed her true feelings. "The Hall of Nobles has for centuries remained free of such degradation and to begin now is–"

Chapter Thirty Three

Suddenly it was Lord Bransen's turn to be cut off, this time by the low, clear tones of another Chime of Attention, struck with considerable force. Everyone reflexively looked at either the source of the sound or the Warden, whose job it was formally to acknowledge the one wishing to speak. The Warden hesitated only briefly. While he did agree with some of Lord Bransen's opinions, though not as vehemently, the way in which the Count had violated protocol by speaking without due notice was a far worse crime in his mind. "The Conclave recognises Lady Alice Ntakani, Baroness Holden," he announced.

The dark woman stood and saluted the Thrones, then faced Lord Bransen, seated below her. "My Lord," she said, in tones of complete and utter disdain, "you are completely, absolutely and unequivocally wrong, and the manner in which you have displayed your ignorance, bigotry and stupidity is an insult and a source of shame to all the Nobility, and indeed all the citizens of Atlantl."

A gasp echoed throughout the Hall. For a Noble to use such open disdain, especially to a higher ranking Peer, was unheard of. On the other hand, many of the Nobles present had been equally dismayed by Bransen's outburst. That, added to the fact that neither the Diarchs nor the Warden appeared about to reprimand the Baroness, had the Nobles seated around the Count edging away, attempting to isolate themselves from the source of the Royal displeasure.

"I call you a bigot because of your small-minded, narrow views on love and those who share it," Lady Alice continued. "I call you stupid because of the inconsiderate and disrespectful way in which you have chosen to express your hateful opinion. And I call you ignorant because it is obvious that you have absolutely no grasp of the lack of truth in your words. The Hall of Nobles is not now, nor has it ever been, free of the 'degradation' that you claim. I know this from personal experience. *I* am a lesbian. And I am not the only one. I will not reveal the identities of the others in this Hall, because it is not my place to do so. For centuries we have hidden ourselves, for reasons that have just become painfully obvious. Well, my future Diarchs require someone to stand for them today, because they cannot hide as we have. Nor should they have to. And so I am no longer hidden. I will support their union with all my power, alone if I have to." By now the Baroness was shouting, and she took a moment to catch her breath. "Your Highness, Lady Alleandre, Your Majesties," she said in a calmer voice, "I offer my apologies for any . . . inappropriate words I may have spoken today."

"Lady Alice," the King said in a deceptively mild voice, "I do not think *anything* you have said here today is inappropriate." He looked significantly at Lord Bransen in a way that boded ill for the Noble's future.

There were a few moments' near-silence, as the assembly came to grips with what had just occurred. Then the quiet was broken by another Chime of Attention.

The Warden, inwardly shaken but outwardly unflappable, announced, "The Conclave recognises Lord R'Tannis Intelezi, Count Techis."

The Count was a grizzled old warrior with only one arm and one eye, legacies of his involvement in the Second World War. He was brash, abrasive, irreverent and more than a little vindictive, and Evelynne disagreed with him on just about every topic they had ever discussed. "Yer Majesties, Yer Highness," he said, his slightly slurred voice a result of more war wounds. "Lady Alice, ye've made some interestin' points, but there is one on which yer mistaken. Yer not standin' alone, an' neither are Princess Evelynne an' 'Er Lady. I am a lover of men and I support 'em also."

Evelynne gasped, echoed by almost everyone else present. Almost before the commotion died down, yet another Chime rang out, and another Noble stood. "I am Fatima, Countess el-Assan, and I am a lesbian."

And another. "I am Herold, Baron Dre'Kir. I am gay."

And another. And another. Lord Uther, Baron Y'Heldis. Lady Yvonna, Baroness Niblin. Lord Thibald, Baron i-Hul-Kan. Lord Tenocl, Baron Flactonu. Lady Mbalani, Countess nec-Bordo. Lady Hildegaard, Baroness Jern. Lord James, Baron Westerlake. Lord Jikel, Baron Durando-mar. Lord Henriss, Baron Marionne.

At last the Chimes fell silent and the waiting assembly held its breath to see what would happen next. A moment later, a single Chime rang out clearly.

"The Conclave recognises Lord Thomas Baker, Duke Avalon."

The Duke got stiffly to his feet, leaning on his cane. "Your Majesties. Princess Evelynne and Lady Alleandre. Fellow Nobles and Citizens." He smiled wryly. "It appears that Lord Bransen's . . . objections have been quite amply dismissed as . . . ill-considered." He didn't even bother looking at the Count, whose normally florid face was very pale and who was trying to sink through his own seat into the floor. Bransen was also trying to stay as far away as possible from Lady Mbalani, whose large figure was still standing at her place right next to him. "It appears that the 'homosexual problem' is not simply a 'concern for the lower classes', as I have heard it put. I think that the events of the last few days have shown that love knows no boundaries, even amongst the highest of our classes." He smiled at Evelynne and Ally. "Those who happen to love their own gender exist in all areas of society. *We* exist in all levels of society." There was a hush as those listening suddenly realised what the Duke had said. Lord Thomas pulled himself as far upright as his age and condition would allow. "I am Lord Thomas, Duke Avalon, and I am a homosexual." He smirked at Lord Hassan, who looked completely stunned. "I have had few regrets in my life and one has been that I have been unable to marry anyone whom I truly loved. My inability to publicly declare that commitment has caused more than one suitor to leave." A deep, old pain lurked behind his eyes. "I refuse to stand by and permit such a thing to happen to these two wonderful young women or any others that come after them. I have remained silent for far too long. And so, I formally Refute the Objection of my peer, Lord Hassan. I find no Moral Questionability. This marriage should—*must* be allowed to take place." With that, and a final reassuring smile at the two women in question, he slowly lowered himself back into his chair.

As more furious whispering broke out throughout the Hall, Evelynne could only look blurrily at those who had risked their reputations and even titles to support her, blinking back her tears. At that moment, the Lord Bransens and Lord Hassans of the Conclave meant less than nothing.

Now that two of the Dukes had formally expressed their positions, attention turned to the third, Lord Marsden, who was sitting with a deeply contemplative expression on his face. He remained that way for several minutes, ignoring the heated rumble of debate going on around him, before slowly and deliberately striking the Chime of Attention in front of him. As the echoes of the sound died away, dead silence reigned as the assembled Nobility and Citizenry strained for his every word.

None were more anxious that Evelynne and Ally. This man before them now held in his hands the ultimate future of their relationship.

'Whatever happens,' Evelynne said to Ally, unheard by any around them, *'I want you to know that I love you. That will never change. And I have no regrets . . . about anything.'*

'I love you too,' Ally replied, sending as much love as she could through their link, as she could feel her lover doing. *'No regrets.'*

"The Conclave recognises Lord Marsden Hallack, Duke Hy Braseal."

The Duke stood for a moment before speaking, his mellow, pleasant voice carrying to every corner of the Hall and beyond, over the airwaves to every television in Atlantl, as well as millions of others around the world. "Your Majesties, Your Highness, My Lords and Ladies. I believe it goes without saying that the past few days have brought to light several topics that many of us are, frankly, reluctant to deal with and discuss. Many of those gathered here would like nothing better than to have those issues ignored and forgotten. But we cannot afford to do so. Her Highness' relationship with Lady Alleandre is only a part of a much more extensive social change taking place throughout the world. And the thing about social changes is that they are completely and absolutely impossible to stop, even if we desire to do so. So, as much as certain members of both the Nobility and citizenry may wish to hide their heads in the sand, it behoves us to discuss this issue." He smiled with sympathy at the entire assembly.

"Change is always difficult, both for its supporters and opponents. It is difficult for its opponents because of the fear of the unknown, of the uncertainty of what the change entails, of the loss of the old, comfortable ways. I can sympathise with these fears. Here in Atlantl we have a wonderful society: prosperous, vibrant and healthy. The system we have now is the reason for our success. I fear what may happen when that system changes.

"Change is also difficult for its supporters and not only because of the struggle they have in pressing forward against those who oppose them. Those are mere practical difficulties. The true pain that the revolutionaries face is that change never happens fast enough for them, no matter how swift it may appear to others. They want a new world and they want it now. Alas, they are often just as blind as those who oppose them. For as history has shown us time and again, whenever change occurs overnight, it is always accompanied by periods of intense, destructive strife. It is this conflict that often destroys the very thing that the proponents of change were seeking to create. Yet change is always a necessity. Otherwise, we stagnate, unable to cope with the realities of the environment we find ourselves in."

The Duke sighed. "However, these are philosophical ideas, abstract concepts and we must deal with the reality of our current situation. The reality is that Princess Evelynne, the Heir to the Throne of our Kingdom, wishes to marry Dame Alleandre Tretiak. She has also raised the possibility of Dame Alleandre's legitimacy as co-ruler, with the result that, for the first time in our recorded history, we may face two female Diarchs seated on the Twin Thrones.

"I am aware that many of those who know me consider me to be an eminently practical man, not prone to allowing personal considerations enter into my decisions. I would imagine that those attempting to predict my response here today have wondered whether I would allow the certain political and social friction that would arise from allowing this marriage to take place to override the possible future happiness and governing ability of my future Liege Lady." He cast a sidelong glance at Lord Thomas, who responded with a slight nod of acknowledgement at the words. "However, what they have likely not considered is another issue, secret until now, that has both practical *and* personal implications for me." Marsden took a breath. "It is well known that my son and heir, Henrit, has been aiding me in the ruling of the Duchy of Hy Braseal for several years now. There have even been occasional rumours of the possibility of a union between my son and

Princess Evelynne. I believe I may say without excessive parental boasting that he is intelligent, charismatic, a gifted administrator and a just and fair young man. He is also homosexual." Another collective gasp and renewed murmuring echoed throughout the Hall. Lord Marsden raised his voice over the sound. "This has been a well-kept secret for a number of years, for obvious reasons, just as Lord Thomas has kept his own preferences concealed. But now Henrit has asked me—ordered me, in fact—to let him 'out of the closet', as I believe the term is used. My son has also suggested to me several times that if it came to a decision for him to hold his title or abdicate in order to marry some man he truly loved, I would be forced to Confirm his younger sister as heir in his place.

"So I must make a decision as well, although mine must be made here and now. Do I avoid the political and social strife that will arise if I set a precedent by allowing this marriage to take place? Or do I allow my son, Princess Evelynne, Lady Alleandre and who knows how many others to both express their love as they see it and also use their considerable talents for the good of Atlantl? I do not know if Lady Alleandre will make a good Queen . . . or King. I do not know her well enough to make such a decision at this time. But that is not the issue at hand here today. I believe time will tell. I have the power today to bestow that time. So, Princess Evelynne, Lady Alleandre, I believe congratulations are in order. I hereby formally Refute the Objection of my peer, Lord Hassan. I find no Moral Questionability."

❦ ❦ ❦ ❦ ❦

"Thanks, Maï-ma," Evelynne said sincerely as the lady-in-waiting prepared to leave. "We just need a few minutes."

"You take as much time as you need," Maïda replied, smiling up at her young ward. There were tears in her eyes. "You've really grown up, haven't you?"

"I have," Evelynne said, smiling back. "But not too much, I hope."

"Oh, you'll always be my little princess." The older woman looked at Ally standing nearby. "Now I have two." She surprised the taller woman by reaching up and wrapping her in an intense hug. "Now you take good care of my Evelynne, you understand?" she whispered. "Just remember that her body isn't the only thing that needs protecting with those gifts of yours. She's given her heart to you for safekeeping. I know it will not remain completely unbruised, but please don't break it."

"I won't," Ally promised in an answering whisper. "She has mine too."

"I know that, dear." With a final squeeze, the older woman left the room, dabbing at her eyes. She closed the door behind her ensuring the privacy of the two women inside.

Evelynne immediately turned and grasped her fiancée in a fierce embrace. She buried her face in the hollow under Ally's chin and sighed heavily, feeling some of the tension of the past few days seep out of her in her lover's arms.

Ally shivered at the breath on her neck, but focussed enough to ask, "So is that it? We can get married?"

"That's it," Evelynne replied, her voice muffled. She pulled her head back slightly. "Oh, Lord Thomas' and Lord Marsden's Advisory Councils could petition to overrule their decisions, but I think the chances of Domdom's Advisors doing that are zero. Marsden is not the type of man to make a serious political decision, even one this personal, without knowing he had the full support of his own Council. It's possible that the Marriage Equality Decision could be overturned, but after today I think that's unlikely. So that's it." She pressed her face back into Ally's neck. "We're getting married." Unable to resist the warm skin beneath her lips, her tongue snaked out and lightly tasted the slightly salty flesh of Ally's neck.

"What about—oh, God," Ally began, her eyes fluttering closed. "You know I can't think when you do that."

"So then don't think," Evelynne mumbled, moving up to the point behind her lover's ear.

Though sorely tempted to give in, Ally retained enough self-control to pull away before she got completely lost. "First there's something I need to know," she said, looking into Evelynne's pouting face. "This thing with me being King or Queen. What will happen with that? It's just that I'm holding on by a thread here, and . . ." She trailed off, a hint of genuine fear in her eyes.

Evelynne gently stroked Ally's face. "You don't have to worry about that for a while," she reassured her lover. "The ultimate decision is up to you and the Hall of Nobles as a whole. They can Revoke your right through a system of votes. Or you can simply choose to refuse the Crown. In either case, that will be a few years from now at the very earliest. So for now you can just enjoy being engaged. You're not having second thoughts, are you?"

Ally sighed and drew Evelynne close to her again. "A few," she admitted finally. "But it's just—it's all happened so fast and the way that I'm in the middle of public scrutiny all the time now . . . and then the whole King issue . . . But being engaged to you? Loving you? Not at all. Sometimes I wish—I wish we were just a couple of normal women, with normal lives and normal

chapter thirty three

jobs. But then, we wouldn't be who we are now, would we? I wouldn't be me, you wouldn't be you and who knows whether we'd actually even like each other?"

"I understand that," Evelynne said, running a soothing hand up and down Ally's back. "I'd like to think that we would still be as much in love as we are right now, but who knows? I know it's been hard for you and I promise I'll do whatever I can to protect you when the world gets to be too much. I also want you to know that whether you decide to become my King or not, I will accept your decision. For the record, though, I think you'd make a great Diarch."

Ally chuckled. "You know, whenever I hear someone talking about me becoming King I get this flash of me sitting on the Throne in full drag. Goatee, oiled moustache, gold chains, the works."

Evelynne laughed. "Have you ever done that?"

"No. Well, there was a time when I was about twelve or so when I dressed up as a man for Hallowe'en. There was a time when cross-dressing for Hallowe'en was the 'thing' to do. I was desperate to do anything I could to fit in. You know, it's ironic. Cross-dressing to fit in with popular society."

Evelynne was giggling uncontrollably. "Oh, I can just picture you. I have just got to see photos. I'll bet your mother has some stashed away somewhere."

"No, she doesn't," Ally said quickly. Too quickly.

"Of course, dear," Evelynne soothed. "They were undoubtedly thrown out years ago." She knew no such thing had happened. "But when people talk about you being King, I get an image of one of the regal ancient Egyptian kings, who happened to be a woman. Their law explicitly stated that only a man could become king. So a few enterprising females took the logical course of legally identifying themselves as men. They wore false beards and were referred to using exclusively male pronouns in official records. So there actually is a precedent of female kings in history."

"Well, I'm just glad you didn't have to use that argument in my case. Hallowe'en costumes aside, I really have no interest in dressing up as a man."

"I'm glad. Although, I think you'd look incredibly sexy in one of those plaid shirts. And nothing else."

"Well, actually, I have a few at my house in Outremer." Ally blushed.

"Really. It seems we might have to make a little stop on our way back to the Summer Palace once we've dealt with all the rest of the Conclave business."

"Um, okay. So what happens now?"

"Well, now that the minor matter of who I may and may not marry is out of the way, if not out of people's minds, the Conclave can get down to the business of actually running the country. New laws and amendments will be proposed and debated; old laws struck down; reports on the status of the economy, environment, military, education system, research and development, agriculture and whatever else anyone happens to have an interest in. And a few things they don't; censures and commendations for Nobles and citizens; foreign affairs meetings. You know. All the niggling little details."

"Ah. That stuff. You know, I noticed that the American delegation wasn't looking too happy," Ally mused.

Evelynne smirked. "No, they weren't, were they? You and I have effectively taken the entire spotlight off them and their first state visit here in thirty years. Now, though, every reporter in the States is only asking what the President's response is to knowing that the next ruler of his biggest competitor in world affairs is a lesbian. So far he hasn't said anything."

"My heart bleeds for him," Ally said wryly. "I think someone needs to smack him upside the head."

"Are you volunteering?"

"Sure. Just give me a line of sight and he won't know what hit him. Literally. Of course, if you decided to project into his mind, you could make him think he was going nuts."

"I think he has enough voices in his head already," Evelynne said with a smirk. "Okay, enough of that. We have to meet his Secretary of State in a few hours. Actually, he's not so bad. Even though I don't agree with most of his ideas, I always got the feeling that at least he's honest. Maybe this time you can let me know whether he really is or not."

"Oh, I see how this is going to go," Ally said with a smile in her voice. "You just want to marry me for my mind."

Chapter Thirty Four

"Thanks a lot, Boss. You have no idea how much this means to me. To us."

"Taldas, stop it," Ally protested as she led Taldas Islin, Laura McGarrity, Marjorie Melan and Rina bel'Oman along the hallway, accompanied by her now ever-present Guard detail. "I do know how much this means to you. Evelynne wants to meet you guys as well. God only knows why." She smirked.

"Yes?" Rina asked hesitantly, her eyes wide. "She knows us? She knows who we are?"

"Of course. I had to tell her so that she would know who to have beheaded." Rina's eyes widened even further. "Relax, Rina, I'm just kidding. It was a joke. Really, she's interested in the work we've been doing at Aztlan."

"She's interested in you, you mean," Laura said dryly. "And you just happen to work at Aztlan."

Ally blushed. "Well, yeah. But she is interested in you, really."

"Not as much as she is in you," Laura teased. "And really, Boss, you should do something about that blush. You are marrying her, after all."

"I'll do my best. I'm sorry this will be such a short meeting," Ally continued, "but with all of the stuff happening this afternoon, the King and Queen and Evelynne don't really have a lot of time. I'll see about maybe arranging something more once the Conclave is over. She wants to come out and see the site some time soon."

"Well, we'll have to be sure to clean the place up for her," Taldas joked. "Can't have Her Highness tripping over broken statuary with her Royal feet." He paused. "Although *you're* going to have Royal feet one of these days." He shook his head as if to clear it. "That's still weird. No offence, Boss, but I just can't picture you as the Royal type."

"That's okay. I really can't see myself that way, either. Well, here we are." They stopped just outside a set of elegantly carved doors.

Sir Arthur was waiting with three other Guards. "Lady Alleandre," he said formally.

"Sir Arthur, this is Taldas Islin, Rina bel'Oman, Marjorie Melan and Laura McGarrity. My team."

The Guard nodded his head. "*Isi, eni,* if you would stand here for a moment?" He gestured to the side and one of his Guardsmen produced a handheld scanner. "We just need to scan you."

"Sorry about this," Ally apologised. "Everyone's a little jumpy right now and this meeting is kind of last minute."

"No problem," Taldas said, submitting willingly to the search. The scan quickly turned up his pocket change, watch and cellular phone. Searches of Rina, Marjorie and Laura turned up similar items.

"That's quite a PDA," Sir Arthur commented as he inspected Laura's handheld device.

"What can I say?" Laura said wryly. "I'm a technogeek. I have a friend in the computer industry in the States and he's always sending me the latest stuff they're working on. This model is one of his latest projects. It's not *quite* illegal for me to have it, since it's past the prototype stage, but it isn't in full production yet, so I'd appreciate a little discretion about who you talk to about it."

"Of course, Ma'am," the Guard said, running an eye over the PDA once more before handing it back to its owner. "Well, everything seems in order."

"Thanks, Sir Arthur," Ally said, smiling. Turning to the door, she opened it and led the way into an informal sitting room, where Princess Evelynne, King Jad, Queen Cleo and Lord Thomas were seated.

The three Royals stood as their guests entered and Ally walked immediately over to her fiancée, stopping to give her a brief kiss and whispered greeting. Behind her, Taldas, Rina and Marjorie bowed deeply. Laura paused a moment before doing the same.

Turning back to her guests, Ally introduced them.

"Pleased to meet you all," King Jad rumbled moving forward to shake their hands. His greeting and actions were echoed a moment later by Queen Cleo and Lord Thomas smiled and waved a greeting but did not rise from his comfortable chair.

"And, of course, this is Princess Evelynne," Ally continued.

"Of course," Taldas murmured, casting twinkling eyes in Ally's direction. "Your Highness," he greeted, bowing over her hand.

"I'm really glad to meet you all," Evelynne said. "Please, come and sit down. I'm afraid we only have half an hour." Once everyone was seated she leaned forward conspiratorially. "So tell me, what's Ally *really* like when she's not around all us stuffy Nobles? No, wait, let me guess. It's all wild parties, drinking and carousing, right? Dancing girls and staying up 'till all hours?" Her warm, informal manner let them all relax a little.

chapter thirty four

"Why, of course, Your Highness," Taldas agreed. "Why, the number of times we've had to pour her into bed in the wee hours of the morning . . ." He shook his head sadly while the subject of this blatant untruth made inarticulate sounds of protest and everyone else stifled outright laughter.

"Of course," Lord Thomas intoned gravely, shaking his head in sorrow. "I knew she was a troublemaker from the first time I set eyes on her."

"I knew it," Evelynne proclaimed in mock triumph. "I knew she couldn't be as decent as she always appears to be. But that's all right." She patted Ally's red face. "I love you anyway."

Ally sighed. "Damnit, you guys were supposed to be on my side. You're all fired, the lot of you."

❧   ❧   ❧   ❧   ❧

"Sorry we had to drag you in today, Chorus," Colonel MaecDonaeld of the Guard Cryptography Unit apologised as he led the young man through the perpetually busy Communications Office. It was even busier today, with the heightened security surrounding the Conclave. "I know you'd rather be with your friend, Lady Alleandre. Tell her congratulations from me when you get the chance, okay?"

"Sure thing, Padraig," Chorus agreed. "Don't worry about bringing me in. I'll have plenty of time to tease—I mean, congratulate Ally later. She'll still be engaged tomorrow, which is more than we could have been sure of yesterday. Besides, she and Princess Evelynne are probably still making goo-goo eyes at each other and won't even notice I'm not around."

Padraig chuckled and shook his head, still unused to the young man's irreverent attitude towards such august personages. "I wouldn't be surprised. I remember when my wife and I first got engaged. Well, I remember *her*, I just don't remember much else."

"I'll take your word for it. Since I've never been engaged and don't plan to be for quite some time." Reaching his desk, Chorus sat down and logged on to his computer. While he waited for the myriad security checks to process, he asked, "So, what's the news?"

MaecDonaeld took a seat opposite and leaned back. "We intercepted a couple of new transmissions from Unknown Thirty Seven late last night."

Chorus raised his brows as the screen before him cleared and he immediately opened the new files waiting for him. "Last night? Why didn't someone come and get me then? You know it helps if I see it as soon as possible after transmission." His eyes were already scanning the lines of encoded gibberish scrolling across the screen.

"Sorry," the Colonel apologised again, "but we've been following up on a rash of anonymous tips that have been coming in since midnight. The entire staff has been going non-stop and someone only remembered to check that tap an hour ago."

"That's okay," Chorus dismissed. "I know you're always busy." He continued scanning the lines of code. There was a pattern there and he could almost see it, almost see the rules of grammar, syntax and vocabulary that made up any language. All a code did was add another layer of complexity to the underlying meaning. But even the most intricate code was still based on certain self-consistent laws and rules of translation, and as such could be treated as any other language. Still, it remained maddeningly out of reach, like an itch at the back of his brain.

"So, Nostradamus, you picking up anything?" Padraig asked.

Chorus frowned, then sighed. "No, nothing. It's there, I know it, but it's hideously complex. I would love to meet whoever created this thing. Although I don't know if I'd shake his hand or punch him in the face. Maybe both. Still, since I'm here I'll hang around a while, maybe try a few different visualisations." He smiled at his companion ruefully. "This was not how I was planning on spending my day."

"Well, I appreciate it," MaecDonaeld said, rising. "Yell if you need anything. I've got to get back to tracing down bogus leads. Of course, it'll be the one that we *don't* track down that will blow up in our faces. I tell you, it's like someone is deliberately trying to drive us nuts."

"Will do. And I–" Chorus broke off abruptly, his face going utterly and completely still.

Later on, he would never be able to pinpoint exactly what MaecDonaeld had said to provide the final clue, the key piece of context that suddenly and unexpectedly allowed his Savant mind, operating on a level unknown to most humans, to unlock the final solution to the code. All he knew was that at that moment, the answer seemed to unfold gently in his mind, although with a suddenness that made it seem like an explosion. Whirling back to his monitor, he scanned the lines of code again and this time instead of gibberish, it was as though he was reading a simple e-mail. And what he read made his black skin pale noticeably.

"Oh shit." It was almost a whisper.

"What?" Padraig asked, startled by the sudden movement and expletive.

Chorus ignored him. He was too busy calling up all the past intercepted messages, their secrets now completely open to him, skimming through them as fast as he was able and by the time he was done he was an alarming ash-grey colour.

Chapter Thirty Four

Looking up at the Colonel, he said without preamble, "I need to talk to the General. Now." The urgency in his voice was unmistakable.

MaecDonaeld hesitated. "Are you sure? It might take a—"

"No. Now," Chorus said flatly. "Do whatever you need to. What's your highest priority alert?"

"What? Er, Alert Code Deluge. Imminent Invasion."

"Good. Use it."

"What? You don't joke about this. Abuse of Deluge nets me five years hard time. I can't just—"

"Damnit, Padraig, this is *not* an abuse. Do you understand me? This is real and we don't have time to confirm it independently."

This time it was Colonel MaecDonaeld's turn to pale, as the meaning of Chorus' words sunk in. Without further delay he grabbed the phone on the desk and punched the large red button that connected directly to General Danun's office. "This is MaecDonaeld, Communications and Cryptography, 985345. I need the General, now!" The person on the other end began to object, but he overrode them. "Alert Code Deluge. I say again, Alert Code Deluge."

There was a gasp from the other end, echoed by several others in the room as they overheard the Colonel's declaration. There was a click on the line as he was transferred directly to the General herself.

"Damnit, this had better be good," Danun snarled into the phone, obviously stressed to the limit by the demands of co-ordinating security for the Conclave.

"General, Colonel MaecDonaeld, ComCrypt. I am reporting a possible Alert Code Deluge. The information is credible and current."

"Who?" Danun asked, her tone going from peeved to businesslike in an instant.

"Civilian Chorus Tladi, Ma'am. He claims to have broken the code." There was no need for him to explain which code he was talking about.

"Put him on," the General ordered. Padraig handed the phone to Chorus immediately. "Talk to me, Chorus."

"If I understand this right, there are already guerrilla fighters in the city and possibly in the Palace and Conclave Hall itself. Although they claim to be HBLA, they're actually foreign soldiers. I don't know from where, because it's never explicitly stated. Actually, the entire HBLA is just a front for this group and is not a domestic terrorist organisation at all. But they're well armed and their mission is to eliminate the Nobility, including the Royal family. Execution orders have already been given."

"Chorus, I need some kind of confirmation. I can't give the go-ahead for the kind of action you're looking for on just one source's information. Not even yours."

"Listen, does the access code X-Ray Tango Four Seven Two Bravo Zulu Eight Six mean anything to you?"

"Where did you hear that code?" the General asked, her voice deadly.

"It's in one of the latest messages. The soldiers are supposed to use it to gain access to the Palace."

"*Tae'e-haka!*" Danun swore. "That's a high priority access code dedicated to the Royal Guard. I'm coming down and activating Code Deluge." Without waiting for a reply, the General hung up.

She flipped open a small, nearly invisible panel set into the surface of her desk. Within was a single large red button. It, or something like it, had been a permanent fixture of every Guard Director's office since before the Second World War and in all that time it had only been pressed twice. The button was connected to a simple transmitter that would send a signal to a receiver in every military base, Naval ship, Guard post, intelligence agency, police station and emergency service in the country. It meant one thing: Imminent invasion. Prepare for possible martial law.

The first time the button had been pressed had been shortly after the outbreak of World War Two, when the Italian navy had attempted a sneak attack on the Atlantlan islands. Alerted by covert intelligence sources, the hastily assembled Royal Atlantlan Navy had managed to ambush and eliminate the attacking ships.

The second time had been during the North Atlantic Standoff in the early 1970's, when the United States had tried to blockade the nation, ostensibly as a way to force social reform in the Kingdom. The blockade had been in place for less than two days before the combined diplomatic pressure of nations on both sides of the ocean had finally forced the Americans to withdraw–although officially the blockade was still in place, only pulled back to a "less aggressive" distance of one thousand kilometres.

The third time the button was pressed, it worked perfectly. The signal went out on its dedicated, top-secret frequency and throughout the country alarms began to wail as startled security personnel scrambled to respond.

Unfortunately for them, the frequency was not as secret as the Guard had believed and the intended receivers were not the only ones tuned to it. In military installations, police stations and Guard posts throughout the Kingdom other, non-official receivers also heard the call. These were not connected to alarms, however. They were connected to detonators and what should have been the most secure signal in the spectrum set them off.

chapter thirty four

Nearly simultaneous with the sirens came the explosions as the small but incredibly powerful charges hidden in otherwise innocuous objects detonated. Not all of them exploded. Some were too well shielded by their location or environment to receive the signal. Some had degraded over the time—years in some cases—since they had been installed. A few simply malfunctioned, either through damage or imperfect construction. But those accounted for less than ten per cent of the total, which left over six thousand bombs to do their deadly work. None of the people they were aimed at knew they were there until it was far too late.

In a police station in Outremer, a coffee maker exploded, instantly killing a quarter of the force and starting a fire that soon threatened to consume a whole city block.

On the aircraft carrier *RANS Enki*, a heating unit produced a blast so strong that it ruptured the hull and only the quick actions of the ship's engineer, sacrificing himself by sealing the emergency hatches from the inside, prevented her sinking.

In a Guard post in the outskirts of Jamaz, the microwave that Major o-Miltay was using to reheat his late lunch was next to a small toaster oven and the interference it produced was the only thing that scrambled the signal enough to prevent the explosive planted in the oven from detonating.

In the main armoury of the Ru'en Army base, the blast from an air conditioning unit installed only a few months before created a chain reaction in the stockpiles of ammunition and explosives stored there, ultimately destroying half the base and flattening buildings in the nearby town.

Similar scenes were played out with incredible variety, throwing the entire nation into chaos in a matter of seconds. In a few cases, "tainted" objects that had been meant to go to military or security locations had inevitably made their way to civilian homes and businesses, and more people died as their own tools turned on them.

And in the heart of the Common Guard Headquarters, the signal was received by a small device expertly concealed in the computer of General Danun's secretary. The resulting explosion destroyed four offices, killing everyone inside. Including General Danun.

ත ත ත ත ත

"But what does Alleandre think?" Queen Cleo asked, looking in Ally's direction.

They had been discussing theories related to the actual construction of the ancient city of Aztlan and Rina had been explaining her own theory on advanced metallurgical and construction techniques. Everyone had been listening and adding their own input with varying degrees of interest.

"Oh, now the *Boss'* theory," Taldas interjected, "is a little more, er, controversial. She thinks that the ancient Atlantlans utilised some kind of collective psychic power to help them move those huge stones."

Ally blushed as a number of questioning looks were directed at her.

"I never explicitly said 'psychic power'," she protested, carefully avoiding the eyes of anyone who knew her secret. "I just said that the properly focused collective will of any group allows it to do things the individuals can't. Now whether that includes displays of unconventional ability, or just a drastic increase in efficiency is open to debate."

"Ah yes," King Jad said. "Your–what did you call it? Emergent spiritualism? I seem to recall discussing the parting of the Red Sea with you in that context."

"Yes, Sire. While my personal belief is that psychogenic ability is a real phenomenon–"

She broke off suddenly as a sensation suddenly rippled across her consciousness and she realised it was coming from Sir Arthur, standing discreetly in the corner. Her eyes snapped to the Guard, taking in his unfocused gaze, obviously fixed on something the rest of them could not see. It only lasted a moment and then, with an almost dreamlike motion, his hand reached for the gun resting on his hip. Sir Adun, the King's personal Guard, and Dame Ilanna, Queen Cleo's, saw the movement and reacted as well, mouths opening to ask a question.

Before they could, however, Arthur bellowed, "Moebius! Zulu! Zulu! Zulu! I say again, Moebius Zulu!" Caught by his collar-mounted mike, his words echoed to every Guard in the Conclave Hall and Royal Palace and throughout both buildings Guardsmen reacted with varying degrees of alacrity as the codewords were recognised. Adun and Ilanna reacted with barely a millisecond of hesitation, displaying the kind of instantaneous response that had led to their Royal assignments.

Zulu: Subject in imminent physical danger. Use of deadly force authorised.
Moebius: All Guardsmen, all subjects.
Moebius Zulu: Widespread imminent threat to all protectees within range. Implication: Large scale assault in progress. Full combat alert.

Although it was part of every Guard's training, Moebius Zulu had never before been enacted in reality. It was that training that gave them a chance, giving them a full ten seconds to respond before the chime of Alert Deluge sounded over their radios and the explosions began. Ten seconds after *that*, realising with the premature detonation of their surprise blasts that there was no longer any need for stealth, hundreds of well-armed, well-trained soldiers–heretofore disguised in Atlantlan military uniforms–attacked.

chapter thirty four

The group in the sitting room only knew that three highly trained Guards were suddenly interposing themselves between their wards and the rest of the room, bustling them away from the windows. Two of those Guards did not know exactly why they were suddenly on high alert, but Adun and Ilanna had worked with Sir Arthur long enough and trusted him enough to take any of his declarations on faith.

The rest of the room's occupants reacted with varying degrees of bewilderment as the tension suddenly skyrocketed. Ally abruptly found herself separated from her fiancée by a very forbidding Sir Arthur. A moment later, the door burst open as the rest of the five Guard details—the King's, Queen's, Heir's, Duke's and Heir Consort's—who had been on the other side of the door burst in, weapons drawn and seeking threats.

"Status, Sir?" Major Nixon was the first to ask as she took up an alert position by the doors, opposite one of Lord Thomas' Guards.

Before any of the Master Guards could reply, they all winced sharply as the alarm of Alert Deluge sounded in their earbuds. The drawn-out wail was carefully designed to be the exact frequency required to revive even the most comatose Guard. Simultaneous with the alarm, a low rumble filled the air, followed several seconds later by a vibration in the floor. Ally risked a glance out the window, her eyes widening as she saw a column of flame and black smoke erupt over part of the distant Conclave Hall.

Hands went to concealed controls as the Guards acknowledged the signal, but they made no move to inquire after details from Headquarters. Deluge assumed that friendly communication channels could be compromised by hostile forces, automatically minimising radio traffic.

"Sire, we are at Alert Deluge," Sir Adun announced, his eyes never ceasing to scan the room, as if he expected gun-toting commandos to burst out of the walls. "We need to get you to Elysium."

Elysium was the codename for a specially constructed hidden bunker, from which the King and Queen could take control of the island once again. There were actually several such bunkers scattered throughout the islands and no less than three in various locations under the Palace and Conclave Hall.

"Closest?" Sir Arthur asked brusquely.

"Kappa-Four," Dame Ilanna replied. "Section Forty-four."

"Good," Sir Adun said. "We'll move together to the arms locker in Section Twenty-eight, then split. Odin will go to Kappa-Four." He indicated his own team. "Hera and Daedelus will proceed to Kappa-Three." Dame Ilanna and the Master of Lord Thomas' Guard both nodded. "Phoenix and Sorceress will move towards Lambda-One." Sir Arthur and Captain el-Jahir signalled their agreement.

"Civilians, Sir?" Nixon asked, her eyes flicking to the other people, who were looking more frightened by the moment.

Sir Adun hesitated. "You, with me." He pointed to Marjorie. "You, go with Hera and Daedelus. That's Queen Cleo and Lord Thomas." Rina hesitantly moved over to them, reluctantly letting go of Taldas' hand. "You two, with the Heir and Consort." Taldas and Laura hurried to Ally and Evelynne. The King's Guard looked at them sternly. "Keep your heads down and do *exactly* what you're told," he ordered. "You are *not* a priority." The words were harsh but true. Each Guard detail's primary focus was the safety of their immediate ward. Civilians took a distant second place.

"Ready?" Adun asked. He keyed his mike. "Point teams, move out."

Two Guards opened the doors and went through, guns drawn and ready to fire, inching down the corridor outside, taking cover behind statues and decorations as they went. When they had secured a length of hallway, one radioed back. "Go," she said.

The remaining Guards hustled their wards out of the room and the small group–thirteen Guards and nine civilians–began its journey towards the hope of safety.

More than a little frightened, Ally moved closer to her lover and caught her attention with a raised eyebrow and touch to her own temple.

'Ally? Are you all right?' Evelynne asked, her own worry washing over the link.

'I don't know. What's going on? I know that Sir Arthur had a flash of something, and that's usually bad. And I saw smoke out the window.'

'Wait a moment, I'm going to ask him.' There was a moment of disconnection, as though Evelynne had put her "on hold" while she switched to another "line". A moment later she came back. *'It's an invasion,'* she said, shock and disbelief echoing through her thoughts. *'He knows somehow that there are enemy forces in the Palace and Conclave Hall itself. Every Guardsman is on alert. He doesn't know what caused the explosions, though.'* She paused, listening to some silent conversation. *'And he wants me to stay out of his head. Apparently it's too distracting. Although he wants to know whether you can sense anything. Central communications are down, so he doesn't know where the enemy is.'*

'Damn, why didn't I think of that? Can you keep me on track for a minute? I've never done this while trying to walk before.'

Without bothering to answer, Evelynne tightened her hold on Ally's arm as they continued to creep forward, ready to keep her balanced while the Adept was focused elsewhere.

Ally slowly slipped into altered consciousness. While remote viewing was never easy for her, this time it was especially difficult, as the effort to

chapter thirty four

remain walking, the constant worry and fear, and the sounds of the people moving around her conspired to disrupt her concentration. Finally, with disconcerting slowness, she felt her awareness expand outwards, no longer relying on her mundane senses to provide information. As always, the alien sense of being able to see everything simultaneously caused confusion, as her sensory processing ability, trained only to deal with a single perspective, sought to handle the input overload.

Vaguely aware that her body was beginning to shake with the strain, Ally cast her mind forward, beyond the vicinity of their little party, up the corridor and further than the conventional sight of the Guards. Her sight was limited in range even under the best circumstances, but she was still able to see at least fifty metres ahead, past where the hallway took a sharp turn. At first she was relieved to find the way clear, but then a group of people seemed to burst abruptly into view. Although they were wearing Atlantlan military uniforms, Ally somehow knew they were not friendly. Tightly focussed hostility rolled off them in waves.

The suddenness and shock of the revelation caused her tenuous hold to snap, catapulting her consciousness back into her body with a speed that had her clutching Evelynne's arm desperately as she retched helplessly. She ignored the attention of those nearest to her, striving to control her rebelling stomach and speak to Evelynne at the same time. *'Soldiers,'* she gasped mentally. *'In the corridor ahead. Not friendly. Ten or twelve, I'm not sure.'*

'I just told him,' Evelynne said. "Are you all right?" She kept her voice low, stroking Ally's back comfortingly. Rina hesitantly patted Ally's arm on the other side.

Ally nodded shakily as she straightened, trying to ignore the smell of vomit.

The procession, which had halted when Ally had begun to retch, prepared to move forward, but paused when Sir Arthur held them back. He appeared to be having some kind of discussion with the other Guards in a coded sign language. Ally couldn't decipher what was being said, but the signals for "ahead", "twelve" and "weapons" were easy enough to comprehend. Sir Adun and Dame Ilanna looked as though they desperately wanted to question Sir Arthur on the source of his information, but valiantly restrained their questions.

Turning back to the civilians, Sir Arthur said in a low tone, "Get against the walls and stay down. We have company coming." He fixed a piercing stare on Ally. "Stay close to her." There was no question which "her" he was referring to.

Ally nodded firmly, wrapping her arms around Evelynne and hunkering down behind a large planter. Lord Thomas was helped down stiffly and painfully beside her and she did her best to interpose herself between him and the corridor as well.

Firmly ignoring her lingering nausea, she cleared her mind, focussing her thoughts and then channelling power into them, wrapping her thoughts around herself, enhancing her aura, just as she had done nearly a year ago in Marseilles. As she felt the protection settle into place with an almost audible snap, she had a moment to lament that she had yet to discover the trick for wrapping a similar field around another person. Thrusting aside the doubts, she carefully moved so that she was between Evelynne and as much of the exposed expanse of corridor as possible.

It was just in time, as the first of the enemy soldiers of the "Hy Braseal Liberation Army" came around the corner, alert but confident. That confidence proved their undoing. They had been expecting to encounter mostly light, if determined, resistance, counting on the surprise explosions and suddenness of their attack to confuse any defenders, especially ones who didn't even know they were there.

They had not anticipated running head on into five of the most highly trained units of the Atlantlan Guard—thirteen of the best warriors the Islands had to offer, fully alerted to their presence by the incomparable vision of an Adeptus Major. While the Guard had only small sidearms, they were able to hold their fire until it could be most effective, turning what had been a scouting mission by the enemy into a total ambush. The initial surprise was complete and five of the invaders went down before they knew what hit them, all with fatal wounds. Another three were more lightly wounded, staggering back from the incoming fire with cries of shock and pain.

However, the enemy force possessed a full arsenal of submachine guns, assault rifles and high-calibre weapons. Even with eight down there were still four left to hastily return fire at the Atlantlans. Though they were almost completely surprised, they were still professional soldiers. Sir Adun's two subordinates went down nearly simultaneously, one dead from a bullet in her head and the other dropped by wounds in his shoulder and leg. One of Dame Ilanna's Guards took a barrage of bullets square in the chest and even though his body armour prevented them from penetrating, it could not fully disperse the kinetic energy of the impact, which was enough to pulverise his rib cage. Major Nixon nearly dropped her gun as a bullet passed through the flesh of her upper arm, but she gritted her teeth, switched to the other hand and continued firing, taking down her opponent with a shot through the throat.

chapter thirty four

Ally winced as she felt a ricochet enter her aura, nearly sighing with relief as the psychokinetic field robbed the projectile of energy, bringing it to a halt millimetres from her skin. Her lower back and shoulder ached in sympathetic memory of a similar experience almost a year before and she had a moment to give thanks that these weapons lacked the awesome power of the sniper rifle that had penetrated her defences in Marseilles.

Despite the initial ambush, the tide was turning against the defenders, as superior firepower took down three more Guards and Ally could hear one of the attackers calling for backup. Shouts from the other side of the enemy soldiers' positions left her fearing the worst. She pressed Evelynne more tightly to her. However, the burst of automatic gunfire that erupted was not directed at the beleaguered Guards, but at the enemy, cutting them down from behind. The fierce firefight continued for a few more excruciatingly long seconds before abruptly ceasing.

The Guards didn't let up on their vigilance for a moment. "Identify!" Sir Adun yelled down the corridor.

"Gamma Six-Five," a voice shouted back, and a slight waver in it could be heard, despite the owner's obvious struggle to suppress it. "Blue Two One Delta. Sigma Three."

Sir Adun looked at Sir Arthur and raised an eyebrow in question. The confirmed presence of enemy soldiers within the Conclave and Palace grounds themselves was an unprecedented occurrence. All the Guards had come to the same conclusion: even with the enemy dressed as Atlantlan soldiers, the infiltration could only have occurred with inside help. That meant that all access and identification codes and communications were considered compromised, and all contacts potentially hostile.

Ally saw Sir Arthur close his eyes briefly, then was surprised to feel the Guard awkwardly reaching out with his mind, the sensation brushing lightly against her own awareness, but not concentrated on her. It was surprisingly similar to what she would feel when her mother used her empathic sense. *He's an empath too?* she asked herself. Intrigued, she cautiously extended her own empathic senses, feeling forwards to the unknown people ahead. Focusing on the nearest mind, she briefly sensed fear, caution, determination, outrage, battle lust and nausea in a nearly overwhelming rush of emotion. But no focussed hostility or active aggression.

Opening her eyes to find Evelynne looking up at her fearfully, she managed a somewhat reassuring smile. Out of the corner of her eye she saw that Sir Arthur had apparently made the same discoveries that she had and he nodded at Sir Adun. The Master of the King's Guard looked at him oddly for a moment, but then shouted, "Alpha One. Approach! Keep your hands in the air!" Despite the assurances of a Guard he trusted implicitly, he was still taking no chances. However, Sir Arthur also appeared to be less than completely convinced by what his extended senses told him, maintaining a highly vigilant attitude. Ally could only approve, since the life he was primarily protecting was her lover's.

"Understood," the unseen voice called back and there was a combination of surprise and relief in it. "Five individuals. We're coming out."

The unknowns came into view, walking in single file with their weapons held high above their heads. In the front was a Guardsman in the uniform of the Palace Guard and Ally knew enough of Guard insignia to recognise him as a Corporal. His uniform was torn and bloodstained, and there was a long gash down the side of his face, which was white with pain and stress. Behind him came a second Corporal, her uniform in much the same condition, although she appeared relatively unhurt, and two Privates walked behind. Another officer, this one in a naval uniform bearing the insignia of a Captain, was the last to appear.

Sir Adun recognised the newcomers, and signalled the Guards to relax their vigilance. They went back to covering the hallway ahead. "Corporal, Captain," the leader of the Guards greeted as the newly arrived combatants sought cover near him. "Good to see you. Report. Where's the rest of your team?"

"Sir, Corporal Rupert Gyrus, Palace Guard. This is Captain Benson." The blonde Captain nodded. Her eyes widened as she recognised the King, nearly hidden behind two Guardsmen several metres away. "We're all that's left, Sir," Gyrus continued. "We were assigned to escort the Captain to the Conclave Hall. She was supposed to talk to the Defence Council." He shook his head, his eyes haunted. "They came out of nowhere, Sir. Sergeant al-Hamman never knew what hit him. Iglesias and I only survived because we were the rearguard. We managed to get Captain Benson down. We wanted to resist them, Sir, but there were too many. Corporal Ramaani covered us while we retreated. He didn't make it. We were on our way to Rendezvous Seven when we heard you."

Sir Adun swore. "How many were there, Corporal?"

"I'm not sure, Sir, but at least twenty five or thirty. We heard other engagements, so there are more around."

"Right. Corporal... Iglesias? You've just been drafted into the Queen's Guard. Gyrus, you're with the King's Guard now." Sir Adun looked at the Corporal's bleeding head wound. "Can you still fight?"

"Yes, Sir," Gyrus replied instantly. "A bullet hit a pillar I was taking cover behind. A piece of marble did this."

chapter thirty four

"Good. Captain, you are with the Heir and Consort. You two, you're with the Duke." The Guard looked down the hallway. "We're going to strip the enemy of their weapons and then keep moving to the weapons locker. I want body armour for the protectees."

"Unwise," Sir Arthur said, shaking his head. "Whoever they are, they've managed to get a very large force into the Palace grounds themselves. And it wasn't through a frontal assault. The only way to do that so stealthily is if they have fiendishly good intelligence. Which means—"

"Which means that they probably know the location of every weapons locker in both buildings." The superior Guard swore again. "And they know that's where we'll be heading. Okay, change in plan. Screw the weapons locker. We're cutting straight to the nearest Elysium. They haven't got in there, I don't care who they are."

Elysium and its defences were a completely autonomous division of the Atlantlan military, one that answered only to the King and Queen. It was they who ultimately decided, with the assistance of Elysium Guard advisors, access codes and procedures. Not even the Master of the King's Guard could enter without a member of the Royal family, since *anyone* attempting to enter would be killed without hesitation. The Guard units protecting the bunkers literally lived in them for months at a time, in a manner similar to the nuclear missile silos in other countries. They were the final line of defence for the Atlantlan Royalty.

The plan set, Sir Adun nodded to the other Guards and they moved forward with practised ease, some providing cover while the others quickly stripped the fallen soldiers of their weapons and wounds were swiftly and efficiently dressed. Major Nixon, her wounded arm preventing her from carrying one of the captured assault rifles, was reassigned to a position closer to the princess.

Ally looked up at the Guard from where she was sitting, Evelynne's face pressed into her shoulder. "I'm sorry," she whispered to the Major. "I wish I could have . . ." She trailed off helplessly.

"Don't be," Nixon replied in a low voice. "*She* is the reason we do this." She indicated the princess, who was crying softly into the crook of Ally's neck. "You save your talents for her." She shifted her newly bandaged arm, wincing. "This is what I was trained to do."

Ally nodded, but didn't say anything more. In her hand she held the bullet that only the power of a thought had prevented from seriously wounding her. It was still warm to the touch and she carefully slipped it into a pocket. She turned her attention to the sobbing woman in her arms. "Evy? Are you . . . hurt?"

Evelynne sniffled a few more times, and then looked up at Ally with watery eyes. "No, I don't think so. I'm just—I was so scared." She wiped her eyes with her sleeve. "You probably think I'm a wimp."

"Hardly," Ally said gently. "I'm terrified myself."

"You don't look like it."

"I've had a bit more experience in situations like these. Well, not exactly like this, but . . ."

Understanding dawned in Evelynne's eyes. "When you were doing your Guardian Angel impression with the drug raids."

"Yeah, that. And a couple of other times I've been way too close to guns going off. I'll tell you about it. Later." The implied promise that they'd both survive to share the tales was clear.

"I'll hold you to that. I'm beginning to realise just how many of these stories you haven't told me." Evelynne pulled Ally's head down to kiss her hard. "Later," she promised. Taking charge of her emotions and reactions once more, the princess turned to Laura and Lord Thomas, who were huddled nearby. "How are you holding up?"

"I'm getting too old for this kind of nonsense," the Duke replied, his face twisted in discomfort as his aged body protested the abuse it had been receiving. "But I'll get by."

"I've got him," Laura said. She looked up to where Sir Adun was signalling the rest of their group. "I think we're moving again."

The group set out again, in much the same manner as before, but with more speed as they raced for refuge. It was still slow going, however, as they now had wounded to move. In the distance they could hear sporadic gunfire and explosions, signalling that the battle for the control of the Palace and Conclave Hall was still ongoing, but the hallways remained remarkably clear of other personnel. Twice they came across the signs of combat, spent shell casings and pockmarked walls indicating the conflicts that had taken place. Occasional bodies also marked the halls, both Guards and uniformed soldiers, although how many of the latter were actually enemies was impossible to tell. Thankfully, only two civilians, Palace servants by their attire, appeared to have been killed in the fighting.

The hallways all seemed to blur into one another in Ally's mind as she inched ahead with her lover, her mind as open as possible to approaching threats ahead. It was too difficult to fully engage her remote sight, so she settled for opening her mind to the hostile emotions of the enemy, consciously blocking out the thoughts of her fellow refugees. It was still hard going and she could feel a massive headache building behind her eyes, but she persevered.

Chapter Thirty Four

Suddenly realising that they had stopped, Ally came back to her physical surroundings, shaking her head to clear it of the stray thoughts she had been picking up. There was a vague feeling of threat permeating the mental plane, but with the stress and alertness around her it was impossible to pin down. She looked up to see Major Nixon looking at her worriedly.

"Are you well, Your Ladyship?" the Guard asked.

Ally managed to smile wryly. "Define 'well'."

Nixon gave her a crooked grin in reply and even Evelynne couldn't hold back a strained chuckle. "Sir Arthur is asking you to come forward," the Guard continued. "There's a point up ahead that he would like your input on." She looked at Ally meaningfully.

"Okay," Ally agreed. She gently pried off the death grip Evelynne had on her arm, then leaned down and kissed her. "I'll be right back." She looked to Laura McGarrity. "Take care of her."

The secretary's face was solemn and there was an almost deadly light in her eyes. "I will," she promised, moving closer to lay a hand on the princess' shoulder.

"I'll be right back," Ally promised. With a last caress of her fiancée's cheek, she turned to make her way to where Sir Arthur and Sir Adun were crouched behind the cover of a large marble column, Major Nixon escorting her.

"What's up?" Ally asked in a low voice.

"I have informed Sir Adun about certain aspects of your abilities," Sir Arthur said without preamble. His expression was focused but mildly apologetic. "I'm sorry, but I didn't have much choice. We need you to tell us just what is waiting up there." He leaned out around the column to indicate the hallway junction ahead.

Ally glanced ahead herself and, even without any military training, could immediately see the concern. Five wide hallways radiated outwards from a common centre, a large, open area lit from above by a huge stained glass dome. Under other circumstances it would have been a lovely architectural feat, but right now the only thing on the minds of the Guards was its potential for a four-way ambush.

"We can get to Elysium through either of the two passages directly ahead," Sir Arthur continued quietly. "The problem is that we've been hearing fighting in this area and we don't know which one, if either, is clear." He shrugged. "That's where you come in."

Ally nodded. "Give me a moment." Ignoring Sir Adun's sceptical expression, she closed her eyes, trying to reach out with her perceptions once more. It took longer this time, the already difficult set of mental machinations made even harder by her growing fatigue and stress. Eventually, though, Ally felt the sight fall into place. She sent her consciousness ahead, seeking those who might threaten herself and her companions. The sight was oddly erratic, giving the impression that she was trying to watch a static-filled television picture, but she persevered, striving to maintain her focus through her growing headache.

She "turned" down the first corridor, her impressions of its physical characteristics both more and less real than her more mundane senses would have detected. The sheer volume of sensory data she was processing made her infinitely more aware of physical objects, while the radically alien method of sensing baffled her conscious mind's comprehension.

Ally didn't have time to dwell on the dichotomy, because only a few dozen metres down the hallway she saw soldiers. Lots of them. At least a dozen commandos dressed in Atlantlan uniforms, but radiating the predatory intent of the invading forces lay silently in wait, concealed behind whatever cover they could find. Cursing mentally, Ally sped her consciousness back to the junction and down the second branching hallway, only to find more soldiers waiting there. The final two corridors revealed even more. They all appeared alert, confident and well armed. Ally felt a heavy lead ball of dread form in her mind.

Pulling herself back to her waiting body, she focused once more on her conventional senses, shaking her head to clear the customary dizziness and wincing as the throbbing headache made itself very well known. "Soldiers," she rasped hoarsely, pressing her fingers to the middle of her forehead. "I don't know how many exactly, but it's at least fifty. They're in all the passages. There's no way we can–"

She broke off suddenly, her head whipping around to look back down the corridor where the rest of the group was waiting, drawn by a sudden spike of pain and terror lancing into her mind from a very familiar source.

"Ally!" *'Ally!'*

Everyone else's attention was also grabbed by the scream and they were stunned for a moment as they took in the improbable scene. For a brief, insane moment Ally thought that Lord Thomas was trying to attack Evelynne, who was being held from behind by the surprisingly strong form of Laura McGarrity. Then she realised that Evelynne was struggling ineffectually against the other woman, who was expertly keeping her off-balance. Major Nixon was lying on the floor, blood on her scalp. The Duke was attempting to pry the princess from Laura's arms, until she ended his rescue effort with a brutal kick to the chest, knocking him backwards and onto the floor. It was

chapter thirty four

an impressive manoeuvre, coming from a woman who was now using her captive as a human shield, held tight to her own body.

All of the Guards acted on instinct and training, multiple weapons being brought to bear on the two struggling women.

"Freeze!" Laura shouted, her eyes intent and focused, showing no fear despite the guns pointed in her direction. "Shoot and she dies!" Now Ally could see that she was holding something small and metallic to Evelynne's throat and for a moment thought that it was a knife, before she recognised the shape. Laura's ever-present PDA was now sporting a thin, razor-sharp needle protruding from the side. "This needle is filled with one of the deadliest neurotoxins known to man." Laura's eyes cut to the electronic device. "There isn't much, but it's enough to kill her within three seconds." She wiggled it slightly under Evelynne's chin. The princess had stopped struggling and was now looking at Ally with pleading, terrified eyes.

"Laura, what the fuck are you doing?" Ally asked desperately.

"What I'm doing," the erstwhile secretary said, inching down the corridor past the impotent Guards, who tracked her every move with dangerous, hungry eyes, "is walking down this corridor, where I will meet up with my friends who are waiting up ahead. Your Majesties—" Her voice was mocking. "—you will both follow me, unless you want to lose your Heir. Once we are all safe and sound we are going to go for a trip. So—" Laura's eyes went to the King and Queen, who were watching with fearful expressions. "—let's move. I'm going to go now. If you don't come along... Well, you may never know what happens to her."

Ally couldn't believe what she was seeing, and, judging from the expressions on Taldas', Rina's and Marjorie's faces, they couldn't either. This was *Laura*, their friend; the woman who kept their project running; who took their anti-American jokes in stride and countered with her own anti-Atlantlan ones; who patiently collated and organised Rina's notorious jumbles of data into something they could use; who was always able to find what they needed; who was always jotting down notes into her PDA, which she refused to let anyone else touch...

Ally opened her mind to the other woman, barely noticing the strain of bridging their two minds, desperate to know why this person whom she trusted was doing this. She didn't know what she'd find. Part of her was hoping to discover the chaotic thoughts of a serious mental condition, something that Laura couldn't control that was causing her to act so out of character. What she found was the opposite. Laura's thoughts were incredibly tight and structured, alertly but calmly keeping track of her surroundings, calculating possibilities, ready to react at any moment. There was a coldness to them, a lack of emotion, either fear or pleasure at how she'd apparently fooled everyone. There was no guilt, no feeling that the people around her were even *people*. Ally realised that the other woman *did* in fact have a serious mental problem: she was a sociopath. Even with that realisation came another: their minds had touched before. Nearly a year ago, when Ally had reacted instinctively to a sensation of danger and had found herself nearly looking through another set of eyes as they sighted down a high-powered sniper rifle, preparing to squeeze the trigger and extinguish the life that was now being held in the would-be assassin's arms. There had been the exact same lack of remorse or anything resembling human compassion then as well.

"You . . ." Ally whispered. Her voice rose. "You! You were the one who shot Evelynne. Who shot me." She was pleased to see a flicker of surprise in Laura's eyes. Ally slowly stood, ignoring the frantic gazes of the people around her. Her shoulder and back, where the bullets had hit her before, burned with remembered pain and she could feel something dangerous, something primal, waking in her mind. Her hand reached into her pocket and, almost of its own accord, wrapped her fingers around the bullet she had placed there earlier. Some part of her was vaguely aware that the soldiers who had been waiting in ambush up ahead were moving towards their position. A snippet of information gleaned from Laura's mind told her that they had been signalled by a transmitter hidden in the PDA now pressed against Evelynne's neck.

"I think you should sit down, 'Boss'," Laura said, still backing down the hallway. "If everyone's smart, you might see your fiancée again. But that's not my problem. I'm just being paid to deliver her. After that, it's not my problem."

"Maybe not," Ally said, her eyes flashing as she continued to stalk towards them, sending a wordless signal of support and reassurance to her lover. "But right now *I'm* your problem." She halted, drawing her hand out of her pocket, the bullet clasped tightly in her fist.

"And what are you going to do? If any of these Guards shoot me, assuming they miss their princess, do you really want to risk that this needle will move and she'll be scratched?"

"Then I'll just have to make sure it doesn't move," Ally said calmly.

And she threw the bullet.

A professional baseball pitcher has the ability to throw a baseball at speeds nearing one hundred sixty kilometres per hour. Ally's psychogenically enhanced arm, capable of buckling ten centimetre steel beams, easily outmatched that. And for a pitcher, once the ball leaves the hand it is out of control. Ally's control of her projectile did not stop at the end of her fingers. Instead, a mind capable of exerting almost fifteen hundred Newtons of force—enough to lift a three hundred pound man into the air—accelerated it even further. Minute control over the bullet's flight turned it from a ballistic projectile into a tiny guided missile.

A guided missile that struck Laura McGarrity between the eyes with incredible force, snapping her head back and causing her to slump to the floor before she even knew she had been hit. There was a gasp from the onlookers as the deadly needle which was pressed against Evelynne looked about to plunge into her neck, but Ally's mind was there also, halting the movement of the needle nearly instantaneously. A moment later, Ally was there in body, wrapping a supportive arm around the princess and carefully moving the PDA away from its lethal position.

Evelynne clutched Ally tightly, in too much shock to even speak. Ally guided her carefully back towards the relative safety of the group, lowering her to the floor behind the reassuring bulk of Sir Arthur just as the enemy soldiers ahead moved into the star-shaped junction.

"You there!" A voice from down the corridor announced that the enemy soldiers had spotted their party. "Lay down your weapons and surrender! You are now in the custody of the Hy Braseal Liberation Army." The words were oddly stilted Lantlan, with an accent unlike any Ally had heard before.

Ally glanced at Lord Thomas, who was gasping for breath in obvious pain in the arms of one of his Personal Guards, his eyes closed and his skin ashen. As though sensing her eyes on him, the old Duke opened his own and an unfathomable look passed between them. Ally gave a short, nearly imperceptible nod.

She looked at Sir Arthur, who seemed torn between gaping at the events that had just occurred and charging out to protect his wards. "Do whatever you have to," she said. Then she looked back down at the woman in her arms and her voice gentled. "I'll be right back." She lifted her hands to cup Eveleynne's face, bending her head and kissing her lingeringly. Gently but firmly she removed her lover's near-desperate gripping hand before kissing the palm and rising slowly, deliberately, to her feet.

"Ally, no," Evelynne whispered.

Ally looked down at her and gave her a reassuring smile. "Don't worry. I'm not going far." Then she turned and slowly began to walk towards the junction. Evelynne could almost see her lover wrapping herself in her power like a cloak.

Sir Arthur made a move to stop her and drag her back into safety, but was stopped by the princess' hand on his arm. "Don't interrupt her. She needs to concentrate right now."

As Ally walked forward, she felt as though she and everything around her was moving in slow motion. She could see and comprehend her surroundings, but it seemed as though all was underwater. Contrary to what her perceptions appeared to be telling her, only her reaction time was faster than usual; her physical abilities were still bound by the limitations of her flesh and bone.

Fortunately, she was not relying on mere physical matter.

Wrapped in a near-impenetrable cloak no thicker than a thought, Ally saw several of the soldiers ahead raise their weapons threateningly and heard, as though from far away, their orders for her to surrender. When she ignored them, more guns swung in her direction, until one soldier, unnerved by her steady, fearless pace, fired a single round from less than ten metres away.

With time to prepare, Ally's aura was more refined than it had been a year earlier in Marseilles. She no longer attempted to stop the incoming bullet though sheer blunt opposition. Instead, her aura twisted and bent the projectile's path, sweeping it around her body like a twig swirling past a rock in a stream, to impact the stone wall behind her. It missed by mere millimetres, but that was no concern—a bullet that misses by an inch is as harmless as one that misses by a mile.

The soldier's shot acted as a signal for the others to open fire. In an instant Ally was at the centre of a tornado of bullets, in the eye of the storm, where nothing seemed to be able to hurt her.

The Adept halted in the exact centre of the junction and raised her arms to her sides.

There should have been *more*, Evelynne thought later. There should have been lightning, rumbles of thunder and coalescing clouds overhead. Ally should have been wreathed in a glowing nimbus of light, her eyes shining and crackling with power, arcs of electricity jumping between her fingertips. The earth should have shaken, the walls should have cracked. There should not have been simply a tall, thin, brown-haired woman, glasses perched on her nose, hair dishevelled by her run through the Palace. There should have been *something* to indicate the immense amounts of power that she was about to unleash.

Instead, there was near silence as the echoes of gunfire faded away, the soldiers staring dumbfounded, as Ally stood untouched before them. There was a pregnant pause as Ally gathered her focus, reaching out for the tools she needed. Then she twitched her fingers, using the small physical gesture

chapter thirty four

as an aid to her focus. Suddenly a small marble bust of King Eldin deMolay (1644-1676) flew off its pedestal towards her, only to stop equally suddenly a centimetre from her palm. As the statue began to orbit her head, a pair of ancient sabres decorating the wall sailed towards her as well before joining in the deadly ballet.

Evelynne was immediately reminded of the first time her lover had deliberately demonstrated her abilities to her and she vividly remembered the gentle way in which the books Ally had been manipulating settled into her lap.

This was anything but gentle, however, as the objects circled faster and faster, until they exploded outwards towards the Adept's enemies. King Eldin would have been pleased to know that his likeness was the first thing to lay low an enemy soldier, as the bust struck the man who had first fired on Ally full in the face. Evelynne barely had time to gasp before the two sabres suddenly lost their scabbards in mid-flight, turning two projectiles into four, which felled another four soldiers. Even then, Evelynne noted that the weapons had struck with their pommels, rather than their still-sharp blades and she knew that had been no accident.

Then Ally was in the middle of another tornado, this one of her own making, as sculptures, vases, and decorations were turned into a hail of weapons that struck down the enemy soldiers. A tapestry, held by a power that made it stiff as a board, slammed into four soldiers, knocking them off their feet and then smothering them against the floor. A short length of heavy ornamental cord, decoratively weighted on both ends, spun down the hall like a bola, and with equal effect. A set of medieval plate armour provided a veritable magazine of projectiles, seeming to explode in slow motion. When Ally seemed to have run out of ammunition, those enemy soldiers still bearing weapons suddenly found their guns torn from their grasp, only to see them reversed to deal their erstwhile bearers a blow that, in many cases, knocked them unconscious. They could not escape, as the projectiles seemed to hunt them down even behind the scant cover available in the hallways.

Then, as suddenly as it began, it was over. Near silence reigned once more, broken only by the faint groans and feeble movements of the enemy soldiers who were now lying strewn about the junction and corridors.

Ally lowered her arms and drew in a long, shaky breath, then turned and walked back towards the small group still huddled behind her. Evelynne almost broke cover and ran towards her lover when she saw Ally stumble. The Adept's eyes were bloodshot and her face was drawn and shadowed, looking like she had gone days without sleep.

"The hallway's clear for at least a hundred metres ahead," Ally murmured distractedly to a conspicuously stone-faced Sir Arthur. She sniffled slightly and then dabbed at her nose with the back of her hand, not terribly surprised to find it coming away stained with red. Her eyes tracked back to Evelynne. "Are you okay?"

Evelynne could only nod shakily before grabbing her fiancée in a crushing embrace. They stayed like that for a moment, until Ally pulled back slightly to kneel next to Lord Thomas who was being cradled in Major Nixon's arms. "How's he doing?" Ally asked.

The Guard's voice was surprisingly, almost overly, calm. "Not good. She broke at least a half dozen of his ribs and I think one has punctured a lung. If we can get him to medical attention right away he might pull through."

"But then again, I might not," Lord Thomas spoke up, his voice weak and raspy. His eyes opened to direct a clear look at the Guard holding him. "Correct?" Nixon hesitated, and then managed a brief nod. "Very well, I will shut up. I am in quite a lot of pain." He smiled at Ally. "I don't suppose you can do anything about that?"

"Sorry," Ally apologised. "That really isn't one of my talents."

"No matter," Thomas murmured. "You were quite magnificent, you know. I'm glad I got to see that."

"You're not going to die on me, are you, Domdom?" Evelynne asked, taking his hand, her eyes bright with tears.

"I'll do my best not to," he whispered back, coughing slightly. "I have a wedding to see, after all." He closed his eyes. "For now, though, I am going to rest."

"You do that, my friend," King Jad replied, resting a hand on the Duke's brow.

epilogue

"So what do we know?" Evelynne asked from her seat on the couch as King Jad, Sir Arthur and Sir Adun entered the small, utilitarian sitting area.

Ally, who had been resting curled up against her fiancée with her head on the other woman's shoulder, started to move away, but Evelynne gently but firmly drew her close again.

King Jad didn't even flinch at the intimate display. Then again, he had far more important things to worry about. "It's not good, Evy," he said bleakly, sitting down heavily in a nearby chair and displaying every ounce of his weariness. "We finally have confirmation on all the Nobles. They were hit just as they were starting to head back to the Conclave Hall." He sighed, rubbing a hand across his eyes. "We lost over three quarters of the Nobility."

"Oh, Isis," Evelynne breathed and it was Ally's turn to silently hold her tightly as tears leaked out from behind her eyelids. "And civilians?"

"We don't have exact numbers, Your Highness," Sir Adun said quietly. He was just as tired as the King, having had to keep up with his ward constantly over the last three days. "However, we're still looking at over fifteen thousand dead and Osiris knows how many wounded, mostly in the vicinity of Ru'en Base. We were incredibly lucky, considering..."

Evelynne nodded, her eyes still closed, although she felt that "lucky" was an extremely inaccurate word to describe the events of the last few days.

After Ally's spectacular elimination of the enemy soldiers blocking them from their goal, the group had finally managed to reach the safety of one of the bunkers, buried deep below the Royal Palace. Alleandre's actions had left some Guards looking at her as though she was some goddess come to earth to be worshipped. Others as though she was the greatest threat they could possibly imagine facing or both. The unending stares were one reason she and Evelynne were hiding out in this spartan sitting room, communing silently through Evelynne's gift. As for the King, while he remained uncertain about the ultimate implications of Ally's abilities, the fact that she had employed them in the defence of his daughter could only be a good thing in his eyes. Besides, as a young man he had studied for a time with the Templars, with their long tradition of esoteric practices, so the sudden and dramatic demonstration of her "supernatural" abilities did not come as a total shock.

The medical teams at the bunker had managed eventually to stabilise Lord Thomas, but he had slipped into a coma from which they were uncertain he would recover. Given his age and the extent of his injuries, the chief doctor had quietly suggested removing him from life support. Alleandre had sat with him for over an hour, unmoving, her hand on his forehead and her eyes closed, and when she finally stirred she had ordered the machines left on. Nobody had argued with her.

Ally's parents were also safe, which had been a major source of relief for both Ally and Evelynne. Maïda had been visiting with them at the time of the attack–a "meeting of the mothers"–and had remained with them throughout the subsequent events. As an adjunct to Ally's new Guard detail, the elder Tretiaks had also suddenly inherited a couple of agents of their own. When the explosions and chaos had begun, they had been in their hotel room and the Guards had performed perfectly by barricading the door and not moving until they could verify that the situation was safe–or nearly so. The reunion had been a four-way embrace that had not budged for over five minutes.

Sir Arthur's reunion with Maïda had been slightly more reserved, at least when everyone else was looking. The two had nevertheless been fussing over each other ever since, although they tried to make it look as though they weren't. They were fooling nobody.

Chorus had also survived. The explosion that had killed General Danun had been–through sheer chance, as far as anyone could tell–the only one to hit the Common Guard Headquarters and had been far enough away that he wasn't in any direct danger. He had actually been of great help to the surviving intelligence forces as they re-established communication and control over the confused Guard teams.

The events throughout the country had completely stunned the nation. The hidden explosives had done their jobs almost to perfection, throwing the entire country into chaos, as the very services that would have best responded to the damage were the most heavily hit. Still, it said something about the character of the Atlantlan people that rather than panicking and adding to the disorder, citizens had banded together almost instinctively to help each other, putting out fires, aiding the wounded and maintaining order as best they could until the professional services could be restored. The individual and group acts of heroism were almost literally beyond counting and the Diarchs had stated their intention to attempt to single out each and every one for recognition.

epilogue

The total disorder and anarchy that the invaders had most likely been looking for had never materialised, at least not for any extended period of time. Even before the first day had ended, they had found themselves hounded and hunted by an increasingly coherent resistance. By now, the entire force had been captured or killed, with the possible exception of a few small groups that had managed to fade away before the Atlantlan forces. Allied troops from Portugal, Spain and Morocco had arrived swiftly, called by long-standing mutual defence treaties and alliances. More from France, Cuba, Canada, England and a dozen other allies were ready to be called on at a moment's notice.

Even America had offered its own "peacekeepers", but nobody in the Atlantlan government was particularly inclined to accept any offers of aid from that source. The US Secretary of State had escaped back to the American Embassy, thanks in no small part to the efforts of a detachment of Palace Guard who had taken it upon themselves to protect the dignitary. However, Americans were not the favourite nation of the Atlantlan government right now, since the identity of the invaders had become known.

And they *were* invaders, despite the speculations of some global media to classify the attack as a "revolution" or "popular uprising".

"What about the HBLA?" Evelynne asked, wiping her eyes as Ally brushed the hair away from her face.

"HBLA? Ha!" Sir Arthur barked a short, unhumourous laugh. "There *is* no HBLA. At least, not in any real manner, except name. Nine out of ten were–are–foreigners. And fifty per cent of *them* are American. Not to mention almost *all* their officers. With what intelligence we've been able to gather, none of them are officially US troops, although some of them are certainly ex-military. The rest seem to be a combination of mercenaries and so-called 'survivalists' from a dozen different countries."

"But why?" the princess asked, her voice baffled. "I mean, Isis knows the US has been supplying, training and funding terrorist groups for decades–hell, half the first world countries have–but those have all been foreign groups. Why send their own people?"

"Intelligence has put together a few scenarios," Sir Adun said. "It seems unlikely that this attack had anything to do with any officially sanctioned American scheme. Oh, there are undoubtedly members of the American government who were aware of it and facilitated it, but the chances of it having any legitimate backing are slim. It could have been some kind of rogue operation, but it lacks the signature of any of the known agencies. The actual fact that the American connection is so strong suggests that someone wants us to blame them. No, this was put together by someone else."

"Who?"

"We don't know. However, as well as we are able to guess—and a lot of this is guesswork—the plan was to infiltrate the mercenaries into Atlantl, where they would begin a terror campaign under the guise of the 'Hy Braseal Liberation Army', intent on liberating the 'poor, oppressed' Atlantlan people from their 'aristocratic, totalitarian regime'. Then, at the proper time, they would stage a 'revolution' and take control of the country. However, all of this was pure show, for the benefit of the international community."

"I don't get it," Ally spoke up for the first time.

"Well, if you don't," the King remarked, "then it's unlikely that the average citizen would, either. However, if we, as a nation, have a group of 'rebels' attempting to 'free the people', then there must be *something* that we are doing to 'oppress' them, mustn't there? And if they are 'desperate' enough to instigate a full-scale 'revolution', then, by definition, we must be truly evil, as 'everyone's known all along'." King Jad was making exaggerated quote marks with his fingers, a sign of his frustration and underlying anger.

"But the so-called rebels would never be able to keep control, even with the numbers they brought along. Even as disorganised as things were, our military could still fight them off. They did." Evelynne frowned.

"And when that revolution manages to kill the entire ruling body, effectively beheading the nation? Then nobody will be around to object when someone or some group begins implementing a change in government, likely to some more 'democratic' system, which is by nature infinitely more susceptible to control by special interest groups. With the international pressure and 'assistance' available—especially if 'peacekeepers' from other nations are present to 'help maintain order'—since the old regime was obviously evil and oppressive, it would be easy."

"But who would want to do all this to begin with?"

"Come now, Evelynne," King Jad chided. "Do you need me to make you a list? There are plenty of interests on both sides of the Atlantic that would love to have a lot more influence over our resources and trading routes. The effects of a 'modest' reduction in tariffs through our territorial waters alone are enough to make any country's economists drool. We're also strategically placed so that any nation would dearly love to be able to position troops and ships in our territory. Those are simply foreign concerns. Let's not ignore the incentive of the power that would be available to those within our own country should the Hall of Nobles fall. Suppose only a handful of Nobles 'fortuitously' survive the rebellion? Then who better than one of them to take up the reigns of the inevitable 'interim government', and then to run for office during the next election? Or even a restoration of the Diarchy

epilogue

and who better than one of the old Nobles to become the first of the new Dynasty?"

"You're right. I'd say an alliance of both foreign and domestic interests," Evelynne mused. Her father waved at her to continue. "Resources. I can only guess at the money that was required to set everything in motion in the first place. Smuggling the mercenaries in, equipping them. Keeping the Guard off the trail for so long definitely points to an internal source. But I know the Guard keeps an eye on large monetary transfers, so the funding had to go through outside channels and the sheer volume of funds is too large for any one interest to front alone."

"I agree and so does Guard Intelligence. Needless to say, there is going to be a very thorough investigation. And it's going to take years."

"I know," Evelynne said.

"Do you?" the King asked. "This is far more than a single assassination attempt. Some person or persons were not only able to infiltrate close to five thousand foreign troops onto our soil; not only smuggle in enough weapons to arm them all; not only plant hidden explosives throughout the country, linked to a signal controlled solely by the Director of the Guard herself; not only provide sufficient passcodes and information on Guard details to allow them access to the Royal Palace and Conclave Hall itself. They were able to get an assassin close enough to the Royal family to almost eliminate us entirely. This tells me that whoever it is, is placed very highly in the government structure. The ease with which he or she has managed to manipulate things so far leads me to believe that it would be easy for whoever it is to manipulate the investigation as well. Simply put, we don't know who to trust." He sighed wearily.

"You can trust Sir Arthur, Sire," Ally said quietly. "And *he* can tell you who else to trust."

"Using his . . . talents, I believe you called them? Perhaps. But as I understand it, *you* possess more skill and experience in that regard and yet you were still unable to detect McGarrity for what she really was. Why is that?" The King's voice was carefully free of condemnation.

"Because I had no reason to suspect her," Ally said simply. "It's not as though I go around scanning every new person I meet. Even under the best circumstances, that kind of wholesale thought sharing is . . . unpleasant. She gave off absolutely no subconscious clues that may have somehow alerted me. She was like a chameleon. I almost think that until she had to do what she had to she honestly believed that she was who she pretended to be. Do you know who she really was?"

Sir Adun shook his head. "Guard Intelligence is still scraping for information and trying to sort themselves out, but it's likely that she was a hired assassin. Do you remember what she said? 'I'm doing what I was paid to do.' And assassins for hire of her obvious calibre are notoriously difficult to identify."

They were referring to the woman who had called herself Laura McGarrity in the past tense, because she was, for all intents and purposes, dead. Ally's thrown bullet had struck her between the eyes and the resulting shock and concussion had caused sufficient brain damage that it was unlikely she would ever wake up. Even if she did, it was uncertain how much mental capacity she would be left with.

"In any case," Ally continued, "Sir Arthur can at least tell you who to use to create your investigative agency. You won't find a better lie detector during interrogations. Especially since they won't know they're under a lie detector."

King Jad looked up at the Guard in question. "Sir Arthur, are you willing to use your talents in this area?"

"Of course, Sire. My mind, as well as my body, are at the service of the Crowns. It is no less than my willing duty."

"Good. Now, there is something else." The King looked at Evelynne with sorrowful eyes. "Argyle died about an hour ago."

"Oh, Isis," Evelynne cried, turning to bury her face in her lover's shoulder.

Ally's own eyes were wet. While she had only met Evelynne's cousin a few times, he had seemed a pleasant, friendly person. She looked at the King, silently asking whether he should be the one to comfort his daughter, but he shook his head briefly. After a time, Evelynne cried herself out and raised her head, unceremoniously wiping her face with the back of her hand.

"I hate to bring this up now," Jad said, "but because of Argyle's death we must consider a particular issue. Specifically, the Germanin Protocol."

"The what?" Ally asked.

"The Germanin Protocol," Evelynne explained, sniffling a few more times. "With Argyle and Reylinn gone, I am now the sole remaining member of the line of Succession. With the Kingdom in a state of emergency, the Protocol makes provisions for me to go into hiding, in order to preserve the Succession."

"Yes," the King agreed. "However, there is a problem. On the few occasions that the Protocol has been invoked in the past, the Heir has been secretly placed with one of our allies in a foreign country. However, right now we simply can't trust our allies with something this important. Whoever orchestrated this attack is still out there and we can't trust that they can't

epilogue

penetrate whatever secrecy we place around Evelynne. Which leaves one option . . ."

"No, *za*!" Evelynne interrupted. "You *can't* make me do that. I *can't* stay in Elysium for however many months or years it will take to make things safe again! I just *can't*." Her eyes were pleading, begging.

"Evy, do you think I *want* to? Patrick is already safe in Europe and his primary protection is probably the fact that he irrevocably abdicated the Throne. However, we *can't* keep you safe outside of Elysium. There's nobody who can—"

"I can." The interruption came from Alleandre.

"Alleandre, I appreciate your unique talents, but even you can't . . ." The King trailed off when he saw that the two young women were gazing into each other's eyes, communicating on a completely private level. The princess' expression changed from questioning, to shocked, to speculative as they communed silently.

Finally they broke contact and Evelynne looked at her father. "Ally has an idea," she said. She took a breath. "You make all the arrangements for me to go to Europe somewhere. Let me finish! You make all the plans, all the false leads, all the covert arrangements. You arrange for me to go to several places, without revealing which one I'm actually going to. Each location will think that I went to one of the others. While the people trying to kill me are tracking down all the leads . . ." She took another deep breath. "Ally and I disappear. Just us. No Guards, no covert protection, nothing."

"After all, tracking down two ordinary women among the three billion others on the planet is much harder than trying to find the Heir to Atlantl among the societies of Atlantl's allies," Ally added softly.

The King's first instinct was immediately to object, but he restrained himself, forcing himself to look at Sir Arthur and Sir Adun instead. He was both reassured and disturbed at the speculative looks on their faces.

"It's . . . feasible, Sire," Sir Adun said finally. "Of course, it would be safer to send along a small covert Guard detail to—"

"No," Alleandre interrupted. "I can get Evelynne and myself past just about any surveillance or border easily. I can't do more than one. Not nearly as easily, anyway."

"But—" Sir Adun started, halting when he saw Ally's firm expression. Part of him was dying to know exactly why she was so sure she could avoid leaving a trail. Another part was strongly rebelling against the idea of leaving a member of the Royal family with only a single woman for protection. Then he remembered that same single woman taking out an entire squad of enemy soldiers with no assistance.

"They should do it," Sir Arthur said suddenly, his gaze unfocussed. He shook his head to clear it. "I don't know why, but they should."

Ally looked at him calculatingly and then she nodded.

The King's expression was less sure. "We'll discuss it."

☙ ☙ ☙ ☙ ☙

Seven people congregated in a moonlit garden to see them off. William and Catherine Tretiak, King Jad and Queen Cleo, Maïda, Sir Arthur and Chorus Tladi were all present. Ally was currently embracing her parents in a three-way hug as Evelynne did the same with her father and aunt.

"Now, you keep each other safe, you hear?" Catherine whispered fiercely, her voice hoarse. "And more important, keep each other happy." William squeezed his daughter harder in agreement.

"We will," Ally promised, reluctantly breaking free from the embrace. She turned to Chorus.

"What they said, Ally," the young man said wrapping her in a bear hug.

Ally managed to chuckle. "I will," she promised again. "Now, you take care of Lord Thomas' Duchy until he recovers, Mister Aide. And also my cat. She'll keep you on the straight and narrow."

"I promise."

With a final rib-cracking hug they parted, leaving Ally face to face with King Jad. "Well, Alleandre, years ago when I thought about having a daughter-in-law, this was certainly not the way I ever imagined it." His face finally broke into a fond smile. "Now, I couldn't think of a better choice." This time, Ally was almost smothered by his massive arms.

"Thank you . . . *za*," she managed to say past a tight throat and tighter chest.

The King's voice lowered. "Just remember that if anything happens to my daughter I will hunt you down, Adept or not."

"If anything happens to her you won't have to," Ally replied in a matching tone.

Finally finishing their goodbyes, the two young women moved together into each other's arms. "Time to go," Ally said, drawing Evelynne back with her into the shadows, where their matching black outfits made them almost invisible. "We'll be back." Suddenly her eyes widened. "What's that?" she asked, pointing.

Everyone whirled to look, only to find nothing there. When they turned back, Ally and Evelynne were gone.

Chorus chuckled. "Damn it, Ally, you had to make a dramatic, mysterious exit, didn't you?"

epilogue

King Jad was staring speculatively at the sky.

"They'll be all right, Jad," William said, standing next to him.

"Oh, I know," the King said, not removing his gaze from the stars. "They'll be more than all right. One day, they're going to change the entire world."

        ം   ം   ം   ം   ം

"'Tis not too late to seek a newer world.
Push off, and sitting well in order smite
The sounding furrows; for my purpose holds
To sail beyond the sunset, and the baths
Of all the western stars, until I die.
It may be that the gulfs will wash us down;
It may be we shall touch the Happy Isles,
And see the great Achilles, whom we knew.
Tho' much is taken, much abides; and tho'
We are not now that strength which in old days
Moved earth and heaven, that which we are, we are—
One made equal temper of heroic hearts,
Made weak by time and fate, but strong in will
To strive, to seek, to find, and not to yield."

~Alfred Tennyson, *Ulysses*

the end

glossary

LANTLAN

A note on pronunciation:

All Lantlan words and phrases in the story have been transliterated directly from the Atlantlan alphabet. Lantlan writing includes 33 phonetic characters, most of which have direct counterparts in the Roman alphabet. Most exceptions are characters which are "compound characters" in English, such as the Lantlan letter *"tla"*, which transliterates to "tl". For example, "Atlantl" actually has 5 characters in Lantlan: *A tl a n tl*.

The two remaining characters are transliterated as the apostrophe (') and hyphen (-). These represent clicks. The "high" click (') is made by placing the tongue near the front teeth, while the "low" click (-) places the tongue nearer the centre of the palate.

Words

Atlantl	Atlantis
bona	good
ca'era	An expression of respect, literally "My soul" (is honoured).
cer'ant	A liqueur, traditionally made in Cere County.
ekani'is	okay, fine, well
e'met	amazing, awesome
eni	gentlemen
Enku	A title of high respect (masculine).
fretin	fucking
ilasi	A fruit, somewhat similar to a pineapple.
Ishta	A title of high respect (feminine).
isi	ladies
k'kela'i	An unusual word which is a pure insult. Unlike most insults in other languages, it has no secondary meaning.
medo'nta	elephants (plural)
moru	consort, lover

ney'rad	ocean spirit
paka	shit
sa-kima	unicorns (plural)
salê!	hail!
sekema	mountain lions (plural)
sekheru	gryphon
tae'e-haka	Another "pure" expletive, like k'kela'i.
tali	Atlantlan currency. Singular = talen (Ŧ1 ≈ £1) Divided into celi, singular = celen (100c = Ŧ1)
teki'a	evil people, traitors
tiama'apep	dragon
tyl'kas	coronet
ur-	high, great, ultimate
Ur-mata	Royal Highness, Crown Princess (title)
va'wer	living room
vei'Chel	A popular board game in Atlantl, similar to chess.
Viamadi	Life Debt. From via = life + madi = blood. The two words are joined together linguistically in such a way that they are understood to be inextricably combined.
y'ek'sal	misfit, outcast
za	dad (a more formal term is zazu)
zhaniyye	a magical being, similar to an elf or fairy (feminine)

Phrases

A mak pro'phes Dusan Collins.	I am Dusan Collins
Bon'gier'a	Good day.
Del mek si'aerat on pellk	She sees things we never have
Eta-o?	Is that you?
Et hura'i o si arra'at.	I am very pleased to meet you.
Ki so liver'o Setswana?	Who taught you Setswana?
Mi Alleandre re-al'a wei arat.	Alleandre taught me a few words.
N'amassa.	No problem.
O'derenn mai-lata presh ala-at.	You look very beautiful this evening.
Pole'can war esse tolu'a mens.	The doors of my mind are suddenly opened. A phrase similar to "Eureka!"
Yvis.	I see.

SETSWANA

Dumela.   Hello.
Ga gona mathata.   No problem.
O tsohile jang?   How are you? (literally, How are you going?)

Ke tsohile sentle   I'm fine. (literally, I'm going well.)

Also available from Cavalier Press

T. NOVAN AND TAYLOR RICKARD'S
WORDS HEARD IN SILENCE

In the midst of the Civil War, two people come together to establish what will become a Southern dynasty…

The fall of 1864 was a dark time in the once bustling town of Culpeper, Virginia. Feisty Rebecca Gaines, widowed by the conflict that had torn the nation apart, struggles to single-handedly manage the family farm. Life is hard in the beleaguered South, so when a troop of Union soldiers rides in to winter over on her property, Rebecca is grudgingly glad of the extra income.

Their dashing commanding officer, Colonel Charlie Redmond, is courteous and gentle in his dealings with her, and she is drawn to this intriguing professional soldier. But he is still the enemy, and Rebecca finds it difficult to come to terms with her feelings. For his part, Charlie is alarmed to realize he is becoming romantically involved with the lovely Southerner, for he hides a secret that, if discovered, would mean social disgrace and the end of a distinguished military career. For Charlie is really a woman.

In this meticulously researched novel, **T. Novan** and **Taylor Rickard** have captured the agony of the War and its impact on soldiers and civilians alike. With its moving love story, powerful scenes of battle, and memorable characters living in and around the war-torn community, WORDS HEARD IN SILENCE is an enthralling work that lays the foundation for the rest of the Redmond family saga.

At your local bookstore, Amazon.com,
Barnes & Noble, and other fine bookstores, or
contact us at www.cavalierpress.com

Also available from Cavalier Press

Blayne Cooper & T. Novan's
Madam President

Devlyn Marlowe, the first woman President of the United States, has just been elected. Breaking with the tradition of hiring a political writer to chronicle her administration, President Marlowe selects one Lauren Strayer, a professional biographer with a reputation for absolute honesty. There's a slight problem with Devlyn's plan, though. Lauren wants nothing to do with what she sees as a political hack job.

It takes some serious persuading, but the Commander-in-Chief is an eloquent negotiator, and Lauren reluctantly agrees to take the job, provided she truly has editorial freedom. So armed with her computer, her incredibly ugly Pug, and a fair bit of trepidation, Lauren finds herself in residence at 1600 Pennsylvania Avenue.

There, amidst the harrowing and demanding life of the First Family, Lauren begins to understand and eventually love the complex woman who is both leader of a great nation and loving single parent to three rambunctious children.

Funny, realistic, romantic, and endearing, **Madam President** is rapidly becoming a modern classic, with thirteen months on the Open Book Best Seller list.

At your local bookstore, Amazon.com, Barnes & Noble and other fine bookstores, or contact us at www.cavalierpress.com

Also available from Cavalier Press

Blayne Cooper & T. Novan's

First Lady

Blayne Cooper and **T. Novan** continue to chronicle the lives of Lauren Strayer and Devlyn Marlowe in *First Lady*, the eagerly-awaited sequel to their thirteen-month best seller, **Madam President**.

Planning a wedding is never easy. However, most brides don't face the challenges that Lauren Strayer does. Her beloved comes with a ready-made family, something the biographer never imagined for herself. In addition, Lauren's estranged father thoroughly disapproves of her future mate, who just happens to be the nation's first female president.

Lauren tackles the perils and pleasures of parenting and the tension between her private nature and her new, very public role. At the same time, Dev, a dedicated public servant, struggles to find the balance between managing the nation's interests, her family, her fears, and her stress, while continuing the development of her relationship with Lauren. The result is an action-packed, amusing, and tender tale of the sort that fans of Cooper & Novan have come to love and expect.

At your local bookstore, Amazon.com, Barnes & Noble and other fine bookstores, or contact us at www.cavalierpress.com